The Time Is Out of Joint

Shakespeare as Philosopher of History

Agnes Heller

ROWMAN & LITTLEFIELD PUBLISHERS, INC.
Lanham • Boulder • New York • Oxford

With thanks to Marcia Morgan and Katie Terezakis

ROWMAN & LITTLEFIELD PUBLISHERS, INC.

Published in the United States of America
by Rowman & Littlefield Publishers, Inc.
4720 Boston Way, Lanham, Maryland 20706
www.rowmanlittlefield.com

12 Hid's Copse Road
Cumnor Hill, Oxford OX2 9JJ, England

British Library Cataloguing in Publication Information Available

Library of Congress Cataloging-in-Publication Data

Heller, Agnes.
    The time is out of joint : Shakespeare as philosopher of history / Agnes Heller.
        p.   cm.
        ISBN 0-7425-1250-9 (cloth : alk. paper) — ISBN 0-7425-1251-7 (pbk. : alk.
paper)
        1. Shakespeare, William, 1564-1616—Contributions in philosophy of history.
    2. Literature and history—England—16th century.   3. Literature and
    history—England—History—17th century.   4. Shakespeare, William, 1564-
    1616—Knowledge—History.   5. Shakespeare, William, 1564-1616—Philosophy.
    6. History—Philosophy—History—16th century.   7. History—Philosophy—
    History—17th century.   8. Philosophy in literature.   9. History in literature.   10.
    Time in literature.   I. Title.

    PR3014 .H45   2002
    822.3'3—dc21
                                                                    2001019599

Printed in the United States of America

♾ ™
    The paper used in this publication meets the minimum requirements of
American National Standard for Information Sciences—Permanence of Paper for
Printed Library Materials, ANSI/NISO Z39.48–1992.

The Time Is Out of Joint

In memory of
Reiner Schürmann

Contents

Part III: Three Roman Plays

13   Julius Caesar   311

14   Antony and Cleopatra   337

     Postscript: Historical Truth and Poetic Truth   367

     About the Author   375

Introduction

"The time is out of joint," says Hamlet. The time is out of joint in all the Shakespearean tragedies and history plays, and in many of the comedies as well.

In the great tragedies, and in some of the history plays (in *1*, *2*, and *3 Henry VI*, for example), the time is out of joint *absolutely*. One can be born to put it right. At least, one can believe that one is born to put it right, as Hamlet and Henry VI do. Or one can willingly assume the responsibility to put it right, as Cordelia does. Yet, all these approaches will fail. For *heimarmene*, the blind and irrational fate, rules here. Freedom-for-the-good, freedom-for-justice, and also freedom-for-evil (as in the case of Macbeth or Edmund), all fight a losing battle. However, time is only out of joint in some of the history plays (such as in the three Roman plays). Time is heimarmene for one actor, whereas it is *sors bona* or *pronoia* (providence) for another. Although time is not set right in the sense of being returned to its former place, "new men" usher in new times (as does Octavius Caesar in *Antony and Cleopatra*). Only in some comedies (*As You Like It, Much Ado about Nothing*, and *A Midsummer Night's Dream*) will time be set right to everyone's satisfaction—sometimes even for the villains (as in *As You Like It*).

"All the world's a stage. / And all the men and women merely players. They have their exits and their entrances, And one man in his time plays many parts." Thus ruminates the melancholy Jaques in *As You Like It* (2.7.139–42). The actors—Shakespeare among them—enter and exit the theater stage. The theater stage is home to another, four-dimensional stage. It is the stage of history, the world stage of historical time; it is the stage of life, of a lifetime. In the history plays and in some of the tragedies and comedies, it is the stage of political time. Finally, it is the stage beyond the stage, the stage of the naked existence where there is no time.

No one will solve the riddle of the sphinx called Shakespeare. This book does not entertain such high ambitions. In what follows, I will make only another attempt to penetrate the absolutely unique combination of the

1

four stages (historical, personal, political, and existential) and the four ways to cope with time being out of joint. These include facing heimarmene in Good or in Evil without taking up the responsibility to set the time right; facing it and taking up such a responsibility simultaneously; transforming history into politics, *sors mala* into *sors bona;* and finally, setting right the time out of joint. I do not need to demonstrate the absolute uniqueness of this combination. It had not existed or been attempted before Shakespeare (in Greek tragedy), and although it has been attempted after him (in the *tragédie classique* or in modern tragedy), the attempts have not been success- ful. Shakespeare's dramas present their own philosophy of history, political philosophy, and philosophy of (im)moral personality.

Understanding Shakespeare's work—and others' as well—as a philoso- phy of history, a political philosophy, and a philosophy of personality is not tantamount to bestowing on Shakespeare the dubious honorary title of philosopher. Many of Shakespeare's plays contain significant philosophical reflections, but almost all of them are concretely situated. They are also acts, most of them not only illocutionary but also perlocutionary. Philosophical thoughts and reflections are uttered by certain characters in certain situa- tions. They are not the philosophical reflections of Shakespeare but of Hamlet, Horatio, Henry VI, Richard II, Brutus, or Prospero. It never would have occurred to Shakespeare to let Talbot, Kent, or Octavius Caesar speak philosophically. "The philosophy of Shakespeare" is like "the language of Shakespeare." Every Shakespearean character speaks his or her own lan- guage. Some of them (like some soldiers or generals) are witty and yet rude, others (like successful politicians) are prosaic and logical. Yet others (men and women of great emotional density) are poetic, rhetorical, and flowery (like Antony). Some speak in a playful and refined manner (like Beatrice and Benedick), while some (skeptical and contemplative heroes) develop a reflective style. I could go on and on, making many other distinctions. Still, it is not absurd to speak of Shakespeare's language. The divine gift of pre- senting all his heroes and heroines with their distinct, unique language is Shakespeare's language. Very similar things can be said about Shakespeare's philosophy of history, politics, or personality. Shakespeare bestows on (almost) all his characters a great moment of insight, a moment *(nunc stance)* where the curtain of transcendence is lifted and the very heart of exis- tence—personal, historical, and ontological—suddenly appears. Consider, for example, Henry Hotspur, the typical man of the battlefield: he is brave but narrow-minded, traditional yet mildly disloyal. His forte is his physical courage. He never reflects; he is the man of the sword. But Shakespeare sud- denly offers him a magnificent gift—one of the most dense, riddlesome, and deeply philosophical reflections: "But thoughts, the slaves of life, and life, time's fool, And time, that takes survey of all the world, Must have a stop" (*1 Henry IV* 5.4.80–82). And listen now to Macbeth, another "hotspur," who never thinks before acting. (He belongs, in fact, to the very few about whom Hannah Arendt's idea that evil comes from thoughtlessness might be true, or at least partly true.) "Had I but died an hour before this chance, I had lived a blessed time, for from this instant / There's nothing serious in mortality. All is but toys. Renown and grace is dead. / The wine of life is drawn, and the mere lees / Is left this vault to brag of" (*Macbeth* 2.3.90–95). Both reflections are given by nonreflective characters, yet both are uttered in a *borderline situation.* Hotspur is dying, and Macbeth becomes a murderer. Both Hotspur and Macbeth have been cheated and defeated by fate without repair: the first out of life, the second out of the meaning of life. I mention only parenthetically that there is a second and very signifi-cant place (aside from *Macbeth*) where Shakespeare seems to support Arendt's philosophical conception, and this is in *Hamlet.* In his first meet-ing with Rosenkrantz and Guildenstern, Hamlet says, "[T]here is nothing either good or bad but thinking makes it so" (*Hamlet* 2.2.251–52). This is a general statement and Hamlet believes it to be true; and it is. However, it is again contextual. The evildoings of Guildenstern and Rosenkrantz are in fact rooted in thoughtlessness. But not all evil in Shakespeare, or even specifically in *Hamlet,* is rooted in thoughtlessness. Certainly, the evildoings of Claudius are not rooted in that way, and the evil doings of Richard III are, to the contrary, evils of reflection.

There are only a few characters of Shakespeare whose philosophical reflections, at least at first glance, are not situated. Such are the Stoics, like Horatio or Brutus. This is precisely how Shakespeare presents the essence of Stoicism. Stoic philosophy molds characters so that they remain the same in all possible situations. Cicero has no "situation" in Shakespeare; and Cas-sius, the Epicurean, will change his philosophy because of the impact of the evil turn of fate *(Julius Caesar).* In this broader sense, all philosophical man-ifestations are contextual.

The character "philosopher" also appears in *Timon of Athens,* where Ape-mantus remains, similar to the Stoics, always true to himself. Yet, he is an altogether different type of philosopher. He is a cynic, a dog that unmasks the vanities of the world while constantly pricking and nagging its fools. There is a touch of the madman in him, molded with a base plebeian self-righteousness. He is clever and mostly in the right because he sees things without interest, without compassion, merely "intellectually." He is the par-ody of the kind of man who was described later by Nietzsche as the ascetic priest.

King Lear calls Edgar (who plays Poor Tom, the madman) a philosopher four times at the peak of the tempest scene (*King Lear* 3.4), even though Tom utters only seemingly nonsensical sentences. Is this Lear's folly, or is it his greatest wisdom? Is it the coming of wisdom? Is it not the poetic way to express the reversal of sense and nonsense, of opinion and true knowledge? Is truth not in the nonsense? Is the opinion, this nonsense of an evil world, not madness? Is it the gift of Shakespeare presented to an old fool who becomes wise in suffering and in madness? Is not Poor Tom indeed the symbol of the philosopher, or at least of the kind of philosopher who is situated in an absolutely evil and mad world?

According to the general perception, it is Hamlet who is the most "philosophical" of all Shakespearean characters; but Hamlet's philosophical reflections are strictly contextual. For example, Shakespeare has Hamlet, in the company of Horatio, meet the clown (another philosopher!) in the cemetery (5.1) to create the most proper situation for the second round of Hamlet's ruminations on mortality. This is a reflection utterly different from the first one. It happens during these ruminations that Hamlet resigns to providence. There is no remaining freedom of choice, no "to be or not to be," as in the first existential soliloquy; the hero subjects himself to the unknown director of the world of *vanitatum vanitas*.

Shakespeare presents many of his heroes, deserving and undeserving, with philosophical reflections. But those characters can do different things with this rare gift. I do not speak, of course, of the dying heroes who receive the gift as a farewell present, such as Hotspur or Othello. I speak only of those who go on living and acting for some time. This gift is akin to drawing a lucky card. The lucky card can be misused or squandered, or it can be used to win the jackpot of a good life, grandeur, or the ability to become a new person. It is as if Shakespeare has put his own characters on trial, as if he himself wants to find out what a person would do with such a moment of sudden and deep insight. Edmund becomes a villain; Shylock remains the same. But Lear and Richard II become new men: they win the prize of a present time that has never been their past. What a person does with the great moment of sudden insight belongs to the contingent elements in Shakespeare's stories (as constituted in his history plays and political dramas, among other works).

Shakespeare's regard is cold; yet, this coldness is not that of *impassibilité*. It is rather the cold but passionate desire to understand everything. In fact, he understands everything, even the greatest extremities of human character. He is not astonished by anything. He observes the world stage, he shows grandeur through pettiness, he points exactly to opportunities either missed or seized. He is infinitely interested in the struggle between a human being and fate; in chances either taken or not; in the cycles of history, politics, and life; and in the intrinsic and complex relation between morals, politics, and luck. To this extent, his interests are like Machiavelli's.

Shakespeare lived in the world of Machiavelli. It is irrelevant whether he read the works of the Florentine historian or not. We know that Marlowe read some of them, but we do not know if Shakespeare did. Machiavelli's name is mentioned by Gloucester (in *The Tragedy of Richard III*) in the spirit of a one-sided and—for a long time—commonplace understanding of Machiavelli as the father of Machiavellianism. Shakespeare's political dramas are Machiavellian in another, deeper sense. They are far closer to our modern reading of Machiavelli's works than to their reading in his own time.

As is well known, Machiavelli distinguishes between well-exploited and badly exploited cruelties. In the seventh chapter of *The Prince*, he writes: "Well committed may be called those (if it is permissible to use the word well of evil) which are perpetuated ones for the need of securing one's self, and which afterwards are not persisted in, but are exchanged for measures as useful to the subjects as possible. Cruelties ill committed are those, which, although at first few, increase rather than diminish in time." This is also the way that Shakespeare portrays the use of cruelty in politics. Cruelty in itself is morally evil and remains morally evil even if used well; but it can be used well, nonetheless. How does the rule of King Henry IV begin according to Shakespeare, for example? Listen to *Richard II* (5.6). Northumberland enters: "The next news is, I have to London sent / The heads of Salisbury, Spencer, Blunt and Kent" (5.6.7–8). Fitzwater enters: "My lord, I have from Oxford sent to London the heads of Brocas and Sir Bennet / Seely" (5.6.13–14). Compare these executions with the first acts of cruelty committed by Regan and Goneril in *King Lear:* they consist solely in not letting their father keep his entourage in their house. And even Macbeth killed just one single man "at the beginning." Yet Henry IV has stopped committing further cruelties after the murder of Richard, and according to the dramas of King Henry (*IV, 1* and *2*), he became a fairly good king. Shakespeare's worst political villains are the ones who use cruelty "badly," who cannot refrain from doing evil but rather escalate in murderous deeds and become despots. As Macbeth (who knows this only too well) says: "It will have blood, they say. Blood will have blood" (*Macbeth* 3.4.121).

Machiavelli discovered the multifaceted significance of time in politics. Time was politicized in ancient Greek thinking in the sense of *kairos.* The man of action has to grasp the proper moment in which to do something; for if it were done earlier or later, the mark would be missed. Machiavelli, in addition, already knows of the time out of joint. If time radically changes, a successful man of politics can perish for having failed to notice that everything got out of order. This also happens with many of Shakespeare's political actors (with Richard II, for example, who identifies the reason for his fall with missing the broken tune).

Machiavelli asks whether worldly events are governed by fortune or by God—that is, by necessity or chance on the one hand, or by providence on the other. He says, in the twenty-fifth chapter of *The Prince*, "that fortune is the ruler of half our actions, but that she allows the other half or thereabouts to be governed by us." But what is the greatest gift of fortune? "He is happy whose modes of procedure accord with the needs of the times

... for fortune is a woman and it is necessary, if you wish to master her, to conquer her by force." That Shakespeare shares those views is self-evident, for they constitute the very structure of his history plays, tragedies, and also most of his comedies. Without fate or providence there is no context. There are no constraints on, and therefore no possibilities for, action. Freedom is freedom against and for something; the constraining conditions can be used for the better or for the worse. They can be "raped" or they can be accepted in resignation. Time is the ever fluid opportunity, the great unknown. It brings the "change of fortune," or the change of the right or wrong fit between situation and character. Whoever rides the crest of the waves will be carried on, either to victory or to defeat.

Shakespeare's heroes take sides in the Machiavellian discourse by verbalizing the relation between freedom and fate. Cassius, for example, speaks out against the omnipotence of heimarmene and so does Edmund in *King Lear*. Yet to side with fate as a "raping wench of fortune," or on the contrary to oppose it, rarely determines independently whether a Shakespearean character will act or not. Moreover, this choice has even less effect on the direction of the action. Different characters' similar convictions about fate and freedom can result in entirely different kinds and directions of actions.

It seems that faith in divine providence, although it might strengthen a character's moral resistance (as in the case of Isabella in *Measure for Measure*), would diminish the appetite for action and for taking initiatives altogether. One can rape fate, but one can only acquiesce in the ways of providence. Although Machiavelli does not make this distinction, Shakespeare does, even if Shakespeare's historical actors sometimes take fate as providence itself. Take the example of Julius Caesar as he walks to the capitol unconcerned about the ides of March. In Hamlet's case, fate and providence are mutually exclusive. To be born to put time right is Hamlet's fate, his destiny. He is an actor who has to answer the call of destiny. There is choice, there is a free space to act, there is resolve. One must take up the gauntlet. Facing providence is altogether different.

In his famous monologue, Hamlet puts the question of "to be or not to be" in the following way: "Whether tis nobler in the mind to suffer / The slings and arrows of outrageous fortune, / Or to take arms against a sea of troubles, / And by opposing, end them" (*Hamlet* 3.1.59–62). Here one can choose between life and death. But if one faces providence, one has no choice. Hamlet says to Horatio: "Not a whit. We defy augury. There's a special providence in the fall of a sparrow. If it be now, tis not to come. If it be not to come, it will be now. If it be not now, yet it will come. The readiness is all" (*Hamlet* 5.2.165–68). Hamlet walks into the trap with the same lack of concern as Julius Caesar. I have already mentioned that in the cemetery scene we witness a deep change in Hamlet's innermost soul. It becomes slowly, if not suddenly, obvious that Hamlet has given up the struggle, that he has entered a stage of melancholy resignation. Yet, he is not resigned to fate; he is resigned to providence.

I cannot answer the question of whether Shakespeare—contrary to Machiavelli—attributed decisive importance to the distinction between *fatum* and *providencia,* or whether he just characterized the innermost spiritual change in the life of his hero (Hamlet) as a move from *fatum* toward *providencia.* The differentiation points, however, to a broader issue.

It was Machiavelli's idea that there is no universal, abstract "good politics" or "bad politics." Even the best needs to be specified. For example, one type of politics is needed if rule is based on tradition and legitimacy, and a different type is needed if power is simply seized. Different kinds of politics are needed when a new constitution is introduced and when an old one is restored. Different kinds of politics can be good or bad prospectively in a monarchy and/or in a republic. If one casts only a cursory glance at Shakespeare's plays, one finds the corroboration of Machiavelli's wisdom. In the Roman plays, politics means something different for the patricians and for the plebeians, for the triumvirs and for the tyrannicides. Yet, in comparison to the perception of politics of English kings, dukes, and the citizens of London, the perception of politics of all the Roman actors appears to be very similar. Machiavelli says that neither the saint nor the devil can be good at politics. In fact, both goodness and wickedness result in political disaster. So it happens in Shakespeare. Henry VI (the saint) and Richard III (the devil) together will ruin England.

Machiavelli speaks of personal character traits, emotions, and passions as representative, accidental factors in political history. Opinions, judgments, and passions can be separated only superficially and artificially. They are normally indistinguishable, whether to the better or to the worse. Jealousy, envy, fear, the desire for power, wealth, flesh, and revenge are almost always as indistinguishable from the capacity to judge, from a healthy sense of danger, from good and bad judgment of character as are compassion, forgiveness, sense of loyalty, and love. In Shakespeare this indistinguishability is not merely articulated and described; rather, this creed is embodied in the characters—in their actions, wisdoms, follies, and fates. What was "prior" in Othello's tragic fate: his lack of judgment or his jealousy? What was prior in Edmund's wickedness: his ressentiment, his cleverness, or his hunger to be loved? And what was prior in Rosalind: her sense of justice, the independence of her mind, her wit, or her great capacity to love and to understand others? In Shakespeare one can never distinguish between emotion and cognition or volition. While reading Shakespeare, one immediately senses the superficiality of all such psychological distinctions.

The vision of politics is not to be conflated with the content of politics. It never occurred to Shakespeare that the "people" could be wiser, better, or more noble than its leaders, notably its kings and dukes. Machiavelli was a republican who well understood politics in a monarchy; Shakespeare was in favor of a peaceful and "liberal" hereditary monarchy, but he well understood politics in a republic.

The root of all this is Shakespeare's absolute sense of *history*—a sense that characterizes him alone, none before him, and none after him. His Roman patricians are Roman patricians, his English dukes are English dukes, his Roman plebeians are Roman plebeians, and his English rabble is English rabble. Moreover, they could have lived only at the very concrete historical moment when they lived, neither before nor after.

Once, one of Hume's friends expressed his desire to meet a real Roman. Hume answered that nothing is simpler than the fulfillment of this wish. His friend should walk into the pub on the street corner, and there he will meet real Romans. If one reads Shakespeare, this will sound true; however, the opposite is also true. One meets real Romans who are concretely Romans and entirely different from all of our contemporaries. Yet, if we go into the pub on our street corner, we will meet exactly the same persons. Coriolanus, for example, is a Roman patrician through and through. He could not have said what he said, he could not have done what he did, except in the exact historical constellation where his tragedy is played out. I do, however, have a friend who is just like Coriolanus. He is in fact Coriolanus, absolutely, without mistake. And this is Shakespeare's unique secret.

Shakespeare lived in the world of Machiavelli, but he also lived in the world of Montaigne. We know that he read some Montaigne. One can hardly miss the very concrete allusions to Montaigne's essay on friendship in Shakespeare's portrayal of Horatio and of the Horatio–Hamlet relationship. Machiavelli—who in this respect remains true to ancient historians— left a space open in political philosophy and historiography for personal stories and vicissitudes. And Montaigne, whose main interest was to understand characters and personal relationship and to ruminate on existence, life, and death, left a space open for historical and political vicissitudes. Machiavelli's philosophy is a philosophy of action; Montaigne's philosophy is a philosophy of reflection, of a thoughtful and highly individualized, "subjective" contemplation. Both are present in Shakespeare's dramas.

Shakespeare's most significant heroes are subjective, in the sense that they deepen, by constant reflection, the so-called internal space of their personality. Shakespearean characters are multidimensional; one of their dimensions is the internal space, another is their situatedness, their historicity or temporality. Some aesthetic theories contrast Shakespeare's dramas, as "character dramas," with the Greek tragedies, as "tragedies of destiny." As Hegel observed, being a character is not identical with being an individual. The Greek heroes had individuality. Hegel puts the works of Shakespeare into the cluster of romantic (Christian) art, because in Shakespeare spirituality breaks the strictness of the form. Shakespeare is indeed a romantic author in this sense, although not in any other. His dramas are certainly character dramas insofar as the characters become the authors or the coauthors of their own destinies and are not simply the manifestation of their destinies. This is how and why history and character as historicity differ entirely from myth and mythic individuality. Shakespeare's heroes and heroines are entirely different from all other characters (frequently also from their other, former, or later selves), yet they are also always historically concrete. But how can this be? I can recognize my friend in Coriolanus, but I do not think that any one of us would recognize her neighbor in Electra or Antigone. Mythical heroines and heroes can be individuals, yet they are neither historical nor personal. They do not belong "there," nor do they belong "here." They are individuals through the portrayal of their scene of suffering, their recognition scene, and *dianoia* (as Aristotle observed it); but they are never invented or reinvented because they never invent or reinvent themselves. There are borderline cases such as Euripides' Medea, but Euripides is in many ways out of touch with his own tradition. Many of the Shakespearean characters are constantly inventing and reinventing themselves, although Shakespeare borrows their raw portrayal and their stories from Holinshed, Plutarch, and others. Shakespeare has them invent and reinvent themselves, in the sense that he transforms individuals into multidimensional characters, into persons who are historical. Yet, these persons are also our next-door neighbors, they are—let me spell it out—*ourselves*. We are not Antigone, neither are we Oedipus (even if we are suffering an Oedipal trauma), and none of us is Clytemnestra or Orestes. But we are Shakespearean heroes and heroines; Shakespeare reinvents us as well. Harold Bloom expresses the common experience of all lovers of Shakespeare in the introduction of his book *Shakespeare: The Invention of the Human*. He addresses the readers with the following words: "We need to exert ourselves and read Shakespeare as strenuously as we can, while knowing that his plays will read us more energetically still. They read us definitively."

The internal space is unlike Pandora's box. It can be opened and locked up again. The spectator (the audience) observes the actors on the stage and hears their voices. The contents of the internal space are not fixed once and for all. Something might suddenly appear as the essence of a man that was never there (in the internal rooms) before. But how can something appear that was not there, even in the form of *dynamis* or potentiality? Something is in constant flux in the internal rooms of Shakespearean characters. We could perhaps speak with Husserl of a halted stream of consciousness whose appearance is caused repeatedly by acts of intentionality. The internal space manifests itself in action, but one cannot know for sure whether or not it is an authentic manifestation, whether action masks or unmasks the actor. Sometimes not even the actor can be sure. But there are moments when he or she seems to be sure, perhaps sure about uncertainty. This happens in the festive moments when the actor, the character, discloses himself to the audience.

There is no soliloquy in Greek tragedy. Ideas, thoughts, and convictions clash in dialogues. It is mainly in dialogues that characters disclose themselves. This happens frequently also in the dramas of Shakespeare. Transparent characters—for example, moralists like Horatio and Brutus—have no monologues: they can disclose themselves in dialogues. But, if the internal space is not transparent, even the fully conscious character does not need to present himself entirely in a dialogue. Frequently, the character presents his personality in a monologue or a dialogue (or a few dialogues): the characters appear from different perspectives, different also for themselves, and the images do not always match. Just as the same character can be or appear as a different character in dialogue with different interlocutors, and not just for the interlocutors but also for himself, so can he be or appear different when speaking to himself. The role of soliloquy is central. Not all Shakespearean heroes are given the gift of soliloquy, the possibility or the need to speak with themselves, to think in solitude yet also to take the spectators into their confidence.

Soliloquy is in general the manifestation of the multidimensionality and modernity of Shakespearean characters. Still, there are as many kinds of monologues as there are reasons one can have not to disclose oneself to others. It can mean absolutely different things to disclose oneself. It happens that a character cannot disclose his plans because they are evil and must be concealed in order to be carried out successfully, as in the grand monologues of Richard, the Duke of Gloucester, both in *3 Henry VI* and in *Richard III*. In another type of monologue, the character presents himself with different options for action and ruminates about his choices. This inner dialogue is similar to the Aristotelian *boulesis:* there are two persons in one, and the two persons entertain different opinions. Different emotions or passions can fuel both options (as in the case of Antony). There is a kind of soliloquy where two heterogeneous persons are battling within the soul of a man. One of them might be the impartial judge, the conscience, as well as a provider of alien truth or opinion (e.g., Hamlet and Richard II). There is a merely reflective soliloquy: a man takes respite from the tumult of the world, withdraws, thinks about existence, takes the position of a spectator (as does Richard II). Sometimes, although very rarely, a person exclusively assumes the position of a spectator. This person has many monologues and only a few dialogues (such as Jaques in *As You Like It*).

The position and formal structure of a monologue can serve us only as a compass in the jungle of Shakespearean complexity. For instance, when two persons in one conduct a monological dialogue about something done that cannot be undone, this "something" can be a missed opportunity, a fatal mistake, a sin, a lucky resolve, or many other things. The conviction that what has been done cannot be undone can also be false, as in *Cymbeline* or in *The Winter's Tale*. Some monologues are means of characterization, but there are as many different characterizations as characters.

I will discuss Shakespeare as philosopher of history and political philosopher in two different steps or approaches. In the first part, I unpack the sentence "The time is out of joint" in general. What does it mean that the time is out of joint? What are the manifestations of this disjointed time? In the second and third parts, I continue by offering my readings of a few Shakespearean political dramas. In Part II I choose *Richard II, Henry VI (1, 2, 3),* and *Richard III* from the English history plays; and, in Part III, *Coriolanus, Julius Caesar,* and *Antony and Cleopatra*—all three Roman tragedies. I proceed with my discussion following the actual historical sequence of the times covered in the plays, rather than in the order in which the plays were written. Although *Henry VI* and *Richard III* belong to the earliest dramas by Shakespeare, I will discuss them after *Richard II*. Similarly, I offer the reading of *Coriolanus* first, although it was written near the end of Shakespeare's authorship. When possible, I avoid making references to Shakespeare's time and the political function of some of the history plays in the context of his own time (too obvious in the case of *Richard II*), because if one focuses on the conflation of "being modern" and "being historical" as I do, any age in the modern world can take the place of Shakespeare's. As Queen Elizabeth and the theatergoers of London recognized themselves in *Richard II,* so theatergoers in the 1940s identified Richard III with Hitler and, a decade later, with Stalin. Hence the felt horror as well as the expectation of the despot's inevitable doom. Shakespeare was and remains our contemporary.

PART I

THE TIME IS OUT OF JOINT

1

What Is Nature? What Is Natural?

One can only agree with E. M. W. Tillyard's observation in *Political Shakespeare* that Shakespeare hardly mentions the cosmic order. The cosmic order was taken for granted. Neither has Shakespeare created a metaphysical space or a metaphysical order. His sense of order, particularly his sense of spatial order, is closer to the Renaissance than to the baroque. His tragic vision is not apocalyptic but strictly historical. Unusual and menacing events, natural catastrophes, or irregularities such as tempests and miscarriages are frequently read by the Shakespearean characters as *signs* of current political evils or *signals* of forthcoming historical change, but they have no cosmic significance. True, Ulysses (in *Troilus and Cressida* 1.3) refers to the cosmic hierarchy. But he does this only to support his commitment to social hierarchy, to the order of subordination/superordination that must be obeyed: tradition is here presented as natural. Mainly superstitious men, and not even very clever ones, believe in superhuman cosmic–divine intervention in the case of an inexplicable or extraordinary natural event (such as Cinna in *Julius Caesar*). Ghosts, witches, fairies, and elves intervene in human action; their interventions frequently have political significance for the actors and thus trigger sequences of political actions. This happens in tragedies like *Hamlet* or *Macbeth*, in comedies like *A Midsummer Night's Dream*, and in romances such as *The Tempest*. The fairy-tale-like forest in *A Midsummer Night's Dream* appears malevolent and wicked to the lovers; but it is enchanted by Puck, the cosmic impostor who can also extract its magic. The tale includes all the tragic matters that can only be placed in a politicohistorical drama: a royal wedding, paternal tyranny, conflict between the king and queen, revenge, and extreme humiliation. I agree with Jan Kott, who writes in *Shakespeare, Our Contemporary,* that *A Midsummer Night's Dream* is a story of extreme terror. All the same, it is surrounded by an aura of lightness. For the bad dream is just a dream, and if one wakes up to a life of happiness, the dream is "so musical a discord, such sweet a thunder" (*A Midsummer Night's Dream* 4.1.117) that it can also remain beautiful in our remembrance.

The time is out of joint. This is, however, only historical time and not cosmic time. There is no cosmic or divine intervention in the Shakespearean theater. This sounds perhaps a bit odd. Shakespeare's tragedies are, after all, telling us stories of retribution. They show us crimes that are met by punishment; they portray sinners who end their miserable lives as victims of their own sins. They allow us to listen to curses that fall upon the heads of the guilty. I do think, however, that the acts done by Shakespeare's heroes tell us more about the fictions created or believed in by the characters themselves than about Shakespeare's own vision. It is true that almost all the murders will be avenged either directly or indirectly, the tyrants will meet their violent death sooner or later, and the curses will take effect. The evil individuals face retribution; at least, this is what the spectator perceives. However, many curses in Shakespeare do not take effect. Several predictions never come true; and although the murderers meet a violent death, so do many innocent men, women, and children. Goneril and Regan perish, but so do Cordelia and the young princes, who have done no harm. The good die along with the wicked. In a sense, Shakespeare's dramas force the attentive spectator to face the old paradox of divine providence, familiar since the prophet Amos. Why does God allow the innocent to suffer and perish along with the wicked? Shakespeare does not ask this question. His history is not providential; in his history, contingency rules amid regularities. In his history there is nothing paradoxical in the suffering of the innocent; it is the result of human wickedness, of tough luck, of the unhappy coincidence of heterogeneous factors. There is no meaning here, only misery. Such is the world. This is history. Such is human character.

Several predictions in Shakespeare's plays come true—for example, Henry VI recognizes in the young Richmond the future redeemer of England. Such predictions were important for Shakespeare's audience, as they are also for us, if not exactly for the same reasons. We love to listen to predictions that we know will come true. We love to listen to curses that we know will take effect in due time. We love to know what the actor hopes and desires; and we love to indulge in the sense of fulfillment when the actor is still lingering in the state of expectation. This is why we, the spectators, do not hear, or rather do not notice, those curses that will never take effect or those predictions that will never come true. Why does Shakespeare do this to us, or rather allow his characters to do it to one another? Why does he put curses in someone's mouth if he knows, just like all his contemporaries, that those curses will fail to take effect? Likewise, why does he allow his heroes to predict or prophesy events that will never come true?

Had he put into the mouths of his heroes only prophecies that were later confirmed, he would have made a case for the total predictability of history. The false prophecies are there for a purpose; they testify to the unpredictability of the historical future. Shakespeare is not ready to sacrifice something that he believes to be true about history for the sake of rhetorical effect.

Furthermore, the predictions and prophecies in Shakespeare's history plays serve a purpose beyond the satisfaction of the spectators' desire to be confirmed in their expectations: they characterize the interplay between actor and situation. In despair and extreme distress, men and women prophesy the downfall of their enemies and the victory of their own cause, simply to vent their rage or indignation, to strengthen their resistance, to amass courage in the face of death. In extreme situations a man can raise himself up to a higher level of insight. The strong desire for revenge or justice or the vindication of one's honor and name is translated into the language of prophesying, cursing, or solemn prediction. Men and women who are on the verge of death, who are devastated or impoverished or in utmost misery, are like beggars asking for alms. They beg the future to grant them the foresight of vindication and satisfaction; they beg the future to grant them not just some alms but full satisfaction.

It also happens in Shakespeare's history plays that a political event looks so important for a character that he begins to celebrate it as a great turning point in history that everyone will remember. Some of these rhetorically celebrated events, in fact, will be remembered as historical turning points. Yet not all of them are. And we fail to react in Shakespeare's plays to the same rhetoric if the celebrated event comes to naught. This is also "human, all too human." One always needs to keep in mind that in Shakespeare history is not neatly rational. If all predictions were to come true, one would get the false impression that there is regularity in history, that there are "laws" of history. Shakespeare does not entertain such an illusion.

Still, one is justified in speaking of Shakespeare's vision of history. Although there is no grand narrative, Shakespeare does something more in his history plays than merely to stage single histories. First, his stories are sequels that cover crucial historical periods chosen by Shakespeare with a historopoetic purpose. The English plays cover the Wars of the Roses from their prelude to their end (not to *Henry VIII,* but to the conclusion of *Richard III. King John* does not belong to the sequence). One could hardly speak of a linear history here, for there is no accumulation of either the good or the bad. Nor can one speak of a cyclical history; there is no *corsi e ricorsi.* At the end of *Richard III* we do not return to the first act of the story of *Richard II* where everything began. Some lessons can, however, be drawn. One can no longer conduct politics as if the Wars of the Roses had not occurred. Shakespeare would not fully subscribe to Hegel's dictum that the sole thing one learns from history is that nothing was ever learned from it. Although he was a skeptic, Shakespeare believed that by presenting stories about the past he could warn the queen so that she could avoid repeating her predecessors' mistakes.

Even the Roman plays form a sequence, although this is less obvious than with the English chronicle plays. It is in *Coriolanus* that the plebeians first appear on the scene as political actors. In *Julius Caesar* their rioting takes events in the opposite direction after the murder of Caesar, and they chase the tyrannicides out of Rome. And finally, in *Antony and Cleopatra* it becomes clear that the clever and cold politicking of Octavius Caesar meets the approval of the already pacified plebes, who are by then more interested in looting foreign countries than in republican freedom. This sequel also leads somewhere, for we do not return to the beginning. The very questionable freedom of the plebeians (questionable for Shakespeare, of course) is, on the one hand, preserved but, on the other hand, destroyed. The world of patricians is entirely past and buried. Histories lead in a direction in both the English and the Roman plays, and one thing in the outcome is welcomed by Shakespeare: peace. Richmond ends the tragedy of *Richard III* with the declaration that "peace lives again," and Augustus promises peace with the end of the civil war, the world where Christ was born.

Constructing history in the sequences of histories gives Shakespeare the opportunity to distinguish between history and politics. One can fail politically yet win in the long run. A defeat can become a lesson, and a lesson can turn into a defeat. Politics counts in a short-term victory; history is a long(er)-term vindication.

On the level of personality portrayal, Shakespeare presents two metaphorical ladders: the ladder of grandeur and the ladder of morality. One can be placed high up on the one and still be placed on a lower level on the other. For example, in *Hamlet* Hamlet is at the top of the ladder of grandeur, whereas Horatio is at the top of the ladder of morality. In *Julius Caesar* Caesar is at the top of the ladder of grandeur, and Brutus is at the top of the ladder of morality. One can observe similar hierarchies in comedies, although here the two metaphorical ladders frequently merge into one, for grandeur is measured by a different yardstick in the tragedies and history plays.

Shakespeare's characters can also occupy different places on another pair of metaphorical ladders: those of history and politics. One can stand high on the ladder of history yet occupy a low rung on the ladder of politics, and vice versa. For example, Richard II is placed higher on the ladder of history, Bolingbrook on the ladder of politics; Coriolanus on the ladder of history, Menenius on the ladder of politics. Here, too, the two metaphorical ladders can merge, and in a few plays no single character ends up at the top of any of the ladders—"ends up," indeed. For Shakespearean characters are never ready-made: they slide down or climb up; they turn around; they can be alienated from themselves. On which step of those ladders the

Shakespearean characters are placed is known only when it is all over.

Neither the long-term historical vindication of political failures nor the short-term political victories, however, are attributed to providence or any kind of divine intervention. The sequence of events as well as historical memory evaluates, distinguishes, judges, and vindicates in a nonmoral sense. There are no signs in Shakespeare of a *deus absconditus* working behind the scenes. While "secularizing" the paradox of the unfathomable divine justice (the innocent perish along with the guilty), Shakespeare writes the dramas of an almost unpredictable history.

But if history is unpredictable, why did I compare Shakespeare to Machiavelli? Machiavelli has established, after all, some regularities in political history. And if there are regularities in political history, then one can predict certain developments by employing the scheme of conditional necessity ("if this is the case, then this will in all probability follow"). Certainly, these kinds of regularities can also be observed in Shakespeare. But Shakespeare is less interested in regularities than in the uniqueness of an action, in personal (chance) encounter and interplay, and in the impact of personalities on one another and thus on the development of events. Shakespeare's use of a historical microscope and telescope is crucial in his distinction between history and politics—for example, between long-term vindication of an act or idea and disastrous political defeat. Politics is always measured by the results of actions, history by their quality. But there is no return to the beginning, and one cannot trace a unidirectional motion in the sequence of events.

Let me spell out what the secularization of the paradox of divine justice and the absence of even a deus absconditus means for the dramatic structure of Shakespeare's history plays: nothing in history depends on divine presence or absence. This is one of the crucial differences between the Greek drama and the Shakespearean. This is strange, for even much later, for example, in Molière's comedies such as *L'Avare* and *Tartuffe,* Providence appears sometimes as deus ex machina to cut the Gordian knot that no character can disentangle.

In spite of his absence as actor from the structure, action, and development of a Shakespearean drama, God can still be a strong presence in them. His presence manifests itself in and through the faith, imagination, and morality of the characters who believe in him. It is also made manifest through the voices of their consciences, their grief, and their repentance. Yet there is only an earthly stage: the historical, political, personal stage. The stage is down here, in our midst. The success or failure of actions is decided on this stage. Yet one can act here in very different ways, depending on whether one lifts one's face upward or casts glances down to the earth alone. In politics, Shakespeare believes, one should not lift one's face only up to the heavens, because the political stage is down here, not up there.

But it is better to lift one's face upward from time to time, to measure one's action also by the laws of the King of Kings, the Judge. There is no transcendent stage, no divine theater; yet there is an absolute Measure and a just Judge beyond the historical stage. This is how (and perhaps why) the most significant Shakespearean heroes have the privilege to appear and to play their act in another theater, the theater of *the naked existence*.

Machiavelli constantly distinguishes between the politics of a legitimate ruler and those of an illegitimate one. The legitimate ruler has a smoother part to play because he is supported by the power and inertia of tradition. There is no single Shakespeare play where the legitimate ruler can rely successfully upon tradition or inertia. There is a legitimate king (Richard II) who is forced to resign, another (King Lear) who resigns, one (King John) who is excommunicated by the pope. There are many legitimate princes (mainly in comedies and in nontragic dramas) who miraculously escape death, are forced into exile, and at the happy end return to power even more miraculously. The illegitimate ruler who grasps power by force, violence, and evil design is most often the brother of the legitimate ruler (Claudius in *Hamlet* and Antonio in *The Tempest*, Frederick in *As You Like It*). And one can wonder why fratricide or attempted fratricide (the Cain–Abel pattern) is so central in Shakespeare's fantasy—far more central than patricide. Among the English kings who rule successfully until the end of their days, only Henry V can raise a claim to legitimacy; but his is also a weak claim. His father seized the crown of England by force from the legitimate ruler, and he himself was considered by his father to be a misfit. The time is out of joint. The usurpers of the English throne grasp the crown by ruse and force, and they know what they are doing; yet they want to preserve semblances. Every usurper has his own genealogy ready, his own so-called true claim to the royal title.

There are two rights, and those two rights clash. Neither is taken for granted by all the actors. There is the naturally given right of a man who is as shrewd as a fox and brave as a lion (or so he thinks) and who is better fitted to occupy the throne than the anointed king. And there is the right of the anointed king (even if he is unlike a fox or a lion) who has inherited the crown from his father and the father of his father. The usurpers raise a claim to the throne by *the right of nature,* the law of nature, because the best (the fittest) has the right to rule. Still, the claim of tradition is powerful, so the self-made kings must shape their ambitions to fit this claim. They refer to obscure genealogies, to their ancestral rights. Shakespeare stresses this point superbly, for example, in his little satire play inserted into the story of King Henry VI, the Cage rebellion. Cage—who is in Shakespeare's portrayal just a stupid brute—also raises "legitimate" claims to the throne on the basis of his forged descent.

The time is out of joint, yet even while it remains so, claims of legitimacy, themselves based upon genealogy, prevail. Two kinds of rights confront one another. One can justify one's ambitions either by the first or by the second, but not by both. Many Shakespearean characters will indeed attempt to use both. The crisis of legitimacy is the crisis of the *double bind*.

At the end of the Wars of the Roses cycle, the audience listens to entirely different music. Richmond, Henry VII, promises liberty and justice since he has called men in arms against "the wretched, bloody, and usurping boar." And then he adds, "All for our vantage, Then in God's name march! —true hope is swift and flies with swallow's wings; —Kings it makes gods, and meaner creatures kings" (5.2). *Sors bona, nihil aliud!* There is no legitimacy claim to rule, but a legitimacy claim to dethrone the bloody tyrant: legitimation through liberation. This is how the cycle of the double bind can end: in a new arena where the issue of *what someone is going to do* with his power will outweigh the question of *how he has grasped it*. This is why Shakespeare could not write a tragedy about history after *Henry VII*. The latest history play, *Henry VIII,* could not possibly be a good one. The double bind, the insoluble tension between two legitimacy claims, the clash between the premodern and the modern world, is the tragic situation that Shakespeare found, explored, poetized, and eternalized. In the Roman plays the question of legitimacy appears as the conflict between justifications and rights. The old (traditional) rights, justifications, and institutions clash with new ones in *Coriolanus* and *Julius Caesar,* whereas in *Antony and Cleopatra* Shakespeare adds a new dimension to the conflict: the irreconcilable clash between the East and the West. Yet in all these cases (as also in tragedies like *Hamlet, Lear,* and *Macbeth*) the tragedy unfolds around the conflict inherent in the double bind. Is it natural to have an illegitimate son? Is it natural to treat him as if he were legitimate? Is it natural to introduce draconian legislation against nature (as in *Measure for Measure*)? Is it natural to serve a wicked master or a foolish master, or does acting naturally mean loyalty at all costs? Is it natural when a woman incites her husband to murder out of love? Is it natural when a girl obeys her father and betrays her lover? Hamlet accuses his mother—among others—of being unnatural for preferring an ugly, undignified swine to a chivalrous and beautiful man (her husband). Laertes does not suffer under the double bind, but Hamlet does. Lear offers legitimacy to two of his daughters and disinherits one. All three daughters are untraditional: they live according to the law of nature, and in this respect there is no difference among them. The only difference is that Cordelia is good "by nature," whereas Goneril and Regan were born evil. Is Love the law of nature, or is it rather power or sex? These are the questions. The same questions will be repeated many times after Shakespeare—by Rousseau and Sade to name just two.

The time is out of joint. Shakespeare portrays the double bind and the tragedies revolving around it. The double bind is not just a personal matter, although it can tear a person apart, as it does Hamlet. The double bind is historical and becomes the undercurrent of politics in many Shakespearean plays (including many of the comedies).

In the history plays, the question of what is natural revolves first around the conflict between the right of nature and the inherited rights; but Shakespeare never stops at this level. Whenever the question of the right of nature is raised, the question "What is human nature?" must also be raised. The foundations of the other right (what legitimacy means, what tradition is) can be known, or at least explored and deciphered. So can the ways to live up to the obligations resulting from traditional rights. In Shakespeare's moral code, living up to the obligations that follow from traditional rights boils down to maintaining and defending one's honor. For a soldier, fighting well is the traditional obligation; if he fights valiantly, he preserves his honor. For a republican (like Brutus), remaining true to the virtues of the citizens of the old republic, dying virtuously, is a matter of honor. It is easy to repeat the old wisdom of Aristotle: nature is what different people with different constitutions all share. The desirability of living according to tradition was a commonly shared conviction in Shakespeare's time; but he had eyes for the uncommon. The uncommon was challenging, new, interesting, dynamic. And the uncommon posed unanswerable questions to the poet. If one strips away tradition, what remains? What is under the garment? What is human nature? What is the human nature to which one refers so lightly when speaking of "natural rights" or "the laws of nature"? What are they? On what ground can one take them as if they were granted in the same manner as matters of tradition and honor? In both his tragedies and his comedies, Shakespeare confronts the *whatness* of human nature, the whatness to which so many references are made but which itself is shrouded in darkness. Shakespeare lights some spots in this darkness. He explores the extremes. He knows that for men and women everything is possible, that all "combinations" are options, that there are perhaps no limits. Or are there limits? I think that there are and that Shakespeare will make us turn back to face those limits again and again. Shakespeare confronts honesty with honor; honesty is a matter of conscience, of obeying the call of conscience. But what is the content of conscience? What does *conscience* know? And how does it know what it knows?

The double bind is not ethically evaluated, nor is the commitment to both or the commitment to one or the other of the clashing concepts of nature. Many Shakespearean heroes are great—among other things—because they cannot choose between the two rights, the two interpretations of natural, or because they choose both. This is the case with Hamlet and Lear, with Queen Margaret, and in another context with Antony. There are as many entirely different kinds of entanglements and entirely different ways to cope with them as there are characters. Some other Shakespearean heroes and heroines, however, choose—and sometimes they choose absolutely. The choice is not presented as a choice between good and evil, but as a choice between different kinds of good and evil, different interpretations of virtues and vices, between falling into or avoiding different pitfalls.

Men and women who are inclined do to evil will interpret both natural rights and traditional rights—whichever they choose—as permission or legitimation for doing evil, whereas men and women inclined to decency or goodness will interpret either natural rights or inherited rights as permission or legitimation for acts of goodness or decency, as a support of honesty or honor. Shakespeare does not disentangle interpretation or self-interpretation from moral or immoral desire. "Which comes first?" is but a theoretical question. And nothing is fixed as "first"; there can always be surprises.

There is an important difference, however, between choosing inherited rights and the concept of natural law. Tradition offers less space for doing something new or reinventing one's character. A purely traditional man, whether good or evil, will therefore not occupy the central place in Shakespeare's dramatic compositions. Yet, a traditional man also needs good moral luck in a world where time is out of joint, since the price for naïveté can be high. Here is Adam, the most loyal servant to Orlando in *As You Like It*. Orlando says: "O good old man, how well in thee appears / The constant service of the antique world, / When service sweat for duty, not for meed!" (*As You Like It* 2.3.57–59). Adam is a good, loyal character. But he also has good luck: his master, Orlando, is an honest man, and as a result his traditional ("antique") service is not misplaced. Villains can also have loyal servants. After all, Rosencrantz and Guildenstern served Claudius, and did so loyally, as did Polonius. The sadistic torturer Cornwall's servant, however, rebels, and he rebels with words that reconfirm tradition: "Hold your hand, my lord. / I have served you ever since I was a child, / But better service I never have done you / Than now to bid you hold" (*King Lear* 3.7.70–72). For this greatest service he pays with his life.

Strong desires and passions less frequently motivate crimes or evils based on, or resulting from, the traditional perception of being "natural." Crimes and evils that result from the absence of thinking or from taking everything for granted are more typical here. For someone who obeys without thinking, someone who does something because others are doing it, without asking whether it is right or wrong—for this man Denmark is not a prison.

I said previously that Shakespeare never presents the choice between two concepts of natural as the choice between good and evil. Now I would like to pose the question, With whom does Shakespeare side in the conflict between the two conceptions of the natural? Does he side with the concept of natural as it appears in the ideas of natural right, or with the concept of natural that identifies nature with tradition? I think that Shakespeare is first and foremost curious, that he wants to get to the bottom of things, never presenting an argument without the man or woman who defends it with his or her life. Still, the fact that the heroes of his tragedies (and most of his comedies) are men and women who cannot escape the double bind, and who interpret and invent themselves with the help of the idea of both tradition and natural right, intimates that Shakespeare finds characters subject to the double bind the most interesting and their secrets most worthy of exploration.

Let me return briefly to the two concepts of natural. The first concept identifies tradition with nature. It is natural that daughters obey their fathers (thus Ophelia and Miranda behave "naturally," whereas Desdemona, Juliet, and Cordelia do not). It is natural that wives subordinate their wishes to their husbands' (thus Titania offends tradition in refusing to grant Oberon's wishes). It is natural that brothers should love one another (the hatred between Henry VI's uncles is unnatural) and protect their sisters (Laertes behaves naturally, Claudio unnaturally). It is natural that estates and titles should be inherited by legitimate sons, that men and women should live out their lives fully, that young men should die on the battlefield fighting the enemy of their country or grow old and die a natural death. It is natural to use one's power absolutely, yet it is unnatural to misuse it. It is also natural to forgive. "Natural" is thus identical with a hierarchical order where the God-anointed king sits on his uncontested throne, where everyone has a place allotted by birth. Once born into a social role, one does everything in one's power to do well what one should, until death. All these are also natural to Shakespeare.

According to the second concept of natural, it is natural that everyone succeed according to his talents and not according to his rank. Our body is *as it is* natural, as well as our spirit. So also are our ambitions natural, and our resolve to make a place for ourselves with the help of our naturally given talents. It is also natural to follow our desires, to love someone whom we desire and who pleases us most. Freedom is natural, for we are born free. "Natural" is the contingent gift with which nature endows the individual. All these are also natural to Shakespeare.

Order is natural, but so can disorder be; tradition and loyalty are natural, but so is the quest for personal freedom and the self-realization of one's best capacities. *Everything is natural for Shakespeare—and nothing is.*

The dialogue between Perdita and Polyxenes in *The Winter's Tale* formulates Shakespeare's deepest convictions about nature. Perdita: "For I have heard it said / There is an art which in their piedness shares / With great creating nature." Polyxenes: "Say there be, / Yet nature is made better by no mean / But nature makes that mean. So over that art / Which you say adds to nature is an art / That nature makes. . . . This is an art / Which does mend nature—change it rather; but / Art itself is nature." Perdita: "So it is."

Polyxenes: "Then make your garden rich in gillyvors, / And do not call them bastards" (*Winter's Tale,* 4.4.87–98).

This is the philosophy in Shakespeare's poetry: there is no human nature without art; yet art is human nature, provided that it changes nature by means of nature itself. There is a limit to art, and this is nature; and there is a limit to nature, and this is art. Each and every flower is the garden of the world, and history is both nature and art.

There can be beautiful "bastards" (the concept of natural right), as we also encounter a metaphorical royal garden unkempt and uncared for by a legitimate king. Thus we learn in *Richard II:* "[O]ur sea-walled garden, the whole land / Is full of weeds, her fairest flowers choked up, / Her fruit trees all unpruned, her hedges ruined, Her knotes disordered, and her wholesome herbs / Swarming with caterpillars?" (*Richard II,* 3.4.44–47).

Whatever Shakespeare's personal judgment was, his most fascinating heroes and heroines are the nontraditional ones, be they evil or good, comic or tragic. They question, confront, and ridicule at least one crucial thing, and quite often absolutely everything that is believed to be natural in the traditional order. In what follows, I will briefly illustrate the modern natural law or natural right theory with the words of three of their most determined Shakespearean advocates: Falstaff, Juliet, and Edmund.

Listen to Falstaff who, while on the battlefield, makes a few comments on the main traditional virtue of the feudal order. He speaks about dying for honor's sake: "[H]onor pricks me on. Yea, but how is honor prick me off when I come on? How then? Can honor set a leg? No. An arm? No. Or take away the grief of a wound? No. Honor hath no skill in surgery, then? No. What is honor? A word. What is in that word "honor"? What is that "honor"? Air. A trim reckoning. Who hath it? He that died o' Wednesday. Doth he feel it? No. . . . Honor is mere scutcheon. And so ends my catechism"(1 *Henry IV,* 5.2).

Listen to Juliet speaking on the balcony: "'Tis but thy name that is my enemy. / Thou art thyself, though not a Montague. / What's Montague? It is nor hand, nor foot, / Nor arm, nor face, nor any other part / Belonging to a man. . . . What's in a name? That which we call a rose / By any other word would smell as sweet. . . . Romeo, doff thy name, / and for thy name— which is not part of thee— / Take all myself" (*Romeo and Juliet,* 2.1.80–91).

Listen, finally, to Edmund: "Thou, Nature, art my goddess. To thy law / My services are bound. Wherefore should I / Stand in the plague of custom and permit / The curiosity of nations to deprive me / For that I am some twelve or fourteen moonshines / Lag of a brother? Why 'bastard'? Wherefore 'base', / When my dimensions are as well compact, / My mind as generous, and my shape as true / As honest madam's issue? Why brand they us / with 'base', base bastardy. . . . / Legitimate Edgar, I must have your land" (*King Lear* 1.2.1–16).

As far as the analysis of this passage is concerned, one might as well disregard Edmund's wickedness. Edmund as much as Gloucester uses the theory of natural law to justify his evil design. It is not because Edmund is born a bastard that he is evil, as it is not because of his legitimate birth that Edgar is good. (For example, in the tragedy *King John* the bastard is a loyal and attractive character, whereas the wicked Goneril and Regan are very legitimate daughters of King Lear.) Deep down, Edmund is motivated by envy and jealousy. He is jealous of Edgar not because he is legitimate but because he is good. Edmund sublimates his envy and jealousy, his strongest passions (after the desire to be loved), into rationalization. In Freudian terms, Edmund has no superego and his ego is weak; yet he is cursed with strong and self-destructive desires and passions. He is, however, also very clever and superbly intelligent. He is good at rational argumentation. He uses this cleverness to buttress his weak ego. He succeeds in strengthening his ego with the forceful justificatory argument just quoted. I defend this interpretation on the ground that Edmund (unlike Gloucester) does not justify doing evil. He justifies robbing his brother of his estates and making himself the only master on the ground that estate, rank, and power are *due* to him (by nature), that robbing his brother by slander is just. Interestingly, Edmund even throws his father's love into his basket of self-justification.

All three passages are *arguments* that justify an action. Yet they justify not merely an action but also a general attitude to life, a way of life that defies tradition. The arguments prove that it is not rational to play, or continue to play, a traditional role. They are nominalistic arguments. *Words* like "Montague" or "bastard" or "honor" are just words. They are not the real thing. The real thing is the nature one can grasp: the leg, the arm. It is the nature one can see: the body; the nature one can display: the intellect; the nature that one feels: desire. The desire to live, to love, to gain wealth and power. The past with its customs, preferences, enmities, and friendships is dismissed. For them there is no past. There is only the future, the future of life, love, and power. The act of today is dominated by the future. The three arguments dismiss *causa efficiens,* such as "I was conceived out of wedlock, *I am* a bastard," or "*I am* a daughter of a Capulet who hates the Montagues," or "*I am* a squire who is in duty bound to live and die in honor." This is *not* what they are. They are just *themselves,* their innate potentials and qualities and their resolve to live up to them, to become what they are. But they judge others also according to the others' presumed innate qualities. For Juliet, Romeo is no more a Montague. For Falstaff, Prince Hal is not a prince. For Edmund, only Regan and Goneril exist, who are—as he believes—like himself. Of the three, only Falstaff misses the mark. Juliet and Edmund will be confirmed and Falstaff betrayed.

Juliet, Edmund, and Falstaff employ rationality as a delegitimating device. One can delegitimate something only if one legitimates something else. All three legitimate nature, the law of nature, the right of nature, in their own manner and way. Their rationality differs from that of their environment. Men and women of tradition let themselves be guided and fooled by specters, by mere names such as family, honor, and loyalty to the master.

Argumentative justification of actions and decisions *(dianoia)* is as frequent in Shakespeare as it was in ancient tragedies. Without dianoia there can be no drama as we know it. In Shakespeare, such justifications or rationalizations (be they dialogical or monological) are custom made. Shakespearean characters frequently use symbolic words and value terms ("mere names" in the nominalist interpretation) as argumentative devices, as cards one can always play with the hope of success, as means for their own advancement. (I have mentioned already the typical case in history plays: to forge legitimacy for the hunger of power). Some Shakespearean characters argue exclusively in situations of choice. Others rationally justify themselves retrospectively, in self-defense. Juliet differs from most Shakespearean young women in love. She does not employ mere names for self-justification but stands up against them absolutely. In *All's Well That Ends Well,* Helena manipulates tradition and uses it with the help of her future mother-in-law ultimately to gain the prize she seeks: the love of her beloved. Margaret and Suffolk (a self-made woman and a self-made man) keep up the appearances badly. Their relation is too transparent, but they adhere to the traditional appearances. Juliet and Desdemona, however, throw away all appearances: they wed secretly, without parental permission. Desdemona justifies her marriage after her father has no choice. And there are other kinds of justification. Many a nobleman who behaves like a coward on the battlefield justifies his lack of honor with honor. There are several clever villains in Shakespeare, some of them self-made men, some offspring of royal blood, some men with low ambitions (like Iago).

The most complex Shakespearean characters do not completely accept the natural law argument, nor are they purely traditionalists. They suffer and act under the weight of the double bind, perhaps for moral reasons, perhaps because of their unique responsibilities, perhaps because both arguments are too simple for them to accept. In Hamlet's case all three "reasons" coalesce. The most brilliantly intelligent hero of Shakespeare is by far not the most rational one.

The time is out of joint. There is always reason and unreason in histories. Time is out of joint when reason and unreason are heterogeneous, when actors do not understand what they are doing and understand even less what others are doing or have done.

Shakespeare's history plays are not detective stories, although there are murders everywhere (both actual and potential) and almost everyone is an actual or potential victim. The motives that prompt one man or woman to become a murderer and not another are never clear, nor are the reasons for becoming victimized. The role of accident, chance, or contingency becomes inflated. Contingent acts frequently begin a chain of events, and in this sense the events have no causes. However, the development of the chain of events accelerates toward the end. The chain of events that defies the present and the past as nothing can also end in nothingness. Listen to the way Macbeth, after having named the Thane of Cawdor and having been cheated by the pagan witches, speaks to himself: "My thought, whose murder yet is but fantastical, Shakes so my single state of man that function / Is smothered in surmise, and nothing is / But what is not" (*Macbeth* 1.3.138–41). "Nothing is but what is not" is the strongest possible statement ever made against the past in the present, against the chain of determination, an absolute statement for absolute freedom and absolute nihilism. But we know that nothing came to nothing, that this "nothing is but what is not" is the absolute self-delusion, the absolute betrayal. (Coriolanus will also discover this truth in act 5 of *Coriolanus*.) Never was a great Greek hero betrayed by Apollo or Pythia to the extent that Macbeth is betrayed by the witches. For no promise of a Greek god or goddess has ever stirred the fantasy of absolute freedom, of creating oneself ex nihilo, for nothing is but what is not. In the case of the artist, the *creatio ex nihilo* disregards but does not annihilate. Yet creatio ex nihilo where creatio ex nihilo is also annihilation *and* self-annihilation is absolute irrationality: neither *causa efficiens* nor *causa finalis*. There was no murder more meaningless than the murder of Duncan by Macbeth. True, it was not at the outset meaningless for Lady Macbeth. For her, the deed lost meaning not suddenly, not at the moment of having been committed, but in time.

And this is decisive. For even if there is no full account of the why and the "what for" (why *X* became a murderer and not *Y*), every character is *branded* by his acts: how far a character goes, at which point a character stops (in murder, betrayal, lying, using others, and so on), has absolute significance. For there is a point of no return. A person can invent and reinvent himself or herself. His or her character unfolds, and he or she can start again. Yet after a point (and there is such a point in every Shakespearean tragedy) the character goes into free fall: the acceleration. There is no return from the moment when the free fall begins. This is why Lukács said in the essay "The Metaphysics of Tragedy" (in his *Soul and Form*) that the tragic hero is dead at the moment that he appears on the scene. I on my part do not think so. I think that Shakespearean characters can reinvent themselves to a certain point. Where this point is located in the structure of the drama is another matter. (It is, for example, in *Macbeth* and *King Lear* already in the first scene, but in *Othello* it is only in act 3.) Yet when there is a point of no return, it is the beginning of the free fall. When the acceleration of the free fall begins (and *if* it begins, because it does not always do so), tragic heroes are—in the Lukácsian sense—already dead on furlough. They are as good as dead.

Shakespeare's history dramas and tragedies are similar to detective stories only in a subtle sense, just as a few centuries later Dostoyevsky's novels are. There are crimes and criminals, there is "evil under the sun," there are—to quote Horatio—"unnatural acts" (measured in both senses of the word "natural"). There is blood, cruelty, torture; there are victims, both guilty and innocent. There is also retaliation, revenge, punishment, and sometimes even justice. Yet Shakespeare's tragedies and history plays also differ even from subtle detective stories, because, unlike detective stories, here everything is or at least can be contingent; there is no logic. Although, for a while, we do not know with certainty which of the Karamazov brothers in Dostoyevsky's novel is the patricide, we understand why old Karamazov was (or could be) the victim of murder. But there is nothing in the character of Richard II and Henry VI (not to speak of Macduff's wife and children!) that made them likely targets of vicious murder. To quote Horatio again: "So shall you hear / Of carnal, bloody, and unnatural acts, / Of accidental judgements, casual slaughters, Of deaths put on by cunning and forced cause; / And, in this upshot, purposes mistook / Fall'n on th' inventor's heads" (*Hamlet* 5.2.334–38). Horatio stresses the accidental, casual, and unnatural character of the tragedy. This is not a detective story; this is history.

If the murder is premeditated, the spectator is generally informed about the project far ahead of its execution. If the murder is not premeditated, the spectator is in the position of both the murderer and the victims: he is initiated in the act by the actors. If the murder has taken place in the past, the spectator and the actors are normally in a similar position. Neither of them can know for sure, in some cases, whether the murder took place or, if this is generally known, who the murderer was. To establish the fact of past murders is in Shakespeare's plays almost never possible. It is unimportant, more precisely, to establish them *as facts.* One can call as a witness in the case of Shakespeare Agatha Christie's master detective, Poirot: it is not the facts that are important, but the "little grey cells." Tolstoy did not understand this when he criticized the irrationality of the Shakespearean plots.

Whether the spectator is initiated by the murderer, whether he is an eye-witness, or whether he is a detective participating in unearthing past crimes, he will never find a satisfactory answer to the simple questions about why a certain man or woman becomes a murderer and another the victim. The veil is never entirely lifted. We all know that Shakespeare's dramas are inexhaustible, for no interpretation is final. What is, perhaps, less self-evident, is that we *share the feeling of the hopelessness of final interpretation with the characters of the Shakespearean dramas.* The passionate Hamlet reinterprets his mother's acts at least three times during their confrontation (and

he could go on). Even the cool and constantly politicking Octavius interprets and reinterprets at least three times Antony's and Cleopatra's motivations and personalities. And here the play ends. Even within one single
scene the act and the word of a hero can be interpreted by another in several ways. Othello uses the few minutes before his death for his final self-
interpretation, but this is final only because he dies. We do not know
whether Iago, who at this stage decides to remain silent, accepted this self-
interpretation. We do not even know whether the Venetians surrounding
him did. We who are now alive can accept it and also reject it; we can go
on reinterpreting (reinventing) Othello. We do not need to accept the self-
interpretation of a character at its face value, even when the character seems
as entirely rational and open as Richard Gloucester in his monologues.
Men and women interpret themselves as well as their acts several times, and
always differently. There is no final self-interpretation.

In Shakespeare's vision of history it is not the facts that are important,
but the little grey cells: the way to understand, to think, or imagine the
facts. The worst historiography would be for Shakespeare to believe in one
single interpretation of a fact as in something final. This is the lesson of the
kerchief story in *Othello*. If one sees a handkerchief, one sees this handkerchief. A handkerchief is a thing, a fact. It is here or there; it is in the hand
of one or the other person. To notice the handkerchief and to take it into
account is not yet bad historiography. It is bad historiography to attribute
one single interpretation to a fact (in this case, that Desdemona gave the
handkerchief to her lover), because in doing so, one identifies the fact with
this interpretation and with a theory. And then, finally, in all probability, one
will get the fact wrong. To understand how the grey cells were working in
the mind of an Iago or a Desdemona would have been for Othello good
detective work. Instead, he believed in the single interpretation of a fact
that turned out to be a nonfact. This made him a murderer and led to his
downfall.

How things "really" happened is a relevant question for Shakespeare's
characters and for Shakespeare himself. But "really" is not a fact; it is a space
that allows several interpretations. That Richard Gloucester, later to become
Richard III, was a devious murderer remains no secret as the play (*The
Tragedy of King Richard III*) begins to unfold. At the end of the drama this
fact becomes absolutely clear to everyone, first and foremost because
Richard (at least in Shakespeare's drama) does not even take care to cover
up the traces of his criminal deeds. Shakespeare makes this case absolutely
clear because he wants the spectators to accept his interpretation, which is,
this time, very strong. Shakespeare, however, limits even here only the interpretability of acts, not of motivations and of character. As far as motivations
and character are concerned, Shakespeare makes great allowances for the
free play of our imagination. But *Richard III* is an exception among Shake-

speare's plays. In almost all the others many things remain unresolved, open, uncertain, unfinished—not only for the spectators but also for the characters of the play.

Let us begin with the beginning. The chain of events that continues with the Wars of the Roses is triggered by an accusation. Bolingbrook accuses Mortimer of the murder (or killing) of the Duke of Gloucester, uncle to the king. He also intimates, without spelling it out, that he holds the king responsible for instigating the foul act. Mortimer is accused of murder in the presence of the king. Mortimer defends himself and declares his innocence. The issue is never decided in the drama. We will never get to know the truth about Gloucester's death. Moreover, in the first scene of act 4, the scene from the beginning of the play almost repeats itself, this time before King Henry IV and in an almost comic orchestration. Aumerle (denounced by Bagot) is accused of the same crime. Mortimer is dead, and there is no witness alive—only earls and dukes who believe (or want to believe) in some version of the story.

Here comes the importance of the grey cells. Shakespeare portrays men and women who act on the grounds of their beliefs and pretended beliefs. They perceive as truth what they desire to be true: this is the truth for them. If one hates Mortimer, one believes that he murdered Gloucester; and conversely, if one surmises that he murdered Gloucester, one hates him. The appearance of truth is the truth for those who believe in it. Very few things can be established beyond reasonable doubt, and nothing can be established without doubt. Hamlet is the only representative Shakespearean character who wants to have the whole truth; he does not tolerate the merger of fiction and fact. He is the exact opposite of Othello: he wants to have the "truth" without interpretation; he wants absolute verification. His intellectual absolutism is as absurd as Othello's foolishness. We, as spectators, know this only too well. Without having been taken into the confidence, together with Hamlet, of Claudius's mind (by witnessing the self-indulgent king in his solitary prayer), we could never know whether he was guilty of old Hamlet's murder. *The truth of fact hinges on a silent confession that neither Hamlet nor we could possibly hear.* Shakespeare presents the past in the present, and thought in speech. This foul king in foul prayer is just another specter. But is this important? Claudius is a murderer because he becomes one. And because he becomes a murderer, he is—and has always been—a murderer. The telos of the character is all.

2

Who Am I? Dressing Up, Stripping Naked

The time is out of joint.

The chief characters in Shakespeare's history plays and tragedies problematize their identity. Some do not know exactly who they are, others are torn apart by two or more identities, some others shed their natural identity to become a new person, while yet others assume a new identity to a greater or lesser extent. The same characters also problematize the identity of others. They cease to take the virtues of others at face value, they doubt their loyalty, they need proof in order to trust anyone, and they put their friends (and enemies) on trial. Their greatest treasure is a reliable knowledge of human character. And this treasure is rare.

The Aristotelian concept of substantial identity is not of great help here, because the essence of what we are talking about is not substantial in the Aristotelian sense. According to Aristotle one can attribute everything to an *ousia* (the substance), but ousia cannot be attributed to anything else. Men are finite individual substances. Our substantiality is our identity; and indeed, every person is unique and his uniqueness cannot be attributed to anything else. Moreover, through all change, a person remains identically the same, at least in a biological sense (fingerprints, for example), but also partially in a psychological sense. Yes, *I am I* and *not not-I*. I am Richard, born the son of a prince. I am Henry, born the son of a king. This is not my identity, however, but the raw material of it. What belongs to my identity? What is my substance? Of what does my uniqueness consist? Does my identity include my birth as the son of the Black Prince? Is this essential or accidental? *Can* the fact that I am born the son of the Black Prince be my identity, although I can lose it, while *my substance* is what remains constantly *me? What* remains constant in me, what remains constantly me, if I lose my throne? What remains constantly me if in old age I lose everything I have believed in, and lived for, during my whole life? What am I if I cannot recognize myself in myself? What remains "identical" in King Lear in the tragedy *King Lear?* What makes the "thatness" of this man? *Is* he a king ("every inch a king"), or *is* he a man? *What* man *is* he? In the "human substance" (ousia) one pre-supposes several potentialities (*dynamei*) that are either actualized *in time* or not. Yet in Shakespeare there are sudden changes in a human character that cannot be traced back to previous potentialities. One is normally entitled to believe that potentialities, particularly strong ones, indicate the possible future of a man who becomes what he already is. But this is not the case when time is out of joint. Several characters in Shakespeare, among them Richard II, Macbeth, and Lear, do *not* become what they had (potentially) been. Suddenly Macbeth, the hero, becomes a murderer. Suddenly Lear, the self-indulgent father-tyrant, alienates himself from everything that he ever was.

Every categorization violates the Shakespearean universe simply because in this universe in a crucial sense *identity reigns supreme.* Each Shakespeare-an character is identical with himself or herself. No character is ever repeat-ed; none even closely resembles another Shakespearean character in anoth-er play. It is precisely the complexity of identity constitution, along with the problematization of this identity by the characters themselves and by oth-ers, that allows for unpredictability, diversity, and uniqueness. There can be no token figure in Shakespeare. No person simply represents a cluster of people (the servant or the naïve daughter, for example). Neither can there be individuals who mainly represent a virtue or a vice or a social role alone (for example, the traitor).

Aware that I am guilty of crude simplification, I will try to show that there are, at least structurally, three kinds of personal identities in Shake-speare. The first two identities can be described roughly by the Aristotelian concept of ousia, whereas the third can be described by the Leibnizian con-cept of individual substances.

The first two character types preserve their identity through change. This means, as we know, that there are different potentialities in each person. Some of these potentialities will develop in time, while others will not. In this scenario every present has been a future (of the person) in the past; every present is a present viewed from the future by, and of, the person. One need cast only a glance at the Shakespearean portrayal of Marcus Bru-tus, and it will register that whatever he will do has been preformed already as a potentiality in his character. He has a *heksis,* a firm moral constitution, and this moral constitution limits the ways he may act in the future or react to future vicissitudes. His present has been the future of his past. Horatio will not surprise us, nor will Polonius or Talbot or Malvolio.

I enumerated quite different personalities, both tragic and comic. By comic person I do not mean one who plays a part in a comedy (many per-sons playing parts in Shakespeare's comedies are far from comic, and several persons who play a part in a tragedy are) but a person whose substance—that is, whose identity—is comic. Both Malvolio and Polonius are comic persons, and the identity of both follows the Aristotelian pattern. A person is a comic substance if that which remains identical throughout the changes in their character is the foolishness that inheres in a basic vice. It needs to be mentioned, although I cannot pursue the matter any further, that folly and foolishness are very different in kind, at least in Shakespeare; there can be sacred folly, but not sacred foolishness.

Whether the Shakespearean characters are tragic or comic, the Aristotelian kind of substance identity is constituted in two different forms. First, a person's identity can be preserved through changes in the case of a traditional personality formation, where identity is constituted primarily through the position that the person occupies in a relatively fixed world order. This is the case with Talbot in the tragic pole of characterization, and with Polonius in the comic. In the second type of character with a relatively stable personality core that is preserved through change, identity is constituted primarily by the weight and the morality of the character in question. This is the case of Horatio in the tragic pole of characterization, and Malvolio in the comic pole.

In Aristotle, substance and attributes (subject and predicates) occupy different levels on the scale of being. Substance is a primary being, which is there and cannot be predicated of another being. Yet other kinds of being, such as quality, quantity, space, time, and relation, can be attributed to the primary being. What changes in the primary being is not the first category of being-as-such, but the other categories attributed to the being. If "royal" is a quality of the man, the man can still remain identical, whether he is young or old, naïve or sophisticated, on the throne or in the Tower or on the battlefield. Understood in such a way, the attributes are just accidents *(symbebekoi);* they are accidental to the primary being. All the previously mentioned Shakespearean characters can be described with this pattern.

The Leibnizian concept of individual substances is different. In the philosophy of Leibniz the accident is in the substance, as the predicate is in the subject (this is the principle of *in esse*). Every moment of its life, the individual substance—for example, a man or a woman—is faced with infinite possibilities, with infinite different worlds. In every choice and action, the man or woman dismisses infinite possible worlds and realizes one world among all of them. Yet in the next moment, he or she again faces infinite possible worlds, that is, infinite contingencies. After the individual has chosen or acted, the act itself will inhere in the person. But it does not and cannot inhere in the person before the act. Thus the person never becomes what he already was, since he becomes what he will be. Several Shakespearean characters, such as King Lear, Macbeth, and Richard II, follow this identity pattern.

I now return to an earlier remark: it is not just Shakespeare who problematizes the identity of his chief characters; they themselves will problematize it at one point in their drama. Shakespeare problematizes the identity of his characters frequently through the portrayal of their own self-problematization. The content of self-problematization is most frequently given by the double bind (the conflict between the two concepts of nature and their consequences), yet their kinds and their weight can be very different. Sometimes the collapse of the world conditions the falling apart of the ego; sometimes it happens in reverse. Yet even if the falling apart of the ego results from the collapse of the world and not the other way around, the world—and along with it the ego—collapses *not just because something terrible has happened but because this terrible thing is beyond understanding.*

The weight of self-problematization is least when characters succeed in living with the tensions of dual identity, with the question marks that they carry inside. They can still function well as father, as king, or as wife, as long as they can live with the internal split. Moreover, this internal tension makes them more interesting in their own eyes. The greater the tension that results from sudden or steady loss of the balance of a person's identity, the more it triggers a decisive turning point in his or her world understanding. As a result, the character's actions themselves become unpredictable, not only for the others, but also for the character himself or herself. Finally, a disturbed ego can fall apart entirely; a person's whole life and world can crumble. Sometimes the identity of the self and the identity of the world collapse simultaneously. This is madness. It can be temporary madness if, after the total crisis of identity and the collapse of the world, a man can recover himself from shambles to the point that he can put together another world, although it will be a brittle world. Or, it is possible that the man will uncover a new Archimedean point in the world that can rescue him from madness. Madness can also be permanent, as in the case of Lady Macbeth or Ophelia. One may wonder about the fact that they are both women.

Since categorization always does injustice to Shakespeare, I will instead briefly illustrate the three kinds of identity disturbances—problematizations, disorder, and world loss—identified with three characters from two plays that are not analyzed elsewhere this book, *Henry V* and *Hamlet.*

In *Henry V* the king is in disguise and speaks about himself as if he were not himself. This circumstance is important. Kings normally vent their feelings in monologues about the tension between being a king and being a man. Kings can never speak directly to their subjects thus: "Look, I am just like you!" Shylock could address Venetian Christians who were commoners just like him with such words, but kings cannot do this. Royalty is not just a garment that a king randomly wears. When a king begins to reflect on his royal essence from the viewpoint of natural right alone—when he thinks of royalty as nothingness, vanity, and an empty title—then his whole world has already collapsed. As long as someone is aware of the significance of being a king—as Henry V is and remains—he can think of his royalty in terms of natural law, but only secretly, alone in his private chambers. To be a king is truly not simply to wear a garment. In the medieval tradition that survived the Middle Ages the king has *two bodies:* the body of the king and the body of a man. A body is not a garment. This is why a king cannot address anyone as a king by saying directly, "I am just a man by nature. I have but one single body, my own, and it is just like your body."

When King Henry V speaks in disguise about himself in the third person singular, he can do something that he could not do if he addressed his soldiers directly as their king: he can dismiss the first, royal body of the king and speak about the king as if he had only one body, his natural body. The king speaks (about himself) to his soldiers: "For though I speak it to you, I think the King is but a man, as I am. The violet smells to him as it doth to me; the element shows to him as it doth to me. All his senses have but human conditions. His ceremonies laid by, in his nakedness he appears but a man, and though his affections are higher mounted than ours, yet when they stoop, they stoop with the like wing" (*Henry V* 4.1.100–107). The first body of the king, the royal one, is at least in this address identified with ceremony. A ceremony does not touch the inner regions of one's soul; it is merely external. Only high affection makes the king (not as a king, but as a man) superior to his subjects, and high affection is also human.

Close to the end of his admonition to his soldiers, Henry V says something else, something that seemingly has little to do with his earlier, indirect admission that he is just a man: "Every subject's duty is the King's, but every subject's soul is his own" (*Henry V* 4.1.175–77). This Henry V speaks as though he has perhaps visited the University of Wittenberg or studied *Leviathan* by Hobbes, which was not yet written. This passage contains a shorthand theory of the *inalienability of conscience*. Surely, in Shakespeare this shorthand formula was also meant to be an intervention into daily politics—a Lutheran statement translated into the language of political rights, the freedom of conscience. The king speaks as if he were a general and not a king, as if he had only one body (the natural one), but also as if he still had the full authority to command. In person, he is responsible for the evils of war because he is the commander in chief. Yet every soldier is responsible for what he is doing, for the good and evil alike. This Henry V also could have been Napoleon, a modern Machiavellian king.

In this address there is no sign of the double bind. The king speaks about the king (himself) just as if he were speaking about a man who is surrounded by ceremonies. The king follows closely the arguments of natural law: not the ceremonies but one of his natural propensities (higher affection) lends the king the true power to lead and to command.

Yet Henry sings another tune when he is alone and continues with a rumination, a dialogue with himself. Suddenly, instead of giving merry and confident reports about the human essence of the king, he is plagued by what seems to be self-pity and doubt. If one listens only to the so-called essential content of the monologues, one will find many similarities between the ruminations of Henry IV (2 *Henry IV* 3.1), Henry V, and Henry VI. All three are complaining about the burden of royalty and envy the peace of mind of their subjects. Yet the similarities are superficial both because the messages are to be understood in their respective contexts and because our interpretation of the monologues is just one moment in the interpretation of the character who speaks. Knowing the previous history of King Henry IV, we are not very much touched by his complaints about the burdens of ruling. We hear the melody of an unjustified and pathetic self-pity. After all, Bolingbrook did his utmost (including letting the legitimate king be murdered) to grab the crown, whose weight he now finds too great. In Henry V and Henry VI we encounter rulers who were born to be kings. Listen to the way in which King Henry V talks to himself: "O hard condition, / Twin born with greatness: subject to the breath / Of every fool, whose sense no more can feel / But his own wringing. What infinite heartsease / Must kings neglect that private men enjoy? / And what have kings that privates have not too, / Save ceremony, save general ceremony? . . . O ceremony, show me but thy worth. / What is thy soul of adoration? / Art thou aught else but place, degree, and form, / Creating awe and fear in other men? / Wherein thou art less happy, being feared, / Than they in fearing. . . . No, not all these, thrice-gorgeous ceremony, / Not all these, laid in bed majestical, / Can sleep so soundly as the wretched slave / Who, with a body filled and vacant mind . . . / Never sees horrid night, the child of hell" (*Henry V* 4.1.230–68).

Do we believe this man? The question is not whether we agree with what he says or whether we believe that it is "true," but whether we believe that his monologue is authentic. Can a king like Henry V (the former Prince Hal, Falstaff's pal) feel like this? Does this king interpret himself and his feelings here in such a way that we can accept his sincerity?

The reader can have ears directed only to commonplaces. Power does not bring happiness, so those who fear me (the king) are happier than I am. One is inclined not to give credit to such commonplaces. One is suspicious: if being powerless makes the man happier than possessing supreme power, why does he keep this power? But even such commonplace questions cannot be answered easily in the context of the life story of Henry V, certainly not in historical or political terms. Yet the ideas and acts of kings cannot be discussed unless one also discusses them in these terms.

We learned from the history of Henry V that the king does not simply imagine but knows from experience how men with little political power feel. As Prince Hal, the prodigal son who bears the weight of his father's shame, as the buddy of whores and thieves, he shared the virtues as well as some (if not all) of the vices of the "low" world. In fact, he felt happy in this world. Prince Hal had a good night's sleep and pleasant dreams. Prince Hal had no responsibility; he lived a carefree life, living only for the present, in good humor and wit. Since he once tried to choose the life where there was no power except the power of personality, he felt himself very much at home there.

But the contemporary spectator will raise further objections. Henry has willingly accepted the crown, he has sent his old friend Falstaff into exile, he has changed exactly into the man-of-the-ceremonies whom he now abuses. In political terms such an objection is meaningless. If there is a kingdom, there are kings. Either Henry will be king, or his younger brother will become one. Someone has to wear the crown. Here enters the issue of the double bind. Prince Hal was very much aware that his father was a usurper (he also looks to Heaven for pardon), and he knows that a kingdom can only be secured from civil war if legitimacy is preserved, at least from now on. He cannot possibly resign to let his younger brother rule without guilt. This would be, indeed, the gravest irresponsibility. On the other hand, he knows that if someone acquires some knowledge about human character in the ranks of the lowly, he will be able to profit from it up among the mighty. This is not the case because, after having shared the vices of the base ones, he can now shine in the rays of the virtues of the mighty ones. Whoever interprets Hal in this manner has not understood his references to natural right (we are all equally human). Perhaps the opposite interpretation is true, or at least more true. In experiencing and learning the lowly virtues and lowly vices, which are but trifles, he can now better understand the high virtues and the abominable and dangerous vices of the mighty—since among the mighty, virtues may be shinier, yet vices are more diabolical. Unlike Harun al Rashid, Prince Hal does not need to walk in disguise among the people to find out their wishes, fears, and injuries. Prince Hal knows these things already because he once lived the life of his subjects. Yet, why did he betray Falstaff? Is it true that a king cannot be a king in the company of Falstaff? Why those ugly words of ingratitude, those so well known words, the biblical words that stand for betrayal: "I know thee not, old man" (*2 Henry IV* 5.5.47)? Falstaff's buddy, Hal, could never become Henry V. There was a choice, and Henry chose politically. He chose a historical role and a historical responsibility. He betrayed the man, as he also turned his back on his own self as a young man. It is at this point that he accepted the double bind. Henry played the game according to the rules of Machiavelli. He instrumentalized Falstaff. He needed to present himself as the representative man, as the public figure. And he could present himself as a public figure, as the man of ceremonies, exclusively by dismissing from himself the merely private man along with a part of his self, as well as his old pal Falstaff—the witness and company to this private life. He had no other choice as a king.

Henry accepts the tension between the two conceptions of nature, the two rights, and the two responsibilities, the split in his personality, at the moment when he takes up the royal garment. He comments: "This new and gorgeous garment, majesty, / Sits not so easy on me as you think. / Brothers, you mix your sadness with some fear. / This is the English, not the Turkish court" (2 *Henry IV* 5.2.44–47). He is aware that this garment does not yet fit him well. But this is the English court where Harry follows Harry, which allows legitimacy to be established.

Taking up the new garment, "dressing up" as a king, transforms Harry into another man, into a cruel man. His address to Falstaff is cruel: "I have long dreamt of such a kind of man, / So surfeit-swelled, so old, and so profane; / But being awake, I do despise my dream" (2 *Henry IV* 5.5.49–51). "Awakening" is a religious metaphor for becoming another man. In becoming another man, Harry despises Falstaff. And, although he does not spell it out, he intimates that he also despises his former self. He breaks away from what he was, yet never entirely. He says (to Falstaff), "Presume not that I am the thing I was, / For God doth know, so shall the world perceive / That I have turned away my former self" (2 *Henry IV* 5.5.56–58). The main theme in this sentence is "so shall the world perceive" it. For in public life, as against the private, the most important thing is *how the world perceives.* Harry was cruel. This was the case of the well-committed cruelty. Henry was from the beginning a Machiavellian king.

Yet he never eliminated absolutely his old self. Otherwise, one could hardly understand why he refers to the signum of royalty with the word "ceremony." Otherwise, one could not understand why in his soliloquy he speaks contemptuously of gold and pearls, of the throne, of the titles and the pomp. But is Henry V really jealous of the commoners' peace of mind? Does he really desire peace and the good night's sleep allotted to "private men"? The rhetoric of the text points in this direction, but its music does not. If one listens to the music of the text, one will hear that Henry V does not at all mind suffering horrid nights on the majestical bed, since he suffers on the majestical bed. And he does not really envy the lackey who sleeps in Elysium, because he is a lackey. Public life, burdened life, torn life is the life of grandeur. The happy men have vacant minds and only their bodies are full, whereas grandeur does not go with a full body but with a mind full of pride, ideas, and plans. The body is never full, but the mind is. The tension is life itself. It is better to command than to obey. Henry V in his soliloquy quoted above defies happiness, satisfaction, peace of mind, and a good night's sleep. He has exchanged them all for grandeur's sake and for the sake of history. Henry thinks, with Hegel, that world history is not the territory of happiness. And Henry loves to dwell in this territory.

In his monologue, although he speaks of royalty, Henry contrasts the private and the public. He contrasts private happiness with public greatness. It is a self-indulgent speech veiled as complaint. Still, it is not a speech of self-pity, as it was in the case of Henry IV. Is Henry V sincere? He is, in the manner that he thinks what he says, for he says what he says ironically, or at least also ironically. He is not sincere in the sense that he does not mean what he says literally. Only Henry VI will mean what he says literally, because he wants to shed public responsibility altogether.

Henry V is a historicopolitical drama but not a family drama (even the king's courtship is ceremonial). It is not a tragedy either, for Henry can cope with the double bind. There is a tension in his soul between Hal, the natural man, and the English "Harry, Harry's son"; his second identity will set the limits of his first. This is how Henry reinvents himself.

Henry reinvents himself only once. Then he develops his abilities, he becomes what he was. His *dynamis* becomes *energeia*. Hamlet's double bind is far weightier. He lives in constant tension, he follows at least two masters simultaneously, he reinvents himself constantly. In fact, he reinvents himself in almost every scene prior to the cemetery scene. He surprises his mother, Ophelia, us, and himself. (Only Horatio is not surprised, because he is not surprised by anything.) It is after the cemetery scene that Hamlet finally becomes a person who does not reinvent himself any longer but subjects himself to providence.

Can we imagine Prince Hamlet in Wittenberg? Perhaps we can. In the play, we encounter him immediately in the state of shock, in a grave nervous tension due to a traumatic experience, in an episode of depression. Since he is so much unlike his old self in the eyes of the royal couple, his beloved, and the courtiers, we can assume that he must have previously been a young man of good humor, a brilliant intellect, a good swordsman, who was elegant, merry, and certainly not inclined to melancholy. This is how Horatio, Rosencrantz, and Guildenstern, the play actors, and Ophelia remember him. Listen to Ophelia: "O what a noble mind is here o'erthrown! / The courtier's, soldier's, scholar's eye, tongue, sword / The glass of fashion and the mold of form . . . quite, quite down!" (*Hamlet* 3.1.153–57). That Hamlet studied in Wittenberg is also of some significance. The city of Wittenberg stands for Luther and Lutheranism. It was Luther who never ceased to speak about the internal chambers of the human soul, who never ceased to describe men as *sive iustus et peccator,* who taught that the more one inspects one's own soul and the more virtuous one is, the more vices, the more horrible evils, will he discover hidden deep down in his character and his mind. If we can believe the recollections of his young buddies and young lover after the curtain raise, the Wittenberg study years have not changed Hamlet's soul essentially but perhaps have conditioned the character of his reaction to his trauma. I think of the spiritual condition of a Lutheran young man, ready to problematize not just the world but also himself, to see vices where there are but faults, and to discover foul play when no one yet registers it. This is the spiritual condition for the psychological reversal of moral sequences observed by Freud: to become guilty in order to be temporarily liberated from the irrational sense of guilt.

Add to this spiritual condition a drama where public and private vices are indistinguishable. The family drama of a royal house is a public drama. Everything that happens here is a matter of state. Yet Hamlet's family is not just a ceremonial institution; it is filled with sexual and emotional tensions and conflicting commitments. This drama is also private or intimate. And it is also obscure: both evil and good acts remain hidden, and so do desires and suspicions. The private life of the royal pair is secret; no third party can have insight into it. Yet, the sexual attraction between Claudius and Gertrude is essential to the drama *Hamlet*. Gertrude is the only creature Claudius loves; one can presume that it was for her possession and not for the throne that he became a fratricide. But it is also out of his love for Gertrude that Claudius does not murder young Hamlet, the lawful heir to the throne, immediately and quickly in a Machiavellian manner. It is also obvious that Gertrude is sexually dependent on her second husband, that she is sexually addicted. Hamlet, with his deep insight into human character, notices this addiction. This is why he suggests that his mother should take a sexual detoxification cure: "Refrain tonight, And that shall lend a kind of easiness / To the next abstinence" (*Hamlet* 3.4.152–54).

Needless to say, no Greek tragic author hinted at sexual attraction, let alone dependency, between Clytemnestra and Aegisthus, or between Oedipus and his mother, Jocasta. Greek tragedies—with the exception of a few dramas by Euripides—did not see tension between the private and the public. In fact, the Greek *oikos* was not a private, much less an intimate, sphere in the modern sense. But in Shakespeare's time, the intimate and private sphere assumed a relative independence. For example, in Shakespeare, publicly displayed love is merely ceremonial—as in the case of Henry V— whereas nonceremonial love and desire of public or political figures are portrayed essentially as clandestine, obscure, illegitimate, and subversive forces. The collapse of nonceremonial, essentially private, intimate tragedies and public ones, while concentrating on the conflicts between the two spheres, is infrequent in Shakespeare; it will be typical only later in the *tragédies classiques* (see, e.g., *Le Cid, Bérenice, Britannicus*). In Shakespeare, it is perhaps only in *Hamlet* and *King Lear* that the tragedy takes place on all levels. In those dramas Shakespeare amplifies the tragedy that takes place in the private–intimate sphere with the tragedy in the public sphere, and vice versa. It is because of this reinforcement or amplification that the tragedies of Hamlet and Lear are so absolute, and so modern. But even in these dramas the main conflicts are not between the private and the political.

In Shakespeare there are two *symbols* of personality: the *name* and the *face*. They are not merely symbols but also signs. Everyone knows that they are signs. One can encounter someone on the street and recognize her by her face. If one hears a mention of someone, one identifies this person by her name. In the great recognition scenes of Greek tragedy, brothers and sisters (for example, Orestes and Electra, or Orestes and Iphigenia) recognize each other by signs. But the signs lead them to the recognition of the name. You are Orestes, my brother; you are Electra, my sister. In Shakespeare similar recognition scenes are frequent in comedies and nontragic dramas. But for Shakespeare name and face have a broader, symbolic significance; for they are not only symbols of identity recognition but also guidelines for self-identification. Shakespeare plays around with these symbols in many dramas, but *Richard II* stands out among all of them. I will discuss this drama separately. Yet also in Hamlet's case one can hardly miss the significance of the identity game.

Generally speaking (but not always and not in every text), a name stands for the right of tradition in Shakespeare, whereas a face stands for natural right (just as in the case of Romeo and Juliet or of Edmund, as my earlier quotations indicate).

Harry is the son of Harry, Fortinbras is the son of Fortinbras, and Hamlet is the son of Hamlet. With a name one inherits the *legitimate succession*. What is true of Harry and Fortinbras is also true of Hamlet. He is, as he therefore should be, the legitimate heir to the throne. The ascension of Claudius (another name!) has already challenged the inherited right. Hamlet notices this, and it worries him. He *is* his name. Yet he *is not* just his name. He is also his *face*. Hamlet was never to *face* the choice of Harry: to *change face,* to become someone else in order to live up to the full significance of his name. Likewise, Henry was never *to face* the ascension of his uncle to the throne, his mother marrying his uncle, or finally, the strong suspicion that his uncle was his father's murderer. Perhaps Hamlet would have become some kind of Henry in Henry's situation, although he would never become a Fortinbras. Fortinbras—as far as we know him from Hamlet's reflections—never experienced the double bind. He was a Fortinbras, the son of Fortinbras, a "name," a straightforward traditionalist, a man of war and of honor, one-sided and one-dimensional. Hamlet's thoughts about Fortinbras, which he also expresses to Horatio, his other self, are very similar to Henry's ruminations about his lowly subjects who have a good night's sleep. The words suggest the wish to be in the place of the other, yet they are uttered with a grain of irony. As Henry would never have preferred to have a good night's sleep without grandeur, so Hamlet would never prefer to keep the honor of his name and sacrifice conscience, intellect, introspection, complexity.

Hamlet, as we learn at the end of the play, would have become a good king. He would have been a king unlike Fortinbras, perhaps a deeper, more reflective Henry. But this was not to be.

At the beginning of the drama Hamlet is caught in a double bind. He is not allowed to become a private man (to return to Wittenberg), yet he cannot step into his public position (to become king) either. The double bind is here not both an opportunity and a burden; it is only a burden. We meet Hamlet when *he has already reinvented himself* like Henry, but in a far more "modern" way. Henry is responsible for the name, lives up to this responsibility, and hides his face. Hamlet is also made responsible for his name; he fails to live up to this responsibility, for he becomes more and more his face, the face of a *melancholic.* Yet being more and more his face, he hides his face. Henry controls the double bind. The same double bind tears Hamlet apart.

All interpreters of Hamlet point out his inclination for introspection, his never-ending soul searching, his passion to know himself and to know himself truly. Hamlet is always preoccupied with the question of "who am I?" This question implies, however, two questions. I am Hamlet, the son of Hamlet. What duties and responsibilities follow from being myself? Yet I am also just what I am, this specific man with these specific inclinations, virtues, and vices. What are the duties or obligations of this man? What are my obligations to others and first and foremost to myself? Hamlet is the person who wants to follow the obligations put on his shoulders by his name, to preserve his honor, to avoid shame. Yet he is also a man who wants to follow his internal voice, the voice of conscience, alone. Yet, the voice of conscience has nothing to do with honor and everything to do with honesty. And what about the face, which all others can see? This is Hamlet's face, it is himself. But others cannot see what is inside, they *cannot read* his face. They *should not read his face.* To read a face means to read the secrets of the dark regions of the soul. We observe Hamlet and discover that *he has in fact a privileged access to himself,* that he can read himself without a looking glass.

Hamlet indulges in this discovery in the first three acts of the drama. Hamlet always sees in himself simultaneously the sinner and the righteous person (sive iustus et peccator). But he does not see himself as a guilty man in the sense that we are all guilty. The question for him is, guilty how? And of what? He deciphers his guilt, he reflects upon the furniture of his internal chambers, he wants to know desperately what or who he is. But he will never know what or who he is through introspection, first, because he is constantly changing and, second, because he is also changing under the torturous practice of introspection.

The central schism in Hamlet is the schism of the double bind around which all other schisms (and there are plenty) revolve. He is a man of conscience who knows that while relying on his conscience alone, he ceases to be a man of honor. He was *born* to set right the time out of joint, because he was born Hamlet, the son of Hamlet, the prince of Denmark. Yet *"conscience does make cowards of us all"* (*Hamlet* 3.1.85). No other Shakespearean hero tortures himself with such angry introspection. "O, what a rogue and peasant slave am I!" (2.2.552) he cries out, and in the same soliloquy calls himself an ass. He calls himself a villain, he calls himself a coward after the actor's scene (*Hamlet* 2.2) Is he all these? He is all these measured by the simplistic, one-sided yardstick of honor, which is also his own. (Conscience makes him a coward.) Yet he is a man of conscience, a specific man, who must think about justice and injustice, right and wrong, and about himself. He must know himself.

Hamlet speaks to Ophelia: "I am very proud, revengeful, ambitious, with more offences at my beck than I have thoughts to put them in, imagination to give them shape, or time to act them in" (3.1.126–29). Is he all these? Certainly yes, if measured by the yardstick of his conscience alone. Hamlet describes the chaos of the soul—a chaos that everyone who ever cast a sincere glance at himself recognizes in himself.

Self-torture or self-debasement is a sign of self-alienation. One of Hamlet's selves is alienated from the other, and all his lonely attempts to put them together, to mend the self thus torn, are in vain. They are in vain because he himself breaks the thread to sew the selves together. Hamlet cannot gather together his personality by his own effort. By gathering together I do not mean the termination of self-torture and even less so of self-searching, but simply becoming capable of coping with suffering and terror while staying relatively sane and alive. At certain junctures of the play, Hamlet's self seems to be entirely alienated—alienated from itself (his other self) and from the world. In these moments his state of mind is close to madness.

A man sees himself in the mirror of others. If all the mirrors show him an ugly and mad face, it will be almost impossible for him to disregard the distorted image entirely. This almost happens to Hamlet. The whole court finds his behavior abnormal even before he pretends to be mad; this is difficult to survive with a sane mind. The certainty that I alone am normal, that I alone know what is right, that I alone know the truth—the truth I have learned from a mere specter who could have also been sent by the devil—is a brittle certainty and can easily fall apart. The question of whether Hamlet plays mad or *is* mad is a wrong one. If one plays mad, if one chooses to appear in the disguise of madness, this is already a sign of world alienation. Surely, Hamlet defends himself against total self-alienation through world alienation: this is why his madness is pretended. But he conducts a friendly dialogue with madness, and this is in a sense already madness. Whenever he gets enraged, he shows signs of episodes of madness; for example, when Hamlet sees the ghost of his father in the rage scene with his mother, it is surely an illusion. But episodes remain but episodes, and Hamlet is not mad. Moreover, as the play unfolds, he becomes more and more sober. In the last act, close to his death, he is entirely sober. I have already suggested that after the cemetery scene Hamlet reinvents himself again. But this new reinvention has a prehistory.

Hamlet protects the secrets of his soul with all his might. He does not allow others to glimpse into his internal chambers. Pretending madness is also self-defense in the literal meaning of the word. He defends his self from intrusion rather than his body from injury or death. All the same, Hamlet cannot live entirely incognito. He must give a hint. He gives hints even to the lowliest and most narrow-minded courtiers, like Polonius, who cannot miss the system in Hamlet's mad talk. Pretending madness through alternating self-closure and self-disclosure, rationality and irrationality is also a game, but not an innocent or aimless one. In playing the game, Hamlet frees himself from the name of Hamlet, prince of Denmark. A madman may do what he pleases. He does not need to comply with ceremonies, he can express his spite and contempt without restraint. Hamlet plays the madman and is in a way also mad for the sake of his freedom and autonomy. A madman can shed all obligations except the obligations that he alone knows about, the obligations to his conscience. Still, although Hamlet liberates himself from the name of the prince of Denmark, he can play his game only *as* Hamlet, the prince of Denmark, as the son of Hamlet, nearest to the throne.

But Hamlet is blessed with a nondistorting mirror, which rescues him from the night of madness. This mirror is the friend, the better part of his own soul, Horatio.

One can listen to the first words Hamlet speaks when he meets Horatio for the first time, almost at the very beginning of the drama: "I am glad to see you well. / Horatio!—or I do forget myself" (1.2.160–61). ("Or I do forget myself": the expression can be interpreted as "if I ever forgot you Horatio, I would be myself no more." And it can also be read as, "Horatio, you are myself, if I ever forgot you, I would forget myself—my better self.") Horatio: "The same, my lord, and your poor servant ever." Hamlet: "Sir, my good friend—I'll change that name with you" (1.2.162–63).

The central point of this riposte is the name exchange. Again, Hamlet rejects his name as a name of honor, a name of tradition. He suggests one of two things: he exchanges the name of the prince for the name of the poor servant, for he is gladly Horatio's poor servant. Yet this also means to exchange the name of friend, for the exchange of the name of friend is friendship. There is no master–servant relationship in friendship; there are just friends.

It is Horatio who pulls Hamlet back from the abyss of madness. Hamlet takes him into his confidence. Something happens here that is very rare in

Shakespeare: the audience is not initiated into this great testimony of friendship; we get to know about it through a retrospective reference made by Hamlet before the mousetrap scene. Horatio becomes a fellow witness.

Indubitably, Horatio is the absolutely trustworthy friend. He can be trusted blindly. His loyalty is the loyalty of a best friend, not the loyalty of the subject. He stands by his friend, he does not obey him. Neither is Horatio's loyalty granted to moral perfection or right: he does not ask first whether Hamlet is right or wrong and accordingly grant his loyalty; rather, his loyalty comes first. When he sometimes does ask the question of right or wrong, his friendship remains intact irrespective of the answer. He is the best friend of Hamlet as Hamlet *is*, because he has absolute trust in Hamlet. This is a certainty that withstands every trial and challenge. Horatio does not accept every act of Hamlet, but Hamlet himself is accepted, and accepted absolutely. One could say that this is first friendship, *pro te philia,* in an ancient sense. But Hamlet is the modern hero par excellence, and this ancient friendship is also modern. Horatio refers to himself as a Roman. But a Roman is a *republican.* A republican is the best friend of the prince: their relationship is *existential.*

Horatio is the mirror Hamlet so dearly needs. And Horatio knows Hamlet better than Hamlet knows himself. In fact, Hamlet's story is told by Horatio. Hamlet's mask is lifted. We witness his silent ruminations because Horatio tells us Hamlet's story, and we know it as Horatio tells it. The dying Hamlet implores his friend to stay alive and to tell his story: "O God, Horatio, what a wounded name, / Things standing thus unknown, shall live behind me! / If thou didst ever hold me in thy heart, / Absent thee from felicity a while . . . To tell my story" (5.2.296–301). The dying Hamlet is blackmailing Horatio with love ("If thou didst ever hold me in thy heart . . ."). Yes, things "standing thus unknown," it seems that a madman, a bloodthirsty, ambitious youth has destroyed a flourishing kingdom that is, as a result, occupied by the enemy's army. "The rest is silence," says Hamlet (5.2.310), but he implores Horatio to speak. And Horatio must speak, for the terrible noise of the arms and trumpets of the victorious Fortinbras can be silenced only by storytelling. As long as the story is told, the audience sits in silence. Horatio possesses inside knowledge because he is not just an observer but also Hamlet's other, better, self. *Hamlet* is the only drama by Shakespeare that is told by one of the characters in the drama.

While Hamlet jealously defends his secrets from all intrusions, from the hostile and alien eye, he also has an opposite desire: his mania to disclose himself, to make himself known, to make himself understood. We know that he disclosed himself to Horatio. But there is deep down a forceful motive in Hamlet to disclose himself to women, or at least to disclose his relationship to women. *All three rage scenes concern women.* They are violent scenes: his encounter with Ophelia, his nightly altercation with his mother, and his "forgetting himself" (as he later expresses it to Horatio) at Ophelia's grave. In all these scenes he rages against the other (Ophelia, Gertrude, Laertes); yet his accusations are coupled with self-disclosure, in the third case even with public self-disclosure. Soul-searching introspection turns into exhibitionism in the Ophelia scene. Self-torture and the torture of the other can hardly be distinguished here. It is as if the torture of the other reinforces Hamlet's self-torture and vice versa. In speaking of his mother's sexual lust, Hamlet certainly wounds himself and makes himself suffer, with or without Oedipal connotations. Clearly, the last, public, rage scene differs essentially from the other two. In the Ophelia scene and the fight with his mother, Hamlet's torture and self-torture are those of a naked man, of a man stripped of all ceremonies and majesties. There are a lover and a beloved who have betrayed him, a son and a mother who betrayed his father. But in the last rage scene, a public spectacle in which Hamlet leaps into the grave, he not only speaks as Hamlet the naked self but also declares his royal name: "This is I, Hamlet, the Dane."

In Shakespeare's portrayal rage is not madness. The raging Hamlet is not mad, although in rage—as Shakespeare portrays Hamlet—a person is also alienated from himself; someone who is not himself speaks in him. This is how Hamlet apologizes in the next scene to Laertes; he in fact blames his own madness for offending Laertes: "Give me your pardon, sir. . . . Let my disclaiming from a purposed evil / Free me so far in your most generous thoughts / That I have shot my arrow o'er the house / And hurt my brother" (5.2.172–89). He apologizes without apologizing, for he is not guilty. Shakespeare stresses Hamlet's incapacity to offer a real apology for sending Rosencrantz and Guildenstern to their death in cold blood. They deserved it: "they did make love to this employment," Hamlet says to Horatio. This is true. Hamlet does not apologize for killing the old fool, Polonius. Then he was also in a rage; he has not acted in cold blood. But he does not say he was sorry even afterwards.

There is a feature in Hamlet that is common in both of his selves, a feature that reinforces both: his immense pride. He is immensely proud as only a royal prince can be, and he is immensely proud as only a man of absolute intellectual and emotional superiority can be. He, in fact, despises everyone—save Horatio. He ridicules them, he mocks them, he leaps over their living bodies as well as their corpses. He knows that as a prince he can toy with Polonius or Osric, the fools; and as a person he can play with those who love him, his lover and his mother, the moral failures. Certainly, they are all inferior, and therefore Hamlet's contempt is justified. This pride carries him to the top of the ladder of grandeur, yet for the same reason he will never reach the top of the ladder of morality. It is the torn personality, the intellectual refinement, the passionate and raging nature, and the pride all together that make Hamlet a charismatic personality.

Yet this charisma is not felt by the contemporaries, the actors in the story. With the exception of Horatio and perhaps Ophelia, everyone in the drama is immune to Hamlet's charisma. Hamlet is not attractive to them. This is how the spectator is pushed into the position of Horatio, into the viewpoint of the man who tells the story. We assume Horatio's perspective, the vision of the best friend. It is through Horatio's magic that Hamlet becomes charismatic. And since we see Hamlet through Horatio's eyes, he is charismatic for us. Yet Horatio is not a man in a double bind. He is a modern man who assumes the costume of a Roman; he is a self-made man designed by Montaigne, from Wittenberg, without raging passions, and without immense pride. He is our eyes. He is also the mirror. We all become Horatio when we look at Hamlet. We are the modern mirrors. Hamlet seems to be a modern man to the spectator because he is mirrored in the eyes of a modern man, and there are no other mirrors.

Henry never loses himself entirely; he changes himself from Hal to Henry. Hamlet reinvents himself three times; he almost loses himself, he splits himself, he recovers himself, and he loses his life. Ophelia will lose her life without recovering herself. Hers is the story of total self-alienation. Lady Macbeth's is another story of total self-alienation, but she is not a victim. Ophelia is a victim, although she is also guilty. But there is no proportionality between her guilt and her punishment. She exemplifies in her short life how the innocent perish together with the guilty; her destiny testifies to the injustice of history, to blind fate, and to irrationality.

Madness from which there is no return is the final stage of a personality's total alienation. The madwoman is alienated from the world and also from herself. Some believe that in Shakespeare self-torture and morbid self-investigation are the fertile soils of madness. Yet the opposite is the case. Lady Macbeth and Ophelia—the paradigmatic cases of total self-alienation —are women *totally incapable of introspection*. This is the common feature of the two, who are so different in all other respects. They have no identity problems; they do not question their own actions. In his once famous book, *The Divided Self*, the antipsychiatrist R. D. Laing discussed Ophelia's fate as a case study: absolutely obedient girls, Laing said, very easily become schizophrenics. Yet Lady Macbeth was not an obedient woman and she was not a traditionalist. However, she became totally self-alienated and committed suicide just as Ophelia did. Because I rely more on Shakespeare's wisdom than on anyone else's, I am inclined to accept that the total absence of self-reflection and self-scrutiny, as unproblematic self-identity, can result in total madness. Certainly, this is the case only in a world where time is out of joint and where all "external" expectations fail. Lady Macbeth is a Machiavellian. She is certain that her husband must commit a crime but that this crime will pay. After the crime is done and done with, Macbeth and she will have a happy life together. But Macbeth is not a Machiavellian, and Lady Macbeth has ceased to understand the world. She never asks questions about herself. She feels guilt, perhaps, because she failed, but we see her only in two extreme situations: identical with herself and nonidentical with (out of) herself.

The same is true of Ophelia. Either we see her as identical to herself, or (in the madness scene) we see her entirely alienated, abruptly out of herself. But we never see her asking questions about herself. In her soliloquy she speaks of her Hamlet, she registers the change in Hamlet, but she does not look into herself. It never occurs to her that she betrayed her lover to her father and to the king, because she did it without knowing it. She was obedient to the father, to the king, to the brother, and also to Hamlet. But she was absolutely a traditionalist, for her obedience to the family and to her sovereign king came first. She never questions the priority of her loyalties. One can guess from the madness scene that she feels guilty because she has a love relationship with the young prince. At least in his film *Hamlet* Kenneth Branagh makes us believe that this is so. This is a matter of interpretation, but if one concentrates on the similarities between Ophelia and Lady Macbeth, it might be a good guess. Since Lady Macbeth acts out her murderous deed (washing the nonexistent blood from her hand) in her state of total alienation, so perhaps Ophelia in her piquant erotic song is acting out something that she has in fact done. Yet, perhaps she is acting out what she wishes to do but has not in fact done. This is all guesswork. What is not guesswork is, however, that Ophelia never asks questions about her own identity; she only asks about the identity of Hamlet.

Ophelia becomes mad and dies because she cannot understand the world anymore. Shakespeare knows quite well what Nietzsche later said, that men can tolerate suffering if suffering makes sense, if there is meaning in it. Ophelia's father was killed by Ophelia's lover. This in itself is a terrible trauma. But it is not impossible to cope with this if one tries to understand the reason behind what happened. What was in Hamlet's and Polonius's minds? What kind of man was Polonius, the father, and what kind of man is Hamlet? But Ophelia does not understand anything. There is for her no meaning in anything. Events happen over her head, not because she is stupid or naïve, but because she never asks questions concerning meaning, right or wrong, or her world and herself. She accepts whatever ready-made meanings are handed down to her. There is no sign of her distancing herself from her father's or brother's constant nagging, advising, warning, or remonstrations and teachings. She takes their commonplaces at their face value as much as she takes Hamlet's protestations of love at their face value.

The fact that *Hamlet* is (like *King Lear,* only more so) a tragedy in which the family tragedy and the historicopolitical tragedy merge, makes of Ophelia (in Shakespeare's world) *the most paradigmatic innocent victim of his-*

tory. She is a victim of history and politics in a double sense. First, the acts and events she does not understand are mostly political. She understands hesitantly what her father says, namely, that the prince stands above her rank; but she does not understand the political motivation behind the king's spying on Hamlet. (Polonius is also spying on his son, and not for political reasons.) Laertes' rebellion against the king is an act of political subversion. But the political is in this case also essentially personal. Laertes wants to avenge his father's death. Ophelia is torn between her love for her father, her brother, and her lover. (It is important that she has no mother.) Yet—and this is the second sense—time is out of joint not only in politics but also in the family. What kind of family is Hamlet's family? What kind of love is the love between the king and the queen? This is the absolute contrast. On the one hand political loyalty, honor, and family are all in shambles; the whole world becomes a lie. On the other hand, there is a young girl who takes the duties of honor, family, and loyalty seriously as if they were intact, as if they were true. She has not the faintest idea with whom she speaks; she does not understand a word. She trusts everyone she loves by duty or choice, the trustworthy and the untrustworthy, the simple soul and the complicated mind. She has no sense of complexity. She does not understand Hamlet's questions ("Are you honest?" [3.1.105]; "Are you fair?" [3.1.107]), and she lies to Hamlet out of filial duty (Hamlet: "Where is your father?" Ophelia: "At home, my lord" [3.1.132–33]).

There is meaning in Hamlet's sufferings. He renders meaning to them repeatedly, new and different meanings, yet his sufferings are all the same. His torturous introspection and reflections on the world, human character, and the times, as well as the constant move from action to reflection and back—as much as Horatio's friendship—all return him to sanity. Yet there is no meaning in Ophelia's suffering. She cannot render meaning to it, because of her innocence and ignorance, for her innocence is ignorance. She is unlike the so-called baser natures, who, as Hamlet says about Rosencrantz and Guildenstern, come willingly "Between the pass and fell incensed points / Of mighty opposites" (5.2.62–63). Ophelia does not mingle, she does not interfere, she does not mediate, she just exists. Can innocence or ignorance be guilt? This is an old theological question, and like so many other old theological questions, it is asked again by Shakespeare. Shakespeare points his finger to the question. The paradigmatically innocent victims of politics and history are those who have to undergo immense suffering, although they believe that they have done nothing wrong. (Still they are guilty of ignorance/innocence.) They are those who do not understand anything that happens to them regarding their beloved ones and their world. These victims float on the waters of history, covered with flowers as long as we remember them.

Is the place that a person occupies in the hierarchical world order just a garment or a name—as Juliet, Falstaff, Edmund, Shylock, and so many other Shakespearean characters declare? Is it not a leg, an arm, skin, an eye, or any other part of man? Can one be stripped and remain just a leg, arm, skin, eye, or some other part—and still remain oneself? Does one become himself if he has the courage to strip himself of all ceremonies, fancies of the world, honor, title, and family—and stay there, as at the moment he was born, naked? I gave my personal answer to this question at the beginning of this chapter. I think that Shakespeare does not generalize. The answer to the question is given by each and every tragic character, and they give different answers to the question according to their character. We never see, for example, Henry V "naked." Rather, he changes costumes. He exchanges the garment of Hal for the royal cloak. Whether he finds it a comfortable fit or not is another question. But with the royal cloak, he also assumes responsibility for everything the cloak stands for. The ugly betrayal of Falstaff is the epilogue of the costume change. The prologue takes place when Henry puts the crown on his head while his father is still living. He apologizes by saying that he means no harm, he is just trying its weight. Yes, he is simply trying on the crown as someone tries on a dress at the tailor's. Expressed in the language of the world theater, it is a dress rehearsal. That Harry tries on the crown tells a complete story: for Harry his royal crown, cloak, and scepter were like a period costume or like a nightgown tried on by a young boy who has been chosen to play the role of a girl in a comedy. Henry has his dress rehearsal. He also needs to learn how to walk and speak like a king—how to play the role before entering the stage, the theater stage as well as the stage of history. After entering the stage, he will play in a show for which he is properly dressed. And he is going to play the role *of* his dress *in* his dress.

Most characters in Shakespeare change costumes, many undress themselves, and a few stand there naked at the moment of facing death. But being stripped naked is not the same thing as feeling the *vanitatum vanitas* at the moment of death; this is not the macabre dance, this is not a medieval mystery. The *danse macabre* is the end itself. One does not find one's identity but rather comes to terms with one's own nothingness. And these are entirely different existential experiences. Being stripped naked can be the final stage in the *search for identity*. The person stripped naked has to recognize his real self in his nakedness, and he must continue to live for a while in the awareness of his nakedness. This is not because he remains naked, since no Shakespearean character remains entirely so, but because the experience of having been stripped naked once, of having recognized oneself in one's nakedness, is the *ultimate existential experience*. A naked person experiences the nakedness of human existence. He experiences contingency in its fullness; he experiences himself as a *throw of the dice*. This is the story of King Lear. (Ian Holm, playing King Lear at the Royal National Theatre, in fact strips naked.)

I cannot discuss here Lear's metamorphoses in all their complexity; I will concentrate only on the process of his striptease from the abdication scene to the storm where he finally stands naked. The abdication scene is not only dense and complex, but it also allows for an interpretation that, at least at the level of sheer existence, would annul everything that I am going to say about the process of stripping naked. It is possible on the existential level to read *King Lear* as the story of a *beggar of love*. If Lear abdicates as a beggar of love, then his story resembles more the story of Edmund than the story of Gloucester. The evil Edmund and the fool Lear are both beggars of love, and both die with the felicitous feeling that they *have been loved*. Shakespeare here again, as in so many other dramas, goes to extremes. He grants a happy death to these two beggars of love, to the wicked bastard and to the foolish king. I am inclined to this interpretation. Yet King Lear's parallelism with Gloucester and his with Edmund are played out on two different stages. The parallel story with Gloucester runs on the stage of politics and history, that with Edmund on the existential stage. Yet—and this is again a manifestation of Shakespeare's courage—when the politicohistorical parallel figures (Lear and Gloucester) are thrown down into the abyss, they also ascend to the existential stage. When Jan Kott (in *Shakespeare, Our Contemporary*) compares Shakespeare's Lear to Beckett's Godot, he has a point, but only if one has the existential stage alone in mind. There is no other stage in Beckett; but there are two stages in Shakespeare's *King Lear*. I speak now only of the transformation of Lear on the historical stage; how does he—while stripping himself—ascend to the existential stage? I could speak also of Gloucester, but there is an immense difference between Lear and Gloucester. Gloucester is blinded, he does not blind himself (as Oedipus once did). Metaphorically speaking, he is stripped but does not strip himself as Lear does.

Perhaps Alan Bloom is right when he writes in *Shakespeare's Politics* that Lear has been a good king who made his country prosperous. At any rate, he must have been a traditional king. He is not reflective; he never asks "Who am I?" for he takes for granted that he is a king and that this is not just all, but more than all. "Every inch a king," he says even in act 5. It never occurs to him that power and authority are not identical. They were traditionally identical. It never occurs to him that a man who abdicates his legitimacy in order to exercise power as his privilege will also abdicate his ability to exercise power as violence, to compel others to do something he wants them to do although they are not willing to do it. By abdicating his power, he also unwillingly and unknowingly gives up his authority. Time is out of joint. "Unnatural" things happen: sons rebel against their fathers, and so do daughters. Cordelia's actions also seem unnatural in Lear's eyes. She fails to bow before the authority of her father.

Cordelia is certainly the true rebel who takes the risk of rebellion. She rebels against her father while Lear can still exercise his full power. Cordelia's love is not ceremonial. It is a feeling that cannot be expressed in a declaration of love; it is something one cherishes inside, it is natural in an entirely different sense from what natural means for Lear. Lear begs for love from his youngest daughter, but he also insists that she resign her deep commitment to the right of nature. Lear commands love, but love—in the sense of Cordelia's concept of nature, which is repeated by Immanuel Kant— cannot be commanded. That is, the two concepts of nature already collide in the first scene of *King Lear,* but not in Lear's mind or soul. There is no double bind as yet for him. Or if there is (perhaps his love for Cordelia is already the voice of another nature), he does not accept it but protests against it. Perhaps this is why he needs the protestation of love, not to be obliged to face a new, untraditional, and—for him—irritating love that cannot be commanded, which is not obedience to an authority. Lear is a tyrant even if he is a good king. He becomes a tyrant because he does not tolerate freedom. He does not tolerate the freedom of goodness. He will pay for this by being pushed to face the freedom of wickedness.

Lear, as a traditional king without the capacity of self-reflection, cannot notice that time is out of joint, that de jure power is not de facto power; he is not aware that once he abdicates the de facto power, he also loses de jure power that he has not freely abdicated. He will be forced against his will because he has lost the privilege and the capacity to employ force. He will be at the mercy of the de facto power in spite his de jure power. Time is out of joint. Lear, this stubborn, obstinate, self-righteous, and naïve old man could have noticed the change of times by the resistance of his favorite daughter. But he becomes rather obstinate in his ignorance. At this crucial moment it is folly to remain unthinking. Lear is a fool; yet he is not foolish in the same way that Polonius or Malvolio is. In his folly there are no comic features. It is a dangerous folly, the folly of blindness. Only his Fool, who is not foolish, and his loyal knight can tell him this to his face.

When Kent offers his services to the already abused king, the king asks him who he is. And he answers, "A man, sir" (*King Lear* 1.4.9) Kent is just another person who knows nothing of the double bind; there is only one nature for him, and this is tradition. The sentence "A man, sir" is important because it is the reversal of the general meaning of the same sentence, since in Kent's case "being a man, just a man" means being in disguise. He is the earl of Kent; this is what he *is.* But now he appears in *the disguise of "a man."* When Lear asks him why he has offered his services to him, Kent answers that he sees something on Lear's countenance that he could call master. "What's that?" asks Lear. Kent answers with one single word: "Authority." For Kent, Lear has not lost one bit of his authority by losing his de facto power. He remains what he was: the king. And Lear behaves as if he were still one. He abuses and strikes his daughter's servant. He does not control his royal rage.

Yet when facing Goneril, *he begins to understand that he does not understand.* This is where Lear first raises a question about his identity: "Doth any here know me? Why this is not Lear. / Doth Lear walk thus, speak thus? Where are his eyes? . . . / Who is it that can tell me who I am?" The Fool answers: "Lear's shadow" (*King Lear* 1.4.208–13/Quarto 220–26). The Fool's answer is prompt and accurate. Lear questions his identity at first because he does not live up to his royal manner. In this sense, he is Lear's *shadow*. This is still true when we consider the last sentence of Lear's address to Goneril: "Thou shalt find / That I'll resume the shape which thou dost think / I have cast off forever" (Quarto1.4.302–4). Here he still believes that he will turn from the ghost of a king back into a real king.

To become a shadow of a king at first means for Lear to lose himself (he *is* the king). Losing himself means losing the world. He can surpass the limit of total self-alienation, madness: "O, let me not be mad, sweet heaven!" (Quarto 1.5.45) Lear prays. "Now I prithee, daughter, do not make me mad" (Quarto 12.2.376). Thus he speaks to Goneril later in Regan's house, and when Regan turns him out he says, "No, you unnatural hags!" (*King Lear* 2.4.437) And he again addresses himself to the fool, "O Fool, I shall go mad!" (*King Lear* 2.4.445) It is thus that he leaves in the middle of the storm. It is not just a storm. It is a symbolic storm (just as in *The Tempest*). *The man who exits from the tempest is not the man who has entered into it.* Lear has been turned around. As if by divine grace, he becomes another man.

In the previous scene (3.3), Edgar, escaping the manhunt, chooses the disguise as Poor Tom. He says, "Poor Tom! / That's something yet. Edgar I nothing am" (King Lear 3.3.186–87). Russel Frazer, the editor of the Signet Classic edition, explains this sentence in the footnotes thus: "There is a chance for me in that I am no longer known for myself." This means two things: others will not recognize me, and neither will I recognize myself, for what has been myself is nothing. This is the sentence of stripping. By taking a disguise so lowly that neither he nor himself would recognize the legitimate son of the earl of Gloucester anymore, Edgar has already been stripped. This is how Lear will understand (see) Poor Tom. Here, contrary to Kent's identification as a man, *being a man is not a disguise, as in the case of Kent, but Edgar's essence.* The storm scene takes place on the existential stage. Storm and tempest—Lear is enraged; he curses his ungrateful daughters. Yet he says, "I am a man more sinned against than sinning" (*King Lear* 3.2.60). This is the first sentence in which Lear questions himself. Although he says that his daughters have sinned more against him than he has sinned, he knows that he has sinned. The next sentence is uttered by Kent: "Alack, bare-headed?" (*King Lear* 3.3). First the head remains uncovered; the stripping begins. "My wits begin to turn," says Lear. He does not understand.

But there is more to it. It is the first time that Lear feels compassion: "Poor Fool and knave, I have one part in my heart / That sorrows yet for thee" (3.5.73). The breakthrough comes in 3.4. 25–33. Lear discovers the truth of nakedness: "Poor naked wretches. . . . O, I have ta'en / Too little care of this. Take physic, pomp, / Expose thyself to feel what wretches feel, / That thou mayst shake the superflux to them / And show the heavens more just." Here, we feel, Lear strips himself of the remnants of his royal garment. And then enters Edgar, who is disguised as a madman. Lear speaks: "Thou wert better in grave than to answer with thy uncovered body this extremity of the skies. Is man no more than this? Consider him well. Thou owe'st the worm no silk, the beast no hide, the sheep no wool, the cat no perfume. Ha! here's three on's are sophisticated. *Thou art the thing itself.* Unaccommodated man is no more but such a poor, bare, forked animal as thou art" (emphasis added) (tearing off his clothes). And then it comes: Lear calls Edgar "philosopher" four times; he needs him, he needs his company. Interestingly, now his friends no longer understand him. They believe that he has lost his mind; they do not understand that he has finally found it. Lear, the king, asks questions of "the philosopher" who is but "the thing itself." "First let me talk with this philosopher. / What is the cause of thunder?" (3.4.141–42). Then: "I'll talk a word with this most learned Theban. / What is your study?" (3.4.144–45). "Noble philosopher, your company" (158). "I will keep still with my philosopher" (3.4.163). "Come, good Athenian" (3.4.166). No one understands. We do. Here are two naked men looking mad because they have stripped themselves naked; but in fact they are men becoming sane, the only sane among all the characters, because they know what they are. *They are "the thing itself," man naked.*

3

Acting, Playing, Pretending, Disguising

One should never forget that Shakespeare wrote plays, not novels, and that he wrote English dramas, not Greek ones. The spectator has a very strong feeling that the Shakespearean historical characters—and to a lesser or greater degree all Shakespeare's characters—*play* their roles. One feels this way especially about the historicopolitical dramas. Henry V plays the role of Henry, son of Henry, the English king; Margaret plays the role of the queen mother avenging the murderers of her family; Anthony plays the role of the triumvir torn between love and duty, between the East and the West. Shakespeare wrote plays for the stage. This means what everyone knows: Henry V, Macbeth, and so on, are roles, and actors play them. The body of the actor who plays Henry V is not the body of Henry V. Henry V speaks of his body as Juliet speaks of hers: they insist that their bodies are not identical with their names. But the actor's body is not identical with King Henry's body (decomposed long before the spectacle), and the body of the actor who plays Juliet is not the body of Juliet. Thousands of actors—all different bodies—play the role of someone who identified himself or herself with *his or her* body. The actor is not the king of England, the actor or actress is not a young patrician girl from Verona. They have to play *to be what they are not*. Or, rather, they have to be transmuted—while playing—to become what they are not. The ancient Greek dramas were also played, but the actors were wearing masks. The actor in mask is in disguise. His face, that is, his *identity,* along with his name, is in disguise. In Shakespeare the actor has a face; he is a face. The face is a significant aspect of anyone's identity, particularly in Shakespeare. This means that the actor admixes a foreign identity with his identity. He offers his face as if it were the face or identity of the character whose personality he embodies. Perhaps no other playwright was so deeply aware of the role that the theater plays in the presentation of the dramatis personae as Shakespeare, the actor. Many of Shakespeare's heroes, first and foremost among them Hamlet, also disclose their opinion about playacting. And the aged Hamlet, Prospero, takes off his nonexistent mask, his role, to ask the spectator's understanding and forgiveness for having been what he was not.

But Shakespearean drama is a play not only because it is played by actors but also because the roles of the historical and quasi-historical characters are not fixed, particularly at the beginning of a play. As I have emphasized, Shakespeare's heroes constantly invent and reinvent themselves. They play their own roles, sometimes one role, sometimes many serially, sometimes several simultaneously. They are like actors. Here again I quote the words of Jaques, the melancholic: "All the world is a stage." Indeed, Shakespeare gives us the impression that it is. The world is a stage where we enter with a name and a body and where we invent ourselves, not entirely, but against the background of our inherited name and personal face. (The English language aids an understanding of this point because the play*actor* on the stage and the historical *actor* on the world stage are both called *actors* in English. In most other languages this is not so. But Shakespeare wrote in English.)

In the historical drama we enter the world stage. The actors of a Shakespearean historical drama play the roles of men and women just now on the absolutely present stage, roles that were played once upon a time on the world stage. The Shakespearean historicopolitical actors bring two concepts of *representation* into play. Moreover, they play with them—with the traditional/medieval concept or the ancient mythological one. Representation therefore means that the single person acts according to the rank he or she possesses or according to the essence attributed to him or her by a myth. The representational role is and remains repeatable, even if it is not a mythological one. Every monarch is anointed by God and thus embodies royalty. This identification of person and representation is constantly repeated as long as traditional monarchy exists. Mythological figures also replay certain traditional roles. This kind of essentialist repetition was beautifully portrayed by Thomas Mann in his Joseph novels. Eliazar, the servant of Jacob, assumed the role once played by another Eliazar, the servant of Abraham. Being a servant to the tribal father of Israel was an Eliazar role.

Yet there is a second meaning of representation, and the Shakespearean heroes, even the traditional ones, are representative in this sense. They represent options, avenues, models, paradigmatic acts, paradigmatic victories, and defeats. To be paradigmatic means to embody a lesson, a warning, a promise, a test case, a model, or an ideal to an extreme degree, so that one stands out and can be seen in the distant future as well. To put up a show on the world stage is to put up a representative show, and the actors themselves are aware of this.

A play goes on in a dual sense. There is a written drama that gives the impression that it has been written by the actors of the drama. For they play, they have their dress rehearsals as much as their premieres and final shows. They can end on the peak of life, but they can also fail. There are good plays, honest plays, and foul plays. There are also contingent elements in those plays. Finally, there are the actors of the theater who are playing those players, who assume the character and the garment of men who have already assumed a character, a costume—perhaps two or three of them. They embody a personality that perhaps changes personality. This is the game of the Shakespearean theater; it is a wonderful ball game. The actor of the theater plays ball with the actor on the world stage, and both play ball with the author, who permits the actors on the world stage to reinvent the role they play. However, this is also a game of hide-and-seek. Between the historical actors and the theatrical actors stands the *text* of the drama itself, the result of constant reinventions and the source of infinite inventions. In a short study on Shakespeare's composition, Lukács said that Shakespeare's heroes have no motivation whatsoever, and this is precisely the reason why interpreters can always attribute motivations to them. I add to his point that, first and foremost, it is the theatrical actors who do just this. For one cannot play a character without making sense of his actions; one needs to attribute certain motivations to him. Interpretation is mainly the imputation of certain motivations.

Action in a drama includes speech acts, debate, argument, command, conversation, and reflection. In Shakespeare the monologue, too, can be of all sorts. Yet there is also the *mute* act, which may also be accompanied by speech and is mostly preceded and followed by speech. Every act of murder is, for example, a mute act; so are the battle scenes, which are quite frequent in the Shakespearean historical plays, and many other violent acts. Other kinds of mute acts are kissing, caressing, kneeling down, bowing, putting on or tearing off the crown, serving, eating, even capsizing a ship, among others. Dressing and undressing are mute acts, as well as walking, running, pleading with hands, dancing, and so on. There are far more mute acts in Shakespeare than in the Greek dramas, yet perhaps fewer than in some modern dramas. What is important in Shakespearean tragedies is that the mute acts are normally very significant; they are rarely trifles.

Speech acts, as I have noted, quite often accompany mute acts. More often than not the former precede the latter, but many times it is the other way around. Speech acts (in the understanding of action through speech) "surround" mute acts. Speech acts are frequently reversible, although this is less the case with dialogues than with monologues. What someone has uttered has been said once and for all; it is there and remains there whether it hits another person or continues to linger in the *intermundii* between persons. If a word strikes a person hard, the person who has been hit can forgive the other, but he rarely will, and he will not forget. Take, for example, the vicious altercation between Winchester and Gloucester at the very beginning of *1 Henry VI*. They cannot control their mutual hatred; as they proceed to verbally abuse each other, it becomes a game of catastrophic consequences: the victory of the house of York, which neither of them wanted. Yet it happens that even words that are uttered rashly can be made relatively reversible, for example, through the speech acts of asking for forgiveness. According to Hannah Arendt in *The Human Condition,* it is precisely forgiveness that can outweigh two essential features of action: its unpredictability and its irreversibility. In support of Arendt I would refer to another Shakespearean scene of mutual abuse, the scene (in act 4 of *Julius Caesar*) between Brutus and Cassius that ends with reconciliation: the two old friends ask each other for forgiveness. This reversibility is, however, only relative.

Shakespeare likes to characterize his actors, particularly the historically significant ones, through the relation of their speech acts and mute acts, especially the violent mute acts. One of the main characteristics of Shakespearean military figures, whether generals or simple soldiers, is the absence of any discrepancy between their speech acts and their mute acts. Soldiers are not pretending (either before others or before themselves); they are not planning things that need to remain hidden from anyone but the common enemy. They are straightforward. The time elapsed between the speech act and the mute act does not leave any traces on their personality. It has strategic significance exclusively in war—depending on the circumstances, the movements of the enemy, and the commands they receive. Their main speech acts are not self-reflective. They are mainly commands or the words of obedience; sometimes they are plans (war tactics), and they usually accompany action itself (for example, they talk while fighting). They can comment on what they are doing, stir their courage, abuse the enemy, and so on. In the case of simple soldiers or traditional generals, even retrospective speech acts are normally not self-reflective. Soldiers are certain that whatever they have done (killed the enemy, conquered a foreign territory) was proper and right; there is not much to think about it in retrospect. They tell stories of their past fights; they boast of their courage or praise the courage of others, depending on their character.

It is obvious to Shakespeare that this kind of simple soldier or traditional general does not make a good politician. For good politicians keep a distance between their speech acts that prepare their mute acts and the execution of the acts themselves. And after mute acts are done, politicians normally do not tell stories but reflect on their decisions, analyzing them and putting them in historical perspective. In Shakespeare's dramas, Henry V and Octavius Caesar are the most typical political (Machiavellian) actors of this supreme kind.

What is problematic for Shakespeare politically, and usually also from a moral point of view, is the hybrid case: someone rebels against the tradition, recognizing the "laws of nature" alone or for the most part, and then, in retrospect, the selfsame character construes the relation between his speech acts and mute acts as if he were standing firmly in tradition. This kind of character does not think over what he is going to do before embarking on an action, although he is not relying on the crutch of ancient customs. If someone breaks with the tradition or rebels against it, he must first consider not just whether what he is about to do is right or wrong but also whether he is able to do it and what consequences such an act may have for the development of his own self. Macbeth, for example, acts unthinkingly. He is a soldier, and as a soldier he never puts a distance between decision and action. While fighting a war, such a distance would lead to disaster or be a sign of cowardice. One kills the enemy, one wins the battle as Macbeth did, and there is nothing to regret. The personality is confirmed and strengthened. Macbeth, the soldier, kills his king as if he were in the situation of a soldier. He decides to commit the crime, a deed absolutely out of order and supremely illegitimate. Yet, after having decided this, he carries it out immediately. Moreover, in a way, his decision also follows traditional patterns: he obeys the suggestions of the witches, the command of his wife, the signal of the dagger. Doing his crime unthinkingly, he will regret it in the moment of execution. It is then that he becomes aware of having undone himself and realizes that he will be unable to live after his crime. Macbeth *seems to think* in his soliloquy (*Macbeth* 2.1), but he does not think. Rather, he obeys the command. Who commands? It is Lady Macbeth in Macbeth's own heart, the vision of the bloody dagger in his own vision. He knows that he does evil. But since he follows the dagger, he *must* do the deed. Listen to Macbeth: "Whiles I threat, he lives. / Words to the heat of deeds too cold breath gives, / *A bell rings.* I go, and it is done. The bell invites me. / Hear it not, Duncan: for it is a knell / That summons thee to heaven, or to hell" (2.1.60–64). But at the very moment that he murders, he already knows that "Macbeth shall sleep no more" (2.2.41). Macbeth will never become a man of conscience. But his personality will be in shambles. He becomes a bloody tyrant out of his unspeakable feeling of guilt. Lady Macbeth notices this immediately and does not understand: "These deeds must not be thought / After these ways. So, it will make us mad" (2.2.31–32). So it does.

In *Measure for Measure*, when the provost seems to be reluctant to execute Claudio the next day, Angelo becomes furious: "Did not I tell thee, yea? Hadst thou not order? / Why dost thou ask again?" The provost answers: "Lest I might be too rash. / Under your good correction, I have seen / When after execution judgment hath / Repented o'er his doom" (*Measure for Measure* 2.2.7–12). Angelo wants the rash to be done: Claudio should be executed immediately. Command needs to be followed directly by its execution. Yet the provost does some thinking. Why the rashness? Why so sudden? (We know the story: the play can have a relatively happy ending only because the provost has only seemingly followed the order and has rescued Claudio.)

Hamlet is in this matter, as also in many others, a kind of unity of opposites. His constant ruminations bring him not closer to, but further away from, the mute act of revenge (the killing of Claudius) to which he has committed himself at first. (Perhaps he has already at that moment committed himself to something else, yet he was not yet aware of this.) But in the state of rage he never thinks twice about what he is doing; he abuses himself, Ophelia, and his mother. And—also in the state of rage—he can draw his sword and kill. (Alas, he could have looked behind the curtain.) I have an even worse suggestion to make about his act of sending Rosencrantz and Guildenstern to their death. It is part of a game. Hamlet plays a cat-and-mouse game with the two petty rascals, and this "ending" of the game seems to him suddenly the artistically right one. He is, after all, a stage manager. But in the end he ceases playacting.

Shakespeare, the author and the actor, plays around with role-playing. All his characters, and particularly all characters from historicopolitical dramas, play their own game. Sometimes they play the same role or a similar one differently, sometimes similarly two or more entirely different roles. Finally, every actor, from the main characters to the minor ones, has his specific role and his unique relation to his role.

Some players have a deadly seriousness: they make strenuous efforts to play according to their historical script. Other players are clownish: they exhibit a playful relation to their own role, and they play also with others. This has nothing to do with the difference between comedy and tragedy. Richard III plays his role as a clown, while Malvolio takes his role utterly seriously.

One can take up an inherited role, one can create a new role, one can change one's role, one can try to rid oneself of all roles. Historical actors who accept the roles handed down to them by their ancestors, traditionalists who are guided by the system of inherited rights, normally identify themselves with their role and keep little or no distance from it. Still, they often play this role. They normally overdo their task of representation. They are very much aware that they are representing the tradition; they declare this conviction, they emphasize it. Traditional roles need to be played by traditionalists, especially if they face powers who deny the legitimacy or weight of their identity. Henry Hotspur is a case in point. Listen, for example, to what he says after the king tells him to forget Mortimer: "In his behalf I'll empty all these veins, / And shed my dear blood drop by drop in the dust, / But I will lift the downfall Mortimer / As high in the air as this unthankful King, / As thus ingrate and cankered Bolingbrook" (*1 Henry IV*, 1.3.131–35). Hotspur, as his nickname suggests, is of a sanguinary disposition: always angry. Yet, he also plays the angry nobleman to live up to the image of an honest, straightforward—and not very clever—warrior knight. Hotspur plays the role of a man who never pretends to be something other than what he is. But he not only *is* this role, he also *plays* this role. To change their roles, characters must suffer a shock or a bewildering experience. They can change entirely into a new or different person, as King Lear does; or else they can change into a person who plays multiple roles, as does Richard II. They can get to know themselves, as well as others, better than they did throughout their entire previous life (as Gloucester does in *King Lear*); or they can just let a self-assumed and protective role fall away from them (as in the case of Beatrice and Benedick in *Much Ado about Nothing*).

Not all Shakespeare's characters are just playactors; a few of them are also stage managers, or perhaps coauthors. They coauthor, or rather comanage the stage. They set traps for others, they try them, they put them to the test; they ridicule them, they expose them, they make them become what they are not; they humiliate others or let them humiliate themselves. To be a stage manager in a Shakespeare play is in itself neither the sign of wickedness nor of goodness. More precisely, perfectly good people are never stage managers in Shakespeare because they never use other people as mere means. They do not humiliate even the wicked individuals, even those who deserve ridicule and suffering. Horatio is not a stage manager; neither is Brutus or King Henry VI. The most representative stage managers in Shakespeare are perhaps Hamlet, Richard III, the Duke (in *Measure for Measure*), Prospero, and Puck.

Stage managing is not exhausted by pretending, appearing, and acting in disguise, although it has to do with any of these things. Pretending to be someone else, playing a strange or foreign role, can also be misleading. Such devices normally aim at misleading others, but they aim at something; they want to achieve something. Thus, disguise is a means to an end. To this I will return later.

Stage managing also entails devices that can be described as means to an end. The mousetrap scene in Hamlet serves the end of finding proof of the king's guilt. Needless to say, the mousetrap scene does not serve this end alone. It is also an end in itself. Hamlet wants to see the king in the state of terror, he wants the "scene," he wants theater to unfold not only on the stage but also in the audience. Hamlet loves to make fools of Polonius and Osric. They are both fools; yet they are also his servants, his subjects, and, as such, proper objects of his playful spirit. He wants to make them uneasy, to make them fall out of their roles, to shock them, or at least to embarrass them deeply. It is true that they are not only fools but also lackeys, and this treatment is what they deserve. Still, there is a kind of self-deification in assuming the role of the stage manager. After all, it is God who manages the historical stage. As already touched upon, it was Hamlet's stage-managing impulse that sent Rosencrantz and Guildenstern to their death. Here I return for the last time to the radical change in Hamlet's character in act 5. He also ceases to be a stage manager. Hamlet is Shakespeare's character with the deepest and most sincere self-knowledge. Although he never admits his guilt to others (his pride is immense), he does not particularly like himself. By giving up the role of the stage manager, Hamlet resigns from all roles. In this respect he becomes similar to Lear in the tempest scene: he strips himself roleless, naked.

The case of Hamlet already testifies that stage managing is a play that is also an end in itself. And in this deepest sense, this is a play, a game, pleasing for the person who is playing yet frequently painful for those who are being played with. Hamlet plays with the fools and the guilty individuals. Richard III plays with everyone. It is not pleasure enough for him to kill; he enjoys the game played with his targeted victims. He is a sadist. Most of his victims are also guilt ridden and wicked, but not all of them are. I will come back to Richard's story in part II.

In the usual interpretation, the Duke (in *Measure for Measure*) returns to Vienna in disguise to figure out whether Angelo makes a good deputy. This is, in my understanding, only half the story. For, after becoming aware of Angelo's crimes, the Duke could have immediately disclosed his identity in order to fix matters; but he first wants to put everyone on trial and to make decisions about the future life of his subjects as if he were writing a play. Take the example of Mariana, who is written to make love to the Duke and wed him after several scenes of misunderstanding and confusion. While the Duke plays the friar, he decides to marry the novice. The Duke obviously enjoys the fear and trembling of the characters in his drama; he lets them suffer, although he already knows the end of the complications, for he himself will end the story. Letting the characters act under delusions is a self-serving game.

The stage managing of the Duke can have two opposite readings. One can take the story at its face value. If so, the Duke is morally as dubious a character as Angelo, his deputy, a mere spectator who plays God with his subjects, who ties and unties. Yet one can offer another reading. The Duke is just like Prospero. Like Shakespeare himself, he allows the characters to act as they want to act, putting them into situations and letting them become what they are, yet also what they never have yet been: wicked, egoistic, coldhearted, rotten, or just ridiculous and frivolous. He then comes and says, "Let us forget it, we forgive. Those who passed the trial with flying colors, the good and the decent ones, have to forgive. You see, this is the human race. And after all it was I (the Duke) who let these characters loose. I wrote the play in a way as Shakespeare is writing his; I brought the characters together in a situation of my choice—just as my master, Shakespeare, does—and watched them while they were acting. Normally I (and my master Shakespeare) let men and women follow their characters directly to a terrible end. But now I see my responsibility as the stage manager. And thus I offer a relatively happy ending, as happy as these characters deserve, no less, no more. For none of them is guiltless, not even Isabella. I am a just an author, although I made Isabella a heroine of forgiveness, not of justice."

Puck is a stage manager in a comic vein. Putting the juice of the magic flower into the eyes of the four Athenian youths, seemingly by mistake, as well as in the eyes of Titania, on Oberon's order, he simply lets loose the game of love. And he enjoys it. For he also knows, of course—as the non-tragic stage managers always know—that the play will have a happy ending and that we can just sit back and enjoy what happens in between. What happens in between is foolishness, suffering, humiliation and self-humiliation, the senseless and wounding games of love and jealousy. If your lover of yesterday says during the night that he hates you, you no longer understand the world. Yet, is this stage managing not just the author's trick again, making characters show what they are or what they could have been? Was not Angelo (in *Measure for Measure*) declaring his love to Mariana, whom he does not recognize anymore? Is it merely the magic ointment that makes Lysander, the lover of Hermia, hate Hermia and love Helena? Is the magic here not just the modification of the time element, so that what would have happened in two years happens here in two hours? Perhaps Bottom, the wise ass, utters the wisdom of *A Midsummer Night's Dream* properly at the moment when Titania first professes her love to him, to the lad in the image of an ass. Titania: "I love thee." Bottom: "Methinks, mistress, you have little reason for that. And yet, to say the truth, reason and love keep little company together nowadays" (*Midsummer Night's Dream* 3.1.134–37).

Let me now quote from the conversation of Beatrice and Benedick from *Much Ado about Nothing* (5.4.73–78); they are the most adult, most sincere, and truest love pair in Shakespeare's oeuvre. Benedick: "Do not you love me?" Beatrice: "Why no, no more than reason. . . ." Beatrice: "Do not you love me?" Benedick: "Truth no, no more than reason."

To be a stage manager is an essential feature of the characters of *Hamlet* or *Richard III*. But these characters are not only stage managers, they are also actors. Puck and the Duke are only stage managers, for stage managing is their sole "action." But these plays in their entirety are not only about stage managing. *The Tempest* is, however, a *play about the stage manager written by the stage manager.* Prospero is Hamlet, yet he is also the Duke, and also Puck. He is not Richard III, although he tyrannizes both Ariel and Caliban. Yet Ariel and Caliban are Prospero himself. They are the two elements in Prospero's soul that are also forced into order and obedience by Prospero as a stage manager and author. He masterminds all scenes, all encounters in *The Tempest*, beginning with the tempest itself. Like the Duke of Vienna, Prospero knows the outcome of the play before it unravels, because he writes the beginning of the play from the viewpoint of its end.

The play is the temporal unfolding of simultaneous divine foreknowledge. Howmever, the actors do not know the script, and therefore both those who are innocent and those who are guilty tremble in fear. The stage manager plays God. Of course, he plays with men and women who are just fictitious characters—actors on the world stage played by actors on the theater stage. *The Tempest* is the mirror image of stage managing and of authoring. After playing their roles, the actor who plays Hamlet, the one who plays Claudius, and the one who plays Ophelia will all stand up and bow before the applauding audience—if they play well. *The Tempest*, just like *Measure for Measure*, is a play where no one dies. In Shakespeare's tragedies, where every significant character dies, in fact, also no one dies.

In *The Tempest*, Prospero is not an actor. Yet, on the other hand, he is. The actors who symbolize the stage manager are magicosymbolic. I have commented, along with several interpreters before me, that these are the primordial elements (instincts, desires, and so on) in Prospero's own soul. The stage manager, the author, claims both the barbarian and the winged fantasy as his own. Prospero says about Caliban: "This thing of darkness I / Acknowledge mine" (*Tempest* 5.1.278–79). And in the epilogue the actor/author turns to the audience: "Let your indulgence set me free" (Epilogue 20). Prospero's last words in the play are addressed to the winged fantasy, to Ariel: "Then to the elements / Be free and fare thou well" (5.1.321–22). But both the barbarian in us and our winged fantasy need to be kept under control. Who controls them? Reason? Hardly. Rather, it is *order* that controls them. And it is also *wisdom* (in Caliban's words: "his books"). There must be *order in a play.* There must be a beginning and an end. The stage manager allows the characters to invent themselves, to live out their wisdom; yet he also allows their folly, their vices, and perhaps also their virtues, to fail. Still, he is the stage manager. He must force them; he must make them obey.

Measure for Measure ends with (problematic) justice. The end of *The Tempest* is forgiveness, not only in the sense that Prospero forgives, but also in a deeper sense. Consider the sense in which Gonzalo speaks of the story's happy ending: "and all of us [found] ourselves / When no man was his own" (*Tempest* 5.1.215–16). What does it mean to find ourselves? For Gonzalo it means that "ourselves" is that which is the best in us. *Finding ourselves means to find our best selves.* This was said by a good man, for Gonzalo is a good man. Still, this is Shakespeare's last answer to the question, "Who am I?"

And *The Tempest* is about forgiveness in another, equally deep sense. Prospero, or rather the actor who plays Prospero, or rather the author who creates Prospero, the stage manager, says: "As you from crimes would pardoned be, / Let your indulgence set me free" (Epilogue 19–20).

There are only a few stage managers in Shakespeare, but there are numerous characters who pretend to be what they are not. This is not the same thing as role-playing. If one plays a role, one does not necessarily also pretend. One can identify oneself with one's role and make it more poignant. One can also overplay one's role. And one can distance oneself from one's role, change the role, or play more than one role. Furthermore, one can try to get rid of all roles and "just be oneself." In contrast, one can be something else, somebody entirely different from the role that one plays; one can separate being such and seeming such. In this latter case, role-playing, even without pretending, can overemphasize the difference between being and the essence of being without pretending. Pretending is not playing on the tension between the being and the essence of being but playing on the difference between semblance and being (or the essence of being). Hamlet clarifies this distinction succinctly in his first verbal exchange with his mother. Speaking about death, the queen turns to her son with the question, "Why seems it so particular with thee?" And Hamlet answers: "Seems, madam? Nay, it is. I know not 'seems'." After enumerating all the outward signs of grief, Hamlet continues: "These, indeed 'seem', / For they are actions that a man might play; / But I have that within which passeth show— / These but the trappings and the suits of woe" (*Hamlet* 1.2.83–86).

Although pretending is not merely role-playing, it can appear as a kind of secondary role-playing. One can play the role of what one is, or what one desires to be, and also what others expect from one and what one is not. These three kinds of role-playing can hardly be kept apart. A role-player is certainly not always aware of playing a role, unless he is overplaying it. The one who pretends, however, knows that he pretends, that he is in fact playing a role. If one pretends, one plays someone else's role, a role that is not one's own. One wants to be seen as someone who one is not; one wants to be misread and misunderstood by others; one wants to deceive, and one knows whether one has succeeded or failed in deceiving.

Shakespeare's comedies are full of double role-playing. For example, the actor (a young boy) plays a girl; the girl plays herself. She also assumes the shape and the personality of a boy; she pretends to be a boy. Yet s/he overplays the role of the young boy, although s/he is constantly falling back into the role of the girl. A beautiful woman falls in love with him/her (*As You Like It, Twelfth Night,* etc.). The double game creates odd and awkward situations that are both erotically dense and playful.

These lighthearted yet not innocent games about the sexes are missing from Shakespeare's tragedies. However, the duplication of role-playing is structurally significant in Shakespeare's stories of politics, history, public victory, and defeat. For example, the actor plays the son of the Earl of Gloucester, who plays first the role of Poor Tom, then again the role of the earl, and at the end the role of the ruler, the future king of the realm.

I already mentioned that the warrior (soldier, general, warlord) and the man of politics, or rather the man who is good at politics, are in many respects essentially different character types in Shakespeare. Generally, although not always, the great soldier is a traditional character. (The obvious counterexample is Henry VII.) But whether traditional or not, a soldier pretends or uses a disguise only to cheat or to mislead the military enemy. He does not pretend before his own comrades in arms; he does not want to deceive them. He knows no civil enemies, or if he does, he confronts them directly. This is why Volumnia's argument to persuade Coriolanus to practice political hypocrisy is a fake one. Volumnia asks with seeming naïveté why, since Coriolanus has no moral problem with deceiving the Voices on the battlefield, he has second thoughts about playing someone that he is not for the plebeians. Volumnia's argument is merely formal and does not hit home. Cheating the military enemy is one of the oldest games. Cheating the public enemy, the civil enemy, is a new game, however; it is not traditional, and it seems wrong. Cheating the military enemy enhances a man's honor, whereas cheating his own fellows (even those whom he despises) dishonors him. In war one does not hide one's motivation, for the motivation is perfectly clear: victory. One can only hide strategy or tactics. The political person, however, also hides his motivation. The traditional man of honor does not fit into this role. If he tries to play it, he does it half-heartedly and makes constant mistakes; and instead of becoming inscrutable, he becomes transparent.

In Shakespeare, strategy in war and strategy in politics are different in kind, in spite of their formal resemblance. And, what is more important, good strategy in one or the other requires different kinds of personalities. In Shakespeare a good man of politics is normally also good at war, yet the good swordsman or military leader will often be a poor political strategist. These Shakespearean insights are also very close to those of Machiavelli. A man of politics, of political shrewdness, is not a traditional but a modern character. Men of politics (or of politicking) are new characters who have developed an ability to choose the most able military men for the right posts on the basis of of their skill alone. In all likelihood men who are good at politics will win all games. If one is a good fox—as a politician must be—one can also be a good lion, or at least hire a good lion. But a good lion is rarely also a good fox. In Shakespeare a good soldier can do either much good or much harm to his countrymen. He can be a selfless hero, or cruel, bloodthirsty, and tyrannical; yet a hypocrite he will never be. A man of politics (church dignitaries included) can do much evil (like Winchester) or much good (like Octavius); but he is always also a hypocrite.

Hypocrisy, particularly political hypocrisy, takes diverse forms in Shakespeare's plays. Every Shakespearean hypocrite is a hypocrite in his own way. For as I said, Shakespeare—unlike Molière—never portrays men as embodiments of vices or virtues but always as complex, manifold characters who in the last instance resemble no one but themselves.

After having advanced my apologies for the impossibility of standardizing or classifying what remains individual and unique in Shakespeare, I will still try to classify the great variety of hypocrites in Shakespeare's political world theater.

Shakespeare's greatest and most successful political hypocrites do not hide their personality. They do not pretend to be what they are not. They are goal-rational actors. They know the goal they want to achieve. In order to achieve this goal they use several more or less dirty means. They need to hide their motivations, the steps they are going to take. Thus they are hypocritical to this extent and for as long as hypocrisy is, in their judgment, necessary for achieving their goals. To speak with Kant: they hide the maxims of their actions not just from their enemies but also from their friends. Yet these goal-rational hypocrites are normally cold men; they do not act cruelly out of revenge, hatred, or spite. Every act of cruelty needs to have its aim and necessity. I have already mentioned Henry V's ugly farewell words to Falstaff as the typical case of a well-committed cruelty. Octavius, the most cold-blooded hypocrite in the Shakespearean gallery of politicians, frequently acts cruelly, although he is not a cruel character. Neither is Henry V. They commit cruel deeds, they betray their friends only for a purpose. This purpose includes, of course, maintaining their power and might, yet not only this. They strongly believe that their own power serves their country best, that they are somehow the executors of historical or divine destiny, that they are men of destiny, men who stand precisely where they stand because they cannot do otherwise.

A totally different kind of hypocrisy is that of Iago. Iago pretends to be someone other than who he is. He hides both his personality and his motivation. He is a man of the laws of nature, just like Edmund. But he is petty. Whether his pettiness is due to the pettiness of his conditions is a question no one can answer, for Shakespeare portrays this time a dangerous and wicked hypocrite in a lowly situation in a limited space of action. Shakespeare is here playing again with the relation between the political man and the military man. Iago is a military man; this is the role he played in the past. We do not even know whether soldier was a primary or a secondary role for him. Whether his being a good soldier was also an act of hypocrisy before the story of our drama begins to unfold, or whether he played his own role then and has built up the personality we are confronted with only later, is a matter of guesswork. Perhaps Othello's confidence in Iago is not as naïve and misplaced as it seems; perhaps Iago was a different man in time of war than the man he became in time of peace— perhaps. But at the moment that our drama begins, Iago is already the lowly politicking man appearing in the disguise of a simple and honest soldier—a politicking man and not a man of politics. Perhaps, if Iago had

had the chance to get mixed up with politics, he would have exercised his ability to pretend, appearing in disguise and leading others by their nose in the arena of grand history just like Richard III. Yet Iago is a base man in a humble situation, dependent on his general, and not even second in rank to him, for this is denied him. He lives by his ability to politick, he exercises his talent to dupe others solely to destroy their lives. Iago's ability to politick takes an evil turn, yet he can wrong only a few, he can destroy his victims only in the private theater. He cannot make any difference in the politics of Venice. He makes Othello a murderer, Desdemona a victim of murder; he lets Rodrigo be killed, kills his wife just to serve his own pleasure and satisfy his resentment. For Iago does not do what he does primarily for gain, not even for revenge, but for sadistic pleasure. There is also a Machiavellian wisdom in the story. A person who commits cruelty for the sake of a constructive goal will cease to be cruel after achieving his goals. One can be a great political strategist; yet if one has no constructive goals, the strategy will be exhausted in the game of sadistic pleasure. This is political capacity wrongly applied. It comes to naught, and everyone will pay—the guilty and the innocent alike, as it happens also in *Othello*. True, the petty politicking character needs fairly naïve enemies to win. And he can still fail to win if there are men and women of a new kind of civic courage who stand up in defense of the selected victims. There is no doubt that in *Much Ado about Nothing* Claudio believes the bastard, Don John, rather than his beloved Hero. And Hero would be lost unless Beatrice and Benedick played a trick on Claudio to rescue the humble (and old-fashioned) innocent girl. Emilia, another woman–rebel, the plebeian alter ego of the patrician Beatrice (in *Othello*), comes too late, and she also becomes a victim.

All kinds of Shakespearean hypocrites, whether men of politics or of politicking, world-historical significance or lowly and petty characters in a limited situation, are frequently also *cynical*. The most wonderfully portrayed blend of hypocrisy and cynicism will be discussed later: the gigantic figure of Gloucester, Richard III. Shakespeare also portrays *fanatics,* both harmful and harmless ones; yet he suspects that fanatics, ascetics, and self-righteous characters are deep down also *hypocrites*. The fanatic misanthrope, Jaques, is, for example, accused of hypocrisy by Duke Senior in *As You Like It*. "Most mischievous foul sin, in chiding sin / For thou thyself has been a libertine, / As sensual as the brutish sting itself, / And all th'embossed sores and headed evils / That thou with license of free foot hast caught / Wouldst thou disgorge into the general world" (*As You Like It* 2.7.64–69). But whether Jaques is a hypocrite is a matter of interpretation. In *Measure for Measure* Angelo is a hypocrite, but in all probability not from the beginning of the play. He is first a fanatic and later becomes a hypocrite, whereas Jaques is (if indeed he is) first a hypocrite, to become later a fanatic. Shakespeare (perhaps because of his own political convictions) never credits a high church dignitary with sincere religious feeling or humble devotion. Such dignitaries are slightly or grossly hypocritical and cynical. For Shakespeare, truly religious men are humble and good, and they are without exception hopeless and thus harmful in politics. Here Shakespeare, far more than Machiavelli, gives his own vision of the dawn of the modern world a Weberian turn. He believes in the plurality of modern deities and in the relative independence of the spheres of politics, religion, the art of war, and the art of fiction, respectively.

I have distinguished thus far between grand politics and petty politicking; scheming for success, scheming to achieve goals in the world theater, on the one hand, and, on the other, scheming to destroy others, conspiring, and taking pleasure in private. But in the comedies, the nontragic dramas, and the romances, men and particularly women can conspire for the sake of justice, to rescue others, to rescue themselves, sometimes absolutely without hypocrisy and even without appearing in disguise. In *The Merry Wives of Windsor* two women make a fool of the old, fat, conceited womanizer, Falstaff, and of a jealous husband by playing tricks on them. Thus is Malvolio fooled, moreover betrayed. This constant hide-and-seek game, which is one of the strong spices in the dramatic art of Shakespeare, distinguishes his dramas from all ancient tragedies. In Greek tragedies gods play the tricks, not men. In Shakespeare men and women play entirely different tricks on one another. Puck and Ariel are also very human and lovely tricksters in our dream world.

Appearing in disguise is not hypocrisy. Moreover, those heroes of Shakespeare who in fact play a role in disguise are normally not cynical or hypocritical. Many interpreters will challenge this point. For example, the Duke in *Measure for Measure* can be also interpreted as a hypocrite. This is, however, not my interpretation, as is obvious from the comparison with Prospero. One can appear in disguise because of magic (like Bottom, the ass), to spy on the opinion of others (Henry V among his soldiers), for loyalty's sake, to protect a respected or beloved person from danger (Kent in *King Lear*), to gain one's beloved (Helena in *All's Well That Ends Well*), to survive the consequences of injustice, and to do justice (Hermione and Perdita in *The Winter's Tale*), to start a new life after having been rescued from a disaster to gain the love of one's own Duke (Viola in *Twelfth Night*), to protect oneself from being murdered (Edmund in the guise of Poor Tom in *King Lear*), and so on. Moreover, one can be, live, and exist in guise (disguise) without changing robes, voice, beard, or countenance. Madness can also be a disguise. The use of madness as disguise is Hamlet's specialty.

Men and women in disguise are normally fooling others for the sake of something good or something evil, yet sometimes they are the ones who are fooled and put to ridicule, just as Rodrigo is by Iago, or Falstaff by the merry widows of Windsor.

Every person appears in disguise who hides his person, his identity, and not just his plans, acts, and emotions. To be in disguise is a kind of self-alienation (not just in the case of playing the mad person or the fool); yet it is a self-alienation where the self is itself aware of its situation and remains ready and able to shake off the guise if circumstances allow. If one cannot shake off a borrowed guise, one has lost one's self or else gained another. To be "a man" can also be a guise (as we have seen in the case of Kent), and to be naked can also be one. Yet all possible guises will not do in all cases. The wolf can take up the guise of the lamb, but the lamb cannot appear clad as a wolf (for then it would cease to be a lamb). The high can take up the guise of the lowly, but if the lowly masquerades as high, he will become ridiculous.

One does not hide oneself just by changing one's name (as in the case of Edgar and Kent, the Duke, Prospero, and so many other Shakespearean heroes). One also has to hide one's face and "internal chambers." One cannot hide one's internal chambers simply by taking up another garment. One needs to protect oneself against those who want to play their tune upon the instrument of one's soul.

In the great plays of Shakespeare everyone is a stranger to everyone else, at least at the beginning of the drama. (Exception: Horatio and Hamlet). Yet as the drama unfolds, some will get to know one another, get a proof of loyalty or disloyalty, of humanness or brutishness. Whether one remains a stranger in this world or finds one's way in settling in it, the memory of the trial will not fade. And this is the case not only in the tragedies but also in most of the comedies. There is in Shakespeare's plays a dual movement of making ourselves known and understood and hiding ourselves, protecting our innermost soul from intrusions. The drama makes the naïve characters shake off their total confidence, yet it also makes characters who are always on guard shake off their all-consuming skepticism and misanthropy. *Timon of Athens* is the most extreme example of this theme. For here you have a character who begins with absolute naïveté—believing everyone and doubting nothing—and ends as a character who abuses everyone and believes no one. But Shakespeare's characters rarely vacillate from one extreme to the other, from absolute trust to absolute mistrust.

The most subtle kind of hide-and-seek play is Hamlet's game. His role as stage manager serves him as a vehicle of disguise. His playing with others also belongs to his art of disguise. He does not need another robe for disguise—just another smile, another intonation, another sentence. He can make others not understand a word about him without changing his name or his face, his outward appearance. True, he hides himself once by exhibiting his madness through a disheveled appearance. We know that the garment, as much as the facial expression, is just what "seems" and what can be pretended. What one is, one cannot pretend, but one can hide. Hamlet wants to hide what he is. Twice he employs the metaphor of the musical instrument for his innermost soul. Hamlet says to Rosencrantz and Guildenstern: "Why, look you now, how unworthy a thing you make of me! You would play upon me, you would seem to know my stops, you would pluck out the heart of my mystery, you would sound me from my lowest note to the top of my compass; and there is much music, excellent voice in this little organ yet cannot you make it speak. 'Sblood, do you think I am easier to be played on than a pipe? Call me what instrument you will, though you can fret me, you cannot play upon me" (*Hamlet* 3.2.351–60).

Men and women in a drama can enter it in the dark. They know little about the world, they do not know themselves. They know little about trust and distrust. The tragedies as well as the comedies and romances are dramas of enlightenment. One gets to know something more about oneself, something more about the others as the drama unfolds. Yet there are also opposite moves. Men are born to believe that they know the world and their surroundings, but as the drama unfolds, they learn that they know nothing—neither themselves nor the others. Both processes develop simultaneously in most Shakespearean dramas. One should not forget: time is out of joint. Hiding, taking up disguises, and disclosing ourselves are moves in the chess game of the knowledge of the world and of ourselves. One plays this game with others; it is a social game. Others play with us or against us; they want to know us, our hidden selves, in order to betray our hopes and our trust, or to help us, or to present us their own souls on a platter. One cannot understand men in guise and disguise without disclosure and vice versa.

The plot of the drama is the game. The knowledge and ignorance of human character, the knowledge and ignorance of ourselves, either support one another or are at cross purposes. Yet they are always connected. We are all strangers in the world, we are all betrayed, and we betray others. Yet we can also be friends, and there are gratifications. Still, strangers we remain.

As Albany says when he realizes that he must become the king of the orphaned and devastated realm (because Kent, the loyal squire, will follow his master, the dead King Lear into his grave): "The weight of this sad time we must obey, / Speak what we feel, not what we ought to say. / The oldest hath borne most. We that are young / Shall never see so much, nor live so long" (*King Lear* Quarto 5.3.318–21). *King Lear* ends in utter resignation. For one should not forget: these are the words of a man who lived in the disguise of the naked fool, Poor Tom, "the thing itself," and who will wear the symbolic rags of Poor Tom underneath his armor as long as he lives.

But one can also look at the world of falsity and betrayal with the eyes of Duke Senior, banished from his throne by his younger brother. Amiens, a loyal friend, is singing the most consoling and cheering song: "Blow, blow, thou winter wind, / Thou art not so unkind / As man's ingratitude. / Thy tooth is not so keen, / Because thou art not seen, / Although thy breath be rude. / Hey-ho, sing hey-ho, unto the green holly. / Most friendship is feigning, most loving, mere folly. / Then, hey-ho, the holly; / This life is most jolly" (*As You Like It* 2.7.175–84). Yes, most friendship is feigning, most loving mere folly—but not all, not all. Life is jolly—as it is in the enchanted forest, and for some but not for all. Not for Jaques, the misanthrope. Shakespeare does not take sides—or does he? One has the impression that in this crucial case he does. He sympathizes with the skeptics, he deeply understands men in deep despair. Yet he keeps the misanthrope at arm's length.

4

The Absolute Strangers

I strongly agree with Geoffrey O'Brien when he says in his review of
Alan Bloom's book that playing a drama changes the drama. The recent
Budapest performance of *The Merchant of Venice* directed by Robert
Alföldi changed this drama for the spectators. I went to the theater without great expectations and I left it with a new and different *Merchant of
Venice* in mind, one that hit me as authentic and true. No one single word
was changed (although there was a new Hungarian translation of the drama
that got closer to Shakespeare's use of language than the previous, more
beautifully worded but poetically homogenizing translation). Now that I
am going to speak of the absolute stranger in Shakespeare, I cannot forget
this Shylock, I cannot rid my memory of this performance. I never would
have thought of this interpretation if I had not seen it. Yet after having seen
it, it became self-evident to me.

The stranger or alien—the refugee, the homeless, the outcast, the man in
search of safe haven—is perhaps the most traditional character of tragedy. In
Richard Sennet's view, the drama *King Oedipus* is essentially not a family
drama but the tragedy of the stranger. Oedipus is also a stranger in Colonus.
Orestes is a refugee, Electra is a stranger in her own city, Iphigenia is a
stranger both in Aulis and in Tauris, Prometheus is an outcast, Dionysus and
his cult are constantly referred to as "alien" in Euripides' *Bacchae*—I could
go on with the enumeration. These strangers are, however, not absolute
strangers. They are cast out from their home, but they can also return home,
as Orestes and Iphigenia did in their bodies or Oedipus did in his grave.
There are no absolute strangers there, with perhaps the exception of Medea,
but even Medea suffers the woman's lot and not first and foremost the
absolute stranger's lot. Shakespeare—perhaps without being aware of it—
stands here in the Greek tradition. But he also changes it.

In his book *Shakespeare's Politics*, Alan Bloom assigns a central place to
Othello and *The Merchant of Venice* in Shakespeare's vision of politics. I do
not share his view. Shakespeare's historicopolitical imagination does,

indeed, center around the stranger. It does not center around the absolute stranger but around the conditional stranger, the stranger-in-a-situation. Men and women who get caught in the double bind are always conditional strangers. Torn by two concepts of nature, they are strangers among those for whom tradition is binding, and also among those who are committed to the right of nature alone. When a Shakespearean character perceives something done to him or her as a thing out of order, unexpected and incomprehensible, he or she will be estranged from the world. But only those characters can be estranged from their world who have once belonged to this world and have understood it (as Coriolanus will be alienated from Rome). One can also be estranged from the world if one feels entirely betrayed, like Timon of Athens. Antony is a Roman who understood everything that the Romans were doing but all the same felt himself estranged from Rome after falling in love with a stranger and, through her, with the East. Yet he is—as a Roman—still not a stranger. Neither is Cleopatra a stranger in her own world: she is very much at home in Egypt; she is a stranger to the Romans and would be entirely estranged in Rome, and not just as the exhibit on a triumphal march. There are in Shakespeare many estranged lovers; a man or a woman who becomes estranged is not an absolute stranger.

To be or to become estranged means also to act strangely, in a strange way. A person acts strangely when others do not understand him or her, when an act crosses all expectations and defies the usual explanations. Yet men or women who act strangely are not absolute strangers. Their strange behavior is a puzzle to be solved. The entourage of an estranged character is interested in solving his or her puzzle. Hamlet knows that his enemies try hard to open the hidden chambers of his soul. He is strange, he behaves strangely, but he is not an absolute stranger. Behaving strangely can also mean to behave ridiculously. Yet ridiculous behavior is not always strange. If men of lower ranks use "elegant" or "foreign" words without knowing their meaning, if they argue in an illogical manner and speak English improperly, they are ridiculous, yet there is nothing strange about them. They become strange (in Shakespeare) whenever they get mixed up with actions outside the scope of their comprehension, or whenever they accidentally cross into a territory that they do not understand. Take the example of a scene in *Much Ado about Nothing* where the ridiculous and honest officers who are philosophizing a lot of nonsense discover and unveil a conspiracy. This is indeed a strange coincidence of accidents and character roles. Yet neither Bottom nor Dogberry nor even Trinculo (from the *Tempest*) is a stranger. They belong to the places in the social hierarchy in which they normally move; they take each other seriously and they know roughly what to expect of each other. They are ridiculous if seen by members of higher strata or classes (and the spectators who are sometimes like them), but one knows what to expect from them as long as they stay in their own situation. Surprises come only if they cross the borders, as in *The Tempest*.

The conditional strangers are chief characters in many of Shakespeare's political dramas. Yet there are only two absolute strangers in all the plays of Shakespeare: Shylock and Othello. Interestingly, both stories take place in the cosmopolitan city of Venice. Of course, Shakespeare has inherited the stories. But he was the one who chose exactly these stories from among many others for his dramas. I think this fact is significant. Absolute strangers are not estranged from their world because the world where they live has never been theirs. They are not strangers because they act against the expectations of others; it is precisely the contrary: they are strangers just because they are expected to act as strangers. Their relation to their world is accidental, for the territory of their actions has nothing to do with their roots, upbringing, or tradition. Moreover, the whole world around them, with all its ranks and classes, is alien from their tradition. There is no second Moor in the play *Othello*. Although there is another Jew besides Shylock in *The Merchant of Venice*, we do not see Shylock's behavior in the company of Jews (Shakespeare has him mention that he is going to meet them in the synagogue); rather, we see him only in the company of Venetian gentiles.

The absolute stranger is an absolute stranger first because he *is employed as a stranger,* for doing certain things that the natives of the cosmopolitan city would not do. Othello is a condottiere of sorts who hires out his services for foreign cities, this time for Venice. The city hires him to perform dangerous tasks: to fight with the Turks and risk his life, to do things that the hedonistic young people of Venice are unwilling to undertake because they want only to enjoy the sweet fruits of victory. He is hired, but he is also used; he is hired for as long as he is useful. He will be immediately dismissed from his generalship after having won the decisive battle. (This happens, as we know, while the Venetian patricians are still ignorant about the fate of Desdemona.) Shylock is used in the same fashion as a moneylender. The merchants of Venice, who believe that it is beneath their dignity to accept interest on a loan, take Shylock's loans and still harvest a greater profit after having paid the interest. It is obvious that Shylock's profession is despised but also needed. Shakespeare makes it obvious that Shylock, although he lends for interest, does not hurt the economic interests of the merchants of Venice but rather furthers them. The merchants are adventurers whose ships take risks at sea, who can win immense fortunes if they are successful. Those ships are busy robbing the native people—as we learn, people from the East—and trading in slaves. All this they can accommodate within their pure Christian conscience. The people with whom they trade in the East are also strangers. The merchants of Venice may behave fairly toward their own folk, but not toward the strangers. All of this is frequently neglected by interpreters of *Merchant,* although it is in fact emphasized in the play. Very similar things can be said about *Othello*. The war is fought against strangers (mainly against the Turks), that is, against people from the Orient; the Oriental Othello is used by the cosmopolitan Venetian patricians to fight against Oriental people.

If there is a political message in these dramas of Shakespeare, it is an unusual one. The typical politicohistorical dramas are dramas of monarchy and dramas of the republic. Here we encounter the dramas of cosmopolitanism. Shakespeare, who wanted to explore the essence of human characters in all significant situations, finds in Venice a new situation and the new character of the absolute stranger. Normally, Shakespeare throws his characters into situations where they touch the border between the traditional and the modern. But in cosmopolitan Venice the old has already disappeared. In the world where the figure of the absolute stranger appears, the cards have been dealt in a new way.

Othello and Shylock are absolute strangers because of their absolute rootlessness in the world that employs and uses them, and because their employment is their subsistence. Moreover, they serve employers who legitimately despise them. For there is no doubt that Othello, the hired gun, is as much despised by the Venetians as Shylock, the usurer Jew. Both were seen as pagans and non-Christians and as such entirely different, entirely other. There is an important element in Shakespeare's portrayal of the essence of the absolute stranger, namely, that the stranger's environment is not interested in understanding him. The environment is not interested in the person of the stranger, just in his (despised and useful) function. Desdemona, one of the most beautiful and most betrayed girl-rebels in Shakespeare, is unique because she is the only one in *Othello* for whom Othello was not a function but a man. In *The Merchant of Venice* there is no single person who is even for a single minute interested in Shylock as a human being. Shylock as a man does not exist.

Of course, one can employ someone in service only if the service is offered. Furthermore, one can offer one's service just as a service. But one can also hold higher or different expectations. One can claim that through having performed a service, one becomes similar to those for whom the service was done. One can think that after having served Venice well, one is already a Venetian—or at least can become a Venetian. This is what both Othello and Shylock think. They believe that the services they keep rendering to people who are not better than they are but just different suffice to make them part of the world to which they have rendered their services. Othello and Shylock do not see themselves as inferior to others. They are the kind of strangers who want to be regarded and respected as natives. But they also know that they chase a vain hope. The tension in their character, their extreme irritability, their constant swinging between humble behavior and rage, are psychological manifestations of this tension between situation and claim. In the case of Othello, his assimilationist illusions can be seen in the text of the play. In the case of Shylock, this is a matter of interpretation. In my interpretation (which is also the interpretation of the Budapest performance of 1998), Shylock is also an assimilationist. The whole performance is built around one significant and often neglected sentence. In act 4, when Portia enters the scene as the Doctor of Law and for the first time encounters Antonio and Shylock, she first asks: "Which is the merchant here, and which is the Jew?" (*The Merchant of Venice* 4.1.171). Obviously, by sight she cannot tell one from the other. Shylock looks like a merchant of Venice, he wears the clothes of a Venetian patrician. Neither his stature nor his look, perhaps not even his face, shows the Jew. Why is he then a Jew? What makes him a Jew? But even if Portia cannot tell by sight the merchant from the Jew, the Venetian merchants, the Doge, and all other Venetians know which is the merchant and which is the Jew. *They see it because they know it.* They see it because they expect that a Jew will behave as a Jew normally behaves, and that a Venetian patrician will behave as a Venetian patrician should behave. They know that Jews and patricians are entirely different. They know that Antonio is one of them and that Shylock is entirely alien. Everyone hates Shylock *because* he is a Jew.

If one expects men to be different, they are different. In the case of Othello the difference shows in the color of his skin. No one would ask which is Cassio and which is the Moor because they can be distinguished at first glance. Othello's desire to assimilate has already been frustrated by the color of his skin, but he fails to recognize this. His naïveté, his total ignorance of human character, his irritability and vulnerability play a great part in his crime and undoing, though they are certainly not their causes, just their conditions.

Since in Shylock's case one could *not* tell the merchant from the Jew, the *knowledge* that he is a Jew determines the behavior of the Venetian and the knowledge of his profession. He is employed as a moneylender; he has no ships to send to the Orient and no arms with which to rob other people of their wealth or to acquire slaves. In short, he is not able to engage in adventures. As a Jew he practices a profession regarded as unworthy for and by the Venetian patricians. The Venetians believe along with Aristotle that money should not beget money, that money that begets money is unnatural. Obviously, they see nothing unnatural in sending ships to trade in gold, spices, or slaves. These are regarded as noble things. Masters need slaves: this is a noble thing. Masters treat slaves as slaves: this is a noble thing. Adventure is noble. Risking wealth is noble. This is a merchant class that believes there is a kind of wealth that does not debase a person, and one can gain enormous riches and still remain a decent man and good Christian. Yet the one who gets rich in an unnatural way deserves contempt.

However, in Shakespeare there is another aspect in which Shylock *is* a

Jew. He looks like a Venetian, he behaves like a Venetian, he smiles like a Venetian, but he prays like a Jew. This is the meaning of the short scene between Shylock and Tubal, the other Jew in the play: "Go, Tubal, and meet me at our synagogue. Go, good Tubal; at our synagogue, Tubal" (*The Merchant of Venice* 3.1.119–21). When Shylock is compelled to become a Christian near the end of the play, he is killed, whether or not he is in fact killed by the mob. In all probability he is lynched, since in the last scene of the play his testimony is read.

Thus Shakespeare portrays Othello and Shylock as absolute strangers in the process of (failed) assimilation. Of course, they could not have been portrayed any other way. For Shakespeare could not have set the dramas in a Moorish or a Jewish community. And if he had, these would not have been plays about absolute strangers.

In most of the political and historical plays of Shakespeare, two worlds enter into conflict and neither assimilates the other. This is also the reason why among all the strangers there are but two absolute strangers. Absolute strangers must lose. They are characters of the dramas of failed assimilation. But it is not only absolute strangers who try to assimilate in Shakespeare's plays. Some bastards try to assimilate into the world of their natural fathers. Sometimes they attempt this directly by gaining the respect of the world of the fathers, at other times they attempt it indirectly by occupying the place of the legitimate world of the fathers. The two absolute strangers of Shakespeare are, however, engaged in a hopeless venture: to preserve strangeness (religion, skin color) and to be accepted completely. I do not say that this is always an illusion, but for a long time it was. And Shakespeare presented it as a representative illusion.

Before I saw the new Budapest performance, I believed *The Merchant of Venice* to be an impossible drama. It coheres three stories with the help of a single character, Portia. Two of the stories are parables or, rather, fairy tales. First there is the story of the three caskets (the golden, the silver, and the leaden one) and the suitors who have to choose among them to get the hand of Portia and her enormous wealth. The story is not original, and Shakespeare does not make a grand effort to make it more interesting than it is. At the end comes the story of the ring, and with this story the expected happy ending. It seems as if the drama of Shylock and of Antonio, the merchant of Venice, is sandwiched between these two fairy tales. The title of the drama, however, does not refer to Portia but to Antonio, for he is the merchant of Venice. Still, the reader is not interested in him. Whenever Portia and her parables do not dominate the scene, Shylock does. This is why it is so frequently believed that Shylock is the merchant of Venice indicated by the title.

Nearly as difficult as giving an account of the structure of the play is giving an account of its genre. What kind of drama is this? For a long time it was played as a comedy. But it can be played as a comedy only if the spectator sides entirely with the Venetian golden youth in excluding the stranger. If the regard is one-sided, then Shylock is just a wicked comedian. He is wicked, for he wants flesh, although he likes money best; and he is comic because he loses, because he falls victim to the trap he himself laid. The good conquers and the lowly, petty evil is vanquished. There is then reason for laughter and for celebration. *The Merchant of Venice* then becomes a Carnival play that thematizes the defeat of the devil and the triumph of life with song and dance.

This interpretation is now out of fashion, and not just because of Auschwitz. If the double bind is a constitutive structural element of the Shakespearean drama, one can take the stance that the double bind exists in *The Merchant of Venice*, all the more so because the natural right argument voiced by good and evil characters alike—by Edmund and by Juliet, but also by Henry V—is voiced by Shylock as well. Even if the cards are dealt anew and there is no tradition left, the world of domination can continue to be challenged with reference to natural rights. One can take seriously a recurring Shakespearean theme and assume that it has a structurally constitutive role in this drama as well.

It is true that *The Merchant of Venice* can hardly be played easily as a tragedy like *Othello*. This is not just because Othello is a general and, as such, noble and well suited to play a tragic role, whereas Shylock is a moneylender, a civic figure who does not take risks and whose lowly trade does not fit into the tragic role. First and foremost it is because in *Othello* the innocent Desdemona and Emilia die as a result of Othello's jealous folly. However, no one is hurt in *The Merchant* except Shylock himself. Thus *The Merchant of Venice* is neither a comedy nor a tragedy. It is not a romance in the sense of the later Shakespearean plays, either. It seems as if in the structural heterogeneity of the play—the impression one gets that it is glued together loosely from three different fairy tales—the second fairy tale, that of the evil Shylock, got out of hand and became more forceful and more significant than other elements of the play. It is clear here also that Shakespeare lets his characters create themselves, not just in the moments of their soliloquies, but also in their intercourse with others.

According to the usual interpretation of the play, Shylock, the moneylender, is interested in money alone, whereas the young people of Venice, although not faultless, are involved in far more noble things like love and friendship. The play's central message, according to this interpretation, involves the conflict between justice and forgiveness. Portia speaks the rhetoric of forgiveness, Shylock speaks up for justice and fails to forgive. If read in this way, *The Merchant of Venice* becomes the companion piece to *Measure for Measure,* for there, too, the final showdown is played out between the principles of forgiveness and justice.

My interpretation will be different. The contrast between the base moneylender and the decent youth is absolutely not borne out by the text. The forgiveness/justice contrast, however, is shown in Portia's argument to persuade Shylock in *The Merchant* and Isabella's argument to persuade the Duke in *Measure for Measure*. Yet in Shakespeare an argument is never just a philosophical and religious statement. All arguments are arguments in a context, they are actions. Isabella implores the Duke for mercy and *is* merciful; Portia reasons against Shylock for mercy but *is not* merciful. The truth of reasoning is in both cases beyond doubt, but in a drama the truth of an argument depends also on its truthfulness. And there is no parallel between the two plays in this matter. A plea for mercy from the mouth of someone who will turn out to be unmerciful (Portia) is hypocritical, and such a plea from the mouth of someone who used to be unmerciful but became merciful (Isabella) is a gesture of penitence. Portia and Isabella are saying the same thing, but they are not doing the same thing.

In my interpretation of *The Merchant of Venice* it is not Shylock who is obsessed by money but rather the whole of Venice. The play begins with Bassanio blackmailing Antonio for money with love: "And from your love I have a warranty / To unburden all my plots and purposes / How to get clear of all the debts I owe" (1.1.132–34). He needs money to get Portia, and with her still more money. The plot could not start to unfold without Bassanio's insistence on getting his money while Antonio's ships are still at sea, and without Antonio's desire to satisfy his beloved in everything he wishes.

Antonio is well known for his hatred of Jews. The Jew is generally despised, yet Antonio's hatred is personal. He hates Shylock for lending money for interest and not just as a friendly service, but his hatred grows until it becomes entirely irrational. Antonio despises Shylock not because he despises the stranger, as everyone else does, but because he is an anti-Semite, and his anti-Semitism becomes an obsession. Antonio, the merchant of Venice, is an irrational man. His love of Bassanio is also irrational, yet this love motivates him to the greatest generosity, to be ready to die for his friend and lend him money to marry a woman, which means also the end of their relationship. That this is a homosexual relationship is only hinted at by Shakespeare, and another interpretation is possible. But that Antonio is in love with Bassanio and promotes his marriage against his own strongest feelings cannot be doubted. Yet as much as his love for Bassanio motivates Antonio to do irrational things and take irrational risks, so does his hatred of Shylock assume an entirely irrational form, as all obsessions do. For the merchant of Venice, this play ends with a Pyrrhic victory. He can satisfy his hatred, but not his love. Moreover, he is the one who loses through Portia's winning of her plea. For it would have been better for him to become a victim of Shylock's knife than to see Bassanio happy in the arms of a very wealthy woman, to see that his lover does not need either his love or his money anymore.

Let me return to my point. From the first scene of the drama everyone is obsessed with money. Nothing else is on the agenda. Even love is always coupled with, or subjected to, the hunger for money. The difference between Shylock and the rest of the Venetians is *not* that the rest are uninterested in wealth and Shylock simply their opposite. Although Shylock is interested in interest, which is a matter of rational calculation, he becomes irrational in his confrontation with Antonio. He becomes like Antonio. In their personal showdown, their personal fight for life or death, both are interested only in flesh. The fight is the showdown between the irrational anti-Semite who rejects the Jew's drive to assimilate, who makes it clearer than anyone else that Shylock is not welcome in Venice, and the Jew who hates Antonio personally, beyond all measure. The idea of getting his interest not in money but in a pound of Antonio's flesh shows that Shylock is "outside" himself, that he is no longer interested in gain. Shylock is obsessed with taking Antonio's flesh as much as Antonio is obsessed with having Bassanio's. These two actors stand in the center, obsessed, ready to kill or to be killed. They are the only ones who no longer care for money. All the other actors, who still care for money, become grey and of secondary significance, spectators of a grand duel. The genius of Shakespeare is not in the portrayal of the Jew but in the portrayal of an alien who will transform himself into a native through the *radicalization of evil*.

The phrase "radicalization of evil" is taken from Sartre, who says that the oppressed are determined by the gaze—the regard— of their oppressors and must accept the roles their oppressors determine. The oppressed can liberate themselves only while accepting themselves as they are and immediately turning the tables on their oppressors. Through this reversal the oppressed will treat those who have hitherto treated them as objects as their own objects instead of as subjects. Sartre says in his preface to *The Damned of the Earth* that the radicalization of evil is the only way for the oppressed to liberate themselves not just politically but also psychologically and that the radicalization of evil implies acts of violence; it happens, in fact, through violence.

I do not accept this last conclusion. I quote Sartre only to show that this is exactly what Shakespeare portrays. Shylock, with the knife in his hand, in a state of rage, is indeed ready to cut out the heart of his enemy, Antonio. The knife is there and he who has never killed wants to kill. A man who plays a humble and subservient role, who is pleased to be tolerated, suddenly behaves like a gentile who never permits injury to go unavenged. But Shylock is a Jew, and he would never infringe the law. He does not lend an ear to his enemy's plea for mercy, for mercifulness is a Christian virtue. Yet to obey the law is a Jewish obligation. The moment that he realizes that the law is against him, he drops the knife and signs his own death certificate. (The parallel with Coriolanus's decision not to go against Rome is striking.) For, after a moment of grandeur, the moment of the radicalization of evil, he falls back into the role of the humble Jew who accepts everything that others tell him, the role of the object constituted by the regard of his enemies. Yet after the radicalization of evil, things cannot remain the same. Shylock becomes a shadow of his former self.

But how does Shylock come to the moment of the showdown, to the radicalization of evil, the sole tragic and wicked moment of his life? When will the Jew be enraged to the extent that he abandons even the pseudo-humility of his self and radicalizes the evil with a knife ready to strike? This does not happen at the beginning. At the time of the contract Shylock assumes that Antonio's ships will safely return and that he will get back only his money without interest. He claims the pound of flesh as interest to show Antonio that he is his equal: not money but flesh is what verily counts. He never thinks for a minute that he will really cut out a pound of flesh from the body of his hated enemy. But then Shylock's daughter, Jessica, elopes with a Christian, with a Venetian. She is not only kidnapped, but she also takes her father's money on the Christian's advice. Jessica is a little girl. Her elopement is considered rape. Now, let us imagine for a moment the father whose only child was raped, was taken away to elope, and was persuaded to take a part of her father's treasure with her. For what is a Jewish girl worth without the money of her father? This is the situation of Rigoletto the clown, and as we know, Rigoletto uses his knife. Shylock does not. Shylock hears of the loss of Antonio's wealth after his daughter has been kidnapped. It is then that he decides to take revenge, and it is then that he uses the natural right argument. Listen to Shylock speak about Antonio: "If it will feed nothing else it will feed my revenge. He hath disgraced me, and hindered me half a million; laughed at my losses, mocked at my gains, scorned my nation, thwarted my bargains, cooled my friends, heated mine enemies, and what's his reason?—I am a Jew. Hath not a Jew eyes? Hath not a Jew hands, organs, dimensions, senses, affections, passions? . . . If you prick us do we not bleed? If you tickle us do we not laugh? If you poison us do we not die? . . . If a Jew wrong a Christian, what is his humility? Revenge. If a Christian wrong a Jew, what should his sufferance be by Christian example? Why, revenge. The villainy you teach me I will execute, and it shall go hard but I will better the instruction" (3.1.49–68).

Now let us cast a glance at Antonio's mock trial. The Duke acknowledges the validity of Shylock's bond, yet asks him to be tender. Tenderness is a catchword in Shakespeare; it is frequently claimed in the execution of justice but rarely granted. Shylock is in a rage, he is not tender, he is ready for cruelty. But what is more important, no one expects anything else from him. They expect him to be like Turks and Moors and not like civilized

Christians. None of those who are witnessing the trial believes that the Jew is capable of acting in a gentle way. The only thing that they presuppose is that if they offer him increasingly more money, he will yield. They do not see that by offering him more money in an attempt to make him change his mind and spare Antonio, they are pushing him into more of a rage because they are determining him (in Sartre's sense) with their regard as an absolute alien, a man unlike them, one who is merely a Jew. Consider the text. Bassanio asks, "Do all men kill the things they do not love?" Shylock replies, "Hates any man the thing he would not kill?" Then Antonio intervenes and says, "I pray you think you question with the Jew. / You may as well go stand upon the beach / And bid the main flood bate his usual height; / You may as well use question to the wolf / Why he hath made the ewe bleat for the lamb. . . . You may as well do anything most hard / As seek to soften that—than which what's harder?— / His Jewish heart" (4.1.65–79). What is interesting here is that Antonio offers a natural right argument. But he uses it for the opposite purpose than Shylock. Shylock says that we are by nature all alike, Jews and Christians, and that the difference is just in the gaze or regard. Yet Antonio the racist says that it is by nature that the Jew differs from the Christian, that it is by nature that he has a hard heart and by nature he is like a wolf. Antonio's argument causes Shylock to remain in the state of the absolute alien. And the more he is kept there, the more he desires to turn the tables and kill. It is at that point that Shylock speaks of the hypocrisy of the world that surrounds him: "You have among you many a purchased slave / Which, like your asses and your dogs and mules, / You use in abject and slavish parts / Because you bought them. Shall I say to you / 'Let them be free, marry them to your heirs. / Why sweat they under burdens? Let their beds / Be made as soft as yours, and let their palates / Be seasoned with such viands?' You will answer / 'The slaves are ours'" (4.1.89–97). Here Portia arrives and makes her plea for mercy. Mercy mitigates justice. It is a beautiful argument. Portia turns to Shylock and asks him to be merciful. Yet Bassanio, her lover, immediately intervenes. He tells her that they have already offered thrice the sum of the money Antonio owes him, yet he has not accepted this. "And I beseech you, / Wrest once the law to your authority. / To do a great right, do a little wrong, / And curb this cruel devil of his will" (4.1.211–14). Now this is a dialogue from which Shylock is excluded. They offer him money and he refuses it. They ask him to be merciful and he refuses that. But while they are doing all this, they continue to abuse him. Again, they determine him as someone who "by nature" cannot deliver the things that they insist he should deliver. And when Portia's shrewdness makes Shylock lose his case, the storm breaks loose. Everyone who pleaded for mercy begins to act in the most cruel way. It is not enough for them that Shylock does not receive the so-called interest that is his revenge. They also take away from him—at this stage against the letter of the law—his own money. They divide his wealth among themselves, in fact giving half of it to the man who raped and kidnapped his daughter and robbed him. Antonio does not hide this at all when he says that Shylock has to leave half his wealth after his death "unto the gentleman / That lately stole his daughter" (4.1.381–82). (What gentleman steals a girl?) After having annihilated Shylock, Portia asks, "Art thou contented, Jew? What dost thou say?" Shylock says, "I am content" (4.1.390–91). Portia speaks, of course, mockingly. And it is of some interest that she—as well as most of those who are present—almost never addresses Shylock by name but calls him just "Jew." And after Shylock is forced to do everything against his will, including becoming a Christian, he says: "I pray you give me leave to go from hence. / I am not well. Send the deed after me, / And I will sign it" (4.1.394–95). Shylock dies; there is no question about this. In act 5 they read his testimony. But in the 1998 Budapest performance a pogrom breaks out after his last words and he is beaten to death. If one reads the text attentively and imagines the way in which hatred gets out of hand in a scene of collective revenge, this interpretation seems very much appropriate.

I dwelled at some length on the 4.1 scene in order to show the way in which the dramatic intercourse between the absolute stranger and the world develops. The two contradictory reasonings on the ground of natural law (Shylock: Jews are like gentiles by nature; Antonio: Jews are another race, entirely different and worse by nature) indicate the spatio-ontological position of the absolute stranger. In the case of a conditional stranger, identity becomes confused, and the two concepts of nature (by tradition or by right of nature) either collide or are in a state of discrepancy. But in the case of the absolute stranger there is no tradition; the traditional concept of the natural is missing. There remains only "nature," but nature itself is divided into identity and nonidentity. In *The Merchant of Venice* Antonio will be estranged despite his love for Bassanio, and he therefore remains alone. Jessica also remains alone, the betrayer of her father and another fool of love like so many of Shakespeare's characters. In a way Jessica remains her father's daughter. Her case is also that of failed assimilation. For what Christian girl of honor who has been stolen from her father would be persuaded to steal another's wealth? Her act casts a shadow on her future that remains hidden on the stage. However, Portia is neither a fool nor a fool of love. She is in control of the play. She cheats (also in the game of the caskets) because she always bends the law to her own will. She is a borderline case in Shakespeare's female pantheon. She is a Rosalind on the one hand and a Margaret on the other. Independent, stubborn, and cruel, Portia is not just a modern woman, she is also a female Machiavelli. She is a woman of politics, but she is still a woman. Her stake, as well as her victory, is private.

The Merchant of Venice, like *Othello*, is a drama about absolute strangers.

Yet it is also a drama about the modern world Shakespeare could not see but could only feel. For on the borderline between the premodern and the modern, two concepts of nature (the traditional and the natural right concept) collide. Yet in the modern world only the natural right argument justifies rights. But the right of nature can be interpreted in two opposite ways: as a claim for equality and a claim for inequality. This time inequality is not inequality by tradition but inequality by nature: it is inequality by race. The world of the French Revolution and the world of colonization are dawning simultaneously.

I have already hinted at several similarities between the treatment of Othello and Shylock by the Venetians. The resemblance is also striking if we consider the modes in which the two men are addressed. Just as Shylock is normally addressed and referred to as "the Jew," so is Othello normally referred to as "the Moor." Even Desdemona speaks twice about him in act 1, scene 3, as "the Moor." And how is Othello first mentioned? This happens when Iago alarms Desdemona's father: "Even now, now, very now, an old black ram / Is tupping your white ewe" (1.1.88–89). The racial difference is again intimated with reference to the animal kingdom, as it was by Antonio. In *Othello*, as in *The Merchant*, "nature" as such (without tradition) is the protagonist. Brabanzio is certain that his daughter is the victim of sorcery because it is absolutely impossible for him to believe that Othello could have won Desdemona without magic: "To fall in love with what she feared to look on! / It is a judgment maimed and most imperfect / That will confess perfection so could err / Against all rules of nature" (*Othello* 1.3.98–101). Desdemona has fallen in love with Othello's *stories, not with his body*. She has fallen in love with him *because he is a stranger,* an absolute stranger so different from all the gentlemen of Venice she knows. This is also the pitfall in regard to the absolute stranger: to fall in love with the type and not with the man. Desdemona does not know Othello when she falls in love with him, she knows only his stories, his image, his pathos, his lack of resemblance to the golden youth of Venice.

Whether one hates or loves Shylock and Othello, the Jew and the Moor, it is all the same. For the Venetians, they appear not as individuals but as representations of their race, of absolute otherness. For to understand the individuality of a man one needs to know the man in his *own context*. If one knows many Jews, one can also know Shylock as a specific man in his uniqueness, not as "the Jew." And if one lives among the Moors, one can get to know Othello as an individual person and not as "the Moor." But the fate of the absolute stranger is that he is living and dying with a collective and not an individual identity, and this is true even for those who are closest to him, who love or hate him.

The absolute stranger is a *type* in his surroundings. This is why there is the temptation to depict to him as a type. In the case of Shylock it is the man who is hungry for money; in the case of Othello it is the brave but naïve soldier. But Shakespeare beats the system. Even if in the eyes of the Venetians Shylock is just "the Jew" and Othello just "the Moor," this is not the case for Shakespeare. He brings the greedy moneylender into a situation where his irrational passion supersedes his greed, and he places the naïve man and good soldier in a situation where his irrational jealousy will annihilate his dignity and pride. Moreover, neither will "represent" even his irrational vice. Othello will not become the embodiment of jealousy, nor will Shylock become the embodiment of cruelty. Needless to say, there is an enormous difference between the two figures. Shylock falls back into the state of humility, whereas Othello judges himself. *Othello* could not have been played as a comedy.

5

Judgment of Human Character: To Betray and to Be Betrayed

The "natives" need to know the absolute strangers only to the extent that they can be properly employed. It is enough for the Duke of Venice to know that Othello is a good warrior who will fight well for Venice. Yet Iago needs to know a little more about him because he wants to use him in another—nonfunctional—way. He wants to use him in such a way that he destroys himself. No deep knowledge of Othello's character is required to destroy him, just enough to play a deadly trick on him. Iago sees Othello's Achilles' heel, his vulnerability. And he also knows that Othello is a naïve and unsuspecting man. He says: "The Moor is a free and open nature, / That thinks men honest that but seem to be so, / And will as tenderly be led by th'nose / As asses are" (*Othello* 1.3.391–94). Othello is a soldier; he knows about the difference between seeming and being only on the battlefield.

It is Iago's general strategy to find out a single weakness or passion in a person's character and manipulate that person by using it. He knows that Cassio behaves irrationally under the influence of alcohol and that Rodrigo lusts for Desdemona. Iago plays on these weaknesses to catch his victims and play cat-and-mouse games with them. Iago is a good strategist because he discovers that by playing upon a single vice or weakness of character, a person's character will turn into its opposite: the courteous Venetian gentleman will behave as a rude drunken sailor, the stingy patrician will throw his money out of the window for nothing, and the trusting Moor will become mad with jealousy. Iago does not need to be an all-around good judge of character to follow this simple strategy. He needs something else to succeed: the trust of those whom he betrays. He must choose as the objects of his deception bad judges of character like Othello, or the kind of Venetian patricians for whom he is simply a nonbeing and who would not make the slightest effort to get to know him. Iago needs to play only a little theater for Othello, since in Othello's eyes Iago exists.

He is not a nonentity but a fellow soldier, and as such is considered trust-worthy. At the very moment when Iago lets his calumny loose, Othello ruminates, "This fellow's of exceeding honesty, / And knows all qualities with a learned spirit / Of human dealings" (*Othello* 3.3.262–64). Othello says two things in one sentence: I trust this man because he is a soldier, naïve and honest; yet this man knows Venice far better than I do. I have to give credence to everything he is saying. He understands Desdemona bet-ter than I do, for I am black and I am old, and I am a stranger who does not understand. "Haply for I am black, / And have not those soft parts of conversation / That chamberers have; or for I am declined / Into the vale of years" (3.3.267–70). The fate of Iago is sealed—and this is very typical in Shakespeare—by misreading a single character. Most generally the deceiver will be deceived by another wicked player. (See the Regan/ Goneril/Edmund trio in *King Lear* or Buckingham in *Richard III*.) Yet in *Othello* the deceiver is deceived not by wickedness but by goodness. Iago has his own anthropology. He is convinced that all men are wicked or fool-ish or power seeking; he does not believe in the existence of selfless, self-sacrificing decency. He is convinced that all women are actually or at least potentially whores, Desdemona and Emilia included. He does not know his own wife, who will rebel against him in a selfless gesture of righteous-ness, who will cross all his plans, and whom he will kill in vain.

In a world of constant playacting, deception, and betrayal, the good judg-ment of human character gives a man a lead in the game. The good judg-ment of character is in itself morally indifferent. It depends on the content and the objective of the game played by a good judge of character whether his good judgment promotes virtue or vice.

In Shakespeare the judgment of character—good or bad—plays just as important a role in the political theater, in both the strategy of attack and defense. Love, hatred, sex, jealousy, envy, lust, ambition, greed, and venge-fulness are the chief passions on the Shakespearean political stage. I will return to this issue in the following chapters.

There are no general schemes by which to classify the good and bad judges of character in Shakespeare. Since every Shakespearean character is entirely unique, so is every case of a good or a bad judgment of character. In the tragedies, the worst judges of character are Othello and Lear. Both tragedies (*Othello* and *King Lear*) hinge entirely on the thread of a fatally bad judgment of character.

One could perhaps add *Measure for Measure* to this list, although it is a romance and not a tragedy. One can say that the Duke left Vienna in the care of Antonio because he misjudged the character of Antonio. But one can also say—and this is my own understanding—that the Duke is not guilty of a total misjudgment, for Antonio's character has changed under the impact of his lust for Isabella, and this could not have been foreseen.

As Isabella says in her plea for mercy, "I partly think / A due sincerity governed his deeds, / Till he did look on me" (*Measure for Measure* 5.1.442–44). Yet, one could also say that Isabella was too generous, for strict self-righteousness is always bad counsel, and thus the Duke could have been forewarned of such a danger in Antonio's character. Everything depends on the interpretation.

In *The Tempest* Prospero attributes his vicissitudes to his bad judgment of character. He says, among other things, in act 1, scene 2, "I, thus neglecting worldly ends, all dedicated / To closeness, and the bettering of my mind / With that which but by being so retired, / O'er-prized all popular rate, in my false brother / Awaked an evil nature; and my trust, / Like a good parent, did beget of him / A falsehood, in its contrary as great / As my trust was" (1.2.89–96). I have quoted Prospero in order to show the similarity of his speech to Isabella's plea in *Measure for Measure,* though his speech appears in a more complex orchestration. There was originally a bad judgment of the brother's nature, yet the brother's nature became evil through, and partly because of, Prospero's absolute trust. Prospero's neglect of the affairs of state was politically wrong, and seen in this light, his loss of power, although morally undeserved, was politically warranted. The end of the play, the pardon, is already prepared by Prospero's story. Still, only the prehistory of the drama and not the drama itself has been triggered by a bad judgment of character. On the stage, Prospero's actions are motivated by a good and fairly skeptical, yet not misanthropic, judgment of character. The Prospero of the play is no longer the victim of his wicked brother, because he is now another man; he is now a good judge of character who has learned self-control and gained political wisdom.

The best judges of human character are good politicians, such as Henry V, Octavius, and Menenius Agrippa. They never fail in their judgments. However, they are not interested in the human character as such, but only in the political significance of certain characters. As long as he was still Prince Hal, Henry displayed a strong interest in human character as such, but after becoming king, he assumed the attitude of a successful politician, and his interest became restricted to the political function of characters. Richard III, who never made any single mistake in his judgment of character—or if he did, he could handle and remedy it successfully—could be best described as an antipolitical man.

After having said all these things, it would be a considerable mistake to come to the conclusion that blind trust is portrayed as sign of stupidity or narrow-mindedness in Shakespeare's dramas. There is stupid blind trust, but there is also generous blind trust. The best judges of human character are able to trust one or two men blindly. Great friendship, *prote philia,* as we have seen in the discussion of the Hamlet-Horatio relationship, is based on blind and absolute trust. It is an enormous risk to trust blindly without good judgment of human character, and it normally ends in disaster. But it also courts disaster to distrust blindly. At the start one keeps one's eyes open, yet one can become blind both in trust and in distrust. One can shut one's eyes after one has already seen something. Blind trust is normally also love. In *Twelfth Night*, the wonderful comedy about trust, distrust, and betrayal, the suffering of Antonio, who believes himself to betrayed by Sebastian, is all the greater because Antonio loves him (a hint of a homoerotic relationship makes Antonio the sea captain the fellow sufferer of Antonio the merchant, although he is a better and a purer character than the latter). It turns out in the end—something that the audience knows from the beginning— that Antonio's trust was well placed. There is one single man in the comedy, Malvolio, who is really betrayed. He is tricked by the merry women of Illyria exactly as Brabantio is tricked by Iago: he is misled through an ugly feature of his character, his vanity. Perhaps we pity him a little because he is betrayed. But in Shakespeare vanity, unlike jealousy, is a base vice. A jealous man can be comic, yet a vain man cannot be tragic. There is justice in this judgment.

There are in Shakespeare extremely good judges of character who are passionately interested in the characters themselves. They want to understand their "instruments," why the strings of their soul sound. Since they are actors and not just spectators, their judgment of character and their passionate interest in the human animal inhere in their actions. Judgment of human character can be their weapon of self-protection or their instrument to unmask others, or both. Yet, knowledge of human character can also be an end in itself. Needless to say, the best judges of human character have a high appreciation for other men and women of good judgment of human character; in their mind bad judgment is a serious character failure. Such great judges of character are the stage managers, the poets, and the historians. Among them the greatest are Prospero, Hamlet, and Julius Caesar.

Since Prospero's character is "ready" at the beginning of the play (this is why he is solely the stage manager), he cannot be betrayed, he cannot be mistaken in principle. Yet Hamlet is not only the stage manager, and Julius Caesar is not a stage manager at all but a political actor and a historian. Julius Caesar is the sole great politician in Shakespeare who has a passionate interest in the strings and the springs of the human soul.

Yet in Shakespeare there is no such capacity as all-around good judgment of human character. First, even the best of judges, be they decent or wicked, can fail at least once, and such a single mistake can be grave enough to lead to their downfall, to change their life, or to put them on trial. And second, judgments are mostly fragmented and passed in an ad hoc manner. Someone passes judgment upon a character and forgets many things he already knows about the character. And he may be right or wrong; it depends. Sometimes bad judges of character can absolutely hit the jackpot of good judgment by mere chance. Everything is possible, and everything happens only once.

In *Hamlet* there are two good judges of character: Hamlet and Claudius. Both of them want the other dead, but in a proper way, in their own way. *Hamlet wants the truth and nothing but the truth, and Claudius wants the untruth and nothing but the untruth.* Hamlet wants his deed to appear in the light of day as the clear case of retributive justice, and the king wants his deed to be hidden so that it remains entirely in the dark. The king almost succeeds, since Hamlet is saved by blind chance: the pirate attack. It is perhaps surprising that the best judge of character, Hamlet, needs a *fact*—the letter of Claudius to the king of England—to realize why he was sent to England. It is perhaps even more amazing that after having proof of the king's resolve to have him killed, Hamlet remains unsuspecting before the duel. This is exactly what Claudius knows about Hamlet. He is sure, as he tells Laertes, that "He, being remiss, / Most generous, and free from all contriving, / Will not peruse the foils" (*Hamlet* 4.7.107–9). And he is right. The king speaks of Hamlet in a way similar to the way Iago speaks of Othello. He is free of contrivance and generous. And Claudius says all this about a man who has suspected him from the beginning of foul murder, who has laid traps for him. Sure, Claudius prepares himself and not Laertes for a duel with Hamlet; who is better at laying traps? As it turns out, both of them will be losers. For Claudius—just like Iago—made a crucial mistake in his judgment of character: he did not know his wife, the only creature he loved, well enough. He did not suspect that Gertrude would be able to say no to him, something that she never did while alive. Just remember that Gertrude is shaken by Hamlet's accusations, yet soon afterwards her sexual dependency on Claudius will prove stronger. She can deliver herself from this dependency only by delivering herself from life. Claudius has not suspected that she was able to die for her son, whom she abandoned for her husband.

Thus both Iago and Claudius lay traps, both judge their adversaries as unsuspecting, remiss, and generous. The traps they lay are absolutely unlike the mousetrap Hamlet lays. Hamlet lays the trap to amass evidence, to bring the truth into daylight for everyone to see; Claudius and Iago lay traps to destroy their enemies so that their deeds can remain in the dark and they can avoid responsibility. This is why I said that Claudius wanted nothing but the untruth. Yet still, if Hamlet falls into the trap, why have I said that he is perhaps the best judge of character in all the Shakespearean dramas whereas Othello is perhaps the worst?

Hamlet interprets all facts through character; he reads the facts from faces, eyes, smiles, and intonations. Facts as facts do not tell him anything. This is why he is not a man who peruses the foils. Just consider what he does after the encounter with his father's specter. He lays the mousetrap in order to see how the king will behave. To see his eye, the color of his face, is to glimpse his soul. Hamlet could not hear what Claudius said in his prayer of insincere repentance, for it was a soliloquy (only the audience could hear it). But he has seen Claudius kneeling before the Savior on the cross, and he saw the movement of his lips, perhaps even his face. These are the signs he, the great judge of human character, could well read. Othello is the very opposite of Hamlet. He believes the feigned facts because he believes only in facts; he cannot read a face. He cannot even read Desdemona's face; moreover, he does not try to. He cannot read signs. It is obvious from Othello's narrative in act 1 that Desdemona made the first move in their love affair. Othello has not noticed how Desdemona was attracted to him or to his stories until she—a rebellious girl like Juliet—expressed her emotions as clearly as decency allowed. Not much later, in his jealous rage, Othello recollects Desdemona's deed as a *fact* (Desdemona betrayed her father), totally abstracting the fact from the character, face, gestures, and so on. He does not trust her because he does not trust himself.

Hamlet is capable of absolute trust; he trusts Horatio absolutely. He also trusts himself with certain things but not with others. As I discussed in chapter 2, he is the man of self-reflection, the man of Lutheran Wittenberg who knows himself only as much as a man can know. He never surprises himself because he knows himself as a man full of surprises. His good judgment of human character is the other side of the coin. He constantly reflects on human character, on the character of certain others (for only a few men and women interest him that much), yet he also possesses an almost unerring ability to read the souls from eyes and faces.

There are three crucial scenes in *Hamlet* where the play between Hamlet's reflection and intuition is best displayed: with Horatio, with Rosencrantz and Guildenstern, and with Ophelia. In his first encounter with Horatio (*Hamlet* 1.2), Hamlet asks, "And what make you from Wittenberg, Horatio?" (1.2.164). Horatio replies, "A truant disposition, good my lord" (1.2.168). Then Hamlet says, "I would not have your enemy say so. . . . I know you are no truant" (1.2.169–72). The emphasis is on "I know." He *knows* what kind of man Horatio is. In his first encounter with Rosencrantz and Guildenstern (2.2) Hamlet begins the conversation mockingly; they speak as they used to do in college. The change comes after Hamlet asks, "What have you, my good friends, deserved at the hands of Fortune that she sends you to prison hither?" (2.2.242–44). Here the mocking style ends. Hamlet becomes suspicious. The conversation turns serious. Hamlet needs corroboration. Thus he asks the same question he asked Horatio, this time directly: "What make you at Elsinor?" (2.2.272). Rosencrantz answers: "To visit you, my lord" (2.2.273). Now Hamlet feels perhaps a little pain, the pain of being betrayed. Yet he goes on, for he needs the truth: "Were you not sent for?" The courtiers do not answer directly. And then Hamlet says (and here comes the end of his camaraderie with Rosencrantz and

Guildenstern), "You were sent for, and there is a kind of confession in your looks" (280–81). The minor pain of having been betrayed is now gone. Confidences with the former buddies end. The old friends are from now on worse than enemies, for they are lowly: spies, informers, rats. A look at the faces of Rosencrantz and Guildenstern suffices: Hamlet sees through them, he knows them once and for all.

There is a similar turning point in the great love/hate scene with Ophelia. Here, just as in the encounters with Horatio and with Rosenkrantz and Guildenstern, Hamlet asks a test question: "Where's your father?" (3.1.132); Ophelia answers, "At home, my lord" (3.1.133). This is the most blatant lie. Hamlet is again betrayed. But this treason hurts, and will not cease to hurt. What follows is Hamlet's first rage scene (which has nothing to do with his feigned madness, or near madness). I have already made the point that all three rage scenes of Hamlet are related to women, and two of his fits of rage occur in the company of women. Hamlet is a person who is not betrayed because of his lack of knowledge of human character, as Othello and many others in the Shakespeare's gallery of characters are, but because he discovers treason fast and early, precisely because of his good judgment of character. Perhaps the treason of Ophelia would have been better not to discover, yet for Hamlet nothing is more important than truth.

If one understands Hamlet as I do, the two best *Hamlet* films do something that seems entirely unnecessary and may even be a mistake of interpretation. In both Olivier's and Branagh's films, Hamlet notices the king and Polonius behind the curtain; thus he gets the facts and this is how he realizes that Ophelia was lying. But this interpretation, in my mind, does not do justice to Hamlet. For Hamlet reads the truth not from the stirring of the curtain but from Ophelia's face and eyes. He sees the betrayal while looking at Ophelia, and this is how he knows it; *he knows that he is spied upon without seeing it.*

Let me return now to the relationship between judgment of human character and politics. Although every case is unique, Shakespeare has some strong convictions about this relationship that run through his oeuvre. Proving everything with mere facts is foolish; there are never pure facts, since every fact is interpreted. It is foolish to identify one interpretation with a fact. Good judgment of human character is the precondition of good politics. It needs to be a simple knowledge, a little more than functional, but not much more. One needs to know character to the extent that one can find out roughly what to expect from others, or can influence the will and the position of others. For example, one needs to know the main virtues and vices of one's political friends and enemies, for it is through vices and virtues that they can be trapped, changed, made friends instead of foes, and so on. However, one does not need to find out everything about "vice" and "virtue." Moreover, one does not need even to assemble an all-around image of the other, and it is superfluous to get an insight into the innermost regions of another person's soul. Overreflexivity, the passion for knowing the truth about others and about ourselves, weakens the force of rational decision concerning goals and means; it is also a superfluous luxury if the goal is to devise strategies of action. It is obvious from all this that the most successful men of politics are *not* the most interesting men in Shakespeare's world of characters.

There is an exception, however: Julius Caesar, the greatest political figure in Shakespeare's arsenal. (Since, in the third part of this book, I will discuss the drama *Julius Caesar* in some detail, I will give only hints here about Caesar as the best judge of human character.)

Julius Caesar was a historian and is portrayed by Shakespeare in this way. His judgment of character is as good as Hamlet's, yet entirely different. Hamlet judges man in relation to himself. He distinguishes his friends from his foes, the base from the noble, the hypocrites from the sincere and open-minded, the appearance from the essence. Julius Caesar judges characters politically. He knows well who is dangerous politically and who is not by making a good assessment of people's characters as a whole. He is not interested in the discrepancy between appearance and essence; to unmask the deceiving character is of secondary importance to him. His mind, I repeat, works like the mind of a historian. He wants to understand the temperament, the character, the morality, the ideas, the psychology of a man in its entirety. He is not motivated by the passion for truth but by *curiosity*—by the passion to understand, to put things in their proper place. He is not a hero of Machiavelli, but Machiavelli the historian *himself.* Certainly, he is also an actor. Yet, whether the actions of a character touch him personally is not the chief question for him, as it is for Hamlet. This is so, among other reasons, because in Shakespeare's portrayal Julius Caesar's actions are not just political but also historical. His personality is historical. He is wise as a political actor will never be. His perspective stretches beyond his own life, for his fantasy stretches beyond the present. Shakespeare's distinction between politics and history, between political significance and historical significance, is the most succinct in this drama (and in *Henry VI*).

Listen to the way in which Julius Caesar draws the portrait of Cassius for Marc Antony. It is important that this is no soliloquy; Caesar gives a historical lesson to Antony, and a lesson about character, to show him who is dangerous and why. Antony is naïve; he needs to be instructed. But Caesar is not just warning Antony about Cassius, he also draws Cassius's portrait, which is an excellent one. One could even say that he gives a "definition" of Cassius, starting with the *genus proximum* and finishing with the *differentia specifica*. "Let me have men about me that are fat / Sleek-headed men, and such as sleep a-nights. / Yon Cassius has a lean and hungry look. / He thinks too much. Such men are dangerous" (1.2.193–96); "Would he were fatter!" (1.2.199); "He reads too much, / He is a great observer, and he looks / Quite through the deeds of men. / He loves no plays, / As thou dost, Antony; he hears no music. / Seldom he smiles, and smiles in such a sort / As if he mocked himself, and scorned his spirit / That could be moved to smile at anything. / Such men as he be never at heart's ease / Whiles they behold a greater than themselves, / And therefore they are very dangerous. / I rather tell thee what is to be feared / Than what I fear, for always I am Caesar" (1.2.202–13). Almost the whole of this splendid characterization is Shakespeare's invention, based on a few sentences from Plutarch's *Brutus and Caesar*. And even these sentences are entirely changed in meaning by Shakespeare. In Plutarch (in *Brutus and Caesar*) Caesar says that he fears most the pale-visaged and carrionlike people such as Brutus and Cassius. Yet Shakespeare's Caesar does not fear anyone, and he speaks only of Cassius and not of Brutus. There is not even a hint in Plutarch that Caesar, the excellent judge of character, also considers Cassius a good judge of character—not of his own (historical) kind, but of a narrower, merely political kind. Cassius, Caesar says, looks through the deeds of man; he cannot be misled; he sees the motivation behind the act and therefore cannot be deceived. And Cassius will live up to every bit of Caesar's characterization in Shakespeare's play.

Does Caesar belong to the excellent judges of character, although he will be betrayed all the same? It is normally suggested that Brutus has betrayed him. I do not think that Shakespeare sees this in the traditional light. It is frequently remarked that Caesar's last sentence, as we know it from Suetonius, "Et tu mi filii, Brute?" appears in the short version, "Et tu, Brute?" in Shakespeare. This version expresses astonishment rather than the desperate cry at the moment of betrayal. If Brutus is against him, then let Caesar fall. The sentence is uttered on the world historical stage and not on the fairly sentimental family stage as the "my son" (mi filii) would suggest. And, apart from this, Shakespeare gives the spectator the impression that Caesar fulfilled his historical mission precisely by getting himself murdered. Politics and history have parted ways.

6

Love, Sex, Subversion:
Political Drama, Family Drama

In Greek tragedy, political drama is for the most part also family drama. The wife murders her husband, the son his mother, the father his daughter, the uncle his niece, the son his father, the brother his brother, the father his son, the mother her son, the husband his wife. But in the material of the myth there is no distinction between the private and the political, at least not before Euripides. The private is not the opposite of the public, it is public. Prior to Euripides, whose dramatic art was regarded not just by Nietzsche but already by the Greeks (for example, in the comedy *The Frogs* by Aristophanes) as the decadent and corrupt version of tragedy, it is only Sophocles' *Antigone* that could possibly be understood as representing the collision between private and public. This is the way in which Hegel interpreted it. Still, even in this interpretation private is not private in the modern sense, not even in the sense of Shakespeare. Hegel spoke of *theomachia,* the struggle of gods, between the gods of death, the underworld represented by the family and the sister on the one hand; and the gods of light, of the public, of the political, the state, on the other hand.

The Greeks set the tone for tragedy, and tragedy could never detach itself entirely from the family drama, as it could never detach itself entirely from the political drama. In the *tragédie classique,* tragedy normally unfolds through the conflict between private and public, more precisely through the conflict between love and obedience (normally to the father), and political exigency and duty. The best of the works of the *opera seria,* and particularly the opera of Verdi and Puccini, like the most significant dramatic works of German classicism, particularly of Schiller, frequently follow this pattern.

There are no patterns in Shakespeare. The conflict between love and obedience occurs also in his dramatic art. But perhaps Antony is the only Shakespearean character who is torn between love and duty, and even his conflict is more complex than this. Juliet and Romeo are not torn between love and obedience because they readily choose love. Ophelia is not, for she is just obedient (if this is her decision at all). Neither is Isabella, since she does not hesitate for a moment to give precedence to her vow of virginity against her sisterly love. Shakespeare's most interesting characters throw themselves into a stream where they courageously swim toward their goal, or where they will be eventually carried away toward self-destruction. They make a conscious or unconscious commitment, and they rarely behave like Buridan's ass.

The most significant Shakespearean history plays are family dramas— dramas of the tragic conflicts between the family of Lancaster and that of York, two branches of the same family tree. Two of his great tragedies (*Hamlet* and *Lear*) are also family dramas, but other tragedies are family dramas only in part (*Othello* and *Coriolanus*), and a few of them are not family dramas at all (*Macbeth, Antony and Cleopatra, Julius Caesar*). The intersection between the private and the public, between the intimate and the political, is, however, of great significance in all of them. This is also the case in most of the comedies and romances, whether the conflict is played out within a family (as in *Cymbeline*) or not (as in most of the rest of them).

This is how historicity constitutes the internal organization of the drama. History is a flow of simultaneous and subsequent political acts; it is a web of acts, a web folded and unfolded through increasingly new acts. Men and women enter and exit this web, they spin it and untangle it. *The Shakespearean stage is itself historical, with the constant entering, exiting, and reentering of the players.* It is not an epic theater but a historicopolitical theater, for everyone who enters and reenters will participate in the spinning and unfolding of the web. The web of the play makes every player an actor, a historical actor. This is also the case in all private scenes—the scenes of love and sex and of the conflicts between parents and children. All of them are, even if entirely apolitical, of historical significance. Every scene is historical simply because the actor and the actress who play the lovers enter the stage. Everything that is going on—as long as it is "on" the stage—is of historical significance. One should not forget Jaques's already quoted words: "All the world is a stage." They can be read also in reverse: all the stage is a world. The stage is essentially historical. Thus, history is the *medium* of the Shakespearean history plays, tragedies, and certain romances and comedies. It is a homogenizing medium only in a very broad sense, in that nothing can be present. Nothing "presences" itself on the stage in the tragedies except the historical.

I do not want to give a definition of the historical. I only describe what historical means as the medium of the Shakespearean tragedies, history plays, and some romances and comedies. I mentioned the simultaneous and subsequent web of actions, that is, of actions that code themselves in memory, imagination, and expectation. Earlier, I made mention of dianoia, one of the major characteristics of drama according to Aristotle, which plays as important a role in Shakespeare as it does for the ancient philosopher. Yet, I spoke also of the soliloquy that is so characteristically Shakespearean. I also mentioned the constant recurrence of prophecies, predictions, and curses, as well as the repetitious references to bygone acts, to the never-forgotten sources of mutual accusations, legitimacy claims, and the constantly recurring reinterpretations of the past. What happens in those language games, such as cursing, prophesying, predicting, and warning? History is created and re-created in them. It is in those language games as verbalizations of remembrance, plans, fears, and hopes that past, present, and future actions become coded and/or recoded.

Let me refer to Hannah Arendt's concept of action as the essence of the political. Action is a new beginning; it always introduces something entirely new, ex nihilo, into the world. It is, in Arendt's words, natality. Yet, she adds to this that without chroniclers and the writing of history, actions would never be kept in remembrance; they would disappear without a trace. In tragedies, including Shakespeare's, actions are always speech acts. However, in Shakespeare the speech acts through which actions become coded are also reacted, recoded, and precoded by the actors themselves. In Shakespeare one does not need the historian, for actions present themselves through the words and minds of the actors. Shakespeare is not just a chronicler; he is not just a person who eternalizes the great deeds that should be kept in remembrance. He does more than this: he presents the thing itself—history—which is in his presentation the web of political and nonpolitical acts in their mostly contingent coincidences, together with their codings. Political actors act freely out of nothing; yet they also enter, exit, and reenter the web. They must somehow understand the code that they will decode or recode. The story of history is not mythological, because it is written entirely by the actors themselves. But the new beginning itself enters the continuity of the web. It codes anew, it decodes anew; it untangles the threads of the webs, it spins them anew.

In Shakespeare, both family dramas and nonfamily dramas are historical dramas. The webs are, however, different. For as I mentioned at the beginning, there is no grand narrative in Shakespeare; he rather presents many different and unique histories. History as such cannot be dramatically presented. I mention only parenthetically that such a presentation was attempted, for example, in the second part of Goethe's *Faust* and in the *Tragedy of Man* by Hungarian playwright Imre Madach. Whatever the poetic merits of those plays, one cannot read and watch them as dramas.

Thus, in Shakespeare's history plays, tragedies, romances, and in some of his comedies, everyone who enters the stage enters history. It makes no difference whether the actors perform a love scene, a sex scene, an altercation scene between brothers, a war scene, or a scene in the parliament; they are all historical. To be historical and to be public are, however, not the same. In Greek tragedy everything was public, the conversation between sisters and brothers no less than between gods and demigods. In Shakespeare's plays one encounters many a private scene among lovers. By private scenes I do not mean scenes of conspiracy, but scenes that are not meant to meet the scrutiny of the public eye because they concern the lovers alone. The soliloquies are by definition not public. Frequently, the actor talks to himself because his thoughts concern only himself or because they are just floating ideas or expressions of desires, suspicions, fears, and hopes that entered the character's mind from the hidden, sometimes unconscious, regions of the soul. Whatever is played out in the heart of one man is not public unless it discloses secrets that directly concern the public. This is also true of love scenes. But even the private is historical, for it participates in the spinning or untangling of the web of significant actions. Even entirely intimate scenes with entirely idiosyncratic personal fears become historical.

The political/public stage is just one dimension of the historical stage. The historical stage is not only broader, but it happens very frequently that the political and the historical significance of an act are bifurcated. The conflict is often played out not between the private and the public but between the historical and the political. The political is by definition public; the historical, however, is not. I have already mentioned the case of Julius Caesar. It was politically unwise of him to go to the *capitolum* on the ides of March. But this politically unwise step made him a legend. The fears of Calpurnia are woven into this web. I will come back to the discussion of the divergence between historical and political significance later in the book. Now I will only speak of the significance of this divergence for the development of love stories. For example, Romeo and Juliet are children in love. Their passionate love concerns only them; it is unique and irresistible. Yet, since they are the children of two warring families of Verona and their love is forbidden, their love becomes historical. Everything is contingent here, nothing is necessary, neither planned nor even likely to happen. But history in Shakespeare is always a history of contingencies. Here history destroys the lovers, but because it was history that has taken them in, their life and death will become representative. It will be a monument, a memento, and their names code words in the life of remembrance.

Hegel pointed to the special significance of brother-sister relations in the ancient tragedies. Love in these works is first and foremost sisterly or brotherly love, although sometimes it is the love of a daughter for her father. And, of course, there is also love among friends. In Shakespeare, the brother-sister relation does not play such a central role. This is so for several reasons, one of which was first mentioned by Hegel. There was generally no split or contradiction between the two concepts of nature in Greek tragedy.

Brothers and sisters were tied by blood (naturally), yet they were of the opposite sex; this tie was not freely chosen. The passion of love appears only in Euripides. In Shakespeare, sexual love is the intimate passion between the two sexes. That is, *the intimate passion between the sexes, the freely chosen untraditional love, is the natural bond between the sexes.* It is more "natural" than the blood relation that ties brother and sister together. This is what Hamlet cries out at the grave of Ophelia: "I loved Ophelia. / Forty thousand brothers / Could not, with all their quantity of love, / Make up my sum" (*Hamlet* 5.1.266–68). This quotation shows that as far as love is concerned, the normal balance between the two concepts of nature leans toward natural law. This is not only in the case in *Hamlet*, but in Shakespeare's works in general. Love can also be homoerotic (as in the cases of the two Antonios) and, as love in general, natural in the sense of natural right. It is remarkable that although the ancients presented homoerotic love as love par excellence in Plato's dialogues, Greek tragedy knew nothing of this. One needed a Shakespeare, who wanted to understand all human passion, to give homoeroticism its place in the world of human drama.

The balance between the two concepts of nature is never permanently biased in the other representative "family drama" types of Shakespeare, the conflicts taking place between fathers and sons, fathers and daughters, mothers and sons. (The mother-daughter conflict, although it happens, is not representative.) It is unnatural that children turn against their fathers, but it is natural for them to claim their rights, particularly their right to love whom their heart has chosen against the tyrannical wishes and whims of the father. A very special case is the portrayal of incestuous relations or incestuous dreams between father and daughter. I mentioned already that I agree with those who interpret Caliban (in *The Tempest*) as the barbarian in Prospero's own soul. Caliban desires to rape Miranda; this is the way to disclose the father's repressed and unconscious desire. The drama *Pericles* begins with the story of incestuous relations between father and daughter, and Pericles himself leaves his newborn daughter in foreign lands until her wedding day, in order not to be tempted by her! The fear of the "natural" in the second interpretation of the word is here obvious. Shakespeare tells us an entirely new story, the story of individual love, of passion, and of sexual desire, including sexual dependency and sexual repulsion, which are almost entirely independent of social status. Titania, enamoured of an ass, shows the extremity of the blindness of sexual passion, although just in a dream. But the dream frequently signifies in Shakespeare, as in Freud, repressed desire. The entanglements of passionate love and sexual desire or obsession are of great historical significance. So are passionate hatred, jealousy, and ambition.

Sibling rivalry is mostly rivalry between brothers (but sometimes between sisters too, as in the case of *King Lear*). Deadly hostility normally develops between brothers, and fratricide is the most frequent variety of political murder in Shakespeare. Attempted fratricide is in his book also a case of fratricide, because the resolve (and not just the wish) to kill amounts to having killed as far as conscience is concerned. If one considers the cases where younger brothers fraudulently occupy older brothers' thrones, one may wonder why brotherly love is so underrepresented in Shakespeare's plays. Perhaps this is because of his sharp historical observation, perhaps for personal or dramaturgical reasons. Needless to say, sibling rivalry between brothers, competition for the throne, enthroning and dethroning of the older brother, fratricide and attempted fratricide, are all politically significant actions. They are played out on the political stage. To stress the political dimension of the historical stage in any system of rule but the republican, Shakespeare had recourse to two kinds of family drama: sibling rivalry and father-son conflict. In those conflicts—contrary to the dramas of sex and love—historical and political dimensions of the stage can only slightly part ways.

Sibling rivalry is of political significance, and it is always politically dangerous and subversive. Passionate love and sex are apolitical yet historical, and they can also become—and often are—politically dangerous and subversive.

When intimacy enters history in an unusual, unexpected, and nontraditional way, the political life as such can become endangered. Sibling rivalry, passionate ambition, jealousy, and hatred are traditionally subversive; everyone knows that they are. Passionate love or sex can be subversive, but in unexpected ways. The passion of hatred, particularly the hatred of a brother, is always evil; all its fruits are evil. But love is different. Passionate love, sexual desire included, can be both good and evil. But whether good or evil, it can become subversive because it is unexpected and nontraditional.

Harold Bloom states that Shakespeare was unsympathetic to passionate love, and particularly to sexual love, that his greatest lovers are also evil creatures. I cannot agree with him. Obviously, all great lovers are representatives of the second concept of nature. Their creed, commitment, and choice lie in their passion. Love is for them the drive of nature, and the drive of nature must be followed; desire stands higher than anything else, be it tradition, cleverness, or exigency. What is true in general about all actors who follow the second interpretation of nature is absolutely true about the great lovers. They can be evil creatures, but they can also be attractive or morally indifferent. Whether they are evil or good depends entirely on their nature (for it cannot depend on tradition).

It is true that the great passions of love, including the sexual passions, are for the most part politically subversive in the Shakespearean dramas. It is likewise true that passionate love and sex are disorderly inclinations, particularly because they do not know external limits. But from this it does not follow that they are necessarily also evil. In general, and not only in the case of passionate love, subversive acts and passions can be morally evil, good, or neutral, or all of these when seen from different perspectives. The conspirators' decision to kill Caesar was subversive in the extreme and was also carried out. However, contrary to Dante, neither Brutus nor Cassius is portrayed by Shakespeare as evil. Brutus is even the model of virtue, although he kills Caesar, who for his part is portrayed as a great, although not especially virtuous, man. The love of Romeo and Juliet is politically subversive, as is the love of Macbeth and Lady Macbeth. In loving one another, Romeo and Juliet wanted to do no harm, whereas Claudius's love for Gertrude made him a murderer and brought about the destruction of Denmark.

Although passionate love is not always evil or politically subversive, passionate lovers are always discredited as political actors. Passionate love might be of the greatest historical significance, but it is bad politics. This is made clear by Mark Antony in *Antony and Cleopatra*. Why is passionate love, like the love of Antony and Cleopatra politically dangerous and also lethal for the lovers? It is not just because it is love or is a new kind of love, but because it is passionate. It is one of Shakespeare's firm convictions that although great passions and desires can usher new and great things into history, both good and evil, no great amorous passion can guide a man well in the pursuit of political endeavors. Politics, particularly good politics, is rational or close to being rational; it tolerates only the passion of ambition, and even that only in its cooler, controlled version; it must recognize both internal and external limits. Love and sex are not rational, however, for they are warm passions; they do not recognize limits, at least not external ones.

Shakespeare rarely portrays chaste love, secret or silent love, or romantic love. He shows unrequited love, with its lovers haunted by the desire to make their love requited or to possess their lovers. Love is also sexual desire, whether this is spelled out or not. Normally, if Shakespeare portrays lower-class characters, the text abounds with rude sexual expressions. When he portrays nobles or patricians, sexual purposes are more veiled; they are merely hinted at in verbal acrobatics, allusion, or pun.

When love is coveted without being requited, Shakespeare's value judgments are stronger than usual. Coercing someone into love is always low, ignoble, and disgusting, although witty courtship and seductive behavior are pardonable. Yet the most beautiful love is the free mutuality of attraction and desire. It is low and base to covet someone's love as a means to acquire wealth; it is noble to covet it for the beloved's beauty or for the sake of character. There are as many love pairs as there are loves. The interpretation of *The Taming of the Shrew* is, for example, particularly difficult, because Petrucchio is not just coercing Katherina into marriage with the help of her father or with threats, he is also "taming" her, that is, he is making her submit herself to him of her own will. This is seduction. But Petrucchio decides to seduce Katherina not out of desire for her body but out of desire for her money. One can play *The Taming of the Shrew* as a comedy, but also as a dark play, as the story of the victimization of an independent-minded girl. There is no ambiguity in the story of Imogen, the daughter of Cymbeline who is in love with Posthumus. Cymbeline is coerced into a marriage against her will (unsuccessfully) by her father and stepmother. One of the fine points in Shakespeare's portrayal of sexual subversion is that, close to the (happy) ending of the play, the queen, for whose sake Cymbeline misused her daughter, says, "she confessed she never loved you, only / Affected greatness got by you, not you; / Married your royalty, was wife to your place, / Abhorred your person" (*Cymbeline* 5.6.36–39). Reference is made here not only to the motivation of the wicked queen's second marriage but also to her sexual disgust with her second husband, whom she married for the sake of her equally wicked son. Angelo of *Measure for Measure* is placed on perhaps the lowest level: the pit of sheer madness of unrequited desire. He commits only a single wicked act, and even this is not realized; but this one act is blackmail, rape, cheating, and murder all combined into one. However, his crazy desire is not mixed with other kinds of covetousness. Perhaps this is why he can repent and be forgiven. In Shakespeare desire and love are usually not separated, but certainly not in Angelo's case. He could not distinguish one from another, and neither can we.

It seems that I have agreed with Harold Bloom that Shakespeare distrusts sexuality and lacks sympathy for passionate love. But I do not think so. I would refer back to my analogy of the parallel ladders of grandeur and morality and the historicopolitical in Shakespeare's dramatic world. One character is on the top of the ladder of grandeur and another on the top of the ladder of morality; one is on the top of the ladder of historical significance and another on the ladder of good and successful politics, frequently in the same play. But this is not a pattern, for in Shakespeare there are no fixed patterns. Some passions, love among them, have an affinity with one of the top positions and not with the other. Men and women possessed by passionate love can easily end on the top, or close to it, of grandeur and of historical significance.

All attentive spectators sense the strong sexual attraction and tension between Hamlet and Ophelia. And we must take at face value Hamlet's confession of his passionate love in the rage scene at Ophelia's grave. For Hamlet can play around with others, but he never lies. Why should we believe that the love of Claudius for the queen was more passionate than the love of Hamlet for Polonius's daughter, just because Claudius killed his brother for the undisturbed enjoyment of the bed of his wife and Hamlet has not killed for love? Hamlet would have been ready for all sacrifices except the sacrifice of his own soul ("Woot weep, woot fight, woot fast, woot tear thyself . . . I'll do't" [*Hamlet* 5.1.272–74]), or for Ophelia, had Ophelia been as loyal to him as his mother was to Claudius. Hamlet acted mad in the rage scene with Ophelia because he discovered her disloyalty, the absence of her commitment to love as passion. He does not understand women. How could his mother remain loyal to a scoundrel? How could Ophelia betray him? Hamlet discovers that Ophelia is no Juliet, and this enrages him. However, it *only* enrages him: his love has not turned into hatred or the desire for revenge. He never would have killed Ophelia as Othello killed Desdemona. Can all this be read as the absence of passion, or perhaps as the sign of a less egotistical passion? In love, Hamlet knew limits.

In his discussion of Shakespeare, Harold Bloom presupposes that amorous or sexual passion by definition knows no limits. Shakespeare does not believe this. I will try to reconstruct later in the discussion of *Antony and Cleopatra* how Shakespeare weaves the relationship between a passionate man and woman, and everything they do and feel, into a fine tapestry. There are limits for Antony and Cleopatra, as there are limits for Romeo and Juliet, although their passion goes beyond all conventions. Convention is only one of the limits; others are morality and regard for the other person. There are contradicting passionate commitments, or even obligations or promises, in Shakespeare's plays.

But what is love? When can one speak about love as passion at all? There are a few absolutes in Shakespeare's portrayal of love. One of them I have already mentioned: there is only requited love. This is how Romeo gives account of his passion for Juliet. And the story repeats itself. Whether evil, wicked, good, partly conventional, or entirely unconventional, love is in Shakespeare always mutual. There is love only when there are two lovers. Rape or even coercion will most certainly never be called "love." When we know nothing of the inclination of one of the parties, we hardly speak of love. For example, at the end of *Measure for Measure,* the Duke's decision to marry Isabella does not impress us as love. Where there is disloyalty, there is no love. The great lovers of Shakespeare, be they wicked or good, will not betray one another. They remain loyal: they live for each other, they fight for each other, they can also die for each other.

The different kinds of love in Shakespeare stretch from one extreme to the other. There are so many kinds, and each is so unique, that I can give only some meager hints at their historicopolitical significance. One of the extremes is occupied by the kind of love I would call "secondary." This is the love of convenience, for it normally ends in a marriage of convenience. "Convenience" stretches from dynastic interest to the desire for wealth. There is no passion here, although there is courtship. Courtship can be witty or charming, the exchange of bons mots between men and women, and its presentation promises a good match. But even the most ceremonial courtship is love if it is mutual. This is so in the case of Henry V and Katharine, the princess of France (dynastic marriage), and in the case of Bassanio and Portia (the mixture of love and desire for wealth).

I think that the "political" and "historical" part ways at this point. Politically, the dynastic marriages are the sanest. They are never subversive; rather, they bring stability for the realm and support the man's political ambitions. Antony's mishandling of his marriage to Octavia for Cleopatra's sake was one of his most apolitical acts. Historically, however, it is precisely this apolitical act that will have great significance.

I do think that the other kind of love, mere convention, where not dynastic interest but only wealth plays first fiddle, is portrayed by Shakespeare with an unsympathetic eye. I have never found a single dynastic love scene in Shakespeare where after a scene of ceremonial courtship love itself would have ended in disaster. Yet there are a few of them in the comedies where convenience has no political tint. One does not need to think of coercion (as in *The Taming of the Shrew*), for a far more terrible combination of courtship and coercion is portrayed in *Richard III,* where, at least seemingly, the dynastic interest is at stake. But I now speak of mutual love, of mutual attraction, love par excellence in Shakespeare. In *Much Ado about Nothing,* Claudio decides at first sight that Hero will be his wife. She is, as he ascertains himself, Leonato's only heir. Benedick's question, "Would you buy her, that you enquire after her?" is quite appropriate (1.1.170). Very soon Claudio's love will not stand the first trial.

Merely conventional love for a woman is not always motivated by love for wealth. Conventions can also surround superficial erotic attractions or take the external signals of "being in love" at face value, as in *Love's Labor's Lost.* Biron will confess, or rather apologize, to Rosalind when he begins to understand what love means: "The ladies did change favours, and then we, / Following the signs, *wooed but the sign of she*" (5.2.468–69, emphasis mine).

In Shakespeare, women are more frequently unconventional and rebellious in their love than men. They mostly rebel against their fathers, like Hermia in *A Midsummers Night's Dream* or Célia in *As You Like It.* Frequently, there are two pairs of lovers (for example, in both the above-mentioned plays), but their love is not equally subversive or believed to be subversive by the tyrannical ruler or paterfamilias. When Celia refers to Fortune's gifts, Rosalind replies, "Her benefits are mightily misplaced; and the bountiful blind woman doth most mistake in her gifts to women." Celia says, "'Tis true; for those that she makes fair she scarce makes honest, and those that she makes honest she makes very ill-favouredly." Rosalind replies, "Nay, now thou goest from Fortune's office to Nature's. Fortune reigns in gifts of the world, not in the lineaments of nature" (*As You Like It* 1.2.3–41). The strong natural right argument cannot be missed here, in Rosalind's thinking.

In this most serious and lightest of plays, political subversion is complicated with sexual subversion in two ways. First, the love of Rosalind is itself rebellious. And second, she dresses like a boy, which subverts her sexual role and results in several erotic misunderstandings. However, political and sexual subversion in the end are not subversive at all. Rather, it is with their help that justice and legitimate rule are restored. Very similar things happen, in this respect, in *A Midsummer Night's Dream*. It is not written in the stars that whenever lovers follow the laws of nature, disaster will result. If this is true, it is true only at the top of the historicopolitical hierarchy, in the world theater.

Whether subversion is fatal or beneficial also depends on the order that will be subverted. In *A Midsummer Night's Dream* a tyrannical, patriarchal order is subverted by the true lovers, and an order on a higher level will be restored, whereas in *As You Like It,* the time is out of joint at the beginning of the play when the legitimate duke is exiled by his younger brother, and it will be subversion through love and passion that will set time right. When time is already out of joint at the beginning, subversive action may perhaps set it right. Yet, this happens only in comedies.

The portrayal of Beatrice and Benedick is exceptional and fascinating in several ways. The lovers are not just unconventional, they dismiss all conventions of love as being phony. For them, conventional love means three negative things: empty ceremony, sexual and emotional dependency, and a cover-up for greed. To this one needs to add the spice of resignation: they are no longer young, they have lost hope of finding anyone who could match their high ideal of a lover, who is their equal in independence, morality, and wit. Their story is old and always amusing. They believe that they are adversaries and do not notice that they have already fallen in love. But it is not the naked plot that is exceptional. What is exceptional is that Shakespeare portrays here an entirely unconventional kind of love that is, however, not subversive. For the resistance met by the lovers, the power they need to overcome, to conquer, or to subvert is not external but internal: it is their disrespect for eros. They do not conquer one another, but love (eros) conquers them. This is the rare occasion when Shakespeare dwells on the development of love. Love is not there at the beginning on either side, nor does it appear immediately. Or if it is there, it remains unconscious and becomes conscious in a crucial moment when the lovers display their solidarity against brutishness and injustice. Beatrice and Benedick are the ones who set the time—which in the meantime gets out of joint—right again. Is this love passionate? Is it sexual? As I noted in an earlier chapter, the lovers understand their passion to be in harmony with reason. Is it for that reason less a passion? Not at all. Perhaps Benedick and Beatrice were able to develop a rational passion of love because they did not need to subvert external powers. It is not their love but the love of Claudio and Hero, this very conventional love, that has subverted the order of justice. It has also turned, thereby, entirely irrational at the moment when the chips were down. I here again refer to Shakespeare's deepest conviction: great love is mutual and withstands trials. This is the case with the love of Benedick and Beatrice, as well as with the Mozartian Tamino and Pamina. Whether the lovers are good or wicked, rational or irrational is of secondary importance from this perspective, but not from all other perspectives.

The great, passionate, and highly sexual love of wicked men and women is placed at the other extreme in the line of Shakespearean lovers, opposite merely conventional love. I have tried to show that in Shakespeare passionate love, and particularly sexual attraction, is by no means wicked as such. However, Shakespeare offers a special gift to a few wicked characters in his arsenal: he gives them great love. Yes, there are wicked men and women who are capable of feeling great love and who remain loyal to their beloved. As I mentioned in an earlier chapter, Shakespeare also portrays the beggars of love. Men (and sometimes, although rarely, also women) can do something entirely foolish and irretrievable to get proof of love, which does not in fact require proof. Lear is an example. Or they can maneuver themselves deeper and deeper into the pit of evil, motivated by their hunger for love, as Edmund does. The beggars of love in Shakespeare play a subversive role without exception.

Here I will speak about lovers whose hunger is satisfied, who know themselves to be beloved, and who are wicked or become wicked. Wicked, passionate love is the most dangerous kind in Shakespeare's book, but there is no causal relationship here (as there is no causal determination in Shakespeare altogether). Although Claudius killed his brother so that he could possess his wife, this was not the cause of the murder. Although Macbeth committed murder under the persuasion of his lady, this was not the cause of his murder. The long-lasting love relationship between Margaret and Suffolk was certainly not the cause of Gloucester's death. But these relationships all contributed to the crimes. They were—among others—the conditions under which those crimes were committed. Thus, justice, law, legitimacy, morality, life, and security were annulled and subverted.

The three above-mentioned cases (two of them crucial in Harold Bloom's discussion) are, however, entirely different. I have briefly dwelled on the difference between the two kinds of sexual subversion. One can speak of sexual subversion when passionate love or sexual relationships subvert tradition, the political order of the state. One can also speak of sexual subversion when the sex roles themselves are reversed. In the second sense one can say that Rosalind or Viola (in *Twelfth Night*) are "guilty" of sexual subversion when playing the role of a boy, although they do not subvert the political order. But in the first sense of "sexual subversion," one can say that Cleopatra and her love of Antony become politically subversive in Rome, although Cleopatra does not subvert sexual roles at all. She is rather the quintessence of seductive femininity. Let me briefly scrutinize the three cases of great passions of wicked lovers from this angle.

We do not witness any outspoken love scenes between Claudius and Gertrude. They always appear together in public. We learn of Claudius's passion from his own confession, and we learn of Gertrude's passion rather indirectly, through the accusations of Hamlet. Hamlet speaks to his mother as a woman addicted to having sex with Claudius. This is the reason that Hamlet recommends a detoxification cure. We may or may not believe him. Yet Hamlet's interpretation sounds accurate, for Gertrude follows her husband blindly even after the brief episode of her catharsis during the altercation scene with her son. But there is no indication of sexual subversion in the second meaning of the expression. Gertrude is a woman through and through who never assumes the position, function, character, or even the garment of a man. She is addicted to Claudius, she cannot get rid of him. This is a usual feminine malady. Sexual subversion is here political: there is a political crime committed by passionate lovers. One can surely say "committed by lovers," even if Gertrude had no idea of the crime when it was being committed. Yet when she learns of it later from Hamlet, she still does nothing. Her passionate love for her second husband (the murderer of her first husband) does not change. She does not want to find out whether Hamlet's accusation is true; one may guess that she had always suspected that Claudius killed her first husband and that she wanted to protect her outward ignorance. This kind of psychological resistance is well known to anyone who has ever lived in a totalitarian state.

In *Macbeth* we encounter both cases of sexual subversion. Without the passionate love between Macbeth and Lady Macbeth, King Duncan would not have been murdered and the traditional legitimate order would have prevailed in Scotland. Gertrude follows the lead of Claudius, but in *Macbeth* the sex roles also become reversed: Lady Macbeth becomes the man and Macbeth the woman.

Lady Macbeth makes an existential choice here, just like Richard III. She chooses herself as a man ready and able for all cruelty: "Come, you spirits / That tend on mortal thoughts, unsex me here, / And fill me from the crown to toe top-full / Of direst cruelty. Make thick my blood . . . / That no compunctious visitings of nature / Shake my fell purpose, nor keep peace between / Th' effect and it. Come to my woman's breasts, and take my milk for gall, you murd'ring ministers, / Wherever in your sightless substances / You wait on nature's mischief" (*Macbeth* 1.5.39–49). We do not know what kind of woman Lady Macbeth was before receiving Macbeth's report; we first meet her at the very moment that she chooses herself as a wicked man. But one may say that Shakespeare knew everything about an existential choice; here one chooses what one is, to become what one already was.

Lady Macbeth has chosen *herself* and her destiny as a person who does not yield to any law or any right. She not only challenges the legitimate order but also the right of nature. By nature she is a woman. Nature makes women, and perhaps even men, compassionate. Pity is a natural feeling. But Lady Macbeth decides to get rid of them all. I repeat: she eliminates duty and legitimacy, but also the natural order and conventional virtues as well as natural feelings.

Still, one could object that Lady Macbeth is a "normal" rebel who clings to nature as against convention. After all, that the female sex is subject to the male sex is a convention. Women who behave like men can be the rebels of nature. They *can* be rebels, but this is not so in Lady Macbeth's case, because she does not choose herself as a man to claim independence and freedom She chooses herself as a man who is committed to use independence and freedom in a certain way—in an *unnatural* way.

For compassion and pity are not only female virtues in Shakespeare, but also male. In the world of Shakespeare, tenderness, pity, and forgiveness are among the chief virtues; and a man who lacks those virtues is not more manly but less. As Macbeth himself says before he becomes a murderer, still resisting his wife's insistence that he should kill and be a man instead of being a coward, "I dare do all that may become a man; / Who dares do more is none" (1.7.46–47). There are cruel men in almost all tragedies and in many comedies of Shakespeare, yet they are not portrayed as manly. True, in Shakespeare's book cruel women are worse than cruel men, for men's business is to fight in wars, and wars involve a certain amount of cruelty. Women are spared these lessons in cruelty; no business requires cruelty of them. But unnecessary cruelty, like the absence of compassion and of tenderness, is always a sign either of wickedness or of pettiness in Shakespeare's plays.

And if we listen carefully to Lady Macbeth's soliloquy and to her first words to her husband, it turns out that she has unsexed herself only in one sense: she chooses herself as one who has become immune to the natural impulse of compassion. She decides to become a murderess and make a murderer of her husband because she is in love with her husband and is certain of his love. She chooses to become a man of cruelty in order to help her husband ascend to the throne. In fact, she fulfills a traditionally female role. Read her first words of address: "Great Glamis, Worthy Cawdor, / Greater than both by the all-hail hereafter" (1.5.53–54). There is a double play here with Lady Macbeth's sex because she "unsexes" herself but remains a member of the female sex. She relates the acts of cruelty to her femininity. Her imagination is so extremely cruel precisely because her fantasy remains feminine: "I have given suck, and know / How tender 'tis to love the babe that milks me. / I would, while it was smiling in my face, / Have plucked my nipple from his boneless gums / And dashed the brains out, had I so sworn as you / Have done to this" (1.7.54–59). No Richard, no Edmund, no Iago, no man could invent or imagine an act of such extreme brutality. Lady Macbeth blackmails her husband with love as many women do. "From this time / Such I account thy love" (1.7.38–39). Murdering Duncan remains the only proof Macbeth can give of his love.

That there is a sexual tension between Macbeth and Lady Macbeth has always been noticed. That there is love between them that frequently surpasses the conventional attachments in marital relations is clear from the text, if only from the passage where Lady Macbeth successfully blackmails Macbeth with love. Some interpreters believe that Macbeth yields to his wife because of his sexual impotence, for which he haS to make up by so-called manly deeds. This is, of course, just an interpretation. Shakespeare can be interpreted here, as in all other cases, in so many different ways because he doesn't provide any causes. It is precisely because he does not present any causes—as Lukács observed—and brings together different characters in extreme situations to find out for himself how the chemistry among them will develop and what actions will occur as a result, that so many different interpretations of "causes, motivations" can be made equally plausible.

I cannot continue here with the interpretation of Lady Macbeth's character, but one thing is still so important to the present discussion that I cannot omit it: the rearrangement of the sexual relations between Macbeth and his lady after the murder. On the one hand it is Macbeth who suffers under the weight of guilt, whereas Lady Macbeth would be ready to forget the murder and live happily ever after. It is Macbeth who cannot rid himself of murder; it is because of his sense of guilt that he will murder again and again, until his death. Lady Macbeth, who has buried weaknesses like the conscience in her soul, would stop killing immediately after having ascended the throne. Without a sense of guilt, nothing necessitates that she go on to commit murder. Lady Macbeth, one of the cruelest of all Shakespearean figures, could have been, in fact, a perfect Machiavellian. Since she was able to murder in cold blood, she would have been able to stop killing. But Macbeth was unable to stop. The same thing that made him resistant to murder for a while made him much more responsible for murder than his lady. He does not even disclose to his wife his resolve to let Banquo and his son be assassinated: "Be innocent of the knowledge, dearest chuck, / Till thou applaud the deed" (3.3.46–47). Yet, after the deed new waves of guilt emerge, and new crimes, and so on. Lady Macbeth continually repeats her accusation of unmanliness. What she terms here unmanly is irrationality. Neither guilt nor the envisioning of appearances or ghosts is rational. Now Lady Macbeth also begins to behave cruelly to her husband, whom she loves, in order to turn his mind toward rational indifference: "O, these flaws and starts, / Impostors to true fear, would well become / A woman's story at a winter's fire / Authorized by her grandam. Shame itself, / Why do you make such faces? When all's done / You look but on a stool" (3.4.62–67).

What happens with Macbeth and his lady is entirely different from what happens with other wicked pairs who experience passionate love and sexual dependency in Shakespeare. Their love is in shambles after Macbeth has "proven" his, after having murdered in order to show it. Through Macbeth's guilt love itself comes to naught. When Macbeth learns of his wife's death during the final battle (5.5), he has only this much to say: "She should have died hereafter. / There would have been a time for such a word" (5.5.16–17). This is Lady Macbeth's obituary.

Yet no common guilt could tear Suffolk and Margaret apart. The passionate love of Suffolk and Margaret (from *King Henry VI*) is perhaps the most complex portrayal of the grandeur of love in wickedness ever presented by Shakespeare. I think that to dismiss *King Henry VI* as a weak drama written by a beginner is foolish, if for no other reason than this. Since I will discuss the three *Henry VI* tragedies in the second part of this book, I will speak now just about one love scene from Suffolk and Margaret's love story.

It is a long, full love story told from beginning to the end. We witness its beginning when Suffolk casts his first glance at the young princess, Margaret, and we follow it until the death of Suffolk and through Margaret's never-ending grief. The story consists of various episodes of subversion. That Suffolk made his lover the queen of England because this was the only way to keep her in his company constantly and to possess her was one of the crucial politically subversive steps that led to the War of the Roses. Political subversion was decisive right at the beginning of the love drama. The young Henry VI offended the dynastic principle by entering an unwise marriage against the counsel of his older family members; this mistake was never forgotten. Furthermore, the lovers Suffolk and Margaret— a self-made man and a self-made woman of sorts—conspire constantly. The House of York, their enemy, will in the end profit from the conspiracy. Also belonging to the stuff of political subversion is the well-known fact that the queen kept a lover. The other aspect of sexual subversiveness, that of "unsexing," did not fully develop in Margaret as long as Suffolk was alive. In relation to Suffolk she was always a woman, even if an independent-minded woman with a tendency to cruelty. But this cruelty could have been interpreted as a reaction to the hostility of the court. Margaret was the stranger, the alien, the "French woman" whom no one accepted and everyone except her husband despised. In her relation to her husband, Henry VI, whom she also loved, Margaret played a motherly role at first. Later, however, her cruelty gained the upper hand and she assumed more and more of a manly role. She was the one who fought the battles and left her husband at home. This is the purest case in Shakespeare of the appearance of both kinds of sexual subversion. And still, this is the work by Shakespeare where we gain insight into secrets of the lovers' love. One of the most wicked pairs in Shakespeare's world is portrayed more than once in a private and intimate setting, where they protest their love and express it. We see an honest and deep love, a love never betrayed, never even doubted, forever cherished. Shakespeare has offered such a bountiful gift not to Romeo and Juliet, or Antony and Cleopatra, but to Suffolk and Margaret—these two murderers.

Let me quote a few passages of the farewell scene between Suffolk and Margaret after Suffolk has been banished. This is their last encounter. It is important to read the entire passage. Queen: "Give me thy hand, / That I may dew it with my mournful tears; / Nor let the rain of heaven wet this place / To wash away my woeful monuments. / [She kisses his palm] O, could this kiss be printed in thy hand / That thou mightst think upon these lips by the seal, / Through whom a thousand sighs are breathed for thee! / So get thee gone, that I may know my grief. . . . I will repeal thee, or, be well assured, / Adventure to be banished myself. / And banished I am, if but from thee. / Go, speak not to me; even now, be gone! / O, go not yet" (*2 Henry VI* 3.2.343–57). And listen to Suffolk: "If I depart from thee, I cannot live,/ And in thy sight to die, what were it else/ But like a pleasant slumber in thy lap? Here could I breathe my soul into the air, / As mild and gentle as the cradle babe / Dying with mother's dug between his lips; / Where, from thy sight, I should be raging mad, / And cry out for thee to close up mine eyes, / To have thee with thy lips to stop my mouth, / So shouldst thou either turn my flying soul / Or I should breathe it, so, into thy body— / And then it lived in sweet Elysium. / By thee to die were but to die in jest; / From thee to die were torture more than death. / O, let me stay, befall what may befall!" (3.2.392–406). Suffolk speaks here to Margaret as if she were his mother. One needs to notice the words "mild and gentle." We have never seen Margaret mild and gentle except in her relation to Suffolk. This is one noticeable instance in Shakespeare where the characters become entirely different in their relation to different others. Who was Margaret? one may ask, for there were many of them. But even after having seen Margaret with the kerchief smeared with Rutland's blood, and after having seen her as the ghost of old Nemesis cursing Richard III, we will not forget Margaret the lover, who could kiss the hand of her beloved and remind him of a gentle mother taking the head of a son desirous of peaceful death into her lap.

What I want to show is that Shakespeare frequently pairs the subversion of sex roles—whenever a female assumes the role of a male—and wickedness. In all such cases, women who assume a male role identify the characteristics of this role with extreme cruelty. Other female characters who are witty, lovely, and kind can also assume male roles, but they do not take up male or allegedly male characteristics, for being a male is perhaps only a garment. But it is a rather significant garment. Clad in this garment a girl can play the role of an independent and free young man. A girl can become a decent, tender, and witty young man, like Viola or Rosalind. But sometimes lovely women do what normally only men practice even without appearing in disguise. Helena (from *All's Well That Ends Well*), for example, practices the male profession of doctor with great success. One should not forget that at this time Elizabeth I was the queen of England.

7

The Sphinx Called Time

Time is a sphinx in Shakespeare's plays, but a sphinx whose secret will never be known, whose riddle will never be solved. Thrown into the deepest pit of misfortune and despair, at the moment of triumph, in the heat of action and in its aftermath, while reflecting as spectators or relating as narrators, in tragedies and in comedies, representative heroes and heroines, and sometimes even less representative ones, address themselves directly to the sphinx called time. They constantly interrogate it, for they want to decipher its secrets. And they always interrogate it in vain, for the secret of time is the meaning of life. A life has no meaning except the question concerning meaning itself.

If we study the list of representative passages in Shakespeare's dramas where time indeed appears as a sphinx who offers her riddles for tragic or comic—but equally unsuccessful—solutions, we will discover something unexpected: time is not addressed as a riddle in any of the Roman history plays, but it is addressed in this way in all dramas of English history, as well as in the great tragedies where the double bind—the two contradictory concepts of nature—tears men and women apart. *Time becomes the sphinx when and where it is "out of joint."* Time is also out of joint in the Roman plays and in some romances and comedies, but although men and women reflect on time as much as on their day and age, the puzzle of time is not interrogated. This is particularly the case in the Roman plays and in a few romances that take place in the fictitious "ancient" world. It is the *place,* the question concerning the right or the wrong place, the fear of being displaced, of being exiled, that is the focus. Being in this place or in no place at all (utopia), that is the *where,* assumes in those dramas a far greater significance than in the English dramas or in the great tragedies, except for *Othello* (the drama of the absolute stranger). In the English dramas and great tragedies, as in many comedies, the representative history takes place "at home": in England, in Scotland, in Denmark. Even the scenes in France in the history plays are in fact English scenes because the place is in English territory or else used to be, or is planned to become English, and the characters with few exceptions are also Englishmen. The traditionally misunderstood Aristotelian requirement of great tragedy, the so-called unity of place, is far more absent in the Roman plays and romances than in the history plays, tragedies, and even most comedies. Coriolanus does not only fight in foreign territory, he stays there; he becomes a hero in a foreign land. He can ask the question: where am I at home? Where is home? The sons of Cymbeline are brought up in the wild bush, where Imogen likewise takes refuge. The story of *All's Well That Ends Well* moves from one place to the other together with Helena. Perdita goes from Sicily as far as Bohemia. Pericles wanders from island to island, and Prospero lives on an island. And where is Antony at home? In Rome or in Egypt? Among the Roman history plays, only *Julius Caesar*'s spatial arrangement resembles that of the *Richard* or *Henry* dramas. However, neither Caesar nor Cassius nor Brutus addresses himself to the riddle of the sphinx called time, least of all at the moment of his death. Time—whenever it appears in the Roman plays as a central issue for reflection—is either the time the Greeks called *kairos* (the time for something that one can catch or miss) or *moira fatum* (time as the executioner of a hidden design). For example, for Julius Caesar kairos appears at the ides of March, and for Pompey in *Antony and Cleopatra* at the banquet on the boat. The fate of Roman history hinges on those moments. Had Caesar decided otherwise, had Pompey decided otherwise, Roman history would have taken another turn. Kairos, however, is not presented as a riddle, for both Caesar and Pompey are cognizant of its presence; the first decides to accept fatum, the second decides to let the moment—which would have made a murderer of him—pass unused.

To find out what the future brings, what fate has in store, to peer into the consequences of actions, is certainly as important to the Romans as it will be to Englishmen fifteen hundred years later. But future time is a riddle just because it is in the future. In the future it will be known, for the future will soon become past again. Yet time as such is not a riddle, for when time as such becomes the riddle—should I repeat it?—life itself together with its meaning becomes a riddle. And life, the meaning of life, was not a riddle for the heroes of the Shakespearean Roman plays.

In this sense also Shakespeare was a splendid historicist. It is of no importance whether he was aware of the fact that he was, but he was. He attributed to the heroes of the Roman plays concepts of time, interpretation of time, and reflection of time that in fact existed in Greece and Rome prior to the emergence of Christianity. If there is anachronism in Shakespeare it is always factual. And we know that as far as historical truth is concerned, he never attributes importance to mere facts (as, for example, a handkerchief). The repeated striking of the clock in *Julius Caesar* is anachronistic factually but not poetically. In the latter sense it is absolutely in the right place.

Only where the double bind (of the two concepts of nature) tears men and women apart, only at the borderline between the premodern and modern, will time become a sphinx, because only then will the question of the meaning of life (and of the universe, and morality, and everything else) be raised and left—in the main—unanswered by those who ask the questions.

One cannot enter the discussion of time as a sphinx in Shakespeare's great tragedies and history plays before scrutinizing, even if only superficially and still approximately, temporality as a constitutive organizing principle in Shakespeare's plays. (To do this in a less superficial way, one needs to offer a broad structural analysis of Shakespeare's dramatic art, which would go far beyond the limited topic of this book.) Time is, to my mind, the essential organizing principle in (almost) all the Shakespearean plays, and not just in those where time is out of joint or where the chief characters are subjected to the double bind.

I would not call Shakespeare's theater epic theater. There is perhaps only one single play by Shakespeare, *Pericles,* in which he structures time in an epic manner. Shakespeare employs here a chorus (a person called Chorus) whose task is to relate the story of all the things happening between two scenes. The scenes themselves, which take place not just in different countries but also in different times, are sewn together by the text of the chorus. This chorus only remotely reminds us of the ancient chorus, for it performs the function of the narrator rather than the coplayer. So he (the chorus) says, "The unborn event / I do commend to your content: / Only I carry winged time / Post on the lame feet of my rhyme; / Which never could I so convey / Unless your thoughts went on my way" (*Pericles* 4.2). That is, to make the connection, the listener has to follow in thought the narrator's recited text, which, although resembling only lame feet, is still the carrier of winged time. But in the Shakespearean drama, it is not the lame feet of the narrator that carry the winged time, if for no other reason than that the "winged" time is just one metamorphosis of time. The epic time (at least in Shakespeare's time) could be "winged time" carried by narration. However, the time that undergoes constant metamorphoses—sometimes it may become lame in need of a walking stick!—cannot.

Since Shakespeare became a cult figure—on the Continent, particularly in Germany, from Lessing to Goethe—his unique treatment of time has always been discussed. Shakespeare did not follow the allegedly Aristotelian norm of the threefold unity (unity of time, place, and action), for there is unity neither of time nor of place in most of his dramatic works. And since Lessing soon refuted the accusations that Shakespeare neglected the three unities, the question was raised in a modified manner. That is, how has Shakespeare secured the unity of time when his dramas (unlike Greek tragedies) always cover more than twenty-four hours—sometimes a year, sometimes ten years? (Sometimes we do not even know how long.)

That every work of literature compresses time is a commonplace in the philosophy of art. Since to play a drama takes normally three to four hours (to read it perhaps only two), and the inherent time of a tragedy is at least twenty-four hours (as in Antigone), there could not be an essential difference between an ancient tragedy or a play by Racine or by Shakespeare in this respect, for they all compress time. The person who enters into the world of the drama will "live" there for at least twenty-four hours (twenty-four hours in three hours), but she can "live" there for fifteen years (fifteen years in four hours). This is in itself not an essential difference, as it does not distinguish the temporality of a drama from the temporality of another work of literature. One can read the story of David Copperfield from his birth until his second marriage in two days; one can "live" a whole life in two or three days.

Now I speak only of the drama, and especially of the Shakespearean drama. As we know, the Greek drama compresses time geometrically; it describes a circle. Twenty-four hours is a perfect circle, from dusk to dusk, from dawn to dawn, and so on. This is mythical time: time as a unit—the time of repetition and repeatability. Historical time is not circular and neither is it linear, at least not quite. To display it graphically, I would choose an EKG graphic. Yet this would still not be ideal. For historical time is also linear. The heartbeats do not repeat themselves in the same way, the rhythm changes, there is more than one rhythm, and the rhythms may have a tendency, pointing at something they do not reach. The graphic presentation of historical time is unlike a healthy heartbeat. It is also frequently pointed out that historical time, in the form of linear time, appears first in the Bible, especially in the Book of Kings, where the events constitute time.

The temporality of the Shakespearean dramas is historical. Here, as in all cases of historical time, the events—especially the density of the events—constitute time. But Shakespeare was the first great tragic playwright who consistently and continuously abandoned all mythological topics (which are inherited together with mythological time) and replaced them with historical topics that lend themselves more easily to organization by historical time. Nature here loses its organizing power. From dawn to dawn, from dusk to dusk, from spring to spring, and so on, these are *natural organizing* times. They are also mythological. Festivals, celebrations of nature, as religious festivals and holidays, repeat themselves every year. In Shakespeare the unrepeatable events do not follow natural regularities of any kind. The rhythm of events, of actions, that constitute the inherent time of his dramas is never natural but historical. Everything that is historical "compresses," but it compresses in a manner other than the mythological. There are at least five main time-organizing elements in Shakespeare's dramas: density, speed, tension, swing, and pause.

- *Density.* Density can be emotional, reflective, and action bound. For example, one assumes that a soliloquy as an internal abbreviated speech act takes place in a split second, but not for us, because the actor will spell out the reflections of the hero slowly. Or many single things happen as "pure acts," abruptly but simultaneously. A man gets killed. There is the man killed not in one stroke but in many, there are the men who killed him, there are the onlookers—they are all doing something. See the murder of Julius Caesar. Great density expands time rather than compressing it. But time can be expanded in a drama because it is essentially compressed. Pause is necessary for creating density.

- *Speed.* Speed is the tempo of the sequences of events. It can be rapid as well as relatively slow (although never entirely slow), accelerating and decelerating. Normally, events are slow in the first act and accelerate rapidly in the fifth. The relative slowness of the sequence of events coincides with the presentation of different characters in concrete situations. Whenever the special chemistry among the characters starts to work, acceleration begins and culminates in the consummation of the tragedy (heaping up of corpses) or comedy (accumulation of joyful events). But there is also a rhythm of acceleration and deceleration within the play. Although it is true that in Shakespeare all scenes move the drama forward (this is why his drama is not epic theater), different things can move forward with different speed, and the heterogeneity of actions, in addition to the uniqueness of the actors, contributes greatly to the amount and kind of acceleration or deceleration. Some happenings push the drama ahead in a slower tempo than others. If this were not so, Shakespeare would characterize all his heroes and heroines in the same way, or at least to the same extent. But this is not what Shakespeare is doing. He slows down the speed of an action sequence just to illuminate one aspect of one of his characters whom he loves (or whom he dislikes). The cemetery scene with Horatio, Hamlet, and the clown is a typical case of slowing down the rhythm of events before beginning the final sequence of acceleration. The love scene between Margaret and Suffolk is also a characteristic scene of deceleration. Here, too, immediately afterwards, events begin to accelerate. The structuring of these plays shows that acceleration will, perhaps, not have the same density of temporality without a previous scene of deceleration.

- *Tension.* The two previous dramatic uses of temporality, density and speed, are not unknown to Greek tragedies, although they never assume as strong and idiosyncratic an organizing power as they do in the Shakespearean dramatic art. What I call tension or reduction is, however, entirely absent. With the exception of the end of the last act (accumulation of corpses or of joy), scenes of the greatest tension are normally followed by a reduction in tension. The time is not the same for all of us. It is fulfilled time for one, empty time for another; it is fearful time for one, light time for the other. The heterogeneity of time experience is built into the structure. There can be no heterogeneity of time experience if time is mythical, but there can be when time is historical. One of the most tense and compressed scenes in *Macbeth* is 2.2. Macbeth has just killed Duncan: "I have done the deed," and his deed immediately "sticks" in "his throat." He is tormented by the avenging ghosts who cry, "Macbeth shall sleep no more." Lady Macbeth goes to smear blood on the body of "sleeping grooms"; she returns and someone knocks at the door. And then in 2a (the following scene), the porter enters to open the door. The grumbling porter's monologue is one of the most comical soliloquies Shakespeare ever wrote. Macduff enters and no one knows anything yet. This is just one case of a strong tension reduction that is followed by a scene of renewed tension when the murder will be discovered. There are a few similar instances in comedies.

- *Swing.* Tension and tension reduction can also be described as a case of swing. There are different kinds of swing in Shakespeare. There are extreme swings in the emotional state of a character, of his or her mood (for example, from rage to tenderness and vice versa). For example, Cleopatra is portrayed as a woman who is always in the state of such a swing. There are moral-ethical swings (for example, from revenge to forgiveness). There are extreme swings of fortune: of victory and defeat in war, vertical changes of power and status. All these can be relatively slow and cumulative, or entirely abrupt. There are extreme swings in human relations: a friend turns into an enemy and vice versa, allegiances made and—perhaps suddenly—broken, and so on. Almost all types of swings point to the unexpected and sometimes also to the undeserved. In Shakespeare they are only real swings. There is no deus ex machina; no good fortune appears without a prehistory.

- *Pause.* Since there is no narrator in Shakespeare's representative dramatic art, and this is why he cannot omit the portrayal of happenings (if something happens, it must happen on the stage), he must cross out time itself. We do not need to know how much time was crossed out or omitted precisely because time itself has been crossed out, and there is neither "much" nor "little." We know that time has elapsed between Hamlet's going to England and his returning to Elsinor. But we do not know how much. It is of absolutely no significance because it is a pause. The pause is time, however, to the extent that it is coded by someone. Hamlet, for example, tells Horatio the story without referring to the time element. The pause has temporal significance because what has happened then is happening here and now. The pause is then a significant break. As far as the history plays are concerned, we learn from history books and from footnotes how many years Henry VI lived and reigned. We have the precise chronology. This chronology, however, is empty knowledge because it is not constitutive of the play. In the history plays as much as in the other dramas of Shakespeare, the pause is a break, and it is to this extent a temporally significant pause because it is carried on in coding, in memory traces, in consciousness. Whatever has happened before act 1, scene 1, is not a pause, it is not a time-constituting element. In Shakespeare, just as in Greek tragedy, characters frequently recall histories of yesteryear and of ages bygone.

Beside the time-constitutive pause, there is the meaning-constitutive pause, which must remain hidden. Density (that is, time expansion) is an absolute requirement of the tragedy. However, composition and density can only exist together through the presence of the hidden pause. The pause is (in the drama) nothing, and yet it is the openness of interpretation. *Every interpretive staging* (and every staging is interpretive) *mainly interprets the pause.* For example, in Hamlet, how does the specter of Hamlet's father move? What are Hamlet's gestures? How do the characters look in the first place? Is Hamlet kissing Ophelia or hitting her? What is not in the drama is in fact there. We must guess what is there.

I mentioned the five main time-organizing elements in Shakespeare's dramatic art. These five elements organize the plot, and also, through and in the plot, the chief kinds of time and temporality that inhere in the plots. *Yet the enumeration and discussion of the organizing elements of temporality do not yet indicate which kinds of time will be organized through these elements in the plots; it does not even give a hint of what those time experiences are.* I will now turn to this issue.

In his brilliant book *The Ethics of Time,* Wylie Sypher distinguishes between four time experiences in *Richard III* alone. He discusses a few other kinds of time in other dramas by Shakespeare, and he also makes the observation, based on Heidegger's understanding of time, that one needs to distinguish in Shakespeare between temporality of *Umwelt* (world of the environment), *Mitwelt* (world of togetherness), and *Eigenwelt* (internal world). I will include many of Sypher's remarks in my own discussion of time by Shakespeare.

Sypher speaks of four kinds of time: *the time of the chronicle, the cycle of fortune, the time of retribution, and the time of psychic duration.* I will add to this list: *time as time for something (kairos), time as irreversibility, time as change (as betrayal of expectations), time as rhythm, time as "times" (our times),* and *time as beginning and end.* First I will discuss these concepts of time. Then I will return to the issue raised by the title and the opening sentences of this chapter: the "interrogation" of the sphinx of time by the characters of the plays themselves.

The Time of the Chronicle

The time of the chronicle (I use the term in a broader sense than Sypher) is objective time. Whether Holinshed, Plutarch, or some other author is Shakespeare's source, he uses them—among others—to date certain acts or events. When one asks the question, "Where are we now in the story?" one may find in Shakespeare temporal road signs for orientation. The time of the chronicle is *linear.* Things happen before and after, and the temporal sequence cannot be reversed. When two scenes take place in two different loci, we will find out which of them happened first. The road signs may legitimate the dating exactly with their banality or insignificance. They have nothing to do with the plot; they fulfill only the function of a road sign. Sypher gives a good example from *Richard III* when, just before dispatching Hastings to his death, Richard turns to the Bishop of Ely and asks him to send some of his excellent strawberries. The bishop exits and then enters again to say that he has already sent for the strawberries. Such entirely insignificant details of dating have a time-organizing aspect; they also reduce tension (just like the scene with the porter in Macbeth). Tension reduction of these sorts is also a way to duplicate or desynchronize the rhythm of events. The moment that will be of life and death for Hastings is just the time to send strawberries for the bishop. Moreover, the scene emphasizes the already mentioned difference between natural time and historical time in Shakespeare. In nature there is late spring or early summer, the most beautiful season of the year; in history there is darkness, the worst season called tyranny.

The Cycle of Fortune

The cycle of fortune preserves cyclical time. Cyclical time is the traditional (Greek, Roman) dramatic time. Its fullness is circular. In fact, the circle is not always closed, not always a full circle. Aristotle says in his *Poetics* that the tragic hero must undergo the absolute change (turn) of fortune: he must fall from the top to the very lowest of points, or be elevated from the very bottom to the top. Several heroes and heroines in Greek drama such as Iphigenia, Orestes, and Oedipus go through the whole cycle, from the top to the bottom and back to the top, although not necessarily in the same drama. Most of the romances of Shakespeare preserve the ancient Greek model of the full cycle of fortune. These are like fairy tales. They corroborate Lukács's idea that the romance, as a kind of fairy tale, is a secularized transformation of the myth. I would add that this is true not just of the Greek myths. Although biblical history is essentially unilinear, it is also familiar with the cyclical time of the myth. However, it is not the wheel of Fortune but the guidance of Providence that is at work: it is the cycle of punishment and forgiveness, or the cycle of trial and elevation. (Take the example of Job.) Since the Shakespearean romances (contrary to the tragedies or comedies) are also moralizing, at the end the good and decent person—and never the wicked or the indifferent one—will once again be elevated. The wheel of fortune acquires a somewhat providential character in his stories, though the outcome will normally not negate its original contingent character. In *Richard III*, for example, almost everyone whose fortune changes abruptly from good to bad deserves it. But it is through Richard's acts that they will meet their deserved fate.

The Time of Retribution

I have mentioned already the frequency and the importance of curses, prophecies, and predictions in the Shakespearean tragedies. They have manifold temporal aspects. They increase tension, and by increasing tension they contribute to the density of the scene and also to an upward swing. Prophecies, curses, and the like increase expectations; we keep them in mind even if the actors of the play seem to have forgotten them; we become involved. Those who prophesy (institutionalized soothsayers excluded) are normally in a state of heightened emotional or spiritual sensibility. We assume that they see further, that they feel more intensely than anyone else. This emotional and spiritual tension is a way to create an upward swing. Their temporal significance is, however, not in their present but in their future. There is a minor riddle that will be solved in and through the changes that follow them. Old philosophical wisdom says that change is time. But one expects not only change but change in a certain direction. One expects that the truth of a sentence will be corroborated in time. Since one cannot make true or untrue statements about historical events of the future, the prediction is true if it becomes true. The curse takes effect when it has already taken effect. That is, the changes, where the proofs of the prediction are "ripening," take place during the *pause*. Someone prophesies or predicts something, someone curses someone, and at some point in the play, or perhaps in the following play, the pause is lifted. The prophecy will return in the present as the event. Curses return from the pause as maledictions take effect or are recalled and acted upon. Something forgotten is remembered and enters the present through the minds of the actors. But is it forgotten? The spectator does not forget it. Prophecies, curses, and so forth are like knots on the handkerchief; they are signs of a beginning, of something that will ripen and take effect. Yet spectators might believe that the actors have forgotten them, because they sometimes do not mention them or act upon them until the chips are down. They also might believe the contrary. They might sense a meaningful silence lingering in the air. I mentioned in the first chapter that in Shakespeare's plays not all predictions come true and not all curses take effect. Now I have to come back to this issue. In such cases curses, predictions, and the like manifest not the time of retribution but the time of the chronicler. They corroborate that this has happened then, that this was said then. Curse and prediction serve then—in their contingency—just like the strawberries of the Bishop of Ely; they serve as road signs signifying objective time.

Prophecies, predictions, and curses are all future-oriented speech acts. They are (mostly) effective speech acts. They all need the temporal arrangement of the pause. However I will discuss them separately, since prophecies and predictions on the one hand and curses on the other have a different moral *valeur*. The first two utter statements of fact about the future, that is, they presuppose the possession of a kind of rational human or divine foresight. The latter utters a retributive (moral) statement and presupposes the magic potency of words—either their direct power (the words of an unjustly treated man own such a power), or their indirect power (the cries of offended innocence reach God and he will make the curse take effect).

That many predictions are quite reasonable and in no need of the power of divine foresight is noted by many shrewd characters of Shakespeare's plays. Those who are good at politics particularly do not attribute such a divine potency to foresight. Whereas superstitious men tend to attribute superhuman power to soothsayers and the like, politically acute actors operate normally with if-then likelihood. They believe in regularities in histories, in rational prediction, including possibilities of error. Listen, for example, to the discussion between Warwick (a prototype of the successfully politicking man) and King Henry IV (in *2 King Henry IV* 3.1). King Henry IV recalls the prophecy of Richard II that Northumberland, unfaithful to him, will also betray Henry: "'The time shall come'—thus did he follow it,— / 'The time will come that foul sin, gathering head,/ Shall

break into corruption;' so went on, / Foretelling this same time's condition, / And the division of our amity" (*2 Henry IV* 3.1.70–74). Warwick
the realist answers: "There is a history in all men's lives / Figuring the
natures of the times deceased; / The which observed, a man may prophesy, / With a near aim, of the main chance of things / As yet not come to
life, who in their seeds / And weak beginnings lie in treasured. / Such
things become the hatch and brood of time; / And by the necessary form
of this / King Richard might create a perfect guess / Would of that seed
grow to a greater falseness, / Which should not find a ground to root upon
/ Unless on you" (75–87). What is the mysterious power of prophecy in
the eye of Henry is a politically sound guess in the eye of Warwick. Warwick argues here with the Aristotelian categories of *dynamis* and *energeia*
that Northumberland's treason was present in his character. He was potentially already a traitor to Henry, where he in fact betrayed Richard for the
sake of Henry. Warwick does not say that if someone betrayed a person, he
will also betray another. Had he said this, he would have been a politically unsound man. Yet interestingly, the king simplifies Warwick's sound
judgment, transforming his sentence from a hypothetical to a categorical,
from a probability to a necessity: "Are these things then necessities? / Then
let us meet them like necessities." (*2 Henry IV* 3.1.87–88). Interestingly, the
next scene among the rebel army echoes the same theme. When Mowbry
declares that the times lay a heavy and unequal part on his and his friend's
honor, Westmoreland answers: "O, my good Mowbray, / Construe the
times to their necessities, / And you shall say indeed it is the time, / And
not the king, that doth you injuries" (*2 Henry IV* 4.1.101–4). In other plays
of Shakespeare, predictions based on analogy or repetition can prove
entirely false (see the interpretation of Desdemona's betraying her father
by Othello). Still, normally and in the main, one can make fair guesses
about the future acts of a character. Such prophecies manifest a sound
knowledge of human character (one may be reminded of Julius Caesar's
understanding of Cassius, although Caesar has not prophesied anything
concrete).

The expression "time of retribution" is perhaps not entirely fitting to
such cases of prediction, for beside the dark predictions (predictions of
doom) there are also shining ones (predictions of grandeur, success). When,
for example, Henry VI predicts that the boy Henry Tudor will become the
great king of England (*King Henry* 6.3), we rejoice in the expectation of a
happy ending. But the temporal structure is the same: someone utters a passionate statement in the future perfect tense, as if it had been already realized. Mostly, since we are talking about history plays, we know that they in
fact have been. But we are placed back into the past. The past is our present, and it is now that something has been predicted, and only tomorrow—another now of the play—that it takes effect like any other human

plan or goal. We decide that we are going to do this or that, and the decision, as a *causa finalis* of sorts, guides our action. In the case of prophecies, however, it is not the same man who prophesies and who makes the prophecy take effect in the future. He does not make a statement about his goal but about a *futurum perfectum* certainty. The prediction takes effect as a conditional certainty. A strong statement uttered with confidence, even if it does not satisfy the criteria of a sound prediction in the understanding of Warwick, impresses men and women as if it were a kind of goal. It has been raised, it is there, it operates from the hidden, from the underground of the not-yet. Men and women tend to believe in predictions. If they are actors of the play, they contribute—already through their belief—to the realization of the predicted event. This is also a way that the pause accompanies action; it can be the unconscious dimension of an action. But unconscious is perhaps the wrong expression here. For predictions are coded in memory, and what is coded in memory remains omnipresent even if is pushed back—in a pause—into the unconscious regions of the mind.

Curses (and blessings) have the power of appeal; they appeal both to this-worldly and to otherworldy agencies of justice. Their taking effect is the proof of a moral order. If they do not take effect, this is the proof of the dissolution of the moral order. Since in Shakespeare both curses and blessings appeal (directly or indirectly) to divine justice, their coming true is a kind of theodicy. The time of curses and blessings can legitimately be called the time of retribution or the time of redemption. This is obviously not so in the case of predictions or prophecies. The moral order does not depend on whether Northumberland will betray Henry VI or whether Henry VII will become the blessed king as Henry VI has predicted. But that Richard III or Macbeth meets an ugly and desperate death is the proof of moral order, whereas Cordelia's death might indicate that there is no such order. In my mind *King Lear* is Shakespeare's darkest play. (It takes place in a still-pagan world.)

When an innocent curses the guilty, the temporal order of the drama and that of the world must coincide. Justice must be done before the end of the drama. The time of retribution and the time of the play must coincide. This is not necessarily so in the case of a blessing. In a very simply constructed tragedy like *Richard III,* curses and blessings are seemingly simultaneous. The ghosts of the murdered souls turn toward Richard and curse him, and then they turn toward Henry and bless him. Yet whereas the curses are the repetitions of previous curses uttered by almost the same victims when still alive, the blessings are uttered for the first time. (It is not only the offended innocent who curses his offender. In Shakespeare, nothing is as simple as that. It happens many times, particularly in *Richard III,* that it is not the offended innocence that curses the evil, but the fellow evil that curses the radical evil—just as the evil betrays also the evil and not only the innocent one. The temporal structure is, however, generally the same, although the moral contents might differ widely.)

The Time of Psychic Duration

The time of psychic duration is one of the main ways of Shakespearean characterization. Shakespeare presupposes the flow of experiencing, the constant flow of unintended and unarticulated lived experiences of every human creature. What becomes articulated and how are presented as the chief manifestations of the temperament, the moral character, and the psychological character of an actor. Quick and abrupt articulation is a matter of temperament as much as that which is slow. In the first case, for example, what appears in the mind appears vehemently and is immediately translated into action. There is no pause between idea (goal) and deed. In this respect the same psychic duration characterizes Hotspur and Macbeth. But their moral as well as psychological characters modify strongly the typical pattern of psychic duration. Whereas Macbeth is constantly reflecting post factum, his psychic time is that of the expanded experience of irreversibility, and as such is dense. Nothing like this happens with (or in) Hotspur, with the sole exception of the moment of his death, which I have mentioned earlier and to which I will return shortly. Briefly, the more the psychic state of a hero changes, the more unique the moments of the articulation of the flow of experience become, the more dense and intensive will be his time experiences, as in the cases of Hamlet and King Lear.

Kairos

Kairos, the proper time for something, the time one has to catch, the "just now" of action, is *political time proper,* although not by any necessity is it also historical time. I mentioned right at the beginning of this chapter that in the Roman plays of Shakespeare, kairos is the overarching concept of time and the main time experience. In the history plays and great tragedies this is not so, yet kairos still has significance as the political time proper. The sense for the "just now," for the "act now" or the "jump now," is more than a political talent. Some catch the time, some fail to catch it. The great man of politics knows when time must be caught, and he never misses the right moment for acting or jumping. In this respect, but only in this respect, politically significant actors are in control of time. They govern time, for they ride on it like a horse (they sense when and where to jump). Governing time, controlling time, may also mean to govern fate or to be in control of fate. Whoever is raping time (kairos) has also coerced fate. But

fate and the time to catch one's fortune are not identical. Shakespeare is
true to Machiavelli: one can coerce fate with the greatest probability of success if one catches the right time. But one does not necessarily govern fate
through catching time. Not even the shrewdest and coldest politicking
actor can eliminate the other players and the multifarious accidents from
the game. Fate cannot be conquered, not even by catching the right
minute. But political freedom widens, and the actor conjures up fate with
a greater probability of success if he never misses the proper time of action
(or of staying put). And this is so also in the history plays.

Time as Irreversibility

In politics, "missing the proper time" is an *irreversible* failure. If one misses
the proper time to do a thing of political exigency, if one hesitates, if one
lets opportunity go unused, similar opportunity will not present itself
again. There is no second time or third time; there is only once. Brutus has
rejected the proposition of Cassius to get rid also of Marc Antony. This was
his grave political mistake, entirely irreversible, and has contributed grossly to the defeat of the republican cause. Had Hamlet been a politician, he
would have killed Claudius at the moment he was praying alone, and he
would have ascended the throne with popular support, would have set time
right and become a great king. He missed this opportunity, and similar
opportunity does not present itself again. Almost three centuries after
Shakespeare, Talleyrand described the political failure of missing the proper time as "more than a crime, a mistake." Shakespeare is more complicated. In political terms and in general, missing the proper time is a mistake.
However, it can also be a crime. But the opposite is also true: catching the
proper time can be politically right but can still be a crime. And in most
cases, crime itself is the worst mistake. Macbeth had one great opportunity to become a king. Lady Macbeth was politically right: if you want to be
king—and Macbeth wanted to be the king—such a splendid opportunity
presents itself only once in a lifetime. The king was sleeping in their castle.
Macbeth could easily kill him and ascend the throne—either now or
never. And Macbeth catches time, but what is the result? The crime itself
becomes his gravest mistake. For in order to catch the time politically, one
needs to be a political character. It is just as Machiavelli describes it: one
must be daring yet rational, hard on enemies, yet never transgressing if not
necessary. Neither Hamlet nor Macbeth is a political character. Hamlet
knows himself fairly well; premeditated murder without proof of guilt is
not in his character. He obviously rationalizes his decision not to kill
Claudius on the only occasion he could have done so in a politically sound
manner. He misses the opportunity by good instinct. Why was his instinct

good? Let me repeat, had he caught the opportunity he could have become the king of Denmark and also a good king. But he would not have become Hamlet. The greatest—perhaps the only—telos of Hamlet is to become himself. And he becomes himself in making his downfall irreversible. Hamlet did not catch time, whereas Macbeth did. In Macbeth's case catching the time was irreversible. He becomes a murderer, and he cannot wash his hands clean. Neither can Lady Macbeth, as we see in her madness scene.

David Roberts called my attention to the circumstance that the main constitutive difference between the Shakespearean tragedies on the one hand and the comedies and romances on the other hinges on the *irreversibility or reversibility* of an act or of a few acts. In the introduction to this book I quote Hamlet's famous sentence "The time is out of joint" and add that time is out of joint in almost all Shakespearean plays. In the tragedies and most of the history plays, time cannot be set right; no one can set it right. But in the comedies and in the romances time is in fact set right. This is the main manifestation, or rather meaning, of (ir)reversibility in Shakespeare. Let me add that the difference is not between nonhistorical and historical time, or between political and nonpolitical time. There is a historical dimension in all plays of Shakespeare, and there is a political aspect in almost all of them (for example, *Cymbeline, Measure for Measure, As You Like It,* and *Much Ado about Nothing*). It has been mentioned by many interpreters of Shakespeare that in several of his comedies and all his romances, there is a moment where the plot can still develop into a tragedy. This moment is the point where reversibility and irreversibility are parting ways. Reversibility (to set time right) involves first and foremost the very thing that Aristotle claims is essential to tragedy: someone at the height of good fortune is pushed to the very bottom, or someone on the bottom is elevated to the very top. What happens in most—although not all—Shakespearean comedies and romances is that *both parts of the movement take place:* innocent men or women are pushed to the bottom and then, finally, elevated again to the top. But this happens also in almost all, although not all, Shakespearean tragedies. Malcolm escapes to foreign lands but will be king at the end; Edgar, the naked "thing itself," also ascends at the end to supreme power. The difference—and this is an enormous difference—can be detected easily: in the tragedies or in the history plays the main characters who are at the top of the ladder of grandeur never go through such a double movement. (In *Henry V* the first movement is missing.) But then the question must be raised: is anyone in the comedies or the history plays placed at the top of the ladder of grandeur at all? Does not the structural constitution of (ir)reversibility hinge upon the characters themselves? Since it is also a traditional approach to speak about the Shakespearean dramas as "character dramas" as contrasted to "dramas of fate," one cannot avoid the

question of whether the (ir)reversibility of fate rests solely on the characters. In both cases fate is relativized, made conditional on the characters
themselves, so much so that characters press themselves upon the drama. As
we saw, *The Merchant of Venice* is a borderline case because the character of
Shylock does not strike us as comic; *Timon of Athens* is also a borderline
case, for Timon strikes us also as ridiculous.

Since there is no deus ex machina in Shakespeare, there is also no God
intervening in human affairs. But indirectly, through the beliefs, desires, and
pleas of the actors, fate is carried by the actors—never by one single actor,
but in the relation between them, in their chemistry. If one disregards politics and identifies the essential difference between tragedies and history
plays on the one hand and comedies and romances on the other as both a
matter of irreversibility and reversibility, one needs to point again to the
role of *contingency* in the Shakespearean plays. One will not find the same
schema twice in Shakespeare. Contingency is the "throw," yet this time it is
neither God nor nature but the author who throws different characters
together and finds out along with us how they develop their characters in
their interaction with one another and how they will finally decide about
reversibility or irreversibility. The original story of King Lear ended happily. However, Shakespeare's characters—and their chemistry—decided for
irreversibility. In the original story Macbeth has a legitimate claim to the
throne and a legitimate grievance against Duncan. But in Shakespeare,
Macbeth's encounter with the witches and his wife's character suffice to
develop the irreversible tendency of the plot. I mentioned Shakespeare's
structural employment of the temporal acceleration: where irreversibility is
absolute, temporality gets denser and the development of the plot accelerates. In comedies where time is finally set right, temporal acceleration rarely
occurs: the sequences of knotting and unknotting can proceed at equal
speed. Yet whatever becomes knotted or unknotted, the love story will
always play a major part in the sequences of waves. The fall from the top to
the bottom of the pit, and the restoration from the bottom to the top, happens—if it happens—also in love: the hero or heroine despairs of their love,
they are betrayed or mistakenly believe that they are, their love remains
unrequited or they falsely believe that it is. Time is to be set right in love,
sexual subversion is to be reversed: the lover is loved or becomes loved
again, the betrayal turns out to be a misunderstanding or will be forgiven,
girls shed the male garment and become girls again, desperate women like
Helen and Marian regain their identities, and Bottom regains his human
face. True, *The Taming of the Shrew* makes me shiver. And in *Troilus and Cressida* Shakespeare makes the question mark explicit: time is in fact not set
right in this play.

Let me return to the "throw." Shakespeare normally throws different
kinds of characters into plays that are supposed to develop as tragedies and

those that are supposed to develop as comedies, according to his narrative sources. The choice is not necessarily related to grandeur itself but to the quality and kind of grandeur of the characters. Shakespeare's dramatic art also essentially differs here from ancient Greek drama. Aristotle's dictum that tragedy imitates great characters and comedy base ones is not true in Shakespeare. I agree with Harold Bloom that Rosalind is one of Shakespeare's greatest characters. But her love of life, the beautiful balance between her emotional world and her reason, her unfailing sense of justice, her humor, her easy reliance on her good instinct, do not make a tragic character. Yet they do not add up to a comic character either. Rosalind is simply a beautiful character who is born to set time right. Shakespeare is courteous enough to offer her the kind of fellow characters—her father the exiled Duke, Celia her friend, and Orlando her lover—who will give her the opportunity to play a major part in setting time right and contribute to the happy ending. Rosalind, like a few other women characters, such as Viola (young women clad as young boys!), receives a great bunch of flowers from the playwright, a present he is normally reluctant to offer to any of his characters.

Although time is set right in the romances too, and the tragic tendency is portrayed here to be as reversible as it is in the comedies, they impress us—with the exception of *Measure for Measure*—in an entirely different way because of the *pause.* Generally, in the romances much time elapses between time getting out of joint and time set right, and normally, although not always, *action is replaced by the pause.* In *The Tempest* we watch only the setting right of time; everything else is past and gone, just memory, or a vicious act carried through only in the feverish minds of the actors, in bad dreams. As far as the fate of the kidnapped princes is concerned, the same is true in *Cymbeline.*

Reversibility is—even in comedies and romances—relative. Not everything is reversible. Moreover, to set time right *does not make time itself reversible; it makes fate or bad luck reversible or more precisely turns it back before fate could take its final effect,* turning *sors mala* into *sors bona.* Time is by definition irreversible, and in Shakespeare it is not just by definition. For in the romances, and sometimes also in the comedies, the world where time gets out of joint and the world in which it will be set right are not the same world. The world has *changed.* Men and women go through an experience; they emerge changed from this experience. Men and women who can distinguish between the faithful and the unfaithful, between semblance and essence, do not remain the same men and women that they were before their long trial. Men and women who learn to revolt or to forgive, or to love or love well, are not the same as before their trials. Men and women who begin to understand themselves, see their mistakes and follies, are not the same as before their trials. The characters—with the exception of the stage managers—are not the same at the end of the play as they were at the beginning. Some characters act as if the others should change. Perhaps they do, perhaps not. Perhaps those who want others to change will themselves change. This is a merry-go-round of changes. But the merry-go-round is not always merry. A play is a sequence of trials and errors, of fear and trembling, of hopes, of unexpected betrayals and fulfillments, of amusements and of lessons, of tests and antitests, and so on.

In comedies and romances many things are irreversible, even if fate can—in the sense discussed above—be reversed. In tragedies, in the genre of irreversibility, there are reversible acts and developments. Lear and Cordelia love each other *at the end of the tragedy again*, thus the father's curse is reversed. Edgar *again* becomes the real son of his father, who does not see the truth as long as he has eyesight and will see it only after becoming blind. In fact, love and hatred are the most frequently reversible feelings in tragedies. The dying Hamlet and Laertes are reconciled in forgiving one another.

Time as Change

Time is change, change is time. The change of the characters and of the positions they occupy is time; time is (also) identical with this change: change to the better and change to the worse, change understood or misunderstood. There is also change that elevates and change that frightens. And the most frightening change is the change where someone or something gets out of tune or out of time. Listen to Ophelia: "O what a noble mind is here o'erthrown! . . . / Now see that noble and most sovereign reason / Like sweet bells jangled, out of tune and harsh; / That unmatched form and feature of blown youth / Blasted with ecstasy" (*Hamlet* 3.1.153–63).

The Shakespearean characters reflect on change constantly—on the change of times, on the change of characters, and on the change of the fate of characters. And they prepare themselves as well as others for changes. Both fear and hope are vested in change. When time is out of joint, almost all certainties are lost. Almost everything can happen, almost everyone can betray expectations. The double bind is one of the major manifestations of the unpredictability of change.

Time as Arrhythmia

The other major manifestation is *arrhythmia*. Listen again to Ophelia's lament. She compares Hamlet's madness to "sweet bells jangled out of tune and harsh." In Shakespeare, man, as well as the times, can go mad. There is a kind of music in man, as in the world. Music consists of melody, rhythm, and harmony. Unpredicted and unprecedented events are like dissonant voices. The world gets out of tune, it becomes arrhythmic like a bad heartbeat. The arrhythmic, atonal world is mad because it has no measure; it is beyond all measures. The theme of Plato's *Philebus* returns here: the unlimited needs the limited, for only the limited determines. Without the limited there is only bad infinitude, hence no music, no language, no writing; nor is there human sociability, repetition, or repeatability. Needless to say, the meaning of measure in Shakespeare is not orthodox Platonism. For Shakespeare one can transcend old measures and establish new ones; one can create new norms and from then on one will follow the new ones. Hamlet compares himself more than once to a delicate musical instrument that hides its melodies from the intruder. He says: "That they are not a pipe for Fortune's finger / To sound what stop she please" (*Hamlet* 3.2.68–69). Yet the possibility of repeatability must remain, otherwise there is neither rhythm nor tune. It must remain either as a repeatability of the act itself or as repeatability of the act through speech act or thinking, in understanding and conceiving. (Hamlet discloses his rhythm and music to Horatio.) "Madness," the loss of measure, of tune or rhythm, can be absolute; there is no melody or measure left in Richard III nor in his world. But the loss of measure or melody can also be conditional: someone will become unable to understand the rhythm or the melody of a mind. Ophelia understands Hamlet less than Polonius, who in fact notices the rhythm of Hamlet's pretended madness: "Though this be madness, yet there is method in't," he says (*Hamlet* 2.2.207–8).

Of course, the tune can alter, as well as the rhythm of a man's soul or of the times. That one needs to be able to follow the rhythm of time is an old wisdom. This simple wisdom might suffice to conduct a good life where the rhythm remains steady. However, this is not so in times out of joint. To notice that the rhythm of time and its tune has been changed is of chief significance. In one of his great monologues about time, Richard II confesses that his worst shortcoming is having failed to take notice of the change of the rhythm and tune of his time: "But for the concord of my state and time / Had not an ear to hear my true time broke" (*Richard II* 5.5.47–48). In Shakespeare, good politicians do not merely catch the proper moment for action, they also understand how to accommodate to the ever changing rhythm of time. They notice when the tune is broken and the sweet music gets sour, and they use this knowledge for their own purposes. But successful politicians are not always the same men who bring the music of time out of tune, who change the rhythm or make the world arrhythmic. So also do the villains, as in the Wars of the Roses or in most tragedies. When I said that in the great tragedies time is never set right, I referred first and foremost to the irreversibility and the accumulation of sinister acts. But I may add to this arrhythmia. Certain kinds of sinister acts push time out of tune. The rhythm will not become restored. Either there will be a new rhythm and a new tune, as in the happy ending of *Richard III,* or no new rhythm or tune will replace the old, as in the end of *Hamlet,* which is (let me now repeat myself) no end but the beginning of the repetition of the story itself. True, sinister acts are not the only kinds of acts that may break the tune and rhythm of time; Brutus and Cassius, the tyrannicides, were not sinister characters. The sole Shakespearean character who breaks the tune and still rides confidently on his self-created wave of rhythm is Julius Caesar.

Time as the Times

The music that sounds as madness, as the broken tune, may also sound as the triumphant new melody and new rhythm in the ear of others; this is the music of *the times.* Shakespearean characters constantly refer to the time or the times. Shakespearean plays are plays about certain times. For Hamlet says, and Shakespeare with him, that the purpose of playing "both at the first and now, was and is to hold as 'twere the mirror up to nature, to show virtue her own feature, scorn her own image, and the very age and body of the time his form and pressure" (*Hamlet* 3.2.21–24). Let us pay attention to the change of the metaphor. Hamlet (or Shakespeare) speaks of the theater play as the mirror of nature, virtue, and vice. This is a traditional metaphor stemming from Plato and employed in various interpretations. Obviously, Hamlet (or Shakespeare) means here a clean, true mirror that shows nature's own proportion. But when he continues and speaks of the "age and body of the time," he uses the metaphor of form and pressure. Time or age is a body that leaves its pressure, its cachet, its stamp, its seal—on what? On the play, on the whole play. And on whom? On the age, the time itself. On itself. The drama is stamped by the age in which it takes place, by the age in which it is written, and by the age in which it is played. Historicity is not a mirror, for it is not concerned with virtues and vices as such, with the constant elements of human nature. It stamps them, it seals them three times, it knots them, it is a body whose weight is carried by all of them. This weight can be heavy, but it can also be light. The characters of Shakespeare are obsessed by their times. They complain that they are born in wrong times. They see themselves as either well fitted or badly fitted to their times. And as they are obsessed with their times, they feel themselves to be chained to those times. And perhaps this is why they are *not* chained to their times at all. For their times are also our times. The third dimension of time is the time of the performance—the ever changing, ever new times. To this question I will return.

Time as Beginning and End

Where does a play begin and where does it end? Goethe said that tragedy ends with death and comedy with wedding. This is not true of ancient drama, but it is mainly true about Shakespeare's dramatic world. Shakespeare's drama is historical through and through. One can paraphrase Hamlet's above-quoted sentence in the following way: *history, the times, stamp existence, but the mirror mirrors existence itself.* The end is either wedding or death: both are existential ends as limits (*peras*). Consummated love and death are both natural ends; however, as merely natural ends they are not existential proper. *They will be existential because they are historical.* Nature becomes existence through historicity. Historicity is the historicity of *dasein.* Here I return to the beginning of my ruminations. The main characters of Shakespeare are contingent or become contingent. The choice of the double bind, the commitment to the rights of nature, makes a person contingent. Contrary to the heroes or heroines of the later modern drama, Shakespeare's heroes and heroines make themselves contingent, they *choose their situation as thrownness.* They choose themselves as naked existences. And they become what they have chosen themselves to be; a wedding or a death is the consummation of these choices. Noncontingent characters also marry and die. These are the ones who follow tradition alone. They are never the chief characters, but they are important for the drama. It is against them, in perfect view of them, that the existential heroes and heroines of Shakespeare choose themselves to follow their own path because, as Luther said, they cannot do otherwise. Hamlet needs a Fortinbras and a Laertes, he needs a traditional contrast to follow his own path.

The temporality of the exister and historical times are interwoven, yet they also differ. For example, the meaning of *power* becomes twofold. Aristophanes in his comedy *The Frogs* makes the distinction between being happy and being powerful. He says through his mouthpiece of Aeschylus that Oedipus was unhappy while in power and became happy when he blinded himself and lost his throne. In Shakespeare happiness is very complex: it is not associated with being in power or with being virtuous or escaping guilt. I will turn to this question shortly. In Shakespeare it is not happiness and power, but power itself, "being in power," that goes through a process of bifurcation. The more a person becomes himself, the more he is in the fullness of his powers. This can happen also in the moment of death, if one becomes oneself in death as in *Othello* (not just for Othello, but also for Emilia). Looking at political power from the angle of the power of the exister, political power looks as *vanitatum vanitas.* But it is still *not* vanitatum vanitas. Political power and the power of the exister rarely coincide. Yet they can coincide (as in Henry V and Julius Caesar). But even if there is a tension between them, they are not necessarily also contradictories, either in good or in evil. Prospero returns home as a prince. The self-chosen wickedness of Gloucester peaks when he ascends to the royal power, and his power begins to shatter while he is still in power. But without having aimed at the supreme power, Richard could not become himself absolutely wicked. The end is either death or a wedding. Where is the beginning?

It is easy to tell where the end is: where the limit of the drama and the limits of the characters coincide. The limit of the drama is the end of the plot, the time where the first and second time dimension ends, and the only remaining time will be the third, namely, the presence of the performance. Then it is time for the allegorical or real curtain to fall; thus it is also the closure of the other space. The spectator can still stay in the times of the play and also in its space, the stage—or rather in Venice or in a royal castle, or on a deserted island—at least in his or her mind. In the case of a comedy, he or she can fantasize about the future of the characters. But the play is limited (peras), and the unlimited *(apeiron)* needs to be sought within the limited itself.

It is harder to determine where the beginning is. Obviously there is the formal beginning of the play: the allegorical or real curtain is lifted, the spectator steps into another time (two other times) and other places. But Shakespeare's plays are here also unlike the ancient drama. There is normally no one beginning in a drama, but there are more—at least two of them. To simplify, there is a tension between the beginning of the plot for the spectator and that for the exister whose fate is going to be consummated in the plot. One can hardly notice any "regularity" here. *Romeo and Juliet* has two very separate beginnings: first when the play begins, second in Juliet's monologue on the balcony. So does *King Lear.* The second beginning is the tempest scene when the king strips himself naked. This is the place where the existential stage is opened within the historical stage. The same "delay" before the second opening can also be noticed in comedies like *Much Ado about Nothing.* In *Hamlet,* as well as in *As You Like It,* the two stages roughly coalesce. In *A Midsummer Night's Dream* the existential stage is the dream stage. The *before* of the beginning (things or stories related by the actors on the stage) can be eminently important historically and politically (for example, when Antony relates the victories of Julius Caesar before the Roman crowd). They can also *stamp* the existers by putting a task, a weighty responsibility, on their shoulders (like the ghost on Hamlet's shoulder), but *they do not play a constitutive role in the historicity of the existers, in that they would become the persons they chose themselves to be.* This is also true of Hamlet.

For the characters of the play, especially for the chief characters, the beginning is not the beginning of the play and the end is not the end of the play. They are not players of the play, they are actors on two other stages: the historical and the existential. They are both the actors and the spectators on the historical stage, yet on the existential stage they are but actors. Kierkegaard suggests that the small theater is the divine theater. Shakespeare does not suggest this, but he does not exclude it either; he simply presents it.

The historical stage is the stage where time gets out of joint, and characters are born to set it right. They either do it or fail to do it. The existential stage is set by the "throw," where characters choose themselves and either live up to their chosen destinies or fail to live up to them, to the best or to the worst, to the good or to the evil. Different kinds of power are at stake on both stages. Life and death are at stake on both stages—different kinds of life and different kinds of death. Love is at stake on both stages— different kinds of love. *The chief characters of Shakespeare act on both stages in constant disharmony, tension, friction, and conflict.* This is why they are obsessed with and fascinated by time, this is why they turn to the sphinx called time to extract her secrets. This is a hopeless venture, since there are no such secrets. It seems as if in Shakespeare the secret of time, as the secret of our times, was the meaning of destiny that becomes fatally unfathomable and unaccounted for in the wake of the discrepancy between the two stages. This is because whenever the two stages miraculously harmonize, the sphinx disappears. For Julius Caesar time is not a sphinx. *For he is time and the times simultaneously.* And so is Rosalind. This is the miracle of the unique grandeur. However, there is another miracle: the state of grace, as it may happen in the fairy tales of the romances.

"The rest is silence," says the dying Hamlet. And even if in the following moment the stage will be filled with the noise of an intruding army, for Hamlet the rest is silence. But Hamlet does not address the sphinx of time at the moment of his death; he turns to his friend in order to clear his name for *posterity.* His last wish is to be justly judged and understood by posterity. Although the time once out of joint could not be set right on the historical stage, Hamlet reaffirms his complex and torn life as his own life, on the existential stage, and puts his trust in the narrative, in the ever present *future times.*

The end confirms or questions the beginning. The characters who question their "beginnings," the characters who never choose themselves or who consider themselves existential failures, interrogate the sphinx of time. So do those who were strangers in their own times, as well as those who missed its tune and constantly failed in their sense for time's rhythm. For all of them time remains a riddle. They always get time, as much as their times, wrong. Time is then the protagonist of all history plays, as well as political plays. Richard II addresses time three times in his tragedy—and every time in a significant dramatic moment. Henry VI's great soliloquy is a monologue about time. I will discuss in the second part of this book the various manifestations of the sphinx of time in their proper place: the context of concrete dramas.

But let me scrutinize for a passing moment a failed existence such as Macbeth's. The fascinating thing in Macbeth's story is that the very moment that he commits his crime and launches his destiny on an irreversible path, he already knows clearly that the path is irreversible and that his choice is fatal. His life has lost all meaning. It is here that he first speaks of time: "Had I but died an hour before this chance / I had lived a blessed time, for from this instant / There's nothing serious in mortality. All is but toys. Renown and grace is dead. / The wine of life is drawn, and the mere lees / Is left this vault to brag of" (*Macbeth* 2.3.89–95). For the exister called Macbeth, the existential beginning and end coincide, that is, the beginning is the end. The totally, absolutely meaningless death is already given at the beginning. The unusually accelerated tempo of the tragedy signals the rare discrepancy between the historical and the existential stage: the story develops on the historical stage perhaps for years, whereas on the existential stage it is over and done with in one second: the very second that Macbeth becomes a murderer. Macbeth's soliloquy at the end of the play is but an echo of his monologue at the very moment of Duncan's death: "Tomorrow, and tomorrow, and tomorrow / Creeps in this petty pace from day to day / To the last syllable of recorded time, / And all our yesterdays have lighted fools / The way to dusty death. Out, out, brief candle. / Life's but a walking shadow, a poor player / That struts and frets his hour upon the stage / And then is heard no more. It is a tale / Told by an idiot, full of sound and fury, / Signifying nothing" (*Macbeth* 5.5.18–27). A godforsaken world, a man-forsaken world, a meaning-forsaken world, where only one kind of time remains: the monotonous recorded time. Time is only *objective,* year after year, generation after generation, where men after men, shadow after shadow make their short performance on the stage of fools. (Here I would like to remind the reader that Shakespeare uses the stage metaphor repeatedly. In fact it is not a metaphor. Another reminder is that the shadow is here Plato's shadow, but without the ideas whose shadow it might be.) There was perhaps a moment in the life of many of us in which we felt like Macbeth. We can feel it again when tasting and quoting his sentences. It is a passing moment only—subjective time. A passing moment is not something final. Only a few of us have lost life forever while still young and very much alive. For them Macbeth's words could be the truth. But they would not understand them. For the passing moment of despair becomes life fulfillment for Macbeth only in and through Shakespeare's deed. The succinctly expressed absolute despair of the wicked is perhaps also a kind of theodicy.

It is not only tragic and historical heroes who are obsessed by time. Many characters of the Shakespearean comedies are as well. Forgive me if I choose again one of my favorite comedies, *As You Like It.* What immediately meets the eye is that melancholy Jaques, the misanthrope of the play (in fact he somewhat resembles Molière's misanthrope, although Jaques is a spectator and not a real actor), says things about life and death that are very similar to what Macbeth says. But all this sounds topsy-turvy coming from Jaques's mouth because he does not speak of his own life but of the lives of others whom he chides for the gusto taken in living and loving and merriment and pleasure, and in spite of betrayal, disappointment, and ugliness. In Jaques's mind the lovers of life are wrong and superficial. Disgust in life is deep, true, and real. He will be constantly rebuked. We are dwelling here in the beautiful utopia of the Forest of Arden. The Forest of Arden is not a utopia in the sense of not existing anywhere. It is a utopia in the meaning of *at times being everywhere.*

Jaques tells of his real or imaginary encounter with the fool in the forest: "A fool, a fool, I met a fool i'th' forest, / A motley fool—A miserable world! . . . 'Good morrow, fool,' quoth I, 'No sir,' quoth he, / 'Call me not fool till heaven hath sent me fortune.' / And then he drew a dial from his poke, / And looking on it with lack-lustre eye / Says very wisely 'It is ten o'clock.' / 'Thus we may see,' quoth he 'how the world wags. / 'Tis but an hour ago since it was nine, / And after an hour more 'twill be eleven. / And so from hour to hour, we ripe and ripe, / And then from hour to hour we rot and rot; / And thereby hangs a tale.' When I did hear / The motley fool thus moral on the time / My lungs began to crow like chanticleer, / That fools should be so deep-contemplative, / And I did laugh sans intermission / An hour by his dial" (*As You Like It* 2.7.12–33). The melancholic Jaques says no to life; he keeps himself in a constant state of moral indignation and is longing not just for the motley, the costume of the fool, but also for the fool's status. He is translating Macbeth's vision of time into the language of comedy. Macbeth makes himself a blood-soaked fool by destroying meaning; his time is objective time where we are born to die senselessly. It is the tale told by an idiot. Jaques wants to be and to act as a fool himself, for the fool—himself—is superior to all others because he knows something that the "clever" ones do not know: that there is just the objective time, and that life is meaningless and senseless. He comes back to his favorite topic very soon in his story about the world as a stage with men and women as players who have seven ages. He describes the seven ages of men and women—from the cradle to the oldest age—as ridiculously disgusting. The text is composed on the analogy of "hour after hour." It continues monotonously, without surprise, contrast, change of tempo, rhythm, or point, without the reduction or reversal of the tension.

Rosalind's comic ruminations on time are, in fact, the counterpoint. Rosalind contrasts "subjective time" to "objective time": the time of expectation, the time of ennui, the time of hope, of waiting for love, the time of hopelessness. These are all different kinds of time; their meaning dwells inward. Time cannot be measured by hours. Time is carried by meaning or the lack of meaning, or by personality or the lack of personality. There are different actors in different times. Rosalind (disguised as a boy) enters into dialogue with Orlando, her lover. Rosalind: "Then there is no true lover in the forest, else sighing every minute and groaning every hour would detect the lazy foot of time as well as a clock." Orlando: "And why not the swift foot of time? Had not that been as proper?" Rosalind: "By no means, sir. Time travels in divers places with divers persons. I'll tell you who time ambles withal, who time trots withal, who time gallops withal, and who he stands still withal" (*As You Like It* 3.2.296–304). Between the marriage contract and "the day it is solemnized" (307-8), she says, even if the interim is but seven nights, "time's pace is so hard that it seems the length of seven year" (308–9). Rosalind lives for a while among the shepherds, but her time is not the shepherds' time. About the shepherd's time we shall hear in the story of King Henry VI.

8

Virtues and Vices:
Guilt, Good, and Evil

Shakespeare is no moralist, but some of his characters are. Take, for example, Jaques the melancholic, Apemantus the cynic (from *Timon of Athens*), Angelo from *Measure for Measure*. The moralists condemn the whole human race; in their eye all men are traitors and all women whores. Moralists are self-righteous, for they obviously make exceptions of themselves; they occupy the place of the judge, and for this reason alone they are suspect. As the Duke senior remarks to Jaques: "Most mischievous foul sin, in chiding sin" (*As You like It* 2.7.64). The senior Duke is neither "right" nor "wrong," he simply defends the merry face of life, giving allowances to human weaknesses, to the "sin" of the flesh and other senses. If the moralist is a commentator or a spectator—like Jaques and Apemantus—Shakespeare presents men as they present themselves. There is no judgment in the plot, no aletheia. The moralists are not "unmasked" by the author but by other characters—most of them also controversial. Yet, where the moralist is also an actor (as in the case of Angelo), the plot utters the judgment; Angelo unmasks himself not just as a hypocrite, but as a hypocrite who is ready to commit the cruelest crimes to satisfy his desire and to preserve appearances simultaneously. Yet not all moralists are hypocrites. Brutus (in *Julius Caesar*) is also a moralist, but not a hypocrite. A few interpreters of the Shakespearean play emphasize his self-righteousness. He is an actor, not a commentator or a spectator (just like Angelo), yet he absolutely lives up to his own absolute moral standards (contrary to Angelo). He is still the most sympathetic moralist in all the Shakespearean plays. Shakespeare's historical sense is perfect here, too. The kind of moralism Brutus represents belongs to the ancient republic, not to the modern world. When it appears in the modern—ethically far more complex—world, it becomes suspect.

Moralists are not curious, and they have no interest in the uniqueness of personalities. Their knowledge of human character is weak, for they think and judge in generalities (*all* women are whores; *all* men covet wealth, power, luxury, and lust; *everyone* will betray you if his interest so dictates). Moralists in Shakespeare are also kind of cultural critics. They are judges of their times, of the alleged corruption of mores; their age is the age of sinfulness. Although the great Shakespearean tragedies suggest something very similar, for the times in *Richard III, Hamlet, Macbeth,* or *King Lear* are indeed the times of sinfulness and extreme corruption. But whenever the great tragic heroes of Shakespeare speak the language of melancholic misanthropes, there always emerges a Shakespearean "counterpoint." When Hamlet begins to speak the language of the misanthrope, he admits that he speaks the language of a melancholic, that he is (now) one of them. If there is a man who is by no means self-righteous, a kind of antimoralist, it is Hamlet. Still, when he finishes his misanthropic exclamations with the words, "Man delights not me—no, nor woman neither" (*Hamlet* 2.2.310–11), Shakespeare has Rosencrantz raise the counterpoint, "if you delight not in man, what lenten entertainment the players shall receive from you" (2.2.317–19). And the players (who are men, too) delight Hamlet. Although the Shakespearean counterpoint breaks the rhythm of Hamlet's rhetoric, it is by no means an unambiguous counterpoint. The players as players (as *playing* men, not as *being* men) delight Hamlet.

Shakespeare is no moralist. He is too passionately interested in the operation of the finest springs of the human soul to be a moralist. Still, the fantastic thing is that the development of his plots, whether of comedies, tragedies, or romances, is also a moral judgment. Moreover, it is a moral judgment that we modern viewers can accept. I mean *we* modern viewers. This is interesting from two seemingly contradictory standpoints. As we well know, many of Shakespeare's contemporaries and, especially, successors—and not just in England—considered his plays immoral, blasphemous, or even barbaric. The ending of the plays was often changed in order to correct the author's moral failure and bad taste. The Shakespeare cult that began with the romantic movement started to change all this. By now, one would not even think of changing a Shakespearean plot, and especially not a Shakespearean ending. One could say that this happened because the modern taste excludes morality, because the moderns are not interested in the moral of the play. This might be true, but one-sided. For the plots of Shakespeare indeed develop in a moral way. They are far more moralistic in a deeper sense than the modern reader would expect. Even if a whole world stumbles into a grave, the grave is well deserved and the punishment will be just. No one could raise doubt about the villainy of the Shakespearean villains. No one would defend Angelo or Macbeth, or Claudius or Iago. In making Rosencrantz and Guildenstern the main characters of his paraphrases, Tom Stoppard diligently tried to change the moral hierarchy of Shakespeare's Hamlet. However—at least in my mind—he has not in fact done so. Shakespeare makes us accept that his wicked characters are wicked and that his good characters are good; yet he also makes us accept certain crimes, misdeeds, and "grievous faults" through the acceptance of the character who committed them. We accept that wicked persons can display great virtues, and good ones manifest fatal vices, which means that we accept the wickedness of the wicked in spite of their virtues and the goodness of the good in spite their vices. We accept the heroes' *felix culpa* if Shakespeare develops the plot so that guilt turns out to be "happy." I mentioned many times that one can easily detect a moral hierarchy of the characters in each and every play. I also mentioned that the hierarchy of grandeur differs from the hierarchy of morals. The morally best persons may also lack the virtues in which the less morally splendid characters excel. Still, in spite of the always unique and perhaps even vague mixture of grandeur and morality, guilt and innocence, good and bad, in spite of Shakespearean characters' flexibility, complexity, and constant change or modification, there is a moral seriousness in Shakespeare one can give account of only with great difficulty or not at all. One can only mark it.

Still, I try, although hesitantly, to say something about Shakespeare's moral vision. I would distinguish between four different issues. First, are there certain acts or passions that are vices or result in vices practically without exception in Shakespeare? Is there a difference between vice and sin, between vice and guilt? Second, what are the main virtues for Shakespeare? Are there general virtues or specific virtues? Do virtues develop differently in different contexts? Third, are consequences or motivations the main depositories of ethical *valeur*? Fourth, is there evil and radical evil in Shakespeare? What is evil? What is radical evil? Is goodness virtue? Is evil vice or something else? It is difficult to discuss each of these questions separately, for they are almost always intertwined in the plays. I can offer only very vague exploratory remarks.

The betrayal of trust is always a sin or moral failure in the sense of *culpa*. Betrayal is ugly; it is also a lie. It is a lie just like perjury, because trust is built on oath or on blind faith, which is even more sacred than a ceremonial oath. In Shakespeare's mind, life would collapse without trust, without confidence. The trusted man or woman, or cause or commitment, is the only solid ground in life. One can trust God only if one has not betrayed the trust of others.

There is a whole gallery of characters in Shakespeare who have all betrayed a trust. They are all very different. Despite the uniqueness of them all, the two mythological models—that of Judas and of Peter—serve as points of orientation for Shakespeare. And there is, finally, the model of felix culpa. Betraying a person is a far graver sin for Shakespeare than betraying a cause. To be a turncoat, to change allegiances a few times (as, for example, Warwick did) cannot be compared to the treason of Enobarbus. He was after all a personal, trusted friend of Antony and not just his follower. To betray a friend is always a graver treason than to betray an authority. On one hand Ophelia and on the other hand Rosencrantz and Guildenstern, have betrayed their lover and friend respectively. Their loyalty to their king and father did not annul their guilt. To betray a friend out of cowardice or desire is almost the worst kind of betrayal: yet even worse is to betray for the sake of profit or power a man or woman who trusts you. (Like Antonio in *The Tempest,* Caliban betrays Prospero not as friend but as master who does not trust him at all.). But the worst of all is to lie about love and loyalty with the hidden purpose of betraying others for the sake of power and profit, and to destroy those who trusted you most. Thus did Goneril and Regan betray King Lear; Edmund, his father, Gloucester; and Richard III (Gloucester), both his brothers. This is evil.

In Shakespeare's unfailing moral judgment (which is in fact the judgment of the plot), everything except evil can be put right. The barbarian (in us) must be tightly controlled. The Peter figures can put right their momentary moral collapse or their change of loyalty sooner or later, and even absolutely. After asking for forgiveness or saying "I am sorry," they can restore the sense of loyalty and trust (as does Clarence for the cause of York in *King Henry* 6.3). True, normally the blot remains, and villains can use it for their own purposes. (Richard III does in the case of Clarence, and so does Iago, who is constantly playing the tune that Desdemona once betrayed her father's trust.) The Judas type can also repent and get absolution, but only in death. For even if the betrayed forgive, the traitors will not forgive themselves. Enobarbus repents, he confesses his guilt and dies after having witnessed, or rather suffered, the magnanimity of the man whom he betrayed. Yet the ones who lie absolutely, who take an oath of allegiance and express their love and then betray this trust of love, will never be forgiven, either in life or in death. Evil in Shakespeare is man beyond forgiveness.

But what about felix culpa? Betrayal is in Shakespeare a lowly and base sin. But what happens if a lowly, base person is being betrayed, or what if betrayal serves a higher purpose? Is there such a thing as higher purpose, or perhaps higher value? Cornwall's loyal servant stands up against his master with moral indignation when Cornwall cruelly puts out Gloucester's eyesight. The servant is here noble and the master base. Henry V's betrayal of Falstaff is in Shakespeare's view a kind of felix culpa, because it serves not personal but political purposes that are finally crowned by success. To be a turncoat, to pretend, to fake allegiance, are mostly cases of felix culpa in politics and belong to the politician's skills in the Shakespearean drama. Here Shakespeare is very much in tune with Machiavelli. In *Othello,* the Doge uses the Moor to win a brilliant victory against the Turks. Othello is instrumentalized and in this manner also betrayed. The Doge has practiced his political skills. Othello lacks such skills. (Interestingly, the Doge plays a similar politicking role also in *The Merchant of Venice*.) Still, betrayal is lowly and remains lowly even if it turns out to be a kind of felix culpa. Felix culpa, the vice with good consequences, does not elevate the politician into the rank of great tragic hero. As I mentioned, the two great politicians in Shakespeare who are also central tragic characters are Henry V and Julius Caesar. In the Shakespearean version of the story of Julius Caesar, not even a single felix culpa is portrayed.

If betrayal is the basest vice in Shakespeare, *envy is the basest passion*. The thirst for power can be attached to grandeur, whereas the lust for wealth (sometimes even money grabbing) and the lust for lust (sometimes even debauchery) can turn out to be pardonable vices, particularly in comedies. Envy in Shakespeare has many colors. It can be coupled with vanity, as in the case of Malvolio, or with jealousy, as in the case of Iago. It can express political ressentiment, as by the Roman plebeians in the three Roman plays. It can accompany constant frustration, as in the case of the Cardinal Winchester or Eleanor, the Duchess of Gloucester (both from *King Henry VI*), and also with Edmund. In the last case it becomes evil. Envy can also overdetermine *revengefulness*. If coupled with envy, jealousy, the thirst for power, or lust, revengefulness has an ugly face. But, if retributive justice is on the side of the avenger, if the drive for revenge is rooted in rightful indignation and is coupled with the idea of justice, there can be grandeur in revengefulness. However, in Shakespeare even rightful vengefulness is frequently distorted by cruelty. As I already mentioned, cruelty is a character trait that Shakespeare especially loathes; he likes mildness, gentleness, and, if possible, forgiveness. Cruelty is ugly, but not necessarily also base. In Shakespeare, a few bigger-than-life characters are obsessed by cruel revengefulness. Here, however, Shakespeare becomes slightly Aristotelian, attached to the "middle measure." "Nothing too much"—it is better not to go to the extremes. Crimes need to be avenged and criminals punished, but only punished, without sadistic extravagances, without becoming enlivened by other people's suffering, not even in the suffering of evil. Evil should be destroyed. There is happiness in the fall of evil; still, torture is always suspect. Shakespeare has one Kantian conviction: that in everyone's soul, except for those with hearts hardened by evil, the voice of conscience sounds. There is a repeated scene in his dramatic world: a hired professional assassin takes pity on his victim. The overly dimensioned and romantic-baroque character of Margaret in *2* and *3King Henry VI* and *King Richard III* is the prototype of the excess of vengefulness. She becomes a monomaniac in her furor of revenge.

In Shakespeare sins are single acts, whereas vices are character traits. They can be constant, but also appear sudden; they can harden or slacken while the plot unfolds. Yet neither sin nor vice is identical with evil.

Murder is sin, betrayal and unfaithfulness are sins, false accusation is sin.

In fact, those are in Shakespeare the major sins. They have an affinity to evil, although they do not make the character evil. In the case of evil (and there are several kinds of moral evil), the sin stamps the character. Sins can be forgiven, but wickedness cannot—neither by men nor (in Shakespeare's mind) by God.

Most sins can be forgiven because the sinner can ask for forgiveness. The wicked (in Shakespeare) never ask for forgiveness. I mentioned Enobarbus, the betrayer of Mark Antony who repents and dies in repentance. King Edward repents of his intent to let his brother Clarence be killed. He dies in repentance. The sin of Antonio is forgiven by Isabella and the Duke. *Measure for Measure* is not a tragedy; Antonio can continue living and even marry the girl whom he wronged (and who also forgives him). In the comedies forgiving and forgetting are sometimes even too easy.

All Shakespearean characters act once or twice—even many times— wrongly. These are not sins, for they are simply forgotten. After having made one or two missteps—being guilty of making false accusations, mistrusting the other without any reason, being possessed by jealous fury or by fits of anger—one does not need to ask for forgiveness, since putting things right, admitting foolishness, makes everything good and everyone merry. Even Viola and Rosalind, who are as perfect as Shakespearean characters can be, unwittingly cause suffering and bewilderment simply by getting dressed as boys and making girls fall in love with them. There is no innocence even in the comedies, but this does not make men and women guilty.

In fact, a person in Shakespeare is not guilty as such, but is rather innocent or guilty of something specific. This distinction has eminent importance in Shakespeare's vision of politics. For political actors who are guilty of something are frequently accused of being guilty of something else, although they are innocent of this something else. The game of transporting guilt from one deed to another, in which the character in question is entirely innocent, is the recurring theme of Shakespeare's English history plays and Roman plays. I will discuss this typical game of political demagoguery later. One can also encounter the same political demagoguery in the tragedies and comedies. For example, Iago makes plausible for Othello Claudio's guilt in debauchery by pointing out that he is guilty of drinking and provoking a fight.

Shakespeare is already living in a century where—according to O. Hirschmann's well-known book *The Passions and the Interests*—the contrast between passion and interest became topical. Thus, the relation between passions and reason may develop in at least four different directions and is duplicated in all of them. In his portrayal, but also in the text, Shakespeare differentiates between moral reason and calculative reason. That is, he differentiates between the kind of reason that is identical with the "virtuous" or "the morally good" and the kind of reason that is identical with "useful" and "successful," with interest. Both kinds of reason may control (certain) passions, and they may also develop (certain) other passions; and both may succumb to passions as well. Let me reiterate my analysis of *The Merchant of Venice*. Among the frivolous youth of Venice, calculative reason is stronger than any passion, or becomes a passion; it sometimes mingles with other passions—for example, love. Passions overcome calculative reason entirely in Antonio and Shylock. The Venetians, with the exception of Portia, try to strengthen the calculative interest of Shylock against his passion, while promising him more and more money. On the other hand, Portia argues on behalf of moral reason (forgiveness and mercy). The great heroes of the great tragedies, like Hamlet, Lear, and Othello, as well as many chief characters of the history plays, such as Henry VI, know only of one reason: the moral reason. They are unable to calculate, or if they try, their calculation concerns a "trial" that is again serving a moral purpose, namely, justice. The comedies are, however, filled with characters, especially dowry-chasing young men, who are guided mainly by calculative reason and suit their passions to this reason.

The greatest tragic characters of Shakespeare have great passions. They abandon themselves entirely to those passions. But Shakespeare does not share—as Hegel later did—the conviction that nothing great is ever achieved in history without great passions. Shakespeare's significant political actors are not eminently men of passions, at least not in the sense that Lear and Othello or Hamlet are. Their forte is their calculative reason. Not that they lack passion entirely, but their passion is put to the service of calculative reason and vice versa. One must note that Shakespeare's wicked characters also mobilize calculative reason while putting it exclusively in the service of their passions. Macbeth is constantly calculating and miscalculating. Many of the great passionate tragic heroes cling strongly to moral reason, or make moral reason itself one of their only passions (as Brutus does) or at least one of their great passions (as Hamlet does). However, the significant political actors also put the very moral reason in the service of calculative reason, or at least they do their best to make the two harmonize as frequently as possible (as Henry V does).

Shakespeare is not a moralist, especially not in politics; but neither is he an antimoralist. In his world politics based on morality fails as miserably as politics based on passion alone. Yet, politics that is based on calculative reason alone and cuts the umbilical cord with any other objective but the success of the political actor himself is empty politics. And—whether in the short or the long run—it will also end in failure. Politics is about power, but power is power-for-something. And this something is what eminently matters. This is also the reason why in politics the consequences of actions matter significantly. I mentioned already that Henry IV (Bolingbroke) commits many foul deeds. Moreover, he commits grave sins, among them betrayal and murder, in the moral book of Shakespeare. But somehow he gets away with them. The first reason is because he repents, he suffers pangs of conscience. Second, he stops killing immediately after having secured his royal power. Third, his reign is generally beneficial for the country. And finally, he leaves a good and legitimate heir: a good Harry after the guilty Harry. But as almost always in Shakespeare, the character projects ahead the consequences of his action. Bolingbroke acts like a man of calculative rationality from the beginning. He is shrewd, shameless in lying and double-talk if his interest so requires, good at raising false claims. He is not carried away by passions, his moral sense is weak; yet he is neither cruel nor envious, just power-seeking. Moreover, because of the grievances he has unjustly suffered, he also has some meager claim on justice on his side. Everyone has suffered grievances in Shakespeare's political world, but not everyone can make good use of them or turn them to his benefit. Bolingbroke did, however. One can observe an interesting and narratively justified circularity in Shakespeare's political plays. Certain character traits of political actors already foreshadow the outcome of the plot. They project the consequences, yet the consequences themselves will—above all—legitimate retroactively the character's aims and deeds: the consequences pass the political judgment. *History (and not world history) is also the judge in Shakespeare.* But history judges by a dual yardstick. Success is not the sole beneficial consequence. Historical significance is also such a consequence, even if the actors themselves fail politically. And the actors may also be aware of this double standard of the future, of the chronicler of history.

Let me return to the observation that sin (culpa) and vice are not identical in Shakespeare. For vice and virtue are character traits, not deeds. One can ask for forgiveness after committing a sin, but one does not ask for forgiveness for one's vicious character. Sin is frequently pardonable, vices are mostly despicable. Passionate characters in Shakespeare swing frequently from one extreme to the other. Some of them are very clever (Hamlet), whereas others are not (Othello); but both the clever and the nonclever characters constantly swing from one extreme to the other. Passionate characters are inclined to become possessed by fits of rage, a kind of demi-madness. During a fit of anger they may do things with which they never would have trusted themselves, things that they may also bitterly regret later, when they sober up. Precisely because of the extremity of the swings, sins committed by passionate characters are not—or at least very rarely are—rooted in vices. The noblest of characters can commit sins if they are overly passionate. Othello is generally not a jealous man. His jealousy is not a vice but a kind of madness; it is a state of rage and is as such out of character. The same is true of Hamlet's three rage scenes (all of which are related to women). Rage, a kind of *pharmakon,* is both poison and medicine, for it also can purify from vices. The stubborn old man (Lear) becomes purified of his vice of vanity, and tyranny is likewise purged in the madness scene of the tempest. I can mention only briefly that the passions of comic characters are limited in kind (normally they are love, sex, jealousy, and ressentiment), and so are vices (normally vanity, spitefulness, and envy). Ridiculous vices are not dangerous and are usually based in a comic context.

The politically sound characters in Shakespeare are by no means carried away by fits of rage. They follow their calculative reason, means-end rationality. Every politically sound and successful actor keeps cool and reasons well in terms of this rationality. This, however, does not mean that everyone who reasons well in terms of means-end rationality in Shakespeare is a sound political actor. Iago, Edmund, Richard III, and even Macbeth calculate constantly in terms of this rationality. But for them calculative rationality serves a passion, a mania, an aimless obsession, or a bottomless goal. Iago is jealous. He hates, he is full of resentment, he decides to destroy, and then he uses calculation to achieve his aimless aim (for mere destruction is not an aim). In Shakespeare these kinds of irrational rationalists fail without exception. In Shakespeare destruction as an aim always includes self-destruction. Perhaps self-destruction is just one of the political results of aiming at the destruction of others, since destructiveness, particularly the destructiveness of a tyrant, makes everyone else—including former enemies—rally against the destroyer. Or perhaps self-destructiveness inheres psychologically in the necrophiliac or sadistic drive itself. The answer is decided in every case by the interpreter.

It is true, as I pointed out earlier, that the political man is not a man without passions. His main passion is vested in wielding political power, the highest political power included. Yet other passions (jealousy; vanity; vengefulness; the drive for lust, love, or even parental or filial love; and so on) are never strong in a political man. Nor is there present the desire to destroy, torture, or annihilate anyone without important reasons, particularly not the ones he could possibly win over or buy for himself. This is why I said that calculative reason is by no means always on a collision course with moral reason in the mind of Shakespeare's political men. There can be such collisions, but they do not develop into a state of steady contradiction. There are many politically sound characters of this type in Shakespeare, (Warwick, the Doge in *Othello*); yet only a few assume grandeur (the Duke in *Measure for Measure*), and only Octavius Caesar gains a world-historical significance.

An abyss separates Shakespeare from the ancient, eminently Aristotelian ethics and its modern, rationalist followers, such as Descartes and Spinoza. The Shakespearean tragedies can also be seen as the blatant refutations of the main thesis of ethical rationalists: virtue is happiness, and perfect virtue practiced throughout one's whole life is perfect happiness. The perfectly virtuous men and women of Shakespeare's tragedies enjoy happiness perhaps less than the rest. Could one with a sound mind say that Henry VI is happy, or that Juliet dies happily? Or Emilia? Or Cordelia? Or that Horatio became happy after the death of the better half of his soul? Or Kent, who dies with Lear? Even the few virtuous men or women who remain alive and whose virtue is—finally—rewarded by destiny or fate,cannot be termed happy (Gonzalo from *The Tempest* is, perhaps, an exception.) True, Brutus sees his life confirmed at the moment of his death because no one has ever betrayed him; but his cause, the cause of the Republic, is lost and buried. Could one call this happiness? Will Macduff be happy at the moment of his victory? No one will bring back his murdered wife and children. And even for those who have not suffered irretrievable personal losses, the experience of wickedness and suffering is never to be forgotten. As Albany spells it out as the final résumé of the tragedy of King Lear: "The oldest had borne most. We that are young / Shall never see so much, nor live so long" (*The History of King Lear* 5.3.320–21). Is this the voice of happiness?

In the comedies, however, the virtuous can win happiness. The end of a comedy is marriage (with some exceptions), not death; and the marriage of true lovers is, of course, traditionally identified with happiness. Yet, more frequently than not, the nonvirtuous also will be forgiven; they may also marry, they may also share happiness. Virtue is happiness, yet the lack of virtue can also end in happiness if there are a few virtuous and decent men and women around. Happy endings hinge on a few honest characters, and on mere good luck. By honest characters I do not mean virtuous persons. I mean men and women, mainly young, for whom the world is a happy world, in the Wittgensteinian understanding of the word. They do not want to harm anyone, they love their neighbors as themselves. They look at the world, at the future, and at other persons with trusting eyes, with confidence and faith. If one looks at the world with trusting eyes, the world will turn toward one its smiling face. Shakespeare does not say that virtue is happiness. He portrays young men and women who bear love for the world, for other human creatures, for life. And it is finally this love (and their own lovely nature) that makes them beloved and merry, and also makes others merry who hardly deserve it. There are men and women who are predestined for joy. They need good luck to satisfy their desire, but their desire is an honest, sympathetic, and decent desire. The virtuous men and women of the comedies are not self-righteous; they are just like the rays of the sun. They warm others and make them confident without even being conscious of what they are doing. Their instincts are good, they do not make an effort to be good, they are simply good-natured. Shakespeare loves them, but does he share their confidence and trust? I doubt it. One need only listen to the frequently quoted short dialogue between Miranda and

Prospero in *The Tempest* (5.1.184–88) to doubt it. Miranda: "O, wonder! / How many goodly creatures are there here! / How beauteous mankind is! O brave new world / That has such people in't!" Prospero: "'Tis new to thee." Yet the girls in Shakespeare's greatest comedies are not as naïve as Miranda. They have already seen something, sometimes even frightful things, of the brave new world. But they have not lost their love of life to this world.

True, in an essential sense the old moral order is reconfirmed by Shakespeare; the wicked are never happy in his dramas. The voice of conscience will not be silenced, guilt will not be erased. Retribution comes already in this world. Only the opposite is not confirmed. The virtuous can become unhappy. Yet if this were not so, there would be no virtue, but only calculation. I here speak for Shakespeare with a paraphrase on Nietzsche: the lover of life is a "happy throw of the dice" if she avoids guilt by instinct and has also good luck not just to be ready, but also to be able, to set time—which got out of joint—back again, or if not back, at least to its new and proper place without sweat, in love, humor, confidence, self-confidence, and merriment.

There are as many kinds of goodness, decency, and honesty in Shakespeare's world as good, decent, and honest characters in his plays. There are as many kinds of wickedness or evil in his world as wicked and evil characters in his plays. Everyone who is guilty of something brings on some evil to someone. Evil is undeserved suffering caused by a human actor. Everyone who causes evil, who causes others to suffer without strong justification, has committed a sin or has set free his vices. All those sins, sometimes even grave ones, and all the vices can possibly be forgiven. But evil as radical evil is something different. Radical evil is unforgivable. Derrida used to say that only the unforgivable can be forgiven. But Shakespeare has avoided paradoxes here: radical evil is unforgivable and cannot be forgiven. The radically evil men and women cannot forgive themselves, and no one else will forgive them, not even God. Only the radically good man might. All the curses of the murdered, injured, and humiliated will fall back on their heads. No one forgives Richard III, Claudius, Macbeth, Lady Macbeth, Winchester, Regan, Edmund, Goneril, or Iago. As we know, even when their conscience awakes for one short minute, they do not forgive themselves. They do not even ask for forgiveness, except Claudius (in *Hamlet*), but he also knows that his prayer is fraudulent and that he will not receive God's mercy. To return to Derrida, he says that only the unforgivable can be forgiven, but he adds that the wicked must ask for forgiveness. If they do not, forgiveness cannot be granted. This is precisely why Shakespeare's radically evil characters will not be forgiven. They will not morally regret what they have done. They can perhaps realize, as Lady Macbeth does, that their wickedness has not reached its aim. Or they can realize, as Richard III does, that the whole world (including the ghost of his victims) rallied against him and that he will be defeated. However, they will never regret anything because it was evil, but rather because of its consequences. I stressed that in politics Shakespeare always considers consequences, whether they are beneficial or not. Yet, he considers not the consequences alone—and they are consequences for others, for the citizens and for the country. If the radically evil characters of Shakespeare regret anything at all, it is only because of the bad consequences for them and not for others. This is one of the main characteristics of radical evil in Shakespeare, making it a distinct kind of evil in comparison with all the vices and sins that allow regret and mercy. In this crucial matter Shakespeare is absolutely committed to the tradition of Judeo-Christian moral thinking.

Hannah Arendt made the suggestion in her books *Eichmann in Jerusalem* and *The Life of the Mind* that evil is the state of *unthinking*. Men commit evil, and they are evil, because they do not think for a moment about the thing they are doing. Shakespeare also knows about this kind of evil. After Rosencrantz and Guildenstern say that they do not consider Denmark a prison, Hamlet says, "Why, then 'tis none to you, for there is nothing either good or bad but thinking makes it so" (*Hamlet* 2.2.251–52). Rosencrantz and Guildenstern indeed become willing partners in evil because they act unthinkingly. They are men of many vices, slavish in their behavior. They are flatterers, and they commit a major sin: they betray their friend. But one could fairly say that they do what they do unthinkingly. Perhaps this is why Rosencrantz and Guildenstern are not prototypes of radical evil in Shakespeare. It is true that Macbeth also acts at first unthinkingly, suddenly, and without reflection. But he follows his path later on with reflection, for he knows already that "blood will have blood" (*Macbeth* 3.4.121). Most of Shakespeare's evil and demonic creatures are, however, extremely reflective; they are constantly thinking and planning. That their reason is calculative-instrumental and not ethical does not make them unthinking; they normally know exactly what they are doing. Richard III, Iago, Edmund, Regan, Goneril, and Lady Macbeth certainly do.

Thus I think that there is radical evil in Shakespeare. I think that the radically evil are the wicked men and women whose acts are unpardonable, who never ask forgiveness and who will never be forgiven. The Shakespearean radically wicked characters share, then, the decisive feature of what Kierkegaard called the demonic: they are or become entirely closed to themselves, they do not communicate with others in any proper sense. They speak much, but no one can reach them. Whatever they say is just a cover-up for what they do not say, and in the last instance they remain silent. Radical evil is, then, absolute closure of a man in the anxiety before the good, and this is what one can call, after Kierkegaard, demonic.

One can recall here the story of the wicked love pair, Macbeth and his lady. They trust each other, they love each other. Yet from the moment that Macbeth kills Duncan, there is no longer communication between man and wife, and the love withers. Lady Macbeth does not listen to Macbeth, Macbeth does not listen to Lady Macbeth; both become closed in themselves and entirely uncommunicative. Lady Macbeth—who suffers pangs of conscience but does not ask anyone forgiveness—does not forgive herself either. "What's done cannot be undone. To bed, to bed, to bed" (*Macbeth* 5.1.65) are her last words on the stage. Macbeth has not even time left for himself to understand, because he clings to falsity and remains fooled by the witches until the last minute of his life. Iago speaks of silence: "Demand me nothing. What you know, you know. / From this time forth I never will speak word" (*Othello* 5.2.309–10). Regan, who allied herself against her father and her sister Cordelia with Goneril, is murdered by Goneril. Winchester, the cardinal Beaufort, who was the main mover behind many murders, and among them the most vicious murder of his nephew, good Duke Humphrey, dies in terrible pain. The King (Henry VI) is standing by his bed, and he is praying: "O thou eternal mover of the heavens . . . / O beat away the busy meddling fiend / That lays strong siege unto his wretch's soul, / And from his bosom purge his black despair. . . . Peace to his soul, if God's good pleasure be. Lord Card'nal, if thou think'st of heaven's bliss / Hold up thy hand, make signal of thy hope. *(Cardinal Beaufort dies)* / He dies and makes no sign. O God, forgive him" (2 *Henry VI* 3.3.19–29). I quote this passage at some length to give a brief insight into the *soul of the radically good*. Radical goodness in Shakespeare has nothing to do with justice. The radically good is the one who forgives the unforgivable. However, the cardinal dies without making a sign. Not making a sign—rejection of communication—is the sign of the demonic. God does not forgive, only King Henry VI does.

There is one exception among the radically evil Shakespearean characters, and this is Edmund. I mentioned in an earlier chapter that Edmund is also love's fool; he is a criminal who thirsts for recognition, for the certainty of being loved. The moment he receives the proof (Goneril kills Regan and then herself because of him, for him), he opens up. That is, he begins to communicate and tries (in vain) to undo one of his foulest murders, that of Cordelia: "Some good I mean to do, / Despite of mine own nature" (*King Lear* 5.3.218–19). This is, however, not regret. When Edgar accuses him of betraying himself and his father, of contributing to the brutal blinding of his trusting father, he simply answers: "Thou'st spoken right. 'Tis true. The wheel is come full circle. I am here" (*King Lear* 5.3.164–65). Even the noble and good Edgar would not forgive Edmund, for the murder of Cordelia is an unforgivable sin.

In considering Shakespeare's portrayal of radical evil, one will detect a very important feature that makes Shakespeare a Kantian *avant la lettre* or a

Socratic *après la lettre*: The wickedness of evil characters is not rooted in
their evil passions but in the *evil maxims*. There are many passions in the
Shakespearean characters who may take an evil turn and motivate wicked
acts. I mentioned among them jealousy, hatred, envy, vengefulness, and so
on, yet none of them makes a man in himself wicked. The passionate characters—the clever and the stupid ones alike—can fall from one extreme to
the other, they can be carried away by some evil passions, yet they can also
regret, ask for forgiveness, suffer pangs of conscience, and do some good.
Sometimes a passion carries a man away into a direction his character
would normally hesitate to follow. But an evil maxim is something else. It
guides the character constantly and keeps him constantly on the track of
wickedness. Richard III says, "I am determined to prove a villain" (*Richard
III* 1.1.30). Several contemporary philosophers doubt that someone can
determine to be a villain. They think that the character of Richard is just a
poetic invention. I trust Shakespeare's knowledge of human character more
than anyone else's. But if one listens to the story of Macbeth, one will
encounter another evil maxim which may sound more familiar to our ears:
"Fair is foul, and foul is fair" (*Macbeth* 1.1.10), chant all the witches. And
Macbeth echoes it: "So foul and fair a day I have not seen" (1.3.36). That
the fair is foul and the foul is fair means something other than "You can
murder if it is in your interest." No, it means rather "It is good to murder."
This is the evil maxim itself. And Lady Macbeth immediately adds another maxim: "Art thou afeard / To be the same in thine own act and valour
/ As thou art in desire?" (*Macbeth* 1.7.39–41). This is a frightfully evil
maxim. For even the most decent characters in Shakespeare's plays entertain in their soul bad, even evil, desires. Hamlet—like other characters of
Shakespeare—does not keep secret his own bad or dangerous desires. But
in the soul of a decent man, the road that leads from desire to act is barri-
caded if the act itself is considered wrong or evil. The maxim that this block
should be removed, that one should immediately act upon everything that
one desires, and moreover that it is cowardice to strengthen rather than
loosen the inhibitions, is an evil maxim. Iago says that he is ensnaring Othello, Desdemona, and Roderigo "but for my sport and profit" (*Othello*
1.3.378). This is also an evil maxim, but a petty one.

There are men who act upon evil maxims on a grand scale, and there
are those who act upon them on a small scale. Shakespeare is passionately
interested in both the Iago type and the Richard III or Macbeth or Goner-
il/Regan and Edmund types. The Iago type operates on a petty scale: he
can destroy a few good persons together with the guilty, but he cannot
shake the pillars of the realm. But this begs the question, Why not? The
answer is that his position is lowly and he is living in Venice, in a republic.
One may wonder about Shakespeare's political insight; in no Shakespearean play can radical evil become fatal for a republic. In fact, there is no rad-

ical evil in any of the Roman plays or in *The Merchant of Venice* or *Troilus and Cressida*. The most significant figures of radical evil are bigger than life; they are of royal or almost royal descent. Radical evil as destructive political power has its home in kingdoms. *The royal tyrant is the bearer of the supreme power, which he uses according to the evil maxims against his country, against law and order, against life, security, justice, morality, and internal peace.* The radically evil (the tyrant) is pestilence himself; radical evil is infectious and attracts other kinds of evil. At the end, radical evil must be dethroned. It can be dethroned only by civil war, but a kind of civil war that will become also a kind of purgatory. That is, if evil reigns, good is rallying against evil. Thomas Mann once said that the Nazi era was a "morally lucky" one, because everyone knew exactly which party represented the good. This is true of all Shakespeare plays where the tyrant is radically evil. Those who rally against the tyrant, such as Richmond, Macduff, or Edgar, are the saviors; thus they are politically better than good.

How can radical evil acquire the position of supreme power? (I mention only parenthetically that there are evil tyrants and family tyrants in Shakespeare, particularly in the romances, who are not radically evil, who will regret their deeds and who will be forgiven at the end of the play, such as Cymbeline, Angelo, and Leontes). There is no single recipe. Macbeth grasps the power with one murderous stroke; in Shakespeare he has no legitimate claim, he begins as a tyrant. The legitimate heirs immediately escape into foreign lands. Claudius grasps the power also with one murderous stroke, but he claims legitimacy by means of marriage to the former queen, and he does not yet behave tyrannically. He becomes a tyrant when he begins to smell resistance. Richard III grasps power slowly, with a kind of salami tactic. He slices off from the salami of power all those who were closer to the throne than himself. He is a murderer before he becomes a tyrant. Regan, Goneril, and Cornwall will occupy the supreme power *legally*; they have received it as a present from the king himself. But the motive of tyranny is doubled here: Lear appears as a tyrant the moment he disinherits his youngest daughter. Whether he is a political tyrant or not, we do not know (judging from Kent, perhaps not), but he is a family tyrant. And when a family tyrant happens to be a king, his tyranny can have lethal political consequences, as in the case of Lear's guilty folly. As many interpreters have suggested, Shakespeare is obsessed by this question, How can radical evil get into the position of the highest power in kingdoms? And since there is no recipe, and it can happen in very different ways, there is a terrible conclusion to be drawn. That is, in a kingdom it depends mostly on a contingent factor, namely, on the character of a handful of men or women, or perhaps on the character of a single man, close to the position of supreme power. I think, as I have mentioned earlier, that Shakespeare would not entirely subscribe to Hegel's bon mot that the only thing learned from history is that nothing has ever been learned from history.

Soothsaying, augury, signs, ghosts, magic, and all kinds of superstitions have—among others—an important dramaturgic function in Shakespeare's plays. They present the condition for action; they create the situation. But Shakespeare employs this dramaturgic trick only when and where augury, soothsaying, phantoms, and magic of sorts has an essential link to the character in situation. Lady Eleanor (from 2 *Henry VI*) is often compared to Lady Macbeth. Both desire that their husbands should wear the crown, both try to incite their husbands to murder the legitimate ruler. Macbeth is ready to execute the act of murder (which he has already executed many times in his mind), whereas good Duke Gloucester remains loyal to his king unconditionally, and pays with his life for his loyalty. But Lady Macbeth is a woman of arguments. She accepts Macbeth's trust in the prophecy of the witches just because it suits her plans. She takes the visions of her guilt-ridden husband as the sign of his cowardice. For Lady Macbeth there are no specters. In contrast, Lady Eleanor believes in magic, in casting spells and bewitching (perhaps because there are no other means for her to satisfy her ambition). She gets in cahoots with a witch (who is in fact an agent provocateur) to cast a spell on the queen and help her husband and herself to the throne. She thereby falls into her own trap and carries her innocent husband with her into doom.

Iago amuses himself with ghosts, as does Edmund. Goneril does not cast spells; rather, she poisons. In fact, all the Shakespearean characters who follow the "law of nature" defy augury, soothsaying, bewitching, and magic. The counterexample may be Richard III before his defeat on the battlefield. But his visions have functions entirely different from the specters that witches normally have. They do not offer the "situation" *in nuce,* they are agents of retribution, angels of death. In fact, although they are visions, the most important thing is what they "say"; they speak in the voice of a lost conscience.

Normally, the radically evil tyrants in Shakespeare have one virtue alone: *courage.* The ghosts, appearances, and phantoms constantly question this courage. They make the heart of evil tremble with fear. Why? Because their only preventative medicine against fear is proving impotent *vis-à-vis a ghost*; specters cannot be killed. Moreover, the more men that a tyrant kills, the more specters he creates. It is best to follow the story of Macbeth to determine how the switch from courage to cowardice, and back from cowardice to courage, is linked to the strength or weakness of men's trust in extrahuman or diabolic powers, their own powers included. We get to know Macbeth as the "brave Macbeth" (*Macbeth* 1.2.16), the "valliant cousin" (1.2.24), and the "worthy Gentleman" (1.2.24). He is the warlord, the man of tradition, the Talbot type rather than the Winchester type. But the witches are already in wait. The evil maxim ("Fair is foul, and foul is fair" 1.1.10) has been spelled out. Macbeth always follows signs, extrahuman indications, ghostly creatures of his ambition in his heated, feverish brain. The dagger leads him into Duncan's chamber. At the moment of murder he hears voices crying, "Sleep no more, / Macbeth does murder sleep" (2.2.33–34). And he says:."I am afraid to think what I have done" (2.2.48). When the ghost of Banquo, his murdered friend, appears for the second time, he cries out that his cheek "is blanched with fear" (3.4.115). After the second encounter with the witches, Macbeth receives from the apparitions the well-known ambiguous promises; thus Macbeth lets himself be fooled. In trusting the witches he regains his courage, yet not as a virtue: it is apparent courage based on false self-confidence, on Macbeth's conviction that he can do everything without running a risk. Almost at the end, when he discovers the fraud, he accepts his essential cowardice: he refuses to fight with Macduff. Macduff then says: "Then yield thee, coward, / And live to be show and gaze o'th'time. / We'll have thee as our rarer monsters are, / Painted upon a pole, and underwrit / 'Here may you see the tyrant'" (5.10.23–27). And then, at this very minute, Macbeth recovers his self, his forgotten self, his self as he had been before the first encounter with the witches: "Though Birnam Wood be come to Dunsinane, / And thou opposed being of no woman born, / Yet I will try the last. Before my body / I throw my warlike shield" (5.10.30–33). He dies in his only element, the battlefield. Shakespeare brings the situation of the witches into the plot twice and accelerates its development, perhaps the fastest among all plays by Shakespeare.

However, the second encounter with the witches is not the repetition of the first but rather a swing in the opposite direction. The first encounter is a trial: Macbeth is tempted by the witches and he cannot resist temptation. The second encounter is the act of retribution. The witches are lying to him while telling him the truth. They put the gravest curse on Macbeth, the curse of dependence on false self-confidence that knows no fear. In Macbeth's eyes the witches are diabolical, demonic. But are they? Man, after all, has free will and can resist diabolical temptation. The witches are to me, rather, angels of destiny. There is a crossroads before Macbeth; he is free to choose which road he is going to take.

Shakespeare presents a man of tradition with this choice. For men and women committed to the law of nature are—in Shakespeare—not placed at the crossroads. Perhaps this is because they are not inclined to listen to apparitions but are determined to do what they are doing. And this is perhaps also because traditional moral codes do not bind them. Macbeth was bound to a traditional moral code absolutely; thus, after murdering his king, he cuts all ties to his previous life. He could have remained virtuous in a traditional sense; he was not absolutely predisposed to become radically evil. He was not "by nature" evil, while Edmund, Gloucester, Iago, Lady

Macbeth, and so on could—in Shakespeare's portrayal—not be placed at the crossroads of virtue and wickedness. Yet Macbeth chose to be wicked and became wicked in all possible senses. Macbeth is a modern Nero, whereas Richard III is not. He is, perhaps, if one needs historical comparisons at all, a Hitler or a Stalin avant la lettre.

Radical evil is self-destructive; on the royal throne it is both politically and historically destructive. Radical goodness shines as the Kantian "sacred will," but on the royal throne it also becomes politically destructive, albeit not historically. But let us allow the plays themselves to tell their stories.

PART II

THE HISTORY PLAYS

9

Richard II

Some of Shakespeare's plays have one central character, while others are structured such that all the characters carry equal or almost equal weight. *Richard II, Richard III,* and perhaps even *Coriolanus* belong to the first type; whereas *Henry VI* (all three parts), *Julius Caesar,* and *Antony and Cleopatra* belong to the second.

As Joseph Papp writes in his preface to the Bantam Classics edition of Shakespeare's works, Richard II "dominates" the play because his language controls the play. It is true that even if Richard dominates a play that in the end will turn into a one-man show, without his *Gegenspielers* he never could have been a soloist. Shakespeare proceeds as usual. He brings certain characters together to allow their chemistry to develop, so as to lead to the final outcome. This does not lead imminently to the final outcome in history—which is generally known—but to the final presentation of the essence and shape of the characters, which are Shakespeare's, and mostly also his characters', inventions. The more a character reinvents himself in the plot to become what he has not been or at least has not been known to have been before, the more the balance of all the characters tends toward this particular character's direction in the structure of the play. If one pays attention to the character development of *Richard II,* it is evident that the scale of balance among the characters does not yet tend in his direction until act 3. The first two acts confront us mainly with the political mistakes committed by Richard II during his reign. As so frequently happens in Shakespeare, we get first an insight into the conditions of the existential, historical, and political changes. The plot first develops slowly, only to accelerate from act 3 onward. And as always in Shakespeare, all the conditions of a turn of destiny do not add up to necessity. Most of them are contingent in the well-known Leibnizian understanding, for events could have happened otherwise. But after the initial movements Richard II reinvents himself and confronts his Gegenspielers, among them Bolingbroke and Northumberland, with his newly reinvented self. His fate becomes his destiny, he assumes a new self in consuming his fate, and all previous contingencies become sublated.

Let us take a brief look first at acts 1 and 2, where the conditions of Richard's grandeur and downfall are presented. The first sentences of the play are spoken by Richard, who calls up Bolingbroke to make his appeal against Norfolk, and Norfolk to defend himself against the accusations. I mentioned already that we will never know whether the accusation (Norfolk's guilt in the death of Gloucester) has any foundation. Moreover, it will turn out during the "repetition" of the accusation scene with another cast of characters (with Aumerle in act 4, scene 1) that no one can ever know the truth about this matter. This circumstance has great significance for Shakespeare's understanding of history and politics. First, the truth of the matter is not the most significant political motivation, but rather the belief in this truth. Furthermore, men believe to be true what it is in their interest to believe. The widow of the murdered duke, the Duchess of Gloucester, firmly believes that her husband was killed by Mowbray (Norfolk) with the complicity of the king, or perhaps as an execution of the king's wishes. But whether Bolingbroke, the main accuser, is also persuaded of the truth of his accusations remains an open matter. We will soon see in Bolingbroke the Machiavellian who chooses his conditions according to his political needs. Mowbray already knows him as a Machiavellian before the opening of the play, and as the development of the plot will show, Mowbray sees him well. From this, however, it does not follow that Bolingbroke lies and does not believe his accusation. Shakespeare allows us to guess, insofar as he leaves all questions of truth open in this crucial first scene. This first scene reminds us of the beginning of a detective story, where the main suspects are presented. Yet Richard II is very much unlike Hercule Poirot; he does not even want to know the secret. Is Richard really guilty, directly or indirectly, of the death of Gloucester? It is unlikely, but nothing is entirely excluded. We are presented here with a very young man, unprepared to live up to his position as the king, preferring merry games to serious public responsibilities. Yet this young man is the anointed king, the legitimate heir of his father, legitimately occupying the English throne. He does not feel himself threatened in his majesty; that he is a king is his nature. At the very beginning of the play he understands the word "natural" in this sense. He never reflects on what he is doing. He is certain that whatever he is doing is right because he is the one doing it. His majesty means that he is always in the right, and all his decisions are right. He is in a way irresponsible, just like young Harry, the later King Henry V, will be. Perhaps, sooner or later, he could have become a fairly good king. But his Gegenspielers do not leave him time. Thus, instead of becoming a fairly good king, he loses his kingdom to reinvent himself as a significant, colorful, fascinating historical personality.

The first scene of the drama is of major importance, for here the view-er is thrown in medias res. Mowbray and Bolingbroke fight over the dead body of the Duke of Gloucester. Bolingbroke accuses Mowbray of high treason. This is a blatantly absurd accusation, for he presupposes simultaneously that his adversary did what he did under royal command. Perhaps this is why we are ready to give credence to Mowbray rather than to Bolingbroke. And perhaps this is also because we see on the stage a person who can confess his guilt when he feels guilty. He appears as a problematic, passionate, but open character. He says, "The honourable father to my foe, / Once did I lay an ambush for your life, / A trespass that doth vex my grieved soul; / But ere I last received the Sacrament / I did confess it, and exactly begged / Your grace's pardon" (*Richard II* 1.3.136–41). For a moment, the veil is lifted. The hostility is not a reaction to the fate of the Duke of Gloucester but is rooted in old enmities between two families. It is always an important issue for Shakespeare whether or not a character is ready to ask for forgiveness. Mowbray does, and this is a significant moment, for the king, who intervenes at this point, also reinforces it. Of course, the king follows strictly the obligatory ceremony: before bloodletting, the enemies may still be reconciled, to "forget and forgive." Mowbray refuses because his honor, his spotless reputation, is at stake. Shakespeare makes Mowbray employ the whole vocabulary of the ethics of traditional nobles: honor, shame, disgrace, reputation. There is not a single word about justice, conscience, or honesty. The same vocabulary (honor, disgrace, shame) is employed by Bolingbroke. It is not just Richard who is a traditional king; the whole setting remains to this point superficially medieval. Both Mowbray and Bolingbroke call each other traitors to King Richard and to each other. Both call themselves "loyal" at heart. Yet again, there are indications of Shakespeare's complicity with Mowbray, as when he allows him to speak thus: "As gentle and as jocund as to jest / Go I to fight" (1.3.95–96). We know what magic the word "gentle" has in Shakespeare's vocabulary. Moreover, Mowbray sounds authentically traditional, just like a loyal medieval gentleman, whereas Bolingbroke sounds hypocritical, although we do not yet know that he is indeed a kind of hypocrite. It will soon turn out that he is not the man of tradition, but a "new man." Whether he is ready to show himself as a new man in the first act, or whether he becomes a new man in banishment, *malgré lui,* is again a matter of interpretation. For there are no certainties, nor even probabilities, indicated by Shakespeare. Yet in contrast to Richard, one still gets the impression that Bolingbroke's later development is very much in character, that his later self is entirely precontained in his former ego. He becomes what he always was, a political man and, in this sense, the man of the law of nature.

Richard's first grave political mistake is to throw down his baton. He does not allow God to decide. No one understands why he has not allowed the mighty enemies to fight their duel. An even greater mistake is that,

before uttering his sentence and announcing his act of punishment, he con-
sults with Gaunt. The verdict follows the consultation, and it is bluntly
unjust and unequal. Mowbray is sentenced to lifelong exile, and Bolingbroke, after the king's verbal duel with the father, only to six years of banishment. Why is this so? It is perhaps because Bolingbroke was a member
of his family. Yet, this family connection is exactly what makes him more
dangerous. It is at this moment that the theme—"the time is out of
joint"—first appears in the play. True, it is indicated in pianissimo by Mowbray's lamenting the loss of the mother tongue. His tongue, he says, will be
from now on like "an unstringed viol or harp" (1.3.156), "like a cunning
instrument cased up, / Or, if being open, put into his hands / That knows
no touch to tune the harmony" (1.3.157–59). The motifs of the broken
time and exile (displacement) appear here. An entirely apolitical act follows:
the king makes the two banished lords swear that they will not conspire.
This oath is totally out of place and shows only Richard's lack of knowledge of character. Richard's opinion of Bolingbroke's character, as we soon
will see, is low. He does not perceive him as dangerous, yet Mowbray knows
his man. The famous words Mowbray utters in which he predicts Bolingbroke's future treacherous actions are frequently cited. It is true that this is
not yet an indication of a good judgment of character. For everyone who
suffers injustice will prophesy that the unjust decision will bear the wrong
kind of fruit, at least in Shakespeare. And if the prediction comes true, this
may be mere coincidence. Yet we can also accept that Mowbray has seen
something in Bolingbroke's character, something that Richard fails to
notice. Mowbray turns to Bolingbroke and says, "But what though art,
God, thou, and I do know, / And all too soon I fear the King shall rue"
(1.3.197–98). In fact the farewell scene between Gaunt (the father) and
Bolingbroke (the son) corroborates Mowbray's words. This is not because
they speak openly about the son's designs, for they do not (perhaps Bolingbroke has not yet forged clear plans), but because Gaunt says, "Think not
the King did banish thee, / But thou the King." This seemingly innocent
sentence already plays upon the theme of role reversal and the places in the
earthly hierarchy, conjuring up the gesture of dethronement. Even more
significant is the sentence that accompanies Gaunt's final farewell: "Had I
thy youth and cause, I would not stay" (1.3.268). It is obvious that banishment means something different to Bolingbroke than it means to Mowbray,
and not just because his exile was limited in time. Mowbray complains
about the broken music, his life ended with his mother tongue. Yet, Bolingbroke has youth and, what is more important, a cause. Which cause?
Both father and son surmise what the cause is, even if they do not dare to
spell it out. Allusion precedes open language.

In the last scene of act 1 we see the king among his friends. He speaks
an entirely different language than in earlier ceremonial scenes. He is far

from being majestic, but he is fairly cynical. It is obvious that he has not believed a single word Bolingbroke has said. He is also suspicious. He acknowledges grudgingly Bolingbroke's great political talent in "courting" the "common people" (1.4.23), "Wooing poor craftsmen with the craft of smiles / And patient underbearing of his fortune" (1.4.27–28), "As were our England in reversion his, / And he our subjects' next degree in hope" (1.4.34–35). The king accuses Bolingbroke of hypocrisy. Yet in Shakespeare's play political talent goes along with a proclivity to some hypocrisy. Richard notices that Bolingbroke behaves as if he were the king. But no decision follows from this observation. Here the king decides to go to war in Ireland. But how is he to get the money that is needed? The cynical unconcern of the king knows no limits (it would have been better politically to be hypocritical, following Bolingbroke's example). Thus, when he hears the news of John Gaunt's sickness, he says, "Now put it, God, in the physician's mind / To help him to his grave immediately. / The lining of his coffers shall make coats / To deck our soldiers for these Irish wars" (1.4.58–61). We should not forget that every chief character in this drama except Richard II will eventually be guilty of murder. (In fact, this is another reason not to believe that Richard was an accomplice in killing the Duke of Gloucester.) Richard is no Machiavellian. He is happy to learn that Gaunt dies a natural death because he can thus put his hand on his coffers—not for his own benefit, but in order to finance a war. He should have listened to Machiavelli: you can murder, but never touch another person's property or wife! Richard here makes perhaps his gravest mistake: he touches another person's property. This can never be forgiven. There is also mention of his aggressive and obviously unjust practice of tax farming. Furthermore, one can ask the question: why are the coffers of the state so empty? Is it not the responsibility of the king and his advisers to master the treasury fairly and to keep enough gold to cover the expenses of the war? Was Bolingbroke's popularity with the common folk simply due to his flattery, as Richard wants us to believe? Or is it perhaps also because of several unjust acts approved by the throne? At the end of act 1 there is already the sense that although Richard's rule was firmly rooted in tradition, and although he now goes to war whereas Bolingbroke is still in banishment, Richard will be no match for Bolingbroke. Mild cynicism and shameless hypocrisy here fight their battle. And hypocrisy will earn an easy political victory, all the more so because the cynical king heaps mistakes upon mistakes, although he does not commit any crimes.

The second act immediately introduces two new characters, the "best supporting actors" of this play: York and Northumberland (the second was already on stage, but without an independent role). York is a Polonius type but has a more significant role to play than Claudius's majordomo. He is the loyal man, bound by duty only to the throne. His problems begin when he does not know who is presently sitting on the throne. One could say that he is the embodiment of the eternal opportunist, but he would not have seen himself in this light, for his loyalty is not to a man but to an authority. He is the one who instinctively makes the distinction between the two bodies of the king. He remains loyal to the divine body, whichever empirical body occupies the divine one. In Northumberland's figure we meet a great kingmaker, the forerunner of Warwick, the even more representative kingmaker. (We should not forget that Shakespeare wrote the role of Warwick first.) Northumberland will make Bolingbroke king.

The supporting actors are supporting historical actors. Without them nothing can happen; with them many different things can. Both supporting actors are necessary for the development of the historical plot. How many such characters populate a play can also be of major significance. But if there are relatively few characters employed in a play (as is the case here), one of each type may stand for a whole class, for the class of "the average." In particular, York stands for the average.

The first scene of act 2 is the straight continuation of the last scene of act 1. We cannot even take a breath. At any rate, Shakespeare himself did not divide the plays into acts. As two scenes before (in 1.3), Mowbray predicts Richard's future by foretelling the treason of Bolingbroke, now his sworn enemy; Bolingbroke's father, Gaunt, prophesies Richard's downfall. In Mowbray's understanding Bolingbroke is the cause of the doom, whereas in Gaunt's understanding Richard is responsible for his own doom. These predictions are not prophecies, nor are they curses. For they are based on facts, although the facts are interpreted through heavy biases. Both Mowbray and Gaunt have observed facts through the glass of their biases: their predictions are extrapolations. As Mowbray knows by experience that Bolingbroke is hypocritical and false, so Gaunt knows from experience that Richard has neglected his royal duties and misgoverned his land: "Landlord of England art thou now, not king. / Thy state of law is bondslave to the law" (2.1.113). Although Gaunt's accusations are in all probability correct, his formulation points in the same direction as his farewell sentences addressed to his son: the king is not a real king, for he has not preserved the state of law (tradition) on which his inherited kingdom was based. These two accusations formulate succinctly the conditions under which the destiny of Richard will be sealed. But, as I said, not all predictions will come true. Many other accidental events have to occur to make these particular ones come true.

I mentioned that it is here that two major supporting actors arrive at the scene. The queen enters together with the king, yet she remains for the time being a nonperson. And all the men of the king—called by the dying Gaunt his flatterers—also remain silent. York at first plays the mediator; wants to make peace with everyone. In his very limited mind everyone is always right, except when tradition itself is wounded. The moment that the king declares the seizure of Gaunt's land and all his revenues for financing his Irish war, a design we already know from the previous scene, York protests. This protest is spiced with a prophetic touch. If tradition is wounded at one point, he says, it can be wounded at all points. The wealth of Gaunt must be inherited rightfully by his son, just as the crown was inherited by Richard rightfully from his ancestors. If one breaks with the tradition at any point, the tradition will suffer a deadly blow. After trampling tradition underfoot, as Richard now does, he cannot justify by tradition the legitimacy of his rule, at least not convincingly. Yet, Richard answers with nonchalance and speaks frivolously when he says, "Think what you will, we seize into our hands / His plate, his goods, his money, and his lands" (2.1.210–11). To this, York gives again a destiny-loaded answer: "My liege, farewell. / What will ensue hereof there's none can tell" (212–13). But suddenly, Shakespeare lifts the curtain on a hitherto unknown character trait of the king: his blind trust. In his absence, he makes governor of England the same York who just moments before disapproved of his acts so strongly. Is this king really under the influence of his flatterers? Is this the same king who gives the supreme power to the single person who has not flattered him at all? Or is this just another gesture of negligence? Or is it the manifestation of the kind of leisurely unconcern that characterizes Julius Caesar and Hamlet in the last moments of their lives? Or is it rooted in the anointed king's firm belief that a traditional man will never abandon him?

We can see here again how Shakespeare composes a drama in counterpoint. After Richard has put the supreme power into the hands of his loyal but critical and narrow-minded uncle, the conspirators appear immediately on the scene. The confiscation of Gaunt's land and property brings the conspirators together. The conspiracy is masterminded by Northumberland, who has no personal political stake in this matter except his love for politicking and conspiring, the exercises of his might, and the reconfirmation of his haughtiness. His power, like the power of Warwick later, is in this play the power of kingmaking. However, the main thing is the game and the adventure itself. Conspiracy is now his game, and his goal the deposition of the king to "make" a new king. Northumberland collects the grievances of nobles and commoners; he manipulates and puts many shovels of new remonstrations on the already burning fire of hate. (He does this with exclamations like "Most degenerate king!") But lo and behold, during the scene of conspiracy Northumberland also discloses entirely new information. He has received intelligence from his personal spies that Bolingbroke, armed by the Duke of Britanny, already approaches the shores of England. How interesting! The property of the duke has not yet been confiscated when Bolingbroke sails with his army towards England. Later on,

Bolingbroke will say that he comes only to get back his rightful property. But we know, because Shakespeare has taken us into his confidence, that he had already collected an army before his property was confiscated. His pretext was false. Or was it? Was the confiscation of his rightful property, if not the motivation, at least the legitimate justification for arming himself against his king? These questions are all matters for interpretation, not only for us, but also for the characters in the play. For, in Shakespeare, the plurality of interpretation and interpretability of acts and motivations is built into the play itself. At any rate, the confiscation of Gaunt's property will be the legitimation of the conspiracy for the conspirators themselves, at least post factum. It seems, however, that the apolitical, negligent, self-indulgent Richard had not the faintest idea that he was offering on a platter a wonderful justification for the conspirators by confiscating Gaunt's property. At least, there is no indication in Shakespeare of his receiving intelligence about the treason either before or at the same time as Northumberland. But he could have, or he could have guessed Bolingbroke's intended moves. Or his entourage could have advised him about its possibility. But what is important for Shakespeare's vision of history is that political and historical actions are constantly carried out with false pretenses, among them through the reversal of temporality. The future becomes the past, the past the future, and all appearances will be false. But irrespective of the falsity or credibility of the reasons, the conspirators join Northumberland to embrace Bolingbroke as a man of action and resolution.

To repeat, Richard apparently knows nothing. He is just a self-indulgent, superficial, slightly cynical, self-assured, unthinking youth, without strong willpower or character or significance. This is the Richard known by the other actors of the play, by us, and perhaps also by himself. For the time being, the balance tends toward Bolingbroke's side. At least the swiftness of his action seems to prove that Bolingbroke would make a better king, although no single word is yet uttered about this conclusion. However, not one single person sings Richard's praises.

At this point we feel that the tempo of the plot begins to accelerate. This acceleration commences immediately following the death of Gaunt. Yet there are at least two different kinds of time experiences on the stage, with the audience more in tune with one than the other. The tempo accelerates for Northumberland and the conspirators. Moreover, they put their finger on kairos: now is the time, let's now act! Yet it is not the time for Richard. He gets the money for the Irish campaign; he has time. For him time has not yet accelerated. He remains ignorant of his fate. The audience does not.

In the next scene, however, the speed of action decelerates; time almost stops. We meet the queen in Bushy's company. She suffers from gloomy premonitions, and Bushy, one of the king's men, consoles her. The queen loves her husband and fears for him. It should be noted that Bushy consoles the queen with almost the same sentence that is uttered by Macbeth, yet with reverse meaning: "So you sweet majesty, / Looking awry upon your lord's departure, / Find shapes of grief more than himself to wail, / Which, looked on as it is, is naught but shadows / Of what is not" (2.2.20–24). The queen is not consoled and tries to describe her sadness; this is anxiety, exactly as Kierkegaard described it. "For nothing hath begot my something grief— / Or something hath the nothing that I grieve— But what it is that is not yet known what, / I cannot name; 'tis nameless woe, I wot" (2.2.36–40). At this very moment enters Green, and after the pause the action again furiously accelerates. Green has received intelligence that Bolingbroke has already set foot in the land, and he names all the knights who have already joined the rebels, also mentioning the sympathy of the commoners, whom the politicking Bolingbroke has allegedly constantly flattered. Abruptly, we are thrown into a state of emergency. This is the moment that York enters. It becomes immediately clear that he is the worst possible choice for deputy of the king. He is a typical underling, good only at obeying an uncontested master. But he cannot command, cannot decide, has no ideas of his own. He is also a narrow-minded opportunist whose loyalty is in doubt. "Both are my kinsmen. / One is my sovereign, whom both my oath / And my duty bids defend; t'other again / Is my kinsman, whom the King has wronged . . . Well, somewhat we must do . . . All is uneven, / And everything is left at six and seven" (2.2.111–22). York decides to remain true to his king, but he cannot rise to the occasion. His failure is inevitable.

In this very moment it becomes obvious to all the king's men that their king has lost his case. As always, flatterers become turncoats, and as frequently happens, ugly treason will not pay. This scene has repeated itself throughout history and throughout our experience. We know all these Bushes and Greens and Mamets.

Shakespeare, as usual, distinguishes the typical from the exceptional. The typical is represented by more than one person (here by three), whereas the exceptional is represented by one. Bagot is the exception; he remains loyal to his king and decides to join him in Ireland.

 In the next scene (2.3) we get to know Bolingbroke, the man of politics, better. Before this scene we have met him only once, in the first act. He is returning to England and to the stage, and he is returning with self-assurance, victoriously leading an army rich in rebel forces. Almost everyone yields to him. Why? We do not know the answer to this. Perhaps it is because he has a cause. Now York enters. Bolingbroke immediately shows his sly character. He kneels to York, to make a public show of his own loyalty to his sovereign. He recognizes the sovereignty of the king in York as his deputy. This gesture is both political and hypocritical. Bolingbroke needs to neutralize York. At first York calls him a rebel and a traitor, which he is. But Bolingbroke's answer is full of well-designed sophistry. He has not returned from his banishment before time, for he was banished as Hereford and returns as Lancaster. Then he refers to his legitimate grievances: his traditional rights have been denied. "Wherefore was I born? / If that my cousin King be King in England, / It must be granted I am Duke of Lancaster" (2.3.121–23). Important is the "I am." He is identical with the Duke of Lancaster; this is what he is. The argument is both sincere and fraudulent. Bolingbroke wants to become what he is not (he was not born to be the king). However, he pretends to claim only what is due to him: "And therefore personally I lay my claim / To my inheritance of free descent" (134–35). I hardly understand the interpreters who believe in Bolingbroke's openness and sincerity. It is as if we had not witnessed how the rats have already left the sinking ship before this scene. It is as if we had not heard that most knights and dukes have already switched their loyalty, not from the king to the duke, but from the present king to the future king. For otherwise, none of their acts would have made sense. The acts and choices of opportunists and climbers only make sense in terms of purposive rationality. York, however, waits for these false and weak pretenses. For he—as we know—only pretends to take the king's side, because in fact he does not want to take anyone's side. He just waits until one of them will be the uncontested master. This is why he refers to his weakness and adds, "I do remain as neuter" (158). The next step for Bolingbroke is, however, no longer hypocritical. He wants his uncle to accompany him to Bristol Castle to help him "to weed and pluck away" all the king's men (166).

Everything is prepared, but the last die has not yet been cast. Speaking of the throw of the die, I presume the contingent character of the event. This is, however, also just guesswork. The royal and loyal Welsh army receives a false report of King Richard's death. The army disperses. But who was the source of the false intelligence? Nothing is said about it, but we are pretty sure that Bolingbroke himself implanted the lethal gossip in the rank and file of the Welsh army. The last contingency was planned after all by the skillful, Machiavellian Bolingbroke.

The second act ends with the words of Salisbury, who has not yet acted his part in the story. He performs here, as he does later, the role of the chorus. His words sound like a funeral oratorio for Richard II, the king: "Ah, Richard! With the eyes of heavy mind / I see thy glory, like a shooting star, / Fall to the base earth from the firmament. / Thy sun sets weeping in the lowly west, / Witnessing storms to come, woe, and unrest. / Thy friends are fled to wait upon thy foes, / And crossly to thy good all fortune goes" (2.4.18–24).

This sounds like a Greek chorus, yet the message is modern. We are now taken from the level of politics—from the platform where until now the whole story took place—to another platform on the level of history. The

immediate consequences of an act are annulled, the long-term consequences are grieved. For it is with Bolingbroke's decision that all the events
that finally lead to the Wars of the Roses begin. Until this moment we do
not like Richard II much; we do not yet grieve for him or for his fate. Why
then the simile of the shooting star, of the sinking sun, of the storm to
come? The images of a cosmic apocalypse predict a historical catastrophe
that no one on the stage can know or foresee. For them it is the hidden
future; for us it is the revealed past. We understand.

The funeral oration of Salisbury already buries King Richard II as king.
Yet his lamentations signal a kind of new birth, as well; the future hides war,
murder, slaughter. But it also hides the world of new men. It also signals the
birth of Richard as the man Richard, the man of sorrows. Tradition has
been wounded and will soon burn to ashes. But from these ashes men lead
by a new star of the law of nature, and with them a new world will be born.
It is an ugly new world, but a world with a new kind of grandeur. In acts
3, 4, and 5 it already happens: another Richard appears before our eyes: a
Richard of grandeur.

Act 3 (I must mention again that Shakespeare has not divided his plays
into acts) begins with a long and fairly self-righteous speech by Bolingbroke. He gives his reasons for executing Richard's men. Contrary to
Richard, who banished but has not killed, Bolingbroke feels at ease with
killing. He also likes to rationalize his murders, sometimes in an obviously
fraudulent way. He says, for example, that Bushy and Green must be executed not just because they allegedly misled Richard, but because they
"made a divorce betwixt his queen and him, / Broke the possession of a
royal bed" (3.1.12–13). And after these words are spoken he sends the
queen his special greetings. There is absolutely no indication in the later
encounters between the king and the queen of the slightest breach between
them. Shakespeare here employs the same device as in the case of prophecies that never come true. That is, he exemplifies that most of the accusations of Bolingbroke are superficially manipulative, for he is not interested
even in their possible verisimilitude. In this respect Bolingbroke resembles
Richard III.

Richard II becomes "Richard the Man" suddenly. But when I say suddenly, I do not mean in one step. There are at least three sudden changes in
the character of Richard. He begins to invent himself, but he also experiments with a variety of characters. He invents roles and also plays these
roles. He invents different roles one after the other, and he also plays different roles one after the other. The journey to become himself begins. It
is a strenuous, difficult journey. It pains Richard, but he also enjoys it.

The first thing that astonishes us when we meet Richard II again, in 3.2,
is his language. Nothing remains of the commonsensical, slightly cynical,
cocky language used by the king in his conversation with his youthful

friends. Now his language becomes theatrical, flowery, poetical—rather heavy and emotional. The language seeks itself. Immediately, when the king sets foot in his country, he bends and touches the ground with a prayer addressed to the goddess of the earth: "Dear earth, I do salute thee with my hand, / Though rebels wound thee with their horses' hoofs. / As long-parted mother with her child / Plays fondly with her tears, and smiles in meeting, / So, weeping, smiling, greet I thee my earth, / And do thee favours with my royal hands. / Feed not thy sovereign's foe, my gentle earth. . . . Mock not my senseless conjuration, lords. / This earth shall have a feeling, and these stones / Prove armed soldiers, ere her native king / Shall falter under foul rebellion's arms" (3.2.6–26). Now Richard plays the role of the anointed king. Tradition as such is no longer taken for granted. To be the king now becomes the great role, which Richard begins to play with firmness and dignity. The king of England conjures up the soil and the stones of England to be his protectors and his army. He already begins to poeticize his role; he transforms his earthly political role into a role-in-drama, a role-in-history. I reiterate that he himself writes his role and enjoys playing it. He in fact enjoys every word he utters about his royal dignity, even the words of grief. While indulging in his role, he does not make a single political move to regain his power. He is interested in the power of poetry and not in the execution of political power. He declares that "not all the water in the rough rude sea / Can wash the balm from an anointed king. / The breath of worldly men cannot depose / The deputy elected by the Lord. / For every man that Bolingbroke hath pressed / To lift shrewd steel against our golden crown, / God for his Richard hath in heavenly pay / A glorious angel. Then, if angels fight, / Weak men must fall; for heaven still guards the right" (3.2.50–58). Later, Cromwell could have told him the earthly wisdom that it is not sufficient to trust in the Lord alone, for one additionally needs to keep his powder dry. But for Richard realities are waning; he begins to live in a world of fantasy. The great drama supplants sound facticity—the great drama in which God's angels will fight for King Richard, in which the revelers will go to hell and the knights of God to heaven. But politics is not buttressed by Richard's fantasy. Immediately after Richard's rhetorical image of the avenging angels, Salisbury cools him down with the news that the Welsh army has been dispersed and that Richard came a day too late (2.3).

From the height of enthusiasm Richard immediately plunges into a state of despair, and for a while he vacillates between enthusiasm and despair. He experiments again with a new role. He continues to write his own drama, playing out his daydreams; but his poetry makes sense. He poeticizes his story in an authentic way. That is, he extracts his story from its contingencies and brings it to the level of essence. To use my terminology, he begins to remove his story out of the politicohistorical stage and live it, experience it, on the existential stage, in an existential theater. In his constant references to time he connects both stages. He says, "All souls that will be safe fly from my side, / For time has set a blot upon my pride" (3.2.76–77). The word "time" has here a triple meaning. It means kairos (he missed the proper time to act), "the times" (historical times), and finally and utterly empirically it means the one single day in which he came back too late. Listening to his ruminations, Aumerl warns him: "Comfort, my liege. Remember who you are" (3.2.78). This is a most important sentence, for this is exactly Richard's quandary. Richard does not know who he is; he remembers who he was, but he cannot remember who he will become. So he answers: "I had forgot myself. Am I not king? / Awake, thou sluggard majesty, thou sleep'st! / Is not the King's name forty thousand names?" (3.2.78–79). After the motif of time, the second central motif of the new-man Richard, the motif of name, appears. Then he is informed of his men's execution, and finally of York's change of loyalty. Richard laments: "Cry woe, destruction, ruin, loss, decay; / The worst is death, and death will have his day" (3.2.98–99). This is an important link in Richard's story of self-understanding. And he indulges in it, he works on it. He says first, "Let us sit upon the ground, / And tell sad stories of the death of kings" (3.2.151–52). The introduction is significant. He does not place himself first in the role of the king, but in that of the storyteller. He does not sit on the throne but on the ground, and continues as a chronicler: "All murdered. For within the hollow crown / That rounds the mortal temples of the king / Keeps death his court. . . . farewell, king. / Cover your heads, and mock not flesh and blood / With solemn reverence. Throw away respect, / Tradition, form, and ceremonious duty, / For you have but mistook me all this while" (3.2.156–70). Listen to the way in which the existential stage slowly emerges from behind the historical stage. In spite of the presence of others, in spite of the circumstance by which he addresses others, Richard II's monologue is a soliloquy where he speaks not just in himself but mainly for himself. The question of identity is raised. Who am I? Have I mistaken myself a king? Have you mistaken me as a king? Yet this is a rumination that can also be described with the Greek term *boule*, that ends in *prohairesis*, the resolve; it is the resolution to abdicate. But this is not yet a real-life resolution; it is rather a theatrical one. Richard wants to taste the flavor of abdication as self-humiliation; he indulges in playing this role. It is the moment of an almost masochistic self-humiliation and not yet the moment of victorious self-confirmation. Thus Richard returns at the end of the scene to the historical stage: "Discharge my followers. Let them hence away / From Richard's night to Bolingbroke's fair day" (3.2.213–14).

During this scene we have witnessed how the balance of the weight of the chief characters has tended toward Richard. The victorious Bolingbroke does not change. He remains a Machiavellian; he continues to commit his deeds of cruelty. Yet, while growing in might he fails to grow in significance. But Richard begins to grow; he loses power and he gains more and more significance. From this moment onwards, whoever may occupy the front stage, this drama will become a one-man show.

It is true that in 3.3 it is Bolingbroke who sets the stage. But this is the stage of sheer political theater. Bolingbroke wants to get it over with quickly. Richard should abdicate, and do it smoothly, without much ado. There are ceremonies, but they are fig leaves. Bolingbroke has first to show his allegiance and reverence to the king, in order to make him leave the castle and get things moving in the right direction. He has a goal, and the proper means to achieve his goal are duly selected. Henry has no doubt that he will achieve his goal. But the thing he could not take into account is the personality of his adversary—his new personality. This Richard was unknown to him as he was for himself and for us. Bolingbroke makes a mistake: he organizes the stage for political theater with himself as the ascending star. But in fact he organizes the stage for the world theater where Richard will be the real hero, outdoing Henry, who will shrink to a royal nobody in his presence. Richard steals Bolingbroke's show, and he steals the show knowingly. This is his triumph.

Richard begins to steal the show right at the beginning of the scene. He mocks Bolingbroke's phony gestures of allegiance. He then turns to Northumberland (who was the hidden mover behind the apparatus of Bolingbroke) with a curse: "Yet know my master, God omnipotent, / Is mustering in his clouds on our behalf / Armies of pestilence; and they shall strike / Your children yet unborn and unbegot, / That lift your vassal hands against my head / And threat the glory of my precious crown" (3.3.84–89). We see the same broad, long, and glorious vision as before. In Richard's fantasy the army of angels is always on his side. And God certainly is. But here he does not pray for victory but for something else, for something that is more than victory: "O God, O God . . . O, that I were as great / As in my grief, or lesser than my name, / Or that I could forget what I have been, / Or not remember what I must be now!" (3.3.132–38). He prays for the power to ascend from the historical stage to the existential stage. He prays for the grace to become Richard the man.

Then he begins the striptease—the first, very incomplete one. He begins, just as King Lear will do later, stripping himself not in body but in spirit, in the mind, of his royal costume. However, there is an ambiguity in this gesture of stripping. He cannot decide whether he strips himself because he must, because he is under constraint, or because he chose the action freely. He strips himself, yet he is also filled with self-pity; he plays the theatrical performance of stripping and he feels the intensity of self-pity. At this stage of self-invention he becomes a clown who plays the king and a king who plays the clown. He causes others to weep because he is the majesty, and everything that he says is pure poetry. Similar things are said by a few Shakespearean kings, but in different contexts. None of those kings is like Richard. "What must the King do now? Must he submit? / The King shall do it. . . . Must he lose / The name of King? A God's name, let it go. / I'll give my jewels for a set of beads, / My gorgeous palace for a hermitage, / My gay apparel for an almsman's gown, / My figured goblets for a dish of wood . . . And my large kingdom for a little grave, / A little, little grave, an obscure grave; / Or I'll be buried in the King's highway" (3.3.142–54). Since Richard speaks still from the wall of his castle, Northumberland gets nervous and advises him that the court wants to speak to him: "May it please you to come down?" (3.3.176). This is a wonderful catchword in actor Richard's ears, and he begins to play around with it in gusto, or rather, in self-torture and gusto. There is something masochistic in his answer, but this masochism is—as perhaps it is frequently—also a source of pleasure. Perhaps we could even go further and claim that his mental and spiritual superiority, his existential superiority, is already the source of this pleasure: "Down, down I come like glist'ring Phaethon, / Wanting the manage of unruly jades. / In the base court: base court where kings grow base / To come at traitors' calls and do them grace. / In the base court, come down: down, court, down King" (3.3.177–81). Is this rage? I hardly think so. Maybe it is also rage, but mostly it is the game of cat and mouse. Richard plays around with the reversibility of high and base. Is not the high also in the base? Or is the traitor not base, even if he is sitting up high? Again, the mockery addresses the intricate connection and the contrariness of the historicopolitical and the existential theater. At the end of the scene Richard descends spatially, but not spiritually.

Bolingbroke (the great hypocrite) is a coplayer; yet he is a poor actor who cannot invent a role. When Bolingbroke pretends again to have come only for his heritage, Richard openly exposes his irony; he can be ironical. York weeps (and Richard consoles the old traitor who does not know what he is doing) and agrees in the procedure of abdication. Also, his agreement is formulated in an ironical mood. King Richard: "What you will have I'll give cousin, and willing too; / For do we must what force will have us do. / Set on towards London, is that so?" Bolingbroke: "Yea, my good lord." King Richard: "Then I must not say no" (3.3.204–8).

There is a pause here, and also a scene of deceleration. We are with the queen, her ladies, and the gardeners. The queen does not yet know anything. I will leave out the scene of the gardeners. They are also a kind of chorus, or rather antichorus. They speak of Richard's shortcomings, of his neglect of the realm. They compare the kingdom to a garden. This is one of Shakespeare's favorite metaphors. The whole land, the whole garden, "is full of weeds, her fairest flowers choked up, / Her fruit trees all unpruned, her hedges ruined, / Her knots disordered, and her wholesome herbs /

Swarming with caterpillars" (3.4.45–48). Only the genius of Shakespeare could have inserted this scene (as also the next) between two great performances of Richard. Since we already identify with Richard, we enjoy his irony, his fantasy, his language and enthusiasm. We must be reminded that Richard the king is not yet the same man. He is not the brilliant man losing his kingdom, but the average man who neglected his duties, who was self-confident and cynical, and still politically impotent. This scene ends with the image of the weeping queen. During his great theater performances Richard was not (yet) once thinking of his weeping queen.

Deceleration continues in the following scene, 4.1. It is here that the first scene of act 1 repeats itself. The stake is also the same: who is responsible for the violent death of the former Duke of Gloucester. Aumerle now stands accused. The background interest of the accusation is unclear; Aumerle is the king's man, but he is also the son and heir of the turncoat York. However, it is not only the motivation of the accusation that is unclear; its consequences are equally murky. In fact, the whole scene is not just a repetition, but a comic repetition. It appears as the satire play written on the theme of the first. Too many men throw their gages, too many of them throw empty accusations at each other's faces according to the script. (For example, Aumerle borrows a gage because he does not have one to throw down.) It is typical for Bolingbroke that he never misses an opportunity to excel in hypocrisy. He declares that he will restore Norfolk, his enemy—that he will repeal his banishment. But he must have known what Carlisle knew so well: Norfolk has already died and there are no more witnesses he can possibly call. At the end of this comic scene Bolingbroke turns to both parties to tell them that their differences will rest under gage and that he will assign them to their day of trial. But we never hear anything more about this trial. Perhaps this is because there will be none. Bolingbroke is also a skillful cunctator. But when York enters, the comedy is over. In the second part of scene 4.1, the development begins to accelerate again, and with an ever increasing speed.

It is not only the development of the plot that speeds up. At first, before the grand entrance of Richard, Bolingbroke's character shows itself in an additional light, without changing. He now acts again just as a Machiavellian prince would. He is swift, he does not tolerate opposition for a moment, he behaves tyrannically. Shakespeare allows him to show his tyrannical face before the entrance of Richard, who will put everyone else into the shadow.

York comes and announces that Richard is ready to adopt Bolingbroke as his heir. And as a historically highly placed Polonius he immediately begins to hail the new king: "Ascend his throne, descending now from him, / And long live Henry, of that name the fourth!" (4.1.102–3). Bolingbroke, who has just waited for York's cue, immediately declares, "In

God's name I'll ascend the regal throne" (4.1.104). Ascent and descent are the two spatial movements alluded to here. It is again up to Richard to reverse the real movement, to make his descent the symbol of a much higher ascent. The new man declares himself king. Yet there is a honest and loyal man remaining in the room, Carlisle, who speaks his heart without any prudential consideration: "What subject can give sentence on his king? / And who sits here that is not Richard's subject? / Thieves are not judged but they are by to hear . . . And shall the figure of God's majesty . . . Be judged by subject and inferior breath, / And he himself not present?" (4.1.112–20). And than he accuses Bolingbroke of treachery and prophesies. In contrast to the predictions of act 1, Carlisle's prophecy is not simple extrapolation of the present experience. It is a kind of prophecy that thinks through the possible consequences of certain actions and decrees these possible consequences as being fated. The Elizabethan theatergoer, just like us, knows already that this prediction came true. It could have happened otherwise. (For example, Henry V could have lived a long life, and this could have made all the difference.) Yet, Bolingbroke's act triggered certain events that in all likelihood—although not by necessity—could have led to the consequences to which they indeed have led. Carlisle says: "If you crown him, let me prophesy / The blood of English shall manure the ground, / And future ages groan for this foul act. . . . Disorder, horror, fear, and mutiny / Shall here inhabit, and this land be called / The field of Golgotha and dead men's skulls" (4.1.127–35). Listen to the formulation of Carlisle. He speaks in a hypothetical mood: if you go on and crown this man, these will be the consequences, but you still have time to reconsider. After he finishes this last sentence, Northumberland allows him to be arrested "of capital treason." Bolingbroke stands by and watches. Remember that Richard appointed York, who cursed him before to his deputy, whereas Bolingbroke allows Carlisle, who only doubts his legitimacy, to be immediately arrested. Moreover, although the text only speaks of the arrest of Carlisle, Bolingbroke continues in the plural: "Lords, you that here are under poor arrest" (4.1.149). It is obvious that Carlisle is just one among many. But it is still more obvious that arrest means execution. Richard then enters and wins all; all eyes are glued on him. The abdicating king will be the real king.

The theme of Golgotha, the hill of the dead skulls, has already been intoned by Carlisle. And here Richard appears on his Golgotha, which is a mountain. Richard is at the top of the mountain, and he now reinvents himself as the man of sorrows. He takes upon himself the garment of Christ. Who is an earthly king in comparison to the man of sorrows? Richard strips himself more and more willingly from the royal garment. He leaves behind the politicohistorical stage. He steps upon the mount of the dead skulls, upon the existential stage that is for him the stage of mythology. In Shakespeare's portrayal these are not sequential steps or gestures. It is not the case that there is first a stepping out from the royal garment and then a slipping into the mythological role of the man of sorrows. Rather, these two things happen simultaneously. Richard swings from one gesture to the other; he sometimes plays two roles at once, or vacillates between them. It becomes even clearer than before that although Richard is suffering greatly, he finds more sense in his suffering than he ever found in his royalty. It is in this topsy-turvy way that he also enjoys the suffering that he plays, although he is playing himself and he is really suffering. While playing he is also testing himself, tapping himself, creating himself—his new self. This is not one fixed new self, but a number of new selves connected to one another while not being entirely identical. Richard becomes an *entelecheia* without a previous *dynamis*. He becomes a man that he never was, for he chooses himself as a man entirely different from the man that he was. He "jumps." He has performed the existential leap.

Richard enters, and while he is looking around, he notices all his former flatterers bowing before the new king. At first he makes a remark about the most difficult part of "stripping": he has not yet shaken off the regal thoughts. He then continues, "Give sorrow leave awhile to tutor me / To this submission. Yet I well remember / The favors of these men. Were they not mine? / Did they not sometime cry 'All hail!' to me? / So Judas did to Christ. But He in twelve / Found truth in all but one; I, in twelve thousand, none" (4.157–62). It happens here for the first time that Richards slips into the garment of the man of sorrows. But immediately afterward he begins to ironize and play. He loves to play with Bolingbroke. He is not submissive; he rather plays the ambiguous game of submission. He takes the crown in his hand and asks Bolingbroke to grasp the other half of it. I imagine the scene in the following way: the actor offers the crown for grabs, yet pulls it back mockingly when the other tries to grab it. Otherwise, the next and very irritated sentence of Bolingbroke ("I thought you had been willing to resign"[4.180]) would not make much sense. Richard answers, again in the role of the man of sorrows, "My crown I am, but still my griefs are mine. / You may my glories and my state depose, / But not my griefs; still am I king of those" (4.181–83). Being the king of his griefs is already a new identity. Still, he starts his ironical game again. Bolingbroke does not like all this; he wants to go straight back to business. He asks simply, "Are you contented to resign the crown?" (4.190). Yet Richard does not permit him to go right back to business; instead he continues to tease him: "Ay, no; no, ay; for I must nothing be; / Therefore no, no, for I resign to thee. / Now mark me how I will undo myself" (4.191–93). Now a new step of the striptease scene follows. It is still unlike the stripping of Lear. Lear strips naked before Edgar, before "the thing itself." Levinas would have said that he strips before the "face" of the other. Richard's stripping is serious, but also ironical. For he does not strip before "the thing itself," not before the face of the other, but before himself. He is his own mirror. Richard does not cease to be what he plays and play what he becomes, for he has discovered himself as an actor, as a mirror, and he wants to employ this new talent to in the extreme. Thus he strips: "I give this heavy weight from off my head, / And this unwieldy sceptre from my hand, / The pride of kingly sway from out my heart. / With mine own tears I wash away my balm, / With mine own hands I give away my crown, / With mine own tongue deny my sacred state, / With mine own breath release all duteous oaths. . . . Long mayst thou live in Richard's seat to sit, / And soon lie Richard in an earthy pit. / 'God save King Henry,' unkinged Richard says, / 'And send him many years of sunshine days.' What more remains?" (4.194–212). The enumeration of things he is "giving away" is a ceremony: Richard invents the ceremony of abdication.

The ceremony is played and overplayed, yet there is a basic sincerity in it. The mention of the earthly pit is in the voice of the man of sorrows. Golgotha is the place of death, and of violent death. Richard sees himself as the man who will suffer violent death, and very soon, at Golgotha, to which he is not descending but ascending. But then comes an abrupt change.

Richard's question *"What more remains?"* will be answered: "No more but that you read / These accusations and these grievous crimes / Committed by your person and your followers / Against the state and profit of this land, / That by confessing them, the souls of men / May deem that you are worthily deposed" (4.213–17). Do we know these sentences? Of course we do. The secret police agents and functionaries uttered them during the Moscow show trials and other show trials. Yes, you need to give false testimony against yourself and against your neighbors; you are obliged to break one of the Ten Commandments. King Henry so commands, yet former King Richard will never do it. This he will never do. As in so many cases before him and after him, it is for this very gesture that he will pay with his life—and he knows this. The man of sorrows cannot say that he and his followers were guilty of crimes "against the state." Richard looks around again and says: "Nay, all of you stand and look upon / Whilst that my wretchedness doth bait myself, / Though some of you, with Pilate, wash your hands, / Showing an outward pity, yet you Pilates / Have here delivered me to my sour cross, / And water cannot wash away your sin" (227–31). Again, he is asked to read the articles of self-criticism, but he does not do it. He says, "Mine eyes are full of tears; I cannot see" (234). Northumberland still wants to persuade him to confess his crimes: "My lord" (234). However, King Richard proudly answers: "No lord of thine, thou haught-insulting man, / Nor no man's lord. I have no name, no title, / No, not that name was given me at the font, / But 'tis usurped. Alack the heavy day, / That I have worn so many winters out / And know not now what name to call myself! . . . Let it command a mirror hither straight, / That it may show me what a face I have, / Since it is bankrupt of his majesty" (4.244–57).

What is a man? He is his name and his face. They are the signals, the outer signs of identity. We call a man by his name, we recognize him by his face. Richard has lost his name, one-half of his identity. Now he wants to look into the mirror to see his face and to get an answer to the question, who am I? He is just a man stepping into the shoes of the man of sorrows; he is on his way towards his Golgotha. But still, before being murdered, he wants to know who he, as a man, as a person, really is. They promise to get him a mirror, but everyone is irritated and impatient. Richard has still not read his self-criticism. Richard must read loudly the list of his sins; otherwise, Henry's legitimacy would remain questionable. Let him have his mirror, then; only he should go on. But does he go on? The man of sorrows is still playing cat and mouse with the victorious Henry. He is never going to read the list of his "sins" and the sins of his followers; he will never give false testimony. They urge him to read it, whereupon he answers, "I'll read enough / When I do see the very book indeed / Where all my sins are writ, and that's myself" (4.263–65). How? He reads his sins in the looking glass? "Give me that glass, and therein will I read" (4.266). He makes a fool of all of them. He plays a comedy. They will never get what they want. Richard is ready for Golgotha.

Then a mirror is presented. Richard does not recognize his own face in the mirror. This, he says, is because it still shows the young, carefree man, whereas he has become inwardly an entirely different man. He looks into another mirror. The play, the drama, is—as we know from Hamlet/Shakespeare—the real mirror. Richard's acts are the mirror. He looks away from his time and his political story; he looks at Shakespeare's story. The mirror is the drama. It is this mirror that provides him the looking glass. The real face is inside; yet the drama, Shakespeare's drama, which mirrors vice and virtue, is the mirror of the inside. Here you can see what you cannot see. And then Richard utters the words that will be, almost word for word, repeated by Hamlet: "'tis very true: my grief lies all within, / All these external manner of laments / Are merely shadows to the unseen grief / That swells with silence in the tortured soul. / There lies the substance" (4.285–89). By now it becomes obvious to everyone present that King Richard will not confess to his crime and that of his followers. He must be sent, and he will be sent, to the Tower of London. The comedy is over. The existential game has been won.

Only a few men are left on the scene. Another repetition unfolds. Just as we became familiar with the conspiracy for Bolingbroke in 2.1, so do we get inside information about a conspiracy against King Henry IV. Yet, similar to the repetition of the duel scene, this repetition will also have a comic touch as kind of satire play. Both satire plays have a common essential function: to show Bolingbroke's character, to offer us inside information about the working of political Machiavellianism. It will be obvious that although Bolingbroke prefers to punish, and do it swiftly, he can also exercise clemency if his interests so require. He is a cruel fox, but still not a lion. He does not allow men to kill out of rage, a sense of revenge, or even from weakness, but because of rational considerations.

As far as Richard is concerned, act 5 is his farewell to life. He has chosen his death himself, and he knows it. His fate has already been sealed. Although unusual in Shakespeare, act 5 does not accelerate events. It is the converse that happens here. Henry IV begins to rule. He commands the execution of his enemies and allows Richard to be murdered. Yet, he does all this as a kind of routine, as a kind of technique, as a necessary part of his skill of ruling. This is why he never gets angry. He is always speculating about means and goals. He is rather irritated with Richard's poetic appeal. It is too much, too long, never relevant to the solution of the problem, boring without reason. That a person like Richard chooses to let himself be murdered, after having already resigned his throne, is a kind of irrational stubbornness Bolingbroke can hardly understand. He understands himself, the politicking man, and he is also suspicious, for he suspects others of doing the same thing he is doing, namely politicking. He understands also the Percy type, the narrow-minded man of war, the valiant hero of battles. He does not understand, however, his own son, who is, at that time, also playing theater. Richard is, I repeat, the greatest puzzle for him; but Richard is a puzzle he does not want to understand. He is not much interested in other persons' "substance"; neither is he interested in his own. Later in the drama King Henry IV, particularly in the second part, will be mollified by age through self-pity and worries. But this will be a typical unfolding of energeia from dynamis. The seed of the mollified, self-indulgent, complaining Henry IV is already present in the soul of the early Henry IV, only it has not yet gotten the upper hand. Shakespeare excels in Bolingbroke's portrayal: Henry needs to wrest every political skill in the game to conquer power. But as it turns out afterwards, he is, in the last instance, lazy. Once in power he can relax, and he does, although he goes on to crush his enemies by routine.

But let us return to the beginning of act 5. The first scene portrays the parting of Richard and his queen. Richard must now return to Pomfret, and the queen home to France. We see that their relationship is not entirely ceremonial, that there are emotions between the two but not passions. Richard advises his lady to live in a French cloister and not remain with him. His time on earth is too short for this: "I am sworn brother, sweet, / To grim necessity, and he and I / Will keep a league til death" (5.1.20–22). When Northumberland comes to direct him to Pomfret, Richard predicts his future for him: Henry will deal with him in the same way that he now deals with Richard. In the first part of this book, I spoke about a scene in Henry IV where Henry recalls Richard's prophecy and is deeply shocked that it took effect. However, he is reminded that this was not a prophecy, just a kind of prediction or extrapolation. This time it is not the extrapolation of a fact or an experience, but an extrapolation based on the good judgment of character. We know that Richard had been an extremely bad judge of character in the first three parts of his drama and that his bad judgment belonged to the factors that made Bolingbroke's victory possible. However, after having shed the royal garment, after having invented a new personality (or rather a few connected identities) for himself, Richard has become a good judge of character. He knows for sure that he will be assassinated long before his assassination has actually been initiated by the king.

After the concise portrayal of the tragic farewell between the royal couple, Shakespeare dares to change the mood of the drama not to the comic but to the grotesque. The next scene begins with a straightforward narrative: York tells his wife about the abdication scene. York's narrative, however, differs substantially from Shakespeare's presentation. York already interprets the abdication of the former king as the loyal and blind "sworn subject" of the new one; the falsification of history begins with his tale. This is why the tale is important. The event that—as Shakespeare's gift—was played just before our eyes is here entirely misrepresented. This is not because York's tale is not true; he even pities his former sovereign. Rather, it is because he does not understand at all what Richard was saying; he sees only his weakness, his tears, not his strength. As the audience in the theater, as well as all the other actors, already knows the story, the function of York's narrative is not to tell the story. Shakespeare introduces us to the uncertainty and fragility of the recollection of historical events, which depend on the authenticity/inauthenticity or truth/untruth of the testimonies of great events given by the witnesses. No testimony is true, but the drama is. There is still something in common between Shakespeare's own story—which in this setting plays the role of the "original," of the "real" and the "actual"—and York's narration, which in this setting plays the role of the testimony of one of the witnesses. The commonality is that the abdication scene has been a "theater." Shakespeare presents Richard as the great actor in the world theater; yet for York the real center of the historical theater was his present lord, Henry, the man who did not play. So he speaks: "As in a theatre the eyes of men, / After a well-graced actor leaves the stage, / Are idly bent on him that enters next, / Thinking his prattle to be tedious, / Even so, or with much more contempt, men's eyes / Did scowl on gentle Richard. No man cried 'God save him!' (5.2.23–28). Richard's words sounded to the audience in York's recollection as a tedious "prattle," and the nontheatrical man seems to appear as the new actor towards whom all eyes now turn.

It is now that the grotesque story involving the Duke of York, the duchess, and their son, Aumerle, unfolds. York discovers that his son is party to a conspiracy in favor of Richard and hastens to King Henry to denounce his own son. The duchess offers the best horse to young Aumerle, to overtake his father, arrive before the king first, and ask his pardon. Taken by itself the scene is terrifying. A father denouncing his son, a father killing his son—this will be one of the saddest melodies in the funeral march of the Wars of the Roses. Still, the terrible and the comic merge into one, and their product is the grotesque. The father crying treason is offstage calling three times for what? His boots! He calls his wife "unruly woman," "mad woman" (5.2.110), because she tries to protect her son. Everything in York is excited, exaggerated, and also small. His exaggeration is simply foolish, but what is foolish can also be dangerous.

But, again, the grotesque conflict (which will continue in the next scene) has an important function: it helps us to notice something human in the Machiavellian King Henry IV. The scenes are not just about a conspiracy dying in the bud but also about a king who must deal with conspiracies, and also about fathers and sons. For, in scene 5.3 we see Bolingbroke with Harry Percy already in a role he will take up as king (in *King Henry IV*), the role of the constantly complaining father. Until this moment Henry was constantly acting. He concentrated on facts, power, violence, goals, and means. It is here that we hear him for the first time venting his grief about the demeanor of his oldest son: "Can no man tell me of my unthrifty son? . . . If any plague hang over us, 'tis he" (5.3.1–3). He calls his son "wanton" and "effeminate," and he obviously envies Northumberland for his son, Percy Hotspur. It is at this very moment that another "son," Aumerle, rushes into the room, kneels down, and asks the king for pardon. At this very moment the other father arrives and cries: "Thou hast a traitor in thy presence there" (5.3.38). The king now gets in a state of bombastic righteous indignation: "O loyal father of a treacherous son! / Thou sheer, immaculate, and silver fountain. . . . And thy abundant goodness shall excuse / This deadly blot in thy disgressing son" (5.3.58–64). This bombastic tone does not fit the cool Henry. But at this moment he—the father—identifies himself with the other father. He refers not only to York but also to himself as the "silver stream," whose great merits give pardon to their sons. Aumerle will be pardoned by a mixture of personal touch, clever policy (he denounces readily the other conspirators and is thus useful and can be blackmailed hereafter), and a sense of humor. This is because, when in addition the duchess runs into the chamber and joins the concert, Bolingbroke shows a new feature of his character: his sense of humor. Machiavellians can excel in a kind of dry humor. Henry himself understands the grotesque character of the scene and says (these are the most human sentences he utters in this drama): "Our scene is altered from a serious thing,

/ And now changed to 'The Beggar and the King'. / My dangerous cousin, let your mother in. / I know she is come to pray for your foul sin" (5.3.77–80). One needs to note that in the dramatic art and character of Richard II, sarcasm and irony are always very strongly represented, yet he has no humor. King Henry does.

But in the next, very brief, scene the same King Henry will turn out to be a foul murderer. Shakespeare leaves undetermined whether he has gone beyond the limits of a "necessary" murder in a Machiavellian sense. At any rate, this is a different kind of murder. All his other murders are straightfor-ward executions. True, there are show trials; yet the semblance of the law has been preserved. What happens here is something else. It is the crossroad. And, in Shakespeare, Henry in fact crosses the road; yet he returns within his limits again. What happens? Exton addresses his first man thus: "Didst thou not mark the King, what words he spake? / 'Have I no friend will rid me of this living fear?' Was it not so?" (5.4.1–3). Of course, he means the king in Pomfret. Let us murder the king in Pomfret. This is not execution, but base assassination. Yet after the murder, when Exton comes to collect Henry's praise and his profit, the king says: "Exton, I thank thee not, for thou has wrought / A deed of slander with thy fatal hand / Upon my head and all this famous land" (5.6.34–36). When Exton answers in indignation that "from your own mouth, my lord, did I this deed" (5.6.37), the king retorts: "They love no poison that do poison need; / Nor do I thee. Though I did wish him dead, / I hate the murderer, love him murdered. . . . With Cain go wander through the shades of night, / And never show thy head by day nor light" (5.6.38–44). Hypocrisy? Yes. Pilate? Worse than Pilate. He himself suggests a murder yet does not take responsibility for it, and he pun-ishes the murderer. But he does not do this in order to get rid of his accus-ing eyes or because of the fear of being found out; it is rather because of disgust. The murderer disgusts Henry; he preserves the remnants of his moral taste. Moreover, he has reached his goal, and by now he can throw away the means. These are crucial for a true Machiavellian. Henry ceases to climb because he reaches the top. Let us recall the whole story. Bolingbroke kept cool, he knew his goal (the throne); his game was to reach his goal. But he never enjoyed the game itself. Bolingbroke is a goal-rational hyp-ocrite, but he does not indulge in playing roles. He never even plays cat-and-mouse games with his victims. He is the bad actor who, after achiev-ing fame, will feel at rest. At the end of the play we see Henry growing old, although little time has elapsed. Growing old means losing great ambitions. Why does he need the throne? Just because he is able to reach it, and because he is also convinced that he will be a better king of England. But every usurper thinks so—except Richard III, who is radically evil and never lies. This is why I said that Henry crossed the road when he incited his men to murder Richard—but that he also returned from the crossroads because he threw away the means. He will never again use those particular means. He will never be a great king, but he will be a relatively fair one.

Yet still, the road has been crossed already in the deposition scene. Foul murder follows from the deposition. Tradition is not only wounded (this was already done by Richard), it was also killed so that the league of more or less self-made men will soon occupy the state. The law of nature will be discovered.

It is in the prison cell of Pomfret that Richard discovers his self once again and reinvents himself almost for the last time. Shakespeare normally blesses his dying heroes generously with the special gift of significant and representative speech. Yet among all of them perhaps Richard II is—aside from Cleopatra and Othello—the most blessed. He deserves it because he is a dramatic poet. He creates poetry from his suffering, transforming himself from an average actor of a well-established state into a marvelous inventive player on a self-created world stage. A man who invents himself in language most deserves the gift of high speech.

It is in prison that Richard is finally alone, in both the pedestrian and Hegelian understanding of the words "by himself." Richard is doing thinking; he becomes a thinker. He cannot act anymore; he has no choice. He can reflect: "My brain I'll prove the female to my soul, / My soul the father, and these two beget / A generation of still-breeding thoughts" (5.5.6–8). Richard begins to populate his own world with thoughts; this will be his world from now on. He discovers the life of a philosopher and a playwright, the life of his own father and mother: Shakespeare. Thoughts and words come hard, for a world of thoughts and of words is not a free world either: "Thoughts tending to content flatter themselves / That they are not the first of fortune's slaves, / Nor shall not be the last. . . . Thus play I in one person many people, / And none contented. Sometimes am I king; / Then treason makes me wish myself a beggar, / And so I am. Then crushing penury / Persuades me I was better when a king. / Then am I kinged again, and by and by / Think that I am unkinged by Bolingbroke, / And straight am nothing. But whate'er I be, / Nor I, nor any man that but man is, / With nothing shall be pleased till he be eased / With being nothing" (5.5.23–41). At this moment the historical stage is also waning. There is one stage left, the existential. Shakespeare speaks through Richard, and Richard through Shakespeare.

Yet then something happens. Someone plays music. The sound comes from the world, from outside, from afar. It is not a thought; it is the real sound, a melody played for Richard. The melody opens the historical stage again—the stage of time out of joint. "Music do I hear / Ha, ha; keep time! How sour sweet music is / When time is broke and no proportion kept. / So is it in the music of men's lives. / And here have I the daintiness of ear / To check time broke in a disordered string; / But for the concord of my state and time / Had not an ear to hear my true time broke. / I wasted time, and now doth time waste me" (5.5.42–44).

Richard, who dies willingly because he never read aloud (and never signed) the paper filled with his and his friends' alleged crimes, now confesses to himself his gravest political (and not personal!) fault. He had no ear for the change in the rhythm and tune of Time. He had no ear for the murmuring of the change of the age. Time was out of joint, and he did not notice it before he himself became its victim, before his fate became irreversible. But after he once missed the moment (kairos), his life is no longer measured by historical time alone. His time is the time of all men, subjective time, the time of finitude, of mortality: "For now hath time made me his numb'ring clock. / My thoughts are minutes, and with sighs they jar / Their watches on unto mine eyes, the outward watch / Whereto my finger, like a dial's point, / Is pointing still in cleansing them from tears. . . . So sighs, and tears, and groans / Show minutes, hours, and times" (5.5.50–58). Richard is maddened by the out-of-tune music until he realizes that it is played for him; it is "a sign of love." Now enters the groom. He is his only loyal servant. Yet even the groom brings gloomy news: Richard's favorite horse, Barebary, is ridden now by Bolingbroke. Even his horse has betrayed Richard; the groom has to leave. The keeper appears with the poisoned food, followed by the assassins.

Something happens. In the very last minute of his life Richard becomes another man again—the man of swift action. He does things he has never done and could not imagine doing even a few minutes prior: he beats the keeper and he kills two of the assassins. He was never a fox or a lion, but in the last minute he acts like a lion.

After Exton strikes him down, Richard utters his final words. These words are the words of a believer. He leaves the historical stage and lifts himself onto the world of transcendence. He curses Exton, but he prophesies not earthly but divine retribution. He offers the right to judge to the King of Kings: "That hand shall burn in never-quenching fire / That staggers thus my person. . . . Mount, mount, my soul; Thy seat is up on high, / Whilst my gross flesh sink downward, here to die" (5.5.108–12).

The rest we know. King Henry promises to go "to the Holy Land / To wash this blood off from my guilty hand" (5.6.49–50). But he will never keep his promise. He will meet his death—symbolically—in the Jerusalem room of his castle. History does not follow curses or blessings. Yet Richard's faith is divine retribution, and his salvation is—or becomes—no more or less a "fact" than Desdemona's handkerchief. Richard believes in his salvation, and he believes in the damnation of his enemies. Everyone knows this, or will slowly get to know it. Richard's pointing at divine retribution becomes a historical factor. Henry cannot wash his hands clean: he remains a regicide. God—so the Bible says—punishes the evil until the fifth generation. Historical actors know their Bible. God had to punish the evil done by Henry IV. If it is not on him, not on his own son, then on his innocent and good grandson, Henry VI and on his great-grandchild, Edward, who will be murdered the same way as their forefather allowed King Richard to be murdered. The wheel of history does not follow the rhythm of divine retribution, yet there is a connection. Historical actors legitimate their acts as if they were vehicles of retribution. But justification of this sort is almost never entirely a pretext: it is felt, it is accompanied by conviction. The question is not whether Shakespeare believed in this connection, for he certainly was infinitely interested in it. In this way, he also believed in it. He observed the mechanism of divine retribution in its effects, for only its effects were observable. They all belong to the tragedy of the *comédie humaine*. In the story of roses, the murder of Richard II plays the role of the original sin. The original sin is consummated in history, not in politics. Politically, Henry is successful enough, and his son becomes the shining star of English history. But politics in Shakespeare is of short duration, and history is of long duration. A politically successful act becomes historically catastrophic because an original sin was committed by the politicking Bolingbroke, the new man, against God's anointed king. Men and women could believe that the historical catastrophe was a work of divine retribution because Henry does not kept his promise to go and fight for the Holy Land. Thus he cheats God with a false promise as he once cheated his king, and he never does penance for his sin.

10

1, 2, and 3 Henry VI

Seen from the perspective of the philosophy of history, the stories of Richard II, Henry VI, and Richard III are equally stories of failure and doom. Seen from the perspective of morals, they are substantially different. The first is the story of a man whose guilt consists mostly of faults of negligence, unconcern, and false self-confidence. The second is the story of a completely good man, and the third is the story of a radically evil creature. Seen from the perspective of political philosophy, the first story may serve as a lesson for later political actors, as a warning and analogy. The second and third stories exemplify the frequently mentioned rule of politics formulated by Machiavelli: both radical goodness and radical evil are politically disastrous. The difference between lesson (analogy) on the one hand and rule on the other does not stand for the contrast between contingency and necessity. Contingency plays a decisive role not only in the story of Richard II but also in that of Henry VI; in the story of Richard III, one can observe a break. Before Richard occupies the throne there are still contingencies, although they are not as significant as in the previously discussed plays. Yet after Richard III becomes king, contingencies disappear and give way to the unfolding of the mechanism of absolute tyranny. This poetic solution can also be described as a sound philosophical proposition. Where the king is absolutely good, his entourage could still act in a sound political way and save him, and particularly his kingdom, from the ultimate disaster. Yet, where the head of state is radically evil, everyone who might still be ready to act in a politically sound way will be murdered by the tyrant. In the case of radical evil, politics and history coincide. Here, lesson and mechanism coincide; evil is necessarily tyrannical and necessarily also self-destructive. Unless its working is stopped in due time, radical evil leads with an ever increasing speed toward the ruin of the realm. This is the sole "historical necessity" in Shakespeare.

The three parts of *Henry VI* differ from both *Richard II* and *Richard III* in one crucial dramaturgical fact: they are not one-man shows. One encounters a whole arsenal of significant characters in all three of the *Henry VI* plays, and they are each other's equals, at last insofar as they match one another in the strength of their personalities. There are traditional heroes among them, yet also entirely self-made men; the plays abound in lions and in foxes. In addition, there are the lambs and snakes. Although Shakespeare here does not mobilize similes from the animal kingdom to the extent that he does later (for example, in *Coriolanus*), he still makes good use of them. This I mention only because of the well-known criticism of the alleged primitivism of the language of *Henry VI* in Shakespeare's own age. He was regarded as pathetically bombastic, especially because of his frequent employment of similes taken from the animal kingdom. I mentioned *Coriolanus* to show that this was not the blunder of an unskilled youthful playwright. He used the metaphors of the animal kingdom whenever he saw they fit the occasion and the person. At any rate, I cannot see in *Henry VI,* as so many do, an unripe work of an unripe youth. In my eyes, this trilogy is one of the deepest history plays ever written by Shakespeare, or by anyone else. It has its own shining perfections.

Originally, the three parts were three separate dramas. All of them have their own panoply of characters, and in each of them different characters are closer to the center point of the action, plot, and events. There are extraordinary characters who are on stage in only two of the three parts. Perhaps this is how the chronicle-like composition of the dramas is best preserved. Yet, no part of *Henry VI* constitutes epic theater, nor can all three parts together be called epic. The three plays of *Henry VI* are in my mind the dramatic counterparts of the Balzacian human comedy: historical dramas that explore the extremities of the human character and existence. The historicoexistential panorama is, however, built around two central characters who will remain in the limelight until the very end—the king and queen. But the real protagonist of the play is history itself: war, conspiracy, heroism, treason, civil war. This is why all strata of the kingdom appear on the scene: not only the court, the dukes, and their followers but also rebels, commoners, pirates, citizens of London, mayors, gentlemen. There are not only Englishmen and -women but also the French king, nobility, soldiers, city dwellers, the dauphin, and, last but not least, Joan of Arc, the Maid of Orleans. We may still recall the words Horatio uttered at the end of *Hamlet*. Horatio does not say, while telling the story of Hamlet, that he is telling the story of Prince Hamlet, the king, and the queen. He says, "So shall you hear / Of carnal, bloody, and unnatural acts, / Of accidental judgements, casual slaughters, / Of deaths put on by cunning and forced cause. . . . All this can I / Truly deliver" (*Hamlet* 5.2.334–39). This is history, and this is exactly the story that is truly delivered by Shakespeare in *1, 2,* and *3 King Henry VI.*

Although the three parts of *Henry VI* are three different dramas, each with its own set of characters, it is difficult to consider them separately. In an interesting performance of the Joseph Papp Public Theater in New York, the three parts were played on two successive nights.

1 Henry VI

King Henry VI, Part 1, was written, as we know, after the shorter second and third parts. We well understand why Shakespeare felt it important to add the first part to the drama. The first part presents us with the "sufficient reason," with all the events that taken together became the conditions of the Wars of the Roses. If even one of the conditions had been missing, the Wars of the Roses perhaps never would have taken place. Each and every die was thrown successively from separate dice boxes; they were mostly unconnected. Yet, they all add up to the unluckiest of all historical numbers. None of the throws was in itself unlucky. For example, it is not in itself an unlucky throw to have a radically good man as a king. But taken together with all the other throws, it proves to be disastrous. It is not in itself necessarily fatal if a country loses some of the territories that an earlier king has won. This happens frequently. But together with other throws, the loss of France was one of the unluckiest.

When I said that the dice were thrown from separate dice boxes, I did not mean thereby the absence of interplay between the dice. If one die is already thrown, it might interplay with the next throw of the next dice box. That Richard chose to act in harmony with his good character was one thing. But he had to choose in a world where a few dice were already on the table. These were the conditions of his decisions. In the case of Henry, the interplay between conditions, on the one hand, and decisions that did not react to the conditions but followed from the character of the king alone, on the other, proved to belong to the fatal coincidences. I said that the three *Henry VI* dramas have history as their protagonist because Shakespeare pays such great attention to the connection and disconnection of a great variety of the throws of the dice.

Let me reiterate that the first part of *Henry VI* is about the "original throws" that have triggered the Wars of the Roses, which for its part will be the historical topic of the second and particularly the third part of the drama.

The presentation of the sufficient reason for something (this time, the Wars of the Roses) does not for Shakespeare annul the essentially contingent character of the unfolding of historical events. The sole exception is perhaps the radical evil on the throne, where one can speak of necessity even if the main aspect of necessity—teleology—remains absent. For in this case, as in many other respects, Shakespeare was a good Aristotelian, whether he knew Aristotle or not. Total determination of an event, or of a development of events, will never add up in itself to necessity. Only what can be grasped teleologically is necessary. Events must have an inherent aim. This is the way in which the result of *Richard II* attained a kind of necessity after Richard chose his own destiny and became himself. For then he himself provided a *causa finalis* for the course of events. A tentative teleology might be observed also in the case of *Richard III*. (I will discuss this drama later.) However, there is no teleology in the story of Henry VI. Nothing makes sense because there is no hidden goal or purpose to anything. Shakespeare here has to imitate God from the Book of Genesis. He has to sweep away from the table of history all the chess figures of his "first creation" that have acted under constraint, but without an inherent end or goal. The only exception, as we shall see, is King Henry VI himself. He will be the Noah of Shakespeare's drama. This he will be not in his person, for he will be slaughtered as a lamb, but because it was Henry VI who has "chosen" and blessed the historical Messiah, Henry VII—the dove, the bringer of peace, the liberator. All other figures have to disappear not just in fact but also in type from the chessboard. Henry VII will enter a chessboard that has already been swept clean by Richard III. This takes place after Richard III, after the deluge.

I agree with almost all interpreters that the central figure of *1 Henry VI* is Talbot. Yet it needs to be noted that Talbot first appears only in act 1.4. The first vicious and dangerous die had been cast, however, in the first scene. This is the way that Shakespeare has us enter history in medias res. This is why Talbot's appearance must be postponed.

The play begins with the funeral of King Henry V. Brothers and uncles are returning from the funeral. Immediately, beside the hearse of their brother's and father's corpse, the most vicious fight breaks out between the dead king's next of kin. This is the typical Shakespearean story. In this case it is not the brothers—for the truth of fact cannot be entirely neglected—but the brother and the uncle of the dead king who turn against one another in black hatred. As he does so frequently, Shakespeare portrays the repetition of the first irrational story of biblical history, the story of Cain and Abel. For in all similar mortal fights between brothers, there is a Cain and there is an Abel. Here good Humphrey, the brother of the dead king, plays the role of Abel, and Winchester, who will become the cardinal, plays the role of Cain. The roles are already assigned from the first scene onward, and they will never be reversed; they will never change. Shakespeare indicates some motives for their mutual hatred. Humphrey (Duke of Gloucester) became the protector of the realm, and Winchester, who is older and is a bastard, is disqualified from this office. Winchester is a man of the Catholic Church and, as interpreters continue to tell us, Shakespeare does not entertain sympathy for this church. But again, these and similar motivations do not "explain" either the depth of hatred or the wickedness of acts, as they never do in Shakespeare.

The rift, the wound, the deadly hostility among the closest of kin of the king: this is indeed the first and the most dangerous die to be cast. For if there had been solidarity, love, and understanding within the family of the king, there never would have been the Wars of the Roses. Moreover, the might and power of the Lancaster family never would have been challenged with such a final success by the family of York. The first scene reminds us that Shakespeare has remained in fact true to the Greek model of tragedy. Politicohistorical tragedy is also family tragedy. The rift, the hatred, and the murder first need to be within the family. History, politics, the ties of the blood: all need to reinforce one another so that the tragedy can offer enough space for the existential stage within, or together with, the historical. (The second brother of Henry V, Bedford, the warlord, the regent of France, will play no fatal role.)

During the first exchange of hate speech between Gloucester and Winchester (before the altar!) a messenger enters with the news that Champagne, Paris, Rouen, Rheims, Orleans, and other cities are lost for England. Shakespeare constantly converts objective chronological time into dramatic-historical time. Sometimes one decade is portrayed as if it were but one day, and one day as if it were one decade. Thus in the concise temporality of the drama the dukes receive intelligence of the loss of great territories in France on the very day of Henry V's funeral. Had this been historically correct, Henry V could not have been such a great and uncontested conqueror as he is praised for being, for the loss of large pieces of France could not have been debited to his infant son. But this is for Shakespeare of no avail. We believe him. Henry V was a great conqueror, and the intelligence of the loss of French territories came at the very hour of his funeral. Here we first hear the name of Talbot. We learn that Talbot has lost the fight and is imprisoned, that Falstaff has run away. Bedford goes to France to change the course of the war, and Gloucester decides to crown little Henry as king. The first scene ends with a brief soliloquy by Winchester: "The King from Eltham I intend to steal, / And sit at chiefest stern of public weal" (*1 Henry VI* 1.1.176–77). Thus he decides to become the protector; this is a death knell for good Humphrey.

We turn immediately to France. The tableau becomes very broad; Shakespeare begins to tell us the story of Joan of Arc. Most interpreters suggest that Shakespeare is unjust to Joan, that he describes her with biased English eyes. I do not think so. I would not say that Shakespeare's portrayal of the Maid of Orleans is one of his strongest, but it is good enough. If one believes that Shakespeare identified himself with the English side, one must also believe that Talbot's voice is Shakespeare's voice. In my mind this is a serious misunderstanding. At least I cannot read Shakespeare this way.

Talbot is one of the great men of tradition. He is not just valiant and noble but also narrow-minded, filled with bigotry. He does not understand anything new, unprecedented, surprising, out of tune with the usual. For him Joan of Arc is a sorceress and a wicked apprentice of the devil. He is the one who is biased from head to toe. It belongs to his character to be biased; he has not the faintest understanding of the laws of nature or otherness. And what kind of witness is York? This is a man who soon afterward will murder half the Lancastrian tribe. When York cries out, "Curse, miscreant, when thou com'st to the stake," how strong is the truth content of his voice? When one listens to what Joan herself is saying, or watches the influence that her voice and speech exert, for example, on Burgundy (and this will finally decide the whole war in favor of France), this will leave an entirely different impression. A peasant girl who hears voices and wins battles in men's clothes cannot be anything but a whore, in Talbot's view. But Talbot is not Shakespeare's mouthpiece. My only proof for this, if an interpretation needs to be proven at all, is that these types of Shakespearean characters (Fortinbras included) are never extremely interesting, and thus can never be the mouthpieces of the author.

Listen for a minute to Joan of Arc talking to Burgundy: "Look on thy country, look on fertile France, / And see the cities and the towns defaced / By wasting ruin of the cruel foe. / As looks the mother on her lowly babe / When death doth close his tender-dying eyes, / See, see the pining malady of France. . . . O turn thy edged sword another way" (3.7.44–52). Burgundy feels himself vanquished and asks his country for forgiveness. Now comes the frequently quoted sentence of the maid, "Done like Frenchmen—turn and turn again" (3.7.85), which from the mouth of Joan is just the expression of contempt for turncoats; and finally her address to the "familiar spirits" on the battlefield where France seems to be lost. That the spirits appear but do not speak, cast their heads, and so on, does not make Joan of Arc a sorceress or a daughter of Satan. Spirits appear often in Shakespeare—for example, in Hamlet and Julius Caesar. The main thing is that, in Shakespeare's portrayal, Joan of Arc does everything for her country's sake and not for her own. This is what we now call patriotism. She thus addresses the spirits: "Then take my soul—my body, soul, and all— / Before that England give the French the foil" (5.3.22–23). At the end she denounces her peasant birth and calls herself noble. She, the virgin, says that she is with child—all this just to save her life. Yes, she wants to live; she is human, all too human. Yet, if one compares her weak attempts to save her life in dignity with the coarse rudeness and cruelty of the English nobility watching the young girl's suffering—mocking her, branding her—her superiority stands out absolutely. For example, Joan speaks of herself thus: "I never had to do with wicked spirits; / But you that are polluted with your lusts / Stained with the guiltless blood of innocents, / Corrupt and tainted with a thousand vices— / Because you want the grace that others have. . . .You judge it straight a thing impossible / To compass wonders but by help of devils. / No, misconceived! Joan of Arc hath been / A virgin from her tender infancy / Chaste and immaculate in very thought, / Wise maiden-blood thus rigorously effused / Will cry for vengeance at the gates of heaven" (5.3.42–53). To this Warwick remarks, "And hark ye, sirs: because she is a maid, / Spare for no faggots" (5.3.55–56). He believes this to be a good joke. With the exception of *The Merchant of Venice*, I have never seen such a biased, cruel, barbarian crowd than the flower of English nobility watching mockingly Joan's humiliation and making jokes at her execution. Joan's curses will surely take effect.

The story of Joan of Arc, which runs through the whole first part of *Henry VI,* is also a story of sexual subversion. She is clad in boy's clothing and conducts war as a boy. But she never pretends (unlike Rosalind or Viola) to be a boy. She does the task of men, yet she does it as a woman, as a virgin. She appears to be an absolute rebel, but is she? I mentioned earlier that absolute strangers are absolute strangers because they are never portrayed in the company of their own kind. We do not see Shylock acting and behaving among the Jews, and we do not see Othello acting and behaving among the Moors. However, here we see Joan of Arc acting and behaving among the English, her deadly enemies. But we also see her among the French, whose savior she is. Perhaps this is why we are more inclined to peer into the author's own persuasion. He is an Englishman; how could he take the part of the French? But Shakespeare is here both English and French, and he is both a man and a woman. Let me add something: we do not see Joan of Arc the woman in the company of women. She is a woman, but she is not a woman. She is, in my mind, the most complicated case of sexual subversion in Shakespeare, for many reasons. First, she is a historical figure. Second, her character goes through extreme swings. Third, her image becomes confused in the interpretation or evaluation of men, depending on whether they are French or English.

It is true that the scenes played among the French do not match in substance and beauty the scenes played among the English, and understandably so. The French actors—the characters of the French story—are but one die cast in the whole fate of England. After this die has been cast, the French will disappear as actors and characters, even if France will remain there as a bounty, a memory, a grievance, or a project. The horizon needs to become narrower. One needs now to concentrate on other conditions of the Wars of the Roses, of the destruction of traditional England.

We see how two of the dice were already cast, through the family feud surrounding the infant king and the trouble in France. Although the French connection ends in the first part with the execution of Joan, seemingly a happy turn for the English side, we learn from Shakespeare's text—and not just from our familiarity with history—that the English cause is lost.

Talbot's story is the symbol of the fate of England. Talbot represents the old, traditional, victorious, brave, simple, energetic, narrow-minded, firm, stable England. His self-identity is never called into question. Talbot is Talbot; Talbot's England is the glorious, proud, self-assured England. Talbot is the hero in *1 Henry VI* not just because of his personal grandeur but also because of his symbolic status. Shakespeare needs a counterpoint to his story about the gathering of all the conditions of a self-destructive England. The characters who bring about self-destruction must be contrasted with a character from the world destroyed by them.

We learn that Talbot is taken prisoner. Yet, we meet him first in his encounter with Salisbury after he has been ransomed. The address of Salisbury is immediately representative. He greets him: "Talbot, my life, my joy, again returned?" This is the greeting of a lover: England is in love with Talbot. Salisbury will soon meet his accidental death. Meanwhile, Joan enters Orleans and—as I have already mentioned—Talbot constantly abuses her. The last sentences of act 1 are important, for it is here that Shakespeare places his hero in the midst of traditional shame culture: "O would I were to die with Salisbury! / The shame hereof will make me hide my head" (1.7.38–39). Talbot never hears the voice of conscience. The sole moral authority he recognizes is the eye of his countrymen; the only moral feeling he is capable of is shame. His acts are the acts of loyalty, of heroism, of revenge, and also of gallantry. The scene with the Countess of Auvergne is the traditional Mars-Venus story, the Renaissance and baroque version of which will be recounted in almost all European languages in different variations. Shakespeare portrays not just the gallantry but also the shrewdness of Talbot and presents him as the man of collective identity. The countess, as we know, wants to seduce him with her beauty and take him as her prisoner. Shakespeare emphasizes that this particular Mars is ugly and also small in stature, that he does not seem to match his fame. Yet, when the countess seems triumphant, Talbot lets his soldiers enter. "How say you, madame? Are you now persuaded / That Talbot is but shadow of himself? / These are his substance, sinews, arms, strength, / With which he yoketh your rebellious necks" (2.3.61–64). This little speech underlines Shakespeare's characterization. It is the opposite of the usual natural law argument. Yes, Talbot is the head of the English army; this is his substance. The collective identity is the arm, the sinew, strength. The collective identity, the identity of name, face, nature, and tradition, is firm, without any question marks— for the last time in all the Shakespearean history plays. Talbot does not take part in the announcement of the Wars of the Roses. When he meets King Henry VI in France, the knights already wear the red and white roses. He does not seem even to notice. He just kneels down with the words: "My gracious prince and honourable peers, / Hearing of your arrival in this realm / I have a while given truce to my wars / To do my duty to my sovereign / In sign whereof, this arm that hath reclaimed / To your obedience fifty fortresses, / Twelve cities, and seven walled towns of strength, / Beside five hundred prisoners of esteem, / Lets fall his sword before your highness' feet / And with submissive loyalty of heart / Ascribes the glory of his conquest got / First to my God, and next unto your grace" (3.8.1–12). This man, loyal from head to toe, is perhaps the first to realize the absence in the infant king, not just of Machiavellian skills, but also of traditional know-how to settle the business of traitors politically by murdering them. He says to the king before returning to the battlefield: "I go, my lord, in heart desiring still / You may behold confusion of your foes" (4.1.76–77). But although Talbot fails to notice the gathering storm, it is perhaps because of the already forceful feud between the Houses of York and Lancaster that he did not receive the needed military help. In York's mind Somerset is the traitor; in Somerset's mind it is York. But neither of them cares about France. They were already possessed by their mutual hatred. York speaks thus: "A plague upon that villain Somerset / That thus delays my promised supply / Of horsemen that were levied for this siege! / Renowned Talbot doth expect my aid, / And I am louted by a traitor villain / And cannot help the noble chevalier" (4.3.9–14). But he could go alone, he could help on his own. Lucy implores him: "Spur to the rescue of the noble Talbot. . . . / To Bordeaux, warlike Duke; To Bordeaux, York, / Else farewell Talbot, France, and England's honour" (19–23). However, York does not listen; he leaves Talbot to his death. He says (he lies, of course, as he almost always does): "Lucy, farewell. No more my fortune can / But curse the cause I cannot aid the man" (43–44). In the next scene Somerset uses the same excuse: "It is too late, I cannot send them now. / This expedition was by York and Talbot / Too rashly plotted. . . . York set him on to fight and die in shame / That, Talbot dead, great York might bear the name" (4.4.1–9). In all probability his interpretation is right, but we cannot know this for sure. Lucy then takes over the role of a chorus: "The fraud of England, not the force of France, / Hath now entrapped the noble-minded Talbot. / Never to England shall he bear his life, / But dies betrayed to fortune by your strife" (36–39). Talbot has been betrayed; the old England has been betrayed by the new. All who call each other villains and traitors will recognize his honor, courage, and virtue. But Talbot serves them better in his grave.

And here comes the scene where this simple-minded, old-fashioned man is elevated to the rank of a tragic hero. Yet, in spite of this elevation, Talbot will never enter the existential stage; he and his son will stay on the historicopolitical stage. But this historical stage will assume mythological significance. It will become the restaging of the old story of Daedalus and Icarus. The stage is the earth from which they begin to fly as heroes to the mythological Olympus. Talbot and his son are fighting shoulder to shoulder, and they become each other's equal in their love for one another and in their love for their country, for their honor and bravery. The father tries to save his son's life, the son his father's life, but to no avail. They fly together as two stars. Shakespeare plays around with "flying." John Talbot: " Surely, by all the glory you have won, / And if I fly I am not Talbot's son. / Then talk no more of flight; It is no boot. / If son of Talbot, die at Talbot's foot" (4.6.50–53). Then old Talbot turns to him and accepts his sacrifice that—he understands—is none: instead of flight, flying. "Then follow thou thy desp'rate sire of Crete, / Thou Icarus; thy life to me is sweet. / If thou wilt fight, fight by thy father's side, / And commendable proved, let's die in pride" (54–57). Young Talbot dies first. "Where is my other life? Mine own is gone. / O where's young Talbot, where is valiant John? . . . And in that sea of blood my boy did drench / His over mounting spirit; and there died / My Icarus, my blossom, in his pride" (4.7.1–16). And then he says: "Two Talbots winged through the lither sky / In thy despite shall scape mortality" (4.7.21–22). Yes, Talbot believes in immortal fame for himself and his son, in a mythological fame that befits great heroes of history. But this pathos-filled scene also has its counterpoint. Joan of Arc vanquished the Talbots. The Maid of Orleans has other memories about the fallen hero. Once she encountered him, and she said: "'Thou maiden youth, be vanquished by a maid.' / But with a proud, majestical high scorn. / He answered thus: 'Young Talbot was not born / To be the pillage of a giglot wench'" (38–41). This is how we learn that young Talbot is like his father absolutely. He has to die with his father. In his simple-mindedness, loyalty, and heroism he is his father. He does not belong to the world already very much in the making.

The scene of father and son will have soon a counterpart in *3 Henry VI* (written earlier), where we encounter a father who has killed his son and a son who has killed his father. This does not take place on the battlefield of France but on the battlefield of the civil war in England. Here, too, the father laments the son's death and the son laments the father's death. But the contrast could not be greater between a father and a son who choose to die together, fighting against the enemy of their anointed king, the father and son who are again shoulder to shoulder as Daedelus and Icarus and earning thereby immortal fame, and the son and father killing one another knowing not what they are doing. The family drama remains embedded in the historical drama; the self-destruction of the family is also the self-destruction of the country. In abandoning Talbot and his son to their fates, Somerset and York abandon old England, old virtues, old loyalties. No more certainties remain, only question marks. The state and the life of man have lost their grounding. This is how the abyss opens before everyone's feet. However, they see only the peaks they are climbing; and while looking upward to the royal throne, riches, and fame, they could not notice the abyss that opens beneath their feet.

After this long detour I return briefly to the first throw of the die, that is, to the feud within the family of Lancaster, the burning hatred between Gloucester, the protector of the land, and Winchester, the cardinal. As early as in the third scene of the first act the whole city of London, the citizens, the officers of the law, and the mayor himself get involved directly or indirectly in the family feud. One must note that the hostile parties are already here, clad in different coats. The servicemen of Gloucester wear blue coats, whereas the servicemen of Winchester wear tawny coats (which gives the impression that these servicemen are higher in rank). Gloucester wants to enter the tower, yet the men of Winchester do not let him in. The first altercation between them shows clearly what can be expected next. Winchester calls Gloucester "usurping proditor" (*1 Henry VI* 1.4.31). Gloucester calls his uncle a "manifest conspirator" (1.4.33) and immediately accuses him of conspiring to murder Henry V (which may or may not be true) and claims that he is whoring (which is a crime on an entirely different scale). Winchester says, "Be thou cursed Cain, / To slay thy brother Abel, if you wilt" (1.4.38–39). This is a very interesting retort. We all know, for it will very soon be clear, that Winchester will play the role of Cain and Gloucester will be killed by him. But why does Winchester identify himself with Abel? Do all men identify themselves with the victim and not the murderer, even the murderer himself? This is a highly important psychological question. However, Gloucester answers, "I will not slay thee, but I drive thee back" (1.4.40), something he will never be able to do. Winchester threatens him with the pope, whereas Gloucester cries: "Winchester goose! I cry, 'A rope, a rope!'" (1.4.52). It is also very telling to consider the way in which Humphrey, the "good Humphrey," as people call him, who in fact will never harm a fly, can get out of himself. I mean, for example, the way that he can get mad or can be possessed by a fit of anger. We know this about Hamlet as well. In a fit of rage some men can say things they don't really mean. This is also the case with Gloucester, particularly when he meets his mortal enemy, his uncle.

The verbal abuse, or rather duel, escalates into skirmishes between blue coats and tawny coats. The citizens of London are also involved, some on one side, some on the other. The mayor, who comes to separate the fighting parties, is, however, not neutral. Obviously, he knows his men well. His knowledge of Gloucester's and Winchester's characters goes back "before our times," that is, before the opening lines of the play. He can say something that we could not yet say: "This bishop is more haughty than the devil" (1.483), although he does not utter a bad word against Gloucester. Playing the part of an imaginary chorus of the citizens of London, he says one additional important thing: "Good God, these nobles such stomachs bear! / I myself fight not once in forty year" (1.4.88–89).

Now we arrive at the throw of the third die, in act 2, scene 4, and witness the symbolic gathering in the Temple Garden. This scene is—allegedly—entirely Shakespeare's own invention. It is a concise and graphic account of an event that stands for all the events responsible for triggering the Wars of the Roses. The scene is well known. One has the impression that Shakespeare wants first to introduce the main characters of the play before the action gets started. Here they are in full: Richard Plantagenet (the later York), Warwick, Somerset, and Suffolk. Some other minor characters are also present. We are now listening to a palaver that has begun in the Temple Hall without our presence (as observers or readers). We now have to guess what it is all about from the recapitulations of the standpoints of each of the participants. But we will never know whether the opinions are correctly recapitulated. Obviously, York was the speaker. He made the provocation and the others fell silent, for they were embarrassed. For York's first sentence sounds thus: "Great Lords and gentlemen, what means this silence? / Dare no man answer in a case of truth?" (2.4.1–2). We know from experience with Shakespeare that for him the presentation of a case as a case of truth is always suspect. Those who take the case of truth without doubts, without offering allowances for other judgments, always take the case of untruth. But we do not yet know anything of the stakes. We first get to know Suffolk's confession, which is, as far as we know, at least truthful: "Faith, I have been a truant in the law, / And never yet could frame my will to it, / And therefore frame the law unto my will" (2.4.7–9). So speaks a self-made man, an upstart, a sincere climber. Somerset turns to Warwick, asking him to be the judge. At this point we already surmise that the altercation must have been between York and Somerset and that Suffolk has declined to be the judge. At first, Warwick seems hesitant also. Some believe that their truth is equal, but neither of them accepts the position of the other. Richard says, "The truth appears so naked on my side" (2.4.20), whereas Somerset answers, "And on my side it is so well apparelled, / So clear, so shining, and so evident" (2.4.22–23). Richard continues, "If he suppose that I have pleaded truth, / From off this briar pluck a white rose with me" (2.4.29–30). Somerset goes on, "But dare maintain the party of the truth, / Pluck a red rose from off this thorn with me" (2.4.32–33). To pluck a red or white rose is to pluck a truth. A truth is absolute; there is only one truth. But already there are two truths, one for the red rose and one for the white. The Wars of the Roses begin as a contest of truth. Shakespeare has not read postmodern authors, but he knows well that in politics to fight for an absolute truth absolutely is to run amok. Talbot does not fight for truth, he fights for his country, right or wrong. This is simple. But now a new fight begins, the fight in which truth is pitted against truth. But there is no absolute truth, at least not in history, not in politics, not in questions of legitimacy. This is the lesson drawn from the story of Richard II, a story that will be written by Shakespeare ten years later. It is, however, a story that has happened much earlier and sounds intimately familiar to the protagonists of the Wars of the Roses. Yet we do not know what the truth is. Do those who pluck the roses know? At any rate, Warwick plucks the white one, Suffolk the red. The white one is plucked by Vernon and also by the lawyer. It seems as if York has the majority. Is there in the case of truth a majority decision? There is obviously not, for the scene continues with mutual verbal abuse, with blatantly false accusations (in the name of truth). Warwick then does two things simultaneously: he picks a white rose and commits himself thereby to York and his family; and he prophesies, "This brawl today, / Grown to this faction in the Temple garden, / Shall send, between the red rose and the white, / A thousand souls to death and deadly night" (124–27).

We already guess that proud Plantagenet tries to outdo the king's family, but the reasons are still obscure. In the following scene, we get some insight into the process of Richard's self-justification. Edmund Mortimer is dying, and he persuades Richard—whom it is easy to persuade—that through his own line, it is Richard and not Henry who has a legitimate claim to the English throne. Richard also has a legitimate grievance. His father had been executed by the former king because he took Mortimer's side. Yet the moment Mortimer dies, we can have a glimpse into the soul of Richard, who is both a cynic and a hypocrite. His brief funeral oration at the corpse of dead Mortimer sounds: "Here dies the dusky torch of Mortimer, / Choked with ambition of the meaner sort" (2.5.122–23). Certainly, he considers his own ambition one of the subtle sort.

The next scene is of great importance. It is the first scene of the third act. We are in the Parliament. It is here in the third act that King Henry VI enters the stage. He is still a child. The scene starts with the continuation of the story known from previous scenes: Winchester and Gloucester abuse one another. The York party is amused. The more the Lancasters hate one another, the better for them. It happens here that the young king intervenes.

There are few characters in Shakespeare who are so steady, so unchanging as the character of Henry VI. Only Richard III, in the play named after him, will be his match. The roots of radical good and radical evil are both transcendent. They simply are. There is no explanation why Henry VI is radically good and Richard radically evil. Yet these are the characters who do not undergo essential changes, at least not character changes. Henry VI will have many bitter life experiences, and this will give him new thoughts and new ideas. But his character will remain exactly the same as it was in his childhood. At first his goodness expresses itself in religious terms; later he will discover the moral law, which will a few centuries later be named by Kant "the categorical imperative." But whether he justifies his feelings and convictions with the Bible, with common reason, or with the moral law, his moral constitution comes first and his justifications second, so much so that when he needs to persuade himself that in order to rule better he should not act anymore out of goodness, he cannot do so. He will only become passive, realizing that he can only be good.

When we see Henry VI for the first time, we see him through and through. He is transparent; he has no undercover persona. Sometimes he is accused of being naïve, but he becomes less and less naïve. Still, he can act only as if he were naïve. This is his character.

He now interferes in the ugly and bitter brawl with the following words: "Uncles of Gloucester and of Winchester, / The special watchmen of our English weal, / I would prevail, if prayers might prevail, / To join your hearts in love and amity. . . . Believe me, lords, my tender years can tell / Civil dissention is a viperous worm / That gnaws the bowels of the Commonwealth" (3.1.66–74). This king does not command, he prays; he does not utter imperatives, he tries to persuade. And he believes in love. He turns to Winchester: "Who should be pitiful if you be not?" (3.112). It is Gloucester who yields. The good Humphrey gets easily enraged, but he loves his Henry and knows what is right. Winchester is not angry, he is rancorous, he does not want to yield. But the king turns to him again pleadingly, and finally it comes to the reconciliation between the two fiends. The king is happy as only a child can be. He also speaks as a child: "O loving uncle . . . How joyful am I made by this contract!" (3.145–46). Then comes the petition of Richard Plantagenet. The king is again forthcoming and mild: he makes Plantagenet the Duke of York, returns to him his father's inheritance. Yet all the reconciliations are faked. The hatred between the uncle and the nephew, between York and Lancaster, keeps burning and spreads fast. When the king and the dukes leave for the coronation, Exeter is left behind as the chorus. He knows that the conflict "burns under feigned ashes of forged love, / And will at last break out into a flame" (3.194–95). Here he refers back to an old prophecy (well known in Shakespeare's times): "That 'Henry born at Monmouth should win all / And Henry born at Windsor lose all'" (3.202–3).

In 4.1, in a scene in France with Talbot (which I have already discussed), the peers arrive already wearing white and red roses. This is the first time that the new rift, the novel feud, reaches the king's ear. He turns to the warring lords and says, "Good Lord, what madness rules in brainsick men / When for so slight and frivolous a cause / Such factious emulations shall arise? / Good cousins both of York and Somerset, / Quiet yourselves, I pray, and be with peace" (4.1.111–15). The king fails to command; again he makes just an appeal. To what does he appeal? He appeals to reason. The whole dispute seems sheer madness to him. Those men are all like Fortinbras: they fight and would die for entirely nonsensical issues. We notice for the first time that the goodness of the king is rational. Yet, his reason is not of the instrumental kind. It is not the kind of rationality that finds the proper means to achieve goals. His reason is, rather, a moral kind of reason. It is for him morally absurd for men to fight over trifles. On the ground of Henry's constant appeal to right reason (the *recta ratio* of the Renaissance, so boldly represented by Erasmus), we could place Henry among those who follow the laws of nature rather than those of tradition. Yet this would not really do justice to Henry's way of thinking. For Henry VI—like radically good persons in general—is neither old-fashioned nor new-fashioned, neither traditional nor a self-made man in a self-made world. He is rather, transcultural, transhistorical. True, Henry's moral reasons are not always apolitical. They are fairly sound, as recta ratio normally is. For example, he appeals to the lords to make peace with one another with the following words: "And you, my lords, remember where we are— / In France . . . what infamy will then arise / When foreign princes shall be certified / That for a toy, a thing of no regard, / King Henry's peers and chief nobility / Destroyed themselves and lost the realm of France! / O think upon the conquest of my father, / My tender years, and let us not forgo / That for a trifle that was bought with blood. / Let me umpire in this doubtful strife. / I see no reason, if I wear this rose" (137–52). The whole argument is politically sound, but the picking of the red rose is a grave political mistake. Henry does not see any reason why he should not have picked the red (he could have picked the white), because it is only a trifle in his eyes, a toy. And he is a child. Henry, like all moral rationalists, has no sense of the symbolic dimensions. Political symbols mean nothing to him. They are not rational. But for the dukes who have surrounded him, the king's picking the red rose means to give a sign. (Had he picked the white one, the reaction would have been similar, but in another orchestration.) Historical actors attribute significance to symbols; they often think in symbols. But Henry VI, who is playing on a historical stage, plays a drama that is suited only and exclusively to the existential stage. He has no understanding of historical mythologies. Exeter, who is here still assigned by Shakespeare to play the role of the chorus of the English nobility, also ends this scene with his prophecies and lamentations.

And now, after the predictable loss of France, after the increasing enmity within the House of Lancaster, after the struggle for power between the Lancaster clan and the York clan, comes the last die thrown from the last dice box: sexual subversion. As in the second and the third cases, the child-king's reactions will be entirely unworldly. I would agree with Hannah Arendt that unworldliness is apolitical.

The situation is already dangerous, but this is not perceived by the loyal men of the king, let alone by the king himself. He is still a child; he speaks as a child. However, he is already exactly the same person he will be to the very end of his sad life. When Gloucester suggests that he make peace with France through a good marriage, he answers, "Ay, marry, uncle; for I always thought / It was both impious and unnatural / That such immanity and bloody strife / Should reign among professors of one faith" (5.1.11–14). After the concrete, politically sound marriage proposition is made, he repeats: "Marriage, uncle! Alas, my years are young, / And fitter is my study and my books / Than wanton dalliance with a paramour. / Yet call th'ambassadors" (5.1.21–24). This expression, "wanton dalliance with a paramour," is itself bookish, showing a child without erotic experience. This plan of royal marriage is crossed by Suffolk's design. He falls in love with Margaret in France. He cannot live without her (and we know from the unfolding of the story that this is meant seriously). He must find a way to be with her. Thus he schemes to marry her to the king of England, to make her queen. The plan is sound on the side of Suffolk, but why does young Henry walk into the trap? Sure, these are historical facts Shakespeare could not alter. But he could have provided some motivations. In fact, he does not. For Henry's character itself "explains," if there is something to explain, why he enters this unsound marriage while annulling an earlier obligation. It explains why at this point exactly he does not listen to anyone's advice (except Suffolk's). He says that the reason is that Suffolk described so graphically Margaret's exceptional beauty (5.5). Why does he not change his mind and refuse Margaret? After all, Gloucester, who is his uncle and loyal protector, advises him to change it before it is too late. One cannot explain this, yet one understands it. He is an unworldly youth; he never listens to political exigencies. For him there is only one relevant voice: the voice of the heart. Here the voice of the heart was the voice of love. To fall in love by seeing a person's portrait was common until the eighteenth century—certainly on the stage, but perhaps also in real life. Since falling in love is not rational, it is triggered and not explained. A portrait is as good as the vision of the person. Here, however, Shakespeare presents us with something in between. Henry does not receive a portrait of Margaret; neither does he see Margaret with his eyes. He rather listens to the description of a girl by her lover. Suffolk is in love; he describes Margaret as a lover. Love begets love; it is in a way infectious. Henry becomes infected by the passionate love of the man who describes Margaret. Henry is likewise falling in love with Margaret, and he knows it: "Whether it be through force of your report, / My noble lord of Suffolk, or for that / My tender youth was never yet attaint / With any passion of inflaming love, / I cannot tell; but this I am assured: / I feel such sharp dissension in my breast" (79–84). And when he turns to his uncle, he turns to him as an uncle and not as the protector of the realm; he asks him simply for personal understanding.

Henry's antipolitical decision will be from this moment onward the constant point of reference of his enemies (and some of his friends). He marries a poor girl instead a rich one, he loses territories instead of gaining some. And Margaret is an alien, a foreigner. She is "the French woman," carrying with herself foreign customs and unusual attitudes, claims, and habits. She remains the thorn in the flesh of the English court. And her sheer presence causes a new division among the king's men. Until now it was the hatred and enmity between Winchester and Gloucester, particularly the ambition and the rancor of the former, that poisoned the ties of the family of Lancaster. Now Suffolk's ambition is added to the danger of dissension.

Shakespeare presents this in two brief monologues, both at the end of a scene where the his marriage is discussed and decided. Act 5, scene 2, ends with Winchester's words directed to the absent peers, especially the absent Gloucester: "Now Winchester will not submit. . . . I'll either make thee stoop and bend thy knee, / Or sack this country with a mutiny" (5.1.56–62). And the whole drama ends with the words of Suffolk: "Margaret shall now be queen and rule the King; / But I will rule both her, the King, and realm" (5.7.107–8). Neither of these designs will succeed, but both will do much harm.

Thus the first drama of Henry VI ends with marriage. It is the typical "happy ending" of a comedy. Yet this is the marriage of the gathering storm. We already know that the storm is going to break out soon. We know it even if we have not the faintest knowledge of English history. The gathering storm is "produced" by the play.

2 Henry VI

In the second part of *Henry VI* (which was, as we know, originally the first), a whole gallery of new characters enters the stage, while many characters of the first part disappear for good, mostly because Shakespeare follows closely the "truth of facts" of the chronicles. (For example, we know that Bedford died in France.) Also in part 2, the drama continues to present a broad historical tableau rich in minidramas, minitragedies, and minicomedies. It is frequently considered an oddity that Talbot's name is not even mentioned in the second and third parts of *Henry VI*. Why hasn't Shakespeare let his characters allude to the hero of the first part of the drama, after having reworked the second and third parts? There is no answer to this question, although I do not miss such references. Talbot belongs to a sinking world, to an age before the deluge, with little relevance for the deadly and self-destructive struggles of the families entangled in the Wars of the Roses.

In the final version of *2 Henry VI,* the action begins as the direct continuation of the last scene of *1 Henry VI.* We can hardly take a breath. This is the wedding day of the king: it is the first time that he looks at his queen-to-be, and all his expectations are confirmed. He is in love with her: "Her sight did ravish, but her grace in speech, / Her words clad with wisdom's majesty, / Makes me from wond'ring fall to weeping joys, / Such is the fullness of my heart's content. / Lords, with one cheerful voice, welcome my love" (1.1.30–34). We may wonder, what is happening here? In all the works of Shakespeare, Margaret is the only woman who is deeply loved by two entirely different but extremely significant men. She is loved by the ruthless, self-made man, Suffolk, who is formerly De la Pole; and she is loved by the good King Henry, the son and grandson of King Henry. She is loved by both from the beginning, from the first moment that these men cast a glance upon her, until the grave. Margaret loves them both, although with very different kinds of love. As a passionate, desiring woman she loves Suffolk, and as a caring and anxious mother she loves her husband. We rarely sympathize with her. She is with justification called a tigress; she is ruthless and cruel to everyone except her men (including later also her son). She is ready to assist murder, to torture, and to mock the enemies of her men. But it is not for her cruelty, or her ruthlessness, or even for her absolute loyalty that she is most noteworthy. For one can still speak of the loyalty of a woman who belongs simultaneously to two men. But it is for something else that she must be noted. Margaret has to have some radiance around her, which makes her unlike all the women of England. Perhaps this is because she is a foreigner, with different habits, but perhaps it is also because of her very personal attraction. There is another ruthless woman in this play: Lady Eleanor, the wife of good Humphrey. But she is a straightforward, proud English duchess with no special appeal. Margaret has many faces; she is passionate and unpredictable. If she reminds us of another female character by Shakespeare, it is Cleopatra, the "oriental" woman. But Cleopatra is loved only by Antony, and she is never wicked, only opportunistic. Margaret, whom Shakespeare portrays all the way from her blooming youth to her bitter old age, is one of the greatest female puzzles in his entire oeuvre.

I mentioned that Henry's marriage enrages not only the lukewarm supporters of the king but also his most loyal friends. This includes his protector, particularly because the duchy of Anjou and the county of Maine are released to the father of the bride. Everyone is against this unusually bad business except the king and Suffolk. The king sees no obstacles, and he makes no conditions; he does not notice the resistance or thinks it to be a mere trifle. Gloucester predicts that France will be lost because of this unsound decision. To us this seems unlikely. That the prediction comes true has in itself no significance, for in all probability it also would have happened in the case of a better dynastic marriage. Still, this event in itself will be of great significance for the future. One of the peers whose reactions

Shakespeare presents before our eyes is Warwick. He will turn against the king, he says, because of the king's weakness to the queen. This is what he claims, but how can we be sure? Warwick was the one who won both Anjou and Maine in battle for England. He takes the loss of these territories as a gesture of contempt directed against his own person. The king's unconcerned, unworldly generosity hurts him above all. The future king-maker will from this moment on lend an attentive ear to York's ambitions and designs. Would he have done so without the loss of Maine and Anjou? We cannot know. This is just one of the interpretations of Warwick's change of loyalty. The acts and choices of Shakespeare's characters are interpreted first by the characters of the plays themselves, and in a great variety of ways. There is a continuity of guesswork and of understanding between the characters on stage and off.

For the present it is not yet Warwick but his father, Salisbury, who begins to tamper with the wheel of fortune. The ever growing discord between uncle and nephew, bursting out every other minute in public, first gives plausibility to the idea of replacing the present protector, Gloucester, with York. We, the audience, already know that York's ambition does not fall short of becoming king and that Salisbury, even if he is not familiar with his ambitious design, is already capable of making a decent guess about York's character. A minor alliance is now formed within a broader conspiracy. From this moment on, Salisbury and Warwick put their bets on the rising star of York.

York remains alone in the chamber. This is his finest hour. In this very moment he keeps his finger on the pulse of politics. As a well-instructed Machiavellian, he figures out how to act and behave in order to snatch the crown from Henry, just as once upon a time Bolingbroke snatched it from Richard. There are a few common motives in both plays. For example, Richard considers that although the commoners love Gloucester, they hate Suffolk, the rude and ruthless, and his lover, the foreign Margaret. On the other hand, Warwick and York may get the support of the people, and they may also mobilize the people against their king. As we shall see, this strategy will be crowned with success. York begins to design his own prospects and the best way for him to proceed: "And therefore I will take the Nevilles' parts, / And make a show of love to proud Duke Humphrey, / And when I spy advantage, claim the crown, / For that's the golden mark I seek to hit. / Nor shall proud Lancaster usurp my right, / Nor hold the sceptre in his childish fist, / Nor wear the diadem upon his head / Whose church-like humours fits not for a crown. / Then, York, be still a while, till time do serve. . . . Then will I raise aloft the milk-white rose . . . To grapple with the house of Lancaster; / And force perforce I'll make him yield the crown, / Whose bookish rule hath pulled fair England down" (240–59). This is the first time that this particular pretender to the throne appears—at least for himself—in full armor. However, if we listen to the monologue carefully, we notice that this York is still closer to Henry IV as Bolingbroke than to his son, the later Richard, Gloucester. But as the drama unfolds, York will leave behind the sound, although cruel, Machiavellian design to become his youngest son's father. He will become wicked, even if not absolutely evil. Here he is not yet a model "sitting" for his son. He has an idea about kairos; he is up to grasp his time. He begins to believe that he has a stronger claim to the throne than Henry (a claim that is weak enough, but becomes strong through belief). He believes that he would make a better king, for Henry is unfit for the throne. This is not a bad observation. Henry's speech is church-like and his interest is "bookish." What kind of king reads rather than acts? York's description of Henry reminds us of the self-description of Prospero recollecting his time as a prince: since he immersed himself in reading his books on magic, he neglected his princely duties and encouraged his broth-er to occupy his throne. York argues that the royal scepter goes with royal responsibilities: if someone cannot fulfill those responsibilities, then he had better resign as king. York's soliloquy is no reflection on history, since he has not the slightest historical imagination. It is a political speech and as such it is also fair. We know, however, that York will soon lose his cool compo-sure, and he will not remain a skilled Machiavellian but will become more and more the slave of his chaotic and increasingly bad impulses. This is why it is here that we meet York at his finest hour.

Gloucester, the protector, is the biggest obstacle to York's ambitious designs. But he is also a stumbling block for Suffolk's ambitions. York does not yet fight the next round of the power struggle against Lancaster. But it remains within the family of Lancaster, not just between Winchester and Gloucester as before, since Suffolk, too, enters the ring. Suffolk does not want to be king, but the chief adviser of the king and the mightiest and wealthiest duke of England. From this moment on, everyone—except Henry—will make designs against all the others. At the end, the crisscrossed threads of conspiracy will not lead to a planned result. The actors will out-wit one another—first and foremost themselves.

Events begin to accelerate in act 1. The acceleration of the unfolding of the plot is accompanied by the increase of its density. Or rather, it happens by the impression of greater and greater density resulting from the fast alteration of the crisscrossings of several conspiracies, designs, and plans. Everyone is involved in "politicking," everyone wants to manipulate every-one else. The mutuality, yet not always reversibility, of hidden manipula-tions, undisclosed designs, secret plans, and so on, gives the impression of irrationality. The more hidden designs, the more secret plans, the more cal-culated risks the audience witnesses, the more irrational all the feverish cal-culation seems. It is as if these constantly scheming, politicking dukes are moved by an invisible power, as if they were pulled by the strings of a puppeteer. In fact, although there is no *fatum* here but the offspring of the actors' minds, souls, and actions, the impression of sitting in a puppet theater is not mere illusion. In spite of all this designing and scheming, very soon the actors are in fact led by their blind emotions. Their designs are not truly designs but the manifestations of their passions in their consciousness. The burning ambition of York will not ever allow him to keep cool. The burning jealousy of both Suffolk and the queen will never allow them to measure the strength of their enemies with a cool mind. I have not yet mentioned the madly jealous and ambitious Eleanor. The heat of passions, of all possible uncontrolled passions, fills the air with the scent of irrationality. For we already feel that all those calculations and plans will fail, perhaps because they are only Machiavellian in their outer form. Their content remains suicidal impulse. All the actors of *2 Henry VI* and *3 Henry VI* are possessed by suicidal impulses except the king and Gloucester. Both are helpless, the king because of his absolute goodness, which is apolitical and unworldly, and Humphrey because of his rectitude, which is old-fashioned. Even this old-fashioned rectitude has to face the greatest horror in his wife, this first Shakespearean edition of Lady Macbeth. Imagine a Lady Macbeth whose husband is a man of unbending rectitude, and who loves his wife. Just imagine how the whole ethical universe collapses for this man. His whole world collapses and there is no fundament under his feet, for he knows not the world. If you can imagine this, you will suffer the pains of the Duke of Gloucester. These are pains that are not rooted in his character or in his deeds, which have nothing to do with him as a man and or with his simple loyalty to his nephew, the king. This is the suffering that makes a home in one's soul when one no longer understands one's world.

The experience of the loss of the firm foundation of one's life makes the minitragedy, played out by Duchess of Gloucester and the duke, so important. It is the conflict between an old-fashioned, upright man who believes he knows his duty and who loves his wife, and the duchess, the ambition-haunted, ruthless woman who could not care less for those old-fashioned duties. She turns to sorcery as the means to achieve all that she desired to achieve, to become the queen of England. She does not do this through clever Machiavellian designs but through magic—through the control of nature.

Shakespeare here introduces the female couple of mutual hatred, the female counterpart of the male couple of mutual hatred that is Winchester and Gloucester. Queen Margaret and Duchess Gloucester "repeat" the story of Winchester and Gloucester. Gloucester, the king's uncle, wields the supreme power after the king. Winchester, the bastard great-uncle, has grown dark jealousy in his heart. He believes himself to be better—better fit for the job—and he absolutely resents the contempt expressed by his nephew. Because upright Humphrey is not a saint like Henry, he rarely misses an opportunity to remark that Winchester is but the bastard of his grandfather, whereas he is the legitimate offspring. This story is repeated almost exactly between the two women. Margaret is the English queen; she has the supreme female power. Yet the duchess despises her and does not hide her contempt. The queen is not English, she is poor. One single garment of the duchess is worth more, Eleanor boasts, than all the properties of the queen's father. The queen responds to this contempt just like Winchester: with destructive hatred. She is determined to get rid of the duchess, and no means are too mean for her if only her goal can be attained. She believes that she will never become a real queen as long as the Duchess of Gloucester plays the queen. Her hatred is not just echoed but also fueled by Suffolk, who for his part resents the protector's influence and power. He also aspires to the second greatest power. Thus, we have three men who compete for the second-greatest power in the realm: Humphrey, who has it and does not want to lose it; Winchester, who wants to get it; and Suffolk, who also wants it. In addition to the three men who compete for the second supreme power, there is York, who aspires to the supreme power itself. Furthermore, there are Somerset and Warwick, who want to make him king. We now see the two women. One enjoys the greatest female power—not just of the throne, but also over two men. But she believes that she has no power as long as the duchess, the protector's wife, can tell her how she should behave in an English court. She is used to French customs, however, and the duchess treats her as the usurper of the English throne and as a whore. The duchess wants to see her husband as king, and to this end she first has to destroy Margaret and Suffolk. These are her greatest obstacles.

It is in these circumstances that the minitragedy of the Gloucester family unfolds. I already pointed out the existential importance of this minitragedy: it is about the loss of firm fundaments. Yet this minitragedy also has serious political consequences, for it will lead to Gloucester's downfall.

Once again, Shakespeare does not tell us that the trial of the duchess and Gloucester's downfall are necessary conditions for the Wars of the Roses. He just says that it happened this way, and that at least it can be understood this way. The die was cast this way. Just listen to the story and watch the characters in action.

Immediately in 1.2 we witness the tête-à-tête between the duke and the duchess. The duchess is straightforward: "Put forth thy hand, reach at the glorious gold. / What, is't too short? I'll lengthen it with mine" (1.2.11–12). Her husband answers: "O Nell, sweet Nell, if thou dost love thy lord, / Banish the canker of ambitious thoughts!" (1.2.17–18). He tells his dream. The dream is significant, not because this is actually going to happen (in fact, it does not happen exactly as in Humphrey's dream), but because it echoes Gloucester's fears. He was dreaming that his staff was broken in two (perhaps by the cardinal). On one piece there was the head of Somerset, on the other the head of Suffolk. Yet, after giving a superficial interpretation of the dream that does not interest us here, the duchess draws the image of herself as the queen of England to appeal to her husband. Humphrey not only answers in the negative, his "no" becomes more and more emphatic: "And wilt thou still be hammering treachery / To tumble down thy husband and thyself / From top of honour to disgrace's feet?" (1.2.47–49). For Gloucester, honor is still the highest prize to achieve, but for the duchess honor is just a word while power is everything. She does not listen; she does not yield. It is at this moment that she bemoans her fate of being born a woman. The theme of sexual subversion appears here for the second time in this drama. Both women, who are fighting one another, who will both lose everything, are guilty of the reversal of sexual roles. A few characters in the play also suggest that Henry VI is like a woman. For peacemaking is a woman's task, whereas cruelty and ambition are the stuff of men. Shakespeare portrays this but does not believe it. Listen to the duchess's voice in her sole soliloquy: "Were I a man, a duke, and next of blood, / I would remove these tedious stumbling blocks / And smooth my way upon their headless necks. / And, being a woman, I will not be slack / To play my part in fortune's pageant" (1.2.63–67). Why do I think that Shakespeare does not share the duchess's image of "being a man"? The whole play is witness to the foolishness of the duchess. Here every man (except Henry VI) acts in a way that, according to the duchess, victorious men should act. They all smooth their way upon their enemies' headless necks. And what is the result? That their own necks also become headless. Vanitatum vanitas. True, Henry VI meets the same fate, but he has at least not wronged anyone. He suffers injustice rather than committing injustice. The good man at least does not fare worse than the murderers do.

Among all the men and women sick with ambition, York is the only one who is able, at least for a while, to control his anger, to cover up his designs. This is why in Shakespeare's book he must come out—relatively and temperately—as the victor in the battle for power. Winchester, the duchess, Suffolk, and the queen are not hypocrites. Even if they keep some of their conspiratorial steps in the dark, their feelings, emotions, and ambitions are clear to everyone. Their skirmishes are played out in public, as is the expression of their hatred. Their feelings are written on their faces, in their gestures. In Shakespeare's understanding they must become the losers. The frequently portrayed collision or tension between passion and interest —which I discussed briefly in the first part of this book—appears here in the form of temporalized juxtaposition. One can follow one's interest only on the condition that one controls one's passions. This is what York is able to do, at least for a while, but neither of his competitors can do this. This is perhaps the case because in York's eyes, and in spite of his fraudulent claim of legitimacy, this is a competition, a contest, a game to win. For the others, it is not. They believe themselves superior to all the others either by birth or by personality, and they think that everything is due to them; perhaps this is why they do not for a moment hide their pride, because a hidden pride is no pride.

Consider, for example, act 1, scene 3. It is to be decided who the king wants to be the regent, Somerset or York. The king declares himself neutral. Warwick (of course) suggests York, and Buckingham, on his part, suggests Somerset for the position. Salisbury asks why Somerset should be preferred, and at this point the queen says, "Because the King, forsooth, will have it so" (1.3.118). (The king has no preference, as we know.) Gloucester, to save the situation, says: "Madam, the King is old enough himself / To give censure. These are no women's matters" (1.3.119–20). But Margaret is clever and plays the trump card: "If he be old enough, what needs your grace / To be Protector of his excellence?" (1.3.121–22). This hits home. But then, after Humphrey leaves the room, she drops her fan. "Give me my fan—what, minion, can ye not?" (1.3.141), and she gives the duchess a box on the ear. "I cry you mercy madam! Was it you?" (1.3.142) she asks. This is an unheard-of humiliation for a proud woman! And the duchess answers in kind: "Was 't I? Yea, I it was, proud Frenchwoman! / Could I come near your beauty with my nails, / I'd set my ten commandments in your face" (1.3.143–45). Then the king speaks: "Sweet aunt, be quiet—'twas against her will" (1.3.146). Duchess: "Against her will? Good King, look to't in time! / She'll pamper thee and dandle thee like a baby" (1.3.147–48). The scene discloses, among other things, something essential about the relationship of the main characters. The king is good, yet he cannot behave like a king. For the time being he does not even understand ambition and hatred. They are, so he says, not rational. As I mentioned, the goodness of the king is rational. Why do people hate one another? It makes no sense! Why would they hurt one another on purpose? It makes no sense! Why are they jealous, envious, or rancorous? They do more harm to their own souls than to the others. It makes no sense.

We might now look at the same scene with the queen's eyes. At the beginning of her marriage—this we receive from her mouth—she was disappointed in her husband. Before she met him, she fancied him as another Suffolk, but he turned out to be quite different. However, her disappointment slowly develops into an entirely different kind of love (and this change begins to develop here, as the duchess rightly observes). The king is unlike Suffolk. He is not the man adored and passionately desired. But he is still a man; he is a good son whom she protects as a son and loves as her elder son. She will frequently step into the shoes of the king. She will do things that are considered no woman's business (like taking command of the army) because her husband cannot do a man's traditional business well.

She will always defend her husband as her big baby.

It happened earlier that the Duchess of York decided to use witchcraft as the means to attain her goal of becoming the queen of England. Like all the main characters of the Lancaster house, she is also blinded by passion; her main passions are ambition and jealous hatred. It is easy to unmask and destroy her (along with her husband), with the help of an agent provocateur. It needs to be noted that this particular agent provocateur is employed by the cardinal (a member of the Lancaster family) and by the Duke of York together. The cardinal thus succeeds in getting rid of the duchess and Gloucester, but it is not he who will benefit from his success. The scene with the sorceress (1.4) also has a double function. It is prearranged to prove the wicked designs of the duchess. York will interrupt the session (of course) and ask the duchess with pretended surprise, "What, madame, are you there?" (1.4.43). It is, however, not prearranged that the spirit conjured up in the séance will give—like Macbeth's witches—ambiguous answers to the questions addressed to it. What shall become of the king? the spirit is asked. "The Duke yet lives that Henry shall depose, / But him outlive, and die a violent death" (1.4.31–32). Everyone can interpret this prophecy according to his or her own desires, because it is not sound reasoning but strong desire that creates make-believe. One can face the truth as blindly as the untruth. When the question of the Duke of Suffolk's fate is asked, the answer will be: "By water shall he die and take his end" (1.4.34). About the Duke of Somerset, the spirit says: "Let him shun castles" (1.4.36). The oracle has spoken, and the words linger in the minds of all the murderers and victims of this play. Only the upright Gloucester and the good king will be exceptions: they do not believe in witchcraft.

At the end of the first act, the ring that was formed around Gloucester by his enemies is closed. In the next two acts, the men and women who hold hands in the already closed circle to destroy Gloucester will draw nearer to the lamb that is standing unprotected in the middle of the circle in order to kill him.

True, even before the circle is closed, that is, before the unmasking of the duchess, Gloucester is already under siege. Take, for example, act 1, scene 3, where the commoners hand him a petition against Suffolk. He is then abused by everyone, particularly the queen, and he leaves the scene. Gloucester's leaving the scene at this moment adds an important shade to the portrayal of his character. Although proud and impulsive, he decides to control himself, to exercise his willpower. After returning he says: "Now, lords, my choler being overblown / With walking once about the quadrangle, / I come to talk of commonwealth affairs" (1.3.155–57). The pressure against Gloucester is already great when a comic (or perhaps not-so-comic) scene interrupts the main action. This is not a pause, because the scene will be essential in the continuation of the story. Peter, an apprentice, accuses his master of high treason because he said that York is the legitimate king of England. The master (Horner) denies the accusation. Although the fight between them is postponed for the following act (when the apprentice kills his fraudulent master in a duel or, to be more exact, a boxing match), the accusation is enough to allow Somerset instead of York to be appointed regent of France.

Let me turn to acts 2 and 3, where the ring around Gloucester is already closed (although at the beginning of 2.1 Gloucester is still unaware of it). An idyll opens the first scene of the second act at Saint Albans; the king is hawking for waterfowl in good company. The movement of the falcon pleases the king. He is happy, marveling about God's and nature's miracles: "But what a point, my lord, your falcon made, / And what a pitch she flew above the rest! / To see how God in all his creatures works! / Yea, man and birds are fain to climbing high" (2.1.5–8). But only the king thinks of nature and God. For the others the flight of the falcon is but a metaphor (wheeling up, swooping down) and a good starting point to burst into rage and hatred. The king's reaction to the outburst of rage and hatred is again in character. He does not command but asks, persuades: "I prithee peace, / Good Queen, and whet not on these furious peers— / For blessed are the peacemakers on earth" (2.1.33–34). Hidden from the king's eye, the cardinal and Gloucester challenge each other to a duel. The king seems not to notice: "The winds grow high; so do your stomachs, lords. / How irksome is this music to my heart! / When such strings jar, what hope of harmony? / I pray, my lords, let me compound this strife" (2.1.58–61). The king does not hear music, music serves him as a metaphor (just as the flight of the falcon does for the others). The metaphorical understanding of the falcon's flight is now answered in kind: employing the metaphor of the loss of harmony, of the "irksome music."

Here comes a pause. A comic scene of a phony miracle ends the seeming—because already undermined—idyll. Then enters Buckingham with news of the Duchess Eleanor's conspiracy. The cardinal, who never really wanted to carry on with the duel because he knows what Gloucester does not even guess (he was the one who employed the agent provocateur), turns to him with glee and satisfaction: "This news, I think, hath turned your weapon's edge. / 'Tis like, my lord, you will not keep your hour" (2.192–93). At this point Gloucester's comportment suddenly changes. He now realizes that he has lost, and he is stricken with grief. For he knows that the accusations might be true (remember his scene with his wife). He has not just lost, he is also beaten: "Ambitious churchman, leave to afflict my heart. / Sorrow and grief have vanquished all my powers, / And, vanquished as I am, I yield to thee / Or to the meanest groom" (194–97). And to the queen, he answers with dignity. He needs to carry on with double loyalty: to his king, betrayed by his wife, and to his wife, who perhaps has betrayed her sovereign: "But if she have forgot / Honour and virtue and conversed with such / As, like to pitch, defile nobility, / I banish her my bed and company, / And give her as a prey to law and shame / That hath dishonoured Gloucester's honest name" (206–11).

Suddenly something happens: at this very moment the king grows up. At the beginning of the idyllic scene he is still a boy, but at the end of the scene he will speak as a man. It is not his character that changes. For, I repeat, his goodness—as goodness in general—has transcendent sources and is as unchanging as the wickedness of radically wicked men like Richard III. But from this moment, he is not just good: he has convictions, and he begins to formulate his convictions in nontraditional terms. His commonsensical and naïve rationality gives way to a noncommonsensical and not-naïve principle. I would reformulate all this more drastically: King Henry VI discovers the categorical imperative; he becomes an early Kantian. It is from this moment on that he—as a Shakespearean character—occupies a significant position in history according to Shakespeare, although he remains always and to the end a bungler in politics.

Every "normal" king or perhaps even "normal" man would answer to the news of a conspiracy against his life and power with anger, rage, or even hatred. But not this king: "O God, what mischiefs work the wicked ones, / Heaping confusion on their own heads thereby!" (198). These are the words of a good man, but not of a naïve man. For what he says is true, and it is true in the very context where the words were uttered. It is true about the duchess, but not only about her; it is about all the wicked men in this story. The king imitates Christ. He forgives, as he always has and always will. But forgiveness is one thing, and justice another. As a man, he forgives; but for the king this is irrelevant. For the first time in the story, and in fact both the first and the last time in all the Shakespearean stories of kings and kingdoms, law will become the sovereign of the state. The words of the king will declare: we heard here a serious accusation. We cannot pretend that nothing has happened. Let an impartial court deal with the case. So justice will be done: "Tomorrow toward London back again, / To look into this business thoroughly, / And call these foul offenders to their answers, / And poise the cause in Justice equal scales, / Whose beam stands sure, whose rightful cause prevails" (213–17). A new discrepancy opens up here. This is not the discrepancy between a royal role and a saintly child as a king unfit for the role, but the discrepancy between the perfect Christian prince and the situation in which he was fated to reign. Henry becomes the mirror of the perfect Christian prince, of the authentic and real anti-Machiavellian prince. However, the situation where Henry suddenly grows up to become the mirror of the Christian prince first calls for a Machiavellian prince. But there is none around Henry, not even among his enemies.

But before we next see the king, we are guided to participate in a supper party with a purpose: conspiracy. The dukes conspired earlier, yet now the purpose is clearly formulated and sealed with a symbolic gesture. Warwick and Salisbury, son and father, the "kingmakers," kneel down before York, the pretender to the throne, and hail him: "Long live our sovereign Richard, England's king!" But York, who still seems to be the perfect Machiavellian, warns them immediately, "I am not your king / Till I be crowned, and that my sword be stained / With heart-blood of the house of Lancaster" (2.2.64–66). But at this moment, this is not their task. For the Lancaster family itself will perform the bulk of the bloody work for them: "Till they have snared the shepherd of the flock, / That virtuous prince, the good Duke Humphrey. . . . 'Tis that they seek, and they, in seeking that, / Shall find their deaths, if York can prophesy" (73–76). York prophesied well, although he did not prophesy all. We can again observe the way in which, in Shakespeare's portrayal, the minds of politicking but passion-driven men work. That is, York believes that what he desires is what is true, and he will never consider as a possibility what he abhors.

In 2.3 we are in London at the duchess's trial. The action begins to accelerate. There is no doubt that the downfall of Humphrey will closely follow the downfall of his wife. It is the question of time—a very short time. The king finds Eleanor guilty (she is in fact guilty) and sends her into exile to the Isle of Man after three days of public penance. Gloucester is a broken man. He knows that the judgment is just. We remember that he formulated the phrase previously in terms of whether his wife is proven guilty, but now he admits that she was. "Eleanor, the law, thou seest, hath judged thee; / I cannot justify whom the law condemns. . . . I beseech your majesty, give me leave to go. / Sorrow would solace, and mine age would ease" (2.3.15–21). At this point the king intervenes and asks Gloucester to surrender his office: "Henry will to himself / Protector be; and God shall be my hope, / My stay, my guide, and lantern to my feet. / And go in peace, Humphrey, no less beloved / Than when thou wert Protector to thy King" (2.3.23–27). Thus speaks the perfect Christian prince, surrounded by wolves.

The banished duchess knows everything about the wolves. This is easy for her, as she is a wolf herself. She knows that Gloucester should have defended her at all costs, guilty or not guilty. By being "mild" (do not forget, mildness is one of the greatest virtues in Shakespeare's book!) he becomes the loser: "And fly thou how thou canst, they'll tangle thee" (2.4.56). She is politically right although morally wrong, and Gloucester is politically wrong and morally right: "And had I twenty times so many foes, / And each of them had twenty times their power, / All these could not procure me any scathe / So long as I am loyal, true, crimeless" (2.4.61–64). Gloucester is a coplayer now with the king. Both are acting as if they were living in the ideal kingdom of the Christian prince where justice prevails, where the innocent has nothing to fear. Was Gloucester absolutely wrong?

Was the duchess absolutely right? What would have happened had Gloucester also joined the wolves? We guess that he would have been murdered too, perhaps a little later; and in addition, he would have lost his pride, self-esteem, and honor.

The second act ends with the duchess going to her banishment. Yet something else happens before the last farewell. The herald arrives to summon Gloucester to his majesty's Parliament. Gloucester is taken aback, for it happened the first time that his consent was not asked. He forgot for a moment that he was no more the protector. But then, he wakes up to the dark morning of the present: "Well, I will be there" (74).

Act 3.1 is the very heart of *2 Henry VI*. We are in the Parliament house, and Gloucester has not yet arrived. In his absence everyone abuses him and accuses him of a great variety of different crimes—the queen, Suffolk, and the cardinal alike. They put pressure on the king. They are sure that the "weak" king can be easily influenced, that he will yield. But the king is as strong as steel. However, he has to serve two masters: the course of the legal law on the one hand, and the course of his own conscience on the other. He makes it clear that the procedure of the law will be followed. Where there are accusations, there must be a hearing, there must be a trial. If this were not so, the laws of the state would be in shambles. And Henry is determined to uphold the laws: without the rule of the law there can be no justice. This is the kind of formalism he believes must be observed. Simultaneously, he lets the voice of his own conscience speak, and he speaks according to the dictates of his conscience: "My lords, at once: the care you have of us / To mow down thorns that would annoy our foot / Is worthy of praise, but shall I speak my conscience? / Our kinsman Gloucester is as innocent / From meaning treason to our royal person / As is the sucking lamb or harmless dove. / The Duke is virtuous, mild, and too well given / To dream on evil or to work on my downfall" (3.1.66–73).

Somerset enters and brings news of the loss of all the French territories. Then enters Gloucester, already abused and accused in his absence. The moment he enters, Suffolk arrests him for high treason. And now the accusations are loosed. (The news about the loss of France is new fuel on the already nurtured flames of hatred and wish for destruction.) One groundless accusation after another falls onto Gloucester's head. He defends himself, just as a single swordsman can defend himself against a bunch of robbers and assassins. All the accusations are false; they are slanderous. No one listens. All hell breaks loose, and there sits the king. What does he do? He does not use his authority to interfere. Could he have done so? With what results? These are not questions for Henry. For he is not interested in the consequences of his action or inaction, he is interested in one thing alone: whether his acts can serve as a norm—a model for a better future. Thus he says: "My Lord Gloucester, 'tis my special hope / That you will clear yourself from all suspense. / My conscience tells me you are innocent" (139–41). Henry VI believes in "fair trial," not because he believes that this trial will be fair, but because he believes in a fair trial as such, which cannot be replaced by a commanding voice or the decision of any authority. But he also knows—only too well—that it is unlikely that this trial could be fair. Yet it is still possible. And then he does something that astonishes everyone. Together with Gloucester, who is taken by guards, he stands up and leaves Parliament. He allows the law to take its course. But he must express his deep disgust and distrust to the actual members of Parliament, particularly to the peers. Margaret turns to him: "What, will your highness leave the Parliament?" (197). And the king answers: "Ay, Margaret, my heart is drowned with grief. . . . Ah, uncle Humphrey, in thy face I see / The map of honour, truth, and loyalty. . . . His fortunes I will weep, and 'twixt each groan, / Say 'Who's a traitor? Gloucester, he is none'" (198–222).

Is the king's firmness in permitting the law to take its course compatible with his absolute conviction of Gloucester's innocence? I think, conditionally, that the answer is yes. As we have seen many times, it is not only the audience or the readers who interpret the actors, but the actors also interpret the other actors continuously. So it is after Henry has left the Parliament. The enemies of Gloucester—some of whom are also enemies of the king—wonder whether Gloucester will be acquitted rather than condemned if the law is allowed to take its normal course. The queen, Winchester, York, and Suffolk realize that Gloucester can still be saved and that they need to turn to other, more radical means if they want to destroy him for sure. The queen says, "Henry my lord is cold in great affairs" (224). She means, thereby, that he is not ruthless and cruel, and she comes to the conclusion: "This Gloucester should be quickly rid the world / To rid us from the fear we have of him" (233–34). The cardinal (the most wicked among this bunch of people) adds, "That he should die is worthy policy; / But yet we want a colour for his death. / 'Tis meet he be condemned by course of law" (235–37). Suffolk retorts, "But, in my mind, that were not policy. / The King will labour still to save his life, / The commons haply rise to save his life; / And yet we have but trivial argument / More than mistrust that shows him worthy of death" (238–42). Was the king not right? Was his judgment not sound? If the arguments against Gloucester were "trivial," as Suffolk himself admitted, would he not be acquitted? And Suffolk follows the well-known argument of the story about the wolf and the lamb: "No— let him die in that he is a fox, / By nature proved an enemy to the flock. . . . And do not stand on quillets how to slay him; / Be it by gins, by snares, by subtlety, / Sleeping or walking, 'tis not matter how, / So he be dead." (257–64). Then Winchester, the cardinal, offers him a helping hand: "Say you consent and censure well the deed, / And I'll provide his executioner; / I tender so the safety of my liege" (275–77). The conference concerning the murder of Humphrey ends with the reassurance of the cardinal: "No more of him—for I will deal with him / That henceforth he shall trouble us no more" (323–24). And this takes place in less than a single day.

There is something more. Winchester wishes the death of his uncle, but not the death of the king, the doom of his house. York goes to Ireland with the feigned purpose of bringing down the rebellion and with the true but concealed purpose of using the rebellion against his king. He still seems to be the perfect Machiavellian. He still keeps cool; he can still calculate a few steps ahead in view of the next action. He is not carried away by anything other than his cold ambition. Yet, somehow he becomes the father of Richard III. He does not kill or allow killing just for the end's sake, but also for the sake of the game. He enjoys his ability to fool the unsuspecting ones; he shows some signs of love of cruelty.

Act 3, scene 1 ends with Richard's soliloquy. This is an important moment, for the future appears here as it is present in the mind of one of its planners. The actions and happenings of the scenes that recount the maturation of the king and the final sealing of Gloucester's fate are summed up by a man who looks back to the event from the perspective of his future: "Be that thou hop'st to be, or what thou art / Resign to death; it is not worth th'enjoying. . . . My brain, more busy than the labouring spider, / Weaves tedious snares to trap mine enemies. . . . For Humphrey being dead, and he shall be, / And Henry put apart, the next for me" (333–83). The sentence "Be that thou hops't to be, or what thou art" is the gesture of an existential choice. York has chosen himself as the future king; he has chosen for himself his destiny. But every existential choice that is not the choice of our own goodness can fail. Henry has chosen himself as a man of the "categorical imperative." Richard has chosen himself as being destined to become a king. They are two different choices of the self, two different destinies.

Shakespeare will compose several scenes of assassination in which an innocent man becomes the victim of brutal murder. Here (3.2) he avoids making us witness to the act itself. When the murderers appear on the scene, the act has already been accomplished. However, one of the themes, which will be so important morally for Shakespeare later, is already voiced here, albeit in a shorter version. There are two murderers; for one of them murder is just a performance of a duty or the exercise of a skill, while the other begins to feel the sting of conscience.

The king appears to open the trial of Gloucester: "Go call our uncle to our presence straight. / Say we intend to try his grace today / If he be guilty, as 'tis published" (3.2.15–17). The king here behaves just like a contemporary judge. Gloucester is innocent unless proven guilty. Justice has to take its course. Let me repeat my question: isn't this king naïve? I suppose it depends on what naïveté is. He believes in the sacredness of the law. And he does not believe that the members of his family will be poised to commit

a foul murder. Suffolk, who has already received news of the successful assassination, then pretends to call Gloucester to his trial and returns with the
"news" (it is no news for him) that Gloucester is dead. The cardinal, who in
fact hired the assassins, adds: "God's secret judgement. I did dream tonight /
The Duke was dumb and could not speak a word" (3.2.31–32). The king
swoons. This moment of fainting is, again, filled with meaning. The king
loses consciousness to bear the suddenly understood truth that he is surrounded not just by ambitious and rancorous peers but by evil itself. This is
why he reacts with such a heavy rejection to Suffolk's gesture of comfort:
"Hide not thy poison with such sugared words. / Lay not thy hands on
me—Forbear, I say! / Their touch affrights me as a serpent's sting. . . . Look
not upon me, for thine eyes are wounding— / Yet do not go away. Come,
basilisk, / And kill the innocent gazer with thy sight" (3.2.45–53). Do not
touch me! Do not look at me! The basilisk—as we know—kills with its
look. It kills the body, and perhaps also the soul.

At this moment it will be obvious that the mild and good-hearted king
will not tolerate evil around him, not for a moment. Now comes the
queen, pleading for Suffolk. She also makes a grave mistake, together with
her lover. She believes that since her husband well tolerates Suffolk as her
lover, he will also well tolerate him as the murderer of his uncle. She is,
indeed, naïve. This is Margaret's greatest misunderstanding. She belongs to
the gallery of Shakespearean heroes who have in general a good judgment
of character but do not know the character of their own spouses. Margaret
now thinks that she can blackmail her husband with love: "Be woe for me,
more wretched than he is. / What, dost thou turn away and hide thy face?
I am no loathsome leper—look on me! / What art thou, like the adder,
waxen deaf? / Be poisonous too and kill thy forlorn queen. . . . Die, Margaret, / For Henry weeps that thou dost live so long" (3.2.73–121). Never
was Margaret more mistaken. The mild Henry will remain firm and will
never yield.

Now enter the men of York. This is the time York has long awaited. Now
he can get rid of his enemies. Warwick publicly accuses Suffolk and the cardinal of Gloucester's murder. We know that this is the plain truth. So does
the king. But he does not say so, because no law, no court of justice, has yet
proven it true. So he answers: "That he is dead, good Warwick, 'tis too true.
/ But how he died God knows, not Henry. / Enter his chamber, view his
breathless corpse, / And comment then upon his sudden death"
(3.2.130–33). That is, according to the law of justice, the king orders an
autopsy.

Henry remains alone, and then he prays: "O thou that judges all things,
stay my thoughts, / My thoughts that labour to persuade my soul / Some
violent hands were laid on Humphrey's life. / If my suspect be false, forgive
me God, / For judgment only doth belong to thee" (3.2.136–40). Men

come in carrying Gloucester's body. They reveal the signs of murder on Humphrey's dead body: he was strangled. Then comes the second round of hypocrisy. Suffolk protests indignantly against the accusation of having done what he has indeed done. It is one of Shakespeare's deepest observations: that a man who is guilty as hell can truly maneuver himself into a state of righteous indignation if others accuse him of his deed. Warwick now accuses Suffolk (rightly), yet Suffolk does not show the slightest sign of guilt. He calls his accuser a "blunt witted lord" as well as a bastard. The two men draw their swords. Salisbury enters with the commoners, who all want Suffolk banished or dead. The king then tells them that he has already resolved to do exactly this. Of course, he doesn't mean that he will let Suffolk be executed, but that he will banish him from his lands. This is the first case in which Henry punishes like a king, and this is why he takes an oath. He knows that he will never break a commandment. One should not take God's name in vain. Without taking an oath, he still could have yielded, but he does not want to yield: "And therefore, by His majesty I swear, / Whose far unworthy deputy I am, / He shall not breathe infection in this air / But three days longer, on the pain of death" (3.2.289–92). And when the queen turns to him weeping, "O Henry, let me plead for gentle Suffolk" (293), he answers, "Ungentle Queen, to call him gentle Suffolk. / No more, I say! If thou dost plead for him / Thou wilt but add increase unto my wrath. / Had I but said, I would have kept my word; / But when I swear, it is irrevocable" (3.2.294–98).

And then follows perhaps the most beautiful love scene Shakespeare ever wrote, the love scene discussed in the first part of this book. Suffolk departs to his banishment.

Let me now return to an earlier part of the 3.2 scene. When Warwick and Suffolk stand there with their weapons drawn, the king ruminates in a very unkingly manner: "What stronger breastplate than a heart untainted? / Thrice is he armed that hath his quarrel just; / And he but naked, though locked up in steel, / Whose conscience with injustice is corrupted" (3.2.232–35). For even if every word of this text sounds true, and for the king it does, royalty is not about an "unstained soul." A king is responsible not only for the eternal happiness of his soul but also—first of all—for the well-being of his country. My question is whether the king feels this responsibility or not. The discrepancy between "political" and "historical" appears already at this stage. Politically, Henry would have acted rightly in the Parliament had he immediately banished Suffolk, York, and all their men and defended Gloucester simply with the authority of his royal person. He would have been a tyrant—a politically sound tyrant, but a tyrant nonetheless. But if a king insists that the law and nothing but the law should decide matters of justice and that one first needs to get the facts and only afterwards can judgment be passed, is he actually not acting the way

that a king in a constitutional monarchy should act? Henry presents a
model of a *just* head of state. This is the first time that the king acts in the
spirit of the categorical imperative. In fact, he embraces the maxim *Act such
and decide such as you wish it should be acted and decided always and everywhere
by a head of state.* That is, Henry neglects the context and acts according to
a universal law. For this reason I can hardly say that he neglects absolutely
his responsibility as the head of state, as a person of supreme authority, as a
sovereign. And still, he does neglect his duty, for he is responsible to his
country in a particular historical time, for a particular generation. Henry VI
is a paradoxical character in Shakespeare, in the sense that his personality
and his existential commitment, on the one hand, and his political obligation, on the other, are irreconcilable.

God judges justly. Winchester, the chief murderer, dies in terrible pain
without hope of divine forgiveness, while the king prays for him by his
bedside. Suffolk, the other murderer, will be held for ransom and will meet
his death at the hands of Walter Withmore, the pirate. He will be executed
by popular verdict: vox populi, vox dei. But, unlike the cardinal, this proud,
rancorous, vicious, self-made man and social climber can die such that he
is true to himself. Even in his death he remains a climber. He compares his
well-deserved and undignified death with the death of the greatest heroes
of history: "Come, 'soldiers,' show what cruelty ye can, / That this my death
may never be forgot. / Great men oft die by vile Bezonians; / A Roman
sworder and banditto slave / Murdered sweet Tully; Brutus' bastard hand /
Stabbed Julius Caesar; savage islanders / Pompey the Great; and Suffolk dies
by pirates" (4.1.134–40). It verges on the ridiculous that a man who
climbed to his position as the queen's lover, who has not a single merit or
achievement to his name either in war or in peace (if murder and conspiracy are not counted as achievements), can compare himself to Tullius, Julius
Caesar, Pompey the Great—with the world historical personalities of
Rome! And still, we believe Shakespeare. We believe Suffolk's self-mythol-
ogization; he preserves this inflated self-image until his dying hour. In spite
of the comic elements, there is dignity in this speech. For it expresses Suffolk's dominating passion aside from love: haughtiness. He is a haughty man
and dies a haughty man.

Now (4.2) the tableau broadens once again. After being at the top of the
social hierarchy, we now get to its bottom, to the rabble: John Cade and his
men. The top and the bottom belong to the same political game on two
counts. First, at least in Shakespeare, the Cade revolt is initiated and fueled
by York to weaken the position of Henry and occupy his throne. Second,
down there at the bottom, among the rabble, a satire play of the drama on
the top is unfolding. In the Greek theater every tragedy has its separate satire
play. In Shakespeare, within a single drama both the tragedy and its satire
play can be acted out simultaneously. So it happens also in *2 Henry VI;* Cade,

just like York, claims that his mother was a Plantagenet. Both resolve to kill for the throne, even though their targets are different. For example, Cade decides to kill all lawyers, or all those who can write and read, or all those who can speak French or Latin. When a clerk confesses that he can write his name, all cry out: "He hath confessed—away with him! He's a villain and a traitor" (4.2.106–7). And Cade prescribes his punishment: "hang him with his pen and inkhorn about his neck" (4.2.108–9). The peers are motivated by rancor, pride, and hatred; the rabble by ressentiment. The rabble murder, steal, and flee; that is, the rabble do the same things the mighty dukes are doing. The difference is not between good and evil but between high and base, noble and ignoble. There is a touch of Nietzsche in Shakespeare. It is of the greatest significance for him whether someone acts in a noble or an ignoble manner. But in Shakespeare, the distinction between good and evil will never be collapsed with the distinction between noble and ignoble. Moreover, the evil that takes hold among the nobles is far more dangerous than the evil that takes hold among the rabble. But there is evil everywhere. The goodness of the lowly shines as beautifully as the goodness of the mighty. It is only that the rays of the latter reach farther and illuminate a broader field.

In act 4 the scenes that take place at the top and those that take place at the bottom alternate with one another, and they are unusually brief. This gives the impression of the simultaneity of a great variety of actions, and assumes a staccato character. In the brief 4.4 scene, for example, Margaret enters with Suffolk's head. (Since the nineteenth century, this scene has reminded us of Mathilde de la Mole caressing Lucien Rubempré's head.) Immediately afterwards, the king is informed about the Cade rebellion. The scene is almost absurd. There is a royal pair in the audience while the queen carries her dead lover's head on her breast. (She tells us that she is longing for the body of this head—quite another absurdity.) In the midst of the scene the king turns to the queen: "How now, madame? / Still lamenting and mourning Suffolk's death? / I fear me, love, if that I had been dead, / Thou wouldst not have mourned so much for me" (4.2.20–24). This is the only personal address by the king to his wife in which he ever refers to Margaret's love of Suffolk. She answers, "No, my love, I should not mourn, but die for thee" (4.2.23). This is true, although she will not die. Her grief for the death of her husband will exceed all limits. It will be a boundless, loud, never ending grief. A passionate woman has enough love in stock to pour it on three men passionately. The king's reaction to the Cade rebellion is also representative. His words do not reveal anything new about the king's character but show it in another situation. He says he does not want to send an army immediately against Cade: "I'll send some holy bishop to entreat, / For God forbid so many simple souls / Should perish by the sword" (4.4.8–10). Is he just saintly? Is he also naïve? Or is he just sound?

First, let us see whether a compromise between these three suggestions is possible. One should not let "simple" people perish by the sword. Shakespeare presents the enraged rabble. However different is the king's judgment, so is his perspective. These are his people. When the messenger tells him that the rabble are killing scholars, lawyers, and gentlemen, the king exclaims, "O graceless men; They know not what they do" (4.4.37). Is he naïve, unkingly, or perhaps just wise? We may remind ourselves of what Hannah Arendt said in our own century about evil, namely, that to act out evil is to act "unthinkingly." The words of Christ do not sound naïve or unworldly in the royal mouth. When the king finally sends Clifford with his army against Cade, the army does not start to fight but becomes engaged in persuading the rabble that they should change sides. Buckingham addresses the turncoat rebels with the words "Follow me soldiers, we'll devise a mean / To reconcile you all unto the King" (4.7.224–25). And this is going to happen. The king pardons them all. "And Henry, though he be unfortunate, / Assure yourselves will never be unkind. / And so with thanks and pardon to you all, / I do dismiss you to your several countries" (4.8.18–21). All shout: "God save the King! God save the King!" (4.8.22–23). Meanwhile, Cade himself will meet his death in Kent, at the hand of Alexander Idem, a squire of Kent. In a very short scene this Kentishman is presented to us as a perfect member of the gentry.

Henry VI, in fact, treats this whole difficult and complex situation very well. He remains honest, truthful, and just, the mirror of Christian princes. He succeeds in bringing order to his court, in making the rabble join him. He succeeds in sparing the life and the property of all and in restoring peace to the realm. From the moment of his growing up in act 3, King Henry learns to behave as a great king. But he still does not trust himself. He is full of gloomy premonitions. He feels himself unfit to carry royal responsibilities. Shakespeare inserts a short monologue before the scene that brings Henry recognition and success: "Was ever King that joyed earthly throne / And could command no more content than I? / No sooner was I crept out of my cradle / But I was made a king at nine months old. / Was never subject longed to be a king / As I do long and wish to be a subject" (4.8.1–6). This monologue has at least two connotations. I have already mentioned the first: the king is grasped by gloomy premonition. The second has, however, more to do with Henry's "Kantianism," with his universalism. For him it is not natural to be king. He also could have been a subject. He is longing to be a subject. Thus, when he acts and decides, he acts and decides not just as a king but also as a subject. This means that he has no paternalistic relation to his subjects, to his following, or to his people. He can change places with them in mood and mind; he is one of them. Sometimes, men who do not want to hold supreme power are better and more just in wielding such power than those who want to hold it.

It is here that the unfolding of the plot suddenly speeds up. York, who has meanwhile been involved in Ireland, enters. He returns to claim the throne. Henry, who has dealt with the internal conflicts honestly yet also in a kingly manner, is now pushed into an impossible position. From this moment on he can continue to act in a kingly manner, but then he can no longer act honestly. Or, he can continue to act honestly, and then he will not be able to act like a king. He is destroyed by this contradiction. It is not York, not the party of the white rose, that crushes him, but his incapacity to cope with the dual task. There is no choice for him. Since he can only act honestly, he has to act in an unkingly way. It is not just the king, but also old England, that will be destroyed by this contradiction.

Now we feel ourselves to be witnesses to the repetition of the story of King Richard II. (Since Shakespeare wrote *King Henry VI* first, Richard II's story could also be seen as the repetition of Henry VI's story.) What repeats itself? Repetition repeats repletion. One could say of English history—as it is portrayed by Shakespeare—the opposite of what Tolstoy said about families: every good rule is good in a different way, yet all phony claims to the throne, all conspiracies, all political murders, resemble one another. As in the story of King Richard II, when Bolingbroke returns from Brittany, here too a messenger arrives to declare (in 4.9) that York has returned from Ireland armed, but that he does not entertain dark devices against the king. He wishes only that the king remove Duke Somerset, whom he calls a traitor. This is the first direct challenge of the party of the white rose against the House of Lancaster. One recalls that a few years ago (in Act 2.4 of *1 Henry VI*) in the Temple Garden, Richard and Somerset challenged one another. They have plucked the first roses: the white and the red. Among those who participated in the first conspiracy, only Suffolk of the red roses died at this hour.

We (the audience and the players) have no doubt that York wants the throne and kingdom. Had we not known it before, York's third soliloquy (5.1) makes his designs clear: "From Ireland thus comes York to claim his right, / And pluck the crown from feeble Henry's head" (5.1.1–2). In fact, many interpreters of the drama argue that Henry is "feeble" because York says so. But one does not need to accept York's interpretation as if it were one's own. York's interpretation strengthens his claim: he is strong; this is why he has the right to rule. We are familiar with this natural right argument. By nature Henry VI is unfit to rule because he is feeble; by nature Richard is fit: "This hand was made to handle naught but gold" (5.1.7).

Still, Henry wants to know York's reasons. He sends Buckingham to him: "I pray thee, Buckingham, go and meet him, / And ask him what's the reason of these arms" (4.8.37–38). What does Henry want to hear? York's rationalization? Has he not heard this already? York's immediate rationalization is extremely weak (that he was only after Somerset, and not the king), but it offers for Somerset the rare occasion to show his virtue and worth in a few lines. We know little about Somerset. But now Shakespeare offers him a bunch of roses. Having heard York's fraudulent reasons, Somerset simply turns to the king: "My lord, / I'll yield myself to prison willing, / Or unto death, to do my country good" (4.8.42–43). These are rare words in this drama. In uttering these words, Somerset comes out as a righteous man.

The king says, "Ask his reason." But when Buckingham arrives at York's camp and asks his reasons, York becomes angry. However, he does not feel strong enough to come out into the open. So he continues to play hide and seek, and answers: "Buckingham, I prithee pardon me, / That I have given no answer all this while; / My mind was troubled with deep melancholy. / The cause why I have brought this army hither / Is to remove proud Somerset from the King, / Seditious to His grace and to the state" (5.1.32–37). It is interesting to observe how York takes a further step in the direction of his youngest son's character. The reference to his "deep melancholy" is an act of comedy. He tries to act as a comedian, an act that his evil son will carry toward perfection. To this Buckingham answers that Somerset is already in the Tower. He might have been sincere, for Somerset offered exactly this service to his king and country. But obviously Henry has not accepted the offer. Accepting it would have been contrary to Henry's character. We will soon see—and so will York—that Somerset remains a free man. After having received this information, York dismisses his powers. At least this is what he says, although he does not do so. He also offers his sons to Henry as a surety or hostages. This is the first time that we get to know the sons of York, who will play such a fatal role in the further development of this (his) story.

When Somerset (whom Henry wants to hide from York) enters with the queen (5.1) into an unspecified place, York is seized by a fit of rage. Now he does not pretend anymore; he is furious: "False king, why hast thou broken faith with me, / Knowing how hardly I can brook abuse? / 'King' did call I thee? No, thou art not king; / Not fit to govern and rule multitudes, / Which dar'st not—no, nor canst not—rule a traitor" (5.1.91–95). Needless to say, the king has not promised anything (not in Shakespeare), and we also know that he never goes back on his word. The lie came from Buckingham, and we do not even know whether he lied or was ignorant. But we know that the accusation that the king cannot deal with traitors is in this case also false. For Somerset is no traitor. York is the traitor. To show that he is able to deal with a traitor, the king must learn to deal with York and not Somerset. This is perceived by Somerset immediately: "O monstrous traitor! I arrest thee, York / Of capital treason 'gainst the King and crown. / Obey, audacious traitor; kneel for grace" (5.1.106–8). He is right. York calls his sons as his bail; the queen calls for Clifford. What is the king doing? Where is he? Why is he silent? Richard's sons appear through one door, and Clifford through the other. Something then happens that is—in the tradition of a royal house of legitimacy—the greatest insolence imaginable. Clifford kneels before the king, and then York turns to him with the following words: "I thank thee, Clifford. . . . We are the sovereign" (5.1.123–25). We—the players, the actors, the audience—are all in bedlam. York does not obey. He seemingly calls his sons as his bail, but really as his helpers.

From this moment on, York plays the role of the king, although he acts in pride and anger. He feels himself in a theater where he can play cat and mouse with everyone: Clifford, the queen, and the king. But he cannot do this with Somerset, for he wants to kill Somerset quickly. We are in bedlam, and King Henry also experiences it as such: "Ay, Clifford, a bedlam and ambitious humour / Makes him oppose himself against the king" (5.1.130–31). Salisbury and Warwick, the kingmakers, enter. This is also their game, and they begin slowly to steal the story of feigned legitimacy, the rationale of York's claim to the throne. This moment everything is in suspense. What the king calls bedlam can be also termed the state of nature. There is one legitimate king, one pretender; the first has power no more, the second not yet. Everyone talks at once, things accelerate, but one does not see any direction, other than up and down. The tension of hatred becomes unbearable.

The king does not interfere with the bedlam. He is lost; he does not know what to do. He is a man of the law, and there is no more law. He is a man of goodness, but there is only hatred. At this point he is petrified. Only once, when he sees old Salisbury kneel to Richard, does he begins to reflect on the spectacle: "O, where is faith? O, where is loyalty? / If it be banished from the frosty head, / Where shall it find a harbor in the earth?" (5.1.164–66). And yet there follows a very important, although brief, conversation. The king asks Salisbury, "Hast thou not sworn allegiance unto me? . . . Canst thou dispense with heaven for such an oath?" (5.1.177–79). To this, Salisbury answers, "It is great sin to swear unto a sin, / But greater sin to keep a sinful oath" (5.1.180–81). The queen remarks, "A subtle traitor needs no sophister" (5.1.189). Shakespeare allows his character to play music on all possible instruments, including rancor, revenge, pride, and ambition.

But in the case of Salisbury and Warwick, we see spiders and not foxes or lions. The spider is a rationalist. He can find a good argument for all his misdeeds. This is not the first or the last time that either Salisbury or Warwick does something wrong that is based on a (seemingly) good argument. Obviously, the argument is correct. If you vow to murder someone, it is better not to do it. But allegiance to Henry is no sin. Salisbury never could have supported the major proposition of his syllogism by proving that allegiance to one's sovereign, who has harmed nothing and no one, is a sin. He takes a false proposition as given; and from it, it is easy to draw a logically correct but morally evil conclusion. Shakespeare knew well that the devil has good logic. And Salisbury is not even a devil; he is just a devil's advocate.

The king is silent, but Clifford wakes up and calls his men to arms. It is here that Richard, the son of Richard the later Gloucester and Richard III, utters his first sentence in the tragedy, cynical and blasphemous: "Fie, charity, for shame! Speak not in spite— / For you shall sup with Jesu Christ tonight" (5.1.211–12).

This is *the state of nature.* In the state of nature there is one thing that decides, that is, *strength* in a Hobbesian sense—pure physical strength. There is no morality, no legitimacy, no power; there is not even politics or violence. The whole tradition is in shambles, including all rules and norms. There is no justice, no loyalty, and no honor. The stronger is going to win. But is this really so? Can the stronger win simply because it is the stronger? Does strength have a future? Today strength is here; tomorrow it is somewhere else. As Hobbes says, life in the state of nature is short and dangerous, and no one can live in security where strength prevails. Strength cannot be temporalized; it cannot take roots because it is ad hoc. The stronger today will become the weaker tomorrow, the weaker will become the stronger.

This moment of the state of nature is representative in the Shakespearean vision of history. In his eyes strength is not a historical actor, or even a political actor. It gains some victories, which disappear the moment they have been won. Without constituting another world on the ruins of the old, everything will collapse. Every haughty duke will become a corpse— very, very soon.

From the Castle Inn to the Battle of Saint Albans, York will see his star rising. But no star risen out of strength will remain on the firmament of a state. A steady star needs a rule; it needs a regular path on the sky. Strength is a bad draftsman; it will never sketch such a path.

On the battlefield of Saint Albans, old Clifford will be killed by York. His last words are "La fin couronne les oeuvres." He still dies for something, for someone; his soul is not yet populated by chaos. In killing Clifford, York falls short of traditional chivalry. It is not chivalrous to kill an aged man. However, in the state of nature such rules are invalid. All hell then breaks loose. Clifford's death will infect his son, young Clifford, with the furious passion of revenge. He pledges to respond to transgression with an even greater transgression, and by taking such a pledge he has already transgressed: "York not our old men spares; / No more will I their babes" (5.3.51–52). In all the Shakespearean plays, there is a final limit. One should not murder, but one does. One should not kill old men, but accidentally one does. One should not kill a child. This is really the absolute; it is so absolute that it knows no exception. In Shakespeare, the murder of a child is absolute evil. The moment that Clifford takes the solemn oath that he is not sparing the babes in the camp of York, he already does the same thing that Richard III will do very soon: he chooses to become evil.

York is a good soldier, just like his son. After having killed old Clifford, he kills his archenemy, Somerset, as well. The king and queen appear. As it is, the king is no soldier. He neither flees nor fights. He simply stays where he is and does nothing. How could he flee? This would be to let God have his will; and it would be cowardice: "Can we outrun the heavens? Good Margaret, stay" (5.4.2). How could he fight? This would have meant murder. Henry does not do what a man is supposed to do, and it is now that Margaret takes the man's role, the role of the fighter. She is going to fight for Henry, since Henry will never fight for himself and will never flee by his own will. It is the queen who realizes that they must retreat to London.

Who is the hero of this battle? The king, who has not fought and does not decide to flee, certainly is not. Perhaps it is York, who kills two of his enemies. At least he has profited from the battle. But the real war hero is his young son, Richard, who helped his father three times back to his horse and who saved Salisbury's life. What do we know of Richard, the later Duke of Gloucester, the later King Richard III? We know that he is a cynic, a blasphemous disbeliever. We know that he loves his father above all, and that he is ready to fight for him and fight well.

The battle is won and the drama comes to a close. Just as *1 Henry VI* ended with marriage, which seemed to be a happy ending but in fact was not, so *2 Henry VI* ends with York's victory, which seems to be a happy ending, at least for York, but is in fact not. At the end of the drama Warwick appears to sum up the lesson. This was the lesson drawn by and for Warwick at this time in this place, but it is not the lesson drawn by others. Shakespeare does not draw lessons. He muses on human comedy. He lets Warwick say: "Now, by my hand, lords, 'twas a glorious day! / Saint Albans battle won by famous York / Shall be eternized in all age to come" (5.5.34–36). It will not be "eternized." It will be cursed as a victory of evil consequence. And it will be forgotten as a victory of no consequence.

3 Henry VI

The third part of *Henry VI* is the shortest of the three plays, but it is among the densest and fastest moving. It is the drama of the Wars of the Roses, the suicidal civil war. The death dance, which will end with the victory of Henry VII, begins with the battle of Saint Albans; it will be the impersonal central "character" of the third part of the tetralogy. The drama about the civil war takes place in rapidly changing locations. It constantly moves up and down. It is the drama of the constant change of fortune and of loyalties, including the change of kings and queens. This is one of the most intense and fluctuating dramas of Shakespeare. He takes much liberty with the time element. Many years are portrayed as if they were only a few days. The rhythm of the civil war is sensitized in the *danse macabre*, where the limbs do not obey the brain but move independently of any center, any plan, any purpose. This is history without one single hero. Henry VI remains on the existential stage. As we shall see, he makes his most representative appearance here at the very beginning of the drama, an appearance that also assumes the greatest historical significance. But after his great historico-existential scene, the king, as a historical actor, fades away and disappears in the tumult and the chaos, staggering in the danse macabre of the civil war. The drama is not about Henry nor about Edward, York, or Richard; it is about madness. History and politics are never portrayed as entirely sound business in Shakespeare's works, but an absolute madness like this he portrays only twice: here (the tragedy of *Richard III* included) and in *Lear*.

Scene 1.1 in *3 Henry VI* repeats—on a higher level—the scene 3.1 in *2 Henry VI*. It was in 3.1 of *2 Henry VI* that we saw Henry suddenly growing from a bookish, religious child into a man committed to the universal moral law. This scene took place in the Parliament building. The second scene of this kind (in 3.1) takes place also in the Parliament building, and this is representative. It is in the Parliament building that Henry confirms his absolute resolve to act only normatively, to offer a precedent for all future times, irrespective of the direct consequences of his action. He decides (in the case of Gloucester) that the law should take its course without autocratic interference. I think he is essentially right. Had the conspirators not assassinated Gloucester, the court of law would have acquitted him. (The conspirators knew that this would be so.) Now, it comes to the second round.

The king arrives from the battlefield, where he neither fights nor escapes. What he then does, or rather does not do, is absolutely wrong in a political sense. But considering his character, it is in good moral order. Fleeing is a politically sound thing to do because getting back to London is the only way to save his throne. But Henry is interested in something that he believes to be superior to his throne: he is infinitely interested in being moral. By staying put, he avoids both flight and murder. Nonaction is for him the best action. He believes Socrates' dictum that it is better to suffer injustice than to commit injustice, to be true. At least, it is true for him. He also knows that for the others the opposite is true, but he does not care.

In scene 1.1 of *3 Henry VI*, which directly follows the last scene of the former play, the camp of York is angry because of the king's escape. They also exchange compliments about having killed eminent figures of the enemy camp. Richard the younger is especially complimented by his father. Warwick points to the royal seat (on a platform) and asks York to occupy it: "And this, the regal seat—possess it, York, / For this is thine, and not King Henry's heirs" (3 *Henry VI* 1.1.26–27). Let us see what happens.

Let me say in advance that the whole of 1.1, as it stands, is Shakespeare's own invention. Holinshed writes that York courteously refused to act violently against the king, and that the king and the future protector (York) together worked out the terms of the agreement, which was broken only by the queen.

But let's follow Shakespeare's design. Armed men surround the seat of the throne, which has been occupied by the usurper, York. Then Warwick speaks the representative words: " 'The Bloody Parliament' shall this be called, / Unless Plantagenet, Duke of York, be king, / And bashful Henry deposed, whose cowardice / Hath made us bywords to our enemies" (1.1.139–42). And then he turns to York: "Neither the King nor he that loves him best . . . Dares stir a wing if Warwick shakes his bells. / I'll plant Plantagenet, root him up to dares. / Resolve thee, Richard—claim the English crown" (1.1.45–49). York then seats himself in the throne. Thus, Warwick utters a threat, a terrible threat: if Henry does not yield, this will be called the Bloody Parliament. Warwick shows himself ready to use the highest institution of the English peers as a means to achieve his goal. The Parliament building can become a battlefield, but who cares? The main thing is the result. The second address (he *plants* Plantagenet emphatically here) is also telling. Richard's whole legitimacy claim is sheer nonsense. Better said, it merely serves as the justification of a decision made by Warwick: that he and he alone will plant kings in the English throne. Kings do not grow out from the seeds of former kings, but they are planted by a good gardener. New seeds are planted. The planter plants. Warwick plants. He is the kingmaker. How can one make or plant kings? One can do this by relying on the law of nature, of course. This is the reason why both York and Warwick need to emphasize constantly the weakness and unkingliness of the king. The point is not whether the accusations are right or wrong, but that the accusations are chosen in order to supply the argument of the law of nature for the resolve to plant another family on the royal throne.

Henry VI then enters. He sounds neither unkingly nor cowardly. He is accompanied by his peers, who are all wearing red roses. He speaks accusingly: "My lords, look where the sturdy rebel sits— / Even in the chair of state!" (1.1.50–51). He reminds his peers that the man has slain their fathers. At this moment the men of the red roses become just like those of the white. They are poised for murder. Westmoreland cries out, "What, shall we suffer this? Let's pluck him down. / My heart for anger burns—I cannot brook it" (59–60). But the king, instead of allowing his men to do the bloody work, says: "Be patient, gentle Earl of Westmorland" (61). But

Clifford knows what to do. The men of red roses are in the majority; they thirst for vengeance, they are loyal to Henry: "Patience is for poltroons, such as he. / He durst not sit there had your father lived. / My gracious lord, here in the Parliament / Let us assail the family of York" (62–65). But here the king makes them stop. All their arguments are in vain: *"Far be the thought of this from Henry's heart, / To make a shambles of the Parliament House"* (70–71, emphasis mine). At this moment Henry loses his power and is proved unfit for politics. However, with the same sentence he not only preserves his soul but makes his entrance into history. For it is a *universal law* that one should not make a shambles of Parliament. *For Warwick the Parliament is a means to an end, for Henry an end in itself.* This is Henry's finest hour, but soon afterwards he breaks down. Why does he do this? It is not because of the power of York, but because he realizes that in one critical thing he is in the wrong—not by his own fault, but wrong nevertheless.

Neither the men of the white roses nor those of the red draw their swords. It is Henry who forbids them to shed blood in the Parliament. Instead of a war of blades, a war of words breaks out. Arguments are pitted against arguments, both parties are justifying their claims. The king's men also become possessed by the desire for revenge, halted only by the command of their own king. During the heated waves of altercation, the sons of York become impatient. Richard interferes: "Sound drums and trumpets, and the King will fly" (198). But at this very moment—sitting still on the throne as if he were the king!—York prefers to avoid bloodshed, for he realizes that he can win with words.

I have already mentioned the turning point in the duel of words fought over the entitlements of the two kings. Henry throws in the obvious argument: he is Harry, the son of Harry, who was also the son of Harry, the English king. York interrupts: "Twas by rebellion against the king" (134). At this very moment, the scepter of the deposed and murdered Richard II appears in the Parliament house. This is where Henry resigns because he realizes that he is wrong. In this war of words, where everyone rationalizes his interest or ambition with the usual arguments, justifications are just a cover-up. The wolf is presenting an argument for his right to devour the lamb, something he would have done anyway without arguments. The king is the sole exception. He is sincere. As long as he justifies his claim, he does it out of conviction and not because he needs to legitimize his naked interest, his hatred, or his ambition. When York confronts him with the fact that his grandfather was a usurper who deposed a rightful king, Henry admits that York is right. This is the end of Henry's self-justification. He loses faith in his own legitimacy and says: "I know not what to say—my title's weak. / Tell me, may not a king adopt an heir?" (135–36). This is a marvelous interruption! There is no single person among these rancorous and ambition-mad lords for whom an argument is an argument, who would be ready to admit being in the wrong. But the king does so. He is stricken with the insight that his grandfather was exactly like York, a rebel like York. His title is weak, he admits. When Clifford subsequently assures him that he would defend Henry whether his claims were right or wrong, Henry—although he appreciates loyalty—cannot accept this "right or wrong." York then turns to him and asks him to resign his crown. Warwick threatens him: "Do right unto the princely Duke of York, / Or I will fill the house with armed men / And over the chair of state, where now he sits, / Write up his title with usurping blood" (167–70). He stamps his foot and his soldiers appear. There is no question that the king will yield, and he does yield to a certain extent. He does not yield because of the threat against his life, nor even because of the threat against his men's lives. Rather, he yields first and foremost because he decided earlier to avoid the most dangerous precedent: that no bloodshed should be allowed in the House of Parliament. If he allows this, the Parliament House will be in shambles. In addition—again, prior to the threat—he realizes the weakness of his claim.

Henry is now ready for a compromise, not because of his weakness, but because of his conviction. He is convinced that this time compromise is right. He offers his kingdom to Richard Plantagenet after his death. This is a sound compromise. He does not want to abdicate. Abdication would mean, again, to make it universal law that whenever one is under pressure and threat, one can abdicate. He draws his lesson from the fate and story of Richard II. That a king is free to choose his heir can perhaps also be made a rule or a general habit. Nothing speaks against such a rule, and therefore he chooses it. This turns out to be, once again, the worst possible political move, because it enrages Henry's own loyal men. He has abdicated his son's right to the English crown; he has neglected the interests of his men.

Certainly good politics and human goodness (historical vindication even included) are incompatible here, and as such they are also paradoxical. Paradoxes cannot be "solved." Henry, in avoiding doing something morally wrong, has to do something that is politically wrong. All his enemies do choose, however, the course of action that seems to be politically right and morally wrong. Whether they hit the politically right decision is another matter, yet they try it. History pronounces its verdict. Both parties are buried under the shambles of the building of old England. Both choices prove equally suicidal.

But not yet, not at this point. Henry's offer is painful, but by accepting this offer sincerely, the bloodiest stage of the civil war still could have been avoided. It is true that it is politically unsound. But had it been taken seriously, Henry's suggestion still could have proved historically sound.

Henry asks York to take an oath: "I here entail / The crown to thee and to thine heirs for ever, / Conditionally, that here thou take an oath / To cease this civil war, and whilst I live / To honor me as thy king and sovereign, /

And nor by treason nor hostility / To seek to put me down and reign thyself" (195–201). York answers, "This oath I willingly take and will perform" (202). Does he really mean this seriously, for even a moment? Perhaps, for a moment, he does. After all, in spite of all his mistaken feeling of superiority, or rather his sense of mistaken superiority, he must feel some respect for the anointed king. There is also a grain of sentimentalism in this treacherous and cynical man. This is not a rare mixture in Shakespeare. But obviously he does not belong to those men who—according to Nietzsche—have the capacity to make promises. He has no such capacity, for his memory is weak and short. He could have taken an oath in good faith to forget it tomorrow, if his interest so required and he was persuaded by his sons to do so.

It cannot be doubted that in Shakespeare's understanding a divine act of retribution was at work in York's case. His terrible death was a punishment for his false oath. One could go further and say that God has also punished him in his children and grandchildren, since almost all of them were murdered by Richard, his favorite son. But at this moment Richard has no premonition. The king himself does not need to have any. For Henry never would have broken an oath whatever the consequences, and he puts his faith in divine retribution and wisdom. He knows well that if York betrays this oath, England will suffer immensely. But one does not keep an oath in order not to suffer.

From this scene onward the behavior (and not the character!) of Henry changes once again. He becomes entirely passive. This is at first only because he realizes that nothing depends on him anymore, and because he feels guilty for disinheriting his son. Later on, it turns out that his own loyal men of the party of the red roses will become as brutal and as cruel as the party of the white. Their acts will be as sinister and murderous as those of the men of the House of York. Lancaster will no longer be interested in right or wrong, but in the bloody business of killing. Henry has nothing further to do with them. Enemy or friend, they are alike in his eyes. Moreover, he falls into a moral crisis. This is because, after all, the men of the party of the red roses are his own men; he is responsible for their acts. He should have prevented them from doing what they were doing. He sees that he cannot do anything to stop them. Still, he should have found a way to do so. He tried, but this was not sufficient. Nonetheless, he should have tried harder. Henry does not acquit himself.

First he is confronted with the accusation of Margaret, and she seems to be right. She accuses Henry of being an unnatural father. We again hear the tigress talking here, this time as the defender of her last man, her dear son: "Hadst thou but loved him half so well as I, / Or felt that pain which I did for him once, / Or nourished him as I did with my blood, / Thou wouldst have left thy dearest heart-blood there / Rather than have made that savage Duke thine heir / And disinherited thine only son" (221–26). Margaret remains Margaret. Nothing is of more worth to her than her men. There is nothing worthy of defending, nothing more to cherish and love. There is no country (it is not her country anyway), no Parliament House (it is not her institution anyway), no peace (who cares for peace?); it is her men. King Henry answers: "Pardon me, Margaret; pardon me, sweet son— / The Earl of Warwick and the Duke enforced me" (229–30). Margaret is furious: "Art thou king, and wilt be forced?" (231). She misunderstands because she does not realize that a person can be forced to do something not because he is a coward but because he wants to defend his country: "The soldiers should have tossed me on their pikes / Before I would have granted to that act. / But thou preferr'st thy life before thine honour. / In seeing dost, I here divorce myself / Both from thy table, Henry, and thy bed, / Until that act of Parliament be repealed / Whereby my son is disinherited. . . . Thus do I leave thee. Come, son, let's away. / Our army is ready—come, we'll after them" (245–57). It is now clear that the queen will not obey the act of Parliament. It has no validity for her; she has not taken an oath. She calls her men in arms; she is fighting for the rights of her son. The king is left devastated, but he understands: "Poor Queen, how love to me and to her son / Hath made her break out into the terms of rage" (265–66). But now he is afraid of fateful consequences, and sends Exeter after the queen to help avoid further civil war, if this is still possible.

After this very long scene, very short ones follow until the end of the drama (with a few exceptions). The quick pulsation of the scenes underlines the quick fluctuation between fear and hope, good and bad luck, upward and downward movement, loyalties and disloyalties, and finally life and death.

In 1.2 it is young Richard and Edward who persuade their father to break his oath. It is more than instructive to listen to Richard's words. If in Warwick's case (in *2 Henry VI*) we were made to listen to the sophistry of the devil's advocate, now we begin to listen to the arguments of the devil himself. Just like the devil's advocate, the devil too can make a formally valid argument for every evil design. Whereas power is the ultimate end, and everything else is but a means to this end for the devil's advocate, in the case of the devil's argument power is always associated with murder. The devil's fantasy is not only mad with power, but also sadistic: "An oath is of no moment being not took / Before a true and lawful magistrate / That hath authority over him that swears. / Henry had none. . . . Therefore to arms . . . Until the white rose that I wear be dyed / Even in the luke-warm blood of Henry's heart" (1.2.22–34). York has waited precisely for this argument: "Richard, enough! I will be king or die" (1.2.35). Is it King Henry who could be easily influenced? Or is it rather York? Who is weak in his resolution? we may ask.

The timing is important, for now the messenger arrives with the news

that the queen has taken up arms. It is significant for Shakespeare's understanding of politicohistorical actors to portray the two parties as acting
simultaneously: *neither the queen nor York first takes up arms, because the other
has already done so.* Both take the initiative, yet both will justify their own
act of perjury as if they had only reacted to the perjury of the other party.

The battle begins. It is here (1.3) that we become witness to the absolute
sin. This is the first unforgivable transgression in the whole story of King
Henry VI up to this moment. It is committed by one of Henry's men, not
by one of Richard's. The absolute sin is the murder of a child. Clifford
murders the child Rutland, York's son. In a significant way, this murder happens before it in fact happens. We remember that when seeing the killing
of his aged father, Clifford decides not to take mercy even on a babe of the
family of York. There are designs that one should not entertain, for if something seems to be permitted in fantasy or thought, one can act out this
thought or fantasy if occasion permits. A few hours before—Shakespeare
suggests—Richard voiced his desire to dye his white rose red in the blood
of Henry's heart. He will act according to his desire, just as Clifford now
acts according to his design before thinking it over. Clifford belongs to the
Shakespearean characters who are not devils; he is no Richard Gloucester.
He becomes evil through a self-righteous desire for an act of justified
revenge. He has no idea about justified revenge. His act is an act of
thoughtlessness.

When I discussed the portrayal of evil in Shakespeare in the first part of
this book, I mentioned that there are cases in Shakespeare in which evil is
committed out of thoughtlessness, first and foremost. (I should qualify that,
by far, not all kinds of evil are committed out of thoughtlessness.) Clifford
does not formulate a maxim for his action, not even an evil one. He just
wants to avenge his father's death and believes that to kill a child is the
proper way to pay his debt to his father. There are as many kinds and forms
of wickedness as there are wicked people in Shakespeare.

Clifford is not only unable to distinguish good from evil, but also to distinguish evil from radical evil. When he meets Rutland with his tutor, he
immediately releases the tutor: "Thy priesthood saves thy life. / As for the
brat of this accursed duke, / Whose father slew my father—he shall die"
(1.3.3–5). The tutor implores, "Ah, Clifford, murder not this innocent child
/ Lest thou be hated both of God and man" (8–9). The boy implores, "Ah,
gentle Clifford, kill me with thy sword / And not with such a cruel
threat'ning look. / Sweet Clifford, hear me speak before I die. / I am too
mean a subject to thy wrath. / Be thou revenged on men, and let me live"
(17–21). Imagine a child afraid to open his eyes, for he is afraid to look at
a cruel face. But Clifford answers, "The sight of any of the house of York /
Is as a fury to torment my soul. / And till I root out their accursed line, /
And leave not one alive, I live in hell" (31–34). Do you understand? He

speaks Hitler's language: Kinder werden Juden; the child of York becomes a York. He decides to root out the "accursed line." The boy pleads, "Sweet Clifford, pity me. . . . I never did thee harm—why wilt you slay me? . . . And when I give occasion of offense, Then let me die, for now thou hast no cause" (36–46). "No cause? / Thy father slew my father, *therefore,* die" (47, emphasis mine). What kind of syllogism is this? The boy quotes with his dying lips the verses of Ovid, which he learned perhaps just a few days before from his tutor: "*Di faciant laudis summa sit ista tuae!*" (48). What an ironic sentence from a wise boy's mouth! The gods have indeed granted that Clifford be remembered for this act alone.

After the son comes the father. This is the end of York's short glory. This is vanitatum vanitas. He now knows: "The sands are numbered that make up my life" (1.4.26). Northumberland (one of King Henry's men) would rather be merciful, but Clifford is not, and neither is Queen Margaret.

The last scene of act 1 has been frequently criticized for the rhetoric employed by the youthful playwright. It is true that some of the expressions are too baroque and some figures of speech sound poetically rude, while the similes and metaphors are sometimes too bombastic and loud. For example, some of Shakespeare's contemporaries found a few of the sentences that were meant to be serious to be rather ridiculous. The main culprit was an allusion to Queen Margaret: "O tiger's heart wrapped in a woman's hide!" (1.4.138). As far as poetic sophistication is concerned, the critics may have been right, but not as far as the structuring of the scene is concerned. The portrayal of the ultimate cruelty of the Clifford-queen duo is essentially Shakespearean. I do not see any difference in taste between this murderous game played by Clifford and the queen with Richard York in this play and the murderous game played by Goneril, Regan, and Edgar with Gloucester in *King Lear.* The sole factor that makes *King Lear* even more radical is that in *Lear* Gloucester is entirely innocent, whereas York is not. Shakespeare was inclined to go to extremes, to show human cruelty and ruthlessness in its ultimate manifestations, coupled with sadistic games, because it is only in this way that he could explore the ultimate possibilities of the human soul. Shakespeare was absolutely interested in every possibility of the human animal, and thus he also experimented with the portrayal of the absolute transgression from his earliest works to his latest. (For example, children are also murdered in *Macbeth.*) What brings men and women to the state where they step over the last boundary? In *3 Henry VI* Clifford steps over the last boundary and Margaret remains nearby. One can step over the last boundary, as well as over the ultimate one, in solo as Richard III does, and also in duo or trio as here, in the scene of York's murder, or in *King Lear.* So it happens, and Shakespeare faces the music. Who is a barbarian? Certainly, the author is not.

The brutal scene opens when Margaret prevents York's execution by

Clifford, because she wants to prolong York's sufferings. From this moment on the roles will be recast. As the sadistic game goes on, the cynical, mendacious, power-hungry Richard will be cast into the role of the man of sorrows, the tortured Jesus, Jesus on the cross to an increasingly greater extent. However, he remains York; he will never confess his crimes, he will never forgive or ask for forgiveness. Although he will be *cast into* the role of the man of sorrows, he will *not be* the imitation of the man of sorrows. The contrast between man and situation is blatant, yet at the end the situation will ultimately outweigh the character of the man, at least for the onlookers, and bring even cold Northumberland to weep: "Had he been the slaughter-man to all my kin, / I should not, for my life, but weep with him, / To see how only sorrow gripes the soul" (1.4.170–73). Although York plays the role of the man of sorrows, it is Margaret whom we get to know better, whose character we explore more deeply. The scene—aside from being one of Shakespeare's great psychological showpieces—is in political terms the repetition of Clifford's murder of the child. Here Margaret offers a napkin stained by a murdered child's blood to the child's father to make him suffer. She mocks, she ridicules the unhealing wounds of her enemy: "I prethee, grieve, to make me merry, York. . . . Why art thou patient, man? Thou shouldst be mad, / And I, to make thee mad, do mock thee thus. / Stamp, rave, and fret, that I may sing and dance. / Thou wouldst be fee'd, I see, to make me sport. / York cannot speak unless he wears the crown. A crown for York, and lords bow low to him" (1.4.87–95). (She puts a paper crown on his head.) Shakespeare gives York time and opportunity to speak. His accusations against Margaret of sexual subversion do not interest us here; neither do his insults. (For example, he says that she is ugly, although we know her to be beautiful.) But his curse does interest us. He says, "There, take the crown—and with the crown, my curse: / And in thy need such comfort come to thee / As now I reap at thy too cruel hand. / Hardhearted Clifford, take me from the world. / My soul to heaven, my blood upon your heads" (164–69). Margaret and Clifford kill him; they sever his head and place it on the gates of the town of York. York's curses will take effect soon. I will come back to the point that the two murders (Clifford's murder of Rutland and Clifford and Margaret's murder of York, whom Margaret tortured) first have a politicohistorical significance. For this moment marks the end of the innocence of the king. Murders surround him. His own wife and his own most loyal man are the scum of the earth. They overstep the boundary more radically than the men of white roses have hitherto done. Shakespeare's Machiavellian understanding of politics is written into every line of this scene. Perfect goodness is political disaster, and it can also become an ethical disaster. A man who is absolutely good cannot prevent evil. He will never commit evil, but everyone around him can, because he will forgive and will repent in another's name. A man of politics must be dressed up for the political stage; he cannot remain existentially naked as an actor of the existential stage. But Henry remains naked on the stage. Even if this had made it possible for him to assume a "historical" significance by making a case for universal legislation, in the concrete context he will ultimately and deservedly fail. I repeat, he will fail not only politically but also ethically (even if not morally). Although Christ said that one should not resist evil, the king should have, because his kingdom was a kingdom on earth. Henry, however, could not resist evil.

The next scene takes us to the children of York. They hear the news of the loss of the battle and the terrible death of their father. This scene is again a turning point in the story, although one hardly notices it. From this moment on the children of York (Edward, George, and Richard) will emerge as the main characters of the drama and of the political game. Here we immediately learn something about Richard: he loved his father. His father was the only person he ever loved in his life. Later we shall see that he hated his mother, and that this hatred was as mutual as the love between his father and him. Psychologists may draw some connections between this family constellation and the development of Richard's character. But as I have often mentioned, Shakespeare does not present motivations. He simply follows his heroes' acts and comments in various situations so that we can learn many things about them, and so that we will be able to offer our own interpretations. He allows us to have not one, but many. We also learn something political in this scene. Warwick arrives. For him a lost battle is nothing. One can lose a battle and still win the war. The kingmaker remains a kingmaker. Richard is dead. The next king will be Edward, York's eldest son. Warwick, as always, has set his mind to something and will carry out his plans.

In 2.2 the victorious Margaret solemnly receives Henry VI in the town of York. For Margaret this is a day of great joy. "Doth not the object cheer your heart, my lord?" (2.2.4) she asks her husband. After all, York is dead, and she can put the crown again on this man's head. But Henry feels no joy, only remorse. "Ay, as the rocks cheer them that fear their wreck. / To see this sight, it irks my very soul. / Withhold revenge, dear God—'tis not my fault, / Nor wittingly have I infringed my vow" (2.2.5–8). Clifford becomes nervous: "My gracious liege, this too much lenity / And harmful pity must be laid aside" (2.2.9–10). Now he advises his king to make Edward, his son, his heir. Who is right and who is wrong? Who can decide this? Politically, Clifford is right. But Clifford advises against leniency, and he is a murderer of a child and the torturer of the child's father, who now asks another father to decorate his son. Can his advice be considered sane and clean? Can it be absolutely rejected, if he is right?

Henry does not yield. He knows his Clifford, and he feels the ambiguity of his situation. There will be no more mild Clifford, no more good

Clifford. At the beginning of his speech he does not even turn toward Clifford: "Full well hath Clifford played the orator, / Inferring arguments of mighty force. / But, Clifford, tell me—didst thou never hear / That things ill got had ever had success? / And happy always was it for that son / Whose father for his hoarding went to hell? / I'll leave my son my virtuous deeds behind, / And would my father had left me no more. . . . Ah, cousin York, would thy best friends did know / How it doth grieve me that thy head is here" (2.2.43–55). He is really mourning. King Henry cannot pretend. Dressed as a king, he remains always naked.

Now the development of the plot accelerates even more, and one scene follows another in staccato rhythm. Immediately comes the confrontation between Queen Margaret and Edward York, who claims his father's right. The king wants to yield, but Margaret does not let the king speak. Edward puts an end to the encounter: "Since thou deniest the gentle King to speak. / Sound trumpets—Let our bloody colours wave!" (172–73). At this very moment Margaret also senses the danger. Thus, she cries out: "Stay, Edward" (175). But Edward answers: "No, wrangling woman, we'll no longer stay— / These words will cost ten thousand lives this day" (176–77).

Is the innocent king innocent in the death of those ten thousand? Clifford will accuse him (2.6) before he dies: "And, Henry, hadst thou swayed as kings should do . . . Giving no ground unto the house of York, / They never then had sprung like summer flies; I and ten thousand in this luckless realm / Had left no mourning widows for our death; / And thou this day hadst kept thy chair in peace" (2.6.14–20). The ethics of *Gemüt* and the ethics of consequences are about to collide. If one judges from the ethics of consequences, Henry is guilty of the death of those ten thousand. But if one reads the story from the perspective of personal morality, Henry remains innocent. He never intentionally did anything wrong; moreover, he never even wanted to enjoy the fruits of his power and of the momentary victories won by his wife.

What remains for Henry? It is only one thing: to leave the post of the king, to take up the position of the *chorus of the mourners*. The king does not justify his acts, but he does not rebuke his men either. He could not become someone that he was not; he could not have acted against his conscience. He was never elastic. This kind of failure was also his strength: it was simply his character. But can anyone be sure that, had he acted otherwise, something else, something better, would have been the outcome? But then, perhaps Henry VI would have become another York, or even a Richard III. But he was Henry VI and remained so. The play of the devil was in the cards. Someone else, and not Henry, had to play out these cards.

Thus, King Henry sits on a molehill, alone. He is on a molehill both in a literary and a metaphorical sense. The battle is raging, and no one knows who is winning or losing the war. The mourner, the king, is not interested in winning or losing: "Here on this molehill will I sit me down. / To whom God will, there be the victory. . . . Would I were dead, if God's will were so— / For what is in this world but grief and woe?" (2.5.14–20). And then the king begins to speak about *time,* just as Richard II does in his prison cell. They refer to the same mistake, that they have missed the proper time. But they allude to time through different interpretations, and the difference in their characters shines through their interpretations. Richard bemoans that he had no ear for the history that was out of tune, that he had no feel for the change of time and that he has not grasped kairos. However, this is not what Henry speaks about. He knows that he would have been unfit to grasp this kairos. Perhaps he even had an ear for the unharmonious tune, but he could not restore harmony, because his time was not of "the times"; it was not political time, it was not kairos. His proper time would have been the *time of nature* and not historical time. This is a time during which there is spring, summer, fall, and winter. This is the time when God *sive natura* has ordered things to their proper place, and man has natural obligations to fulfill. "O God! Methinks it were a happy life / To be no better than a homely swain. / To carve out dials quaintly, point by point. . . . So many hours must I tend my flock, / So many hours must I take my rest, / So many hours must I contemplate, / So many hours must I sport myself, / So many days my ewes have been with young, / So many weeks ere the poor fools will ean, / So many years ere I shall shear the fleece. / So minutes, hours, days, weeks, months, and years, / Passed over to the end they were created, / Would bring white hairs unto the quiet grave. / Ah, what a life were this! How sweet! How lovely!" (2.5.21–40). Many English kings—in Shakespeare's portrayal—ruminate about living an honest life like that of their subjects, without worries and royal burdens to carry (for example, Henry IV and Henry V). A few other kings (Richard II, for one) ruminate about time. Henry VI brings them together in one chain of thought. He is the sole king among them all who—again, in Shakespeare's portrayal—really means what he says. Perhaps for a moment Henry IV and Henry V also indulge in similar thoughts, but the moment is passing and they take up their royal tasks again with joy. But Henry VI never wanted to become a king. Royalty has always been a heavy burden to him, and we know that he even felt himself guilty because as a king he could not live up to the obligations of a king. If Henry VI could have lived his life again from the beginning, he would have prayed God to make him a shepherd, that is, as a Rousseauian and not as a Hobbesian man of nature.

Then come the two scenes that resemble a mystery play. Both have their counterpart in *1 Henry VI* where Talbot and his son compete over who will more readily die for the other. In *3 Henry VI* the father kills the son and the son the father. King Henry sits on the molehill and mourns: "Weep, wretched man, I'll aid thee tear for tear; / And let our hearts and eyes, like

civil war, / Be blind with tears, and break o'ercharged with grief"
(2.5.76–78). Again: "Woe above woe! Grief more than common grief! / O
that my death would stay these ruthful deeds!" (94–95). And again: "Was
ever king so grieved for subject's woe? / Much is your sorrow, mine ten
times so much" (3.5.111–12).

The queen takes him away from his molehill to Scotland. Margaret fights
for him; she does not let him die.

While Henry has stolen back to England and is recognized by a game-
keeper, delivered to King Edward, and sent to the Tower, a repetition of a
significant political event is in the making. The last die that offered the sufficient reason for the War of the Roses at the very beginning of the reign
of Henry VI was an act of sexual subversion. Young Henry decided to wed
Margaret, the beautiful lover of Suffolk, and thereby annulled a dynastic
marriage contract negotiated by his uncle. One may still remember that it
was because of this act of Henry that Warwick and his father became interested in the York family and shifted allegiance from Henry to Richard. A
very similar story is going to unfold now. The same Warwick who abandoned Henry, joined York, and made Edward king, travels to France to offer
Lady Bona the throne of the queen of England. Meanwhile, Edward, the
renowned womanizer, covets Lady Grey, a widow who is not ready to go
to bed with him except in holy matrimony. The king yields and marries
her. Warwick is betrayed. While in France, he is informed of Edward's
change of heart, he again does what he has done before. He now turns his
back on Edward and swears allegiance to Henry, whom he promises to get
back his throne.

We know that Shakespeare loves repetitions of this kind, not because he
wants to be truthful to historical facts, which he frequently neglects, but
because he can portray two things at once. First, every historical event is
unique and individual; all conditions are present only once, history does not
repeat itself. Second, there are regularities in history as there are in politics.
Such a regularity is, for example, that taking away the property, particularly
the land, of a subject is a gesture that normally results in disaster. This is, we
know, also Machiavelli's position. In Shakespeare we see a few examples of
this. For instance, it was a serious mistake on the part of Richard II to con-
fiscate John Gaunt's property. We know that the conflict in the first scene in
Richard II, that of the mutual accusations between Norfolk and Bolingbroke, is repeated in act 3 with other main characters. It is still a repetition,
given that the contested issue (the question of who is responsible for
Gloucester's death, a question that remains undecided) is the same. Here in
Henry VI, Shakespeare points out the regularities in two unique events: it is
politically dangerous if the king's personal desire decides the choice of a
queen against the interest of the state. This is why certain patterns repeat
themselves, although every concrete act and event in history is and remains

unrepeatable. In history one encounters the always unique combination of the almost predictable and the entirely unpredictable. This combination interested Shakespeare, I believe, for its own sake, yet perhaps also for concrete practical reasons. He presented, as we all know, his plays in court, mostly before the queen. One can only guess that she found a particular interest in the repeated stories because of the possibility of further repetitions.

To return to our story: Shakespeare deciphers a case of the unrepeatable repetition. Warwick turns around for the second time: "I came from Edward as ambassador, / But I return his sworn but mortal foe" (3.3.256–57). But in comparison to his first sudden shift of allegiance, his maneuvering room becomes incomparably narrow. Still, there is some hope again for Margaret, because his son, Prince Edward, marries Warwick's daughter, Anne. Former enemies are thus reconciled. And Clarence, the second son of York, suddenly decides to marry Warwick's second daughter. The kingmaker also becomes a great marriage broker. To remain close to him, he promises—so it seems—triumph and victory. But the repetition is still partial. Edward is unlike Henry, and Henry has no brother to back him up, not even in his own interest. Edward's youngest brother, Richard, has already shown his teeth.

Richard's first great soliloquy is inserted into *3 Henry VI* as early as 3.2. It takes place at the time of Edward's marriage. Richard expresses hope that no children will be born from this wedlock as additional obstacles to his ascent to the throne, after having gotten rid of two brothers, King Henry and Prince Edward. As we know from the later story, Richard will succeed in ridding himself of these obstacles. We learn further from his utterances that marriage makes him uneasy, for he is fully aware of the ugliness of his deformed body and his unloved self ("love forswore me in my mother's womb"). It is here for the first time that Richard begins to explain his designs with *causality*. He is ugly and cannot be loved; for this reason he wants the throne and the throne alone. We do not need to accept his self-interpretation. In a man's life, nothing can be understood directly by means of a causal explanation, most especially not the goals of a person. This is what Richard is doing here (and is going to do later as well), as if his ugliness would have made his determination to kill everyone who gets in his way. Yet even if the causal explanation of his desire for the English throne must not be accepted, his self-description as a murderous comedian seems to be, in light of later events, accurate. Richard knows himself. As far as the injunction to know thyself is concerned, he gets close to perfection: "Why, I can smile, and murder whiles I smile, / And cry 'content!' to what which grieves my heart, / And wet my cheeks with artificial tears, / And frame my face to all occasions. / I'll drown more sailors than the mermaid shall; / I'll slay more gazers than the basilisk; / I'll play the orator as well as Nestor. . . . I can add colors to the chameleon, / Change shapes with Proteus for advantages, / And set the murderous Machiavel to school" (3.2.182–93). There are only two words in the description that are, perhaps, puzzling: the words "grieves" and "heart." Richard speaks about himself as a man whose heart can grieve. This is not entirely the Richard we will know from *Richard III*. Is Richard's character already fully ready? As I mentioned earlier, just like Henry VI, Richard III will not change character. But still, he speaks about the grief of his heart, and he will never again talk of such grief, although he will constantly speak about himself and no one else.

My interpretation of this shift is based fully on my philosophical vision. At the beginning of *Richard III* we hear a monologue about Richard's existential choice of himself, whereas here he still presents the "self" before the choice. This is the self he will later choose existentially. After he has chosen himself existentially as evil, he cannot speak of his grieving heart, because he has also chosen his heart as evil. But we are still in *3 Henry VI*.

I would return to the main line of the plot. Henry VI is again king of England, but by now his decision is firm: he is unfit to rule, he does not want to govern, he resigns his government to Warwick. "For thou art fortunate in all thy deeds" (4.7.25), agrees Clarence the protector. He wants to remain king, but only in name. In fact, Henry VI discovers a kind of constitutional monarchy: "That no dissension hinder government. / I make you both Protectors to this land, / While I myself will lead a private life" (40–42). But Henry still wishes that Margaret and his son Edward would be allowed to return to England. Here come the famous words: King Henry blesses Henry, Earl of Richmond (the later Henry VII), with, "Come hither, England's hope" (68), and continues absolutely in the spirit of the right "by the law of nature" with which we are so familiar. "His looks are full of peaceful majesty, / His head by nature framed to wear a crown, / His hand to wield a scepter, and himself / Likely in time to bless a regal throne" (71–74).

A brief repetition is again inserted. We always have the feeling of déjà vu, and with good reason when people turn away from a king who has lost legitimacy. This happened also with King Edward, who, however, turned to German and Dutch forces to retrieve his throne (as well as his lands, for just as in the case of Bolingbroke, his lands were meanwhile seized on Warwick's order). Edward wins, Henry loses. Clarence, as expected, is a turncoat again. Now that he returns to the fold of his brother, Edward, Warwick is commanded to yield to Edward also. But the stubborn and haughty kingmaker says no. Edward commands: "Shall, whiles thy head is warm and new cut off, / Write in the dust this sentence with thy blood: 'Wind-changing Warwick now can change no more'" (5.1.55–57). Edward only now minds the blustery wind because it blows in another direction. However, Warwick's fate is still deserved. Henry's reason to elevate him into the position of the governor—because of his consistent good luck—is in the end a mistake.

After having joined Henry, his good luck changes to bad. His funeral oration sounds odd from Edward's mouth: "Die thou, and die our fear— / For Warwick was a bug that feared us all" (5.2.1–2). His death approaching, Warwick discovers the vanitatum vanitas as so many heroes of Shakespeare do: "Why, what is pomp, rule, reign, but earth and dust? / And, live we how we can, yet die we must" (27–28).

The very broad tableau already began to narrow at the beginning of act 5. Now it becomes even narrower. The circle, the stage, becomes smaller. There essentially remain only two royal families on the tragic stage: Prince Edward, Margaret, and King Henry of Lancaster; and King Edward, Clarence, and Richard Gloucester of York. Just as the circle becomes ever smaller, the tragedy intensifies. All the personages on the scene, with the exception of King Edward, will soon die a violent death, but not in this drama. Here there are still victors and victims.

However, even if we consider *Richard III,* there is no balance between the fate of the two families. The Lancaster family does not merely meet a deeply tragic fate. But at least some among them—Henry VI, first and foremost—deserve our empathy as well as the empathy of the storyteller. Even Margaret will step into York's position. As in act 3, York—the Machiavellian, the usurper, the villain—will suddenly be placed in a situation where he can play the role of the man of sorrows. Here Margaret will be placed, although only for a moment, in a situation where she can play the role of Mary: she will be the mother of the man of sorrows. We feel that embracing her murdered son, her lamentations and curses will find their way to heaven, just as the lamentations and curses of the humiliated, mocked, and tortured York do. Is this Shakespeare's justice? For it is not justice. The drama, the tragedy, offers positions and historicotemporal places; and it allows historical actors to play their roles. Even the wicked can move us to tears if they step into the shoes of the vanquished, the downtrodden, the abused, and live up to this role with great passion or dignity. It is not about justice. The two brothers of the York family, particularly Clarence, can be pitied; but their fate will never attain tragic grandeur.

In 5.4 we are before the last battle. Margaret behaves like a king. She is majestic and proud, although she is certain that her war is already lost. This is Margaret's finest hour; she addresses her army: "Lords, knights, and gentlemen—what should I say / My tears gainsay; for every word I speak / You see, I drink the water of mine eye. / Therefore, no more but this: Henry, your sovereign / Is prisoner to the foe, his state usurped, / His realm a slaughterhouse, his subjects slain, / His statutes canceled, and his treasure spent— / And yonder is the wolf that makes this spoil. / You fight in justice, then, in God's name, lords, / Be valiant, and give signal to the fight" (5.4.73–82).

In 5.5 we meet Margaret and all her men as prisoners. Soldiers then enter with young Prince Edward. Prince Edward appears only in a few scenes, but he is a special prince in Shakespeare's history plays. He is the only royal prince who behaves with majesty. We remember that the later King Henry V was far from behaving with majesty in his youth. Young Edward is a strong prince who behaves as an absolute price in the very moment that he is entirely powerless. He addresses the victorious king as "ambitious York" (5.5.17) and as a traitor. The queen cannot help but sigh, "Ah, that thy father had been so resolved" (5.5.22). The "human factor," one of the contingent factors, is once again emphasized by Shakespeare. It was a biological accident that Henry VI is unlike his son Edward. Had son Edward been in his place . . . Shakespeare does not indulge in writing an alternative history, but he again expresses in this little scene his vision of history: nothing is necessary, most things could have happened otherwise.

Then comes the ritual slaughter of Prince Edward. First, King Edward stabs him (he could have died from this wound), and then Clarence stabs him too. Margaret pleads, "O, kill me too!" (41). Richard is ready to finish her off, but King Edward intervenes. Margaret swoons. Richard leaves for the Tower to murder Henry as well.

The Margaret who awakens from her fainting spell is an entirely different Margaret. Within a few minutes, she has grown old. She is now already the Margaret of *Richard III*. She is the Margaret who remembers everything done against her innocent husband and her innocent son. But she forgets what she herself once did when she offered the dying York the kerchief still warm from the blood of Rutland, his innocent son. Now she becomes a Fury, the demon of retribution: "Butchers and villains! Bloody cannibals! / How sweet a plant have you untimely cropped! / You have no children, butchers; if you had, / The thought of them would have stirred remorse. / But if you ever chance to have a child, / Look in his youth to have him so cut off / As, deathsmen, you have rid this sweet young Prince!" (60–66). So it is with Margaret's prophecies, as it is generally with curses and prophecies in Shakespeare. Both Edward and Clarence are going to have children or they have them already, and Edward's children will be killed. However, the children of Clarence will be spared. Margaret appears here for the first time in the role that she will play from this moment on. She was always a passionate woman. She could love and hate; she was full of jealousy and driven to revenge. She could also be generous and rancorous, brave and courageous, for her emotions were always extreme. From now on, all her passions are concentrated into a single passion: hatred. From here on, she will play the role of Nemesis.

Act 5, scene 6 is the end of the tragedy of *Henry VI*. We are in the Tower. Henry reads a book. One should never forget that Henry is a man of intellect. His books are in all likelihood not books of magic (like the books of Prospero) but religious and philosophical works. Interestingly, just before his death, King Henry shows a sense of irony; he now realizes that he participates in a play. This is not because he is a player (he never was), but because he is confronted with Richard, the comedian: "What scene of death hath Roscius now to act?" (5.6.10). His irony is the irony of a fatally wounded man. His irony is the irony of superiority.

The theme of Daedalus and Icarus comes back. We remember that it first appeared in the scene of the common death of the Talbots, where the son died before the father. We had once encountered the repetition of the Talbot scene in the reverse direction. Now we encounter it straightforwardly. We are, however, not on the battlefield but in the Tower. Daedalus and Icarus do not compete to die for their country, but they are both murdered by butchers who are their own countrymen.

Richard mocks Henry, as he also mocked his son. He mocks the story of Daedalus and Icarus (he, just like Macbeth, never had and never will have any children): "Why, what a peevish fool was that of Crete, / That taught his son the office of a fowl? / And yet, for all his wings, the fool was drowned" (5.6.18–20). Henry remains true to himself. He never blames God, nor does he blame fate or destiny or history. This is for him no cosmic history, but a political history. He blames only men who had free will and could have acted otherwise. "I, Daedalus; my poor boy, Icarus; / Thy father, Minos, that denied our course; / The sun that seared the wings of my sweet boy, / Thy brother Edward; and thyself, the sea, / Whose envious gulf did swallow up his life. / Ah, kill me with thy weapon, not with words! / My breast can better brook thy dagger's point / Than can my ears that tragic history" (21–28). And then Henry prophesies that many a thousand will rue that Richard was ever born.

He does something else as well: he provokes Richard. He must provoke Richard to let himself be killed. He wants to die fast. He must make Richard angry, to make Richard stab him, not to extend his tortures. He finds the proper way to make Richard relieve him of his life. He speaks of his deformity, of his mother's pain and loss of hope: "Teeth hadst thou on thy head when thou was born, / To signify thou cam'st to bite the world; / And if the rest be true which I have heard / Thou cam'st" (53–56). The provocation succeeds; Richard bears no more: "I'll hear no more. Die, prophet, in they speech / For this, amongst the rest, was I ordained" (57–58). This is a remarkable sentence. Richard sees himself ordained. Is he ordained by the devil to kill the true, the good, on earth? Or is he ordained to kill everyone, to clear the world from all those who participated in this bloody war? Sure, this sentence appears as a credo of a man of destiny. He is perhaps destined by his birth to be the scourge of the world. This is the prelude of the existential choice of evil. But in order to know his thoughts, we must remain with him alone; and Henry, the last witness, has to die. He reacts to the Richardian sentence of "being ordained": "Ay, and for much more slaughter after this. / O, God forgive my sins, and pardon thee"

(59–60). In his last words Henry presents himself as Christ-like. He asks God to pardon his murderer. He forgives the unforgivable. And this is, to speak with Derrida, the only authentic meaning of the act of forgiving.

Now we remain alone with Richard. Henry is dead, yet he again stabs the dead man. This gesture is diabolic. He stabs a man who is dead and who asked God to forgive him with the following words: "Down, down to hell, and say I sent them thither" (67). He continues, "I that have neither pity, love, nor fear . . . since the heavens have shaped my body so, / Let hell make crooked my mind to answer it. . . . / I have no brother, / I am like no brother; / And this word, 'love,' which greybeards call divine, / Be resident in men like one another / And not in me-I am myself alone" (68–84). This is what I have already indicated: Richard's personality undergoes some changes in *Henry VI*. His character becomes absolutely constant only in *Richard III*.

From his previous monologue we learned that he can pretend to be happy while his heart is aching. It seems as if he knew love and suffering. We cannot doubt that he loved his father. He saved the life of his father, who put him before his other sons. His father's death pained him, and he could not love anyone thereafter. At the moment of his father's death he already reached out for the throne. Must Richard be followed by his son, Richard? Richard Gloucester has never justified his plans with the well-known traditional argument; this circumstance itself could be suspect, but I leave the psychology of Richard aside. Here we meet the rational Richard immersed in his calculations: he has already cleared a few obstacles, like Prince Edward and King Henry, from his way to power; and now only his own family members remain. But this is nothing new. Richard had already resolved in his previous soliloquy to achieve the supreme power, cost what it may. Until this moment members of the York family killed members of the Lancaster family, and vice versa. It is up to the young Richard York not only to murder Lancasters but also Yorks; there are no limits. Until this moment only men were killed, not children and women. The sole exception (and the scandalous sin) was the deed of Clifford, who murdered the child Rutland. For Richard there are no limits; children and women do not make a difference. *This absence of all limits is not merely evil, but radically evil.* That Richard has chosen himself as radically evil was not indicated in the previous soliloquy; he chooses his ends but still not himself. Here, in this soliloquy, he chooses himself as an entirely isolated man away from all human company, a man who does not belong to the human race and who is no brother of the brother. He decides that his soul should match his body. Heaven has given him an ugly body, but he could have chosen a beautiful soul for himself. Instead he has chosen to match his soul to his body. What does it mean that Richard chooses himself as an isolated, absolute loner? It means that radical evil is absolutely lonely. Radical evil can inflict fear, but not love. Is this true? I do not think so. But perhaps, when Richard speaks of love, he speaks of a special kind of love: a love for the being of the other. No man could love him for what he is, only for what he is not. And he means also, perhaps, divine love. God cannot love him, and he cannot love God; nor can he love men or women. Love will therefore always be denied him. This is absolute loneliness; it is an existential loneliness. Richard made an existential choice that was the sole existential choice compatible with the choice of loneliness: to banish himself from the divine theater. There is, however, a tension—or rather a paradox—in Richard's existential choice. He has chosen himself as the devil without God, for he banished himself from the divine theater: the devil of Nihil, of nihilism. But the devil is the Gegenspieler of God; he can play only in a divine theater, he can fight only with God. There is no devil without God.

In the next (last) scene of *3 Henry VI,* King Edward kisses his son Ned. We cannot forget that two scenes before a mother grieved for his son Ned, killed by the same Edward. Edward says that he did everything for his son: "That thou might repossess the crown in peace; / And of our labors thou shalt reap the gain" (5.7.19–20). The brothers kiss their nephew. So does Richard ,who immediately compares himself to Judas. One should not forget that this man—whose character from this moment on will not change at all—loves to play roles and indulges in biblical, mythological, and historical similes. King Edward sends the childless widow Queen Margaret back to France. As we all know, she will not go. It is not important whether the historical Margaret returned to France or not. In the history books she did. In Shakespeare, she does not. But the Margaret who wanders in the royal court is the ghost of Margaret. Whether Margaret herself becomes a ghost who continues to haunt the members of royal family of York to their bloody end, or whether she is the ghost of Margaret haunting the minds of the guilty, makes no difference. She is, as I said, Nemesis itself, who continues to curse the guilty and to punish them with the hand of Richard, whom she outlives.

11

The Tragedy of King Richard III

Shakespeare portrays the logic of tyranny several times. But only in two of his plays, *Richard III* and *Macbeth,* is the tyrant himself the representative of radical evil. Richard is an entirely rational tyrant, whereas Macbeth is an entirely irrational one. Their characters are radically different, yet the *mechanism* of tyranny itself shows strong similarities in both plays. The mechanisms of all tyrannies have certain things in common, and there are even closer resemblances among tyrannies where the tyrant is evil or radically evil. Introducing us into the mechanism of tyranny in *Richard III*, Shakespeare offers an insight into his vision of the mechanism of all tyrannies. Tyranny is in Shakespeare the most abstract form of rule. There can be little resemblance in Shakespeare between one kind of kingship and another (for example, that of Richard II and Henry V), one kind of republic (the Venetian in *Othello*) and another (the Roman in *Coriolanus*); they are concrete forms of rule and government. Yet *tyranny is abstract*. Thus, tyrannies, and particularly evil tyrannies, are very much like all other evil tyrannies. Shakespeare warns against tyrannies, against the danger of plunging into one. For if a tyranny is already established, it will bring the same kind of mechanism into motion as in all previous cases. Tyrannies are disastrous for knights and commoners alike, as well as for the tyrants.

It is because of the abstract mechanism of tyrannies—in Shakespeare's portrayal—that the role of Richard III was so well fitted to Hitler and Stalin alike. One need not modernize the story to have a perfect fit. No strenuous effort was needed to recognize the political essence of the present in the past. Richard III *was* Hitler, and he was also Stalin. He also fits the bill better than Macbeth, for *Richard III* is a far simpler play than *Macbeth*. This is, first, because there is just one Richard. All the others will be his victims and alter egos, since *Richard III* is a one-man show, whereas *Macbeth* is not. At least Lady Macbeth is equal to her husband. This is, second, because of Macbeth's irrationality. A rational—and rationalistic—tyrant like Richard offers a simple, and in this respect also entirely transparent, insight into the working and fate of radically evil tyranny.

Richard III is a simple play, one of the simplest tragedies written by Shakespeare. *Richard II* is also a one-man show, but with an immense difference. Contrary to Richard II, Richard III's character is static; he does not reinvent himself as the play goes on. In fact, in the drama *Richard III,* everything is predictable. Perhaps it is just the simplicity, the straightforwardness of the drama, that has made it so popular. And perhaps it is the static yet complex character of this particular devil that has made Richard III one of the prize roles for noted actors. In one respect, Richard III blends a feature of Henry VI with a feature of Richard II. He is strictly self-identical, just as Henry VI is; but he is also an actor, a player, a comedian, just as Richard II is. Only his game is different. Richard II's game is that of self-discovery and self-invention, finding out what he is. Richard III's game is, at least for a long while, to cover up his essence, to play someone other than who he really is. Both get pleasure out of the game. But for Richard II the pleasure goes with pain; the game can turn masochistic. For Richard III, however, the pleasure of the game remains undiluted; he is sadistic without being masochistic. Richard III plays only with others. The game serves his goal of subjecting others to torture, of misleading them, of causing them pain, and finally of destroying them. There is only one indestructible person in *Richard III,* and this is Margaret, because she is already a ghost, albeit a living ghost who has already lost everything. Richard has no power over Margaret, for he cannot harm her more than he already has. A ghost cannot be killed, blackmailed, or tortured; yet a ghost can torture and kill with curses.

Richard is radically evil because he chooses himself as evil. Shakespeare makes this clear in Richard's last soliloquy in *3 King Henry VI.* Sometimes contemporary performances of *Richard III* begin with Richard's soliloquy from the previous play. This makes sense, although Richard repeats his existential choice of evil in his opening soliloquy in *Richard III.* But his absolute loneliness, this characteristic feature of the demonic, is not accentuated here to the same extent as in *3 Henry VI.* The existential choice is even more succinctly presented in the frequently quoted words "I am determined to prove a villain." This is a precise formulation: Richard does not become radically evil because he chooses evil, but because *he chooses himself as evil.* He repeats here as well what we already seem to know: it is because of his ugly outer appearance that he has chosen his ugly internal essence. This repeated justification is frequently interpreted as the cause or motivation of Richard's wickedness, as if his ugly and "unnatural" appearance, his mother's disgust or even hatred, would have determined the quality of his soul. It is possible that this interpretation caters to general prejudices. Able-bodied men fear the deformed and surmise that a deformed soul might dwell in a deformed body. Shakespeare takes this common prejudice into consideration and plays on it. But he, I think, does not believe in it. He never believes in anything being determined by nature or tradition; he always believes that one chooses one or the other, or both, and one can choose them in different ways. One should not forget that Richard was the favorite son of his father, that his father praised him far beyond his brothers, and that his loyalty to his father was never questioned. These were also very important factors in his life, but why did they not determine him? The answer is that in choosing himself as a villain he could not refer to fatherly love, he could not choose or rechoose the valiant and heroic soldier fighting for the cause of York. In choosing himself as a villain he had to choose his ugly and deformed exterior, the hatred and the disgust of the mother, against the love and praise of the father.

What does it mean that one chooses oneself as a villain? I have already discussed radical evil in the first part of this book. The acts of radical evil are unforgivable, for radical evil crosses all limits. But where are the limits? Who sets the limits? In Richard's day and age, God and his Ten Commandments set the limits. This was the world of the living God; everyone believed in God. By choosing himself as a wicked person, Richard chose to break all commandments, and *he in fact infringed all ten of them*. That is, Richard chose himself as *God's Gegenspieler, as Satan*. Perhaps this was not necessarily "in character," but it was the condition for the drama. I mentioned that even the most lonely characters of Shakespeare need Gegenspielers, for only in confronting a Gegenspieler can a character develop or show itself. Although Bolingbroke is no match for Richard, he can act as Richard II's Gegenspieler. In *Richard III* there is no human Gegenspieler. No one resists Richard. The man who will win the final victory against him is an outsider who never saw him face to face, and he will call him God's enemy: "One that hath ever been God's enemy, / Then if you fight against God's enemy, / God will, in justice, ward you as his soldiers" (*The Tragedy of King Richard III* 5.5.206–8). And those who support his victorious enemy in his battle for liberation are the ghosts, the specters, who cannot be killed, for they are already dead. The specters of the murdered are God's helpers in the battle, and Richmond is the prince of God, as he himself says in his prayer before the last battle. Yes, Richard's Gegenspieler is God himself; he wants to win the battle of the underworld against God. This explains the great number of monologues in *Richard III*: God does not conduct dialogues in Shakespeare's theater. Richard III is the demon, Satan. Can anyone *be* Satan? I hardly think so. But one can play the role of Satan, one can imitate Satan, one can choose oneself as God's Gegenspieler. If someone reads the play attentively, he or she will immediately notice the frequent appeals to the "King of Kings." Only the King of Kings can help, only the King of Kings is a match for this man, only the King of Kings is strong enough to crush the wicked king.

Richard's satanic character explains, perhaps, one of the titles of the play,

The Tragedy of King Richard III. Shakespeare emphasizes in the title that we are watching a tragedy. An absolutely wicked man can also be a tragic hero because he is God's Gegenspieler. Edmund and Iago have no tragedy, and Claudius is not a tragic character. But the wicked Richard is a tragic hero. He has charisma: the charisma of evil.

One could comment that God's Gegenspieler, Satan, from the Book of Job, was not wicked. He just entered into a wager with God betting against man; Job was tried by God himself and not by Satan. However, Shakespeare wrote history plays and not mystery plays. Richard, God's Gegenspieler, was acting not only on the existential stage but also on the historicopolitical stage. The absolute evil is represented as the absolute tyrant. Shakespeare had to present us with the most abstract portrayal of the mechanism of tyranny and with a fairly concrete portrayal of evil incarnate. Richard's portrayal has to become concrete, indeed, to make this drama a real drama or real tragedy, in spite of the abstraction of the politicohistorical mechanism itself. Shakespeare thus *unites* the features of the evil tyrant with the features of Satan from the Book of Job, and with a portrait of a hypocrite and comedian.

Contrary to the Book of Job, it is here Richard and not God who tries men and women to find out whether they can withstand evil, whether they are tempted. Richard plays the role of Satan well; in spite of all the appearances (deformity and hatred of the mother), he has no "inferiority feelings," he has no complexes; he is self-assured in his superiority as the fiend and tempter. He exercises his powers to get everything that he wants. He has the great capacities of the devil, first and foremost, not to recognize any limit. What others may do only in their dreams, he will immediately act out in life. For him there is no difference between a daydream and a goal. *His day-dreams are also his goals.* Everything is possible, everything can be done, everyone can be tempted, every will can be crushed and subjected to his own if one does not know limits at all. This is, first, because knowing no limits means to be without conscience, and conscience (as we know from *Hamlet*) makes cowards of us all. Richard is—in this respect—absolutely courageous. He dares everything, for he lacks conscience. All other capacities of the enemy of God follow from the lack of conscience (and also the lack of the sense of honor and of shame). He can inflict fear, and not just rational fear (since a man without conscience can kill without much ado) but also irrational fear. To inflict fear and to refrain from recognition of any limits form a kind of charisma. But Richard adds something to this charisma. This man without conscience who inflicts fear can also play the *charmeur*. All these capacities together have a demonic effect: Richard III seems to be the perfect tempter. Shakespeare shows us on the stage how Richard employs his capacities to tempt, first in his scene with Anne when he marries the widow of the murdered Prince Edward who hates him and wants him dead, and in the repetition of the scene with Elizabeth, whose children he has killed.

As always, the repetition of a scene serves Shakespeare as both reinforcement and contrast. The repetition of the scene with Anne and with Elizabeth reinforces our understanding of Richard as a tempter and the frailty of women who let themselves be tempted. (However, in Elizabeth's case we cannot know whether Richard really succeeds, or whether Elizabeth yields only seemingly.) Richard tempts. He wants to gain, to exercise his demonic powers; yet he also wants to prove—just like Satan—the truth of the demonic convictions that every man or woman, without exception, can be tempted by evil. But when Richard's conviction is confirmed and he sees how his power to tempt to evil succeeds beyond all expectations, he seems to be taken aback and almost shattered by the result. After his scene with Anne (in which his deformity is no obstacle in winning her love), he ruminates as follows: "What, I that killed her husband and his father, / To take her in her heart's extremest hate, / With curses in her mouth, tears in her eyes, The bleeding witness of my hatred by, / Having God, her conscience, and these bars against me, / And I no friends to back my suit withall / But the plain devil and dissembling looks— / And yet to win her, all the world to nothing? Ha!" (1.2.218–25). That he is fighting against God (and conscience) is clear. What is not absolutely clear is whether he is solely happy about his victory. For this, "All the world to nothing!" is an ambiguous exclamation. This is particularly so if one reads it together with the sentences following it, when Richard compares himself to the murdered Prince Edward and enumerates his serial killings. For it is the exclamation of the triumphal devil, but it is also an exclamation of deep regret. Here Richard resembles closely the Satan from the Book of Job.

One may also wonder whether Richard's acts are indeed the acts of Satan fighting against God, whether they are contrary to God's will or rather executions of his will. Are they not the acts of just retribution? With the exception of the murder of the little princes, one may believe so. After having cursed the whole family of York as the ghost of retribution, Margaret addresses Richard thus: "Richard yet lives, hell's black intelligencer, / Only reserved their factor to buy souls / And send then thither." (4.4.71–73). For Margaret, Richard is the fiend of God, yet at the same time also an instrument in the hand of God. Seen in this respect, *Richard III* is also a play of theodicy. For we may mark the words of Margaret directly following the above-quoted sentences: "But at hand, at hand / Ensues his piteous and unpitied end. / Earth gapes, hell burns, fiends roar, saints pray, / To have him suddenly conveyed from hence. / Cancel his bond of life, dear God, I plead, / That I may live and say, 'The dog is dead'" (73–78). Finally, it will be Richmond, the knight of God, and not Margaret, who will repeat these words: "The day is ours. The bloody dog is dead" (5.8.2). When Margaret speaks, Nemesis, the pagan goddess of retribution, speaks. The ghost Margaret—like the witches in *Macbeth*—here conjures up supranatural creatures and elements. Her curses trespass the historical stage. But the sound and final, triumphal words of Richmond are uttered on the battlefield, on the historical stage. For Margaret, Richard is the fiend; for Richmond he is the tyrant. In fact, he is both.

However, these two elements (fiend and tyrant) together would still yield only an abstraction. Richard is Satan and he is the tyrant; the play is about radical evil and about radical tyranny. This unilinear message is responsible for the relatively simple structure of the plot and the relatively abstract characterization of the main figures. But the drama becomes a drama because of the *concreteness of Richard*. For he is also, as I said, a hypocrite and a comedian. Yes, he is an actor, and he loves acting. He never changes, yet he constantly reinvents not himself but his roles. He is as self-indulgent a player as Richard II once was. But he knows no limits in playing. He compares himself once with a chameleon, for he can change his colors. He plays whatever he pleases. He is simply an excellent actor.

Or is he? An actor is excellent if the audience believes him, if the audience believes that he *is* the one whom he plays. For a while, Richard is an excellent player in this sense. In the first act everyone—except Margaret, of course—believes him; his appearance is taken for his essence. Furthermore, he is not just an actor in the sense of a player, he is also an actor in the sense of a historical actor. An actor who is a historical actor acts not only on the theater stage but also on the historical stage. Richard III, the comedian, carries this tension, this contradiction into the middle of his performances. On the stage of the theater, the historical stage appears, the mechanism of tyranny. As a broker of this mechanism, Richard acts on the other stage. The acts on the historical stage unmask his game and play in his theater as camouflage. Fewer and fewer people will believe him. They will realize that he lies and pretends, that no single word he utters is sincere. They will see the tyrant behind the acts of the comedian, for he behaves tyrannically. Even then, he continues to play. Why? For he is no longer interested in whether or not they believe him. He practices his ability to play out of pleasure. This is perhaps because he enjoys the fact that others do not believe in him but must pretend they do, that his hypocrisy coerces others to speak and act hypocritically, without inclination and without skill. He takes pleasure in his comedies, for as a comedian he is superior to all his enemies and friends. Thus he also plays in order to excel as a good actor among all those bad actors. One never knows which stage one is watching, the historical or the theatrical, whether Richard plays for us or for "them," whether he plays out of spite or for pleasure. Richard's capacity to know no limits in acting makes this devil and tyrant into a frightening but real person, into a complex character one will never forget.

In order to decipher the mechanism of tyranny, one needs to follow the drama step-by-step. Shakespeare designed a very broad hinterland for the

Wars of the Roses. He meticulously presents in the three parts of *Henry VI* all the dice that were thrown, one after the other, to provide the "sufficient reason." Shakespearean scholars usually speak of a tetralogy instead of a trilogy. *Richard III* still belongs to the Wars of the Roses as their final conclusion. In one sense, I would accept this suggestion. After all, the mutual extermination of the grand families of old England is consummated in this drama. It is here that all the actors of the past disappear from the stage. But this is not the only way to interpret the events. Shakespeare has never offered us retroactive "necessities," yet he normally presents the audience with the possibilities of new choices. If one looks at the tragedy of *Richard III* alone, taking away the diabolical figure of Richard and replacing it with another, then we see the Wars of the Roses as a matter of the past. True, King Edward chased women, was suspicious and vain; but so were many other kings, and the young princes are succinctly presented by Shakespeare as able future kings. Edward's and his son's rule could have been peaceful. One should not forget that one of Richard's self-justifications for his evil designs is exactly this circumstance: the new times are the times of peace, of jokes, of music, dance, courtship—not of strife or war. Precisely because he is disgusted by peace, Richard declares war on everyone. One gets the impression—perhaps not just a superficial impression—that in Shakespeare's historical imagination the condition for the tyranny of evil is first and foremost *one single man who is radically evil* and who decides to do evil. An evil character who knows no limits is the indispensable condition of evil tyranny. This is not the historical space in which many single and sometimes equally weighty dice have to be thrown to get a result, because there is one single die here whose importance stands out among all the others. Without this single factor nothing would have happened. Without Gloucester, Richard, King Edward, and his sons might have ruled in peace. Surely, not at every moment and in every place can a demon seize the navigation of the realm. The conditions to accept him, at least in the beginning (for later it will be too late), need to be present. They are present here. At the time of Henry VI's murder, those who remain alive are still full of unfulfilled ambitions and the frustration of unavenged losses. The new sexual subversion (King Edward's marriage with a commoner's widow) has added displeasure to the dissatisfaction already visible in *3 Henry VI*. Moreover, the kinfolk of Queen Elizabeth (the former Lady Grey) were also unwelcome in the court by York's men, and their being in favor is an additional grievance for some remnants of the old nobility. This is particularly so for those who were, or made themselves, into their enemies. To put it simply, there is much unfinished business, and Richard Gloucester is brilliant at playing on it for his own sake. Others' grievances become for Richard the multitudinous instruments of his advancement.

We—the audience, the reader, the initiated—know, of course, that the goal of becoming a king was set in Richard's mind before Edward's marriage to the lady and the birth of their children. We also know that Richard is the man who does not recognize any limits, who does not know the difference between a daydream and reality. Since he already dreamt of himself as the king when not only his own brothers but also King Henry and Prince Edward were still living, the realization of the daydream requires nothing more than to get rid of the rest. There is a kind of madness in the absence of distinction between desire and reality; yet evil is also a kind of madness, at least in Shakespeare's book.

I have tried to show that evil in Shakespeare is a kind of madness. This madness-as-evil includes a lack of knowledge of any limits, of the difference between a wish and a daydream, on one hand, and actuality and action, on the other. We know that Hitler and Stalin were also frequently seen as madmen.

True, one of the most eminent character traits of Richard Gloucester is his rationality. He calculates all his steps ahead of time. In this respect, as in many others, he is the extreme opposite of Macbeth. Is this not a contradiction: a madman who is at the same time utterly rational? I think that Shakespeare's portrayal is accurate in both historical and psychological terms. Madness and purposive rationality do not exclude one another. One can be obsessed by a fixed idea and still calculate all the concrete steps one needs to make. For example, one can have the fixed idea that prostitutes pollute society and calculate in advance when, where, and how one should kill them without being intercepted by the police.

Another misconception is that an evil man, in order to take the wheel of the state, has to be born very close to the center of power. This is certainly not true in the twentieth century, but neither was it entirely true in previous eras. Neither Nero nor Caligula was exactly born to become a Roman emperor. Richard, the third son of a man whose own father was executed as a traitor, who had no title or honor, was certainly not born very close to the fire. First his father and then he himself had to pave their way to power.

I speak of the mechanism of tyranny and of the evil tyrant. Yet Richard III does not begin his career as a tyrant. He begins his career during the last years of Henry VI and the peaceful rule of King Edward. Richard is already at the center of the stage as the embodiment of radical evil before he gets close to the center of domination. He does not yet have political power, and without political power one can be a tyrant only in one's family or close environment. Even the drama *Richard III* can be divided into two parts. The first part tells the story of the Duke of Gloucester, the evil comedian paving his way to power; it is at this stage that he needs to employ his capacities as an actor and as a hypocrite above all. The second part begins when Richard is the protector of the realm and becomes king;

it is the story of Richard III, the tyrant. It is in the second part that we get inside knowledge of the workings of tyranny. In the first part, we are introduced only to the character and to the machinations of the future tyrant. These machinations anticipate the mechanism of tyranny, just as totalitarian parties already anticipate in their structure and functioning the mechanism of a totalitarian state and society before they seize power.

While still striving for absolute power, the Duke of Gloucester murders friends, brothers, enemies, yet he plays the naïve, almost childish, innocent. He overemphasizes his feigned innocence in order to accuse others of the crimes he has committed. He has a double purpose: to rid himself of half his enemies and of those in his way to the supreme power through murder; and to accuse, sometimes with success, the guiltless of murder. He plays with men and women like puppets who allow themselves to be pulled by strings and to be fooled. There are exceptions: he cannot cheat those who already know him from his deeds and not just his words and theatrical acts. In other words, he cannot cheat Margaret and his own mother. In the main, however, he succeeds in his manipulations.

Richard's hypocrisy is not just a kind of Tartufferie. He is not the kind of hypocrite who achieves his goal by pretending to be someone he is not. He does not pretend to be virtuous when actually he is wicked. Richard is a more complicated player. He sometimes plays a role, and plays still another role within that role. Moreover, he overplays his role, and he enjoys not just the game but the overplaying itself. I have mentioned that a tyrant normally has charisma and that he always inflicts terror. This is true of Richard until he seizes de facto, even if not de jure, supreme power. After he achieves the throne, terror will get the upper hand and Richard will be less interested in playing comedy. From then on he can manipulate people because he has the power to inflict terror.

In act 3, Shakespeare clearly draws the line between Gloucester, the evil comedian striving for tyranny, and Richard, who has already set the mechanism of tyranny into motion. Until the beginning of the act, Richard has initiated and ordered murders while pretending to be innocent. From act 3.1—from the moment that he sends the young princes into the Tower—he murders mostly in the open (with the exception of the assassination of the princes and the murder of his wife), while pretending that those he ordered to be executed were guilty as accused. The execution of Lord Hastings is the case that stands for all other cases.

Yet even before 3.1, the gathering storm can be noticed. In 2.4, Queen Elizabeth, after having received the terrifying news that her brothers had been sent to Pomfret, says, "Insulting tyranny begins to jet / Upon the innocent and aweless throne. / Welcome destruction, blood, massacre! / I see, as in a map, the end of all" (2.4.50–53). The queen already sees in the map the whole mechanism of tyranny. But the imprisonment and the later execution of the queen's brothers could be still seen as an act of "normal" Machiavellianism. After all, these men are upstarts, hated in the royal family, and by no means innocent. The queen knows, because her own brothers are the victims. Here all could feel the beginning of the work of tyranny: the introduction of the well-known salami tactic. One takes one slice, then a second, then a third. In the end, the whole salami is devoured. But the second victim is happy as long as only the first victim is sliced, and the third victim will be satisfied while the second one gets sliced. Queen Elizabeth recognizes the tyrant in Richard earlier than others do, because the first slice happens to be her own family. There are no show trials yet. Shakespeare shows the "other side" as well, in the scene where citizens discuss the possible consequences of Edward's death. Among the three citizens, one speaks of Gloucester as a man "full of danger," whereas the others are more afraid of a child becoming king (learning something from the lessons with Henry VI) than of the protector. However, what is commonly observable is groping, unspecified fear: "Truly the hearts of men are full of fear" (2.3.38), says the second citizen. Anxiety is widespread.

But it is in act 3, scene 1, after the young princes have already been sent to the Tower, that the first show trial begins to unfold. The tyrant himself now commands the execution. There is still pretending, playacting. But the protestation of innocence takes a new turn. At first Richard protests his innocence. He has nothing to do (so he says) with the murder of George, his brother, or with the execution of the queen's family. However, he now wields the sword of justice: Hastings is guilty, he is the conspirator. Richard legitimates his murder, he terms it "law." I repeat, this is the moment when the mechanism of tyranny is set into full motion. I think this is why it might have been important for Shakespeare to date this event with the help of the famous strawberry episode, which I discussed in the first part of this book.

Let me briefly recapitulate certain scenes from the first two acts seem to be important for setting the stage for the portrayal of the mechanism of tyranny. The action starts exactly where *3 Henry VI* ends, at the time of Henry's funeral. The first two acts portray Richard and his family to show Richard's ascension to protectorship, that is, to power. (His coronation is just an addition to his already absolute power.) Shakespeare portrays Richard with some gusto. He makes Richard at least three times protest his naïveté and innocence. We see how his brother, the not-very-clever Clarence, believes him, as do some others. Perhaps this is because they buy his hypocrisy, perhaps because they have common enemies and have a vested interest in believing him (like Hastings), or perhaps because they do not really care. Anne (see the seductions scene) will believe also, if not in Richard's innocence—for which he in this encounter does not even want to claim, since his murder of Henry is his pride and also common knowledge—then in his love as his motivation for murder. For everyone who watches this scene, Anne's acceptance of Richard as a true lover appears absurd. It seems as if Richard has gone too far in his game. But he wins with bravado. Offering his sword to Anne to kill him is a calculated risk. Since Richard takes the risk, we may even get the impression that he is ready to die. But the risk is not great; Richard is one of the great judges of character, and he despises women. He is convinced that no woman can resist love, even the love of a murderer, if the murderer assures her that he has murdered for the sake of her love. Shakespeare also plays his trick, of course. He shows us how Richard fools others, but he lets Richard take us constantly into his confidence. Shakespeare gives Richard many monologues. These are monologues in which he not only reveals his otherwise closed personality to us but also takes us into his confidence by telling us his goals, projects, means. We know beforehand what he is doing, what he desires, how he will act; we can follow his designs step-by-step. We are the helpers of Richard in a way, for we are looking into his mind. A loner, a man who does not trust anyone except himself, must trust us, because Shakespeare wants it so. This trick has added to the popularity of this play.

Immediately, in his first, well-known soliloquy, Richard tells us that he is now going to let his brother Clarence be murdered. Everything follows according to his plan. He bids adieu to his brother with the following words: "Go tread the path that thou shalt ne'er return. / Simple plain Clarence, I do love thee so / That I will shortly send thy soul to heaven, / If heaven will take the present at our hands" (1.1.118–21). I have chosen this short passage from among many similar ones because it shows clearly that Richard challenges Heaven, that he plays the devil he has chosen to become, that he has challenged God to a duel. In 1.4, the scene of Clarence's assassination, Clarence answers the challenge, although the answer is not directed to him. For Clarence still believes that he fell victim to his brother, Edward, and that Richard loves him. He turns to the two murderers: "Erroneous vassals, the great King of Kings / Hath in the table of his law commanded / That thou shalt do no murder" (1.4.190–92). But then the murderers justly retort, why has Clarence not discovered this commandment when he was killing others? Clarence answers: "Have you that holy feeling in your souls / To counsel me to make my peace with God, / And are you yet to your own souls so blind / That you will war with God by murd'ring me?" (1.4.245–48). What follows is a familiar Shakespearean scene involving two murderers, one of them unrepentant and the other repentant. The second murderer does not want to touch the murder fee (although he refers to himself as Pilate, not Judas). It is Richard who commits; it is not against Clarence, but against God, that he fights.

In spite of Shakespeare's distinction between the mechanism of evil reaching out for power and evil as the mover of the mechanism of tyranny, there are already tricks played by Richard—in addition to feigning and playacting—that are typical of the mechanism of tyranny. I have in mind *the guilt of speaking in the conditional.* This is where in Shakespeare a tyrant and a king honoring the law part ways: that is, in the interpretation and use of the conditional. This is a matter of modality. We remember the use of the conditional by Henry VI when he speaks of Humphrey's alleged crime, and Humphrey when he speaks of his wife's guilt: *if* this is true, we condemn him or her, but let us first find out whether it is true. The dukes suggest that the accusation against Humphrey is true; but the king says that we cannot know for sure, that we should allow the law to take its course. Here exactly the opposite happens. Richard makes an apodictic statement, and the peers say, "*If* this is true, then . . . "; but Richard does not tolerate an "if." The mere use of the conditional counts for him as high treason. What he says is true, even if it is utterly unbelievable. No if can be tolerated.

We first encounter the tyrannical rejection of the use of the conditional in 1.3, where Richard accuses the queen of evildoing. Richard: "You may deny that you were not the mean / Of Lord Hastings' late imprisonment." Rivers: "She may, my lord, for— ." Richard: "She may, Lord Rivers; why, who knows not so? / She may do more, sir, than denying that" (1.3.90–94). He plays ironically with the word "may" and uses the game as a threat.

When tyranny sets in (after the death of Edward) fear, including the fear of spies and denunciations, becomes widespread. Elizabeth remarks in the same scene in which she speaks of tyranny that "pitchers have ears" (2.4.37). But it happens in 3.1, as I noted, that the mechanism of tyranny is put into full motion. No contrary opinion is listened to, no disagreement accepted. It is either absolute subsumption or death: this is the logic of tyranny.

The tyrant sits in the center of the circle where the mechanism of tyranny is set into motion. The tyrant who sits in the center is also a trainer; everyone within the circle has to practice springing over a vaulting bar. The bar is set higher and higher, since greater crimes need to be committed or approved. This is a moral test for the tyrant's men, although not for the decent men, for they do not even try to jump over the lowest bar. But it is, I repeat, a test for the tyrant's own men. Many of them jump over the lowest bar. The lowest one is to get rid of enemies, to lay traps for them, to manipulate, to rejoice in their death. Four of Richard's men spring over this bar: Hastings, Buckingham, Catesby, and Richard himself. But then the bar, the moral stake, is put higher. Now the princes, the sons of King Edward York, have to be sent to the Tower. They must be disinherited and Richard put in their place. Hastings hesitates; he does not spring over this bar, and thus he will be executed. The next bar is the murder of children. Here even wicked Buckingham hesitates, and for this hesitation he pays with his life. Catesby does everything, not because he is more wicked than Buckingham, but because he is a traditional man of a lower rank. For him the service of the sovereign does not admit any ifs. Richard does not only leap over all the bars, he sets them as well. Setting the bar of wickedness, trying others' resolve to do evil, and killing them if they hesitate: these are manifestations of radical evil. Whoever fails to spring over the bar loses his head. Everyone—bar after bar—loses his head. This is how radical evil remains alone.

In 3.1, Buckingham and Richard send Catesby to Hastings. He has to tell him the good news that his adversaries will be killed tomorrow, and to find out Hastings's reaction to Richard's planned coronation. Buckingham asks: "My lord, what shall we do if we perceive / Lord Hastings will not yield to our complots?" (3.1.188–89). To this Richard simply answers, "Chop off his head" (190). And this is the moment Richard promises the earldom of Hereford, his brother's former possession, to Buckingham. In Buckingham, Richard recognizes his Sancho Panza, his comrade in arms in evil. Buckingham is not wicked by nature, yet he loves the game. He likes to play it for his own benefit: wealth, earldom, power. He climbs through Richard, with Richard, and thus will share his wickedness. This is why Richard, who is always full of suspicion, trusts—as far as he can trust anyone—Buckingham. Buckingham is absolutely dependent on Richard, but now he can play the wicked fool together with him. We may recall that Richard is a loner. When he was just a climber, he took only the audience into his confidence. Now, Buckingham is also his confidant.

It soon turns out that Hastings will not run for the second bar: he does not want to spring over it. He says, "I'll have this crown of mine cut from my shoulders / Before I'll see the crown so foul misplaced" (3.2.40–41). He speaks the truth, although he means to exaggerate. He does not really believe that he will now lose his head after having served Richard so well against the queen and her family. He feels himself safe, and also happy and triumphant: "But now, I tell thee—keep it to thyself— / This day those enemies are put to death, / And I in better state than e'er was" (3.2.98–100). After all, those who will be executed the next day in Pomfret have also felt themselves safe!

Is Richard, the devil, God's executioner? We are at Pomfret, where Richard II was killed. All those who will be killed at Pomfret are guilty of the murder of Henry VI and Prince Edward. All who are now murdered are guilty of being accomplices to murder, just as much as all those who have let them be murdered. However, the men murdered now at Pomfret are repentant: they suffer pangs of conscience, and they regret their sins. Still, the desire for revenge is as strong in their soul as the readiness to confess their guilt. Gray says, "Now Margaret's curse fall'n upon our heads, / For standing by when Richard stabbed her son" (3.3.14–15). Rivers continues, "Then cursed she Hastings, then cursed she Buckingham; / Then cursed she Richard. O, remember, God, / To hear her prayer for them as now for us. / And for my sister and her princely sons, / Be satisfied, dear God, with

our true blood, / Which, as thou know'st unjustly must be spilt"
(3.3.16–21).

Do we remember the fateful dinner in 2 *Henry VI* in which the fate of
Gloucester was decided around the dinner table? We are sitting at a table
again; Hastings wants to discuss the time of coronation. He thinks of the
coronation of the young prince. Then Richard (still the Duke of Gloucester) enters, sending the Bishop of Ely to get him the strawberries. Richard
takes Buckingham aside and tells him what he has just heard from Catesby: Hasting will not approve Richard's coronation. (We know already
Richard's answer, together with Buckingham's: "Chop off his head!") This
is a crossroads. Until now, Richard could still pretend to play his comedy,
for he has not yet put the mechanism of tyranny into motion, or at least it
has been slowly put into motion and many have still not perceived it. Hastings, among them, has not yet perceived it. Hastings takes Richard's fraudulent and hypocritical self-presentation at face value. His own words tell us
how successful a hypocrite and comedian Richard has been during the rule
of his brother Edward: "I think there's never a man in Christendom / Can
lesser hide his love or hate than he, / For by his face straight shall you know
his heart" (3.4.51–53). Now Richard initiates a new game. He still plays,
but now he plays the game of false and absurd accusations. He does not base
his success anymore on his great craft as a comedian but on simple deadly
terror. So Richard asks a "poetic question" that introduces the first show
trial of his tyranny. He asks what should happen with the man or woman
who uses witchcraft against him. "I pray you all, tell me what they deserve
/ That do conspire my death with devilish plots / Of damned witchcraft,
and that have prevailed / Upon my body with their hellish charms?"
(3.4.59–62). To this, Hastings, who does not yet understand that a new poet
has been born and that he will be his first victim, answers: "I say, my lord,
they have deserved death" (66). Richard then comes up with his trump
card: it is Queen Elizabeth and Madame Shore, Hastings's paramour. They
are the ones who conspired against his life. Hastings says: "*If* they have done
this deed, my noble lord" (73, emphasis mine). Hastings utters the phrase in
conditional form. But what if not? Yet there is *no* "if-not." *If* itself casts the
death spell on the man who transforms an apodictic sentence into a conditional one. Richard cries out: " 'If'? Thou protector of this damned
strumpet, / Talk'st thou to me of 'ifs'? Thou art a traitor— / Off with his
head. . . . Some see it done. / The rest that love me, rise and follow me"
(3.4.74–79). This is psychologically a marvelous scene. Since it is obvious
that Richard does not want to allow Elizabeth or Lady Shore to be killed,
he uses their accusation as bait, for he knows that Hastings will bite.

Hastings finally faces the truth, the simple truth all lovers of tyrants who
will become their victims will and must at last discover. "Woe, woe for England, not a whit for me, / For I, too fond, might have prevented this. . . . I

now repent I told the pursuivant, / As too triumphing, how mine enemies / Today at Pomfret bloodily were butchered, / And I myself secure, in grace and favour. / O Margaret, Margaret! Now the heavy curse / Is lighted on poor Hastings' wretched head" (3.4.80–93). So he leaves for his execution.

It is here in act 3, after evil ambition has triggered the mechanism of tyranny, that time will be compressed, actions will become speedier as well as denser. As we know from Hastings's own words, he is executed on the same day as his enemies. We also know (from the earlier scene) that his death was conditionally sealed the same day as that of his enemies. In the next scene Lovel and Ratcliff enter with Hastings's head. Fear becomes terror. The lord mayor is present, since he must retroactively approve the execution. Richard plays his usual games by pretending to have been threatened by a vicious plot, but we feel that the confidence of the audience on the stage quickly withers. All now begin to see the cruel wolf in the garment of the whining lamb. Their eyes will be opened. Richard's comedies will not deceive anyone anymore. It is fear, pure and undiluted, that will make Richard king and temporarily keep him on the throne.

He continues for a while to play the comedian, because he enjoys it. There is another reason as well. At the beginning he needed to pretend to be what he was not. Now he does not need to do this, because he inflicts terror instead. He continues to playact precisely because he knows that no one believes him. Still his audience pretends to believe him because they are afraid not to. He is seconded by Buckingham, the supporting actor, for a time. With Buckingham he is sincere; this is the kind of sincerity that is also like a game, and it lasts only as long as Buckingham seems ready to follow him everywhere. Richard says mockingly, however, that he is following Buckingham. Richard gives his smaller alter ego some lessons: "Come, cousin, can'st thou quake and change thy colour? / Murder thy breath in the middle of a word? / And then again begin, and stop again, / As if thou wert distraught and mad with terror?" (3.5.1–4). And the good disciple answers in kind: "Tut, I can counterfeit the deep tragedian. . . . Intending deep suspicion; ghastly looks / Are at my service, like enforced smiles" (5–9). They are buddies, and are ready to do a joint performance.

Shakespeare shows us one of the joint performances, the one played before the mayor and the aldermen, two bishops, and a citizen to get their support for Richard's coronation. Scene 3.7 can be also read, in a good Shakespearean manner, as a play within a play. Richard and Buckingham are the stage managers as well as the chief actors; they design the act in addition to the roles that they and the others are going to play. But are they acting well? *Richard acts the role of Henry VI.* He pretends to be a good, saintly man, unwilling to take the crown: "Alas, why would you heap this care on me? / I am unfit for state and majesty. / I do beseech you take it not amiss. / I cannot, nor I will not, yield to you" (3.7.194–97). In fact, when Richard imitates Henry VI, he also mocks him. It is a cruel comedy in itself to play the role of the king he has murdered. Buckingham plays his part in the comedy as a fake good Humphrey and finally "succeeds" in persuading Richard to accept the crown. The others remain silent. The mayor approves what he must; there is a hidden threat in the words of Richard, if the mayor fails to approve. Richard and Buckingham are bad comedians, since they cannot identify with the roles they play. What happens on the stage? Good actors must play bad actors, and play them well. This is a double-edged comedy. It is another reason for the play's well-deserved popularity.

Above the comedy played before the mayor and the alderman, the bishops and the citizens, lingers the threat. Hastings was only yesterday sent to his death; the family of the queen has been executed. Richard has shown his teeth. The little Richard, Buckingham, is also feared. But to realize the immensity of terror, one has to join the chorus of women. Four women play the role of a Greek chorus in *Richard III*. These are the widow of Henry VI, Queen Margaret; the widow of Edward, Queen Elizabeth; the Duchess of York (the mother of Richard, Edward, and Clarence); and sometimes also Lady Anne, the murdered Warwick's daughter, the former wife of the murdered Prince Edward, and Richard's wife. It is the chorus of women that accentuates one of the major characteristics of tyranny: the unnatural death of men. These are women whose fathers, husbands, and sons were killed or are going to be killed by the tyrant. They are husbandless and childless women lamenting the fate of their beloved. Their lamentations fill the theater with the voices of the helpless victims, just as in Euripides' play *The Women of Troy*. But at least those men of Troy were killed in war, whereas the men of unfortunate England were the victims of evil. At least the Trojans were killed by the Greeks, by men of another *ethnos*. The husbands and children of these Englishwomen were killed by their own kin, by fellow Englishmen, by members of their own family.

I have said that these women's lamentations fill the theater. So do their curses. No one man is ever cursed by so many women so many times, and so desperately, in any play by Shakespeare, as Richard III.

I mentioned the Greek theater, and at this point *Richard III* gets closer to Greek drama than any other play by Shakespeare. These women in Richard III are truly a chorus, having almost no character, at least in the normal Shakespearean sense. In *Henry VI* Margaret has a character, a very complex one. Here she has none. Here she is the embodiment of grief, revenge, and hatred. She is a ghost and at the same time Nemesis itself. Almost all her curses will take effect, and every victim of Richard will recall them. Margaret's curses sometimes give us the impression that she is right, that Richard is somehow verily "God's informer"—somehow a godsend, the vehicle, albeit unaware, of divine retribution.

Shakespeare avoids going as far as Margaret. Richard allows the two little princes to be murdered. But the two princes are not guilty of anything, they do not deserve punishment. I mention only parenthetically that Shakespeare here reconfirms his vision of history: not all curses will take effect, not all plans will succeed. For example, Clarence's children finally escape murder, and Margaret's curse will not affect them. Margaret's curses are like strong dominating tunes in a piece of music; they are taken up by others. She sings—or rather cries—the theme, and others will slowly take it over. The music of horror and lamentation, the disharmony of the voices, becomes increasingly louder and arrives at its peak in act 4.

But Margaret isn't the only one who has "lost" her character. Queen Elizabeth has no character; neither has Queen Anne. Anne is just a passive creature; she curses Richard like Margaret, her former mother-in-law, becomes a victim of Richard's charisma, marries him and repents, and finally becomes the only woman murdered by Richard. Before her fate is fulfilled, she joins the women's chorus; all the while, though, she is but a voice and not a character.

The only one in the chorus of women who is characterized to a certain degree is Richard's mother, the Duchess of York. She is important in understanding Richard's background. We learn about the hatred against her son from her own lips in this play, although we learn about it from Richard and also from King Henry in *3 King Henry VI*. The only new thing we learn about the duchess is included in one of her answers to the curses of Margaret. She says, "O Harry's wife, triumph not in my woes. / God witness with me, I have wept for thine" (4.4.59–60). At this moment, we see something of the Duchess of York aside from her love for her grandchildren and her hatred of Richard. We realize that this woman can also weep when others suffer. She can empathize—something that Margaret is unable to do. Something is disclosed about the duchess that makes her different not just from Margaret but also from her husband, the former Duke of York.

Margaret remains unrepentant. Queen Elizabeth asks her to teach her how to curse. But no one can curse so well and so absolutely as Margaret. For she has no conscience; her heart is full of revenge, and there is not one grain of love left in it. Margaret remains the only person who is a match for Richard. This is not because she is radically evil, although her torture of York is one of the ugliest scenes in the whole story of the Wars of the Roses, although she is without goodness of any kind. She is going to live as long as any of her enemies. Richard must perish before she does, because she is kept alive by curses. The other women are kept alive by hope. Elizabeth still has a royal daughter, and she has a son from a former marriage. The duchess still has three grandchildren. Margaret is the only one without an heir, without anyone to mourn her. She is a loner, just like Richard. She has not chosen to be a loner; she was made one by Richard. But this is her strength.

The chorus of the women is not the only chorus in *Richard III*. We hear the lamenting voices of the victims, yet we also hear the prosaic voice of the spectator. The spectator does not curse; he observes, takes notes, and describes. He also laments; he laments, not his own fate, but that of his country.

I note here the little scene of the scrivener, who enters the stage with a paper in his hand, the indictment against Hastings. What we hear is, of course, a soliloquy. The scrivener speaks to himself, since what he says cannot be said in public. Only the audience of another age can hear his thoughts, for they are forbidden and dangerous thoughts. There are spies everywhere, one cannot speak aloud. But no one can spy on our thoughts to ourselves: "Here is the indictment of the good Lord Hastings, / Which in a set hand fairly is engrossed, / That it may be today read o'er in Paul's— / And mark how well the sequel hangs together: / Eleven hours I have spent to write it over, / For yesternight by Catesby was it sent me; / The precedent was dull as long a-doing; / And yet, within these five hours, Hastings lived, / Untainted, unexamined, free, at liberty. / Here's a good world the while! Who is so gross / That cannot see this palpable device? / Yet who so bold but says he sees it not? / Bad is the world, and all will come to naught, / When such ill dealing must be seen in thought" (3.6.1–14). The scrivener knows that Hastings's trial is a show trial, that he is indicted before an investigation can take place, that everyone sees through this device but no one dares to say aloud what he sees. This is what the Hastings case, the first show trial of Richard, represents. Shakespeare does not need to portray many such cases; one representative case stands for all. The mechanism of tyranny has been exemplified, and this silences all contrary voices. We have already witnessed the result of Hastings's indictment and execution in the scene with the mayor and the alderman, the bishops and the citizens, in the bad comedy played by Buckingham and Richard.

Richard is king, but he cannot enjoy his power. This could have been foreseen, not only because "sin will pluck on sin," in his own words, but also because he does not take enjoyment in ruling—only in murdering, torturing, playing comedy, and inflicting fear. In 4.2 he discloses his designs to kill his wife, to marry Elizabeth's daughter, and to make Clarence's daughter marry an insignificant gentleman. (This device we know from Euripides' *Electra*.) But a few moments earlier he has taken Buckingham once again into his confidence. He cannot enjoy his royalty, he says, as long as young Edward lives. At first he just hints, and Buckingham pretends not to understand. Afterwards, he expresses himself openly (he has no secrets before his alter ego!): "I wish the bastards dead, / And I would have it immediately performed. / What sayst thou now? Speak suddenly, be brief" (4.2.19–21). But Buckingham temporizes. The bar of wickedness is set too high: he does not know whether he can spring over it. But a moment of hesitation is enough for Richard. This belongs not only to Richard's psychology but also to the logic of tyranny. As there are no ifs, there can be no moments of hesitation. When the tyrant speaks, one has to obey unconditionally, immediately. Buckingham changes (or seemingly changes) his mind and expresses his readiness; but it is too late. For Richard does not hesitate, not for a moment. Seeing Buckingham's momentary reluctance, he drops him and turns to Tyrell, renowned from his close contacts with hired assassins. He makes his decision: "The deep-revolving, witty Buckingham / No more shall be the neighbour to my counsels. / Hath he so long held out with me untired, / And stops he now for breath? Well, be so" (4.2.43–46). This is the moment when the king remains alone; the final loneliness of the evil demon sets in. On the stage, only one embodiment of radical evil plays solo. God can have but one single Gegenspieler who is ready to go to the extreme.

Buckingham decides—after some hesitation—to obey Richard (or pretend to do it) because he remembers that Richard has promised him an earldom and Hereford, and it is time to claim his due. At this moment, we are again getting a good Shakespearean lesson in the psychology of evil and the mechanism of tyranny. Richard does not answer at all; it is as if he has not heard what Buckingham is saying. Buckingham simply does not exist for him. Only at the end of the scene does he deliver a short sentence to his hitherto loyal cobandit: "I am not in the giving vein today" (4.2.119). And it is then that Buckingham understands the mechanism of tyranny in full, and he knows that he will be executed: "O let me think on Hastings, and be gone / To Brecon, while my fearful head is on" (4.2.124–25).

I have said that one does not need to accept Richard's self-justification that he wants Edward dead *because* he is not really king as long as Edward lives. Shakespeare, in fact, makes this explicit. For Richard remembers well Henry's prophecy that Richmond will be king. And if someone believes that Richmond will be king, why should he let Prince Edward be murdered? Yes, "sin will pluck on sin," not because there is necessity in this, but because Richard loves to sin. He has chosen himself as a villain, and without constantly sinning he cannot remain true to himself. This is why he must call for Tyrell and command the assassination of the young princes.

This is the second scene of a secret murder executed by hired assassins in *Richard III*. In other tragedies there is normally only one, and sometimes there is none. The repetition, as always in Shakespeare, accentuates a representative feature of the political system or of a person's character, or both. Here the repetition of murder by hired assassins accentuates that we are witnessing the operation of radical evil. The victim of the first assassination scene, Clarence, is the murderer's brother; the victims of the second are children. Clarence is not just Richard's brother but a brother who loves and trusts him. The young princes are his nephews, and he is their protector. In both cases there is a double transgression. In the second case (the victims are also children), Richard commits the absolute transgression. There are no higher bars of wickedness. Aside from Richard, only Macbeth allows children to be murdered. Only radical evil transgresses the ultimate limit. And this is in fact the last transgression of Richard portrayed by Shakespeare. The rest is unimportant. After the ultimate transgression, one can kill and continue to murder; Buckingham will be executed later. But after the ultimate transgression, one knows everything. Retribution can come only from Richard's Gegenspieler, God, whom he has challenged to the final duel.

In contrast to the scene of Clarence's murder, the assassination of the children is not played before the eyes of the audience. (The portrayal here resembles that of the assassination of Gloucester in *2 Henry VI*.) Moreover, the murder of the children is recounted by Tyrrell, not by the hired assassins themselves, as if Shakespeare wants to spare us the actual scene of absolute transgression. Tyrrell recounts that even the hardened assassins were "melted with tenderness and mild compassion" (4.3.7). One of them almost changes his mind (just as in Clarence's assassination). "Hence both are gone, with conscience and remorse. / They could not speak, and so I left them both, / To bear this tidings to the bloody king" (4.3.20–22). Please note that it is the mafioso, the master of the hired assassins, who calls his king bloody. Shakespeare again demonstrates Richard's sadistic inclinations. He not only wants to have the children dead; he also says to Tyrrell, "Come to me, Tyrrell, soon after supper, / When thou shalt tell the process of their death" (4.3.31–32). He wants to hear the process to improve his digestion.

It is now that Richard decides to marry the sister of the murdered boys. We do not know how much time has elapsed since they were killed, but we assume that it is very little. Perhaps the marriage takes place the following day. This allows enough time for Elizabeth to learn that Richard murdered her sons, but no more. Richard is in a hurry; he wants to execute his plans immediately. As always, the time between plan and execution is representative of a Shakespearean character, as much as the character's resolve to execute a plan. Terrible as it sounds, Richard is a man who has the capacity to make promises. He acts fast and he acts out all his wishes and whims, transforming them into rational plans and choosing their proper means. He acts as quickly as Macbeth, who acts out of instinct, without thinking. As Richard says in 4.3, "Delay leads impotent and snail-paced beggary." It is not only Richard who is in a hurry, but also the play. Richard has just enjoyed satisfaction from the murder of the boys when a war breaks out, threatening his expensively acquired throne (although the costs are paid by others).

The last scene of the lamenting and cursing women is 4.4. The women know already about the death of the princes. Previously, Elizabeth asked

Margaret to teach her cursing. She has learned it, as has the duchess, but the duchess curses no one but her own son.

I mentioned the one sentence of the duchess that I found characteristic: she says that she has mourned the deaths of Henry and Prince Edward. This one sentence is significant to the interpretation of the first part of scene 4.4. The duchess addresses Richard (we do not know why) with the question "Art thou my son?" (4.4.155). She wants to speak with him (why?), and she even adds, "I will be mild and gentle in my words" (4.4.161). To this Richard answers, "I am in haste" (4.4.162). We still do not know, and do not get to know, what the duchess, the mother, wants to tell her son "mildly." For what she now says is far from being mild. "What comfortable hour canst thou name / That ever graced me with thy company?" (4.4.174–75). Now the old tie between mother and son is restored. The mother hates her son, but she wants to continue talking to him. Why? Was our understanding of the mother-son relationship too simple? One has the impression that she remains a mother as she—with her curses—provokes Richard. To what? To stop killing? He has already killed everyone dear to his mother's heart. To confess? To repent? To give at least a sign of his humanity? She must have some reason to talk with Richard, for she is extremely eager to speak. She seems desperate: "Hear me a word, / For I shall never speak to thee again" (4.4.182). Is this a threat? Since the hatred is mutual, Richard could not care less. But does he really not care? Is not one of the secret wishes of this devil to get at last a sign of acknowledgment from his mother? Perhaps, if he achieves everything that his father, his mother's beloved husband, her "man," never achieved: to get a Richard York on the throne of England. If yes, this was his most fateful mistake. That one sentence of the Duchess of York shows her as a mild and loving person. A mild and loving person would never acknowledge the grandeur of a murderer. Her mildness, and perhaps even her goodness, makes her curses more frightful and more extreme. She is, unlike Margaret, not a woman of rancorous passions. And now she does not only curse, she wants the enemy of her son to win the battle! Who cares for the family York anymore? Not the Duchess of York. "My prayers on the adverse party fight, / And there the little souls of Edward's children / Whisper the spirits of thine enemies, / And promise them success and victory" (4.4.191–94). Richard York does his utmost to take the crown from Henry and the House of Lancaster, and his widow now desires nothing but the defeat of York, the succession of a Lancaster. This is the beginning of the end.

I have mentioned the second part of scene 4.4, the seeming repeat of scene 1.2 with Anne. It is up to the interpreters to decide whether Elizabeth has really accepted Richard's offer, or whether she pretends to enter the game to gain more time and opportunity to join Richmond's camp. In my interpretation, the roles have been twisted here. In the end, it is

Elizabeth who pretends successfully, and it is Richard who mistakenly trusts her. This is why he cries out, just as after the Anne scene, "Relenting fool, and shallow, changing woman" (362). The repetition is, however, a repetition in reverse. This does not mean that Elizabeth is not honest. During the whole conversation she remains sincere. Her reference to the King of Kings vouches (in Shakespeare's context) for her sincerity. If we listen to the text attentively, Elizabeth pretends at the end. But she pretends no more than to turn to her daughter and find out her inclination. This is not much, but she can get away with it. And Elizabeth succeeds also in extracting from Richard, the Gegenspieler of God, the devil again. She succeeds not by calling him a devil, which she frequently does, but by making him take a false oath and curse himself, as once Buckingham did, as if this were just a trifle. Richard is again challenging his fate. He curses himself; that is, he challenges once again both the God of Heaven and the goddess of fortune to a duel: "As I intend to prosper and repent, / So thrive I in my dangerous affairs / Of hostile arms— myself confound, / Heaven and fortune bar me happy hours" (328-31). He runs toward his own doom and death. He tries all, and he loses. Does he lose all? Not quite, for he has won first prize for his demonic playacting.

Yet before Richard faces his doom, Buckingham, his last victim, is to be executed. Close to his violent death, Buckingham manifests a rare gift: to tell us succinctly what he has done, what his guilt is, and how evil tyranny works. He also interprets his and Richard's deeds against the backdrop of the work of transcendent powers. He is the one who tells us that he (and Richard) challenged God to a duel. He admits not just that they have lost but also that it was the work of divine justice that they did. This is not just repentance. Buckingham looks at himself from the position of the spectator, or rather the victim—from the position of Margaret. He makes an object of himself, while giving a sincere account of himself and judging himself. This last scene shows clearly that Shakespeare did not want to portray Buckingham as just another petty model of radical evil. He puts his finger on something that is of greater political and historical significance, namely, that radical evil can infect others with its bacillus. In our time, totalitarian rules and rulers have confirmed Shakespeare's observation. Listen to Buckingham: "This, this All-Souls' Day to my fearful soul / Is the determined respite of my wrongs. / That high all-seer which I dallied with / Hath turned my feigned prayer on my head, / And given in earnest what I begged in jest. / Thus doth he force the swords of wicked men / To turn their own points in their masters' bosoms. . . . Come lead me, officers, to the block of shame. / Wrong hath but wrong, and blame the due of blame" (5.1.18–29).

On Bosworth Field the knight of light and the knight of darkness at last meet. But Richard is not just the embodiment of Satan. He is not an abstraction; he is and remains a full-bodied character. This play is, after all, his tragedy. As little as we learn, however, about Richmond as a character, what we know is enough to bring the drama to its close.

Just as the drama as a whole is played on two levels—on an existential-transcendent stage as well as on a historicopolitical stage—so is also the decisive battle acted out on both stages. Henry Richmond is the knight of God, for he understands himself in this way: "O thou, whose captain I account myself, / Look on my forces with a gracious eye. . . . Make us thy ministers of chastisement, / That we may praise thee in the victory" (5.4.61–67).

Richmond is also the liberator, the man of historical destiny who comes to free his country from tyranny and to bring peace. Furthermore, Henry is a new man, "a man of nature," an outsider. He was not born to be king, and he knows this. This is why he sings the praises of self-made men: "True hope is swift and flies with swallows' wings; / Kings it makes gods, and meaner creatures kings" (5.2.23–24). Yes, Richmond is born a meaner creature, and it is hope that carries him now on swallows' wings to become a king.

Two self-made men, two upstarts, meet on the battlefield. Both became kings by choosing themselves. One chose himself as a devil, the other as liberator. They are each other's match.

Richmond himself links the two stages (the existential-transcendent and the historicopolitical) quite closely. He fights his enemy on both stages. He presents this combination succinctly. In addressing his soldiers in 5.5, Richmond begins his speech on the existential-transcendent level and continues it on the historicopolitical level. He first speaks about a murderer, "A base, foul stone, made precious by the foil / Of England's chair, where he is falsely set; / One that hath ever been God's enemy. / Then if you fight against God's enemy, / God will, in justice, ward you as his soldiers." He continues on the historicopolitical level: "If you do sweat to put a tyrant down, / You sleep in peace, the tyrant being slain. / If you do fight against your country's foes, / Your country's foison pays your pains the hire" (5.5.204-12).

Richmond is a simple hero, and we can leave him with his men to rejoice in his triumph. But in contrast to Richmond, who plays on both stages and wins victory on both, Richard seems in his last hours to leave the historicopolitical stage altogether, to meet his defeat and his death on the existential-transcendent stage alone. This is to be alone in a double sense: solely on the existential stage and remaining alone on this stage.

The transcendent stage is set. The souls of the men and women whom Richard has murdered appear in his dream and curse him. They then turn to Richmond, bless him, and promise him victory. Both Richard and Richmond are dreaming. Yet the difference between dreams and visions depends on one's state of mind. Richmond speaks of the "fair" dream that he had.

But Richard has a vision in a dream, although he reassures himself that he was just dreaming.

Richard faces the greatest terror: it dawns on him that his existential choice of himself has failed. All kinds of existential choices face the risk of failure, with the exception of choosing oneself as a good, decent person. One could fathom, however, that the way to choose oneself as a decent being and the way to choose oneself as a wicked being are mirror images, and thus evil incarnate can also avoid or resist existential failure. After all, no special capacity needs to be pregiven in either case (contrary to concrete existential choices, such as choosing oneself as a philosopher or politician, or the like). But, at least in the mind of Kierkegaard, who was the first among the philosophers to break through the jungle of existential choice, there is still an essential difference between choosing oneself as a good person and as a wicked one. For in choosing oneself as a decent person, one chooses oneself back into the human race, whereas in choosing oneself as evil, one isolates oneself from the human race. That is, one chooses the demonic closure of the self.

From all this, few conclusions can be drawn, only that Shakespeare discovered the existential choice and its entanglements many centuries before the philosophers, and that he presented it as a possibility of the human soul and as a puzzle. Since Shakespeare portrays the existential choice of a wicked self through the model of Richard, we have now to follow him closely when, on the battlefield, he discovers the lethal threat of a final existential failure.

One thing I would add to the philosophico-psychological theory of the existential failure in Kierkegaard's terms is that if a person who has chosen himself or herself existentially fails, his or her personality falls apart. The question is whether this is what happened in Shakespeare's portrayal of Richard.

Richard is haunted by the ghosts of his victims, and he wakes up with a start: "Give me another horse! Bind up my wounds! / Have mercy, Jesu!— Soft, I did but dream. / O coward conscience, how dost thou afflict me? . . . What do I fear? Myself? There's none else by. / Richard loves Richard; that is, I am I. / Is there a murderer here? No. Yes, I am. / Then fly! What, from myself?. . . Alack, I love myself. Wherefore? For any good / That I myself have done unto myself? / O no, alas, I rather hate myself. . . . I am a villain. Yet I lie: I am not. . . . Perjury, perjury, in the highest degree! / Murder, stern murder, in the dir'st degree! / All several sins, all used in each degree, / Throng to the bar, crying all, 'Guilty, guilty!' / I shall despair. There is no creature loves me, / And if I die, no soul will pity me. / Nay, wherefore should they?— Since that I myself / Find in myself no pity to myself?" (5.5.131–37).

I said that Richard has no conscience. Now he seems to have pangs of conscience. Again, do we believe him? His conscience tells him that he is a murderer. He is in a state of terror, he is afraid—not of the ghosts but of himself. Why is he afraid of himself? He is afraid because he cannot love himself. No one loves him, and someone who is not loved by anyone cannot love himself. But he has chosen himself as a villain. He must love the one whom he has himself chosen. He must love himself, because if he does not love himself, his personality collapses. As he says, *"Richard loves Richard; that is, I am I"* (137, emphasis mine). This is the very moment of the collapse of the existential choice of wickedness; it is the collapse of the existence, the personality, of Richard. In fact, in this terror-stricken soliloquy, Richard is out of himself; he is no longer Richard as we know him. Although he is Richard, he is also another man. For his personality is split: one half loves the other half, one half hates the other half, one half judges or confirms the other half. Although his personality is split, Richard has no pangs of conscience. This mental and moral "episode" is far more serious and far less ethical. It is more serious, for pangs of conscience normally do not result in the total loss of one's own identity. Remember Buckingham's words before dying. The Richard episode is far less ethical, because Richard is interested only in what *he is*—that is, in the question of his own identity—and not for a moment in the suffering of others. It seems as if Kierkegaard is confirmed. The existential choice of wickedness breaks down, but not in Shakespeare. For in Shakespeare, Richard pulls himself together again; he overcomes his existential crisis.

This is why one can accept the original title, *The Tragedy of Richard III*. Richard overcomes his existential crisis; he returns to himself. But it is no longer important that he has chosen himself a villain. The only important thing is that he reconfirms his existential choice absolutely, and that he will not—cannot—lose himself. In his last words, Richard swears allegiance to the choice of his self. This is the only oath he will keep, irrespective of his wickedness. He chose his wickedness, but now he cannot act anymore as a villain. Nonetheless, he remains true to the gesture of the choice. Be he good or wicked, a victorious king or a tyrant suffering defeat, murderer or innocent—who cares? Richard is Richard. No one loves him. This is what he has chosen. He loves himself, a man whom no other man can love. "I am I." And he will die true to his own choice. After crying: "A horse! A horse! My kingdom for a horse!" (5.7.7)—perhaps the most frequently quoted sentence in the whole drama—Richard chooses to die as a man who confirms his existential choice. His last words are addressed to Catesby, and they are the words of a perfect Nietzschean hero beyond good and evil: "Slave, I have set my life upon a cast, / And I will stand the hazard of the die" (9–10). And *then* he will be killed.

Shakespeare once again makes us face extreme situations—greater than life, souls, and men. Richard gets closest to a human being when he is close to losing himself, when his personality begins to fall apart. But when he pulls himself together again and says, *"I have set my life upon a cast"* (9–10), he tells not just the truth about himself but also why he could pull himself together. When he determined to be a villain, he put his life upon a cast. He is now the loser, but he will never say that God is the victor. No, he is beaten by sheer bad luck, by the hazard of the die. The world is not God's world; neither is it the world of the devil. Who wins—God or Satan— depends on the roll of the die. Richard's defeat is for Richard as contingent as Richmond's victory.

Waking from the beautiful and terrible dream, both Richmond and Richard interpret the world through the voices of the ghosts. A murderer must meet punishment; this is God's judgment. Richmond is the knight of God; he must win, and the dark powers of Satan must lose. Richard hates himself, and he discovers—what he always knew and could not care less about—that no one loves him. It must be noted that already in this scene Richard has left the historicopolitical stage. He never returns to it, not in his last declaration of the rule of contingency. When he cries, "My kingdom for a horse!" he means also, who cares for the kingdom? All these are vanities. He fights the last battle to live up to the hazard of a die. A horse is needed for this, not a kingdom. There is a kingdom left only for Richmond. So he wins on the historicopolitical stage.

What about the existential-transcendent stage? In all probability, Shakespeare sides with Richmond: there is divine retribution, and the devil is punished by the King of Kings. But the last words spoken by Richard about "the hazard of the die" do not vanish. Shakespeare leaves a little window open for another, alternative interpretation. In this play, there is just a little window. In other, later plays, there is an open door. Think of *Macbeth,* think of *Lear.* But perhaps it is because of this simple but strong trust in a just and divine retribution that we love *Richard III.*

The Wars of the Roses have ended. As Richmond says: "Now civil wounds are stopped; peace lives again. That she may long live here, God say Amen" (5.5) This is an historicopolitical happy ending, so rare in Shakespeare's work. Shakespeare hates war, particularly civil war, and he loves peace. But not all kinds of peace in Shakespeare's oeuvre are as promising as the sunny peace at the end of *Richard III.* After having lived through hell, one must believe in heaven on earth.

PART III

THREE ROMAN PLAYS

There are good politics and bad politics. In matters of morality, Shakespeare explores everything; human nature in its infinite variety is infinitely interesting to him. In matters of politics, his judgment is simple. Good politics is successful, bad politics fails. Kierkegaard once remarked that the moment in which a man looks right and left and is concerned with the results is the moment that he is morally lost. A good politician is, however, a man who does look right and left and is concerned with the results. It is in this simple sense—and not because a politician dismisses moral considerations—that politics is external to morality. This is also Shakespeare's understanding of the relationship between morality and politics, as well as Machiavelli's.

One looks for results in a concrete context. Shakespeare understood, much as did Machiavelli, that politics in a republic differs from politics in a monarchy. As I tried to show in the discussion of the the absolute stranger in part 1 of this book, Shakespeare possesses a brilliant historical sense. Human possibilities are always cast differently in a republic than in a monarchy. In matters of politics, this is markedly so. I would dare say that although Shakespeare can portray kings as either good or bad political men, in Shakespeare politics pure and simple appears exclusively in plays placed within the Roman republic. It is in the republican context that politics is always about the constitution of liberties as the invention and establishment of entirely new institutions, and not simply as a better and different way of wielding power.

True, the time is out of joint in all the Shakespearean dramas, and it cannot be set right in any of the tragedies or history plays. On one hand, in the dramas on monarchy, time is out of joint at the very moment the story begins (or two or three plays earlier, as in the history plays on the Wars of the Roses, with the deposition of Richard II). And it is presupposed that in the past, when traditions were still intact, time also sounded like an unbroken tune or rhythm. But in a republic, time itself stands for "being out of joint," for being out of joint is here the essence of political time. In a republic everything is in a constant flow; the rhythm is always broken. In monarchies the essence of politics becomes manifest solely when time becomes out of joint, when legitimacy becomes problematic. Yet, the republic is *about* politics. There is no republic without politics, without the conflict between yesterday and tomorrow, without the collision of interests—not just the interests of a few mighty and ambitious men, but also group interests and the interests of different political ideas. This explains why the multitude plays a different role in the republican plays than in the dramas of monarchy.

I have already expressed my disagreement with several Shakespearean scholars who claim that Shakespeare portrays the republican multitude as the English mob. Shakespeare's historical sense does not let him down. Later, in the context of the plays themselves, I will return to this issue. But here I want to give a bit of a hint: whereas in the English history plays and in some of the comedies the mob is frequently depicted as comic or ridiculous, this is never the case in the Roman plays. The mob can be ridiculous in the English history plays because it is not wielding real power, or because it acts only as an obedient means in the hands of shrewd manipulators. However, in the Roman plays it cannot be ridiculous. The multitude is not always also a mob, and it wields real power even if it can be manipulated (as in *Julius Caesar*). Anointed kings are sacred and are supposed to act by absolute authority. They are absolute princes. But there is no anointed king in a republic, no political power is sacred, and a claim to absolute authority infringes the republican spirit. Politics pure and simple can be portrayed in a world without absolute political authority, where power and domination and the kinds and forms of power can all be constantly queried and put at stake.

Thus Shakespeare's Roman plays are essentially political. It is true that the general Shakespearean distinction between the hierarchy of the ladder of politics and the ladder of historical significance remains in force here as well, just like the distinction between the place one occupies on the political ladder and on the moral ladder. What perhaps strikes us as unique is that there are no radically wicked persons—most are not wicked at all—in the three Roman republican plays. Perhaps this is because the historical material offered a stricter frame for Shakespeare's constitution of characters, although I doubt it. I rather believe that precisely because there is no absolute authority here, there cannot be absolute evil either. In the Roman world there is no Christian God; thus, there is no demonic in Shakespeare's sense, no Gegenspieler.

I will speak of the three Roman plays primarily as political plays, although this is only one of their aspects. Since Shakespeare chose three different stages in the history of Roman politics, I will follow these stages according to their historical appearance and neglect their sequence in Shakespeare's literary oeuvre. Thus *Coriolanus,* the play written last, will be discussed first.

12

Coriolanus

Coriolanus is a tragedy with an unsympathetic but by no means wicked hero. Caius Martius is a man who remains a spoiled child almost until the last moment of his life. Cornelius Castoriadis once told me, in reference to his decades-long psychoanalytic practice, that a person who believes that everyone loves him or who cannot endure it if someone does not love him remains a child and will never grow up. This is a fairly accurate description of Coriolanus. He is an adult man still doted on and lionized by his mother, from whose love and judgment he can never extricate himself. He is a patrician who hates the plebeians but is still deeply hurt when they do not repay his hatred with adoration and respect. He is the warrior who cannot even imagine that his love and respect for fellow warrior Aufidius, a Volscian patrician, is not returned. Haughty and naïve, easily inflamed and cruel, Coriolanus does not seem likely to appeal to a modern man's sympathy. Yet he does. The Hungarian plebeian poet Sandor Petofi, who translated Coriolanus into Hungarian, recognized himself in the patrician hero, although no one could be further from Petofi's political sympathies than Coriolanus. George Eliot simply loved Coriolanus. Likes and dislikes are difficult to explain. This one, however, is understandable. The deserving man, the genius, the outstanding man who is rejected by the mob, whose merits are not acknowledged, who loses out against undeserving competitors only because he cannot ask favors and cannot sell himself, will always sympathize with Coriolanus. The fundamental situation of rejected excellence shines through the play, and so does the "lesson": deserving men should speak for themselves, they do not need advocates. The deserving man hates to flatter, particularly to flatter the one who can do him favors. Haughtiness is certainly not a Christian virtue. But those who sympathize with Coriolanus do not sympathize with a Christian virtue. They identify themselves with genius; their sympathy is modern and romantic. Everyone knows at least one Coriolanus personally. My next-door neighbor is one. He is a philosopher who will never humiliate himself by applying for a job, because the whole world should know that he is the best. He will never ask for letters of recommendation, he will never show his wounds (his list of publications), for these plebeian routines hurt his pride. And if, in the end, a far inferior competitor gets the honor (the stipend, the position, the award), he will be filled by righteous indignation against the irrational mob (academic institutions are also moblike). He will be indignant about those who prefer mediocrity to excellence, who like to be quoted, who are never magnanimous enough to acknowledge a brilliant performance unless the performer flatters their vanity. These kinds of haughty men are also inclined to fits of rage—the anger of righteous indignation—or sometimes even to manipulate their own anger, exactly as Coriolanus does every evening in the theater. Are these lovers of Coriolanus entirely wrong? I doubt it. For, in fact, what they say is true. Average people, if gathered together in a crowd or in a democratic institution, are not in favor of tall poppies. They prefer to cut off the tall poppies' heads. It is more comfortable to live with mediocrity than with excellence, for one does not like to feel oneself to be small. The gesture of self-humiliation was not invented in vain, as it is not practiced in vain in every culture. Self-humiliation—asking for favors or saying "thank you" even where there is nothing to thank someone for—is the traditional gesture of self-protection against envy, jealousy, and resentment. In a world where equality is one of the guiding political ideas, the tendency to press toward substantive equality can become omnipresent. Substantive equality enhances the perception that no single man is better than any other single man, that all merits are but relative. Grandeur, genius, and brilliance are treated with suspicion and regarded as phony pretentiousness. This is even more succinctly the case if the man of grandeur or genius understands himself as such, if he is eminently aware of his own superiority. In monarchies where tradition reigns, it is taken for granted that men are unequal and that there are some who are in all respects superior to others, who cannot even be compared with some others.

Coriolanus takes place in a world that shows many similarities to modern republics and modern democracies: it is a world of ressentiment just like our own world. Our contemporaries who sympathize with Coriolanus support their preference for very different reasons: hostility to democracy, siding with the individual in conflict with the crowd, contempt for ingratitude, and so on. Richard Rorty says, in the wake of Judith Sklar, that in a liberal democracy cruelty is the gravest vice. This, like every similar generalization concerning vices, is exaggerated. One could say with just as much justification that ingratitude is the greatest such vice. For Shakespeare, safe radical wickedness—namely, cruelty and ingratitude—is the gravest vice. I discussed in the first part of this book the scenario of sexual subversion: the cruel woman is for Shakespeare the ultimate barbarian. True, the cruel man is second in line. Tenderness and gentleness are crucial virtues. Many a representative Shakespearean hero praises the virtue of being gentle. Gratitude is in itself not the greatest virtue because it should be taken for granted, but gratitude above the measure of mere reciprocation is a virtue of supreme sublimity. Shakespeare tells us many stories of faithfulness, and also of disloyalty and betrayal. The latter are also cases of ingratitude, different variations on the theme.

Thus, to return to Coriolanus: he is cruel, whereas the multitude is ungrateful. They face each other with their respective vices, not with their virtues. Both Coriolanus and the multitude have virtues. Shakespeare is no Nietzsche, he does not voice his preferences. He portrays a political situation in which both parties are right as well as wrong, a politically unbalanced and dangerous situation. In the collision between Coriolanus and the multitude, there is a balance in vices (ingratitude and cruelty hold the balance), yet not in the scale of grandeur and sound politics. Grandeur is only on one side, the side of Coriolanus; sound politics is only on the side of the multitude, the tribunes. Sound politicking is not a virtue in Shakespeare's book. Still, it is good politics if it yields beneficial results. Grandeur is in itself also no virtue (for example, it can be demonic), yet it is the condition of a tragedy. Coriolanus can be a tragic hero, for there is a certain grandeur in this grown-up child, this cruel man. The grandeur of Coriolanus is rooted in a few virtues, first and foremost the virtue of magnanimity. This is a noble virtue that since Aristotle has stood aesthetically at one of the pinnacles of all virtues. This virtue is also a virtue in a republic or a democracy.

But I reiterate that it is not with his virtues that Coriolanus faces the crowd, for he is far from acting magnanimously toward the multitude; he is magnanimous toward his patrician friends and patrician enemies. The tribunes also turn toward Coriolanus not with their virtues (for example, of rational speech, of reason giving, or of decision) but with their vice, ressentiment.

Magnanimity is the potentiality of a tragic hero, but Coriolanus becomes a tragic hero solely through his final catharsis. The crowd never changes, since this is not a man but a many-faced multitude; yet, the politics of the multitude can change if circumstance so decrees. This happens in the play. Coriolanus, the man, however, can change: in the end magnanimity, accepting the power of reasoning, wins over his enormous pride. His own virtue wins against his own vice directly after the moment in which he, the man of mere instinct, finally succeeds in formulating the principle of his life after banishment, the principle of a modern self-made man: "I'll never / Be such a gosling to obey instinct, but stand / As if a man were author of himself / And knew no other kin" (*Coriolanus* 5.3.34–37). These are, let me repeat, the haughty words of the self-made man, which recall Richard III's last declaration of self-identity ("I put my life upon stake"). Shakespeare sweeps away the historical sources. It is not the patrician man who speaks these words, but the man who made himself—who does not belong to any cast, any people, any family. It is the man who even abandons his patrician instinct and stands before us as his own creature. It is from this height that he will kneel down before his mother and resign. His gesture will be the opposite of that of Richard III. Whereas Richard returns to his existential choice, Coriolanus resigns his—not under duress but on purpose, knowing exactly what he is doing. He knows himself to be lost, but not in the way usually interpreted. It is not just that he knows that Aufidius will kill him but also that he knows he has given up his ultimate pride as an entirely self-made man. It is not the patrician politics, it is not his class, but his chosen self. He sacrifices himself for Rome. This is the absolute act of magnanimity, where gratitude for his home, country, and kin gets the upper hand over his enormous pride and cruelty. This is why I suggested that magnanimity will conquer his pride. Coriolanus does not die as a military hero or as a hero of the patricians, but as the "knight of resignation" in the Kierkegaardian sense of the phrase. In the first step of his catharsis—when he understands himself as the author of himself—Coriolanus ceases to be the blond beast, the man of aristocratic instinct, the cruel man. But the second step follows: Coriolanus resigns himself as a self-made man and—to refer again to Kierkegaard—"repents himself back" into his kin, country, and city and thereby regains himself.

But let me return to the beginning of the story. There is the blond beast on one side and the multitude's ressentiment on the other. The blond beast belongs to a world of substantive inequality, the republican multitude to the world of substantive equality. They represent opposite sides of the same political coin and belong together. Nietzsche, who among the moderns not only discovered ressentiment but also put his finger on its intimate relation with substantive equality, has also described (and presumably also preferred) the blond beast. In Nietzsche, there is a historical sequence between the emergence of the blond beast and the crowd of ressentiment. In the republican/political situation portrayed by Shakespeare, they are coeval and mutually dependent; they complement one another. They are each other's enemies, but they are enemies who live from the very existence of each other. Shakespeare keeps cool as an author. He does not defend the blond beast against ressentiment, or ressentiment against the blond beast. He presents us with the conflictual situation in which both the cruelty and haughtiness of the blond beast, and the cowardly ressentiment of the crowd reciprocally develop and reinforce one another.

Coriolanus is a cruel, haughty, magnanimous, grown-up child. In remaining a child, he is hardly rational; he is easily carried away by fits of rage. Yet he also creates his fits of rage artificially as a means to blackmail (as many children and adults do). Undetermined, weak, and malleable within, he plays the stern man of absolute resolve, the brave and unshakable man of muscle for his Rome and its enemies, that is, for his audience and spectators. He is entirely outer-directed, a man without conscience but with an overgrown sense of shame. In Shakespeare (as already in Plutarch), an internal weakness is compensated for, or rather covered up, by a show of stubborn rigidity. The man can be easily hurt; this is why he hurts others easily. This psychological sketch is also the sketch of a role-player. Coriolanus is entirely dependent on the role assigned to him by his mother. Thus, he is entirely dependent on his mother. He always wants to please her; he wants to appear before her eyes as the greatest. Let me reiterate that the culture of Coriolanus is a pure culture of shame. Only the eyes of others determine for him the difference between good and bad. He constantly watches his mother's eyes, seeking her approbation. As an outer-directed rather than inner-directed man, he is, in the opening scenes of the drama, very far from being a self-made man. He is instead a man made by his mother, Volumnia, guided by her ideal of a patrician male. It is, perhaps, not artificial to contrast the figure of Coriolanus again with the figure of Richard III, who is hated by his mother. Richard desires total power instead of recognition. One of Shakespeare's deepest psychological insights, which he reveals both through Richard and through Coriolanus is, be yourself or else lose yourself. Where Richard chooses to remain himself and dies a wicked death, Coriolanus chooses to lose himself while he regains himself and offers his life as a sacrifice. The man who was beloved by his mother can afford to lose himself, because for him there is something to fall back upon since he can regain his kin through repentance. But the man who was hated and rejected by the mother can fall back only upon himself. Granted, this comparison is one-sided. Richard and Coriolanus do not resemble one another in any other aspect of their actions or lives.

The brief psychological sketch of Coriolanus in Shakespeare is the sketch of a role-player. In the first act he plays solely the role that his mother pressed upon him. As I said, he stands always before the eyes of his mother. When we encounter him, he has already become used to playing this role. Precisely because of his internal weakness and incapacity to reason, he will become unable to change from one role to another. His story first develops as the story of a man whose superego (in this case the mother) pushes him to change from one role to the other, whereas he feels himself already incapacitated to take on and to play the second role. Volumnia, guided by her own ambition, presses the political role upon her son. She does not notice that her son, her male substitute, is unlike her. She does not notice that his soul is not as strong as hers, that he is just playing a role dutifully. He can play no other role. To play many roles one needs to be elastic, and in order to be elastic one needs a hard and immovable core of personality. This is the kind of core that Coriolanus finally acquires, in growing up, almost at the very end of act 5.

Coriolanus belongs to those plays by Shakespeare that, like *Richard II* and *Richard III*, can be described as one-man shows, in contrast to plays like *Julius Caesar* and *Antony and Cleopatra*. The latter, together with *1, 2,* and *3 Henry VI*, can be described as decentered dramas with multiple main characters. A one-man show is not a show with a single hero but a show with only one central hero around whom the plot revolves. We see Coriolanus in relation to his mother (wife and son), to the Roman plebeians, to Menenius, to the Volscians, and among others to Aufidius. Shakespeare does not present Coriolanus with a single soliloquy, although he speaks two asides. Once again, we encounter an exemplification of the existential/sociological handling of the soliloquy in Shakespeare. The demonic character who is unable to communicate, whether wicked or alienated, is presented by Shakespeare always with several monologues; Iago, Richard III, and Hamlet are examples; they talk to themselves, for they cannot talk to anyone else. Yet, Coriolanus cannot talk to himself except near the end of the drama, during his catharsis, when he twice speaks aside.

In the case of Coriolanus, there is a contrast between the weakness of the interior and the resoluteness of the exterior; yet as far as thoughts are concerned, essence and appearance coalesce. This is why we see and hear Coriolanus only as a being related to other beings, that is, in acting. Speech can also be action, but the content of such speech is normally very meager. The important element in Coriolanus's acts is his gestures. Fighting and using the sword are gestures; falling into rage, abusing others, humiliating oneself (before the mother): these are all gestures. Before act 5 Coriolanus is close to being the hero of a puppet theater, for his gestures—theatrical, simple, rigid—are seemingly identical with the man. The gestures are always emotionally loaded, and those emotions are extremely simple. The simplicity of the emotions, emotions as kinds of "acting out," the absence of the difference between external and internal—all these acquire eminent dramatic significance during Coriolanus's fits of rage. He cannot control himself, nor does not want to control himself. He lacks willpower.

These fits of rage belong in an essential way to the very role that Coriolanus plays, to the role of the war hero. As long as he plays this role alone, the identity of internal/external never becomes problematic. Why do I speak of role-playing if internal and external are identical? Coriolanus plays himself, that is, he plays the persona fixed upon his thin identity by his mother. But because he is constantly acting before the eyes of someone (before the eyes of his soldiers, the enemy, Aufidius, and—even while she is absent—before the eyes of his mother), he constantly overplays the role. This is why he also manipulates himself into a state of rage.

The primary role of Coriolanus is that of the soldier, of the Roman army general. In battle, there are some benefits to the soldier's state of rage. The enraged person does not care about himself, he is not concerned about his life or well-being, he does not even notice his wounds. The enraged person is stronger because rage makes men strong. To be inflamed, to lose control, enhances the strength of a soldier in a battle situation. If we read attentively the battle scenes of *Coriolanus*, we will soon notice that Caius Martius wins his battles with personal bravado, through his unconcern for his wounds and with his sheer bodily strength. He is not a strategist; he has no tactics; he does not plan his moves ahead of time. His whole existence as a general has nothing to do with the work of the brain but only with the omnipresence of his body. Caius Martius acts without thinking. Losing his head does him no harm because it improves the use of his body.

Shakespeare's numerous war heroes, soldiers, and generals share certain similarities. As I tried to show in the first part of this book, none of those soldiers and generals makes a good politician. Perhaps they are like lions, but they are never like foxes. Still, as all single persons are different in Shakespeare, so are all single soldiers. Talbot, for example, identifies himself with his army. His victories are, according to his own self-understanding, the victories of a brave army; they should not be ascribed to him alone. He is also a patriot, as is his son. They both die for England. Their loyalty can never be in doubt. There are additionally soldiers—as we shall see while discussing *Antony and Cleopatra*—like Enobarbus, who is ready to change allegiance if defeat is certain. He is also characterized, just like Coriolanus, by his personal bravado. But he is rather a plebeian figure, interested in advancement and in money, and is not a man of shame. I think that it is not worthwhile to continue this line of discourse, to admit the uniqueness of Coriolanus among the soldier-types of Shakespeare. But I repeat that there is a common feature here: none of the soldiers is good at politics. There is a kind of simplicity in all of them that disqualifies them from devising long-term strategies. Yet, in contrast, good political men, although they are not great soldiers, can excel in waging wars because they wage wars with their brains, by devising strategies and tactics, by making alliances and breaking alliances at the right time and in the right place.

The tragedy of Coriolanus begins when he is thrown into a situation alien from the role for which he was trained: he is pressed by his mother to take up a consulship. His character is unfit for this role. The first obstacle is that an irascible man will be bad at republican politics. In addition, since he is transparent, his enemies know about his irascibility and will use his weakness for their own purposes. If one has to fight in a fit of rage, the enemy might succumb. However, if one talks in a fit of rage, one is going to say many things one did not even intend to say. This is because one ceases to think it over. One will expose oneself and will in all probability lose. The identity of appearance and essence in one's convictions makes the person also unfit to carry on with the work of politics. In politics one also plays a role, but the role needs to be modified in any given situation in order to be played successfully. The political role (contrary to the role of the warrior) does not need to be internalized; this is why it can be modified. The roles of the soldier and the politician are played before each other's eyes, but in politics the roles are usually played in a certain disguise and, if not, at least with the attitude of distance. Coriolanus cannot play a role with distance, yet a political man must do so. In act 2, Coriolanus takes upon himself a role (under pressure) that he is absolutely unfit to play.

But why does he do so? He does so for the same reason that he plays the first role, the soldier, which has already become his personality: because his mother wants him to. Coriolanus is on the one hand aware that he is unfit for this role, yet he is also absolutely convinced that he is the best man for the job of consul. This leads to an ambiguity. He plays this role without playing it. He plays it while showing that he hates it, that it does not suit him—that he would rather not play it. Only very bad actors play that way. Coriolanus becomes a very bad political actor, yet he still believes that he is the best actor for this role. Politics appears to him as a reward for his bravery. To make a contemporary analogy, he is like a very rich man without any political experience elected to parliament, or a Communist Party functionary who can hardly read or write but who is put in control of a writers' association.

Coriolanus not only plays badly but also intends to play badly; for in his mind the political role is unworthy of a soldier. When his mother, Volumnia, tries to persuade him that he is mistaken, that the two roles are very similar (for, on the battlefield one also pretends to have a plan different from the one carried out), in principle she is right. But in the case of her own son she is wrong, since, as we know, Coriolanus understands war as a fight on equal terms—when soldier meets soldier, where superiority is qualitative and not quantitative. Even in the war scenes Coriolanus appears to be neither a strategist nor a tactician. He does not pretend or calculate, for he is unable to do so. This is also a sign of his childishness, something that his mother caused but would not notice.

Let us now briefly follow the story. The drama starts with the uprising of the Roman plebeians. Shakespeare, as is well known, fuses two uprisings into one. The plebeians are enraged against Caius Martius (the later Coriolanus), who is their sworn enemy. Already in the first scene, Shakespeare gives the citizens the capacity of speech, that is, the capacity to offer arguments and to discuss matters, even during times of upheaval. The first and second citizens differ in their judgments and express this difference clearly. One notices that this plebeian crowd is not the faceless multitude that we encounter in *Julius Caesar*. In this drama, the plebeians have faces. It is not merely their representatives who have faces but also the individual citizens. Thus, when the first citizen censures the pride of Caius Martius, the second answers in a way that could have been a quotation from Nietzsche's

On the Genealogy of Morals: "What he cannot help in his nature you account as a vice in him" (1.1.39–40). Shakespeare, following Plutarch, at this point introduces Menenius and makes him tell his famous story. Menenius plays the counterpart of Coriolanus. He is a patrician like him, he despises the crowd like him, but he is also a politician. He knows that in politics compromises cannot be avoided, that there are no absolutes but only maximum possibilities. He is ready to protect the patricians and to keep the power of the Senate intact, to enter into a compromise with the citizens; he talks to them and appeases them.

The new institution, the *tribuna plebis,* was established as a result of political negotiations, although—in Shakespeare—without the knowledge of Menenius. As I mentioned, the establishment of this institution is of chief importance to the development of this play. Politics pure and simple is politics of interest, particularly of group interest, of handling conflicts and solving them relatively peacefully; it is also about speech and compromise. The establishment of a new institution is not a temporary tactical compromise but a lasting one. The Senate, as we are informed indirectly from the curses of Caius Martius, accepts the representation of the people by the tribunes. Something new happens here that will last, that will become a historical institution. The political question put to Caius Martius is the following: how will a Roman patrician relate to this new institution at the time of its conception?

At the very beginning, as a prelude to the development of the plot and the presentation of his character, we see Caius Martius facing the plebeians with uninhibited class hatred. First he abuses them, calls them "dissentious rogues," and later calls them rats, just because they are hungry and want corn to eat, and he accuses them in one breath of ressentiment: "Who deserves greatness, / Deserves your hate" (1.1.174–75). Not for a moment does Caius Martius want to hide his hatred and contempt. For, contrary to those of the Nietzschean blond beast, Coriolanus's words express not only contempt but also hate. He feels himself endangered, and this is how an original contempt, which may also be coupled with some kind of pity, becomes transmuted into boiling hatred. He loses self-control because he thinks that he does not need to control himself before the rabble. He does not try to restrain himself while speaking about, and to, nonentities. Although many interpreters of Shakespeare accuse him of misrepresenting the crowd, I believe that the citizens of Rome, in Shakespeare's presentation, practice much more self-restraint and are far more intelligent and understanding than their patrician enemies.

But presently the news arrives that the Volsces are in arms, and Aufidius is leading them. Caius Martius, who entertains nothing but hatred for his Roman plebes, immediately expresses his high respect for the enemy of his country who is, like him, a general and a patrician: "And were I anything but what I am, / I would wish me only he." (231); "He is a lion / That I am proud to hunt" (235–36). The respect seems mutual.

However, it is not in a public scene but in the household of Caius Martius that we get a first glimpse of a blond-beast character befitting Nietzsche's pen. Valeria, the like-minded friend of Volumnia, recites this story not about Coriolanus but about his son. "O' my word, / the father's son! I'll swear 'tis a very pretty boy. O' / my troth, / I looked upon him o' Wednesday half an hour together. . . . I saw him run after a gilded butterfly, / and when he caught it he let it go again, / and after it again, / and over and over he comes, and up again, / catched it again. Or whether his fall enraged him, / or how 'twas, / he did so set his teeth and tear it! O, / I warrant, / how he mammocket it!" (1.3.59–67). I note that in three brief sentences Shakespeare succeeds in characterizing all three women. Volumnia says, "One on's father's moods" (1.3.68). Thus, she praises in the sadistic and cruel boy the father, her son. Valeria says, "Indeed, la, 'tis a noble child" (1.3.69). She expresses her conviction that a sadistic and cruel act becomes a nobleman. And Virgilia (the wife) says, "A crack, / madame" (1.3.70). She does not like to hear what she has heard, but she cannot oppose two powerful matrons, particularly not her mother-in-law. Yet, this mother-in-law dominates the whole scene. She scolds her daughter-in-law because she is anxious about her husband going to war. She should be cheerful. She has sent her son into a cruel war to seek danger and to win fame: "I sprang not more in joy at first hearing he was a man-child than now in first seeing he had proved himself a man" (1.3.15–17). The ancient Roman legend of Coriolanus, even in Plutarch, corroborates that Coriolanus has proved himself a man (although Plutarch speaks of his insecurity, too). In Shakespeare the bloodstained Coriolanus of the battlefield is no man, or not yet a man. For a man is a man of free will, not a dependent and cruel child with adult weapons. In Shakespeare, Coriolanus becomes a man in act 5.

One can ruminate about Volumnia's motives. Since I cannot sufficiently emphasize that Shakespeare refrains from presenting the motives of his heroes, we can attribute to Volumnia many different motives. She is happy to have a man-child, for she was born an ambitious woman who soon found out that there is no place for ambitious women under the Roman sun. She wants to achieve the highest honors through her son. There can also be Oedipal motives. One may recall that when Volumnia addresses Virginia, her daughter-in-law, and scolds her, she says, "I should freely rejoice in that absence wherein he won honor than in the embracement of his bed where he would show most love" (3-5). It will not escape our attention that the mother imagines herself in the place of her daughter-in-law, in her son's bedchamber, making love. But one can also understand her as a widow who wants to replace the missing father, to become the father-mother of the orphaned boy and the mediator of the old virtues of nobility. And these motives, like many others, are not mutually exclusive. Volumnia is, after all, a fairly complex woman. She almost belongs to the Shakespearean gallery of manly women of "sexual subversion"—but not quite. For at the end of the drama she will surface as the mother: as the mouthpiece of the homeland, of the earth, of biological-genetic ties, of the umbilical cord that no one should ever cut—not even her son.

In 1.4 we meet Caius Martius on the battlefield. The army retreats. At this moment the hatred of Caius Martius against his plebeian compatriots breaks out once again ("All the contagion of the south light on you, / You shames of Rome"[1.5.1–2], etc.), and he enters the gates furiously alone. I had, first and foremost, this bravado in mind when I said that as a general, Coriolanus is not fighting with his mind but just with his body. He wins with his bravado and blind courage. Yet the first thing that he does when facing the consul (the official leader of the army, Cominius) is to denounce the plebeians politically: "The common file—a plague! tribunes for them!" (1.7.43). And then he turns to the deserving ones with an appeal to follow him. Blood does not only need to be shed, if it must in fact be shed; one needs to love blood, to love this "paint." I have missed a few important details. One thing must be mentioned, however. Coriolanus is haughty. But haughty men also like to humiliate themselves and can be extremely modest if they face people they acknowledge to be of equal rank, even if not of equal merit. There is a little episode here that again sheds light on Coriolanus's personality, or rather, illuminates even further the traits that we already know. Coriolanus asks, as a gift from Comenius, to spare and to reward a poor man of Corlioles who has treated him kindly. Cominius happily agrees. But when he asks the name of the good man, it turns out that Coriolanus has forgotten it.

We, the audience, also learn something about Aufidius's hatred for Coriolanus. Coriolanus does not suspect this hatred, for he cannot even imagine that someone of his own rank and bravery could hate him. Coriolanus knows hatred and cruelty, but he does not know envy and jealousy. These are vices alien to a magnanimous and haughty patrician. This naïveté will cost him much—in the end even his life.

Coriolanus is in my mind such a thoroughly political play that the politically uninteresting scenes (such as the introductory part of 2.1) also seem dramatically redundant. In my understanding, the second act begins with Volumnia and Virginia joining the tribunes and Menenius bringing the news that Coriolanus will soon return home wounded and victorious. It seems that there is here a touch of irony in Shakespeare's strictly Plutarchian characterization of Volumnia. She thanks the gods for the wounds of her son, a little later: "There will be large cicatrices to show the people when he shall stand for his place" (144–46). When Menenius mentions Coriolanus's nine wounds, the mother retorts, "He had before this last expedition twenty-five wounds upon him" (150–51), to which Menenius adds, "Now it's twenty-seven" (152). After this exchange Coriolanus enters, kneels down before his mother, and leaves to see the patricians. Volumnia's mind is set upon making her son a consul of Rome: "There's one thing wanting, which I doubt not but / Our Rome will cast upon thee" (198–99). Volumnia is certain, for she misreads, as do so many other heroes of Shakespeare, historical time. What would have been certain only a few years before is no longer certain now. Volumnia takes it for granted that whatever the Senate decides is final. But the situation has changed since the institutionalization of the tribunal of the people. The institution is brand-new; one does not yet know its power. This will be the first time (not in Roman history, but in Shakespeare's plot) that the new institution will try out its power, by stretching it to find out how far it can go and what it can achieve. The acceptance or rejection of the enemy of the people, Coriolanus, as the next consul, is a veritable test case. And the tribunes (in Shakespeare's portrayal) are in a political sense absolutely sound to treat it as a crucial test case. It is not just the fate of Coriolanus that is at stake but also the fate of the Roman institutions. The conflict is a politically representative one. The two tribunes are different, yet their commitment is the same. Brutus more frequently uses the language of ressentiment, which is also his own language; yet he also follows the exigencies of a politician of interest. Class (group) interest as the motivation of rational politics is also something new. When Sicinius admits that he might warrant Coriolanus's consulship, Brutus immediately answers: "Then our office may / During his power go sleep" (2.1.219–20), and he is politically in the right. He is a populist politician and he is, indeed, good at his office. His arguments (for he has arguments, indeed) are sound, as are his tactics. He sometimes employs rude rhetoric to persuade people not to elect Coriolanus, but not just because of malice. Rather, it is because he knows how dangerous Coriolanus may become. The content of his rhetoric is not demagogic, for he is right: "We must suggest the people in what hatred / He still hath held them; / that to's power he would / Have made them mules, / silenced their pleaders, / And dispropertied their freedoms, / holding them / In human action and capacity / Of no more soul nor fitness for their world / Than camels in their war, / who have their provand / Only for bearing burdens, and sore blows / For sinking under them" (242–49). In the next scene (2.2) we learn that Coriolanus is going to be elected to the consulship by the Senate. One of the most interesting political debates follows this scene, a debate between two officers. We do not know to which group they belong—perhaps they belong to none—but they are for certain not members of the Senate. Shakespeare shows us here the attractive sides of a republican/democratic decision-making process, introducing two people who discuss the merits and demerits of a candidate very objectively and with a kind of clever superiority. They understand that Coriolanus does not want to flatter the people, but the first officer adds, "Now to seem to affect the malice and displeasure of the people is as bad as that which he dislikes, to flatter them for their love" (2.2.21–23). The two men hold different opinions and exchange them peacefully.

After the Senate's consent to Coriolanus's consulship, one senator turns to the tribunes to ask their consent. Brutus answers: "Which the rather / We shall be blessed to do *if* he remember / A kinder value of the people than / He hath hereto prized them at" (56–59, emphasis mine). This "if" stands for a sound condition put by a man who protects the interests of his electorate.

I think that, in Shakespeare's portrayal, the story of Coriolanus is not a story of ingratitude and popular hatred, a collision between an unthinking mass and a deserving yet proud hero—not at all. It is not a moral but a political story. Politically assessed, the tribunes of the people are sound, and they are absolutely right. It is only that theirs is a kind of politics Coriolanus does not tolerate and the Senate as yet does not know. That the members of the Senate also seek their own advantage in conducting public affairs is natural; but they do not admit it, because admitting it would be unworthy. In addition, the members of the Senate are not good, as Coriolanus at one point says, at using words (he in fact says, "I fled from words" [73]). Menenius is here the exception; this is why he will be the man of compromise. Words are the weapons of politics pure and simple in the republic. Rhetoric, argumentation, and persuasion are republican/democratic modes of speech. The patricians fight wars only with swords, whereas the plebeians fight with words. This is an entirely alien scenario for Coriolanus and his entourage. It is not just that Coriolanus feels himself unfit for politics (and at the same time the sole right choice for office), but politics itself has changed and is still in the process of changing. Just a few years before (in the drama of Shakespeare), Coriolanus would have been elected unhindered to consulship; and he could have become a fair consul, even if not a significant one. Coriolanus is unfit for politics in general (as all the soldier types in Shakespeare are). Yet he is absolutely disqualified from entering politics in the particular time in which he lives and in the particular situation into which he is thrown. His failure is overdetermined. Since Shakespeare here follows his sources, other interpretations are also admissible. The senators who try to persuade Coriolanus to go to the people and ask their favor refer to his predecessors who have all done so; they speak of a custom to be followed. Yet, in Shakespeare the appearance before the plebeians to ask their favors cannot yet be a custom. For Caius Martius hears about the institutionalization of the tribunal just before he goes to war against the Volsces. And he would, if elected, be the first consul after Cominius, the consul during the war.

The whole scene between Coriolanus, the multitude, and the tribunes is, however, Shakespeare's invention. First, we are confronted with a situation similar to that in the earlier discussion between the two officers: the citizens have different opinions, each argues against the opinion of the other. Particularly interesting are the (sometimes funny, but always intelligent) words of the third citizen. First, he warns his fellows against the vice of ingratitude (we know that ingratitude is one of the gravest vices in Shakespeare's book): "Ingratitude is monstrous, / and for the multitude to be ungrateful were to make a monster of the multitude" (2.3.9–11). From this he draws the result: "Are you all resolved to give your voices? / But that's no matter, the greater part carries it. I say, *if* he would incline to the people there was never a worthier man" (2.3.37–40). The "if" lingers in the air. Then Coriolanus enters and does not hide his hateful contempt for the people. He speaks like a racist, as if the plebeians belonged to another race. His abuses uttered against the plebeians resemble the abuses heaped upon Shylock and the contemptuous words addressed to Othello in the two dramas placed in the Venetian republic. Before even talking to the plebeians, Coriolanus says: "Bid them wash their faces / And keep their teeth clean" (2.3.62–63). The plebeians are dirty, they stink. And while Coriolanus is reluctant to ask for the votes of the electorate, the third citizen says something very straightforward and correct: "You must think if we give you anything we hope to gain by you" (2.3.71–72). To this Coriolanus answers by asking mockingly: "Well then, I pray, your prize o'th' consulship?" The first citizen, with a great amount of dignity, retorts, "The price is to ask it kindly" (2.3.73). As we know, at the end of this scene Coriolanus will get the people's voices. However, these voices will be retracted in the next.

It is often said that this happens because of the demagoguery and manipulation by the tribunes. But Shakespeare's portrayal is more complex. The tribunes do not act like (in *Julius Caesar*) Marc Antony; the multitude of *Coriolanus* is not the mob of *Julius Caesar*. The crowd (as many single individuals) is surely always ready to change its mind under the influence of persuasion. But there is a very great difference between the tribunes and Marc Antony's ways of persuading the crowd. There is no hero worship here—precisely the opposite. Furthermore, the tribunes do not appeal to sentiments or to pecuniary advantages. Times are different, as are people and institutions. I cannot stress enough Shakespeare's unfailing historical instinct. It is not simply that the tribunes manipulate people. For several citizens have already noticed that, while asking for their views, Coriolanus is mocking and ridiculing them. It needs to be emphasized that before the tribunes utter one word, the majority of the citizens (two out of three, at this point) know that Coriolanus mocked them, and they begin to regret their vote. It is at this point that the tribunes begin to speak. Brutus, the cleverer of the two tribunes, who uses the weapon of words more skillfully, is the first to notice the change of mind in the majority. His rhetoric is based on this knowledge, as well as on the idea of the majesty of the people. It is a great idea for a tribune of the people. Brutus believes that the plebeians gave their vote to Coriolanus because they are still standing meek before the mighty, because they have gotten used to being humble. He believes that they should overcome their humility. He warns them that Coriolanus has always spoken against their liberties. Those who voted for him fail to cherish these liberties. Sicinius—who is not as good at rhetoric as his fellow tribune but better at sheer power politics—devises the idea to manipulate Coriolanus (and not the plebeians). Sicinius claims that they should create a situation in which Coriolanus would lose his newly won consulship by working him into a state of rage in which he would say things that would disqualify him for the office. The plan is manipulative but not necessarily also evil. For if a man who can be put into a state of rage with the slightest provocation—to the extent that he becomes irrational— is voted in as the consul, he will probably do a very bad job. In particular, he will revoke the liberties of the people, because he perceives those liberties themselves as a state of provocation. Granted, there is a shovel of Machiavellianism thrown into the fire. It is not easy to revoke a voice already granted. Thus, the tribunes advise the people to lie: they should put the blame on them, they must say that they were pressed by the tribunes to cast their vote for Coriolanus. It needs to be mentioned, however, that this dirty, manipulative plan is not executed in Shakespeare. Coriolanus's rage will be sufficient reason.

The third act follows the structure of an ancient Greek drama. A hero who is at the pinnacle of his good fortune—winning wars, becoming exalted as a hero, elected consul—will be thrown from on high into the pit. First he is abused, then put into a state of rage, and then stripped of his honors. Finally, he almost loses his life and is banished from the city. This is a representative nosedive. Most Greek heroes (as also some heroes of Shakespeare—Lear, for example) learn their existential lesson in the pit; others do not. In Shakespeare, for example, Timon of Athens does not learn his lesson, nor does Coriolanus. One can learn a lesson only with the force of introspection, which opens up the internal chambers of a man, divides his self, and makes a naïve, self-righteous, proud, stubborn, or superficial man ready for reflection and self-reflection (such as Lear or Richard II). However, those who do not open up their internal chambers do not learn a lesson. They become rigid in their pride, will merely blame others for their misfortune, and cry ingratitude. Instead of resorting to reflection, such a man becomes obsessed with the hatred of those whose favor was expected, required, and taken for granted. In this sense, the story of Timon and the story of Coriolanus resemble one another. Yet Timon becomes an absolute misanthrope who translates his hatred into curses, whereas Coriolanus, who learns to hate his country and cuts all ties with tradition, translates his hatred into personal ambition. *Timon of Athens* is one of the most hopeless dramas ever written by Shakespeare. This is not true of *Coriolanus*. (One has to presuppose that Timon—in Shakespeare—is already past his fifties, whereas Coriolanus is very young.)

What is immediately interesting at the beginning of act 3 is that Coriolanus, in the middle of civic strife when he has just taken up the consulship, will be obsessed with one man alone, Aufidius. His unfinished duel with Aufidius weighs far more on his mind than his unfinished conflict with the plebeians. Yet his conflict with Aufidius is unpolitical. It is a kind of emulation. Coriolanus wants to be first among equals, and it is Aufidius alone whom he accepts as his equal. He is fixated on Aufidius as much, although not in the same way, as he is fixated on his mother. Where does Aufidius live? Has Aufidius spoken of him? What did he say about him? These are Coriolanus's main concerns before the tribunes enter. His mind is still with Aufidius: "I wish I had a cause to seek him there, / To oppose his hatred fully" (3.1.20–21). Immediately afterwards, he speaks about his contempt of the tribunes. But the despised tribunes confront him with authority. They do not let him pass, for, as they say, the voices of the people were denied him.

It is in this scene that Coriolanus speaks with full openness without a second thought, for the tribunes understand how to rid him even of the weakest attempt at a compromise. By putting him into a state of rage—which is easy—they manipulate him. However, in my understanding, they have not manipulated their own electorate, the plebeians. The tribunes follow a cool tactic; they refer to ancient conflicts between the people and Coriolanus (for example, concerning the free distribution of corn), and their tactic proves successful beyond expectation. They use Coriolanus as a mere means for their goals, and he lets himself be used. Despite the constant interference of his friends, particularly of Menenius, who tries to silence him, who prays him to withhold his opinion and to control his rage, Coriolanus becomes more and more uncontrollable. I agree with the interpreters who (in the wake of Plutarch) suggest that Coriolanus's trouble is internal weakness; his own anxiety that he might let others win him over and change his opinion makes Coriolanus such easy prey to his own rage. He abuses the plebeians, and when Menenius warns him to do "no more" (77), he goes on and on, maneuvering himself into an ever greater fit of rage. No one can control his tongue any longer, including himself. He shouts, for example: "So shall my lungs / Coin words till their decay against those measles / Which we disdain should tetter us, yet sought / The very way to catch them" (81–84). Hearing this, the hated Brutus, who keeps calm, will be in the right when he remarks, "You speak o'th' people / As if you were a god / To punish, not a man of their infirmity" (85–86). But during this unequal altercation the most remarkable exchange of words comes a little later. After the words of Sicinius addressed to Coriolanus as to the enemy of the people, that "It is a mind / That shall remain a poison where it is, / Not poison any further" (89–91), Coriolanus explodes: "'Shall remain'? / Hear you this Triton of the minnows? Mark you / His absolute 'shall'?" (92–94). The injunction "shall" is close to a command; it can be interpreted thus. And who commands? It is only the man born to command; the patrician has the authority to command. All the values are reversed; the table of values is turned upside down when the minnows can say that the giants "shall" be or do this or that. This seems to be the end of the world. And it is, indeed, the end of the world of Coriolanus's childhood and youth. The "shall" reminds him immediately of the Athenian democracy. It is in the Greek democracy that a plebeian who was chosen as a magistrate could address a patrician with a "shall." The stake of the political contestation is well formulated here: it is precisely in regard to the possibility or impossibility of even a restricted kind of symmetrical reciprocity. This is because even in a restricted version of symmetrical reciprocity (restricted because plebeians can enter the state of reciprocity not with their individual bodies but solely through their representatives), the citizens of the same city—whether plebeian or patrician—will be in an equal position to address each other with a "you shall." What occurs to Coriolanus (to Shakespeare's Coriolanus) and what is the target of his growing indignation, is the division of powers. There is no longer one center, but two, "and my soul aches / To know, when two authorities are up, / Neither supreme, how soon confusion / May enter 'twixt the gap of both and take / The one by th' other" (111–14). Since Coriolanus's times (or rather Shakespeare's version of Coriolanus's times), democracies, or even republican governments (in the Kantian sense of republicanism), were constantly attacked by their enemies by bringing about institutional chaos, disorder, and anarchy, ending in the loss of all authorities, and so on. The reference to Greece is a reference to a past historical experience, the interpretation of which is here taken up by Coriolanus. (I mention parenthetically that in the times of the legendary Coriolanus, the Roman population had not the faintest idea about the existence of the Athenian democracy.) As almost always in Shakespeare, it is of no interest whether or not democracy indeed runs amok toward the destruction of the city, whether or not Plato's interpretation, as it was handed down for centuries, needs to be accepted at face value. The main thing is that Coriolanus—as all patricians—believes in the truth of this fact; it is true for him and is not just a phony piece of self-justification.

Indeed, Coriolanus here speaks openly and utters only sentences that he believes to be true. But from this, certainly, it does not follow that in fact they are true and that others share the belief that they are. Shakespeare's political sense suggests that in political speech and argumentation the belief in the rightness or truth of something is one of the strongest motivational forces. What you believe to be the case is the case for you. The belief can change, but then a new belief works the same way. The destruction of the prerogatives of the aristocracy is, in Coriolanus's mind, tantamount to the destruction of the city. Grandeur will be the matter of the past, and the Senate's power will become an empty shell.

Coriolanus (in Shakespeare) is unable to formulate gloomy predictions without abusing his enemies in all possible ways, always pointing to their pettiness, baseness, lack of nobility, and quality. It is the rabble who—as he says—"will in time / Break open the locks o'th' Senate and bring in / The crows to peck the eagles" (140–42). From this point on, the enraged Coriolanus becomes absolutely unstoppable. Now he does not even hear the soothing words of Menenius; he enters the hyperbolic state of rage: "One part does disdain with cause the other / Insult without all reason" (146–47). And he becomes threatening: "At once pluck out / The multitudinous tongue; let them not lick / The sweet which is their poison" (158–60). He then even becomes personal: he abuses the tribunes because of their old age, and finally he questions the legitimacy of their office. He turns to Sicinius, a man elected by the people: "Thou wretch . . . / What should the people do with these bald Tribunes. . . In a rebellion . . . / Then were they chosen. In a better hour / Let what is meet be said it must be meet, / And throw their power i'th' dust" (167–73). This sentence is high treason, and this is what the tribunes were waiting for. Now, finally, Coriolanus is rightly accused of treason, and the tribunes allow him to be apprehended. Even after having been apprehended, Coriolanus remains in a state of choler. He calls the tribune "old goat" (188) and becomes violent. Now he not only wants to hurt with words but also with his hands and with a sword; he wants to beat and to kill: "Hence, rotten thing, or I shall shake thy bones / Out of thy garments" (181–82). Menenius, who is the man of compromises and of good common sense, calls to both parties to control themselves. But it is only Coriolanus who has lost control, for the tribunes remain cool. Coriolanus's naïveté also consists of his belief that his abuses will harm the tribunes; he does not realize, because he is incapable of noticing anything, that it is precisely his abuses that they want. And here comes an extremely important exchange of words between a senator and a tribune. The first senator denounces the act of the tribunes (who apprehended the wrongly elected consul) as an act to "unbuild the city" (197). Yet the tribune (Sicinius) formulates the well-known Aristotelian dictum in the form of a question: "What is the city but the people?" (198). The plebeians echo him: "True, / The people are the city" (199). The first part of 3.1 ends with the tribunes' declaration that Coriolanus deserves the death penalty.

I have dwelled on this tense scene to show Shakespeare's detached rendering of the conflict's development. Who is right and who is wrong?

Either both parties are wrong, or neither. It is here that the men of ressentiment confront the blond beast head-on. The conflict is presented. No side is taken. The interpreter is to take sides. After Coriolanus's exit, Menenius says: "His nature is too noble for the world. . . . His heart's his mouth" (255–57). Many interpreters take this judgment to be the judgment of the author. However, Menenius is a senator, a patrician, and an old friend of Coriolanus and is a kind of substitute father to him. His appreciation of Coriolanus is in his situation and character. There is little reason to think of him as the author's mouthpiece. Yet there is equally little reason, or even less, to think that the author sides with the plebeians. For right is here pitted against right. Menenius still treats Coriolanus as the consul, since he was in fact lawfully elected consul. And the tribunes (the plebeians) do not consider him a consul but a traitor, because he abused the institutions of Rome and its representatives, threatening rebellion in reverse, thereby disqualifying himself from the office of consul. To use a contemporary expression, they have impeached him. The situation—where right is pitted against right—is threatening; civil war may be renewed. Coriolanus would be only too happy to draw his sword, but his mother disapproves.

I think that this exchange between mother and son is of crucial importance. The mother, who has raised her son to be a proud patrician warrior—a haughty and stiff youth who is the embodiment of all manly virtues—suddenly realizes that the product of her upbringing is unable to practice self-control. She notices for the first time the essential insecurity of her man-child. Coriolanus turns to his mother with complete understanding: "I talk of you. / Why did you wish me milder? Would you have me / False to my nature? Rather say I play / The man I am" (3.2.12–14). To this Volumnia answers: "You might have been enough the man you are / With striving less to be so." (18–19). If one plays the man, one is not man enough. Volumnia gives her son some of her wisdom and asks him to think hard: "You are too absolute, / Though therein you can never be too noble." (40–41). It is then that she refers to the similarities between making war and doing politics: one needs to apply tactics in both cases. I already hinted at her mistake; she has sent her son to the battlefield, but she never sees him there. We, the voyeurs, know that Martius has never won a battle by using his head or any special tactics; he has won only by using his anger and bravado. The mother now asks her son to do something that contradicts the character the son has hitherto played: to ask for pardon, to show regret. Volumnia is a Roman woman. Her duty is owed to her city; right or wrong, it is her city. Here for the first time it will become obvious that the doting mother respects the laws of her city above all: "Prithee now, / Go, and be ruled" (90). Coriolanus gives up; he will ask for pardon. But he knows that by doing so he loses himself. He does not lose the self that his mother believes to have brought up but the self that he cherishes as his identity. So he says, "You have put me now to such a part which never / I shall discharge to th' life" (105–6). Volumnia still holds sway over her son, and she will never cease to do so. The son obeys, but there is an internal schism in his soul. For there is an abyss between the man he believes his mother wants him to be and the man whom the mother now expects to act. An outer-directed man becomes confused if expectations unexpectedly change. This happens in Coriolanus's case. Volumnia praises him now: "My praises made thee first a soldier, so, / To have my praise for this, perform a part / Thou hast not done before" (108–9). And when Coriolanus resists, she continues to insist and to blackmail him mildly: "Thy valiantness was mine, thou sucked'st it from me, / But owe thy pride thyself" (128–29). Coriolanus concedes. He gives up and says: "Pray be content. / Mother. . . . Chide me no more. . . . Look, I am going. . . . I'll return consul, / Or never trust to what my tongue can do / I' th' way of flattery further" (130–37). Volumnia, who now notices the child in the man who overplays the man, does not notice that with her praises she is throwing Coriolanus back into his childish state—no longer a firm state, but rather a chaotic, childish state. It is also questionable whether her advice is sound. She acts under the illusion that while asking pardon Coriolanus can still be and remain the consul of Rome. This is an incorrect assessment. Coriolanus humiliates himself in vain—at most he saves his life for the time being— but will not keep the great office his mother's ambition assigned to him.

Act 3, scene 3 is the culmination of the political clash between the patricians and the plebeians. The scene contains, in a nutshell, the free fall of Coriolanus from the height of a consulship down to the pit of disgrace and banishment. The previous scenes can also be described as cat-and-mouse games in reverse. Coriolanus was in a position of power. He was abusive and shouting, he spoke from upside-down; he seemed to be the person launching an attack. In fact he was under attack. In 3.3 he is no longer under attack in fact only but also de jure. He is not just pressed into a corner, but officially charged with "affecting tyrannical power." He is found guilty before trial, but the sentence is still open. It can be a fine, banishment, or death. The tribunes, so it seems, would prefer death. Their tactics remain as before. As Brutus says: "Put him to choler straight" (3.3.25). This is because whatever Coriolanus promised Menenius and his mother, Brutus knows that in the state of rage "he speaks / What's in his heart, and that is there which looks / With us to break his neck" (28–30). The outcome— given the character of Coriolanus—could have been easily predicted. The tribunes and the people first decide to banish Coriolanus. This will be his trial; it will be his moral trial as well. Coriolanus, as always, runs immediately into the trap and loses the trial: "You common cry of curse, whose breath I hate / As reek o'th' rotten fens, whose loves I prize / As the dead carcasses of unburied men / That do corrupt my air: I banish you"

(124–27). He then makes a statement that is fueled by rage; by uttering this sentence he loses, for the time being at least, also his moral trial: "Despising / For you the city, thus I turn my back. / There is a world elsewhere" (137–39). Coriolanus takes the position of which he is accused—not the position of a tyrant (for he lost the opportunity for that) but the position of a traitor. He shows himself to be a man who has placed his own person and pride above his city, for whom it becomes indifferent which city he is going to serve as long as he remains the master. From behind the guise of a patriot the condottiere appears, the man who is indifferent to cause and country, who holds only his own power dear. These are the words he will, in the end, deeply regret and repent.

Perhaps the regard of the others fashions the man. The tribunes and the plebeians called Coriolanus a traitor. Now he has become a traitor. But first he takes leave of his family, mother, and wife. Volumnia curses the plebeians; yet she is also naïve. She does not understand her son, the condottiere. She asks in despair: "My first son, / Whither will thou go?" (4.1.35). It never occurs to her that her son could seek a generalship in the army of his country's enemies.

The danger of civil war is over. The tribunes, who are, as we have always seen, very good at devising political tactics, decide not to push their case further. As Brutus says: "Now we have shown our power, / Let us seem humbler after it is done / Then when it was a-doing" (4.2.3–4). Still, the desperate mother's and wife's confrontation with the tribunes (who are at first cowardly and avoid meeting them) follows. Volumnia accuses them of inciting the rabble and curses them. Her words, "Whom you have banished does exceed you all" (4–5), are not just the expression of motherly love; there is also a truth to them. But exceeding all the others and being in the right against the others are not the same thing. Even in her state of despair Volumnia knows this. She curses the tribunes for their ressentiment and ingratitude; however, she never says that her son was always in the right.

Act 4, scenes 4 and 5, constitute the turning point of the drama: Coriolanus is joining the Volsces. One does not arrive, however, at this turning point unprepared—at least not in Shakespeare's presentation. For we have seen that even at the time of his first clash with the plebeians, Coriolanus's mind was constantly turning toward his relationship to Aufidius. He was always obsessed with Aufidius. One could even say that the outcome of his political conflict with the plebeians, his banishment, offered him the only blessed opportunity to enter into the bond of star-brothership with the only man whom he held in high esteem. We know that Coriolanus's love for Aufidius was as misbegotten and self-defeating a faith or passion as his burning hatred against the plebeian crowd.

Coriolanus's mind is set on treason. But in fact, he does not perceive his joining the army of the enemies of Rome as treason. From this time on he obeys only himself. He becomes the sole master of himself. He has the right by nature to do what his passions dictate. As he says in 4.4, "My birthplace hate I, and my love's upon / This enemy town" (4.4.23–24). It has happened many a thousand times, as it is still happening in our age, that men and women turn their backs on their birthplace and choose another town or country (perhaps the enemy country) as their new home. Whether such an act of reversed loyalties is treason or not—or, if it is treason, whether it is by all means morally/ethically reprehensible or not—depends on many factors. But if personal injury, wounded pride, or the seeking of personal revenge is the sole or prior motivation for the reversal of loyalties, the spectator will not be in great sympathy with the character. It is difficult to portray this act of Coriolanus in a sympathetic light. Yet for Shakespeare, if I may express myself in a simplified manner, this is not a problem. He does not cut the acts and the person of Coriolanus into little pieces, and he does not portray any of them as independent or abstract stories, the moral of which needs to be drawn and the outcome judged. The figure of Coriolanus is carved from one single block of marble. His acts, the very chain of his acts, present him—in conflict with his city's people and in obedience to his mother and to his city's aristocracy—as a whole. Anger and rage are essential to his character. We have seen him in a situation in which he was grasped by a fit of rage. We are not astonished when we realize that his short-term fit of rage does not disappear without a trace. It turns into a chronic malady. His anger and rage, after their hot eruption, like that of a volcano, during his clash with the plebeians, result in his banishment. And they will continue to burn under the surface of his cooler acts and decisions. It is not just hatred, which is always long term, but also rage and fury that can become chronic. In Coriolanus, they turn from a sudden emotional occurrence into a slow and steady passion. Somehow—according to the message of the previous quotation—Coriolanus loses his capacity of reflection altogether. He does not think anything over twice, he acts as if he were under the influence of a hypnotic; that is, he acts blindly. Like a tank, he sweeps away every obstacle. Perhaps this is why he becomes so successful in the short term. First, this is why and how he paves his way into the presence of Aufidius, and later (not much later) this is why and how he acquires the highest military post—on the side of Aufidius—in the enemy camp: generalship.

Coriolanus enters the Volscian camp at Antium in disguise. Aufidius asks his name. He asks his name three times. I mentioned several times that in Shakespeare's dramas a man's identity manifests itself above all in face and name. Aufidius notices that Coriolanus's face "bears a command in't" (4.5.50) but also inquires his name. After the third question, Coriolanus makes himself known: "My name is Caius Martius" (4.5.66), who is also called Coriolanus. And then he continues that his original name, his name of birth, his Roman name (Caius Martius), he from now forsakes and keeps only the name Coriolanus. He now stands before Aufidius "in mere spite" (4.5.83), desiring to take revenge. Aufidius's answer sounds sincere. On the surface he reciprocates Coriolanus's brotherly feelings; but there is something suspect in Aufidius's warm words. They are hyperbolic, exaggerated, too enthusiastic, and too loud. "But that I see thee here, / Thou noble thing, more dances my rapt heart / Than when I first my wedded mistress saw / Bestride my threshold" (4.5.116–19). He addresses Coriolanus as "thou Mars" (4.5.119), reminding him that he has beaten him, "Aufidius," several times in battle. It is not clear whether this kind of artificial exaggeration is just the insincere expression of a very sincere joy at having received the winning card in his war game against Rome for free. Nor is it clear whether his envy and jealousy were at this moment unconsciously repressed, or whether while exaggerating he wanted to cover up his already half-conscious inimical feelings. But one way or the other, Coriolanus and Aufidius are not equal in matters of sincerity. It turns out that Aufidius is far better at politics than Coriolanus. He seeks not only military advantage but also great political advantage in dividing the leadership of his army with Coriolanus for the future of a conquered Rome. The unpolitical Coriolanus does not smell danger. He never does.

In Rome rumors are spread the the Volscian army is planning an attack and that Aufidius has divided the supreme power of generalship with Coriolanus. The patricians are torn between two feelings: joy and triumph on one hand (after all, it is one of them who is treated like a god by the enemy) and fear on the other, for how could Rome withstand such a united power? The plebeians are in a state close to panic, and they manipulate their own memory. They never wanted Coriolanus banished, they say: "That we did, we did for the best, and though we willingly consented to his banishment, yet it was against our own will" (4.6.152–54). Once again, this sentence is uttered in a particular context, and it is fitted exactly to this context.

In 4.7 we are back in the camp of the Volsces. We meet Aufidius in the company of his lieutenant, where he can allow himself to speak more openly. It becomes evident that Aufidius is deadly jealous, that he accuses Coriolanus of using witchcraft. It again remains obscure for the spectators as to whether it is Aufidius's jealous nature or his fear of competition and of being second place that is at work here. There is also the question of whether Coriolanus himself, with his very haughty nature, has put coal on the fire of Aufidius's jealous inclinations. At any rate, a traitor is always suspect. Someone who betrayed his homeland might easily betray his chosen country. Aufidius says that Coriolanus cannot be trusted, and perhaps he believes it. As I mentioned before, Aufidius has far better political instincts than the proud and unsuspecting Coriolanus. So he says: "So our virtues / Lie in th' interpretation of time, / And power, unto itself most commendable. . . . One fire drives out one fire, one nail one nail; / Rights by rights falter, strengths by strengths do fail. . . . When, Caius, Rome is thine, / Thou art poor'st of all; then shortly art thou mine" (4.7.49–57). Coriolanus's fate seems to be settled by Aufidius—both by his envy and by his politics—long before he fulfills the prophecy that he will make a political turn for the second time. Yet, this important disclosure of Aufidius's plans makes one interpretation of Coriolanus's story doubtful. According to this interpretation, Volumnia causes the death of Coriolanus by making him change his mind. But if Aufidius had been keen to carry out his plan, the victorious Coriolanus, after having helped to capture Rome, would have met the same fate: he would have been destroyed together with Rome. If this interpretation holds—and perhaps it does—Volumnia's words do not doom her son, but they save Rome.

The last act is not only about Coriolanus's second change of allegiance; it is also the quintessence of his tragedy culminating in catharsis. It is also the story of Rome's survival and of the reconciliation of patricians and plebeians. Coriolanus's catharsis is frequently compared to Socrates' decision in Plato's *Crito*. Socrates is sentenced to death, and his friends suggest flight. However, Socrates chooses death because he does not want to disobey the laws of his city. Those laws brought him up and made him the man he became. He keeps his allegiance to the laws of the city and drinks the hemlock. In his famous argument for the laws, Socrates says—among other things—that he could have left his country many times, and yet he stayed, thereby restating his commitment to those laws. The story of Coriolanus is essentially different. He did not stay in his country, he joined the enemy camp. He turned against his city because the laws of his city banished him. Socrates is not a tragic character but a moral figure. He undergoes no catharsis; he just reinforces once again before his death his fundamental being and choice. But Coriolanus becomes a tragic figure, and to become one he has to undergo catharsis, the purification of his soul from fear of humiliation and self-pity. He has to stand there and acknowledge his ultimate commitment to his city and to its laws, even to the laws that banished him. For this was his city, his home, his nurse.

Everyone knows the story. One delegation of suppliants after another comes to the camp of Coriolanus to persuade him not to enter Rome, not to sack his own city. He dismisses all of them, including Menenius, his substitute father. But his resolve is already shaken, perhaps because of his love for Menenius, perhaps because he needs to show his loyalty to Aufidius. And perhaps it is because in the deepest regions of his heart this was the only thing he ever really wanted: that his city should ask him, the banished one, for forgiveness. Just like Joseph in Egypt, he wanted to forgive the brothers who sold him into exile, where he grew to the highest office, because he was in the position to destroy them. Has Coriolanus (Shakespeare's Coriolanus) realized gradually that the role of the forgiving hero is far nobler and subtler than the role of the avenging hero?

After Menenius (5.3) enter the last suppliants: Volumnia, Valeria, Virginia, and young Martius. As always, the mother's figure stands out among them. Martius must fight it out with his mother. The fate of Rome will be decided by the verbal battle between mother and son. Knowing the story and knowing the Shakespearean characters, we have no doubt about the outcome of this verbal battle. Still, a fascinating drama is played out before our eyes. This is nearly the only occasion where Shakespeare becomes almost "Greek" (the other might be the altercation between Brutus and Cassius before Philippi). In a Greek type of altercation both parties need to stand for something, and they both need to have their truth, their right. The verbal battle needs to be played out among equals or near equals. Dianoia, in the ancient Aristotelian understanding of the word, is essential in the encounter between Volumnia and her son. The other members of the family act as a chorus. The stake of this altercation is, however, intrinsically Shakespearean: it centers around the interpretation of "nature" or the "natural." The verbal battle assumes a rhetorical character (just like, for example, the verbal exchange between Creon and Antigone). The force of rhetoric is on Volumnia's side; she will, she must, persuade Coriolanus to do what he ought to do. The scene is also a kind of recognition scene, but not in the ancient Greek sense. It is the fatal meeting where everything will be decided, and in a very modern way, through recognition. Although Coriolanus and Volumnia know who is who, they must still mutually recognize the essence of their existence. Coriolanus needs to find again his mother in a Roman matron, and Volumnia must recognize again her son in the Volscian warrior.

Coriolanus is not characterized by monologues, for, as we know, the fairly transparent Shakespearean heroes who always speak their hearts do not need for dramatic reasons to disclose their hidden interior to the audience. Yet, close to the end of the drama, when he sees his mother coming, Coriolanus speaks *aside*. Letting the character speak aside is the vehicle for Shakespeare to present the discrepancy not between plan and words but between the heart's inclination and the words. Coriolanus's words are harsh, yet in his heart he has already succumbed to Volumnia. As he says to himself: "I melt, and am not / Of stronger earth than others. My mother bows, / As if Olympus to a molehill should / In supplication nod" (5.3.28–31). The highly rhetorical and exaggerated comparison (Coriolanus compares his height to a molehill and his mother's to Olympus), shows clearly that the relation of the son to his mother has not changed and remains heavily loaded emotionally. It is here that Coriolanus utters (again aside) the already-quoted sentence "I'll never / Be such a gosling to obey instinct, but stand / As if a man were author of himself / And knew no other kin" (34–37). This is where Coriolanus formulates the second concept of nature in a very radical way. He is—he has become—an autonomous, completely self-made man who has left the instinct of the blood behind. Instinct symbolizes nature, the mother, loyalty to his kin. Ultimately, he will realize that he cannot stand by this resolution. This is the Socratic motive. He is not a man without kin; he cannot be the sole author of himself. His mother and his country have coauthored him. Still, Coriolanus, who—unlike Richard III—is ready in the end to revoke his claim for total self-authorship, will not end an existential failure. He will reconcile and unite in himself the man who is part of a family and a self-made man. This will be an existential mirror image of the political reconciliation between new and old, between tradition and renovation, between the Senate and the tribunes, between the patricians and the plebeians. One reconciliation (the existential of Coriolanus) ends in his death, yet also in the rescue of Rome against its external enemy, the Volscians. The other reconciliation, the political one, ends with the survival of Rome against the internal enemy, the civil war: *peace* is the result in both cases. As we know, this is always a happy ending in Shakespeare's dramatic scenario.

The reconciliation of a self-made man with his own roots, that is, the reconciliation of the two concepts of nature, does not erupt as an *acte gratuite*. For Coriolanus's heart was ready for such a reconciliation from the moment he arrived at the gates of Rome. His above-quoted sentence, which dismisses instincts, was, as the sentence itself suggests, coined by the brain alone; however, no one, especially not Coriolanus, only follows the dictates of the brain. The moment that Volumnia first addresses him, Coriolanus speaks aside for the second time: "Like a dull actor now / I have forgot my part, and I am out / Even to a full disgrace" (40–41). He already knows that he will be unable to play the self-made man's role consistently, as he never played another role well except that of the Roman general. All the other roles were borrowed or came to him in case of emergency, in the wake of loss, carried only by his pride and anger.

Volumnia enters the tent of her son not just as his doting mother. She also brings arguments; she is armed with the weapons of rhetoric. She not only wants to change her son's heart, but also to straighten out his thoughts. In the dramatic scene of the reversal of kneeling (first the son kneels before the mother, as tradition dictates, then the mother kneels down to her son as a suppliant), the gesture counts instead of the "information." Coriolanus knows very well what his mother, wife, and son ask of him and immediately he protests: "Do not bid me / Dismiss my soldiers, or capitulate / Again with Rome's mechanics. Tell me not / Wherein I seem unnatural. Desire not t'allay / My rages and revenges with your colder reasons" (82–86). He knows that he *seems* unnatural. Yet, *is* he unnatural in his own eyes? He protests that he only seems to be unnatural, but he knows that he is unnatural. And he also knows that his mother will no longer talk to his pride, as she always did, but to his reason.

Volumnia proceeds through her rhetorical speech in six steps. In the first step, she confronts Coriolanus head-on: they want him to abandon his military plans against Rome. In the second step, she speaks of the torment of Coriolanus's family, who are torn over their love for him, and appeals to his *sentiments*: "Alack, or we must lose / The country, our dear nurse, or else thy person, / Our comfort in the country" (110–2). In the third step, she speaks to Coriolanus's *imagination*: either he will be defeated and led in manacles through the streets of his native city, or he will be victorious and shed his wife's and children's blood. Volumnia proceeds to the fourth step, and begins to turn to *reason*. As in every case in this play where reasoning takes the leading part, she offers Coriolanus a compromise, in this case a compromise between his pride and his nature. He can avoid disgrace if he reconciles the two parties to end the war: both the Volsces and the Romans will praise and bless him. Then comes the fifth step, a reference to the *ethical*. Coriolanus falsely believes that his rage and desire for revenge are noble, whereas, "Think'st thou it honorable for a nobleman / Still to remember wrongs?" (155–56). In Volumnia's eyes, her son's behavior is base rather than noble. Finally—this is a trump card—Volumnia plays out the card of *filial duty and divine retribution:* "Thou art not honest, and the gods will plague thee, / That thou restrain'st from me the duty which / To a mother's part belongs" (167–69). This last moment ends with a postponed, *suspended curse*: "This fellow had a Volscian to his mother. / His wife is in Corioles, and his child / Like him by chance" (179–81). By postponed or suspended curse, I mean the curse of excommunication. Coriolanus, if he is going against Rome, will be expelled from his family. The essence of Volumnia's suspended curse is bluntly the following: if Coriolanus is ready to destroy Rome, his family will retroactively confirm his banishment and sign the decision of the tribunes and the people against Coriolanus. They will admit that the tribunes were right. This is an argument that Coriolanus cannot resist: "O, mother, mother! / What have you done? Behold, the heavens do open, / The gods look down, and this unnatural scene / They laugh at. O my mother, mother, O! / You have won a happy victory to Rome; But for your son, believe it, O believe it, / Most dangerously you have with him prevailed, / If not most mortal to him. But let it come" (184–90). Shakespeare once more emphasizes that the reinterpretation of natural/unnatural is central to Coriolanus's catharsis. Yet, it turns out immediately that the schism between nature as kin and nature as personal desert reappears in his newly won identity. The reconciliation can succeed existentially, but the man must perish. This is how this irritable and haughty man becomes a tragic character. Coriolanus, for the first time, sees everything clearly. In his soul he serves now two gods (his kin and his own nature), but his loyalty to his kin will cost him his life. He has bad premonitions. He knows—I repeat, he sees clearly—that whereas

Rome wins, Coriolanus will be lost. But he says "let it come" (190); he chooses his choice as his fate. And this is how he achieves the synthesis between the two concepts of nature. He finally wins his existence, and thus he can die.

I indicated above that in Shakespeare's presentation at least the jealous Aufidius would have let Coriolanus be killed, even if he had continued as a Volscian general and had sacked Rome. But this knowledge becomes indifferent here because what has happened, has happened. This is how the destiny of Coriolanus has been fulfilled, as also the destiny of Rome. This is because, as I mentioned, in scene 5.5 patricians and plebeians wait in the state of gravest tension for the news. Then comes the good news. Both Menenius and Sicinius, the tribune, patricians and the people, rejoice together. The crowd hails the ladies of Rome and throws flowers before their feet. The triumphant mother is welcomed with drums and trumpets. The tragedy of *Coriolanus* is settled before the drama comes to a close. The judgment will be executed in 5.6, the scene that is staged by Shakespeare in Corioli. As Coriolanus won his famous victory at Corioli, he also has to be killed in Corioli. The last scene, as a double contrast, is a dramatic gem. It is contrasted with the great victory scene in Corioli, yet it is also contrasted with the scene of Coriolanus's banishment from Rome. It is the sister scene of the battle scene, for the wives and the children, the widows and the orphans of those who were at that time killed by Caius Martius and his army are the rioting mob led by the conspirators against the hero. But it is also the sister scene of the banishment scene, for it is the enraged crowd, this time the unorganized mob both of the nobles and of the lowly classes, who are harassing him. Yet the Roman crowd decreed banishment, it did not kill. Since it was not a mob, it did not riot. It was an organized crowd with representatives, and this is why it finally spared Coriolanus's life. Otherwise, it could not have come to the reconciliation between the plebeians and patricians in Rome. Here, however, without tribunes, without elected institutions, the crowd acts as a faceless mob, ready to kill.

It is also in another respect that the last scene of Coriolanus's life resembles both the battle scene and the scene of his conflict with the tribunes. Coriolanus, who was entirely sober in the dialogue with his mother and has accepted his fate, becomes once again enraged. In the first Corioli scene, Caius Martius is enraged with the bad soldiers who might have let the Volscians win. In the Roman scene the tribunes push Coriolanus into raging choler on purpose. Here, in the last scene, Aufidius, his chosen brother soul who betrays his friendship, puts him into a state of rage as a preparation for his murder. When he calls Coriolanus the boy of tears, the latter maneuvers himself once again into blind fury, this time against Aufidius. This fit of rage is fully justified, for it is not the fiend but the friend who uses him wrongly. Coriolanus now employs almost the same words of abuse he used against the tribunes in Rome: "Measureless liar . . . Your judgments, my grave lords, / Must give this cur the lie" (5.6.10–8). And later: "'Boy'! False hound" (113), and so on. When a lord (similar to the patricians in Rome) tries to protect him, the Volscian conspirators incited by the false friend cry: "Kill, kill, kill, kill, kill him!" (130). And he is killed. He is killed in a state of rage, but this time in a justified state of rage. His death is his own death: he dies in character.

Here the drama ends, but a few sentences are still needed for a proper finish. Aufidius regrets his deed. He regrets it seemingly only because his rage is gone. (As it turns out, all patricians are somehow inclined to be carried away by rage.) In fact, because his hatred becomes redundant, he has achieved his political end. Coriolanus, his competitor, a man better than himself, is no more. He remains alone on the scene to reap the fruits of Coriolanus's proposed compromise. The last words of Aufidius introduce the political man, who allows killing to the extent that he believes it to be useful or necessary, and who can be sorry after the enemy is gone. This is similar to Henry IV. We know—also from Shakespeare—the afterlife of Henry IV's regrets, but we know nothing of the consequences of Aufidius's regret. It is of no interest. We, the audience, witness how Coriolanus will be buried with honor by the Volscians, while Volumnia and the other Roman women will get a statue inside the walls of Rome. These are the monuments of political reconciliation.

This is the play by Shakespeare (based on Plutarch) where a woman (Volumnia) makes good politics as well as history. In the end, one excuses her exercise of tyrannical power over her son and her absurd exaggeration of military valor. One needs to consider that as a woman she can play the great, beneficial, and successful political role that her talents enable her to play only by using men. Her only avenue and opportunity for employing her talents is through dictating to her son. But the best ideas that her son had finally carried through were her own political ideas. Shakespeare suggests that they were historically significant ideas that helped to usher in a new epoch.

13

Julius Caesar

Similar to *Coriolanus* and in contrast to all his other history plays and great tragedies, there is not a single wicked character in Shakespeare's *Julius Caesar*. Virtues and vices, passions and calculations overdetermine one another or clash; none of the characters determines to become a villain, none carries the desire for revenge to the extreme, none is daemonic. They express their ideas and plans in speech, and they mostly follow certain guidelines of ethical behavior amidst political exigencies. The raw material of the Shakespearean dramatis personae is borrowed from "Brutus" and "Julius Caesar" from Plutarch's *Parallel Lives*. Shakespeare, as usual, preserves the Roman/pagan personality of the characters with good historical sense. This is despite his transforming them and making them, in comparison to their models, into more complex—as both more vague and more explicit—modern characters in his unique way. Unlike *Coriolanus,* this drama is not centered around one single character. It is closer in this respect to *Henry VI* than to *Richard II*.

Several interpreters of the drama believe that it is mistitled as *Julius Caesar:* it should have been titled *Brutus* instead. After all, Julius Caesar is murdered in act 3.1, and Brutus remains on the scene until the very end. There are more significant reasons to elevate Brutus to the position of the main character of the drama. I think, first of all, of Nietzsche's strong position in paragraph 98 of *The Gay Science*. Nietzsche writes:

> I could not say anything more beautiful in praise of Shakespeare as a human being than this: he believed in Brutus and did not cast one speck of suspicion upon this type of virtue. It was to him that he devoted his best tragedy—it is still called by the wrong name. . . . Independence of soul!—that is at stake here. No sacrifice can be too great for that: one must be capable of sacrificing one's dearest friend for it, even if he should also be the most glorious human being, an ornament of the world, a genius without peer—if one loves freedom as the freedom of great souls. . . . That is what Shakespeare must have felt. The height at which he places Caesar is the finest honor that

he could bestow on Brutus. . . . Could it really have been political freedom that led this poet to sympathize with Brutus—and turned him into Brutus's accomplice? Or was political freedom only a symbol for something inexpressible? Could it be that we confront some unknown dark event and adventure in the poet's own soul of which he wants to speak only in signs?" (Friedrich Nietzsche, *The Gay Science,* trans. Walter Kaufmann [New York: Vintage Books, 1974], 150–51; in German, *Sämtliche Werke,* Band 3 [München: Deutscher Tascherbuch Verlag, 1980], 452–53.)

These sentences are reminiscent of Kierkegaard's *Fear and Trembling.* Kierkegaard says on the one hand that Shakespeare never portrayed Abraham's anxiety, but he also surmised that Shakespeare himself, as a man, experienced this anxiety.

Nietzsche also makes the point that Shakespeare twice portrays a poet's encounter with Brutus, who twice treats the poet with contempt; for these poets are pathetic, conceited, importunate, as poets generally are. They do not recognize grandeur and cannot even show a commonplace kind of rectitude. Nietzsche seems to discover a kind of self-contempt behind Shakespeare's portrayal of poets. (I would add that, in *Julius Caesar,* the philosopher does not fare better. The conspirators do not even approach Cicero, because they know him as a man who never participates in a venture unless has has initiated it.) This is an extreme and yet wonderful interpretation. Nowadays, the diametrically opposite, and equally extreme, interpretation is frequently accepted. According to this interpretation, Brutus is a self-righteous man, pompous, close to being ridiculous, and is just playing a Stoic act.

I subscribe to Nietzsche's observation that Shakespeare portrays Caesar as the incomparably greatest man, the ornament of the world, an unparalleled personality. I agree also with Nietzsche's remark that Caesar's greatness contributes to Brutus's greatness. But Shakespeare does not portray Brutus as a man who sacrifices his closest friend for his own freedom. This sounds rather like an allusion to the Nietzsche-Wagner friendship. In Shakespeare, Caesar is not Brutus's closest friend or his adopted son. I already mentioned that Shakespeare uses the shorter version of Caesar's last sentence. It is not "et tu mi filii Brute?" but "et tu Brute?" (3.1.76). There is no family drama, no allusion to a sacrificial parricide or fratricide. In Shakespeare's drama, Brutus's act of murder is and remains a political act of tyrannicide. All Brutus's emotions are entirely absorbed by his civic virtues, except perhaps for his love of Cato's daughter. Brutus is not a man without passions but a man whose passions have already been molded into the form of "virtuous character traits" in the vein of Aristotle, such as friendship, courage, magnanimity, temperance, and justice. All of these are crowned by the republican love of liberty. In my interpretation, Shakespeare believes that Brutus indeed excels in those virtues, that his participation in the anti-

Caesar conspiracy is not motivated by resentment, envy, or ambition. Still, I think that Caesar occupies a higher position in the hierarchy of grandeur, even if not in the hierarchy of morality, than Brutus. Better yet, Shakespeare's Caesar is a man who stands above all those hierarchies. He cannot be ranked, measured, or compared; he cannot be numbered either first or second, because he cannot be cast or framed. In my mind, there is an enormous difference in matters of grandeur between Caesar and Brutus, and no love of liberty, no authenticity or autonomy, can annul this absolute difference. Brutus is a Stoic; he follows the moral recipes of Stoicism. Even if one believes completely in his sincerity, virtuousness, or rectitude—even if one does not accuse him of self-righteousness, hypocrisy, or self-aggrandizement—he remains a man who plays a role. He plays the role of the perfect Stoic, and thus the role of the morally perfect republican citizen—the role of "noble Brutus." Brutus is in fact virtuous even if he remains unseen; he follows the voice of his conscience. Yet as a Roman citizen he also plays the role of "noble Brutus," for his virtue is a republican asset. He is inner-directed, yet also a man acting for others; on the historical stage there is no either/or. Brutus is noble, yet he plays a role that is already "there," a role played by others before him, like Cato.

Let us, however, cast a glance at Caesar. He acts on the public stage without playing a role: he appears just as himself. And even more important, he never wants to show himself to be anything but what he is. He does not want to look virtuous. Caesar does not play theater, because he creates his own role; he does not need to show what he is, because he himself is the show. He sweeps aside the Roman images of courage, temperance, justice, and the rest; they are not his virtues. He is courageous, but he does not need to show himself as courageous, because courage is his nature and he relies on his nature. Shakespeare's Caesar is a *man who is never ashamed, who is not shaped or codetermined by the regard of his fellow citizens.* He is thus absolutely undetermined by the others, be they traditions, laws, judgments, or the image that others create of him. This is not because he does not care for others; he can love. It is likewise not because he does not judge others. He is—aside from Hamlet—the most excellent judge of human character in all the dramas of Shakespeare.

Julius Caesar does not act on the world stage because he establishes the world stage. Where he enters, history enters. Although he is killed at the beginning of act 3, the world as it appears in acts 3 through 5 becomes wholly the world of Caesar. Everyone who remains alive faces the dead Caesar, for the dead Caesar is more alive than the living. All faces are turned toward the dead man; all acts are played before him. The specter of Caesar, as it appears to Brutus before Philippi, is unlike the specter of Hamlet's father. Interestingly, in Shakespeare the ghost of Caesar, the vision of Brutus, his "evil spirit," as he himself calls it, does not trigger guilt feelings in

Brutus. Brutus is simply assured that they are going to meet at Philippi, that the last battle will still be fought between Brutus and Caesar. And Caesar will win, for he has already won. It is Caesar around whom the whole story and history is going to revolve. Caesar has made a difference in their world that cannot be undone.

Shakespeare portrays the grandeur of Caesar in the most unexpected and brilliant way. There is a cumulative presentation of scenes and stories in acts 1 and 2. All of them are variations on one major theme: Caesar knew no shame. This is not because he was shameless, but because he was entirely inner-directed. Whatever Caesar does is done in his way; this much suffices. Caesar does not follow any guidelines, philosophies, or ideals. He follows only his own genius.

The first stories about Caesar are told by Cassius. He describes Caesar to Brutus in 1.2 not only with rancor and resentment but also with contempt. Once, thus one of his stories runs, Caesar encouraged him to swim across the "angry flood" (1.2.105) of the Tiber to the other shore. But at one point Caesar could not go on and cried, "'Help me, Cassius, or I sink!'" (113). Cassius continues: "And this man / Is now become a god, and Cassius is. / A wretched creature" (117–19). Further, Cassius says, in Spain Caesar had a fever, and "I did mark / How he did shake. 'Tis true, this god did shake" (122–23). Moreover, Caesar asked for a drink "as a sick girl" (130). Cassius expected Caesar to follow a predetermined pattern: a Roman patrician of honor never shakes, groans, or cries for help or for water. Caesar did all these things, and thus behaved as a base, unworthy man. But Caesar swept away all the "prescriptions," the codes of honor for a Roman gentleman. He could do everything that a real gentleman would never dare to do in the company of others, and despite all this was still regarded as a god—as Cassius admits. He was not a "man of honor," to imitate old clichés, but a *homo novus* through and through.

Soon afterward, after having given a piece of his mind to Mark Antony, Caesar says, "Come on my right hand, for this ear is deaf" (214). Some interpreters suggest that the sentence should be read as "Take care, this is a secret." But I would rather like to take the sentence as it stands. A man who is not ashamed of crying for help, of trembling, of groaning, or of asking for water would have no reason to be ashamed to admit that he is deaf in one ear. This little sentence fits the Shakespearean portrayal of Caesar only too well. It is true that the two interpretations do not exclude one another. For one should not forget that immediately after this scene Casca reports on Caesar's swooning, on his falling sickness. The expression "falling sickness" will be understood both in its literal and in its metaphorical meanings.

In scene 2.2, Caesar twice changes his mind about an essential decision. First he decides to go to the Capitol. Afterwards, under the influence of Calpurnia's dream and request, he decides to remain at home. Finally, under the influence of Decius's reinterpretation of the dream, he decides to go all the same. Who has ever seen an undecided god, who has ever adored a man so easily influenced? The Roman gentleman never changes his mind. Yet, again, Caesar had no desire to fit into any scheme. His slogan is *sic volo, sic jube.* He could change his decisions as many times as he wanted, because they were all were *his* decisions.

I mentioned that there is a main theme with different variations. Indeed, throughout these two acts, Caesar appears as a man with many weaknesses, and even bodily or mental infirmities. But in his case, weaknesses are not weaknesses and infirmities are not infirmities, because they are his own self; they are his manifestations. Shakespeare succeeds in portraying grandeur through his weaknesses, more precisely, through Caesar's total unconcern for his weaknesses. It is thus that Shakespeare conveys to us the strong impression that this man, Caesar, is different from every other man Rome has ever experienced.

Granted, Shakespeare's portrayal of Caesar is not just a kind of negative theology. There are two outstanding virtues in Caesar: courage and honesty. But his courage is not moral courage in an Aristotelian sense. He does not need to overcome fear by following the path of a righteous man. He is simply not afraid at all; he does not even understand the fear of dying: "Cowards die many times before their deaths; / The valiant never taste the death but once. / Of all the wonders that I yet have heard, / It seems to me most strange that men should fear, / Seeing that death, a necessary end, / Will come when it will come" (2.2.32–37). Similarly, Caesar always tells the truth because he does not care for lying. Lying is cowardice; the man who lies is afraid to tell the truth and he, Caesar, is never afraid (or ashamed). When Calpurnia asks her husband to send a message to the Senate that he is sick, Caesar answers with indignation: "Shall Caesar send a lie? / Have I in conquest stretched mine arm so far, / To be afeard to tell greybeards the truth? / Decius, go tell them Caesar will not come" (65–68). This verbal exchange shows the well-known pattern: Caesar does not lie because he is not afraid of being put to shame. Nothing and no one can put him to shame, for he is above and beyond everyone and all shame.

The third positive virtue of Caesar is his exquisite judgment of human character. We have seen already how well he dissects the character of Cassius and how he teaches Marc Antony, his young friend and pupil, to recognize dangerous people when he meets them. Marc Antony learns from Caesar to beware of Cassius. Centuries later Hume agrees: Caesar characterizes Cassius as a man with whom we now would not even sympathize. Yet, good judgment of character, appreciated so highly by Hume, was hardly a Roman virtue. Perhaps it was not a virtue at all, but a kind of excellence. Brutus is a very bad judge of character, and so is Marc Antony.

However, absolute constancy is perhaps the essence of Caesar's grandeur.

Constancy is also a republican virtue, but absolute constancy is not. For absolute constancy means that one does not listen to counterarguments, does not accept good counsel, relies on no other judgment than one's own, and places oneself absolutely above all other men. Absolute constancy is absolute haughtiness. Caesar makes a spectacle out of his absolute haughtiness during the last minutes of his life, when Metellus and Cassius kneel before him and Brutus kisses his hand in supplication to beg enfranchisement for Publius Cimber. We know, of course, that they are just playacting, because they have already decided to kill him. Perhaps Caesar, too, knows then that they are going to kill him: he has not forgotten that the Ides of March are not yet over, and he is a man who can read other men's eyes. But it is unimportant for him whether those men want to kill him or whether they are in fact petitioners, when he answers: "I could be well moved if I were as you. / If I could pray to move, prayers would move me. / But I am constant as the Northern Star, / Of whose true fixed and resting quality / There is no fellow in the firmament. . . . Yet in the number [of men] do know but one / That unassailable holds on his rank, / Unshaked of motion; and that I am he / Let me a little show it even in this— / That I was constant Cimber should be banished, / And constant do remain to keep him so" (3.1.68–73). When he adds the poetic question, "Hence! Wilt thou lift up Olympus?" (74), he already faces his destiny. He shows surprise only when Brutus stabs him, not when Casca does.

There are two examples of homo novus in this play: Caesar and Octavius. Caesar is a statesman, Octavius a politician; Caesar is a genius, Octavius a clever strategist. The first sets in motion the waves on which the second will be able to navigate safely to the harbor of imperial power.

The death of Caesar divides this drama into two parts. Before Caesar's assassination Shakespeare presents the characters of the conspirators and the development of the conspiracy. What is going to happen after the conspiracy is not, and cannot be, directly indicated by the playwright. The audience knows only as much as the characters know or believe. (One can know, of course, the whole story from other sources, without receiving even a hint from the play.) In the mind of the conspirators, the end of the story is the end of Caesar; after the death of the tyrant the patrician republic will be restored. History, if I may use a Hegelian idea, operates behind the backs of people. Only Caesar has ridden the horse of history; the conspirators have no access to it. Nonetheless, there is one thing that ties together the first part (before the death of Caesar) and the second part (from the death of Caesar to Philippi), and this is the complex relation between Brutus and Cassius— both their personalities and the character of their friendship.

The tempo of the plot is in a state of continuous acceleration. After a relatively slow beginning, where Cassius tests Brutus's willingness to join the conspirators and finally persuades him to become their figurehead, the speed of the events suddenly increases. The tempest scene is the watershed. There is an instance of anachronism in Shakespeare's *Julius Caesar* that, in my mind, is anachronism on purpose. I mean the striking of the clock. When the conspirators sit in counsel in Brutus's house and Brutus has just turned down the plan to kill Marc Antony, too, a clock strikes. Brutus: "Peace, count the clock." Cassius: "The clock hath stricken three" (2.1.192). It is then that they decide to have everyone meet at Caesar's house at eight o'clock. During the night, perhaps between four and five o'clock, Brutus tells his wife Portia everything about the conspiracy. He may have slept two hours. While already in Caesar's chambers, before leaving for the Capitol, Caesar will ask: "What is't o'clock?" And Brutus will answer: "Caesar, 'tis strucken eight" (2.2.113–14). Only five hours have elapsed between the decision to kill Caesar and Caesar's decision to go to the Senate. In 2.4 we move to Brutus's house. Portia enters and sends their young servant boy, Lucius, to the Senate house to "bring word" about what happens there, without betraying her knowledge of the conspiracy. Full of nervous tension and complaining about the lot of women who must wait, whereas men do all the acting, she calls a soothsayer. She does this not in order to lift the veil of the future but to receive intelligence about the present. Portia: "What is't o'clock?" Soothsayer: "About the ninth hour, lady" (2.4.24–25). We the spectators realize that Caesar, who left his chambers an hour ago, has already arrived at the Capitol. Shakespeare uses the dramatic device of "counting back." The striking clock is the clock of history. The repeated sound of the clock striking three once, then eight, and then nine, helps to create the required tension as well as the impression that subjective time and objective time diverge. For Portia one hour is eternity. Even Caesar's short talk with Popilius seems unbearably long for Cassius, who fears betrayal and becomes hysterical. What is important, however, *is that the clock does not strike ten.* That Shakespeare mentions the clock in two different scenes—once striking eight and then striking nine, and he never mentions striking ten—is significant. Shortly after nine o'clock Caesar's destiny is fulfilled. Of course, a regular clock does not stop striking, but the clock of history does. After the culmination of the acceleration of speed, clock time becomes insignificant.

Let me return to the conspiracy. I mentioned that it is the personalities of Brutus and Cassius and the special quality of their friendship that bridge the first part (before Caesar's fall) and the second part (after Caesar's fall) of the drama. Brutus here stands for moral perfection—in Max Weber's terminology, for value-oriented action. Cassius represents political exigency and goal-oriented action. Both are men of the same patrician class: both are republicans, both hate tyranny, and after a short hesitation on the part of Brutus, both agree to the necessity of Caesar's assassination. Yet, if one employs Nietzsche's ethical terminology, they are also each other's opposites: Brutus is a noble (*edel*) character, whereas Cassius is a base (*niedrig*) character. Brutus feels ill at ease about the conspiracy. He is torn between contrary feelings and convictions. Even if Caesar is not yet a tyrant, he is like a "serpent's egg" (2.1.32) that needs to be killed in its shell. On the other hand: "O conspiracy, / Sham'st thou to show thy dang'rous brow by night, / When evils are most free?" (2.1.77–79). Cassius urges that all conspirators should take an oath, because he is highly suspicious and has confidence in no one. However, Brutus prevents the taking of the oath, because he believes in the honesty of others: "What other oath / Than honesty to honesty engaged / That this shall be or we will fall for it?" (125–27). One must notice the word "honesty." Honesty, and not honor, is the motivating force for Brutus. And he presupposes the same honesty in others. A man who speaks in this way is hardly self-righteous. Furthermore, in Shakespeare, honesty—contrary to honor—is the moral motivation of the man of conscience. Thus, Shakespeare attributes a kind of morality to Brutus that bears some resemblance to the virtue of Horatio (both of them are Stoics). However, Brutus is—Nietzsche is right— rather a melancholy man, like Hamlet.

Cassius acknowledges the human superiority of Brutus. This shows precisely the complexity of their relationship. He loves Brutus, but he also manipulates Brutus. Nonetheless, Brutus's friendship is more important to him than anything else. Ultimately, it will become even more important than victory and the republican cause. Moral constancy characterizes Brutus, inconstancy characterizes Cassius; Brutus is courageous, Cassius sometimes behaves hysterically. Brutus does not begrudge grandeur, Cassius does; Brutus is magnanimous, Cassius rancorous. The motivations of Brutus are exclusively spiritual, while some of the motivations of Cassius are material. And still, Cassius sacrifices everything for Brutus, while Brutus gives up nothing for Cassius. The virtue of friendship, in an Aristotelian manner, shines through all of Cassius's deeds. His love of Brutus is personal, yet it is also a kind of hero worship. Cassius resents Caesar, for Caesar stands above him; but he does not resent Brutus. It is just the opposite— Brutus stands above Cassius. In his long appeal addressed to Brutus (1.2), all his motivations are mixed: spite of Caesar, love of Brutus, moral indignation, despair about the loss of ancient ways of life, and so on. ("What should be in that 'Caesar'? / Why should that name be sounded more than yours?" [1.2.143–44].) But there is something else that makes the appeal tense with urgency: the recognition of the proper time, of kairos. Cassius now demonstrates good political instinct, as he will also do a few times later on. He feels that Brutus needs to be persuaded now, because it is just now that they can take their destiny into their hands: "Men at sometime are masters of their fates. / The fault, dear Brutus, is not in our stars, / But in ourselves, that we are underlings" (140–42). I add only parenthetically that Shakespeare underlines Cassius's inconstancy in making the very man who has uttered the above words entirely taken in by diverse superstitions later on. Cassius's main virtue is his friendship and love for Brutus. But why do I call it a virtue? After all, Cassius manipulates Brutus in order to make him—a man considered by everyone to be the most important Roman— a party to the conspiracy against Caesar. Nonetheless, Cassius sacrificed the fate of Rome three times for his friendship with Brutus, at least in Shakespeare's presentation.

Marc Antony will be the key figure in the determination of the fate of Rome and of the conspirators/liberators. There will be one moment during which the fate of the world will hinge on Marc Antony's skill and decision. Marc Antony loves Caesar just as Cassius loved Brutus. The conspirators could have expected trouble from his side. Political consideration required finishing off Marc Antony along with his master. This is Cassius's proposal in 2.1, but Brutus completely rejects it, fundamentally on moral grounds: "Let's be sacrificers, but not butchers, Caius" (2.1.166). To this Cassius answers, "Yet I fear him" (183). But he agrees. The story is repeated. After Caesar's assassination, Cassius sends someone to the pulpit to cry out "'Liberty, freedom, and enfranchisement!'" (3.1.80) but immediately asks the question, "Where is Antony?" (3.1.96). Antony enters and finally asks to speak on Caesar's funeral. Brutus agrees. Cassius protests, but Brutus gets what he wants. The results are well known. Far later in time, in scene 4.2, after the altercation scene between the friends, Brutus proposes to march to Philippi, and Cassius says, "I do not think it good" (4.2.249). However, Cassius will yield, and they will lose the battle.

Julius Caesar becomes a thoroughly political play (a play about politics) after the assassination of Caesar. In the first part, we encounter a single man standing against a whole group of conspirators. The assassination of Caesar is a republican, ritual slaughter in the name of liberty, freedom, and enfranchisement. From this moment on, however, the plot turns on political (and military) decisions. Perhaps this is how and why our perception of Brutus may change in the second part (after Caesar's assassination). In the first part, one does not get the impression of a self-righteous Brutus. He is absolutely not contemptuous of others. For, as I mentioned, he presupposes the same honesty in all the conspirators; he believes that they are motivated by high ideals, just as he is. The Brutus of the first part of the drama is a man reluctant to participate in a base act like conspiracy, and he does it only for the sake of public liberty, without the desire for self-aggrandizement. He is not the one who strikes Caesar first. He also feels, like Hamlet, that time is out of joint and that he cannot refuse the obligation to participate in setting time right. And he believes—together with others—that through the act of a sacrificial assassination, time will be set right. But the obligation weighs heavily on him. For he was not born to set time right; he has a choice. Like

Nietzsche, Brutus is a melancholic character. But when it turns out that the single great gesture, the ceremonial sacrifice of a man on the altar of liberty, does not suffice, that time has not been set right—that the world clock has not been set back into the times of the ancient republic—Brutus's character undergoes certain changes. In Shakespeare, a character is always a character in a situation. The situation has changed. It has become purely political. Brutus is bad at politics; he misjudges situations. His task is no longer to kill a great man, a serpent's egg, but to navigate successfully among his friends and enemies—among those who are equals in rank and standing but not in political abilities. In this situation a pure Stoic morality becomes impotent and even dangerous. Brutus might have felt it, but he remained "the noble Brutus." He can only act on moral grounds, although he knows about political exigencies. Thus he does the only thing he is able to do: overplay his morality, use his moral reputation as a political asset. It is then, for example, during the altercation with Cassius (to which I will return) that he says, "For I am armed so strong in honesty" (4.2.123). The passages pointed out as significant by the advocates of the "self-righteousness" theory are spoken at a time when Brutus tells Cassius of his grief about Portia's suicide. He tells Cassius that Portia is dead, and he excuses the outburst of his unjust passion with his suffering. Afterwards Messala arrives with the sad news about Portia. Messala: "Then like a Roman bear the truth I tell; / For certain she is dead, and by strange manner" (240–41). Brutus answers, "Why, farewell, Portia. We must die, Messala. / With meditating that she must die once, / I have the patience to endure it now" (243–44). Some interpreters believe that two versions of the same scene were mistakenly put together later, or that Shakespeare forgot to erase one of the dialogues. Alternatively, this seeming (or real) discrepancy serves as the basic trump card in the "self-righteous" or "hypocrite" theory about Brutus. I do not accept either the first or the second version. Brutus's short exchange of words with Messala does not prove that he lied or that he was a hypocrite. He could have received news of Portia's death without receiving a letter from Portia. He does not mention such a letter to Cassius. However, we know that Brutus was hurt, that he suffered, and yet he maintained (in the dialogue with Messala) his cool. He is, indeed, playing the role of "noble Brutus." He, indeed, pretends to be what he is not. But I would hardly call this hypocrisy. One behaves differently with a close friend than with an ally. In addition—and this is what I accept of the "self-righteous" theory—Brutus knows that his greatest political asset is his moral honesty, and he uses this political asset. He had no other assets at his disposal.

The time is out of joint for Brutus, Cassius, and all the conspirators. Their conviction that it can be put right with a gesture of tyrannicide has been proven wrong. They were the fools of history; the sacrificial ceremony was performed in vain. The ghost of Caesar towering above the second part of the play, and appearing to Brutus in his dream, represents the historical judgment. Yet in *Julius Caesar,* as well as in *Antony and Cleopatra* and to a lesser extent in *Coriolanus,* that time is out of joint means something quite different than in the history plays or the great tragedies of Shakespeare. The Roman plays also tell the story of entering new times, of a new calendar. True, a "new man" may appear also at the end of history plays, and sometimes also at the end of great tragedies; but the institutions themselves never change. Time is out of joint for everyone, and no one can set it right. In the Roman plays, however, time is out of joint for some, but new times are triumphantly setting in for others. This is not because the new man appears at the end (for this happens also in the history plays, and does not happen in *Coriolanus*) but because new institutions replace the ancient ones. This is not the same thing as when a good king takes the place of a wicked one, or vice versa. The men who carry those new institutions on their shoulders, or who embody them, appear at the beginning of the three Roman political dramas and not at the end. *Coriolanus* begins with the establishment of the institution of tribunes. Time gets out of joint for Coriolanus, yet not for the tribunes. They just enter time. In *Julius Caesar,* as well as in *Antony and Cleopatra,* Octavius—the homo novus of politics—will bring the work of Caesar to full fruition. "Caesarism" will sweep away the ancient times. The very circumstance that basic political institutions are changing, and that the men who change them are present at the moment a drama of political struggle begins, is one of the main reasons for calling these three Roman dramas political dramas.

Let me now follow in some detail the development of the political drama proper in *Julius Caesar,* beginning with a scene that became known as scene 3.2 in the Shakespeare tradition: the funeral oration of Brutus and Antony. In the prior scene we see Marc Antony remaining alone with the body of Caesar. He has just received permission from Brutus to speak at Caesar's funeral. Here we witness one of the most touching of Shakespearean monologues. Marc Antony speaks. He is speaking to himself, and yet to the dead body of Caesar. Whatever he is going to do later in this play, here he is portrayed as a young Marc Antony who will become the Antony of *Antony and Cleopatra.* It is amazing—for these dramas were written many years apart—that whenever Shakespeare had an intuition of a character's continuity, he could portray this continuity in two different dramas conceived in different times. Here we have already in the young Antony the more mature hero: a passionate and undisciplined man whose moods quickly change, who can be generous and magnanimous if he follows his passions. He is good at war but stupid in politics. He expresses himself in the most poetic language—it is rhetorical, full of pathos, and with an inclination to demagoguery. He is a man who can love, betray, and suffer; a man of great gestures. He is closest to Othello; he is no stranger but a Roman in a time out of joint.

Antony stays with Caesar's corpse and addresses it in his expressive language. It is the same language that he will employ so many times in another play: "O, pardon me, thou bleeding piece of earth" (3.1.257). He prophesies domestic fury, fierce civil strife, blood, and destruction. And then he makes a political decision, sending word to Octavius not to come yet to unsafe Rome, before he tries in his oration to express the mood of the people. Then follows the crucial scene, which, as it stands, is entirely Shakespeare's invention. The political task of both Brutus and Marc Antony is to appeal to the Roman crowd and to assure their support. These are still the plebeians we know from *Coriolanus*. (We remember that Shakespeare wrote *Coriolanus* later.) These plebeians are, however, not citizens sitting in council. They do not discuss matters amongst themselves, they do not voice differing opinions. These plebeians do not act but *react;* they react to the words of the speakers, to their appeal. They are influenced, but they do not exert influence. Three plebeians react to the speech of Brutus. First, they react in concert. (All: "None, Brutus, none" [3.2.35]), and later "Live, Brutus, live, live!" [48].) Then they speak separately. First Plebeian: "Bring him with triumph home unto his house." Fourth Plebeian: "Give him a statue with his ancestors." Third Plebeian: "Let him be Caesar" (49–51). After the first part of Antony's speech Shakespeare adds another plebeian. The first three have already changed their minds: now they all become inclined to turn against Brutus. In the midst of the second turn of Antony's oration all the plebeians will cry again together: "The will, the will! We will hear Caesar's will" (140). At the end of the oration, the crowd finally becomes molded into an infuriated, irrational, rioting mass: "Revenge! About! Seek! Burn! Fire! Kill! Slay! / Let no traitor live!" (200–201). Shakespeare contrasts two kinds of speech: Brutus's short speech and Antony's long oration. Antony is a master of rhetoric: we see how words can be put to incorrect use, how skillfully words and sentences can be made to inflame. For Antony has no other weapon at his disposal but his words. And it is with his words that he wins against the army of the conspirators. His words inflame the plebes, and the plebes have the power of numbers to destroy the well-armed few. Antony needs the power of numbers, and he needs it only to destroy. For the time being, this suffices. Defeat is not yet transformed into victory, but the other, the victorious party, will be forced to flee.

To the degree that Antony's language becomes inflammatory, the plebeians are losing their own language. At the end, they do not even use language at all. They utter words randomly, inarticulately. Only a master of speech like Antony could deprive the plebeians of even the remnants of the speech they still control. This is and remains Antony's sole political victory. For when he is faced with a man who had powers other than the power of numbers, whose speech cannot be silenced by rhetoric (for it was a strong although entirely different speech, a speech of planning and devising and not poetry), Marc Antony runs up against a wall. Octavius will remain entirely indifferent to Antony's poetic and rhetorical speech; he is interested only in the propositional content of speech. He is not impressed by anthems or by speech acts of any kind, or by the beauty of personal appeal. He has no emotions to which Antony can appeal.

At the outset, Brutus's task is easier than Antony's. He and his friends have killed Caesar; he is the victor, and the crowd normally hails the victor. Brutus is the one who speaks first. He is absolutely sure that his words will be accepted, and they are. However, he is also sure that Antony's speech cannot influence the crowd. But why is this? Cassius knows better. Is Brutus naïve? He is; he believes in the power of the good cause, and he is sure that only his cause is a good one. But there is something more to his striking failure. If one listens attentively, Brutus's speech is also rhetorical. He uses rhetorical tricks. It is not just Socratic dialectics that he employs, but the art of persuasion. What, then, goes wrong in his speech?

First, as I pointed out, here Brutus begins to use his morality as a political asset, although not as clearly as later. ("Believe me for mine honour, and have respect to mine honour" [3.2.14–15].) But then he employs other rhetorical devices: "Who is here so base that would be a bondsman? If any, speak, for him have I offended. Who is here so rude that would not be a Roman? If any, speak, for him have I offended. Who is here so vile that will not love his country? If any, speak, for him have I offended. I pause for a reply" (29–34). And after the crowd's reaction, "None, Brutus, none" (35), he concludes: "Then none have I offended" (36). The speech is prosaic but, I repeat, it is also strongly rhetorical. What went wrong? I think that Brutus addressed his words to the wrong audience. These were words he could have addressed to the patricians. They were the ones who never would have chosen to become bondsmen. He addresses not even the men of honesty, but the men of honor. But his audience this time does not consist of men of honor. Addressed to the crowd, his rhetoric could have only a very short-lived appeal. I think that not even the brilliant rhetoric of Antony was needed this time to change the crowd's mind. One only needs someone to appeal to the crowd's wishes, needs, and desires.

Everyone knows Antony's oration, or at least a part of it, by heart. Thus I do not need to discuss it. I only call attention to a few characteristics of this speech. Brutus never expresses emotions. As a Stoic he despises emotion and particularly its manifestation. To the contrary, Antony not only appeals to emotions, he expresses them as well. And he appeals to the same emotions he himself expresses. He loved Caesar, so did the crowd. He is crying, so does the crowd. He does not fake emotions, for he really feels them. He does not persuade with mere hypocrisy, but with at least partial sincerity. He behaves as a man of the crowd, as a poet of the crowd, who has the gift to express and to formulate in words what the crowd feels but cannot express. True,

Antony also gives reasons. Moreover, he refutes the strongest accusation against Caesar—that he was ambitious—with three examples that strike us as true. Examples, of course, do not replace reasons or proofs. But one cannot prove or disprove in any case whether Caesar was or was not ambitious. Antony employs the device of ironical understatement, as well as the rhetorical conditional. He also uses the device of self-fulfilling prophecy. Caesar's will, if read, he says, will inflame them. After having succeeded in bringing the crowd to the required mood, he postpones the impatiently awaited reading of the testament. Instead he presents the *spectacle*. Without the skillful employment of words, no spectacle could inflame the crowd. But Antony prepared the great spectacle: the presentation of the corpse. The body is first presented in his mantle to show the places of the stab wounds. Then comes *aletheia*, unconcealment as truth. The naked Caesar's body with his wounds: this is the truth. The biblical allusion (Christ taken off the cross) cannot be missed. Antony's speech turns to a mystery play. This is Antony's answer to the ceremonial murder of Caesar. The ceremonial burial, not the ceremonial murder, is the Truth.

The mystery play has its intended effect. The plebeians want to burn Brutus's—the traitor's—house immediately. But then, Antony postpones the act of revenge for a little while, only to make it more devastating: he finally reads Caesar's testimony. And then the spectacle is over. Brutus and his friends flee the city in a hurry. Octavius arrives. Antony goes to see Octavius. Here ends the finest hour of Marc Antony, the politician/poet. From this moment on, poetry and politics will part ways.

Before entering the gate of the new world, Shakespeare condenses the whole terror of the mob riot into a scene borrowed from Plutarch. Cinna, the poet, is murdered by the mob, just because his name is—like that of one of the conspirators—Cinna. Yet, after having entered the gate of the new world, the picture does not change. Now the triumvirs murder, not only as many as the rioting mob, but more. For they murder systematically. They prick the names of those who shall die, among them each other's close relatives. Proscription is a truly Machiavellian act of political murder. It can be stopped. At least, this is what Antony suggests to Octavius at the end of the scene. Now it is time to make enemies friends.

The triumvirs divide the world among themselves. Yet dissension begins right away. Antony starts it; he would like to exclude Lepidus, who is wealthy but stupid. The basic difference between Antony and the teenager, Octavius, can already be traced. Whenever Antony wants to do or to receive something (for example, to treat Lepidus unequally), he shares confidences immediately with another man (here with Octavius) whom he recognizes as his equal. But whenever Octavius wants to get rid of someone (as he soon wants to get rid of both Lepidus and Antony), he keeps his plans and opinions entirely to himself. Octavius has his plans, but does not confide in anyone. The poet/politician, Marc Antony, has pulled the chestnut out of the fire for the pragmatic politician, Octavius. Yet he has still won one-third of the world.

The next scene takes place in Sardis. Brutus is camping here with his army. He collected the army to fight, along with Cassius, the final battle against the triumvirs. The main preparation for the war and the choice of the battlefield will take place here. Clausewitz says that war is the continuation of politics by other means. In Shakespeare only the Roman plays can be fitted into this scheme. Shakespeare tells the story of wars and portrays battle scenes quite frequently, but most of them could hardly be understood as the continuation of politics. War is the continuation of politics only if it has a political purpose: this happens if a political plan or program can be executed strictly through the use of arms. A kind of power is always contested in war, and glory is always sought. But the desire to conquer is not politics. To make a display of one's courage, to excel in bravery, to earn honor, or simply to fight as a sport—these are not in themselves political acts. When a king defends himself against a pretender or a usurper, this is not in itself politics. A war is a continuation of politics if losing or winning the war results in, or is related to, a change in the political order or, in extreme cases, sovereignty. The objective of a war is political, if the balance of political powers and perhaps even the character of those powers are expected to change through the employment of violence. When a king or a royal family is expected to be replaced by another king or family, the purpose of the war is not purely political. *Coriolanus* is a political play through and through. Still, Caius Martius's war against the Volsces is not the continuation of politics by other means, but Coriolanus's march against Rome is. So is the decisive battle in *Julius Caesar,* and so are the battles in *Antony and Cleopatra.* In both cases, Shakespeare portrays the events with the eyes of Cato: "victris causa diis placuit, sed victa Catoni." The victor's cause pleases the gods, the victims' cause pleases Cato. Shakespeare achieves this "effect" in a similar way in both plays. In *Julius Caesar,* Brutus and Cassius—the would-be victims—are friends. Their friendship is problematic. The story of their political failure is embedded in the great and very human drama of their friendship. The victors, the triumvirs, are not friends. They are temporary political allies. No human drama takes place between them. They remain cool in following their purpose: to beat Brutus and Cassius, and thereby also the Roman republic.

In *Antony and Cleopatra,* the two title characters, who are the would-be victims, are lovers. Their love is problematic. The story of their political failure is embedded in the great and very human drama of their love. The friendship of both friends and the love of both lovers are unique to their personalities. (The parallel between the suicides of Cassius and Brutus, on one hand, and of Antony and Cleopatra, on the other hand, cannot be missed.) Antony's and Cleopatra's enemy, Octavius, displays no emotions or passions, however. He entertains only one purpose: to remain alone on the world stage and to substitute the united principality for the republic and for the triumvirate. In both dramas, Shakespeare achieves the Catonian effect by portraying the victims in their emotional/moral complexity and the victors as successful power machines.

Let me return to the crucial altercation scene (4.2) between Cassius and Brutus. We join Brutus in his camp at Sardis. The altercation scene is already set before Cassius even enters the stage. Brutus expresses his suspicion to Lucillus, his follower: "Thou hast described / A hot friend cooling" (4.2.19). Cassius arrives. He enters in a state of controlled anger. His first word is a word of reproach: "Most noble brother, you have done me wrong" (4.2.37). The formulation of the reproach is telling. Brutus is still the "noble brother," both noble and a brother. Cassius is offended, deeply hurt. How can a noble man wrong another? How can a brother do wrong to his brother? Brutus immediately denies having done anything wrong: "Judge me, you gods: wrong I mine enemies? / And if not so, how should I wrong a brother?" (38–39). The words "doing wrong" are employed in a slightly different way by Cassius than by Brutus. What Cassius means by "doing wrong" is not just injustice but also personal offense, whereas in Brutus's mind one can wrong another man only if one is unjust. In this sense, he does not acknowledge the difference between an enemy and a friend/brother, or an indifferent person and a brother. We understand Cassius's growing indignation: "Brutus, this sober form of yours hides wrongs" (40). Brutus catches the meaning of the sentence and becomes more personal. "Cassius, be content. / Speak your griefs softly. I know you well" (42). He then makes an all-important gesture. He sends the witnesses away in order to remain alone with Cassius. He moves the conflict from the public stage to the intimate/personal stage. True, his gesture also has the political purpose of keeping up appearances. The soldiers "should perceive nothing but love from us, / Let us not wrangle" (4.4.45). But it is also Brutus's personal desire to talk to Cassius alone. When friend talks to friend in anger, others should be excluded.

Cassius unpacks the reason for his anger. Brutus condemned Lucius Pella for taking bribes, although Cassius wrote a letter on his behalf. Brutus answers: "You wronged yourself to write in such a case" (58). Cassius replies, "In such a time as this it is not meet / That every nice offence should bear his comment" (59–60). This is the clearest case of the clash between morality and politics. Brutus's moral absolutism does not know about "these times" or "those times." Bribes should not be taken, nor should they be offered. This is an absolute maxim (Kant would say), and an absolute maxim should be followed absolutely. There can be no exceptions. But then a sentence slips from the lips of Brutus that seems unlike him, or at least unlike the picture we have formed of him so far: "Let me tell you, Cassius, you yourself / Are much condemned to have an itching palm, / To sell and mart your offices for gold / To undeservers" (4.2.61–64). This is ugly. Brutus accuses his closest friend, his spiritual brother, of ugly vices before giving him a hearing! What kind of friendship is this? Is there friendship without confidence? Cassius is so hurt by this betrayal of the core of friendship that he cannot even answer. He just exclaims in despair: "I, an itching palm?" (65). "Chastisement?" (69). Yet Brutus is now in a rage, and he rages in the mood of moral indignation: "Remember March, the ides of March, remember. / Did not great Julius bleed for justice' sake? / What villain touched his body, that did stab, / And not for justice? What shall one of us, / That struck the foremost man of all this world / But for supporting robbers, shall we now / Contaminate our fingers with base bribes?" (70–76). Three different emotions and thoughts are mixed in Brutus's angry appeal. He feels now, after the fact, not so sure about having been right in joining the conspiracy. When he joined, he believed that if Caesar were gone, the virtuous and noble days of the glorious republic would return. But this has not happened. And it dawns on him that whether he and Cassius will be the victors, or Octavius and Marc Antony, the hope of returning to the glorious days of the republic has already melted into air. Another world has come into being. Retrospectively, their ceremonial tyrannicide will look like plain murder. Similar feelings have caught the minds of historical actors from Brutus's time to the present day. They are the actors who did something morally reprehensible to usher in an age of political liberty but realize they may in fact have ushered in something else. Bribery is dirty and ugly. The bribery to which Brutus alluded really took place. Brutus cannot tolerate the fact that Cassius defends it on the grounds of political exigency. But Brutus does not stop here. His good moral argument, although not necessarily his good political judgment, serves merely as a prelude to a series of grave reproaches. He immediately accuses his best friend of taking bribes and selling offices. Whether this was true or untrue about the historical Cassius is not Shakespeare's interest. In this drama, it is untrue. In this drama it is a case of false accusation, of calumny. This is why Cassius cannot find words to defend himself; this is why he utters only exclamations of extreme despair. He feels himself annihilated.

When he finally begins to speak, he still shows more friendship than Brutus, and more humanity: "Brutus, bay not me. / I'll not endure it. You forget yourself / To hedge me in. I am a soldier, I, / Older in practice, abler than yourself / To make conditions" (80–84). And then we see two friends, two chosen brothers, shouting at each other in a state of rage. Cassius warns: "Tempt me no farther" (89). But Brutus's choler knows no bounds: his love turns into hatred, his friendship into deadly hostility and aggression: Brutus:

"Shall I be frightened when a madman stares?" Cassius: "Must I endure all this?" Brutus: "You shall digest the venom of your spleen, / Though it do split you. For, from this day forth / I'll use you for my mirth, yea, for my laughter, / When you are waspish." Cassius: "Is it come to this?" (94–104). Brutus cannot stop. Cassius: "Do not presume too much upon my love. I may do that I shall be sorry for" (118–19). Then Brutus shows his trump card, the card that he has not mentioned at all before: Cassius has offended him personally. "I did send to you / For certain sums of gold, which you denied me" (125). The accusation switches from a general moral one to a very concrete one: Brutus shouts at his friend the accusation that he has acted unlike a friend. Then comes Cassius's answer. It is simple: "I denied you not" (137). Brutus insists, "You did." Cassius: "I did not. . . . Brutus hath rived my heart. / A friend should bear his friend's infirmities, / But Brutus makes mine greater than they are." Brutus: "I do not, till you practise them on me." Cassius: "You love me not." Brutus: "I do not like your faults." Cassius: "A friendly eye could never see such faults" (138–44). And Cassius despairs: "Come, Antony and young Octavius, come, / Revenge yourselves alone on Cassius; / For Cassius is weary of the world, hated by one he loves." (147–50). Cassius is still the better of them. He is, in spite of his anger, still human. He still speaks of friendship and love, and he despairs about the loss of love. Brutus is indeed inhuman and self-righteous in this part of the scene, and he does not speak as a moral man. For at first he hides his very personal injury under the mask of universal morality. He is as much hurt in his personal pride and interest as is Cassius. Yet Cassius says it clearly, whereas Brutus plays the role of moral superiority—until this very moment. Here he collapses, and changes. His rage suddenly evaporates. At the same moment, anger also leaves Cassius. Cassius begins to apologize for his ill temper. And Brutus says, "I was ill-tempered too." Cassius: "Do you confess so much? Give me your hand." Brutus: "And my heart too." (170–2). The altercation scene, one of the greatest scenes that Shakespeare ever wrote, ends here. But something is postponed. Brutus has not yet spoken of Portia's death. This is, indeed, noble of him. When he confesses to his ill temper and reconciles with Cassius, he does not seek for himself a mitigating circumstance. Now, when they sit together in Brutus's tent, friends again, it is only now that he confesses: "O Cassius, I am sick of many griefs" (196). And when Cassius reminds him of his philosophy: "Of your philosophy you make no use, / If you give place to accidental evils" (197–98). Brutus replies, "No man bears sorrow better, Portia is dead" (199). Then Cassius cries, "How scaped I killing, when I crossed you so?" (201). Now he understands the unusual irritability of his friend. He has never for a minute ceased to love him: "I cannot drink too much of Brutus's love" (214).

One should not forget the situation in which this daring scene about friendship almost lost and then regained is taking place. The reconciled friends are informed about proscription (the spectators are already familiar with it) and about the political murder of several senators—of Cicero, among others. The political decision is now a decision about life and death. It then comes to the choice of the battlefield for the final showdown. As is well known, the advice of Cassius is politically solid, whereas Brutus's advice turns out to be fatally wrong. Yet Cassius agrees with Brutus only for friendship's sake. Brutus, too, just like Cassius in the first part of the play, points to kairos, the exigency of proper time. He contrasts the choice of proper time with the choice of proper place. In fact there is no such choice, not in the mind of Cassius. Brutus speaks of kairos: "There is a tide in the affairs of men, / Which, taken at the flood, leads on to fortune; Omitted, all the voyage of their life / Is bound in shallows and in miseries. / On such a full sea are we now afloat, / And we must take the current when it serves, / Or lose our ventures" (270–6). Cassius gives up. They meet the triumvirs at Philippi.

This is not an opera, but we still hear music. Brutus asks his favorite young boy, Lucius, to play for him, just like David played for King Saul. Here we encounter once again Nietzsche's Brutus: the melancholy man listening to a beautiful young boy playing music. Then enters the ghost of Julius Caesar, and Brutus repeats to the apparition his farewell sentence to Cassius: "Why, I will see thee at Philippi then" (337). And when the specter leaves or Brutus awakes, the boy, Lucius, remarks: "The strings, my lord, are false" (341). These false strings that are out of tune represent, in Shakespeare, both time out of joint and ill-fated destiny.

We all (the friends, the triumvirs, the ghost of Caesar, and the audience) meet at Philippi (5.1). The political fate of Rome will be decided, so all the actors believe, on this battlefield. Antony and Octavius enter the stage. Octavius observes that Brutus's choice of a battlefield was a mistake for his side. Antony notes that the decision was made on moralistic and not on a strategic grounds: "To fasten in our thoughts that they have courage" (5.1.11). There is a short exchange of words, and we immediately notice the voice of an absolute, and yet cool, authority, that of Octavius, the youth. Antony, the older soldier, offers Octavius the left side of the field. To this Octavius answers: "Upon the right hand, I; Keep thou the left." Antony: "Why do you cross me in this exigent?" Octavius: "I do not cross you, but I will do so" (18–20). This is Caesar's voice: *hic volo, hic jubeo.* All others are silenced when they hear Caesar's voice. One may say that this is Caesar's voice without Caesar's personality, but with Caesar's absolute resoluteness. The difference between Marc Antony and Octavius is very clearly marked by Shakespeare in the short exchange of words between the two parties. Antony indulges in passionate accusations against Brutus and Cassius. He employs several moral terms of abuse: the conspirators are vile flatterers, villains, apes, hounds, and so on. But Octavius speaks politically: "I draw a sword against conspirators / When think you that the sword goes up again? / Never till Caesar's three and thirty wounds / Be well avenged, or till another Caesar / Have added slaughter to the sword of traitors" (5.1.51–55). No hound, no villain, no flatterers, no apes, just traitors and conspirators. This is enough reason to annihilate them. And this is the only (political) reason to do so.

Octavius, Marc Antony, and their men leave the stage. Then comes the farewell scene of Brutus and Cassius. For a moment, everything stands still. There is a pause in the story. Souls are speaking, philosophies are conversing, men are facing their destiny, friends are saying goodbye. Before everything, life or death, the fate of Rome and of the world will be decided; the friends need to reckon with themselves and with their own lives. This is the moment of final reckoning. The future is still open, but soon their destiny will be fulfilled.

But is the future still open? If one listens attentively to the farewell scene of the two friends, one senses that they are prepared for defeat rather than for victory; they are prepared to die rather than to live. They do not believe in their own future. Antony and Octavius do not even consider defeat. But Cassius puts the question to Brutus: "You are contented to be led in triumph / Through the streets of Rome?" (108–9). Brutus answers, "No, Cassius" (110). Soon afterwards, Cassius becomes the victim of a fatal mistake. He believes that Brutus has been defeated when he has not. This is perhaps only because he expected from the beginning that this would happen and no longer cherished any hope in the victory of their cause.

During the "intermission," the pause before the decisive action in which time stands still, philosophical reflection occupies the center stage. Cassius turns to Messala: "Messala, / This is my birthday; at this very day / Was Cassius born. Give me thy hand, Messala. Be thou my witness that against my will . . . am I compelled to set / Upon one battle all our liberties. / You know that I held Epicurus strong, / And his opinion. Now I changed my mind, / And partly credit things that do presage" (71–78). Cassius, who not so long ago defied augury, now begins to look for signs in the flight of birds. To my mind, the two parts of Cassius's brief confession are strongly linked. He defies augury as long as he believes that the fate of liberty depends on the life of one single tyrant (Caesar). But he can no longer defy augury after the fate of liberty is decided by a battle, that is, by an event whose outcome depends on an accident, on good or bad luck. If the fate of the world does not depend on the resolve of men, on their courage and republican spirit, but on an accident, the philosophy of Epicurus (as Shakespeare's Cassius understands it) makes sense no longer. Epicurus says that it is miserable to live in necessity, yet it is not necessary to live in necessity. However, if everything depends on an accidental turn of fate, then it is necessary to live in necessity. For pure accident equals necessity; nothing depends on a single man's resolve. Brutus's philosophy undergoes a similar, although not exactly identical, transformation. He says, "Even by the rule of that philosophy / By which I did blame Cato for the death / Which he did give himself . . . arming myself with patience / To stay the providence of some high powers / That govern us below" (100–107). Brutus rejects suicide and abandons himself (just like the other melancholic, Hamlet) to Providence. He does not reject suicide in general, just suicide before having exhausted all the possibilities still offered by Providence.

Then comes the farewell. Brutus: "But this same day / Must end that work the ides of March begun; / And whether we shall meet again I know not. / Therefore our everlasting farewell take. / For ever, and for ever farewell, Cassius. / If we do meet again, why, we shall smile. / If not, why then, this parting was well made" (113–19). To this Cassius echoes: "For ever and for ever farewell, Brutus. / If we do meet again, we'll smile indeed. / If not, 'tis true parting was well made" (120–22). It cannot be mistaken; this is an opera. The parting of Cassius and Brutus must be sung. It reminds us of a later drama, the parting of Marquis Posa and Don Carlos in Verdi's opera. The last word belongs to Brutus, who gives voice to the thought expressed by many other characters of Shakespeare, among them Hamlet, but in a different orchestration: "O that a man might know / The end of this day's business ere it come! / But it sufficeth that the day will end, / And then the end is known" (123–26).

In 5.2 and 5.3 we are at the battlefield, where speech accompanies or mediates actions. First, Marc Antony wins against the forces of Cassius, and Cassius—mistakenly believing that Brutus is defeated—kills himself. Brutus, who has won against the forces of Octavius, cannot withstand the joined forces of all his enemies after Cassius's desperate and hasty act. One can say that the battle is won by the triumvirs because of Brutus (who chose the wrong battlefield) and because of Cassius (who panicked), and not because of the great military skills of Octavius. For, in Shakespeare, even among the triumvirs, it is Marc Antony who wins (he in fact defeats Cassius), and not Octavius (who was at first defeated by Brutus's forces). Yes, war is the continuation of politics by other means. But victory in war is just an opportunity; on its own it does not determine the result of the political struggle. This single battle does not decide the fate of Rome, as Cassius fears and believes. Rather, it is the political skill of Octavius, who turns the victory of Philippi to his own personal victory and who can safely vacillate between war and peace in order to continue politics in any form or manner.

Shakespeare's Marc Antony is incapable of making this step. Still, this is only hinted at the end of *Julius Caesar*. This is how Shakespeare, not Plutarch, presents the battle and its aftermath. He does not dwell in length on the battle, but on the death of Cassius and Brutus. Yes, victris causa diis placuit, sed victa Catoni. Yes, in this play (certainly not in all his tragedies!), the cause of the defeated pleases Shakespeare. The death of Cassius and Brutus is symbolic: it is the death of the Roman republic. More than politics, history is happening on the stage. In Shakespeare the consummation of history is also the consummation and culmination of the life of the major characters. Death is revealing; it reveals the character and the destiny of a man. It reveals whether there is a schism between character and destiny, or whether the two have been molded into one.

I have mentioned that Cassius's mind is set for defeat, not for victory. He abandons his philosophy, he becomes superstitious, and this day is his birthday. Before finding out about the turn of the battle, we hear Cassius's short soliloquy: "This day I breathed first. Time is come round, / And where I did begin, there shall I end. / My life is run his compass" (5.3.23–24). It is no wonder that he immediately gives credence to the news that Brutus has been overcome by Octavius's forces. Knowing that his fate is sealed, he asks his bondsman, Pindarus, to kill him, after having made him a freeman according to Roman custom. He asks him to kill his master with the same sword Cassius used to kill Caesar: "Caesar, thou art revenged, / Even with the sword that killed thee" (45). And he dies. Cassius dies a very simple death, and he dies by mistake. But his mistake was not just a mistake; it is in character. He always believed in the worst outcome; he was a distrustful man. During the times of conspiracy, perhaps his distrust could have saved the republic. But then the trusting Brutus opposed him. In facing his death, Cassius does not deliver a speech. He does not sum up the lessons of his life; he just mentions the joke of fate that turned his birthday into the day of his death. It is as if everything that happened between birth and death, between the turning of the "full circle," has lost all significance. One gets the impression that Cassius sees his own life as a failure. Or, it is as if the friendship of Brutus alone would have made sense in this life. I think that after the altercation scene, only Brutus mattered. Cassius was dead on furlough the last time he gave in to Brutus out of friendship. He was not a noble man, but he dies—in error—a sacrificial death. Messala soon discovers the error. The words that he utters beside the dead body of Cassius seem a concise yet just funeral oration: "Mistrust of good success hath done this deed. / O hateful Error, Melancholy's child, / Why dost thou show to the apt thoughts of men / The things that are not?" (5.3.65–68). Yes, Cassius became a melancholic man the moment he gave up on his life and cause. He was an emotional man; he was crying inside, he realized that *vanitatum vanitas.*

Cassius's character—in Shakespeare's portrayal—becomes more interesting in the second part of the play than the character of Brutus. Cassius is changing; a man of rancorous ambition is becoming the man of friendly love and melancholic resignation. Caesar's description of Cassius, embodied in his words addressed to Marc Antony, is absolutely accurate when he is giving a lesson about the judgment of human character to his younger friend. The same words would have been wholly inaccurate had they described Cassius at Philippi. Shakespeare portrays Cassius as a man of multiple selves. As the plot develops, his second self replaces his first self. Cassius is never a role-player. He is always too emotional for playing roles, for better or worse.

We saw how dearly Cassius loved Brutus. Now Shakespeare lets us see how Cassius was dearly beloved by another man. Titinius loved Cassius with all his loyal heart, and Cassius knew this. Let us listen to the way in which he sends Titinius into Brutus's camp: "Titinius, if you lovest me, / Mount thy horse" (5.2.15). It was the wrong information about Titinius's fate that made Cassius decide to die. After having returned with good news, and seeing the dead body of Cassius, Titinius kills himself also. Listen to his words, the words of an entirely unselfish, friendly, and loyal lover: "But hold thee, take this garland on thy brow. / Thy Brutus bid me give thee, and I / Will do his bidding. Brutus, come apace, / And see how I regarded Caius Cassius. / By your leave, gods, this is a Roman's part: / Come Cassius' sword, and find Titinius' heart" (5.3.84–89). What does Shakespeare do with this scene? What complexities of the heart can his language express? Titinius says to the body of Cassius: "Thy Brutus," and then addresses Brutus: "See how I regarded Caius Cassius." These little things tell a long story, a story of jealousy, of silent love, of competition. Brutus was for Caius "thy" Brutus, but Titinius is the one who chooses death for Caius, and only for him. Titinius is saying in this scene, "I kill myself with the sword that killed Caesar, although I did not participate in the assassination of Caesar. It is only for my friend, Caius, that I am going to die. You, Brutus, cannot compete with me."

Contrary to the character of Cassius, the character of Brutus remains steady. Yet, is he overdoing his role as a moralist, as "noble Brutus"? Is Brutus overplaying his role for the sake of his own glory, or is he a historical mythmaker? These are very different things. If he is overplaying his own role, he can still be branded with some justification as a self-righteous man. But creating a historical myth is not self-aggrandizement. On the battlefield of Philippi, Brutus steps on the cothurn and takes all his remaining friends with him to the height of the historical stage. He thus creates the myth of the fall of the Roman republic, the myth of Republican virtue and heroism, the myth of Roman virtues in general. He creates a myth that will stay alive until the French Revolution and even longer.

The mythmaking begins at a moment when Brutus is not yet resigned to defeat. For he—unlike Cassius—is resigned to suffer defeat only if everything is finally settled. Without hope and without fear, he remains true to the Stoic creed. Nonetheless, he begins mythmaking beside the bodies of Cassius and Titinius: "Are yet two Romans living such as these? / The last of all the Romans, fare thee well. / It is impossible that ever Rome / Should breed thy fellow" (97–100). We, the audience, who know much about Cassius's character (and very little of Titinius's) are surprised to hear this gross exaggeration. Will Rome be incapable from this time onward of breeding men of such quality? Cassius's character was, as we know, far from impeccable. (Brutus knows this, too.) But all these things do not matter; at the grave of the Roman republic the republican virtue must shine for many generations to come. Cassius and Titinius are now invented by Brutus as the embodiments of those virtues, and this mythologization is effective. For the men around Brutus are going to behave, fight, and die as part and parcel of a mythological truth. Young Cato allows himself to be slain; Luculius pretends to be Brutus to let himself be killed instead of Brutus. At this point in the drama, something interesting happens: Marc Antony joins the chorus. The enemy begins to participate in the mythmaking of his enemies. The myth of the battle between Achilles and Hector returns. Grandeur fights grandeur, hero confronts hero; the battle at Philippi is transformed into a theomachia. When Luculius is taken and brought before Marc Antony in the belief that he is Brutus, Marc Antony says: "This is not Brutus, friend, but, I assure you, / A prize no less in worth. Keep this man safe. / Give him all kindness. I had rather have / Such men my friends than enemies" (5.4.26–29). We then see Brutus finally beaten.

Just like Cassius, he asks his bondsmen to kill him. They refuse. So Brutus completes his own myth, and he completes it not in a self-righteous way. He creates his own myth in a *mirror*, presenting his grandeur in the mirror of his friends: "Countrymen, / My heart doth joy that yet in all my life / I found no man but he was true to me. / I shall have glory by this losing day, / More than Octavius and Marc Antony / By vile conquest shall attain unto" (5.5.33–38). Those who know Shakespeare's hierarchy of virtues know how high a position loyalty, fidelity, and gratitude occupy. None of the main characters, and none of the favorite heroes of Shakespeare, could see themselves so clear, pure, and impeccable in the mirror of their friends. This is because none of them could have truly said at their dying hour that everyone remained truthful to them. Brutus is the only one who can, who does. But is this true? Was no one unfaithful or disloyal to Brutus? We do not know, for we know only the myth. What remains is the act of execution. Just before the execution Brutus speaks and acts as simply as Cassius. His thoughts wander toward a spirit, the same spirit as the thoughts of the dying Cassius: toward Caesar. They wander toward the living Caesar, the murdered Caesar, the ghost of Caesar, and the spirit of Caesar, who will be the real victor of the day. He is the historical, albeit not the moral, victor. He must share his myth.

Marc Antony continues what he began: he contributes to the myth of Brutus, but not to the myth of the last Romans. His narrative offers a historical appreciation of Brutus, yet not a mythological aggrandizement of his cause. Brutus is the exception; Cassius and the other conspirators are the rule. If we listen to the text, we notice that this is not the usual Shakespearean ending in which someone needs to bury the corpse and say some empty yet laudatory sentences about the dead. Octavius will play this part at the end. But Marc Antony does something else. He puts the death of Brutus and the defeat of the conspirators into historical perspective: "This was the noblest Roman of them all / All the conspirators save only he / Did that they did in envy of great Caesar. / He only in a general honest thought / And common good to all made one of them. / His life was gentle, and the elements / So mixed in him that Nature might stand up / And say to all the world 'This was a man'" (67–74). With the exclamation *"ecce homo!"* (which is entirely Shakespeare's invention), Marc Antony takes Brutus out of his historical context and self-created republican mythology and places him in the pantheon of moral men whose virtue was personal, unique, and independent of their cause.

The last words belong to Octavius. He is the one who buries the dead with the usual empty slogans and with due respect for those who were made harmless. Octavius appears at the end of *Julius Caesar* as Fortinbras appears at the end of *Hamlet*. But he is no Fortinbras. He is—unlike young Fortinbras—not a man of traditional honor, the son and natural heir of old Fortinbras, but the man of the future. He is young Octavius, who is just beginning to call himself Caesar, but who will become what he chooses himself to be—that is, Caesar.

14

Antony and Cleopatra

This play is the most complex of the Roman dramas; moreover, it is perhaps the most complex of all the Shakespearean history dramas. It is not the tragedy of one man, but of a man and a woman, of Antony and Cleopatra. However, while this tragedy unfolds, other tragedies are also taking place simultaneously: the tragedy of Pompey the younger, and the tragedy of Enobarbus. Both tragedies perhaps deserve their own separate dramas. But Shakespeare compacts—as in *King Lear*—several tragedies in one single drama. Even in the main tragedy, that of Antony and Cleopatra, several threads are knotted together. Each of those threads is spun from different fibers; sometimes even one single thread is spun from different fibers. The political drama of Rome is not just the political drama of Rome, it is also a clash between two cultures (if I may employ this modern term), that of the East and the West. The whole play is imbued with the contrast between East and West. It is also the story of the decline of the East and of the victory of the West, which might be perceived as a Pyrrhic victory. This is also a drama of repeated betrayals, infidelities, and changes of allegiance, of ups and downs, of the vicissitudes of fortune. Shakespeare's ambition here is to condense into one drama a great variety of heterogeneous factors that contributed to the birth of the Roman Empire from the ruins of the republic. Yet these are not all direct political factors; they can also be indirect ones.

Shakespeare's ambition structures the play. It consists of several, sometimes very short, scenes. Some take place at the same time but in different places, some at very different times. Private and public events cross over each other and overdetermine one another in many of the brief scenes. Men emerge, show their faces and fates, and then go down. But all the scenes are decisive and not episodic. They are not "pauses," for they participate in the mainstream of the world events wherever they are taking place. This is why it seems to me unrewarding to follow step-by-step, scene by scene, the unfolding of the drama; that is, to do the same thing I have done with every other play.

As a love story, *Antony and Cleopatra* is frequently compared to *Romeo and Juliet*. *Antony and Cleopatra* was written by a man in his ripe age who knew more of love than he knew or preferred to know in his youth. In *Romeo and Juliet* love itself is unproblematic. All the conflict, and finally also the tragic end, results from external and contingent causes. But in *Antony and Cleopatra* love itself becomes problematic. This happens not entirely independently of external causes and incidents, yet not simply as their result. This love is inherently problematic. First, the lovers are brought up in different worlds; they carry in their souls and on their bodies the marks of different traditions. They love each other, but they do not read each other well. They are also strangers, aliens to each other. This love relation impresses us as being modern precisely because of the lack of absolute confidence, because passion and knowledge are parting ways, because desire and possession do not meet halfway. And because, the problematic aspects of passionate love notwithstanding, or perhaps because of it, it is a great love story, an immortal love story—a monument of passionate and total love. Love is omnipotent, sensual, emotional, spiritual; it proves stronger than reason, interest, common sense, historical grandeur, success, and glory. Love is worth all the sacrifices made for it.

Shakespeare frequently portrays love as problematic. In part 1 of this book, I discussed some cases of sexual subversion, among them great love stories of cruel and wicked men and women, including the kind of love for which men and women are ready to kill, hate, or destroy. There is, in Shakespeare, sadistic and masochistic love, destructive love. But the love between Antony and Cleopatra, although problematic, is not of this kind. If it is destructive, it is first and foremost self-destructive. Antony and Cleopatra hurt one another, sometimes even viciously, yet perhaps not more than Brutus and Cassius hurt each other at the camp in Sardis. They can abuse one another, spit on one another, hate one another; but they never harm one another on purpose. What is even more important, neither Antony nor Cleopatra is consistently cruel; that is, they are not cruel but in a state of rage. Neither of them murders, neither is guilty of political killing (at least not in this play), neither has acted even once in a sadistic way. Antony and Cleopatra are problematic persons, but not bad persons; they are just "human, all too human." It is Antony who buries the spotless Brutus with the words "ecce homo." At the end of this play we could repeat the same sentence of "ecce homo" before the dead bodies of these far-from-spotless lovers. The passionate, the erring, the naïve, the magnanimous and generous, the repenting, the failing, the sentimental, the honest, the loving, the silly, the unjust, the crazy: the problematic individual is closer to us than the spotless hero. Antony is never in control of himself, yet he never does anything unforgivable, either.

In one significant way the temporality of the drama *Antony and Cleopa-*

tra is a complicated case of irreversibility. The drama's tempo is very fast, and every deed becomes irreversible in the sense that it cannot be undone as far as the development of history—and the fate of Antony and Cleopatra—is concerned. Yet there are no acts, mistakes, or follies of Anthony and Cleopatra that would become irreversible from a moral point of view. Neither of them commits a crime or a sin; in a deeper moral sense neither of them will even be guilty. This is why it can be said that nothing that they have done is unforgivable. The unique combination of political/historical/personal irreversibility and moral/ethical/emotional reversibility is the preeminent feature of the drama. One could reply that there is nothing unique in this reversed mirror image of reversibility/irreversibility in *Antony and Cleopatra,* for this is the common temporal structure of all the Roman plays; there is no positively wicked person in any of them. Still, there are differences. In *Coriolanus,* for example, the hero's betrayal, his joining the enemy's army, is a political act, but it is still reversible. In *Julius Caesar*, the assassination of Caesar is irreversible, but as far as the structure of the play is concerned, the fate of the heroes could have been reversed. They make a few fatal mistakes. But in *Antony and Cleopatra* it is written not in the history books, nor even in the series of mistakes, but in the character of the lovers and their love, that whatever they do in the political arena will become irreversible. They never make an irrevocable decision, they constantly hesitate, their minds turn from one direction to the other, they act irrationally. It is precisely because they constantly take back what they decide that there is no firm purpose in their actions—and if there is, it will soon become unsteady—that everything they do must become irreversible for their own fate as well as for the fate of the world.

Antony and Caesar

The typical Shakespearean characterization through language and speech is extremely strong in this play. The style of Octavius's speech is flat but cutting. Every sentence is aimed at some goal. Moreover, he normally speaks in short sentences. On the other hand, perhaps no other Shakespearean character employs such colorful, poetic, and complex language as Antony. He can play on emotions and also be emotional; his speeches frequently make his soldiers cry. Yet he can also speak the language of pleasure, gaiety, and wit. He speaks in a different language as a lover, as a soldier, as a Roman, but in all cases he plays with language. He never speaks in ready-made sentences. His language is always his own, in courtship and in battle, in political encounters and in private pleasures, in happiness and in rage. His language is a musical instrument on which he can play such different, but always beautiful, melodies. Antony is a character from an opera; he sings duets with Cleopatra, and his monologues are arias.

It is because of Antony's poetic talents that the world stage and the theater stage seem to meld into one, for Antony is always playacting. He feels himself to be always on stage. His most private feelings and passions are played in the presence of a sometimes fictive audience. Listen to him in 1.1: "Let Rome in Tiber melt, and the wide arch / Of the ranged Empire fall. Here is my space. / Kingdoms are clay. Our dungy earth alike / Feeds beast as man. The nobleness of life / Is to do thus; when such a mutual pair / And such a twain can do't—in which I bind / On pain and punishment the world to weet—/ We stand up peerless" (1.1.35–42). The speech is a gesture: he is throwing away everything for love. But this gesture is played on the world stage. Antony speaks about a "peerless" pair and refers to their "world" where they stand up in a peerless way. When he decides shortly afterwards to leave for Rome all the same and curses Cleopatra for holding him back, he mentions that because of young Pompey the world is in danger. Thus he remains on the world stage, although playing another role.

It is clear right from the beginning that Shakespeare's Antony has no chance against Shakespeare's Octavius. Antony's changes of mind are motivated by passions, a sense of duty, sentimentalism, and generosity, whereas Octavius's changes of mind are always of a strategic/tactical character. He does not change his mind on one crucial thing: he wants the power and wants it alone and quickly. Thus every step that he takes, even if seemingly contradictory to other steps he has taken, is completely devoid of contradiction. For every step serves the very same purpose.

Caesar's judgment of Antony shifts a few times. But, in general, Caesar does not appreciate men who are so much unlike him. Habits that are not his habits are despicable in his eyes. As a man of strong convictions and an absolute faith vested in himself, he is also a man of prejudices. Antony's involvement with Cleopatra and his passion are for Octavius signs of unmanliness, weakness, and cowardice. For Caesar, Antony—who is so absolutely manly for Cleopatra—looks unmanly; his ideal of manliness is extremely narrow and strict. Let him speak: "He fishes, drinks, and wastes / The lamps of night in revel; is not more manlike / Than Cleopatra, nor the queen of Ptolemy / More womanly than he" (1.4.4–6). And when Lepidus defends Antony by referring to his bad heredity, Caesar continues, "Let's grant it is not / Amiss to humble on the bed of Ptolemy, / To give a kingdom for a mirth, to sit / And keep the turn of tippling with a slave, / To reel the streets at noon, and stand the buffet / With knaves that smell of sweat" (16–21). But immediately afterwards, hearing about Pompey's strength, Octavius decides to make use of Marc Antony. Caesar is a man who suspends judgment, or shifts it, if tactics so dictate. Antony stands no chance against Caesar.

In fact, Antony himself realizes that he has no chance against Caesar. As early as act 2, scene 4, in his conversation with the soothsayer, he spells it out. But he believes in Octavius's miracles. He thinks that Octavius is constantly winning against him because of his mysterious good fortune, or perhaps even as the result of sorcery, and that he himself loses because of his equally mysterious ill fortune. He is not farsighted enough to realize the truth spelled out by Shakespeare's Cassius to Brutus before Caesar's assassination: we are our own destinies; it is not in the stars thar our fate is decided.

Whether the soothsayer was sent by Caesar himself to make Antony return to Egypt, that is, to act according to Octavius's stratagem, one cannot decide. The text, however, speaks clearly; Antony is open and honest and outspoken, as always. If there is an entirely antidemonic character in Shakespeare, it is Antony. This makes this brief conversation all the more interesting. Antony asks the soothsayer, "Say to me, / Whose fortunes shall rise higher: Caesar's or mine?" (2.3.15). The soothsayer answers: "Caesar's. Therefore, O Antony, stay not by his side. / Thy daemon, that thy spirit which keeps thee, is / Noble, courageous, high, unmatchable, / Where Caesar's is not. But near him thy angel / Becomes afeard, as being o'erpowered. Therefore / Make space enough between you" (16–21). The soothsayer is not a soothsayer. He is a judge of human character. The interesting thing is not what he says about the future (an easy guess!) but what he says about the character of the main historical actors and their relationship. What the soothsayer sees well and points out is that Octavius, who is neither magnanimous nor even courageous, has something Antony is lacking: the spirit of absolute authority. Antony becomes afraid in the presence of this man, whom he regards as mediocre, because he is great in one thing: he is charismatic. His is not the usual kind of charisma, it does not depend on grandeur of character. If this were so, Antony would be the winner. Octavius's charisma is the charisma of absolute resolve, of the strong-willed; it is the charisma of nonlistening, noncaring, nonconsidering. It is the charisma of a new man who does not depend on customs, codes of honor, friendship, or anything else, who knows only his goal and stubbornly follows it. Octavius has in fact a kind of demonic power. This is the power of silence, of nonreacting unresponsiveness. This is not because he does not speak—he does—but because behind his speech there is the silence of the undisclosed absolute purpose. He does not notice the other person as a man or as a woman, only as a means to his strategic enterprise. He is a man who uses argumentative justification for everything that he decides, without listening to contrary opinions. For example, he enumerates Antony's accusations against him in 3.6. Every bit of the charge is entirely true: Caesar betrayed Pompey, Lepidus, and Antony in turn. But Caesar says that Lepidus became too cruel, and that this is why he deserved what he got. He makes an offer to Antony, knowing before-hand that it is an unacceptable one. There is something demonic in this stubborn unswervingness and purposiveness. For such an unyielding man who cheats and lies if needed, without the slightest pang of conscience, is also a loner. But Caesar is not cruel, he does not kill or permit killing without purpose. And he is the greatest judge of character.

Antony stops the soothsayer: "Speak this no more." But the soothsayer says: "To none but thee; no more than when to thee. / If thou dost play with him at any game / Thou art sure to lose; and of that natural luck / He beats thee 'gainst odds. Thy lustre thickens / When he shines by. I say again, thy spirit / Is all afraid to govern near him; / But he away, 'tis noble'" (22–28). The soothsayer says things that would awaken poisonous jealousy in every man but Antony. Antony knows jealousy only in love. He is too noble and too generous to become jealous. Although the soothsayer wants to awaken his angry jealousy, Antony's reaction is very different. Antony takes the advice: he leaves for Egypt. He does what he wants to do anyway, which is to return to Cleopatra. The soothsayer's message is just a pretext. Instead of envy, Antony is grabbed by anxiety—for he, as I said, does not understand the source of Caesar's victories. This source is unfathomable to him because it originates in a different world. His Rome is the world of chivalry; Octavius's Rome is the world of politics. Antony's world is also the world of the Orient; Caesar's is exclusively the world of the Occident. Thus ponders Antony in a short soliloquy (and this soliloquy offers us an insight into his noble heart and also his failure to understand): "Be art or hap, / He hath spoken true. The very dice obey him, / And in our sports my better cunning faints / Under his chance. If we draw lots, he speeds. / His cocks do win the battle still of mine / When it is all to naught, and his quails ever / Beat mine, inhopped, at odds. I will to Egypt; / And though I make this marriage for my peace, / I'th' East my pleasure lies" (30–33).

The game between Antony and Caesar—which is lost for Antony from the beginning—is the main political conflict of this drama. There are many other conflicts and many other characters in this drama, and very represen-tative ones. There is Cleopatra first and foremost but also Pompey the younger and Enobarbus, to mention only the most significant ones. They play a tragic role, just like Antony (and unlike Octavius). Yet, even if their drama is not political, it is intimately connected to the main political colli-sion. Every concrete tragedy is related to the main political drama, be it political in character or not. Cleopatra's fate is inseparable from that of Antony; the betrayal of Enobarbus happens in the shadow of Antony's fate. Pompey alone holds for one moment the possibility of turning the wheel of fortune around. He misses the opportunity. In the end, his fate, like the fate of Lepidus, will also depend on Caesar's decision.

Pompey the Younger

I would like to dwell for a while on the point at which the wheel of fortune could have turned in another direction. Had Pompey decided to act upon Menas's advice, no good luck or clever politics would have saved Octavius Caesar. At this point, it is really good luck that saves Octavius. However, in Shakespeare—and not just in Shakespeare—politics is full of contingent events. That Pompey did not dare to do what he wanted to do (to allow the murder of the triumvirs on his ship), that he knew the ethical difference between doing something and allowing something to happen, that there was a remnant of old Roman republican honor in his spiritual outfit, were merely contingent factors from the perspective of Octavius's destiny. Thus, for a moment, the fate of the world hinged on a very thin thread: Pompey's distinction between doing something and letting something happen. How do we know this? We know it because Plutarch said so. How did Plutarch know it, if no one but Pompey and Menas knew it (and they were going to die soon)? Plutarch played the role of the omniscient narrator, but Shakespeare does not need to play such a role. For the event happens under our nose, on the stage—the stage of the theater, which is simultaneously also the historical stage. The historical stage discloses itself on the theater stage.

The banquet scene in Shakespeare's presentation is crazy, phantomlike. The leaders of the whole world are gathered on a boat; the fate of the world depends on something that will or will not happen on this boat. The phantomlike scene in Shakespeare represents the phantomlike character of history itself: sheer madness and sheer contingency compressed into one small place within a few hours.

Immediately before the banquet scene, Shakespeare offers the spectators the best opportunity to see Octavius Caesar working in his proper medium, politics. Octavius responds briefly to Pompey's long jeremiad complaining of Rome's ingratitude: "Take your time" (2.6.24). This is a brief statement of cold, calculated condescension. Antony and Lepidus talk to Pompey, but Octavius Caesar does not. When Lepidus asks Pompey how he received what they offered him, Octavius Caesar just adds, "There's the point" (31), showing that he will not waste his speech on such a man. Pompey now comes to speak of the triumvir's offer: Sicily and Sardinia. He is willing to take the offer and dismiss his pirates, to disarm himself and put himself at the mercy of the triumvirs. But Pompey is not merely a fool. For if it were for Antony and Lepidus, the promise would have been kept, particularly because Antony is obliged to Pompey and freely recognizes his obligation. However, Caesar is already in business. Pompey, who does not know Caesar, does not sense the trap. But his man, the pirate Menas, does.

He generally keeps his misgivings to himself, but eventually he shares them with Enobarbus, in whom, an honest soldier, he has complete trust: "Pompey doth this day laugh away his fortune" (106). The offer is taken, the agreement settled, and the banquet begins.

This is again a scene from an opera. Mozart should have set it to music. While entering the banquet room, Antony offers a brief lesson in Egyptian agricultural and meteorological practices to Lepidus, who is, however, interested only in crocodiles. It is a telling episode, for it shows Antony's interest in what we now call "otherness." He is not just Cleopatra's lover; his involvement in Eastern knowledge expands further and is authentic. Yet Lepidus, who has already started drinking heavily, makes fun of the East: "Nay, certainly, I have heard the Ptolemies' pyramies are very goodly things: without contradiction I have heard that" (2.7.33–35). Antony is irritated by Lepidus's high and mighty stupidity and serves him with a description of the crocodile full of cutting irony: "It is shaped, sir, like itself, and it is as broad as it hath breadth. . . . It lives by that which nourisheth it, and the elements once out of it, it transmigrates" (41–44). While drinking continues, things move to the above-mentioned scene from Plutarch about the temptation of Pompey by Menas: "These three world-sharers, these competitors, / Are in thy vessel. Let me cut the cable; / And when we are put off, fall to their throats. / All there is thine" (69–72). After Pompey refuses, Menas says aside: "For this, I'll never follow thy palled fortunes more. / Who seeks, and will not take when once 'tis offered, / Shall never find it more" (80–82).

Caesar and Antony portray a world of betrayal. In this drama everyone is betrayed at least once, if not many times, and almost everyone betrays someone else. This is a world without trust, without confidence, a world of suspicion and double-dealing. The master of all these tricks is Caesar. Yet Caesar knows the reason of treason, of broken promises and torn agreements. He knows, for example, that the agreement he made with Pompey is a trap, whereas others incidentally leave the "palled fortune" to join the victors. They are turncoats—what Caesar is not.

The drama is about history and love as well as politics and betrayal. There is betrayal repented and betrayal unrepented. Caesar will not repent his betrayals, for he hardly sees them in such a light. For him these are just political moves. One cannot but betray one's friends. Yet none of the protagonists of this drama are Caesar's friends. They might be his momentary allies; this is all. Caesar has no friends. Whoever is without friends, whoever is without commitment to another person in his heart, cannot be a traitor. In order to be a traitor one must be loyal, one must be a friend of some kind. Only trust can be betrayed, mistrust cannot. Caesar does not trust anyone and does not expect to be trusted. If one trusts him all the same—as Antony, Lepidus, and Pompey do—this is their bad fortune and, seen from Caesar's perspective, the result of their miscalculation. There is no miscalculation on Caesar's part. Still, Caesar sometimes complains about having been betrayed. This laconic man suddenly becomes very talkative when it comes to accusing Antony of betraying Octavia, his sister. Although the marriage of Octavia and Antony is a cunning device on the part of Caesar to secure Antony's military help against Pompey and he does not need this marriage anymore (for he does not need Antony) after he gets rid of Pompey with cunning and without war, there might have been a grain of sincerity in his hypocritical accusation. Caesar might have really loved Octavia, even if he sacrifices her without much ado on the altar of the state. Furthermore, although Caesar never repents of his treasons, his broken promises and tricks, he can feel sorry because of them and exhibit compassion for defeated enemies. He wants to defeat them by all means. But once he has done so, he does not hate them. He can feel sorry for them. In this matter, as in others, there is a continuity of the character of Octavius. Just as Octavius praises the dead Brutus—although in a merely formal manner—and promises to respect his memory, so will he praise the dead Antony and Cleopatra. In this (the second) case, as we will see, his words will be less conventional. After all, he had nothing to do with Brutus. Yet Antony was his ally, although not his friend; they were fighting together. Although he is incapable of real emotion, Caesar experiences some kind of feelings when he repeats in his last sentences of the drama the thought that had been formulated by Antony at the very beginning of it: "No grave upon the earth shall clip in it / A pair so famous. High events as these / Strike those that make them, and their story is / No less in pity than his glory which / Brought them to be lamented" (553). There is a tint of chivalry in this perfect Machiavellian politician.

Enobarbus

The brief but central tragedy of young Pompey represents the age in its historical significance; the tragedy of Enobarbus represents the moral chemistry of the age as a litmus paper. In times of distrust and betrayal even the most loyal man becomes a traitor. The typical soldier is in Shakespeare normally truthful and honest, simple, uncouth, and yet trustworthy: a man of honor. We get to know Enobarbus as just such a man. He is not a general, but the general's second man, not a refined gentleman but an uncouth fellow, open and sincere. He loves Marc Antony, although he sometimes disapproves of his acts or choices. He is a man of honor of the second rank.

In the concert of characters of the drama, Enobarbus belongs to those who play second fiddle. But the fiddle is always present; from the beginning to his end, the voice of Enobarbus is to be heard in the ever changing melody of the play. He enters the chambers of Charmian and Alexas (the ladies-in-waiting for Cleopatra) right after the soothsayer. He is familiar with Egyptian customs. He backs Antony's wishes, even the untold ones, in his rough manner. He teases Antony. He loves to make jokes about women whom he slightly despises. When, for example, news arrives of Fulvia's death and Antony for the first time considers leaving Egypt for Rome, Enobarbus teases him: "Why, then we kill all our women. . . . Cleopatra, catching but the least noise of this dies instantly. I have seen her die twenty times upon far poorer moment" (1.2.125–34). His direct speech is positively vulgar (for example, "when old robes are worn out there are members to make new. . . . your old smock brings forth a new petticoat" (156–60). Jokingly, he always plays into Antony's hands.

Enobarbus accompanies Marc Antony to Rome. First we find him in conversation with Lepidus, the man of trepid compromises. Lepidus speaks the language of differences (differences can be settled) and not the language of force. It is still before the banquet scene, and Pompey invests some of his hopes in the unity of the triumvirs. Enobarbus looks with suspicion ahead to the awaited meeting between Caesar and Antony; he is afraid for Antony, as he also understands the importance of the event. In history, in politics, there are no innocent meetings: "Every time / Serves for the matter that is then born in't" (2.2.9–10). The next, crucial, scene contains the verbal exchange between Antony and Caesar where both Enobarbus and Lepidus are present. Caesar accuses Antony of having broken his oath. Lepidus interrupts him to stop his accusation of Antony, but Antony asks Caesar to go on. He does not like things to remain unsaid; he prefers accusations openly made. After Antony rejects half the accusations and apologizes for the other half, Enobarbus intervenes, turning to Antony and warning him that he is now going to be used against Pompey. However, Antony refuses to listen: "Thou art a soldier only. Speak no more" (112). To this Enobarbus answers, "That truth should be silent I had almost forgot" (113). Enobarbus is indeed a soldier and not a statesman. He is a man of common sense, and perhaps this is why he does not let himself be misled: he knows strategy and tactics when he sees them employed. This is not the last time Enobarbus warns Antony about falling into Caesar's trap. But one cannot persuade a person to act against his character, and Antony's character is open and also trusting. In the following scene, where the marriage proposal between Octavia, sister of Caesar, and Antony is made, Enobarbus remains present. He also remains present during the discussion in the next scene between Agrippa and Maecenas. They, the friends of the bitter and steady Caesar, are hungry for some juicy gossip; they ask Enobarbus about Cleopatra and about Antony's love. And then Enobarbus tells the story of the first encounter between Cleopatra and Antony on the River Cydnus, taken from Plutarch. It is a great ballad that could also be set to music, and it is absolutely convincing that the ballad is recited by Enobarbus, because he can describe the fantastic Eastern pomp and show with adoration but also comment on it in a cynical way. But when Maecenas remarks that now Antony will leave Cleopatra for Octavia, Enobarbus knows better: "Never. He will not. / Age cannot wither her, nor custom stale / Her infinite variety. Other women cloy / The appetites they feed, but she makes hungry / Where most she satisfies" (240–44). That is, Cleopatra is the woman whom one desires even if one possesses her, for in her case alone possession does not quench desire. Enobarbus does not need a soothsayer to foresee what the future will bring.

What is the dramaturgical function of Enobarbus's presence in all scenes preceding the banquet? He is the witness, because everyone confides in him. He even entertains Menas, the pirate, and they understand one another. When Menas complains that the enemies gave up fighting and turned to drinking instead and that "Pompey doth this day laugh away his fortune" (106), Enobarbus speaks his mind and answers, "If he do, sure he cannot weep't back again" (107). Enobarbus also reassures Menas that the marriage between Octavia and Antony will not be a long-lasting matrimony and that instead of sealing a friendship, it will rather cause enmity. This is something, we may add, Caesar also foresaw and promoted.

Enobarbus keeps his frank and cynical mood during the banquet. When a servant is carrying away the stone drunk Lepidus, Enobarbus remarks that he must be a very strong fellow: "A bears the third part of the world, man; seest not?" (2.7.87). He proposes also an Egyptian bacchanal, but what he and his buddies are practicing is rather the merrymaking of Western barbarians: "The holding every man shall beat as loud / As his strong sides can volley" (108–9). Enobarbus constantly plays the role of the honest Western barbarian in which—perhaps most outspokenly in 3.2 of the engagement scene, while showing his disbelief at the comedy of brotherly alliance between Caesar and Antony—he makes half-cynical and half-cutting remarks on the grandiloquence and playacting of the main players of the historical show.

In 3.5 Enobarbus learns something from Eros that he suspected from the start. The comedy of Caesar was just a comedy. He was breaking his promise; he made war against Pompey but did not let Lepidus partake in the glory of the action. Pompey is murdered. Enobarbus draws the conclusion: "Then, world, thou hast a pair of chops, no more, / And throw between them all the food thou hast, / They'll grind the one the other" (3.5.12–14). The final decision cannot be long postponed. Enobarbus goes to Antony.

In contrast to *Julius Caesar*, where Shakespeare fuses two battles into one, here he keeps different battles apart. In 3.7 we are already at Actium. The battle of Actium, which will go down in the history books as the decisive one, is not yet the decisive battle here. It is important for Shakespeare, again, to point to accidental events in the flow and stock of history and to portray foremost what different people can do with such accidents, how can they use or misuse them, how can they turn contingency into their destiny or fail to do so. The capacity to deal with contingency as it increases or decreases, depending on events, is rooted in the character of the actors. A few characters can surprise us, others will not. Antony and Cleopatra surprise us all the time, but Caesar never does.

The battle of Actium will be decisive for the world. Yet it is also decisive in the story and in the fate of Enobarbus. For the idea of switching loyalties, the thought of leaving his master and joining the victorious Caesar, first begins to take shape in his mind right after this battle. He does put the thought out of his mind a few times, but it comes back with ever greater power.

Enobarbus is a soldier, but he is not a traditional soldier-man of English nobility. He does not serve his family or country, or even his traditional master. He serves one single man whom he has chosen as a master and friend, and who has accepted him. His tie to Antony is not an inherited but a chosen one, and whatever has been chosen can also been abandoned. One can change one's own choice. The choice of Enobarbus has fallen on a man whom he regarded not just as powerful but also as strong willed: a good general, an emotional but also clever fellow. The moment he begins to see Antony's character in a different light, he cannot find sufficient reason to remain loyal to a losing, or already lost, cause. If a cause is lost without the failure of the loser, this is one thing. But this cause will be lost, so Enobarbus starts to believe, through the character failure of his master, as a result of his weakness, foolishness, bad decisions, and the like. In addition, Antony has many times crossed Enobarbus's decisions. It is the freedom of choice that makes Enobarbus a traitor. And it is, again, the freedom of choice that makes him regret his treason. For Enobarbus recognizes two things. First, he recognizes that to flee a sinking ship is disgraceful and that nothing can counterbalance such a disgrace. Second, he recognizes that the "weakness" of a character is a very complex thing, that not only cowardice can weaken a man's character, but so can noble feelings and magnanimity. He will soon notice that there is a kind of grandeur other than the traditional heroism of a Roman soldier. This is Enobarbus's story in a nutshell. But the episodes, in the sequences in which the story develops, are more important dramaturgically and poetically than the story itself.

Before Actium, Enobarbus forbids Cleopatra to participate in the battle. It will soon turn out to be in vain. Enobarbus also advises Antony to refuse to fight Caesar on the sea and to prepare to fight on land. However, Antony, under pressure from Cleopatra, decides on a sea battle. In this scene all soldier followers of Antony (Canidius, Scarus) back the advice of Enobarbus. Everyone knows that Antony is wrong. The soldier followers have joined a

great general, not a bungler. As Canidius says to Antony: "Soldier, thou art;
but this whole action grows / Not in the power on't. So our leader's led, /
And we are women's men" (3.7.67–69). The sea fight immediately goes
wrong. Enobarbus is outraged. All the soldiers are outraged. Scarus curses:
"The greater cantle of the world is lost / With very ignorance; We have
kissed away / Kingdoms and provinces" (3.10.6–8). Canidius sums it up:
"Had our general / Been what he knew himself, it had gone well" (25–26).
And then he proceeds: "To Caesar will I render / My legions and my horse.
Six kings already / Show me the way of yielding" (33–35). This is the first
betrayal in Antony's army within the drama (the others to which Camidius
refers have taken place outside the drama). And Enobarbus adds the following comment to Canidius's treason: "I'll yet follow / The wounded
chance of Antony, though my reason / Sits in the wind against me"
(35–36). This "yet" is stylistically beautiful! Is Enobarbus still loyal? Or is he
a traitor on furlough? A traitor in waiting? He speaks about his reason.
What is reason? This reason is Caesar's reason; it is calculative reason, it is
purposive rationality. To follow reason here means to act according one's
interest. We know of several concepts and interpretations of reason in
Shakespeare in addition to those in this drama.

The first surprise is that Antony understands the decision of his traitors.
He knows that he has made the wrong decisions for the wrong reasons, he
knows that he is guilty. Instead of crying ingratitude, he asks his men to take
his wealth and leave him. This is where we first learn about Antony's generosity and magnanimity. Not only does he forgive, but he does not even
see anything that would call for forgiveness. It is rather to him that his disloyal friends should extend their pardon: "It is ashamed to bear me. Friends,
come hither. / I am so late in the world that I / Have lost my way for ever.
I have a ship / Laden with gold. Take that; divide it, fly, / And make your
peace with Caesar" (3.11.2–6). Generosity touches the hearts of all. This is
not the first or the last time that Antony makes his soldiers weep. He is still
the same Antony who wept hot tears while reading the testimony of Caesar and speaking about old Caesar's generosity. When the friends refuse to
flee, he still insists. And his insistence is absolutely honest: "Friends, be gone.
. . . Pray you, look not sad. . . . Let that be left / Which leaves itself" (15–20).
Still, he has not forgotten: it was he and not Octavius Caesar who won the
battle at Philippi.

Antony sends away Caesar's ambassadors and challenges him to a duel.
This is chivalrous indeed, but entirely unfit in a time "out of joint." Enobarbus is flabbergasted at this crazy offer. He comments (aside): "I see men's
judgements are / A parcel of their fortunes, and things outward / Do draw
the inward quality after them / To suffer all alike. That he should dream, /
Knowing all measures, the full Caesar will / Answer his emptiness!"
(3.13.30–35). Antony speaks now as a kind of Don Quixote: he dreams of

a glory that he has no more opportunity to win. The world of honor and of republican virtues is gone. He knew this, but now he forgets it.

This is the second occasion where Enobarbus's loyalty falters. He ruminates (aside, again): "Mine honesty and I begin to square. / The loyalty well held to fools does make / Our faith mere folly; Yet he that can endure / To follow with allegiance fall'n lord. / Does conquer him that did his master conquer, / And earns a place i'th' story" (40–44). At this point, we sense a clash between two kinds of "reason." First: one does not remain loyal to a lost cause, particularly if the man one has served loyally acts foolishly. But second, and to the contrary: the fall of great men is great; history will remember them. And those who remain loyal to them will earn a place in the history books—and a noble place. In Enobarbus's mind, the reason of temporality and the reason of immortality clash. What is more important: to have some good days during the rest of one's life, or to win fame immortal? For the time being, Enobarbus votes for immortal fame.

But then comes the last drop in the goblet. Enobarbus witnesses the reconciliation scene between Cleopatra and Antony after Cleopatra's alleged betrayal. (I will come back to this point.) Enobarbus now begins to hate Cleopatra. She is the bad influence; she gives all the bad advice. It is because of her that Antony never listened to him or to any of his men. Fury, jealousy, and despair are acting together. Finally, Enobarbus makes up his mind: "Now he'll outstare the lightning. To be furious / Is to be freighted out of fear, and in that mood / The dove will peck the estridge; and I see still / A dimunition in our captain's brain / Restores his heart. When valour preys on reason, / It eats the sword it fights with. I will seek / Some way to leave him" (197–203).

Before Enobarbus has found the way to leave Antony, something else happens. In 4.2 Antony stages a great farewell scene between himself and his men. Of course, he plays theater. But just as in his funeral oration next to the wounded body of Caesar, he feels the emotions he plays. He is still a sentimentalist who is constantly moved by generosity—by the generosity of old Caesar and by his own generosity. He sheds tears easily. Thus, he invites his men to a meal and turns to all of them with the words: "Give me thy hand. / Thou hast been rightly honest; So hast thou, / Thou, and thou, and thou; You have served me well, / And kings have been your fellows" (4.2.10–13). Then he turns especially to Enobarbus: "And thou art honest too" (15). He asks his men waiting on him during the night: "Tend me tonight. / Maybe it is the period of your duty. / Haply you shall not see me more; or if, / A mangled shadow. Perchance tomorrow / You'll serve another master" (24–28). Enobarbus, the would-be traitor, asks him not to continue: "What mean you, sir, / To give them this discomfort? Look, they weep, / And I, an ass, am onion-eyed. For shame, / Transform us not to women" (33–36). But this is true about all theater plays. Tragedies make men weep; they transform all men into women. And Antony plays the last act of a tragedy with full conviction.

Night is falling. Antony has asked his men to wait on him during the vigil. The theme of the man of sorrows, the theme we know so well from *Richard II,* makes itself slowly heard. The soldiers hear music from underneath. The music is a sign: "'Tis the god Hercules whom Antony loved, / Now leaves him" (4.3.13–14). Morning breaks. This is the time of truth: dies irae. Antony asks, "Who's gone this morning?" Soldier: "Who? / One ever near thee. Call for Enobarbus, / He shall not hear thee, or from Caesar's camp / Say 'I am none of thine'" (4.5.6–7). We are in the story of the Passion. Enobarbus is Simon Peter; he will say, "I am none of thine." And how does Antony react? He forgives. And he does more than forgive: he acts with never failing love and generosity: "Go, Eros, send his treasure after. Do it. / Detain not jot, I charge thee. Write to him— / I will subscribe— gentle adieus and greetings. / Say that I wish he never find more cause / To change a master. O, my fortunes have / Corrupted honest men! Dispatch. Enobarbus!" (12–17). The last word, the name, he utters, "Enobarbus!" is the cry of sorrow and despair. Marc Antony is no Christ; he is just the last Roman gentleman. No church will be built on Enobarbus the traitor. In him, Peter will play Judas's role. First, Enobarbus discovers his own foolishness, and only then does he discover his guilt.

Caesar deals in a friendly manner with traitors as long as he needs them. But at this point he has already beaten Marc Antony, and only a trifle is left over. Now he does not need traitors and can make them feel his contempt. He treats traitors of Antony just as, in the history plays, Henry IV treats the murderers of Richard II. They will expect their rewards in vain. It turns out here that Caesar is a perfect Machiavellian—even more perfect than Bolingbroke—who does wrong only when necessary. His aim is reached. He will not entertain turncoats. Now, Enobarbus begins to realize this. Alexas betrayed Antony and was hanged by Caesar. And even Canidius and the rest who betrayed Antony "in time," "have entertainment but / No honourable trust. I have done ill, / Of which I do accuse myself so sorely / That I will joy no more" (4.6.16–19). There is regret, yes, but no pangs of conscience. But then the soldier enters with Antony's letter and with Enobarbus's treasure; the betrayed Antony pays the man who has betrayed him. This is the moment of Enobarbus's catharsis: "I am alone the villain of the earth, / And feel I am so most. O Antony, / Thou mine of bounty, how wouldst thou have paid / My better service, when my turpitude / Thou dost so crown with gold! This blows my heart. . . . / I fight against thee? No, I will go seek / Some ditch wherein to die. The foul'st best fits / My latter part of life" (30–39).

We are at a camp before the last battle. Enobarbus nears the camp ("O bear me witness night" [5]). What follows is again an opera aria. Enobarbus, stricken by pangs of conscience, the torments of guilt, is dying. He talks (sings) to the moon before collapsing: "Be witness to me, O thou blessed moon, / When men revolted shall upon record / Bear hateful memory, poor Enobarbus did / Before thy face repent" (7–9). The sentries listen quietly to the penitent's confession to the moon: "O sovereign mistress of true melancholy, / The poisonous damp of night disponge upon me, / That life, a very rebel to my will, / May hang no longer on me. Throw my heart / Against the flint and hardness of my fault, / Which, being dried with grief, will break no powder, / And finish all foul thoughts. O Antony, / Nobler than my revolt is infamous, / Forgive me in thine own particular, / But let the world rank me in register / A master-leaver and a fugitive. / O Antony! O Antony!" (11–22). This "Antony, Antony" is the answer to the exclamation of Antony, "Enobarbus!" Those two exclamations meet in the spiritual sphere; the sorrow of the exclamation of a man who has been betrayed and forgives, and the despair of the man guilty of betrayal who asks for forgiveness. Enobarbus, the rude soldier whose language was always direct, uncouth, cynical, and prosaic, expresses himself now in Antony's noble and majestic language. In his aria of repentance, Enobarbus takes over the melody of Antony.

Cleopatra and Caesar

Cleopatra is not a French cocotte, as she is sometimes played. She is the queen of Egypt—she is Egypt. (Antony frequently calls her "Egypt.") She is the mother of royal children, among them a son by Julius Caesar. She wants to secure the throne for one of her sons. Her relation to Rome is a power relation. She is a woman of some power who has to accommodate Rome's overwhelming power. Since Julius Caesar, Antony, and Octavius Caesar are all Roman statesmen, her relations to them cannot be sheerly personal; they must also be dynastic. She is a passionate, attractive, and seductive woman who uses her power of seduction. She uses it in love and for love. She is in love. Yet she tries to use love also for dynastic purposes. It is very difficult to separate in Shakespeare Cleopatra the queen and Cleopatra the woman. For as a woman she is a queen, and as a queen she is a woman.

Antony, the Roman statesman, leaves Cleopatra for Rome, only to return to her. Shakespeare's Antony is not torn between love and duty (like several heroes and heroines of Corneille and Racine will be); even less is he torn between two loves. Rather, he is torn between love and ambition. However, in the eyes of Cleopatra, Antony has betrayed their love. Cleopatra, too, will hesitate between loyalty to Antony (the living and the dead Antony) and her ambition as the queen of Egypt. After Antony's star goes down (not without her complicity), she has to rely on Caesar for protection. Shakespeare never tells us "the truth" about Cleopatra. We will never know whether she was ready to sell out Antony for Caesar, whether she pretended to do it, whether she playacted to gain time or offered compromise in earnest. It is not just because this truth turns out to be untruth at the end but because there is no such truth. For Cleopatra is always two in one, and even when her queen soul, her monarchic interest, her shrewdness and calculation come into the foreground, her lover soul does not disappear. It is momentarily in eclipse, only to burst out triumphantly on the next occasion. This is why she is never matched with Caesar, not even in the position of a dependent, and not because she is more than twice his age and too old to seduce him. Even had she been sixteen, she would have been unable to seduce Caesar. And even had she been able to seduce him, she would have been unable to benefit from it. Octavius Caesar (in Shakespeare) is a cold fish, and he is not attracted by strange or alien customs. He looks at otherness with suspicion, not curiosity. And he always knows what he is doing.

Caesar's prejudice is the Roman prejudice. The first lines of the play spell it out: Antony cools "a gypsy's lust" (1.1.9), "The triple pillar of the world transformed / Into a strumpet's fool" (12–13). Conversely, Cleopatra (and her friends) detest Roman customs, the epitome of which is Caesar. For Cleopatra, it is Caesar (beside Fulvia and Octavia, the Roman wives of Antony) who represents the alien, the threatening other. The relationship between Cleopatra and Caesar mirrors the distrust between two cultures. But there is also a capillary movement between the two cultures to be noticed. Antony, indeed, moves between two cultures and appreciates both. And, at the end, Cleopatra will die a Roman death in oriental garb.

In the beginning there is just refusal. Cleopatra abuses "the scarcebearded Caesar" (22) and fears for Antony. Immediately, the oriental way of life is presented: Cleopatra in the company of her ladies-in-waiting and attendants. One senses how un-Roman their language and way of speaking is. The scene begins with Charmian's address: "Lord Alexas, sweet Alexas, most anything Alexas, almost most absolute Alexas, where's the soothsayer?" (1.2.1–3). What Roman matron would speak thus? Here there is idleness, pomp, and yet style and refinement. It is a stylized, ceremonially organized, but also deeply sensual world of beauty. It is a world that is attractive to Antony but not to Caesar.

Cleopatra is in love with Antony, yet she, as a queen, would appreciate it if Antony makes up with Caesar, provided that he remains true to her and returns to Egypt. She resents the fact that Caesar has given Antony a choice: either Rome and his friendship or Cleopatra. She wants to reconcile her love and her dynastic interest, and for Antony to return to her as a friend of Caesar would answer both desires. Thus, when the messenger arrives from Rome (2.5), she is ready to receive the good news. (I would add that during the report of the messengers, Cleopatra behaves not just as a jealous woman, but also like an oriental despot. Or are all passionate and jealous women, in their heart of hearts, oriental despots?) "I have a mind to strike thee ere thou speak'st. / Yet if thou say Antony lives, is well, / Or friends with Caesar, or not captive to him, / I'll set thee in a shower of gold, and hail / Rich pearls upon thee" (2.5.42–46). It is then that the messenger has to spell out the news of Antony's marriage to Octavia, the prize of "friendship." Cleopatra draws her knife.

That Antony returns to Cleopatra we know first from Caesar's mouth. That he wants this to happen and also masterminded it is more than a fair guess. He justifies his plotting against Antony with feigned or real accusations. He instructs his sister to divorce and tells her that he pities her, without listening, however, to her defense of Antony. He shows as much indignation as he is able to. His indignation against Antony is sexual, cultural, and political: "Contemning Rome, he has done all this and more / In Alexandria. Here's the manner of't: / I'th' market place on a tribunal silvered, / Cleopatra and himself in chairs of gold / Were publicly enthroned. At the feet sat Caesarian, whom they call my father's son, / And all the unlawful issue that their lust / Since then hath made between them, Unto her / He gave the establishment of Egypt; made her / Of lower Syria, Cyprus, Lydia, / Absolute queen" (3.6.1–11). Although he discovers with satisfaction that his well-prepared plans develop quickly in the direction of culmination, his indignation is also sincere.

And thus we arrive at Actium, at a scene important in the story of Cleopatra and of Enobarbus. Enobarbus asks Cleopatra to stay away from the war. He says, "And this said in Rome / That Photinus, an eunuch, and your maids / Manage this war" (3.7.13–14). One should not forget: a second man, a "vassal" to Antony, speaks thus to the queen of Egypt! Cleopatra's answer mixes hatred against Rome with the pride of a queen: "Sink Rome, and their tongues rot / That speak against us! A charge we bear i'th' war, / And as the president of my kingdom will / Appear there for a man" (15–18). Cleopatra suggests the wrong tactics (fighting on the sea) in order to use her own vessels and also to make her country victorious in the battle against Caesar's Rome. We know the consequences. Cleopatra's ship flees, Antony follows, and the battle is lost.

The new chapter in the Caesar-Cleopatra relationship begins after the lost battle. This is the moment when Antony's men begin to abandon him, when Enobarbus first considers treason. This is thus the moment of truth. Antony and Cleopatra's ambassador approaches Caesar. Antony wants to stay in Egypt, and if this is not granted, to live as a private man in Athens: "Next, Cleopatra does confess thy greatness, / Submits her to thy might, and of thee craves / The circle of the Ptolemies for her heirs, / Now hazarded to thy grace" (3.12.16–19). Is this treason? I do not think so, not yet. Cleopatra does not say that she wants to leave Antony, but she wants the kingdom of Egypt to remain under the rule of her heirs, with some kind of independence for Alexandria. She has not much choice. But Caesar is clever as always. Until this point, he has abused Cleopatra and accused Antony of submitting himself to her oriental influence. Now he wants to get rid of Antony; and for this purpose, he wants Cleopatra on his side: "For Antony, / I have no ears to his request. The Queen / Of audience nor desire shall fail, so she / From Egypt drive her all-disgraced friend, / Or take his life there. This if she perform / She shall not sue unheard" (19–24). Caesar's offer is clear: Cleopatra should not only betray her lover, but preferably also let him be killed; then she will have a hearing. (Of course, we already know Caesar; he lays traps. Even if someone performs the evil deed, the profit will belong not to her but to Caesar, who will always wash his hands of the affair.) This is again a matter of sound calculation. Caesar is not interested in moralistic perspectives. Thus, he turns to his man Thidias and sends him as his ambassador to Cleopatra with the following message, mixing cunning and contempt: "To try thy eloquence now 'tis time. / Dispatch. / From Antony win Cleopatra. Promise, / And in our name, what she requires. Add more / As thine invention offers. Women are not / In their best fortunes strong, but want will perjure / The n'er-touched vestal. Try thy cunning, Thidias" (26–31).

Immediately afterwards (3.13), the ambassador enters the chamber of Cleopatra with Antony. Antony already knows that his very sound request has been rejected, and he also knows something about Caesar's offer to Cleopatra. Antony says bitterly: "Let her know't. / To the boy Caesar send this grizzled head, / And he will fill thy wishes to the brim / With principalities" (3.13.15–18).

Thus Thidias speaks to Cleopatra. Caesar does not seduce with his youthful body; he seduces by blackmail. Thidias wants to speak to Cleopatra alone, but she refuses. She even cares for Enobarbus's company (although he was always hostile to her). Thidias intimates that Cleopatra never loved Antony, and this is why she will willingly put herself under the protection of Caesar. Cleopatra's answer to this insinuation is seemingly humble, but in fact ironic: "[Caesar] is a god, and knows / What is most right. Mine honour was not yielded, / But conquered merely" (60–62). Only those who cannot listen fail to notice the contemptuous irony in what follows. When Thidias continues, it will warm Caesar's spirits: "To hear from me you have left Antony, / And put yourself under his shroud, / The universal landlord" (70–72). Cleopatra answers: "Say to great Caesar this in deputation: / I kiss his conqu'ring hand. Tell him I am prompt / To lay my crown at's feet, and there to kneel / Till from his all-obeying breath I hear / The doom of Egypt" (74–78). But Antony has no ears. He is in a rage. He allows Thidias to be whipped, and whips Cleopatra with crazy accusations. ("You have been a boggler ever" [111].) But are these accusations really crazy? Is it so innocent to yield to a conqueror, even if only apparently, and abandon a conquered, even if only mockingly? Is this not in itself a sign of betrayal, or of a betrayal yet to come? We know from Enobarbus's story how fast treason develops from the first idea to the decisive act. Antony's anger is not entirely irrational; he has reason to be mad. Yet, he also has reason to stop raging and to reconcile with Cleopatra.

This is Cleopatra's first temptation by Caesar. The next temptation will be of a different kind. But first the fate of the war will be decided. Antony wins on land but is forced into a sea battle. The battle is lost, for Antony's boats join Caesar's fleet. And Antony believes, again, that he has been betrayed by Cleopatra. Shakespeare follows Plutarch here. But neither Plutarch nor Shakespeare knows whether there was a betrayal. In all probability, there was not. Since we know from Shakespeare's presentation that Antony's best men left him for Caesar's service after having noticed that his sun was setting, one does not need to plunge into accusations against the queen. The Roman soldiers are leaving the failing cause on their own.

Cleopatra initiates the last temptation herself after Antony's death. And this will also be the last of Caesar's hypocritical tricks. Caesar sends word to Cleopatra: "Bid her have good heart. / She soon shall know us, by some of ours, / How honourable and how kindly we / Determine for her. For Caesar cannot live / To be ungentle" (5.1.57–59). After the Egyptians leave, he immediately turns to his confidant, Proculeius: "Give her what comforts / The quality of her passion shall require, / Lest in her greatness, by some mortal stroke, / She do defeat us; for her life in Rome / Would be eternal in our triumph" (62–66).

With Antony dead, Cleopatra continues the war against Caesar on her own. This time Caesar will be the loser. He could win all his battles against Antony, he could win the world, but he could never win against the formidable woman, Cleopatra. For Cleopatra fights on an entirely different stage with different weapons. Caesar will be defenseless on this stage, against those weapons.

And Cleopatra knows this. Only dead heroes are great heroes, she says. This is because life is still open to vicissitudes, to smallness, to pettiness. Nothing is ready yet: "My desolation does begin to make / A better life. 'Tis paltry to be Caesar. / Not being Fortune, he's but Fortune's knave, / A minister of her will. And it is great / To do that thing that ends all other deeds, / Which shackles accidents and bolts up change, / Which sleeps and never palates more than dung, / The beggar's nurse, and Caesar's" (5.2.1–8). Cleopatra speaks like Hamlet.

But then Proculeius appears and brings the fraudulent promises of his master. Cleopatra says that she trusts him—and she does. But Proculeius is true to his master and lies. Still, Cleopatra has bad premonitions and makes her conditions: she will kill herself unless she receives a promise that she will never be carried to Rome in a triumphal march. Only Dolabella remains on the scene. To Dolabella, Cleopatra sings (because this is an opera!) about Antony's unparalleled greatness (just as Isolde sings about Tristan); and at the end Dolabella begins to second her. Dolabella, the Roman, now understands Cleopatra and feels for her. This is not just compassion but a kind of understanding love. Now Cleopatra seduces someone with her love for another (dead) man. Cleopatra makes use of the situation: "I thank you, sir. / Know you what Caesar means to do with me?" (104–5). When Dolabella hesitates to answer, Cleopatra puts the direct question: "He'll lead me then in triumph?"(107). Dolabella answers: "Madam, he will. I know't" (108). This is also treason, a noble and beautiful treason. Dolabella betrays Caesar's trust because Caesar has trusted him to lie, cheat, misguide. This is the disloyalty of an honest man.

At last it comes to the final showdown between Cleopatra and Caesar. This is their sole personal encounter. Caesar enters; Cleopatra kneels down: "My master and my lord / I must obey" (112–13). Caesar continues lying. He playacts the benevolent, kind overlord. Cleopatra also cheats: she withholds some of her treasures. Caesar's affable and condescending treatment of Cleopatra here has a grotesque effect. For Caesar does not know that Cleopatra knows his plans, and that she does not believe one single word he now utters. Cleopatra kneels again: "My master and my lord!" (186), to which Caesar answers: "Not so. Adieu" (187). He remains secure in his feeling of superiority, because he does not understand that he is, vis-à-vis Cleopatra, the toy of fate.

And then Dolabella, the gracious and honest turncoat, offers his last service: "Madam, as thereto sworn by your command— / Which my love makes religion to obey— / I tell you this: Caesar through Syria / Intends his journey, and within three days / You with your children will he send before. / Make your best use of this. I have performed / Your pleasure and my promise" (194–99).

When Dolabella returns to take them prisoner, all the Egyptian women—Cleopatra, Charmian, and Iras—are dead. Caesar, who wanted them alive, immediately changes his purpose, because he is the man who can always build contingencies into his destiny. He always accepts what cannot be changed. If someone is neither useful nor harmful for his purpose, he can be gracious and just. We see, once again, why he is the mirror of the perfect Machiavellian prince.

This time he sees the corpse of a woman with whom he wanted to decorate his triumphal march. But confronted with the unchangeable, Caesar remarks respectfully: "Bravest at the last, / She leveled at our purposes, and, being royal, / Took her own way" (329–31). Yet after saying those words, his curiosity gets the upper hand, and he immediately continues: "The manner of deaths? / I do not see them bleed" (331–32). After some inquiry, he gets to the fig leaves: "Most probable / That so she died" (347). This is the finishing touch on Shakespeare's portrayal of Octavius Caesar. The practical arrangements then follow for the common funeral of "a pair so famous" (354).

Antony and Cleopatra

Pascal remarks that, had Cleopatra an ugly nose, the history of the world would have turned out differently. The beautiful shape of Cleopatra's nose was contingent on the history of Rome. This contingent thing became the destiny of the world. The love of Antony and Cleopatra was on the one hand accidental, but on the other hand it turned the wheel of fortune in a direction in which it continued to roll for a long time.

For Shakespeare, however, the love of Cleopatra and Antony, this historical accident, is not portrayed as something accidental. Shakespeare could portray the accidental as accidental if he saw it fitting (for example, the epidemic in *Romeo and Juliet*). But this is not what he did in the love story of Antony and Cleopatra. This is not just because an accident can be turned into a destiny, and not just because an event that is accidental from one perspective is the work of fate from another perspective.

Shakespeare goes deeper: he portrays the love of Antony and Cleopatra not as the accidental trigger of a historical destiny but as a historical destiny itself. Antony and Cleopatra's love is imbued with the historical. The drama is not just about two people who meet accidentally and fall in love accidentally. It is the love story of an Egyptian queen, the very embodiment of the Oriental-Alexandrian culture, and a passionate Roman, the very embodiment of Roman chivalry as well as some Roman virtues and convictions. The fascinating element in the love story of Antony and Cleopatra is that the two lovers belong to two different cultures, and that their emerging from two different cultures—their representing two different cultures— inheres also in their mutual attraction and in the problematic character of their love. *Antony and Cleopatra* is also a tragedy of a love between two people who do not understand each other fully, who cannot understand well the signs and signals the other gives, who frequently misunderstand the gestures, the words, and even the smiles of the other. It is almost impossible for Antony and Cleopatra to read each other's minds, wishes, desires, and decisions. No such difficulty arises in the innocent love of Romeo and Juliet or in the guilty love of Gertrude and Claudius or that of Suffolk and Margaret. The love of Antony and Cleopatra is not a guilty love; neither is it an innocent love. It is a love of two great lovers who cannot take each other's gestures for granted, who are and remain lonely in their love relationship, whose sensual passion is never matched by confidence and friendship. This is, if I may repeat, a modern love story. Modern love stories are stories about love between two strangers. The love of Antony and Cleopatra is a passionate love between strangers. In such a love there is no convention, because this kind of love defies all conventions. In such a love there is strong erotic attraction, because strong erotic attraction defies conventions more radically than anything else. In such a love, there is parting, suffering, embracing, recognition; there are constant ups and downs. In such a love, lovers are irreplaceable for one another. Such a love is obsessive and passionate. Such a love comes with mutual dependence—a dependence that also means a loss of freedom. In such a love each lover tries to get rid of the other. The lovers try to get rid of their dependence, of their love, but they cannot. In such a love there is jealousy, yet this is a jealousy of misunderstanding. In such a love there is always reconciliation. Perhaps only the love between Othello and Desdemona resembles the love of Antony and Cleopatra, for they are also both passionate and they also misread each others' signs, signals, and gestures. But Antony and Cleopatra are the strangers who overcome their strangeness in their love. This is their grandeur. They do not kill one another. They commit suicide for each other, and they will be buried together. Love was never so absolutely victorious in Shakespeare as *in Antony and Cleopatra. Omnia vincit amor.*

The first scene between Antony and Cleopatra demonstrates immediately the character of the relationship. Cleopatra: "If it be love indeed, tell me how much." Antony: "There's beggary in the love that can be reckoned." Cleopatra: "I'll set a bourn how far to be beloved." Antony: "Then must thou needs find new heaven, new earth" (1.1.14–17). Antony's answers are telling. He is at first reluctant to express his love in words. Yet, when he speaks for the second time, he speaks in absolute terms. Instead of "how much," he expresses the infinite. When Antony first refuses to receive the messengers from Rome, he exclaims: "Fie, wrangling queen, / Whom everything becomes—to chide, to laugh, / To weep; how every passion fully strives / To make itself, in thee, fair and admired! / No messenger but thine; and all alone / Tonight we'll wander through the streets and note / The qualities of people" (50–56). To wander around the streets, to note the qualities of people! The picture comes from the stories of *A Thousand and One Nights.*

Antony's decision to break "these strong Egyptian fetters" and to become once more a Roman who does politics instead of making love precedes the news of his wife's death. Cleopatra does not know his decision, but she is always afraid of losing Antony. Shakespeare now shows us Cleopatra in the company of her ladies-in-waiting. This is a short scene, but it underlines that Shakespeare presents not "the Eastern woman" in Cleopatra, but a woman whose female cunning and tactics are in her circles generally unaccepted. Cleopatra says: "If you find him sad, / Say I am dancing; if in mirth, report / That I am sudden sick" (1.3.4–5). Charmian answers: "Madam, methinks, if you did love him dearly ... in each thing give him way; cross him in nothing" (6–9). It turns out that nothing depends on the female tactics. For Antony will return to Cleopatra; he must return to her, even if Cleopatra is not sure, even if she is distrustful and afraid. There is another brief exchange of words where the character of Cleopatra appears in full light. Antony tells her about his wife's death. And Cleopatra, who has always been jealous of Fulvia, now, contrary to all expectations, answers: "O most false love! / Where be the sacred vials thou shouldst fill / With sorrowful water? Now I see, I see, / In Fulvia's death how mine received shall be" (63–65). She adds: "I prithee turn aside and weep for her" (76). Next time, we see Cleopatra waiting for Antony. The fate of a woman differs from that of a man, even if the woman is a queen. Antony acts, fights, marries, divorces, gets angry, and does politics; but Cleopatra only waits. She waits for news from Antony, she waits for Antony. Granted, she enriches herself in human knowledge; for example, she asks the eunuch Mardian whether he can feel desire, and he answers in the affirmative. Desire is everywhere, everyone desires; Cleopatra desires to be with Antony. She is constantly dreaming of Antony: "Where think'st thou he is now? Stands he or sits he? / Or does he walk? Or is he on his horse? / O happy horse, to bear the weight of Antony!" (1.5.1–21). In 2.5 (back in Egypt), Cleopatra plays with the same Mardian who, although he cannot satisfy it, experiences desire: "Come, you'll play with me, sir?" Mardian: "As well as I can, madam" (2.5.6–7). To this Cleopatra answers: "And when good will is showed, though't come too short / The actor may plead pardon" (8–9). The scene is ambiguous. Playing can mean playing music, but also some other game. The ambiguity is not only present to the audience; the words sound ambiguous to the players of the drama themselves. This type of ambiguity belongs to a kind of refined and decadent civilization. Then comes the scene I briefly discussed above. The messenger arrives from Rome with the news that Octavius and Antony are reconciled and that Antony has married Octavia. Cleopatra's fury transcends all bounds. She strikes the messenger, allows him to be whipped. Although extreme and irrational in its manifestations, we see reason in this fury: Cleopatra did not foresee that she would be thus betrayed. She did not know the Roman Antony well enough. Jealousy, the feeling of having been abandoned unjustifiably, puts her into a state of rage. She sees no reason for Antony's decision; she has done nothing to deserve unfaithfulness on this scale. (Please note that it is not Antony who sends her the message.) After the messenger escapes her wrath, Cleopatra sends her ladies after him: "Bid him, / Report the features of Octavia: her years, / Her inclination; Let him not leave out / The colour of her hair" (111–15).

Shakespeare lets us partake in the scene of parting and in the grief and rage of the lonely Cleopatra. Now we hear Antony declare his return to the East where his "pleasure lies," but Shakespeare does not offer us direct insight into the triumphant meeting and reconciliation of old lovers. We get the news from Caesar.

Next we meet Cleopatra before the battle of Actium in the company of Enobarbus, who, as we know, wants to keep her and her army far from the battle (3.7). Yet Antony, who joins the conversation, decides otherwise. We know the consequences. After having lost the battle, Antony becomes hysterical. He accuses Cleopatra of having been the cause of his defeat. But Cleopatra pleads with him, not as the queen whose ship in command has fled, but as a lover who has eaten some forbidden sweets: "O, my lord, my lord, / Forgive my fearful sails! I little thought / You would have followed" (3.11.54–56). Antony's answer is absolutely remarkable. For he, the proud Roman general, confesses that he ran after Cleopatra with his own fleet as a lover and not as a general, and that Cleopatra should have known this ahead of time: "Egypt, thou knew'st too well / My heart was to thy rudder tied by th' strings, / And thou shouldst tow me after. O'er my sprit / Thy full supremacy thou knew'st, and that / Thy back might from the bidding of the gods / Command me . . . You did know / How much you were my conqueror, and that / My sword, made weak by my affection, would obey it on all cause" (57–68). When Cleopatra asks pardon for the third time, Antony says: "Fall not a tear, I say. One of them rates / All that is won and lost. Give me a kiss. / Even this repays me" (69–71). Lost is the cause, lost is the world, lost is the Roman honor. But Cleopatra remains. One of her kisses is worth more than victory.

Antony cannot be angry because of a lost battle, or even a lost empire. But when he begins to entertain doubts about Cleopatra's loyalty, he will be filled with uncontrollable fury. The scene of Antony's fury is the mirror of Cleopatra's fury after hearing that Antony has married Octavia. One never asks the question of which rage or fury was based on sound facts and which was not. The feeling, the pain of being betrayed, suffices. The pain was there in both cases, and in neither case was it entirely unfounded. In Antony's case it was, perhaps, unfounded. But the major and constant underlying current of the love relationship is the lovers' inability to read each other's signs properly, even if the messages are straightforward. And perhaps there are no straightforward messages at all. Perhaps there are never such messages. But conventional men and women believe in them; they are capable of understanding each other entirely, although maybe this is superficial. Antony and Cleopatra do not believe in straightforward messages. There are none for them.

I mentioned Caesar's trick to divide and rule and thus offer a seeming compromise to Cleopatra. Antony believes that Cleopatra has accepted

Caesar's offer sincerely, that she has already betrayed him. He turns to Cleopatra: "Have I my pillow left unpressed in Rome, / Forborn the getting of a lawful race, / And by a gem of women, to be abused / By one that looks on feeders?" He continues: "You have been a boggler ever. / But when we in our viciousness grow hard— / O, misery on't!—the wise gods seal our eyes / In our own filth drop our clear judgements, make us / Adore our errors, laugh at's while we strut / To our confusion" (3.13.105–16). All love is taken back; the past is abused. To this Cleopatra answers the only thing she can answer (the same thing that Cassius said to Brutus at Sardis): "O, is't come to this?" (117). Antony's rage turns into questioning love, again: "Cold-hearted towards me?" (161). The genuinely despairing Cleopatra answers, "Ah, dear, if I be so, / From my cold heart let heaven engender hail, / And poison it in the source, and the first stone / Drop in my neck" (162–64). Antony is relieved; Cleopatra loves him. He is satisfied; moreover, his courage to meet Caesar again on the battlefield returns with the love of Cleopatra: "Dost thou hear, lady? / If from the field I shall return once more / To kiss these lips, I will appear in blood. / I and my sword will earn our chronicle. / There's hope in't yet" (174–79). But this hope soon evaporates.

Before the battle there is still an operatic/amorous scene. Antony and Cleopatra are making love. Cleopatra wants him to stay on and on (just like Juliet wants Romeo to stay in *Romeo and Juliet*), yet Antony asks his man, Eros, to bring his armor. Cleopatra unskillfully helps him to fix his armor. Antony chides her mockingly: "Ah, let be, let be! Thou art / The armourer of my heart. False, false! This, this!" (4.4.7–8). Before the battle begins, Antony continues with his amorous teasing. He calls Cleopatra "great fairy, my nightingale and my warrior."

Antony wins on land, but then his navy joins forces with Caesar. Once again, Antony is absolutely sure that Cleopatra has sold him out to Caesar. And again, Shakespeare does not say whether he is right or wrong, but in all probability he is wrong. But Antony's fury knows no bounds. This time it lasts longer and threatens with devastation: "O this false soul of Egypt! This grave charm, / Whose eye becked forth my wars and called them home, / Whose bosom was my crowned, my chief end, / Like a right gipsy hath at fast and loose / Beguiled me to the very heart of loss" (4.13.25–29). It is here and only here that Antony becomes an ugly Roman. He speaks about Cleopatra as the gypsy. It is the stranger, the alien, the non-Roman whore who has ruined him. At first, Cleopatra does not even understand. ("Why is my lord enraged against his love?" [31].) But then Antony becomes even angrier, and he lets loose his aggression against Cleopatra. Could he eventually kill her, as Othello killed Desdemona? Listen: "But better 'twere / Thou fell'st into my fury, for one death / Might have prevented many. . . . The witch shall die. / To the young Roman boy she hath sold me, and I fall / Under this plot. She dies for't" (40–49). Cleopatra is afraid of Antony, not just of the loss of his love but also of his murderous fury. She fears for her life, although Antony is never aggressive, and despite his fury, the character portrayed by Shakespeare could never kill his beloved, not even in a state of rage. Antony is a man who does not even allow the messenger to be whipped, a cruelty Cleopatra is ready to commit. But a raging man who cries betrayal in everything—life, comradeship, alliance, love—who threatens with killing, is dangerous to the other and to himself. Cleopatra seeks refuge; she hides herself. She must wait until the rage is gone. It will be gone.

After Cleopatra sends the false notice to Antony about her death, all fear and doubt disappear from Antony's soul. Just as Caesar never begrudges a fallen enemy, so Antony's love reaches its peak at the mere thought of a dead Cleopatra. From this moment until the end (which nonetheless takes more than one act), the tragedy transforms itself into the tragic opera of *Liebestod*.

Antony "sings": "I will o'ertake thee, Cleopatra, and / Weep for my pardon. So it must be, for now / All length is torture. Since the torch is out, / Lie down, and stray no farther. . . . I come, my queen" (4.15.44–50). Antony asks Eros to kill him. But Eros chooses instead to kill himself. What takes place here is the repetition of the scene at Philippi with other characters: the victor is now the victim. Shakespeare appropriates from Plutarch the story of Antony's failure to commit suicide. Perhaps it is not just for the sake of "faithfulness," for otherwise how could he have devised the poetically formidable *Liebestod* scene between Antony and Cleopatra? The parallel between Cassius's and Antony's suicides is simply that both believed in false information and acted upon it promptly. Still, there is no essential similarity. Without this mistake Cassius's cause might have been won, yet Antony and Cleopatra were both lost with or without the mistake. Only the manner of their Liebestod could have been different.

The duet of the Liebestod scene is not just the final and now irrevocable confession of love; the lovers also voice the final and irrevocable aggrandizement of one another. Their death will assume a cosmic character, as will their love. They are—they become—Mars and Venus, divine stars in the historical heaven. Cleopatra: "O sun, / Burn the great sphere thou mov'st in; darkling stand / The varying shore o'th' world! O Antony, / Antony, Antony!" (4.16.10–12). Antony: "Peace. / Not Caesar's valour / Hath o'erthrown Antony, but Antony's / Hath triumphed on itself" (15–16). Cleopatra: "And welcome, welcome! Die when thou hast lived, / Quicken with kissing. Had my lips that power, / Thus would I wear them out" (39–41).

And now Antony advises Cleopatra to compromise with Caesar, but Cleopatra refuses: "My resolution and my hands I'll trust, / None about Caesar" (51–52). When Antony dies, Cleopatra continues (like Isolde) to

sing: "The crown o'th' earth doth melt. My lord! / O, withered is the garland of the war. . . . The odds is gone, / And there is nothing left remarkable / Beneath the visiting moon" (65–70). She commands her men to
bury Antony in Roman fashion. There is no more distrust; finally, the lovers
understand each other. Roman or Egyptian, it does not matter; they are
united in death.

Act 5 is the act of Cleopatra. She remains alone with her women, as Brutus remained alone with his men. Iras dies before her; now it is time for her
to die. Killing herself, she dies as a Roman, as Portia died, as a wife of
Antony. Yet, she also dies as a queen. Cleopatra: "Give me my robe. Put on
my crown. I have / Immortal longings in me. . . . Methinks I hear / Antony
call. I see him rouse himself / To praise my noble act . . . Husband, I come.
/ Now to that name my courage prove my title. / I am fire and air"
(5.2.275–84).

And then comes the final verdict of Caesar, the winner: "She shall be
buried by her Antony. / No grave upon the earth shall clip in it / A pair so
famous" (352–54). It is not a political verdict but a historical one. Politics is
first and foremost about victory, but history is also about fame.

Octavius Caesar

Can one be satisfied with Antony's historical summary that it is not Caesar's valor that vanquishes Antony, but Antony himself? I doubt it. True, it is
not Caesar's valor that vanquishes Antony, but Caesar's resolution. We who
are sitting in the audience do not like Shakespeare's Caesar. Caesar is not
lovable because he is quite inhuman. He is not adorable because he is not
magnificent, because he lacks the colorful sort of grandeur. But is unilinear
and headstrong resolve not a grandeur of sorts? Caesar is the only man in
this whole play who knows from the first moment onward what he is
doing and why he is doing it. He calculates correctly, he never makes a
wrong step, and he handles contingencies very well. All his traps are working; people are falling into them. Almost all his treasons lead to the required
results. He comes out of all the complex situations victoriously. And at the
end, he remains alone on the scene. Now he is lonely, since there is no
other person remaining who is equal to him.

During the whole play Caesar is constantly acting. He never stands still:
he plans, he devises one step after another, he ties and unties. But now, at
the end, he has reached his goal. He will bring his enemies to Rome in a
triumphal march. However, all the great men are dead: Brutus and Cassius,
as well as Antony and Cleopatra. Even the second-class personalities such
as Pompey and Lepidus have left the scene. The lord of the world remains
in the world with his servants and underlings. And he knows this only too

well while lamenting Antony's death: "O Antony, / I have followed thee to this. But we do lance / Diseases in our bodies. . . . We could not stall together / In the whole world. But yet let me lament, / With tears as sovereign as the blood of hearts, / That thou, my brother, my competitor / In top of all design, my mate in empire, / Friend and companion in the front of war, / The arm of mine own body, and the heart / Where mine his thoughts did kindle—that our stars, / Irreconcilable, should divide / Our equalness to this" (5.1.35–48). The victorious Caesar stops acting for a minute, and for a minute he discovers the poesy of speech. Afterwards, as we know, Caesar continues to scheme; for it is now that he gives the finishing touch to the trap he laid for Cleopatra. But here he will fail. Grandeur turns its back on Caesar.

Whose tragedy is *Antony and Cleopatra*? It is the tragedy of Antony and Cleopatra, the tragedy of Pompey the younger, the tragedy of Enobarbus. And yes, it is also the tragedy of Octavius Caesar. The man who calculates rationally until he becomes the sole ruler of the world pays a heavy price for it: loneliness. The man who weeps real tears for Antony becomes a melancholy man. The united Roman Empire will live in peace. But not only will Caesar trust no one—he has never trusted anyone—but he will never again find a man who could be his match. The man of political greatness will pay the price of his success with two absences: the absence of friendship and the absence of passionate love. For his triumph, Caesar thus pays the heaviest price that can be paid in the world of Shakespeare.

Postscript:
Historical Truth and Poetic Truth

T his is a postscript and not a conclusion, for the presentation of Shakespeare's poetic truth about history speaks for itself; it does not require, or even allow for, a conclusion.

Nonetheless, the expression "poetic truth about history" calls for clarification. Poetic truth about history is unlike factual truth. It is also unlike a theory of history, a historical narrative, or a theoretical interpretation of a historical narrative. The interest of the latter is unearthing and understanding the past from the perspective of the present. The past can be changed. One changes the past not solely by reinterpreting it but also by discovering new facts, inserting them into a theory, revising the theory, or devising—in view of them—a new theory. Historical fictions are approximations. They want to tell us the story as it really happened. One will never know how something really happened, first and foremost because nothing "really" happened in any one fixed way. Everything happens in different ways for different people; thus the "real" happening is not a fact but already an interpretation. Still, one can approximate, in various ways, what really happened. There are many different stories told about the same historical event, although—if they are true—there must also be some agreement among them. One can always write a new narrative about the same event. The past remains always open, *as the past,* in the present and the future. Aristotle was the first to remark that tragedy is unlike historiography, for it presents us with the way in which a thing could have happened or might happen, and not how it happened in fact. This is why tragedy is a sibling of philosophy. The truth of tragedy is *revelatory.* In Shakespeare it is revelatory in a way that is different from that of the Greeks.

What is "revelatory" is the truth that we *accept as it is.* When we read the story of Richard III in a history book, we always ask the question, Did it happen this way or that way? Is it true? But when we watch Shakespeare's

Richard III on the stage, we do not ask this question. For the question itself is external to the play. In historiography or even in the chronicle, the question concerning the truth of facts is, on the contrary, internal to the genre. Shakespeare's tragedies reveal both what has happened and how it has happened. They do not ask the question of why something has happened in this specific way, or what will be the consequences. The categories of causality and determination are alien to the genre of tragedy, and especially to Shakespearean tragedy. The plot develops in this way and that way; the development itself—namely, that men and women of a certain kind are acting in certain ways in certain situations—is self-explanatory. This is one reason why I called the truth of tragedy revelatory.

Philosophers have accounted for the experience of the revelatory character of truth in art in several ways. In the hylomorphic tradition (for example, in Hegel), one could say that the content disappears entirely in the form. In a prosaic manner, one could add that the work of art is perfect, since nothing can either be added to it or taken away from it. But what is the message of such a commonplace wisdom? We know, for example, that many of Shakespeare's plays were staged in shortened versions, and that sometimes even their endings were changed. Yet the revelatory character of the truth of the artwork does not change simultaneously. If one experiences *Hamlet* first in the presentation of Lawrence Olivier's film, one will also feel that the play is perfect in the above-described sense. Whenever we are watching a play, its truth reveals itself. The truth, the perfection, will be exactly what we see and what we experience. The knowledge that something has been abbreviated does not annul the revelatory experience. For it is always there whenever a work and its listener/watcher are tuned in to one another. The truth of an artwork is revelatory, for the artwork has no "before" and "after." It speaks for itself. Nothing can be added or taken away in the *present time,* when we are sitting in the theater and when the truth is going to be revealed. Let me give an example. The first performances of Mozart's *Don Giovanni* in Prague and in Vienna were not exactly the same. Mozart composed an additional aria and left out one scene completely, if I remember correctly. But in both Prague and Vienna, the opera revealed the truth. From this one should not conclude that to return to the original texts of Shakespeare (as we now know them) and to refrain from abbreviating them is futile, or that all possible changes in the text would be acceptable. Not all alterations or changes come across effectively, and some leave the spectator feeling dissatisfied. But this is also true of many presentations of the uncut versions of Shakespearean (or other) dramas.

Since historical truth is about the approximation of "what really happened" from the position of various theories and from the perspective of different presents, the interpretive work of history changes the fiction. However, if one presents a Shakespearean drama on the stage (presupposing that the whole drama is staged and that the end remains unchanged), the interpretive work does not change the fiction but the understanding of the fiction (causes, motivations, characters, and their relations). Moreover, the idea of "approximation" is entirely absent in the interpretation and in the staging of revelatory truth. There is nothing to approximate, because the drama itself *is* the truth. One is confronted with the question of what exactly this truth is, not with the question of whether this is the truth. As a result, all interpretations interpret the *that* and not the *what* of the truth. This has some significance for the question concerning the self-referentiality of the work of art. To remain with the tragedy, and more precisely with the historical tragedies of Shakespeare, the question is wrongly put. Since the so-called plot of Shakespeare's historical tragedies is taken from literary sources—from chronicles or from Plutarch, from historians who wanted to tell us how and what really happened—Shakespeare's historical tragedies are in this sense not self-referential. But as far as truth is concerned, they are. For revelatory truth is self-referential. The truth that is referential is true knowledge or true theory about something that combines and orders the truth of facts interpretively. But revelatory truth is not related to anything external, and as such it is self-referential.

Almost all dramatic theories place great emphasis on the fact of "presencing." The drama does not take place in the past, but in the present. In the historical tragedies of Shakespeare, similar to Greek tragedies, the plot and the material are taken from the past. What the drama refers to has taken place in the past. However, the presentation of the truth of history, that is, the truth of history as it appears in poetic truth, is always in the present. In historical tragedy, the past is presencing. It is not only interpreted from the standpoint of the present, but it *is* eternally present. Any time that a tragedy is staged—or when we read it—it is and will be the time of *now*.

In this sense, historical tragedy, particularly that of Shakespeare, preserves and reinforces one essential feature of *mystery plays*. The truth of the Jewish and Christian religions (and some other religions as well, which have no bearing on my topic) is revelatory truth. One can speak about revelatory truth authentically in one way alone: in revealing it. The repetition of revelation is the presentation of revelatory truth. That is, truth of the past is truth of the present; it is constantly presencing. Jesus is born every Christmas, although he was born two thousand years ago. We know that he was born roughly two thousand years ago, just we know when Augustus Caesar was born or when he became the first man of Rome. But each and every Christmas, the birth of Jesus is repeated. And Christ is crucified every Good Friday, and every Easter he will be resurrected. In the *pravoslav* ceremony, everyone repeats: "Christ is resurrected, he is indeed resurrected," and they kiss one another on their lips. So is it in the Jewish religion. On the Seder evening of Passover, the Haggadah is read. Every year, every Seder evening, the story of the wicked boy is told. The wicked boy asks his father: "How does the whole thing concern me? It happened a long time ago!" To this the father ritually answers that it happens to us, it happens to you, it is now that God liberates us from Egyptian slavery. In the religious festivities, festival, ceremonies, and rituals, truth dwells as revelation. Sure, one can also tell about the same events as historical narratives. One can tell that history has not proved that the Jews were in Egypt at all, or that we are (historically) absolutely sure that Jesus of Nazareth was not born in December, and not in Bethlehem. But the historically important addenda to true knowledge are entirely irrelevant when it comes to truth as revelation. This, however, does not mean that revealed truth cannot be interpreted. In fact, it is always interpreted. It belongs, for example, to the Passover ritual to reinterpret passages of the Haggadah. The priest or the minister constantly interprets the stories of Christ's birth, passion, and resurrection. Those interpretations can differ. They differ less than the interpretations of the Shakespearean tragedies only because there is a religious canon that puts a limit to interpretation, whereas no such canon exists for the interpretation of Shakespeare's history plays. And, of course, Shakespeare's history plays can be staged in every season, and they do not need to be staged every year. (In the case of Greek tragedy, there were still such regular occasions.)

Perhaps it is clear by now why I said that the truth of Shakespeare's history plays (tragedies) is revelatory truth. But the plot of his history plays is neither mythical nor mystical. Neither God nor any deities participate in the action, and no festive occasion colors the fibers of the revealed truth. Truth is revealed about history. Historical events happening, historical characters acting, without any kind of otherworldy interference of protection, will be the carriers of the truth. *Truth about that, not truth about why and what for.*

Shakespeare's history plays (tragedies) are tragedies of revelatory truth about history. They reveal the covering and the hiding, for they reveal the truth that there always remains something unrevealed and unrevealable. The infinite interpretability of the Shakespearean dramas is also connected with this troubling experience. In poetry there is no other truth about history than the one revealed, presenced before us in a history play, but it is revealed *that* there are secrets in history and historicity about which neither the poet nor his characters can speak. Perhaps it is not the cause of events or the motivation of the characters—which become irrelevant in the process of revealing—that remains a mystery, but the internal reserves and sources of the characters and of their actions. Why is one person good and the other one wicked? Why is Cordelia good and Goneril and Regan wicked? To this question no answer is given. We take the men and women as given, we take the characters as they are presented in their relationships to others by the poet. But the characters are just put on the stage; they are presented as the *archai* of a finite world standing for truth as such. It is important in Shakespeare that they are the archai of a finite world. For it is not through the eternal, the immortal, and the infinite that truth about history is revealed in Shakespeare's historical plays and tragedies, but through finite and transient beings in a finite present time. It is through the finite and the transient that truth is revealed to the finite and the transient. In Shakespeare's revelatory truth we can recognize ourselves. We are revealed to ourselves. The truth reveals to the transient its own transience, its own finitude; this is what I meant when I said that it reveals *that* something cannot be revealed, not *what* cannot be revealed. In the latter case, it would be a secret, but in the former case one does not even know whether there is a secret.

This duality of revelatory truth constitutes the doubling of the stages in Shakespeare's tragedies and history plays (but not in some of his comedies). As I discussed at some length in the first part of the book, Shakespeare's characters act on a historical stage and sometimes also on an existential stage. And the most complex characters play their parts on both stages. It may happen that one character makes his or her first appearance on the historical stage and enters at a crucial moment the existential stage (like Lear, Coriolanus, Richard II, and others). And there are characters who play continuously on both stages (Hamlet, Henry VI, Richard III, and so on). But the presence of two stages is all-important in Shakespeare's historical drama. Shakespeare formulates this succinctly in Hamlet's words addressed to the actors: "[T]he purpose of playing . . . was and is, to hold . . . the mirror up to nature, to show virtue her own feature, scorn her own image, and the very age and body of the time his form and pressure" (*Hamlet* 3.2.20–24). Shakespeare makes the differentiation—in Hamlet's formulation—between virtue and scorn on the one hand, and age and the body of time on the other. When presenting virtue and vice, one mirrors nature; virtue and vice present themselves as such on the existential stage. But the play also wears the impress of age and time. And the impress of age and time are not "independent" of the mirrored virtue and scorn. The king's face is pressed upon a coin. One time one king's face, another time another king's face is pressed on the coin. The mirror, the drama, shows virtue and vice, but the pressure of time modifies them. This is how there are two stages.

The two stages together are the revelatory truth, not the existential stage alone. On the existential stage men and women are standing naked, sometimes metaphorically naked, sometimes even literally naked, as in the case of King Lear. History fades away, the stamp or the pressure of time disappears, the form of time becomes invisible. But the truth of history revealed in Shakespeare's dramas points to the moment of nakedness as to exceptional moments. They are the moments of truth about human existence, and as such also moments of truth about history, about its insignificance, about its transience. However, the historical stage also reveals its truth: the truth of the significance of life-in-time. For intemporality makes its appearance in temporality, and time can stand still where there is time, where time and "the times" matter.

The truth of Shakespeare's plays is revelatory. I almost said that the truth in art is revelatory in general. But it is better to stay with Shakespeare. The specificity of Shakespeare's history plays is, as I have tried to show in my interpretation of several of his dramas, that he was conscious of his manner of presenting historical truth. In this he differs from the ancients. In Greek tragedy the question of good and evil, of vice and virtue, of the sacred and the profane, of knowledge and ignorance occupied the center point of the drama. In Shakespeare the axiological center of the drama condenses all the categories of "orientation," such as good/evil, beautiful/ugly, useful/harmful, successful/unsuccessful, sacred/profane, true/untrue. They do not fit, they shift, they contradict one another, they constitute different hierarchies of values, and they can also overbalance one another. I have mentioned that the ladders of grandeur and of morality, of historical significance and of political relevance, are very different in Shakespeare, and that one character can step to the highest rung in one and remain on the lowest rung on another of those ladders. Shakespeare presents heterogeneous slabs of values. He does not present one as the true measure and the other as an untrue one. To the contrary, revelatory truth reveals the complexity and multiplicity of the measures in a finite world of axiological conflicts. All ladders participate in revelatory truth. Perhaps this is why the question of truth will also be constitutive in Shakespeare in the plot of the drama, in the development of characters, and in their relation to each other.

The question of truth appears in several forms in Shakespeare, but it always remains the question of truth. Being and remaining true to ourselves (whether we are good or evil) is a fundamental question of truth. Presenting ourselves as we are (as we believe ourselves to be) or hiding ourselves: this is also the question of truth. Before whom we hide ourselves and before whom and when we disclose ourselves: this is also the question of truth. Whether we are able to disclose ourselves or not: this is also the question of truth. Lying or telling the truth (truthfulness): this is a fundamental question of truth. Betrayal or treason is untruth, whereas loyalty is the truth. The true man is loyal and faithful, the untrue is disloyal and unfaithful. At this point the question of truth becomes the question of the good. But being able to foresee the consequences of our actions is also a question of truth. The knowledge of human character is also a question of truth. The distinction between mere facts, the concern about the thoughtful interpretation of a fact: this is also a question of truth. The ability or inability to understand the stranger is again a question of truth. Curiosity, thoughtfulness, caution, reflection on our situation and our action, mediation between thought and act: these are all questions of truth. To be able to select among information, to determine not to believe anyone but believe someone absolutely: these are also questions of truth. To abstract one's decisions from momentary interest, real or seeming: this is also the question of truth. These and similar questions are presented in Shakespeare, and all of them are decisive in all of his dramas. As I mentioned about *Hamlet* in the introductory chapter to this book, Hamlet and Claudius are each other's absolute opposites, for Hamlet wants the truth and nothing but the truth and Claudius wants the untruth and nothing but the untruth.

I was at first reluctant to bestow the ambiguous title of "philosopher of history" on Shakespeare. Now, I would be less reluctant to do so. Shakespeare's historical dramas (and most of his dramas are historical) reflect on issues and reveal puzzles that would not even be addressed by philosophy for at least another two hundred years. The question of time and temporality would not be reflected on seriously and philosophically before the nineteenth century; the relation between the two stages would not be examined until Kierkegaard; the difference between the truth of fact, theory, and interpretation and revelatory truth would not be considered until the twentieth century. Shakespeare anticipated postmetaphysical philosophy and its central concerns at a time when modern metaphysics had not yet reached its peak. Modernity recognized itself in Shakespeare only from the time of Romanticism, perhaps also because modern philosophy and the speculative self-understanding of modern man in general resigned at that time the ambition of metaphysical system building. It was only around this time that philosophy abandoned fixing its gaze on the eternal, the unchangeable, the infinite, the immortal alone. When modern men began to abandon not necessarily faith in an eternal, timeless, and absolute meaning, but at least in the accessibility of such a meaning, the revelatory character of Shakespeare's tragedies could be grasped by an audience to whom it was revealed. The Shakespeare cults grew out of this experience. This *cultus* might wither as every cultus does. Moreover, there is no revelation without congregation. The revelatory truth of Shakespeare can also prove transient. The audience to which Shakespeare's tragedies, history plays, and dramas reveal their truth is a congregation that bears testimony to an understanding of virtue, scorn, the age and body of time: the human condition as historical condition, the historical condition as modern condition, the modern condition as life lived fully amid the constraints of transience and finitude.

About the Author

Agnes Heller is Hannah Arendt Professor of Philosophy at the New School for Social Research in New York. She was the student and friend of Georg Lukács and a dissident in Communist Hungary. She is the author of more than twenty books, including *An Ethics of Personality, A Theory of Modernity,* and *Beyond Justice.*

	DATE DUE		